Styx & S[illegible]

-:Tales of the *El Defensor*:-
Book One.

A Novel.

2nd Edition Published in June 2020

ISBN-13: 978-1535290708
ISBN-10: 1535290706

Dedication

This book is dedicated to
Nicola, Ryan and Owain.

When I need Inspiration...
You are mine.

I got there in the end!

Prologue

Kerian Denaris pulled sharply on the reins of his stallion, bringing its gallop towards Caerlyon Vale to a thundering halt, his journey across miles of war-scorched land a rushed and anxious one that was finally nearing its end. He was a haunted man, driven not by a noble cause or sense of justice but by the fear of his own impending death.

His horse snorted at the rough handling, pacing backwards and forwards in agitation as its master scanned the twisting path ahead with a military focus, looking for possible ambush sites or other dangers to impede his urgent path. There was a glint of steel and a threat of violence about the warrior's hazel flecked eyes, his scarred leather armour and battle-worn weapons indicating this dark quest had not been a peaceful one.

The fog was thicker here in the vale, its chilling touch wrapping around the mounted knight as he eased his stallion forwards. Tendrils of ground mist coiled about the forelocks of his charger, making the horse step nervously at the unsolicited attention.

"Steady, Saybier." Kerian reached forwards, patting the neck of his steed reassuringly. "I think it would be better if I walk from here." He dismounted carefully onto the slick path below. The fog swirled about his scuffed leather boots obscuring the surface of the trail but the knight never hesitated, reaching out to take Saybier's reins with one gloved hand even as his other rested lightly upon the pommel of his sword. The last time he had left this place he had sworn never to return: now necessity forced him to do so. With a dry throat and a frame barely suppressing the shiver running down his spine, he took a deep breath and stepped further into the gloom. Castle Caerlyon waited below, its evil presence permeating the air, rekindling thoughts of dark secrets and stirring long buried emotions.

Kerian did not want to follow this path, yet he knew, despite his deep-seated reservations, that the dark magic controlling his future would only be broken following the inevitable confrontation awaiting him.

Gnarled roots, half buried and obscured beneath the slick mud of the trail made the descent a perilous one, loops and snarls threatening to trip the unwary and send them falling through the mists to their doom. Brittle-fingered twigs clawed out from the murk to snare Kerian's cloak and catch in his hair making his feelings of apprehension rise in tandem with the agitation displayed by the normally taciturn charger at his back. Trying to seek solace in the confines of his cloak was equally futile, the woollen material already saturated from the long night's travel and enveloping mists. The pathway began to level out and the sentinel trees withdrew from the trail in mock deference as his path dwindled to an end.

Kerian tensed at an alien sound ahead, a cackling echo, distorted by the mists but tinged with an underlying cry of the insane. The sound amplified as he advanced, splintering from its initial origin into shards of sound that appeared to come from more than one source, mocking the knight and raising his sense of hopelessness.

Something was wrong here... horribly wrong. Was he too late? Were the rumours from the roadside true?

Several shapes emerged from the swirling mist. The cackling sounds came from these sinister creatures but they were not interested in the approaching horse and rider, only navigating the shrouded ground, occasionally stopping to jab at unseen objects beneath the veil of mist.

He recognised the creatures instantly. They were the pets of his queen, her eyes and ears to the outside world. However, their appearance outside the castle raised more unanswered questions, making the knight curse the weather and his inability to see things clearly. This was insane, coming back here without scouting the area first. What had he been thinking? These creatures were supposed to be caged and should never have been loose unless they were out scouting for their mistress. What was going on?

One of the creatures caught his eye, its ragged form precariously balanced upon the cross hilt of an abandoned sword, the tarnished blade swaying gently under the weight of the scavenger. It turned to regard Kerian with baleful black eyes before spreading skeletal wings to glide down and join the fevered pecking of its colleagues.

Kerian's eyes narrowed in grim distaste as he realised that further down the now vacant blade, there gripped the unmistakeable remains of a desiccated hand, contorted in the violence of death. Slithers of flesh still dangled from the partly stripped bony fingers, and even as he looked, another black shape hopped over to feast on the remains.

Kerian became aware of a cool breeze that suddenly sprang to being as he took his next tentative step, its draft momentarily shredding the mist, peeling back the layers of secrecy to reveal a bloody morass underneath. Corpses lay everywhere, unseeing eyes staring blankly from sockets that oozed congealing blood and enhanced grimacing death masks. Dismembered limbs lay alongside abandoned tools of war, dropped in terror from nerve-severed hands. Swords and spears lanced the sides of fleeing soldiers, their unyielding steel sheathed in the bodies they had slain. The smell of copper was overpowering, with grasses stained scarlet and pools drying with a crimson crust.

One shuffling scavenger pecked its way across the grass towards the knight, showing no signs of wariness, just a single-minded goal to find the freshest carrion upon which to feast. Kerian's boot lashed out in disgust, catching it unawares and snapping its light bone structure as if it were kindling. All the other pecking and cackling stopped at the explosive sound, feasting forgotten, replaced by a sense of self-preservation as the area exploded into collective flight, skeletal wings scything through the mist, beaks filled with whatever moist prize they could hastily snatch.

Kerian continued to skirt the battlefield warily, noting the armour and uniforms adorning the bodies at his feet. The majority of the dead wore colours that matched those he used to wear. His pulse quickened as he recollected the tales of uprising whispered from gaunt refugees passed along his way. The rebellion against the Caerlyon Knights and the dark queen was much more than half-suppressed rumours, his lover's power had clearly slipped away.

Picking his way through the appalling carnage, he approached another well-traversed path that lead up and away from the battlefield. The littered ground held grimmer corpses, twisted in death and more numerous in numbers, forcing him to step ever more carefully as he tackled the increased hardship of the trail. Castle Caerlyon loomed darkly from the fog, its parapets and gargoyles towering high with overhanging battlements emphasising the ominous tyranny its owner once held over the surrounding lands.

From his poor vantage point, Kerian could see flames flickering from untended fires, the light dancing with shadows at every arrow slit and murder-hole. He hurried on, hunched inside the folds of his cloak, doubt assailing him at each step. He was too late; he should have started back days ago... if only he had not been so proud!

The shadowy ramparts seemed to tower even higher as he ascended the path, the walls blackened with pitch and oil, peppered with catapult shot and scorched with magical flame. Bodies hung from cages stripped of flesh, bony digits hanging free, stretching down to him pleading for release, whilst other, fresher corpses hung as a macabre warning, their necks stretched with the hemp every traitor to the crown earned. His queen had ruled harshly during her years here and even now, after all the fighting, fear of retribution meant her warnings to others remained on display.

The drawbridge hung open, its appearance anything but inviting, the thick lengths of weather-seasoned wood lying smashed and splintered from the invading force that had fought to bring the drawbridge down and gain entry. Any thought of crossing on horseback was a foolhardy option, leaving Kerian little choice but to reluctantly tether Saybier to one of the thick drawbridge chains or risk the weakened wood crumbling under their combined weight.

"Wait here," he whispered, sharing a nervous smile as he reassuringly stroked the stallion's nose. "I'll be back before you know it." With one last tug to secure the reins, Kerian turned towards the entryway, offering a silent prayer to any gods that his last words would prove to be prophetic ones.

The moat churned and bubbled below, as if some unseen force lurked beneath the surface, maliciously digesting the last foolish person who had dared to cross this ill-fated evening. The knight winced at every tortured groan and agonising creak his armoured weight drew from the ruined timbers beneath him as he gingerly stepped from slat to slat. Kerian felt uncomfortably warm, despite the chill in the air, beads of sweat dotting his brow as he struggled to maintain his balance and reach the far side of the ruined drawbridge.

After several harrowing moments, his feet finally touched unyielding stone and he gasped in relief, stealing a moment's pause to gather his breath. His heart pounded in his ears as he took one last glance back at the shadowy figure of Saybier snorting nervously amidst the swirling fog, before he turned to pass under the bared teeth of the double iron portcullis and into the black throat of the castle beyond.

Bodies of Caerlyon knights lay around him, slumped against the castle walls, or strewn across the cobblestones like discarded marionettes, lifeless and limp, their strings cut, with no one left to play with them and bring them back to life. Their presence added further angst to his paranoid thoughts. Someone had stormed the castle, the walls and gates clearly breached. He was definitely too late.

A forgotten torch spluttered into life, spiralling acrid smoke to the ceiling above, its meagre illumination helping to steer the knight deeper into the castle's structure, down twisted stone passageways long committed to memory. Kerian's sense of rising panic helping to ignore the dark haired rats and other less identifiable creatures that lurked and skittered in the shadows about him.

Heavyset doors of the throne room marked his passage, gargantuan in structure, matching the sheer scale of the outside walls in making anyone entering feel small and insignificant. What remained hung forlornly from warped and buckled hinges; the smooth wood blasted with arcane fire, ragged holes still glowing from the fading residual magic that had destroyed them. The throne room was over fifty feet square; the floor littered with more corpses. Firelight danced across cool stone, where vibrant tapestries had transformed into black ash, cooling embers kissed dangling cobwebs and arcing streaks of wet scarlet painted how knights had met their end.

Kerian discarded his torch, placing it into a nearby sconce on the wall, easily retrieved if a fast getaway was required.

'If you even get that far...' his mind taunted.

The knight entered cautiously, the crackling of the fire serving to mask his footfalls as he moved to the right, slowly circumnavigating the room, the wall firmly at his back.

This was all so wrong! The vibrant life of the royal court was gone, wiped away in these images of brutal reality. Memories from a lifetime ago flickered through his mind. A sensual moment in a now defaced alcove; a furtive glance for the great table, where a stolen kiss and an erotic tryst had been taken passionately, breathlessly, with no thought that the exotic beauty writhing beneath him would be his ultimate downfall. Where was the table anyway? It should have been present, here in the centre of the room.

Across the floor, the raised dais and throne from which she had ruled was ablaze. In his imagination, it was still whole, his queen achingly magnificent, her face one of hatred and spite as he had crashed to his knees before her in chains, beaten and bloodied for his betrayal. It was there that she had bestowed her parting gift for his lack of devotion and sealed his fate with her dark sorcerous powers.

Cadavers lay all around, some missing limbs, others appearing to have met their ends in rows, plainly killed on their knees and left where they had fallen, all facing towards the pyre and where their queen once ruled.

Kerian flexed his hand as he took in the grisly scene, affirming the grip he had on his sword. This could have been his fate if he not taken the painful choices he had. His thoughts seethed murkily as he began to understand what had happened here. He would have fought just as bravely, never questioned, never doubted and willing to offer the extreme sacrifice of giving his life in her defence. He shamefully realised that despite all the horror and pain, she still meant that much to him in the darkest recesses of his mind.

The knight took a breath, determined to crush this alien emotion. His being here would have changed nothing. What use would another dead commander have been? He took in the faces of the men around him, comrades he had once shared fireside tales with and sparred on the practice fields. Now all they did was stare accusingly at him with lifeless eyes.

Yet one question remained. If they had all died here to protect his queen… where was her body? Why did her corpse not lie amongst them? This did not feel right.

Kerian slowly unsheathed his sword, a pale violet nimbus crackling up the awakened blade and dancing across the runes etched across its surface. He felt chill, the hairs on his arms rising, as if exposed to a static charge near a lightning storm. His sixth sense warned him there was unseen danger observing him from the shadows.

Choking back his feelings of insecurity Kerian tightened the grip on his sword, taking his time to scan the room, putting the fire behind him so he could take in the charred tapestries, shattered furniture and the painted frescos on the ceiling. His shadow appeared to dance about the ruins in manic glee as he slowly turned around.

Satisfied that no threat remained behind him, the knight walked around the dais, cautiously skirting the fire and it was only then, in the periphery of his vision that he saw her. Initially he refused to believe the grisly scene that his eyes beheld, blinking several times to clear his tear-blurred vision. He was determined to blame this on the wall of heat he approached, rather than the feelings he knew he still held for the woman before him, yet as clarity confirmed his deepest fears and realised the truth of what he beheld, a deeper anguish realised his hopes and dreams had crumbled into bitter ashes of despair.

His queen still sat upon her throne, holding empty court with her returned suitor of one. However, her throne now stood in the centre of the blazing pyre. Smoking eye sockets stared out from within a blackened skull of peeling skin and exposed ivory bone. Dribbles of molten gold traced down the sides of her grisly visage, where the remains of her crown melted upon her brow. Thick chains restrained her arms at her sides, glowing in the heat generated from the remains of the great table used to feed the blaze at her feet. Sentenced with fire for her sorcerous crimes, her throne became the makeshift stake on which she burnt.

Kerian felt his knees weaken at the sight and sank slowly to the floor. The rebellion against the queen had succeeded. Celebrations would be taking place across the land even as he spoke. Bells would ring from church steeples; people would cheer and cry as the throne at Catterick would now receive the new King in waiting. The tyranny and terror of his queen removed forever, swapped for a newer threat as advisors sought to bend the favourable ear of a child not yet able to choose the colour of his clothes, let alone rule a land. Nothing ever changed, life moved on.

However, not for Kerian Denaris...

He heard the drawn out scream long before he realised it was his own. The acrid air stilled as all of his frustration, terror and overwhelming despair finally gave voice. He bowed his head. This could not be happening, not now, not after he had tried so hard to return.

"Why?" he screamed his frustration. "I have your token... his hand reached for a worn leather pouch at his side. "I am here as you demanded... you have to free me from this damned curse!" Tears of frustration tracked down his face as his desperation aired. "You can't be dead... You just can't be."

The knight struggled to control his breathing, he felt like he was drowning, gasping for breath his lungs refusing to inflate and give him the oxygen he needed. His head started to spin, dots dancing across his eyes, even as his mind recognised the signs of panic for what they were. He needed to bottle up the emotions inside him, become a professional soldier once more, get a grip on himself and think. What was he going to do now? Her message had been clear. If he wanted to be free of his curse, he needed to return and present her with her token. The very thought of it at the time had been risible.

Why would he return to this cruel sorceress and her merciless army when he had just escaped from her dungeons and deserted? The decorated walls to the castle were clear as to the penalty for that! Yet as the curse had taken hold over the weeks following his escape and terror had risen at the reflection greeting him every morning, common sense had evaporated. It was clear she had let him escape; clear she wanted him to suffer for doubting her powers. She had wanted him to crawl back to her, begging, grovelling to be free... The logical part of his mind realised he would have faced a long lingering death at her hands if she had still been alive. Unfortunately, with this current situation he was facing the same outcome. It was just going to be a little quicker now.

A dull thud from behind snatched away any further feelings of self-pity, replacing the knight's musings with a sense of sudden danger. He rose quickly, turning sword in hand, a faint violet arc tracing the blade's path through the air as the runes upon its length blazed brighter.

Dark magic was loose in the room.

Narrowed eyes scanned the room, noticing the slight vibration from one of the ruined doors, the flakes of burning tapestry falling to the floor disturbed by something unseen passing. Then Kerian noticed a pooled area of shadow ripple as if it were liquid, before something darted across the wall, heading ever closer with gravity clearly not impeding its path.

A squealing sound like long fingernails scrapping down slate removed any possibility this was just imagination, causing Kerian to set his stance, turning to present his side towards the threat, minimising his exposed surface, his sword low before him.

"Who's there?" he demanded, in a voice sounding more confident than he felt inside. A teasing laugh echoed in answer as the shadow moved again, sliding into the darkness of the dais steps. Kerian's free hand reached towards a dagger sheathed at his other hip, intent on complementing his sword by adopting the dual weapon style he favoured but a loud hissing snap from the fire froze him in mid motion. He turned towards it, marking the edge of the dais with his peripheral vision as he tried to identify the cause of the sharp noise. The charred skull of his queen slowly, impossibly, swung up from her chest, regarding him with ghostly green lights flickering in her fire-cleansed sockets.

The knight gasped in horror, clasping his sword tighter as his terror sought to engulf him. How could she still be alive? No one could survive the heat of these flames, not even someone as powerful as his queen! His heart pounded, his mind screaming at him to run but all the knight could do was stare disbelieving, frozen in place like cornered prey beneath a predator's talons.

A cracking jerk freed one hand from the glowing chains, Kerian following the movement to observe several brittle pieces of bone crumbling to the floor. Her charred arm rose to point towards him, the movement hypnotic almost snake-like.

"You," the skull hissed, the word emphasised with a snapping jerk forwards of the cadaver it issued from. "We were told to look for you."

Kerian was not sure which was worse, the grinning skinless smile of the parody that jerked and crackled before him, or the spectral voice, clearly not that of his queen but something impossibly darker in nature, as forbidding as a long forgotten tomb.

"What has happened here?" Kerian almost stammered the question, his throat uncomfortably dry. "What manner of creature are you?" He took a cautious step backwards towards the edge of the dais.

Further snapping sounds issued as the burning corpse tried to get to its feet, straining against the chains until a brittle snap cut through the air, jerking the creature away from the throne as resistance finally yielded and causing Kerian to jump. The corpse took several unsteady crunching steps towards the knight, the back of the throne crashing to the floor, the glowing chain lying in smoking coils around blackened twig-like metatarsals.

"Where is the rest of the queen's army? The knight continued, edging to the left, the better to bring his sword to bear on the nightmarish figure. He felt the gorge rise in his throat as something wet and smoking slithered from his queen's abdomen to slop onto the marble floor, not knowing if his sword would be effective against this creature but prepared to raise a defence. "What has happened to my queen?"

"Don't take me as a fool Denaris!" The corpse drooled, something dark and congealing dribbling from its jaw. "Your queen stands before you... At least, the remains of her!" It gestured at the body it occupied.

"It seems her tyranny caught up with her at the end but don't worry, she planned ahead for you. She hated that you questioned her ways and turned traitor... that is why she cursed you and then permitted you to run away. Knowing full well that as the curse transpired and you started to age you would have to return begging for the spell to be lifted." The skeleton took another jerking step, fire-brittle joints snapping and popping at each macabre motion. Kerian backed away in revulsion at the travesty before him.

"What's the matter?" the creature taunted. "Don't you want her anymore?" It lifted its arms wide as if to accept the knight in a lover's embrace even as it threw back the head of the skull and issued another sinister laugh.

"Then my queen is truly dead." Kerian muttered to himself, the numbing realisation turning his hopes to dust and his fears to vivid reality.

"Yes. Such a shame," the creature shambled forwards again. "Especially as it means she can no longer lift her enchantment. You are doomed to die before your time... A young man trapped in an old man's body. How old are you now? Late forties? Time appears to be running out fast!"

Kerian stepped back to maintain his cautious distance, knowing in actuality that he had just turned thirty-two years of age, despite his weary and magically aged appearance. He also knew the monster was right; the curse had prematurely aged him to forty-six.

He nearly slipped as his boot came down on the edge of the raised dais making his footing unsteady. The knight checked himself from falling then lifted his head to find himself mere inches from the grinning caricature of his queen.

The stench of roasted flesh assailed his nostrils as the skull head swayed from side to side, the eerie green light in the sockets further emphasising the horror before him. The skull lunged forward, biting the air, causing Kerian to recoil or risk injury from the smoking incisors.

He slipped down to the floor below, bringing his sword up, attempting to stall the creature's advance.

"What in the name of mercy are you?"

"I am one of three," the creature hissed in reply. "I told you your queen planned ahead. You took too long to return and she was losing patience. We have been summoned to hunt you, hound you, make you return here and if that fails... kill you."

"My queen is dead." Kerian gestured, "I am already here. You can't hound me back into her arms."

The skull paused navigating the step down to look up into Kerian's eyes and hesitated, cocking the smoking head to one side as if considering something it had previously been unaware. Then slowly it began to laugh anew, making it perfectly clear the creature had already considered this and already knew the outcome, despite the pretence otherwise.

"Once we are summoned we always follow our instructions to the letter." It continued, "We cannot return to our home otherwise and must remain on this plane of existence until we fade." It stroked a smoke stained bony chin with a charcoal stick of finger.

"So if we cannot hunt, hound or drive you into her arms... there is only one thing left," hissed the cold detached response. The skull jerked forward and screamed, its eye sockets flaring brighter than before, as the nightmare Kerian beheld broke into a shambling lunge towards him. The knight reacted instinctively, military training trying to push down the feelings of horror he felt. He parried the monster's outstretched limbs and then dropped to one knee, swinging his blade in a sweeping arc of destruction. There was a rush of heat, an overpowering smell of burning flesh, then the corpse hit the blood smeared marble floor, its brittle bones shattering in contact with the unyielding surface.

Charred bone fragments skittered across the marble, falling to rest on either side of the knight as he completed his swing, slashing his sword down to protect his right flank as his left hand angled his dagger to protect his other side.

Kerian gasped, releasing a breath he had not even realised he was holding. What was that creature? He looked down at the ruined remains scattered around him and tried to suppress a shudder, nervously double-checking to ensure no physical signs of life remained in the long-dead bone fragments. His sword continued to blaze violet indicating the threat was not yet gone, despite the ruined corpse seeming to indicate otherwise.

Gathering his courage, Kerian returned to his feet, approaching the largest fragment of the corpse before gingerly prodding it with the tip of his sword. The charred skull appeared to mock his actions with its broken smile. The knight realised this blackened bone was all that remained of his past life. His queen had beaten him, her curse now unbreakable in her death. He had months to live rather than years. In a time where it was rare for people to live past forty the thought of aging so fast was terrifying. He brought his sword down on the skull with a snarl, disintegrating its last vestige of humanity into a thousand spinning shards of frustration and anger.

"I swear I will beat you, my queen," He spat at the shattered remains. "You may believe you have beaten me, doomed me to an early grave, but I won't accept this! I will find a remedy! I will find a way to beat you, even if I have to descend to the deepest levels of the underworld and tear the cure from your blackest of hearts!" He turned, striding grimly towards the throne room doors, determined to put as much space between himself and the appalling horrors of this castle before nightfall. There was nothing here for him now, he needed to find somewhere quiet to sit and think, to somehow formulate a new plan and maybe get a stiff drink.

A low hissing sound stopped him in mid-stride.

He turned towards the sound, watching in horror as a sickly green mist began to gather from the remains of the body on the floor. Wisps slid from exposed marrow and roasted flesh, others slipping from the ruined skull, gathering into a pale spectral shape that hovered clear of the floor below it. As the mist continued to collect, features became more apparent, curved horns sprouting from an oval head; long arms with emaciated skeletal fingers adorned with long piercing claws, wings sprouting from a twisted spine. However, it was the eyes that drew Kerian's complete attention, the same piercing eyes that had once gazed from his queen's dead skull.

"So, the hunt begins," the creature laughed. "Run little man, run!"

Part One: - Crossed Paths

"Always show courtesy when meeting fellow wayfarers upon the road. For you never know when your paths may cross again."

Old Traveller's Proverb

Chapter One

There is nothing more exasperating than a locked door when you want to go shopping. Luckily, for Ashe Wolfsdale, he rarely let such trivial obstacles get between him and a good bargain, especially when he did not intend to pay for it!

The Halfling examined the stubborn keyhole before him with a critical eye and quickly rose to the challenge, the final rusty tumbler just about to click into place when he heard horse's hooves clacking on the cobblestones behind him.

With a mere whisper of sound, the little figure dived behind a rotting water barrel and skilfully obscured himself within the shadowy recess it cast. From his damp hiding place he was able to scan the street and see the approaching rider more clearly; he also noticed that in his haste to avoid detection he had left his lock pick jutting prominently from the door and silently bit back a curse, grinding his teeth in frustration as the rider drew closer.

At the end of the road, a rundown tavern filtered shuttered light weakly across the way, illuminating an impressive ivory warhorse, possibly one of the biggest mounts Ashe had ever seen. Muscles rippled at each step and heavily shod metal shoes sparked as they struck the cobblestones. The horse came to a halt and its rider slid from the saddle. He stood beside the stallion, straightening his long black cloak, pulling the hood tighter around his face and tucking in strands of white hair before turning to examine the shadowed storefronts about him.

Ashe forgot his predicament as curiosity tugged at him. This was interesting: who was this mysterious traveller, riding about so late at night, clearly not wanting anyone to see his face? Did he not know that hiding in shadows was something only shady low-down individuals considered?

"Saybier!" the rider tugged at the reins to get his horse's wandering attention. "I need you to wait here and be ready for a fast get away. This place has the reputation for being rough, and things may turn hostile quite quickly." He stroked Saybier's snout and offered over an apple that the horse sniffed once before covering with its huge teeth and lips. A low crunching sound filled the air as the rider turned towards the entrance of the tavern, his cloak a swirl of shadows. Then he paused, as if in afterthought, turning once more to scan the darker shadows of the street. Ashe swore he could feel the intensity of the hooded gaze and struggled to squeeze himself further into his darkened corner.

"Oh, by the way," the rider motioned to his mount. "Keep your eyes on the little man hiding in the shadows by that doorway. If he tries to take anything from my saddlebags you have my permission to bite him." He turned with a chuckle and walked purposefully towards the tavern entrance, pausing to tease open the door and weigh the mood of the crowd before committing himself to action, pushing through the slatted bar doors and letting them swing shut behind him.

The diminutive thief and the warhorse eyed each other suspiciously with only an escaped cloud of bar smoke as company, its swirls eddying to nothing in the cool evening air. Ashe failed to understand how he had been spotted so easily. He stood and brushed himself down, thinking furiously. It had to be the lock pick! He cursed his carelessness, tugging his large floppy hat back into shape before reaching up to check his lucky yellow griffon feather (very rare, one of a kind and a real bargain!) remained secure at the brim. Happy appearances were satisfactory his thoughts returned to the unkind jab sent his way.

What did that man mean by calling him little? At just over four feet high and growing an average of one thumb thickness a year he was practically full-grown! He moved from the water barrel and turned to gaze at the lock and door handle level with his chin. Now, where was he? The shop lock beckoned but... should he now consider the saddlebags of this latest arrival?

He turned back towards the horse, calculating eyes flickering across the secured bundles, noticing several interesting bulges. It would not hurt to have a little look. Obviously, he would put everything not of value back in place after he finished exploring! The Halfling started to step across the road.

Sensing the movement, the stallion turned to regard Ashe's slight figure with a malevolent stare, its albino eyes daring him to approach. The thief paused in mid-step suddenly indecisive as a hoof sparked against the cobbles and a thoroughly ragged apple core covered in slobber flew through the air to land at his feet.

He swiftly reconsidered the situation, suddenly remembering the urgent appointment he had with a certain locked door. He should at least retrieve his lock pick, after all what self-respecting thief left a job half done? Besides the teeth in that mouth were big! Moreover, sharp... Definitely sharp! He tugged the front of his tunic, readjusted his belt and coughed to show he had a pressing engagement. Then he smiled, tipped his hat in apology and edged back into the shadows.

* * * * * *

The *Serving Wench* was a rough establishment, untidy, filled with smoke and a magnet for the undesirable element of town. Battered tables were scattered as haphazardly as the wine-soaked straw littering the floor. Occupants huddled together in secret conversations and cryptic conspiracies, swords and daggers openly displayed, close to hand for ease of use. The open fire spewed more fumes into the room than up the crumbling stone chimney, making the atmosphere thick, heavy and irritating to the eyes and throat. Tallow candles dotted unevenly around, cast just enough light to allow murky shadows room to stretch into far too many areas of the tavern for an honest man to feel comfortable. Although Kerian could have argued that from the looks of the customers, there were not many honest men frequenting the *Serving Wench* this night.

He stood just inside the entrance to the tavern, his senses calculating threats, watching for hands sliding towards blades, hats and cloaks being pulled up or tugged down to hide features or make it easier for patrons to check him out surreptitiously from under the brows of their ragged moth eaten hats. There was also an overpowering smell in the air, which made Kerian realise how glad he was he had already eaten. He feigned indifference towards the attention he was getting and turned his focus to the approach of a short, balding man, whose apron appeared covered with bloodstains and the slimy remains of bird excrement.

"A table and a drink, if you please," Kerian opened, stealing the opportunity for the patron to launch into monotone small talk.

Kerian flipped a silver crown towards the filthy steward. It glinted twice, catching the faint candlelight, before it was snatched mid-flight by the barman's grubby, calloused hand. Within seconds it was tucked away, its existence a fleeting memory for those who had glimpsed its short flight from across the room. The man grunted in response to payment and turned into the room, his sweaty girth weaving a meandering path between tables to a vacant one tucked away in a dark recess, far beyond the warmth of the fireplace.

The barman quickly used his stained apron to clear the table, only to smear something indescribable across the worn and chipped surface. Shrugging, he turned and gestured to the only chair before reaching into his pocket and pulling out a sorry looking stub of candle he lit and stuck unceremoniously in the table's centre.

"Your ale will be brought to you soon" he grinned, showing a set of badly decayed teeth before winking and heading off back across the room, leaving Kerian alone to consider how the barman had decided it was an ale he wanted?

The knight slowly took his seat, positioning his back to the wall so he could take in his surroundings. A further survey showed that a great many customers of the Serving Wench favoured the back-to-the-wall seating plan. He pushed his cloak back over his left shoulder exposing the studded leather armour below, allowing himself freedom to reach for his sword without being tangled. Then slowly, so as not to arouse any reaction from the people near him, he gently freed his blade from the scabbard by the slightest millimetre, ensuring it would not snag if he required its swift use. It was strange how his military training had become instinct, carried out in small ways like this, almost without thought.

The flickering candle flame caught his wandering attention; its hypnotic dance serving to draw him back to haunted memories of the past. The screams of prisoners set upon by his queen's magical creations; the pleading for pity from captured soldiers he ordered slain, no mercy given; seemingly endless bloodshed and the face of his queen burning on her thro... He closed his mind shuddering, gasping in a large breath and licking his suddenly parched lips. His hands were visibly shaking, his heart pounding in his chest. He could not allow himself to be like this... he had to be strong for what was to come. There was too much at stake.

"That's the past!" he uttered angrily, annoyed at how easily he had been distracted. He tried to focus on the bar, staring across the room with smoke stung eyes. The barman was talking to the barmaid gesturing in his direction and showing her the colour of coin Kerian had recently handed over.

The disgraced knight tried to smother a much-needed chuckle as a fake smile slid across her worn features and she vainly attempted to straighten her hair. She provocatively shrugged the dress from her shoulders before setting off across the room with a drink balanced on the tray in her hands, barely disguised greed glinting in her eyes.

He tried to hide his smile further by looking down at the table surface before him, but this only made him feel like a bashful altar boy. A small river of molten wax had tracked slowly across the uneven table, inching ever closer to the edge and the fall into oblivion that followed. Absentmindedly, he began to pick at the wax, lifting tiny slivers with his ragged fingernails.

A small cough made him look up. The serving maid was smiling at him, licking her rouged lips and doing her best to push her breasts as far into his eye-line as possible without actually letting them tumble from the front of her grease-stained dress. She deposited his mug of ale with a flutter of eyelashes and a further enhanced view of ample cleavage. Kerian leaned forward, moving out of the shadows and deliberately let his hood slide from his head. The false show of affection stopped in mid-flutter as the serving maid's emotion moved from financial lust to undisguised revulsion.

"In your dreams old man!" she hissed, turning in a swirl of skirt that almost extinguished the guttering candle. Kerian shared a cruel smile and a wink as she turned to look at him again from over her shoulder, knocking another patron's drink from his hands as she passed.

Kerian used the distraction to slide back into the shadows as voices rose in anger. He wanted to smile but deep inside there was a longing for days past, when time with a barmaid had been a welcome distraction. Now, with the queen's curse rapidly affecting his body, ideas of such dalliance's would indeed remain lost somewhere in his dreams; buried deeply in an airless tomb secured by chains of heavy rusted iron that made acting on them simply impossible.

Sighing despondently, he picked up the cracked tankard and ran his finger around the chipped rim. The liquid inside moved as he watched, revealing a small insect trapped on the surface. No matter how much it struggled to remove itself from its predicament, no matter how hard it tried to reach the edge of the tankard, it appeared to be doomed to failure. The parallel was not lost on his own predicament. It seemed whatever he tried to do, he was always finding that elusive glimmer of hope remained stubbornly just out of reach. He pushed the tankard away, suddenly no longer thirsty and settled back to wait for his target to arrive.

* * * * * *

There was a muffled click as the oak door swung inwards on well-oiled hinges, framing the small-silhouetted figure against the backdrop of the alley beyond. Stowing his lock pick securely alongside his yellow feather, Ashe slipped into the dark shop and gently shut the door behind him. There was another click as the latch fell home. Ashe nodded to himself before turning to examine the shop floor. He took security very seriously in his business; you could not be too careful these days. He was sure the owner would not want anyone walking in off the street on a whim.

Moonlight filtered sparsely through the barred windows, illuminating the contents of glass display cases set around the shop. Dust motes swirled through the air as the diminutive thief set about his nocturnal trade. Small-unguarded gasps of delight escaped him as he tiptoed past numerous gaudy baubles before finding himself focused on the main object of his endeavours.

A long triangular piece of crystal shone softly from within its case on the far wall, its cut surface splitting the pure moonlight into vivid hues of mauve and red that danced and swirled throughout its clear length. Granted the prism was nowhere near as valuable as other items in the shop, but it was unique and it stirred a distant memory in Ashe's mind that he simply could not deny.

The Halfling had asked how much it was and had been laughed at as the item was locked away, the shop keeper saying he should come back when he had the money to buy the crystal... so that was obviously an invitation to return and examine it at a later time without any outside interruptions. Unfortunately, the shopkeeper had not specified what time he had to return but Ashe was sure the man would be happy seeing a contented customer claim his prize.

He padded softly over to the shop counter; his mind completely focused on the crystal lying snugly on its bed of burgundy velvet. Grasping fingers stretched upwards towards the cabinet lock but even on tiptoes, the thief realised he was simply too short to reach his goal. This was so frustrating! He gritted his teeth, looking around to notice a rickety, wooden stool. Just the job for what he required! The thief cursed his luck at being so small before picking up the stool and waddling back across the floor. Why did everyone seem to make things so big and cumbersome? He finally clunked the stool down and wiped his brow, noting his goal was now several steps and a shop floor closer!

Careful not to make any untoward noise, the Halfling positioned the stool and within seconds was standing on tiptoe, nose to glass, like a child gazing in through a sweet shop window. His fingers itched where they pressed upon the glass surface, mere inches from his prize. It was time to get to work and rescue the prism from its glass prison. Ashe paused as the thought flashed through his mind and chuckled at the word play before returning his mind to the job at hand.

He reached up to his hatband and located a smaller pick than his previous selection, plucking it from the sash and adjusting his hat upwards so the brim would not interfere with his vision. Then, tongue sticking out of the side of his mouth in serious concentration, he tackled the lock before him.

The lock signalled its defeat several seconds later, with an audible click accompanied by a small 'ta-dah' from the Halfling thief. The front of the case swung down towards him with minimal resistance until it came up short, bumping into Ashe's forehead.

With an exasperated sigh, the thief moved to the side, squatting down on the stool and trying to squeeze his arm around the edge of the glass frame and into the case, but from his scrunched up position he could not get his arm around at the right angle to gain access.

Ashe gritted his teeth and leant out backwards, away from the stool, letting the glass door edge slowly down his nose as he did so. The stool squeaked alarmingly in protest at the shift of weight but the little thief was completely focused on the object of his desire. The front legs nearest the case slowly rose from the floor as the Halfling continued to increase the angle at which he teetered.

His arm stretched out above his head; his little fingers outspread to reach his glittering prize. It was almost within reach, all he had to do was lean back a little more! His arm angled painfully over the edge of the opening, fingertips brushing the prism but frustratingly unable to find purchase. He stretched even further. He was almost there! With one last mammoth effort, the edge of the glass door finally grazed past the tip of the thief's nose and onto his upper lip.

"At las..."

The stool finally gave up in its attempts to remain upright, shooting out from beneath the little man and ricocheting off the wall with a noise loud enough to wake the dead. Ashe tumbled to the floor with a resounding crash and winced at his clumsiness. It was not just the dead he risked waking, it was equally true of any light sleeping, perpetually nervous, security conscious shopkeeper!

"Oh, mouldy acorns!" Ashe cursed. Raised never to use bad words when cursing, the Halfling had found he could get a lot of angst and frustration out with 'mouldy acorns'! He saved words like 'sausages' for truly momentous occasions. He got to his feet dusting himself down and went to retrieve the stool. Several other strong multi-syllable words sprang to mind as one of the stool legs clattered from its housing. The stool was ruined! He looked up hopelessly at the cabinet, now open, but tantalisingly beyond his reach and bit his lip in frustration at his diminutive form.

Sometimes being small was simply not conducive to his field of work! Maybe he could consider getting stilts... but the problem was he did not have the time to learn how to use them and he needed to be tall right now! Life simply was not fair! How was he going to reach his prize now?

A low growl from behind froze him in mid-contemplation.

Ashe turned slowly towards the sound and came nose to tooth with a snarling set of very large fangs positioned menacingly below two luminescent yellow eyes, narrowed in clear, nocturnal, Halfling shopper hatred.

That was the way with life. Just when you think it cannot get any worse, someone forgets to tell you the shopkeeper has a large, hungry, guard dog!

* * * * * *

The cabin door flew open, bouncing off the wall with a thump, jarring the steady writing hand of the man within. His pen slid across the parchment page, creating an unwanted streak of ink across his immaculate text. Thomas Adams raised his head, his right eyebrow arched in annoyance.

"What can I do for you, Rauph?" he enquired, regarding the stooped eight-foot tall titan who loomed above him who was the sole cause of the interruption.

"Catterick lies off the starboard bow, captain," the chestnut haired creature snorted, as Thomas reached for the bag of blotting sand on the desk's surface. "You told me you wanted to know when we spotted the port."

"Finally," Thomas muttered; his distraction temporarily forgotten. "Progress along the coast and look for a sheltered cove or headland where we can drop anchor. We can send in a small team by dinghy as dusk falls, then follow them in later with no navigation lights or flags raised. We need to avoid anyone discovering we are here; it simply leads to too many questions." He paused as if considering the steps in his mind. "Let the Rinaldo Brothers, Lubok, Abeline and

Plano deal with checking for any harbour master becoming too interested and inform Scrave to ready himself for the row ashore."

Thomas waved his hand in dismissal, eager to return to his ledger and repair the rapidly spreading ink stain. A shuffling of an enormous frame drew the captain's attention to the fact the ship's navigator had not left, as was expected.

"Is something the matter Rauph?" he looked up at the longhaired crewmember and tried to show a relaxed and welcoming demeanour, even whilst, out of the corner of his eye, the ink continued to track across the page.

The hulking creature snorted in what appeared to be embarrassment, if one so large and formidable could possibly display such emotion.

"You... umm... well..."

"Just come out with it Rauph! I haven't got all day!" Thomas scowled with impatience.

"Well last time you promised... promised I could go ashore." Rauph mumbled.

"But this is hardly the time..." Thomas Adams paused in mid-retort, memories of earlier conversations confirming that he had indeed promised his crewman this privilege. He gazed up into two deep brown pleading eyes framed by a gleaming set of polished blackened horns.

The Minotaur's eyes began to water, and his head slumped as he turned to leave, giving Thomas the view of an immensely powerful muscled back and two double handed swords sheathed in well-worn scabbards. The captain swiftly considered his response.

The boat was going in under darkness; the items needed would be considerably heavy. It should be fine if the ship's navigator remained close to shore and did his foraging there, or waited in the boat until his other crewmate Scrave called to him.

"Rauph", he began, halting the creature's dejected departure. "You know I always keep my word... and you are a highly valued member of my crew." Thomas paused bracing himself for the order he was about to give. His mind stunned at the revelation his lips decided to utter. "So... yes of course you may go with Scrave. But you must stay with the dinghy and keep out of sight unless he needs you." Rauph's immense shaggy form began to quiver with barely controlled excitement, his head nodding in speechless comprehension, before the Minotaur headed for the door.

"There's no need to thank me," Thomas mumbled at his crewmember's back. "Just don't tell Scrave, let me do that. Remember... you stay in the boat... and don't slam the..."

The cabin door crashed shut, causing the picture hanging alongside it to tilt dramatically sideways. A lonely lantern burning innocently on a nearby shelf expired in a spiralling puff of exasperated smoke.

"...door!" Thomas Adams looked back at the logbook before him with a sigh and started liberally applying sand to mop up any residue from the spill. The page would need removing, which was frustrating but he always took pride in his work, it was something that would have to be done. His high standards demanded nothing less and the stain was a silent accusation of uncharacterised clumsiness.

Satisfied the sand had absorbed the moisture, he upended the book and poured the grains away, allowing the front cover emblazoned with the name *El Defensor* to catch his eye. She had been his ship for the last five years, and he was as proud of her now as he ever was. Nevertheless, it was a heavy role to preside over. The pressures of keeping the ship sound, whilst balancing the moods of the crew seemed never ending.

The weight of responsibility hung heavily over him. He had to try to be positive, tonight had to go well. If they did not have a successful foraging trip, it could find them marooned here for the near future and that was not going to happen under his command.

He meticulously cleaned his quill and replaced it in the tankard on the desk, before turning his attention to a pile of scrolls and charts, newly acquired from eager vendors during recent landfall. Thomas paused now and again to compare one chart with another, identifying coastlines that were similar in nature, seeking out ports with names that promised exotic adventure.

Star charts showed alien constellations to aid navigation wherever a ship might sail. Writhing sea serpents dotted edges of maps, along with names of cartographers whose sanity and ability to portray creative licence in their creations lay validity and accuracy open to serious questioning. They could have been making these exotic places up for all he knew! None of it made any sense!

Not a single crewmember recognised any of this. They were all totally lost and there was no one they could ask for directions. None of these charts gave the slightest hint of the destination he desired. This quest was becoming more hopeless with each passing day. It was becoming clear he was never going to find his way home.

Chapter Two

Ashe dodged to one side, throwing his small frame through the air as gleaming fangs snapped shut just where his face had been. He careered around the corner, sandaled feet slapping across the wooden floor, ricocheted off the wall and found himself looking back at the huge grey haired hound that pursued him, claws clacking loudly as it struggled to find purchase navigating the floor at speed.

He backpedalled as fast as possible coming up against a display case that clunked loudly as he connected but before the thief could look for an avenue of escape the guard dog jumped at him. There was only one thing Ashe could do. He raised his hands over his head and ducked, just as the animal head butted the display case above him and rebounded back, ending up on its rump, nose smarting and dignity all but lost.

The case tilted backwards at the force of the collision, all of the items inside sliding towards the lowest point of gravity, making it highly unstable, then the whole thing crashed down towards the floor. It came to rest at an angle, before exploding and filling the air with flashing diamonds of shattered glass and baubles.

Ashe's eyes shot open at the cacophony and he instantly saw his way out, climbing up the shattered frame to crawl precariously on his knees upon the glass top of the adjacent cases. The guard dog was now back on its feet, snarling and spitting in frustration; its yellow teeth bared in a wickedly salivating sneer as it realised the thief couldn't remain on the display case forever.

The Halfling tried to stand up, sandals squeaking as the glass began to splinter and crack at the concentrated weight in a smaller area. The dog continued to circle with hungry eyes, licking its lips with a long pink tongue as it anticipated the coming feast. In desperation, Ashe threw himself towards the next display case, twisting his agile body through the air in a valiant attempt to bridge the gap. Jaws snapped shut barely inches below his vulnerable behind. He fell short, just managing to grab the edge of the next case by the skin of his fingers.

The dog barely hesitated before jumping up at the dangling and defenceless Halfling, just as the case Ashe had leapt from collapsed in on itself from the strain of his passing. There was a deafening crash as more shards of glass and broken ornaments knifed through the air and skittered across the floorboards.

Ashe yelped at the crash, his fingers slipping at the shock, sending him tumbling for the floor. The guard dog jumped up as he fell, only to find the little thief falling past his clicking jaws and a glass case right in front of him. There was a dull clunk, as canine encountered glass, then a squeal as it slid down the side and landed heavily onto the astonished thief below. There was an explosive grunt of air, then sudden dazed silence, as the hound shook its head clear and looked around puzzled trying to locate the person it had been pursuing.

A little hand moved, catching the corner of the dog's eye, and it turned to regard the battered appendage sticking forlornly out from beneath its tail. Several muffled groans arose, as the dog regained its feet and circled in place. Then with a blur of ruffled fur, surprised yellow eyes and a great deal of flashing teeth the dog lunged at the newly located thief.

Ashe rolled out from underneath its snout; panic an effective analgesic to the splinters of glass slicing into his hands and knees. He tucked in; diving under the case he had been hanging from and out the other side into temporary freedom.

Loud creaking and cursing above signalled the shopkeeper was awake and the skittering of paws confirmed the dog was in hot pursuit as Ashe headed for the nearest window, shedding fragments of glass from his battered form as he ran. He grabbed the shutters in his tiny hands, throwing them open wide before groaning at the sight of parallel steel bars stretching the length of the window before him. There was no escape this way and the dog was between him and the door!

Panic grabbed him as his mind raced. This was not how he had wanted it to be. This was supposed to be an easy visit. A quick collection and then out again, not flying glass, growling dogs and mass pandemonium! He spun back into the room to see the hound bearing down on him at full stretch, taut muscles rippling in the moonlight, eyes cold and full of menace. Ashe had nowhere left to go and only one thing left to do!

He squeezed his eyes tightly shut and braced for impact!

* * * * * *

Kerian sat toying with his ring as he waited for his target to arrive. He spun it around his finger noticing absent-mindedly that it seemed to have become looser in the last few weeks. He had not noticed he was losing weight but now he thought about it, he had tightened his belt recently. It was probably due to the focus he had been putting on this job. He simply could not allow himself to fail, the outcome was too important, his bounty too vital for his survival.

He focused back on his ring, knowing that engraved inside the time worn, dulled and battle-scarred golden band was his claim to his noble heritage and an estate that was far removed from the dingy tavern in which he sat. He had not checked on his family for years and after the death of his brother at the battle of Verhan's Point, his life had taken a distinct turn for the worst, leaving thoughts of going home nothing but a foolish dream. The journey would cross many leagues and take more time than he was sure he had. Indeed, he did not even know if his family were still alive, or if they even cared if he was.

The ring was practically worthless to him. He would have thrown it away, but he knew that just like his current living nightmare, it would always come back to haunt him if he tried.

The only other jewellery Kerian owned hung beneath his tunic and close to his heart. The silver linked necklace had a locket with the thin sliver of an emerald gem inside. Rumour had it that the gem had been a piece of a holy relic for the goddess of Spring, bathed in a sacred child's tears of laughter, and sealed into the locket with the essence of a dryad's soul.

Kerian did not care much about the history of the piece; he had not even cared about the previous owner who had been foolish enough to not want to give the item up, despite Kerian offering to pay much more than it was worth at the time. He only cared that it was helping him stave off some of the more restrictive side effects of the curse laid upon him. The fact he had left the owner beaten and dying in the gutter for refusing his offer was not important. His need was greater, so he took it, just like the bounty for tonight. Morals and ethics were a nicety he could not concern himself with and certainly not a priority when viewing his current lifespan.

A loud lilting voice came from across the bar, and Kerian looked up to see that his informant's information was right. A tall pale man, with a shock of red hair and a face a mass of freckles, had just entered the bar. His confident swagger was of a youth who thought his father's money could solve all of his problems, whilst the hanging on louts, jostling and laughing behind him, would solve any of the more physical issues that may come up in his life.

Kerian slowly reached for his sword, his eyes taking in facts swiftly. The louts all matched descriptions given, obviously protecting their interest as long as the money and free drinks kept coming their way. The clothing worn by his target was flamboyant matching the latest fashions. It all seemed so out of place in a low-end dive such as this, but Kerian knew Ferdinand came here because he had a fondness for the gambling pits out back, betting heavily on the baited and starved caged animals, kept feral to ensure maximum entertainment when released to rip into their opponents.

Ferdinand gestured towards the barman, who instantly became more attentive; bottles of spiced alcohol appeared from beneath the bar, thirstily snatched up by the group almost as fast as the money thrown on the bar disappeared into the barman's grubby fist.

His colleagues shouldered other patrons away from the bar and took up their favourite spots, whilst the barmaid managed to make another button on her top 'magically' spring free to give a promising and hopeful eyeful.

Kerian hated this open display of arrogance; it was pathetic how others fawned over the dandy. He eased himself out from behind the table and began to make a slow, unthreatening approach towards the rowdy group at the bar, never taking his eyes from the man he was here to kill.

As Ferdinand reached out for his own bottle of liquor, the barmaid fluttered her eyelashes at him.

"Have you any new poetry to tell?" she asked. "Any tales of the struggle?"

"Of that you can be sure." The dandy beamed, knowing secretly that the biggest struggle he ever faced was deciding what outfit to wear on a given day. His cocky smile faded, as the look on the barmaid's face indicated there was a problem.

Ferdinand looked up to see a cloaked figure place a fine parchment letter on the bar surface alongside him. His eyes glanced down at the neat script on its surface and he froze, he saw the family crest on the paper and knew it instantly.

"What's the meaning of that? And who are you?" Ferdinand's face betrayed the emotions running through his mind, initial bafflement, turning to fearful outrage as he realised his past indiscretions were coming back to him.

"Can't you see..." his voice wobbled slightly, as he tried to bluff his way out, "I don't sign autographs... Moreover, my colleagues and I wish to be undisturbed. Do not insult us with such triviality." He swallowed dryly, hoping the implied threat of his associates would cause the cloaked figure to back off slightly.

"I was informed you read poetry..." Kerian retorted in a calm but intense voice. "Surely if you can read flowery prose you can understand this?" He watched his mark closely; the man had beads of sweat forming along his brow. It was clear he knew exactly what this was all about and just did not want to lose face by admitting it. Kerian decided he would help Ferdinand break the story to the people around him, the audience growing as people sensed some additional entertainment was on the bill in the *Serving Wench* tonight.

"The letter you have before you is a contract requesting compensation to the Brewers family whose crest is shown at the top of this sheet. Apparently you, Ferdinand Kepstin promised to wed their daughter, you wooed her, told her poetry and made up tales of daring deed, then stripped her of her honour and innocence and left her with child. Apparently, she has had no choice but to move away to a place of healing in the countryside quite beside herself and the child placed under the care of the church. The family demand one thousand gold crowns for her suffering and the shame brought upon the family, or your head. It makes no difference to me one way or the other.

Kerian smiled as if to rob his words of their implicitly threatening message, even as Ferdinand tried to study his partially hidden face. A lined brow, deep creases indicating a life hard lived, cold hazel flecked eyes and a thin bitter mouth drawn into an insincere expression of understanding. Long grey hair completed the image, pulled back and tied at the nape of Kerian's neck.

A trickle of sweat tracked down the side of Ferdinand's face. His companions sensed something was amiss and began to back away from the bar, slipping into the crowd like rats deserting a sinking ship. The dandy looked back down at the script, licking his lips nervously.

"But..." Ferdinand began, "I don't have this kind of money."

"That's fine by me," Kerian responded coldly. "It makes things all the easier. Believe me when I say it really is nothing personal. You are simply a means to an end."

Ferdinand's eyes flickered from fearful to confident in a split second. The touch of cold steel against Kerian's back announcing the arrival of one of the fop's colleagues, evidently not as keen to desert as first thought and clearly eager to earn his status and gratitude in the group by acting first.

For a moment, it was as if all in the *Serving Wench* held their breath waiting for the old man before them to face a certain grisly demise. The heady anticipation of the final thrust hung unspoken in the silence; one bleeding body littering the straw-strewn floor of a tavern that had seen many such encounters over the years. Yet, in that frozen instant, one figure moved, far more swiftly and with far greater agility than most of the spectators would have given him credit for being able to achieve.

The cold tip of a razor sharp dagger put paid to the henchman's enthusiasm, sliding between the folds of his bulbous neck, to stop just short of breaking the skin. Kerian smirked as he sensed Ferdinand's supporter swallowing hard. It must have appeared that Kerian had some sort of sixth sense, as he had not even turned to be sure of the dagger's placement.

The reflective surface of the polished bottle on the bar appeared to wink in the candlelight, sharing Kerian's secret with no other in the room. He watched the henchman's reflection shifting uncomfortably and allowed himself a confident smirk. This was how reputations were made.

"I wouldn't do that if I were you." Kerian said gently, raising the dagger blade slightly and making the thug go up on tiptoes. "Unless of course..." he paused for dramatic effect, "You'd care to dance?"

The crowd of onlookers suddenly parted, shattering Kerian's premature surge in confidence as two of Ferdinand's lackeys decided to join the proceedings, advancing with swords drawn.

"How many more daggers do you have under that cloak?" one mocked, stepping closer. The whisper of cloth was barely audible as a response, yet the protruding hilt that suddenly appeared in the ruffian's chest seemed answer enough.

"Oh... I have enough." came Kerian's acidic reply, as the man slumped silently to the floor.

Kerian's eyes darted swiftly about the room. Although he still appeared calm to those around him, he knew that if he showed weakness, this crowd would rip him apart like a pack of baying hounds. The situation needed to be resolved swiftly, with a confidence he was starting to believe he did not have.

Ferdinand's reaction to the unfolding drama was one of disbelieving desperation, which was exactly why it caught Kerian completely by surprise.

The dandy's hand swung up from the bar, the bottle of drink that was once Kerian's ally now turned into a makeshift weapon against him. It exploded across the side of the knight's face, temporarily stunning him and making him shut his eyes from the sharp sting of the alcohol and the scratching splinters of glass. A flurry of punches followed, dropping Kerian to his knees as his arms sought to fend off blows he could not see coming but could definitely feel landing. His dagger fell from his hand and slid across the floor.

Red and flushed from his unbelievable luck Ferdinand regarded the slight figure on the floor before him. It was strange how a few seconds could change the perspective of a situation for the better. His would be assailant without his confident swagger looked at least sixty years old. Errant strands of loose grey hair had come free from a dishevelled ponytail, contrasting starkly with the dark lines of blood oozing down his face from where the bottle had connected and indicating the mortality of a would-be killer who was suddenly revealed to be nothing more than an old man, who had apparently forgotten his age.

It gave Ferdinand pause for thought. If this old man had managed to beat him, he would have been the laughing stock of the town. His reputation would have been in tatters, his benefits as a lady's man would have been a thing of the past. His demeanour turned from one of elation at having the tables turned to one of a darker anger. He needed to make this old man pay for his gall, needed to make this an example to others, ensuring no one else had stupid ideas above their station in the future.

Kerian shook his head in an attempt to clear his blurred vision, his hand stretching out for the dropped dagger only to stop inches from the blade as a mud-stained boot pinned his fingers to the floor. Ferdinand was laughing at him now, mocking his situation as his confidence began to flood back. Kerian allowed his head to fall forwards in seeming defeat; with his dagger out of reach and his sword still sheathed he appeared disarmed and helpless.

He scanned the floor around him, eyes still downcast, allowing his peripheral vision to fill in the picture as the mockery rained down from all sides. The boot on his hand released him when its owner realised he had given up on his attempt to retrieve his dagger, so Kerian did what was expected, pulling his hand towards himself as he started to inch away backwards.

The body he had dispatched earlier lay where it had fallen and Kerian winced as his hand encountered the slick of blood pooling beside it. The onlookers laughed louder as he feigned slipping in the mess but as they laughed fresh hope flared in Kerian's heart, his seeking hand landing on the centre of the corpse's still warm chest and closing around possible salvation.

"Now kind sir," mocked Ferdinand, his control and confidence rising higher as he relished being the centre of attention. "Firstly you will do me the courtesy of telling me your name." He slid a jewelled rapier from the scabbard at his side, flourishing the blade to his audience. "And then we shall see whose head is... How did you put it? Oh yes..." He smiled a thin-lipped sadistic smirk. "...Whose head is taken tonight?"

* * * * * *

"Fang! Stop that infernal racket!" The voice paused while its owner surveyed the chaos of the shattered display cabinets now littering the shop floor. "...What in all the Seven Hells is going on down here?"

The guard dog skidded to a halt at the sound of its master's voice, stopping so close to Ashe's face the thief could feel the hot, fetid breath assaulting his skin and nostrils. Its head snapped around to face the night gowned figure standing silhouetted at the top of the stairs, lantern in one hand, wicked looking cudgel in the other.

Ashe dared to crack open half an eye and peered through his fingers at the temporarily halted nemesis that panted in front of him. Far too closely in front of him! In fact, in a real invasion of personal space! As he realised that the disgusting yellow fangs were not actually going to sink themselves into his flesh in the next moment or two the Halfling instinctively took advantage of the situation. He bolted past the dog and dashed quickly around one of the few remaining glass cases that remained intact, heading back to the reason for his nocturnal shopping trip.

There was no point in being quiet anymore so he purposefully shoulder barged the case with the prism inside causing the entire thing to crash to the floor, resulting in a yelp from the dog and a shout of dismay from the shopkeeper. Ashe scooped his prize from its velvet padding and then fled up the stairs directly towards its stunned owner. Cudgel or no cudgel, it was an infinitely better prospect than the dog's teeth. The Halfling's yellow feather bobbed along through the air behind him as if it was some deranged game bird flushed from the brush, pursued ever intently by the closing clatter of dog claws.

"You!" the shopkeeper exclaimed, clearly recognising Ashe as the troublesome customer he had removed from the shop earlier that day. "What are you doing ...?"

"No time!" Ashe interrupted breathlessly, shoving at the startled man, before the shopkeeper had time to raise his cudgel, slipping past him through the doorway at the top of the stairs and into a sparsely furnished bedroom beyond. Ashe tried to bolt the door, closing it on the shopkeeper and hearing an angry thump against its surface followed by frantic scratching at the base of the door.

The shopkeeper barged the door, pushing Ashe further back into the room as the door opened slightly wider. Furious grunts and frustrated snarls showed that neither the guard dog nor the shopkeeper intended to lose interest in the pursuit. Ashe's sandals started to slide across the floor as the pressure on the door increased, his little size slowly losing its battle to contain his foes. The diminutive thief risked a quick glance over his shoulder and came face to face with a similarly attired female version of the enraged shopkeeper. However, this version came armed with a chamber pot that sloshed menacingly as she advanced.

The door slammed into the Halfling and this time Ashe simply had to let go or risk losing his balance entirely. He stepped to the side much like a bullfighter in an arena, minus the red cape: shopkeeper, guard dog and wife coming together in a comic collision. Unspeakable fluids cascaded on the scrabbling heap and an acrid odour filled the air.

Ashe did not wait to see the outcome, nimbly dodging a flailing wild swing of a cudgel and heading for the bed, hopping up onto it.

"I suppose late opening hours won't continue next week?" he quipped, ducking as the now empty chamber pot flew past to clang off the wall. "Be assured, I shall give your establishment a suitable review." Ashe smiled politely, tipping his hat, a gesture he felt the situation clearly merited, before turning to the window, throwing open the shutters and leaping out into the night beyond.

The shopkeeper arrived at the opening and stared out over the two-storey drop to the cobbles below. Of the thief, there was no sign. A sliver of tile fell from above; attracting his attention as it nearly sliced off his rather expansive nose, betraying the escape route of the departing figure. He flung his cudgel in one last furiously futile gesture, its gnarled wooden length whistling through the air barely inches below the scrabbling Halfling's feet, before the little thief disappeared into the shadows that bred thickly amongst the eaves, gutters and chimneystacks inhabiting the rooftops above the town.

If the trader had known the future into which the diminutive thief was heading, he would have had some sense of consolation instead of the irate rage he felt at having his merchandise stolen. Instead, he cursed pointlessly and loudly, kicked his bedroom door, then barked at the guard dog for being useless before hobbling downstairs to see what the intruder had stolen.

* * * * * *

Ferdinand circled his blade inches from Kerian's exposed throat, effectively pinning the old man in his prone position up against the corpse on the floor. He continued to play to the crowd, his restored confidence becoming a magnet for the attention of the customers around him.

"Now, as I requested earlier, old man, your name, if you please." A cruelly satisfied smile slid across Ferdinand's features as he displayed his superiority.

This old man could take mere seconds to dispatch but Ferdinand preferred to make certain that the story of the kill would last that much longer, hopefully guaranteeing more flamboyant heroism on his part with each glorious retelling.

An icy gaze looked up at him, meeting his stare with no signs of visible fear and then the man did the last thing the flamboyant thug expected. He simply smiled. Ferdinand hesitated unsure as to what his foe meant by such an action, his hesitation his undoing.

His downed foe quickly raised a blood soaked hand from the mess of the ruined corpse he leant against, showering droplets of crimson gore across the straw strewn floorboards and splattering the front of Ferdinand's tunic as a glittering bloody blur flew the short distance between them and sliced into Ferdinand's left hand. The youth half spun with the force of the unexpected attack, his palm slamming wetly up against the side of the bar. White-hot pain lancing up his arm as his scream froze every customer in the crowded room.

Ferdinand dropped his sword in shock, the blade clattering loudly to the floor as he reached across instinctively to guard his injury. Excruciating agony dropped him to his knees, but his injured hand remained pinned to the bar, spasmodically flexing in reaction to being pierced clean through by an already bloodied dagger.

The elderly man was on his feet in an instant, hooking a boot under Ferdinand's discarded blade, flipping it up into the air and into his own grasp. The nearest thug lost his left hand on the first swing and his sight with the second, dropping to his knees and screaming out in terror at the deadly kiss bestowed by the whistling blade.

"This sword is nicely balanced." Kerian stated calmly, whipping the sword around in his hand to perform practice parries before turning to face the rapidly retreating crowd. Of the two remaining 'bodyguards' there was no sign; just the creak of the bar doors swinging shut at their passing into the night.

Kerian took advantage of the momentary lapse in danger to take a deep breath, betraying to those paying attention that he was anything but calm. He fought an internal battle to prevent a tell-tale shake from running the length of the steel he held out before him. This was insane! He had been too cocky! Things had gotten out of hand too quickly. Why was he doing this?

Because if he did not he would be dead soon! That was why! His mind left no room for self-pity. He needed to end this quickly and withdraw to the anonymity of the city streets and out of the watchful eye of those around him. If he took much longer, someone was bound to call the city watch and he was in no position to deal with awkward questions at this time. He needed to make his move. Kerian cleared his throat loudly and watched as Ferdinand's attention turned from the pain in his impaled hand to the unresolved threat still standing behind him.

The dandy squealed as he realised the old man was approaching him. How could this have happened? His seemingly vanquished opponent from moments ago was now bearing down on him. He winced expecting a blow to land but instead Kerian calmly smeared the blood from the side of his mouth and returned to the bar, grabbed one of the forgotten bottles from the bar top and downed a good swig of stinging liquor before looking down at Ferdinand and bringing his full glare to bear on him.

Ferdinand whimpered again, only to have the sound strangled off into a choked gurgle, his throat grabbed forcefully. The old man leaned in close and winked into Ferdinand's widely frightened eyes.

"Shall I play to the crowd now?" Kerian whispered, whipping the sword around in his free hand.

"How can you move so fast?" Ferdinand gulped. "You... you are so old"

"They say appearances can be deceiving," the knight whispered back. "You know this really is a nice sword."

With an ice-cold calmness Kerian tapped the sword blade on the hilt of the dagger that pinned his prey to the woodwork, vibrating the weapon and smiling in satisfaction as Ferdinand almost swooned with the new agony that resulted. Then, without missing a beat, he grabbed the dagger and yanked it firmly, freeing Ferdinand's hand with a spurt of crimson and a fresh scream. The grate of steel on bone was clearly audible to the hushed assembly and suddenly the customers seemed to find that looking anywhere but at the bar was an ideal solution to living a long life.

"You asked for my name," Kerian continued, his voice calm and almost soothing in nature. "Those in the know call me Styx."

Whispers rippled through the crowd like a still pond disturbed by a dropped pebble. Styx was a name that inspired fear and respect in equal measures, even in this backwater seaport town.

"Please!" Ferdinand begged his eyes wide with pain and suffering. "How much are you being paid? Allow me to pay you the contract price. I'll even double it. Just let me go."

"I'm a bounty hunter, not a mercenary," came Kerian's acidic reply. "And, from what you've already told me, you couldn't afford my services." He looked down at this pitiful man before him and tried to put the doubts that were forming far from his mind. Tried to justify that this flamboyant thug had been going to kill him scarce moments before without any of the compassion he now found himself considering.

He looked at his own prematurely aged hand holding the ornate sword before him and gritted his teeth. He had set his feet on this path months ago. He did not have time to reconsider his actions and could not go back in time to erase the mistakes he had made. This came down to his own life or death and he did not intend to give anyone the satisfaction of his own demise just yet.

"Then . . . take what I have ... all of it ... and kill the contractor. Please ..." Ferdinand pleaded.

"I'm sorry..." Kerian muttered, not entirely sure if he was saying sorry to the man kneeling before him or apologising to his own conflicting inner morals. The sword swung in a glittering arc and Ferdinand's head parted from his torso to thud wetly to the bar floor below.

Kerian cleaned his dagger on Ferdinand's cloak before re-sheathing the blade with a well-practised flourish and then collected his grisly trophy from the floor. He secured the blood-matted skull in a sack from his pouch and collected the contract he had left on the bar before walking across the barroom and out of the swinging doors.

Ferdinand's head was what his client had asked for; so that was what Styx would deliver!

"Who's going to pay for the drinks?" the barman whined to the suddenly unsympathetic crowd.

Chapter Three

"These tiles are more slippery than they look," Ashe thought to himself, teetering at the precipice of a sagging rooftop. Loose tiles wobbled and cracked beneath his sandals as he gingerly tottered his way to the nearest chimneystack. Wrapping his arms tightly around its warm, soot-stained exterior he finally released the breath he had been sub-consciously holding in, emitting a long and thankful sigh.

The city of Catterick appeared almost magical from this vantage point; the minarets of the Crystalline Palace seeming to rise like spears and pierce the dark velvet sky overlaid with scattering diamond stars that loomed far above the dirty tumbledown skyline of crumbling chimney pots and sagging buttresses. The breath-taking visage captivated Ashe's innocent gaze, making him forget, for the briefest moment, the poverty and depravation that lay just under the surface of the fairy tale image displayed before him.

For Ashe, the view accompanied a feeling of lightness and a lifting of his spirit, as he imagined all the treasures just waiting within the mighty structures before him, each one eager for his appreciative nocturnal attention. There were rumours the throne itself was solid gold and encrusted with hundreds of precious gems, a lifetime of luxury all for the taking, fashioned into a single item of neglected furniture. Okay, so as small as he was he couldn't hope to lift such an item but maybe some of the gems could be loose in their settings, maybe with the right attention he would become rich overnight. Ashe laughed at the thought realising all too well this was nothing more than idle fantasy.

He closed his eyes to dream once more and then shuddered as he remembered, all too vividly, the public execution of the last king to sit upon that throne; the evil sorceress Isobelle had blasted him into a slushy mess during the city's recent bloody occupation, warning all onlookers of the dangers of having ideas above their station.

Even though troops had now reclaimed the city, with current rumour telling of Isobelle's own grisly fate, the throne remained empty of all but a thick layer of dust. Some believed that Isobelle had laid a curse upon its cold gleaming surface, resulting in rumours of having a replacement throne commissioned rather than risk the wrath of a sorceress from beyond the grave. Ashe suddenly felt cold despite the warmth emanating from his silent cosy companion; he hugged the chimney tighter, pressing his cheek to the pitted terracotta and felt his skin tingle at the comforting heat it gave off.

The boy, king now in all but ceremony, had certainly put a stop to Isobelle's plans of domination, gathering armies of volunteers from seemingly defeated and downtrodden areas, bringing peasant farmers and retired knights flocking to his tattered banner. It seemed terror only held the masses in check for so long!

Caerlyon Vale and the surrounding lands fell swiftly in a campaign not won by superior numbers but by the sheer faith the people held in the boy riding valiantly among them. A birthmark... that was all it had taken, that and a legend no one wanted to believe in, or at least hope to believe in without fearing a knock on the door and a time in Isobelle's dungeons with her interrogator.

The coronation was set to be held a week from today in what was sure to be a major display of revelry, reverence and laughter. A new order was about to rise from the ashes of a once proud land; a land whose occupants hoped was destined to be proud once again.

"I wish I could do something heroic," Ashe muttered. "No one would ever make fun of my height then!"

Shouting rose from the street below, shattering his solemn self-pitying thoughts. Reluctant to let go of the warm chimney, the Halfling finally succumbed to his curiosity as the shouting rose in volume. He slid down the tiles to the creaking guttering below, before manoeuvring himself, silently as a mouse, to peek over the eroding edge into the shadow-shrouded street below.

A cloaked figure holding a sack stood outside the inn, turning his head from side to side as if searching for a missing companion. Ashe recognised the profile in a flash as the mysterious rider he had encountered earlier. Whatever was he doing? Ashe leaned over more for a better look. That was it! The horse was missing. That would serve the arrogant man right for his earlier obnoxious behaviour! Ashe allowed himself a small chuckle at the thought.

As he watched from his high viewpoint, the thief became aware of further movement. Something shifted in the shadows at the end of the street but instead of the missing horse revealing itself, four heavily armed fighters stepped into the light.

"Going somewhere?" questioned one of the ruffians.

"Apparently not," came the stranger's cool reply, as another four figures emerged at the opposite end of the street. Eight fighters against one! Ashe shifted his position on the tiles for a better look. This could be exciting!

A brittle snap came from the tile beneath him, freezing the diminutive thief to the spot. There was another explosive crack, followed by another and then the tiles beneath Ashe simply crumbled away. The Halfling scrambled for a handhold only to find his flailing hand grasping a moss covered slate and himself facing a fantastic view of the cobbled street rushing up to meet him.

* * * * * *

Kerian turned first one way and then the other, regarding the thugs that were confidently approaching him, two of them instantly recognisable as Ferdinand's armed cronies from the bar. From the look of their companions,

Kerian judged that Ferdinand's wealth was being spread slightly further than normal this night; they were mercenaries if ever he saw them and from the swagger of one, inebriated swords for hire at that. How ironic that these reinforcements were somewhat belated in arriving.

"Your patron is dead," Kerian snarled in warning, working the numbers and not liking the odds. Where was his damned horse! Saybier was always wandering off when needed the most!

"Then you'll soon be joining him," retorted one alcohol-induced member of the approaching gang, struggling to slide his sword from his scabbard as he advanced.

Kerian reached for his own blade, and then paused as several slivers of moss-covered tile showered down at his feet.

"What the ...?" He looked up, fearing a crossbowman of some sort on the rooftop above even now drawing a more accurate aim and instead came face to face with a free-falling Halfling.

The connecting crunch echoed throughout the street, reverberating back from the closely constructed shop fronts before dwindling away to leave a stunned silence in its place. Kerian went down heavily and stayed there, unmoving, whilst Ashe rolled with the fall, ending up in an undignified heap against the far wall, with his hat all askew and his yellow feather tickling his nose.

The Halfling shook his head, trying to clear his double vision whilst attempting to comprehend where the soft landing had come from. Nimble hands swiftly checked that everything was attached and functioning, whilst shapes came fuzzily into focus around him. He quickly noticed the cloaked stranger lying face down in the centre of the street, his form strangely still with one arm jutting from his side at a bizarre and twisted angle. Then he noticed the other eight figures who had stopped to stare and were even now starting to laugh at the situation before them.

Ashe crawled over to the prone stranger, gently shaking him and then nudging him slightly harder when he gained no visible response. Over Ashe's shoulder, he could hear the thugs deciding if they should let their target recover or simply jump in and keep him down.

"Are you okay?" Ashe asked meekly, concern apparent in his voice, before it became more urgent at the sound of approaching footsteps. He snapped out of his compassionate role with the swift realisation that he had fallen into a potentially deadly situation and shook the unconscious man with increasing urgency. The old man opened his eyes after another more determined shake.

"You," Kerian groaned, in recognition.

"No time," Ashe shouted, shaking the knight harder whilst observing the approaching thugs with ever widening eyes.

"By the love of Adden!" Kerian exclaimed, as everything came rushing back to him. He staggered unsteadily to his feet and almost fell again as a viciously sharp pain raced up his left arm. Horrified, Kerian looked down at the offending limb hanging lifeless at his side, blood slowly dripping from his pale hand to the cobbles below.

Ashe grabbed a loose cobble from the street and turned to throw it towards the closest thug but it fell short with a clatter, skipping across the stones. The man went to jump it and tripped drunkenly, falling to the floor as he tried to avoid it and smacking his head with a crack and a groan.

His companions paused at this unexpected turn; their alcohol fogged minds suddenly aware one of their number had already gone down. It had happened so fast that they were not sure if some sleight of hand or other trickery had befallen them.

Kerian struggled to free his sword from its scabbard, turning determinedly towards the closest members of the mob, guarding his injured limb behind him. As the blade's naked steel slowly slid from its housing, deeply etched runes upon its surface began to emanate a pale violet corona that cleaved the shadows like a scythe and illuminated his pain-etched features as he assumed a defensive stance. His face grimaced anew as fresh pain lanced up his injured arm and the pins and needles sensation of impaired circulation began to dance through his fingers. His arm was broken; all the symptoms were savagely evident. Therefore, the coming fight was not going to be an easy one.

A tugging of his cloak reminded the knight of the Halfling at his side.

"Do you know how to use a dagger?" Kerian enquired swiftly, clutching at straws.

"Of course!" came the small figure's response, as he drew a three-inch blade from his belt.

"I don't mean a toothpick!" came Kerian's acidic reply as he lunged at one thug who had drawn too close for comfort. "Use the one at my belt."

"Really?" Ashe gasped, leaping at the opportunity to draw the weapon sheathed there. "Does this one glow too?" He grasped the hilt of the twelve-inch blade firmly in his hand and chuckled at the absurdity of it all. This was almost a short sword to someone his size! Moreover, *what* a short sword! Intertwining black and gold wire ran from pommel to hilt, where a huge ruby was set deep. Both ends of the cross guard were painstakingly carved into the roaring mouths of dragons, their eyes beset with tiny emerald gemstones. The blade itself was blackened steel, with edges silver sharp in contrast to the rest of the blade.

"Let them get close," the old man advised, warily circling his blade in the direction of the nearest threat. "Don't overextend your thrust or you risk losing the dagger and your life. You are expendable, my dagger is not. It would serve you well to remember that."

Ashe nodded in response to the pause in conversation, not having heard a single word the man had said. Instead, he looked lovingly at the weapon before him and then at the advancing men, desperately trying to look mean and threatening. When he had wished for the chance to do something heroic, he had not considered that the opportunity might arrive so quickly! Did heroes feel this terrified before a battle? His insides were doing cartwheels and a feeling of nausea rose like a tide in his throat.

The Halfling considered the possibility that he might begin his heroic career by throwing up in public! Only momentarily though, because then action exploded at him from all sides, shattering the thief's thoughts in a heartbeat as the little man found himself far more concerned with fighting for his life!

Kerian parried and returned a vicious thrust, slashing through the nearest man's guard and plunging his sword deep into the fighter's chest. Behind him the Halfling's blade parried attack after attack, with far more luck than judgement, as Ashe struggled to come to terms with the weapon in his hand. If the knight had been able to see his smaller comrade's face, he would have seen an expression of sheer terror, punctuated by repeated wincing each time Ashe's blade parried an opponent.

The deafening sound of clashing steel rang in Ashe's ears at each strike and his hands throbbed painfully from the vibrations wrought by each collision of the blades. This was intense. He would probably have enjoyed the spectacle if he had not been the one stuck in the middle of it!

Oblivious to his companion's discomfort, Kerian continued to press the attack, whirling violet streaks flashing through the air at each lightning fast parry, thrust and feint he made with his sword.

The thugs continued to circle, their first attack over as they paused to reconsider and re-examine the possible weaknesses of the two seemingly unlikely allies before them. Loud groaning arose from one of their number who lay on the ground, desperately trying to stop his life from literally running away through his hands. Their next attack was faster and more furious. Three men stepping up and attacking simultaneously.

Ashe moved out to meet one of the attackers, diving under a lunge and slicing a deep gash across the man's unguarded stomach before stepping back into the protective shadow of the fighter beside him. He desperately tried to ignore the haunting imagery before him as his target fought to stem the sudden rushing snake of greyish white innards from spilling out onto the cobbles at his feet.

Kerian was weakening fast. Sweat dripped into his eyes making him blink repeatedly to clear his blurred vision. Each parry was slower than the last, excruciating agony following, as the force of the blows sent cascading tremors along the blade, through his weakened body and down his broken limb. Blood continued to trickle down his hand, turning his sleeve into a sodden piece of material that slapped wetly against his body at every movement and something was grating within his arm. His parries slowed further as, with grim realisation, Kerian acknowledged the precariousness of his predicament. If something did not happen soon, he was going to lose.

Ashe moved around Kerian's legs darting from one side to the other before moving forwards to assist and catching one thug across his sword hand as the thug lunged at Kerian. There was a curse as the hand swiftly withdrew but Ashe wasn't aware, instead he suddenly dropped to his knees and slipped between Kerian's legs, throwing his colleague's cloak upwards to precede his passage and startling a thug who was about to plunge his blade into Kerian's unguarded flank.

The Halfling's dagger swept up, parrying the attack with inches to spare. The force of the clashing blades pushing Ashe back down to his knees as the crossed blades inched towards his diminutive frame, only for the pressure to be suddenly withdrawn as a violet blur whipped over Ashe's head and forced the assailant to retreat or risk losing his head.

Kerian lashed out angrily, this time catching his foe's exposed throat and etching a permanently ghoulish smile there, before whipping his blade around in a waltz of glittering destruction. Below his swing, the Halfling thrust outwards to spear one fighter through the knee, removing yet another participant from the uneven contest.

"That's three for me," Ashe counted aloud.

"Make that . . . three all," Kerian replied breathlessly, sending a head spinning away from a thug's torso with a deadly swipe of his blade. Kerian's breathing was laboured and he was sure the remaining fighters were aware of how badly he was faring. It was just a matter of how good they were: and whether they could worry him down as a team.

The thugs suddenly paused, visibly shaken by how fast their favourable odds had reduced to even ones. The coppery tang of spilt blood hung heavily in the air, almost suffocating in its intensity and the uneven cobblestones were slick with clotting liquid, making footing precariously unsteady and dangerously unpredictable.

They looked at the blood-streaked fighter before then, then at the violet humming sword he held in his hand and finally down at the grisly corpses at their feet. Then as one, they turned and fled up the street and into the shadows that had initially spawned them.

"Come back," Ashe yelled despondently after them, waving the bloodied dagger for emphasis. "I'm only just getting the hang of this." Realising the short-lived battle was over; he turned to his new comrade-in-arms and warmly offered his hand.

"My name ..." he began, pausing dramatically for theatrical emphasis, "...is Ashe Wolfsdale. Who is it I have the pleasure of addressing?" He bowed with an artistically comical flourish of his hat. Kerian smiled at the vision before him and then sank to his knees in exhaustion, groaning in pain as his arm encountered the floor.

"My name is my business little one and not that important," he replied, desperately trying to catch his breath and remain conscious, whilst his exploring hand probed the severity of his wound. "That you saved my life is, however, and for that I am eternally grateful. Therefore, in gratitude for your actions you may take any of the belongings this motley bunch may have about their persons and do with them what you wish. However, do it quickly before the watch come around.

Ashe looked at the desperate figures on the ground and evaluated the meagre offerings they would have, then looked back up at the stranger before him, knowing pickings would be small.

"You may not think your name is important but I like to know the names of the people I nearly died alongside." He snapped indignantly. "And what's more you owe me. You would never have coped with eight fighters in your condition." Ashe shook his head in emphasis, determined this was a very important fact to point out.

Kerian rolled his eyes towards the heavens. Not daring to point out the Halfling falling on him was the reason he was in this mess.

"If you insist..." he paused taking time for thought. Okay let's see if my reputation can work for me, he decided. "... You may call me Styx." He looked on hoping for awe or a thrill of terror to cross the little man's features.

"Sticks?" muttered Ashe. "That's a peculiar name."

"Let's just say that it serves a purpose and that I am comfortable with it." Kerian snapped, disappointed at the lack of recognition and unaware of the misspelling that may have caused this misunderstanding. "Now, where's that damned horse?"

Kerian gasped in another breath and somehow found the strength to whistle one long clear note. A ghostly equine head poked out into the street from a darkened alleyway, several shops down, then looked both ways as if to check for any further risk of danger, before Saybier stepped out from his hiding place and trotted meekly up to the exhausted fighter.

"Where were you?" Kerian asked, scolding the stallion lightly with his tone as it shook its mane in response. "You're supposed to fight alongside me, remember? That's what you are trained for."

A warm unguarded smile flickered across the knight's worn face as the stallion gently nuzzled him, as if apologising for deserting in his hour of need. Kerian struggled to his feet with another groan, and after retrieving the sack from where he had dropped it, pulled himself painfully up into the saddle before looking down at Ashe.

"I must be going now," he stated, swaying a little unsteadily. "But, before I do, I would ask one thing of you."

"Let me guess. I never saw you and I don't know who you are or what did this terrible thing," Ashe offered helpfully. "Don't worry, I won't tell the City Watch a thing. After all, I should not have been here either and my earlier evening's entertainment would hardly put me on their most honoured citizen of the year list."

"Actually," Kerian interrupted, "I would just like my dagger back, please."

Ashe looked down at the dagger now hanging at his belt. "Oh ... this one?" He smirked innocently, shrugging his shoulders as he drew the weapon and offered it up hilt first. "Would you mind telling me why those men were after you in the first place?"

Kerian leaned over, winked and then pulled the Halfling's hat down over his eyes. "That's something you needn't concern yourself with, my little friend." He wheeled Saybier sharply about, the horse snorting in response and rearing up, before galloping off up the street in a manoeuvre that Kerian would pay for later in additional pain.

Ashe jerked the hat from his eyes and found he was suddenly standing alone in the darkness, with only the corpses littering the floor around him for company. He found himself feeling cold and vulnerable, now that the sword wielding Sticks had left the scene. He slid into the shadows, drawing the concealment of the night about him and plunged his hands into his pockets to ward off the sudden chill.

Something cold and hard was in his left pocket. He quickly withdrew the item and discovered it was a scarred golden ring. He bent his head to examine it and was surprised at the thickness of the metal and the intricate carving that adorned its surface. Ashe's finger slid into the ring without difficulty and it was there, on the inner surface, hidden from the eyes of the world, that the thief felt a small engraved script. Angling the ring towards the moonlight revealed very little of the writing presented within the metal band and the Halfling swiftly returned it to his pocket.

"Sticks! What a funny name!" He looked in the direction the fighter had taken and sighed to himself. What a horse that man rode. Ashe set off down the street, jumping from shadow to shadow, eager to be far away before questions were asked and bodies discovered. His life was hard enough without this complication. He allowed himself a little shiver of excitement, as he left the site of the encounter far behind him. Who would have thought being a hero was so scary, or that it would be over with so fast?

His imagination replayed the scenes of the recent battle even as his hand absent-mindedly played with the ring in his pocket. It had been quite an eventful night but now was the time to get back to his home, turn in and get some rest. He would examine his prism once he got back to the safety of his loft and then relive his newly found heroic status from the warmth of his rag-filled bed, embellishing his memories of heroism with the many images of eternally grateful damsels-rescued-from-distress.

As for the writing in the ring, he would examine that by candlelight later.

* * * * * *

Crashing footfalls reverberating through the deck from above, served to remind Thomas Adams of his current responsibilities. He swiftly reviewed the plans for landfall, running through the details and leaving nothing to chance. This midnight entry into Catterick would go well as long as his crewmen could slip onto shore aboard one of the ship's two man boats and the *El Defensor* could then ease in quietly behind once their work was done and simply pick them up.

As confidence steadily grew, the faint sound of Rauph's raised voice reached his ears, turning confidence into concern in mere seconds. Thomas groaned as he heard the sudden raised muffled voices above, one filled with excitement, the other with obvious disbelief and outrage. He cradled his head in his hands as the voices increased in volume, confirming what had obviously happened; Rauph had let the cat out of the bag, dumping it well and truly amongst the pigeons!

There was a lesson here about trusting an over excited Minotaur with the concept of being discreet!

Scrave was not the most amenable of people at the best of times and there was no way he was going to be happy about being accompanied by an eight-foot tall, eager to please shaggy minotaur, a minotaur with questionable intelligence and unlimited enthusiasm at that! The exclamations from above cut through the air like sharpened daggers.

"Oh dear," Thomas muttered, closing his eyes. The cabin door flew open in a direct parody of the navigator's earlier entry, revealing the thunderous visage of an extremely volatile Elf.

"And here it is," the captain concluded, suddenly wishing the floor of the cabin would swallow him up, yet already knowing with his luck it was never going to happen.

"How can I help you Scrave?" he began.

* * * * * *

The clear water in the chipped enamel bowl turned a vivid crimson as Kerian squeezed out the ragged piece of cloth he had been using to bathe his injured arm. He could barely suppress the trembling that threatened to wrack his body, blinking away perspiration that slid into his eyes as he cautiously examined the bloody rent in his pale, stretched skin.

A jagged edge of bone protruded from the newly cleansed area but even as he watched, tiny red blotches began to form again, spreading swiftly and running into each other so that the wound was soon dripping scarlet tears of life. Fighting back the rising bile in his throat he reapplied the damp cloth in an attempt to stem the fresh blood flow, wincing from the pain as he regarded his injury anew. His left humerus had fractured approximately two inches above the elbow; one edge of the lower piece of bone was piercing the skin at a jagged angle of roughly thirty degrees. There was no way Kerian could repair this extensive damage himself.

Cool sea air brought a faint tang of salt into the room through the small open window, its scent helping to dilute the almost overpowering taint of blood and sweat that swam thickly around him in a cloying haze. Kerian cast his eyes around the cramped loft room that had served as his home for the last few weeks, desperate for much needed inspiration.

The full-length mirror opposite captured his attention, reflecting an image of two youthful eyes, trapped within the haggard profile of the old man he had prematurely become. The figure returned his gaze from the edge of a hard wooden bed, his aged torso somehow alien and unreal. The pale skin; blue veins and grey hair completely the opposite of the thirty-three-year-old body he should have seen.

Beads of perspiration flecked his pasty coloured skin, the pale violet glow seeping from the naked blade lying across his knees giving him a ghostly sheen. Studded leather armour lay in a neglected pile at his feet, and numerous discarded empty ale pitchers, some upturned, others lying carelessly on their sides, served to complete the reflected picture presented to him.

His well-worn saddlebags leant at the base of the mirror, normally packed in preparation for a hasty departure but this time the contents were scattered across the floor as Kerian had tried to find items to help manage his terrible wound.

A battered mahogany dresser stood in silent judgement of his attempts at self-pity. On the dresser were two smoking candles, a leather-bound journal and a hand mirror with silver gilt edging. The only door into the room was set back in the right-hand wall, and barred by the last remaining piece of furniture, a rickety wooden chair, whose back was wedged tightly up under the door's brass handle. Kerian's black velvet cloak draped solemnly across the splintered seat, hiding his blood-stained boots and the sack containing Ferdinand's head in the shadows beneath.

A warm trickling sensation focused Kerian's attention as a thin line of blood slowly traced a track down his arm. The cloth was swiftly rinsed and reapplied but it failed to bring temporary respite from the pain.

Movement at the periphery of his vision caused Kerian to turn in alarm. Dropping the bloodied rag, he reached for his sword; trying hard not to jar his damaged arm any more than was necessary. Even so, spasms of jagged pain ran through the damaged bone and flesh, causing Kerian to suck in a desperate steadying breath, temporarily forgetting the reason for his sudden alarm.

This was not a good situation. He recognised the state he was in but his options were sorely limited at this time of night. The alcohol had helped with some of the pain but did not help focus his mind on the important things he needed to resolve. He felt like crying, letting some sign of despair come forth from his taut frame but was worried that opening the flood gates would make him lose what little self-control remained.

His rag momentarily forgotten and sword now in hand, Kerian struggled to remember why he had jumped, then he saw the movement again and was able to identify the source, squinting to focus his pain blurred vision, before noticing a small grey spider hanging from a silken thread. It swung like a pendulum, inches before his face, arachnid legs moving in swift flurries of action as it struggled to ascend its thin lifeline to the relative safety of the wooden beams above. The abdomen of the spider gleamed golden as a newly minted coin, even in the room's sparse illumination, confirming its identification. It was a sunset spider. A species indigenous only to the region of Catterick. This particularly industrious specimen suddenly froze in mid-climb, dangling motionless as if aware of the unsolicited examination it was receiving.

Kerian grinned at the irony of it all and relaxed his grip on his sword. The inn was named after this thumb sized creepy crawly but he had not expected one as his roommate! For some odd reason the notion caused him to laugh aloud, an action that was so absurdly out of character and instantly stalled when he caught a guilty glance at the empty pitchers scattered across the floorboards at his feet.

How many of these things had he consumed? Kerian struggled to focus through the haze of pain and alcohol, only to come to the opinion that he was, in fact, rather drunk.

A knock on the door made him blink and shake his head as if to clear it of the cloying mist threatening to overwhelm him. A further knock, more urgent than the last snapped him out of his repose. He had stated quite clearly that he was not to be disturbed this evening so the knock on the door was out of character for an inn that prided itself on being discreet to its customers.

Kerian rose unsteadily to his feet then gasped as his legs buckled from beneath him, bringing him crashing to his knees. Pain lanced through his wounded arm eating through the protective alcoholic bubble like an acid, causing him to sob as he dropped his sword from nerveless fingers and gripped the injury as if he could physically hold the agony at bay.

The door shook as someone tried to gain entry. Instincts screamed at the knight to get to his feet and fight but the pain was too much. His sword, although mere inches from his hand, seemed to be a continent away. Fumbling anxiously for the hilt, Kerian tried vainly to focus but realised he was simply too drunk to form any kind of defence to whatever threat was approaching him.

The chair squeaked and groaned in protest as the door suffered repeated blows. Raised voices called out something that Kerian's intoxicated mind simply could not grasp. He finally located his sword, grasping it with fingers that had little coordination and felt as if they were on fire with every movement they made. He raised his sword shakily in the direction of the door.

The chair back suddenly snapped as the door flew open. Kerian lashed out at the blurred figures advancing upon him, hearing a loud exclamation, before his vision began to cloud and he felt himself falling. Trying desperately to hold on to failing threads of consciousness, he was aware only that someone was advancing towards him and that he had no strength left to defend himself.

He inexplicably found himself face down on the floor, his new vantage point allowing him to see the swiftly retreating sunset spider scuttling across the floor towards the skirting board. He tried to regain his feet but the effort was more than he could muster.

With a groan Kerian's consciousness failed him, plunging him mercifully into oblivion.

Chapter Four

It was early afternoon before Ashe rose from his slumber and ventured out into the hustle and bustle of Catterick's society. The heat was oppressive and sultry in nature, promising a storm in the near future and making his journey through the dry, dusty streets an uncomfortable experience both physically and mentally, even without the aches and pains that wracked his body from the excitement of the night before.

Ashe finally slipped into a refuse-filled alleyway, slipping into the shadows, lightly stepping over puddles and scaring the rats lurking there. He eventually stopped before a small non-descript door set back into the lichen covered brickwork. A small candle flickered faintly within a niche beside the door making the Halfling smile.

Good! He was not too late. Business was not finished for the day! He checked the satchel at his side and then rapped out a memorised signal on the door. It flew open almost instantly, revealing inky darkness within.

"Hello," Ashe opened. "It's me. I have some items to sell." He reached for the flap of his satchel in forgetful eagerness.

"Not out there, you fool!" hissed a disembodied voice from the funereal depths.

Ashe found himself dragged unceremoniously through the doorway and into the room beyond, the door slamming soundly shut behind him, trapping the thief within. A spark split the darkness off to the Halfling's left and a small candle spluttered to life, illuminating the features of a weasel-like bespectacled old man whose rodent-tailed beard bobbed away hypnotically as he spoke.

"So Ashe, what delights have you brought me this time, eh?" The weasel stretched out a clawed hand ravaged by age and scar tissue. "You didn't take any of this from Atticus's patch now did you? I have enough problems with him as it is, without having his thugs visiting me."

Ashe offered the items from his satchel without pause, shaking his head to confirm he had been nowhere near the violent guild master's patch. He had heard tales about people who had crossed the man and lost limbs because of it. Indeed, Ashe had been dodging Atticus's thugs for some time due to a small misunderstanding about a model of a silver sailing ship that broke when Ashe was trying to examine it. I mean who made statues so flimsy in the first place? And how was he to know it had been Atticus's birthday present anyway?

Ashe careful omitted the cold prism from the takings of the previous evening's escapade. That beautiful crystal was for his eyes only and he had no intentions of fencing the item, no matter how tight his finances were.

"Wait here," the old man wheezed, turning towards the back of the room, the candle flickering and spitting before him. Ashe stood alone in the darkness as the shuffling footfalls of the departing figure dwindled into the distance.

"Don't I get a candle?" he asked vainly to the shadows around him, before fidgeting from foot to foot in barely concealed impatience.

Time passed laboriously within the Halfling's overactive imagination, with minutes seeming to have stretched into hours before the greasy gleam of a half-dead lantern heralded the old man's return as it smeared a sickly light through the darkness before settling on a well-worn bench.

Ashe advanced without invitation; he had carried out business with Boyce in the past and knew that the old man had a flare for the dramatic. Several unenthusiastic hums and tuts arose from the bench as he systematically sorted the knick-knacks from one pile to another. Within minutes, only one item remained on the desk unvalued: The golden ring Ashe had found in his pocket after the brawl.

Boyce's well-wrinkled features appeared to warp even further, his eyes narrowing suspiciously as he regarded the solitary item of jewellery. He held it up to the light of the lantern turning it one way and then the other, squinting with heavy concentration before returning it to the wooden desk before him. There was a long pause as the old man appeared to close his eyes with thought, wracking his memory for recognition of the item before him, then he swiftly snatched it up again and peered within the golden circlet to stare unyielding at something obscured from Ashe's vision. A wry smile slid across Boyce's sly features.

"I'll pay you twelve shillings for all of these trinkets," he gestured, indicating the assorted pile of items that had already been scrutinised. "But I won't offer on the ring unless you tell me how you came by it."

"Why?" asked Ashe, stepping closer. "Is the ring valuable then?" He paused, the initial feelings of greed suddenly subdued as he realised what Boyce had quoted for his ill-gotten gains. "Twelve shillings for three nights' work! You cannot be serious! It's worth at least three times that amount."

Boyce made a calming gesture with his hand in an attempt to subdue the ranting Halfling.

"The ring, my boy..." he prompted. "Where did you find the ring?"

"I'm not sure," Ashe snapped, in a sudden wounded huff. "Twelve shillings indeed."

The old man brought his hand swiftly over to the lantern as if preparing to extinguish the flame in a typically theatrical gesture. Ashe sobered up immediately, realising that if the flame went out so did his chances of closing the deal.

"Wait!" he blurted out. "I think it came from an old man I met last night."

Boyce stared at him coldly, the flame of the lantern reflecting in his glasses, creating a near demonic countenance. Yellowed teeth showed as he uttered a short guttural laugh that echoed menacingly about the darkened room, chillingly reminding Ashe of the guard dog's maw from the night before.

"I treat you like a son, don't I?" Boyce enquired slyly.

"Of course you do," Ashe replied anxiously, suddenly uneasy and unsure of where this was heading.

"Yet you continue to lie to me," the old man snapped. "Now the truth or go elsewhere." His hand hovered by the lantern threatening an end to the negotiations once again.

"It's the truth, I swear," the Halfling stammered, desperation bringing a truthful edge to the tone of his voice.

"Read the writing in the ring," Boyce cackled, flipping the ring across the desk. Ashe snatched it from the air and brought it close to his face, struggling to make sense of the engraving within the scarred golden band. He shrugged his shoulders in a non-committal gesture before flipping the ring back across the desk towards the shady crook.

"So what?" he offered in response.

"I know you can't read." Boyce laughed, amused at the theatrical actions of his pet thief, "I've known for a long time, so you can spare your faked indifference." Flecks of spittle flew from his lips making the candle splutter. "Here's your twelve shillings. Now, take them and go."

A small pile of coins appeared on the worktop, which Ashe swiftly scooped up and secured about his person. The ring remained forlornly upon the desk, its future suddenly in doubt.

"The ring is yours as well," Boyce prompted.

"Don't you want it then?" Ashe asked, slightly bemused. "I thought it was somewhat valuable. Is it a fake or something?"

"Not in the least," came the reply. "It's definitely not a fake as far as I can tell, and in the right hands it would be immensely valuable. However, if the owner was an old man as you state, then he stole it as surely as you did, which gives this trinket a history I want no part of. I am sorry but I will not take this item from your possession, Ashe... It is simply too dangerous for me to move on. And," Boyce studied Ashe carefully in a way that made shivers run up and down the Halfling's spine, "probably too dangerous for someone like you to possess either."

"Oh..." Ashe found himself lost for words. This had never happened to him before. Boyce normally purchased everything he found. "Would you consider taking the ring if I offered some kind of trade instead?"

The room was suddenly plunged into darkness and rough hands grabbed him, propelling the thief from the room to land in a dishevelled heap amidst the refuse of the alleyway outside. Ashe slowly got to his feet, dusting himself off and removing a piece of rotten fish from his left ear. He turned to see the thickset door closing ominously, then it suddenly stopped and something small flew from the darkness to bounce painfully off his forehead.

Looking down, Ashe saw the golden ring lying half-submerged in a murky puddle. He bent to retrieve it as the door thudded closed behind him.

"But the ring *was* his," Ashe muttered to himself as if trying to justify his story to an unseen jury. He turned towards the closed door eager to state his case and realised that business with Boyce was at an end for this afternoon. There was no way he would reopen that door to Ashe now.

Undeterred, he grabbed a soggy box from the nearest refuse pile and dragged it across the cobbles before hopping up onto it and finding himself level with the spluttering candlestick that now burned weakly in the niche alongside the door.

He swatted vainly at the fluttering moths and bugs that buzzed annoyingly around his head, their erratic flights attracted by the flickering flame and lifted the ring up into the light attempting to explain Boyce's uncharacteristic reaction to the item. With a concerted effort, he finally managed to make out the ornate script within the ring.

Denaris 12.06.524

However, as he had not learnt to read, his scrutiny left him none the wiser and he returned the ring to his satchel. The numbers, which he could read, might well be a date, he surmised, jumping down to the cobbles. His mind continued to pursue this thread of enquiry as he made his way back out to the hustle and bustle of the main street. Five hundred and twenty-four... it was now five hundred and fifty-seven so if the numbers were a birth date the owner of the ring would be... There followed several seconds of pained silence, mentally torturing arithmetic, strained expressions and the use of most of the Halfling's fingers ... thirty-three.

"Well I'll be... Boyce was right!" Ashe shook his head in disbelief. The ring could not have belonged to Sticks then... Well, well, he would not have thought the old man had it in him! Looks could be so deceiving!

He jogged through the dwindling crowds; his mind occupied as he headed back to his attic retreat. He swiftly secured his newly acquired funds under a loose floorboard beneath his bunk, and only then let loose a sigh of relief. Financial security! This would keep the wolf from the door, for at least a couple of days... He mentally chastised himself. Okay his landlord... anything with four legs and sharp teeth was better left forgotten as far as he was concerned.

Hopping up onto the bunk, he pulled a moth-eaten blanket up to his chest, before turning to look up at the mouldy ceiling above him. Ashe reached into his pocket and drew forth the golden ring. What was he going to do with this thing? Boyce had made it perfectly clear he did not want it. Other acquisition dealing contacts did not handle solitary items and one-off trinkets such as this one. It was not worth the time, or the risks involved.

The problem was Ashe would soon have to go out again on another job. There was nothing for it, Ashe the thief... wait... now Ashe the *heroic* thief would have to haunt the tiles of Catterick once more. With his newfound heroic status, no one would be safe from his light-fingered clutches. He chuckled before turning over and getting ready to catch a few winks of sleep. If he stole something else worthwhile, maybe he could include the ring as part of the total package.

He tugged the blanket up under his chin, slipping the ring under the covers and holding it close to his chest. If it was truly worth as much as Boyce had hinted at, he for one was not letting it out of his sight!

Within moments, the diminutive figure was breathing steadily, his chest rising and falling in a light slumber. Twilight stretched the shadows across his room revealing a small glimmer of light that began to pulse rhythmically from underneath the blanket that covered the thief, its source: a small golden band that lay clutched within the slumbering Halfling's grasp.

* * * * * *

Kerian awoke to an agonising world of grogginess; his eyes cracking painfully open, only to close tightly again, due to being lanced through the brain by painful spears of piercing bright light. In addition to the pain, he had an unmistakeable feeling he was not alone.

Fighting to clear his bleary vision, he tried to focus on the vague form, his tired eyes allowing him to recognise the distorted features of the 'Sunset Spider's' landlord. The man stood there, all red faced with wisps of stray hair plastered across his profusely sweating otherwise bald scalp and his hands wringing his apron in nervous apprehension.

"At last," Kerian heard him mutter, as he moved forwards to reveal a concerned expression on his face.

Looking past the looming figure, Kerian struggled to take stock of his condition. Clearly, he was still lying in his room at the inn, as he could see the remains of the chair that he remembered forcing under the door handle when he thought he was in danger. He angled his head to view his injured arm, terrified that something untoward had happened to the limb during his obvious period of unconsciousness. The sight of a freshly bandaged wound and not the rounded stump of an amputated limb made him silently offer thanks to gods long ignored. Pain lanced through his head, dropping a veil of red tinged agony across his already compromised vision. Kerian groaned anew, silently uttering an empty promise never to touch alcohol again.

"You have the serving lad to thank for this," the proprietor roared, gesturing at the bandaged arm and laughing loudly. Kerian recoiled back into his pillows as if physically struck, his headache rebelling against the noise. He gestured wildly with his hand in a vain attempt to quieten the over enthusiastic man who was lost in his continuing tale of Kerian's rescue. The knight tried to voice his protest but his tongue felt thick and furry like a dehydrated garden slug, whilst his throat felt like he had swallowed a bucket of broken glass. Oblivious, the landlord continued:

"I've had to reset many a broken bone in my time behind two foot of polished mahogany," the landlord grinned, "but, I must say, yours was one of the best I've seen in a long time. It was pure luck that the blacksmith was in asking about you when the lad came down and told me how sick you looked, else I would have never been able to open your door by myself. Oh ... speaking of the door, the chair we had to break is going on your bill when you leave. And the cost of the lock."

Anyhow," he continued to ramble, "between us, we managed to reset the bone but that blacksmith," the landlord shook his head as if to further emphasis the point, "he was the real expert you know, resets broken bones all the time in his job. I tried several times to reset your arm without much luck but he just stepped in there and snapped it back into place with hardly any pulling or shoving at all." He paused as if reliving the moment, and for a heartbeat Kerian's aching head dared to hope the man had finished his tirade. However, it was not to be. On he went!

"A funny thing that was, too. I still can't understand why it didn't snap apart again, like it did when I tried it." Kerian paled at the thought of the protruding bone ends grating together and then springing apart. Just what had these butchers done to him while he was unconscious? Something about the description was nightmarish and nauseating.

"That blacksmith has sure got the touch for setting bones!" Kerian closed his eyes in despair as the proprietor continued, "But he can't stitch to save his life, which is a real shame," he chuckled, "seeing as how you sliced his arm open like you did."

Kerian flushed slightly at this revelation. He did remember lashing at something before he passed out and mentally registered a need to make remuneration to his impromptu doctor once he had recovered. It appeared he owed the blacksmith dearly.

"I wouldn't suggest too much action right now," the landlord gestured at the arm. "No brawling or wenching, okay?" He chuckled at the expense of his guest and turned to leave. "Just lie there and rest and I'll send up the lad with supper later. I shudder to think what would have happened if he hadn't seen you earlier. He'll be glad to know you're all right. Just make sure you tip him for his service." The proprietor slipped out through the door, still chuckling to himself.

Kerian lay there for a moment, relaxing as the silence left in the wake of the departing landlord washed over him like a refreshing wave, cooling and soothing his discomfort and allowing time for solitary reflection. He re-examined his swollen arm and tentatively flexed it. Red-hot needles of agony raced up and down the limb, making him hold the arm in mid-motion until they subsided, before gingerly lowering it back to the bed with a curse. His arm was next to useless.

Settling back into the pillows, he closed his eyes and tried to quieten his rising angst. Something about the proprietor's conversation felt wrong but he was too fuzzy headed to begin working out what it might be. He grunted to himself, as if discussing the enigma with a silent committee then let exhaustive sleep take him into her comforting arms.

It was several hours later when he finally awoke, his headache little more than a bad memory and his stomach more than ready for a meal. Supper, therefore, was an excellent and welcome affair of spicy exotic vegetables that left a pleasant tang on his tongue, submerged within a delicious beef stew with a rich thick gravy that clung to the meat and simply cried out for the fresh bread to clean the plate. He washed everything down with cold milk, a sentiment to the knight's earlier vow to avoid alcohol, which strangely complimented the meal perfectly, leaving Kerian with the feeling that, with the exception of his broken arm, it was good to be alive.

Kerian sat in reflection, considering the errors in his ways from the previous evening. He had been too confident, an ideal based on an inflated ego that he had paid for in full. It would have been so much easier to wait until the men had left and plunge his dagger into Ferdinand's inebriated back, simple, effective and safer. However, not very stylish or honourable.

His reactions had also been slower than usual and this was worrying. He reached for the necklace at his throat and held it up into the light. Maybe the enchantment set within the stone was beginning to fade; perhaps its ability to combat the ravages of his premature old age was becoming less effective over time. This was a concern; for Kerian knew the re-enchantment of the necklace would not come cheap and the procedure was not always successful.

He generously tipped the serving lad, as suggested by the proprietor but Kerian's coffers were only so deep! He was relieved his previous night's activities had been so successful, in both trophy and hopefully monetary gain!

The knight looked across at the mirror, trying to judge if he was fit to venture out later that evening and smiled at the respectable old man whose heavily lined face stared back at him. He brushed up quite well for a thirty-three-year-old approaching his sixties! Even his arm appeared to be trying to do its bit, with only the occasional painful twinge to mark its movement in comparison to the agony he had suffered earlier. Could he have imagined the severity of his injuries? How much had he drunk? There was something going on here that simply did not make sense!

Outside the window the sky was turning a vivid violet hue, heralding the coming of night and confirming that Kerian had some time before considering any further actions. He piled up the pillows on his bed, plucked the leather-bound ledger from the dresser and settled down to look back on a book that had become both his undying enemy and loyal companion over the previous months.

His book was certainly old in appearance; its scuff marked red leather cover indicating the mileage the book had travelled. Two battered gold clips protected the outer corners of the front cover, whilst the back cover simply displayed two dents that gave clues to past ornamentation that had been lost to the ravages of wear. A small red ribbon poked meekly from the bottom of the book, indicating the progress of the reader through its multitude of yellowed pages. Etched into the front cover of the book, in flaked, peeling, gold leaf was a faded coat of arms, the detail sparse and barely visible.

"Of the House Denaris," Kerian read aloud. "In honour's path we tread." He smiled sadly. "If only they could see me now." He shifted his frame, trying to find a comfortable position that did not put undue stress on his arm and then began flicking through the yellowed pages. Small lines of condensed black script seemed to glint in the light with an underlying golden tint. He turned the pages with his breath held in his throat and sighed with relief when a clean page of parchment and not the back of the book, awaited him there.

"Not today," he whispered to himself before turning back to the earlier pages and allowing his mind to wander. The journal entries laid open for his inspection hid no secrets from their author and were more than just a daily log of his travels. They represented an exercise of tradition and routine whilst offering Kerian an opportunity to cleanse his troubled mind, emptying its turmoil onto the pages before him.

He shook his head silently as he re-read a particularly painful decision mistakenly made in the past. The enthusiastic writing belied the shocks to which it had inadvertently led. Had he ever been that young? Innocent in the ways of the word and eager to prove himself? So many things had seemed important in those days but were now insignificant.

Kerian flicked through further pages. He had been the weaver of all of these tales, baptised in blood on the terrible campaigns of his queen, with no idea how his exposure had changed him into the man he had become. Kerian returned to the blank page, eager to commit his new personal thoughts to paper with the hope its confessional nature would leave him stronger and abler to face the trials of the coming hours: but where was he to begin? He paused to collect his thoughts. Maybe a brief recap was in order to justify his callous actions of the night before and thereby aid his yet undecided plans.

"Write," he commanded.

A small magical flame about half a centimetre high suddenly appeared on the page, its golden light crackling slightly as the flame danced in anticipation of what was to come. As Kerian spoke, the golden flame flickered in response emitting a low hiss as it traced its path across the page. Neat coal black letters now mirrored his verbally uttered statements as the flame chronicled his thoughts on the fresh parchment sheet and his mind began to wander.

Chapter Five

"We're going around in circles you idiot!" Scrave roared in abject frustration at the hulking figure alongside him, his Elven features warped into a snarl that clearly mirrored his growing exasperation. "Stop rowing, this instant!"

A battered wooden oar on one side of the small lop-sided dinghy the two figures sat in ceased to thrash the otherwise calm waters of Chalantear Bay into a white frothy maelstrom, allowing silence and relative calm to return.

"What's the problem Scrave?" asked his large hairy rowing companion; his phrasings stilted and slow, as if the Minotaur found the question embarrassing to ask as he was afraid what the reply would be. He looked up at his Elven associate awaiting a response and instead found a stony silence broken only by the soft lapping of waves against the wooden hull of the boat.

"I can't reach down to the water," Scrave stated from his perching point on the very edge of the boat's rim, indicating the water level several feet below in a matter-of-fact tone of voice. "You're the only one doing any rowing."

Rauph's bovine visage turned suspicious in a second.

"Why is that?" he questioned, his views of the Elf taking unfair advantage of him quite apparent in his open facial expressions. The Minotaur shifted his immense bulk and began to move over to Scrave's side of the dinghy. The small wooden craft groaned in protest and began to rock erratically in the water, threatening to tip both of its crew into the sea at any moment.

"No!" Scrave screamed, throwing himself across to the vacant side of the dinghy in abject terror at the Minotaur's absurd actions, his hasty movement a desperate attempt to counter the weight of his curiously clumsy companion. Rauph, oblivious to the chaos he was causing glanced down at the velvet blackness of the water lapping at the edge of the boat barely inches away from his wide snorting nostrils.

"What's your problem?" he inquired gesturing with huge hands that could snap a spine in seconds. "The water is right there. Why couldn't you reach it?" The Minotaur paused as if formulating his next words carefully then turned to look up at his colleague once more. "You just want me along to do all the work don't you?" he asked in a hurt accusatory tone.

Scrave looked up to the full moon illuminating the night sky above and shook his head in disbelief, wishing that the huge all seeing orb could somehow reach down and tell the Minotaur that it was nothing of the sort. Rauph shifted his weight, causing the boat to wobble once again and Scrave grabbed hold of the side of the boat on which he was now balancing and hung on for grim death, his knuckles turning white in the process. The waters of the bay rippled six feet below him in response to the actions of the Minotaur, totally inaccessible to an oar.

The Elf looked back down at the Minotaur with a stare that could wither small shrubs. He watched amazed as the hulking figure dipped his oar back into the water and began to thrash it about, creating a scene more akin to a pack of flesh eating Wantayhu fish stripping an unwary wildebeest than actually rowing!

The small boat began to turn in a slow circle once more and Scrave watched as the *El Defensor's* majestic silhouette came into view for the twenty-fifth time that evening. The galleon's two main masts pointed to the stars above, and as the Elf watched, the main sail began to unfurl. The ship was beginning preparations to sail. The night was slipping by. He looked back at the Minotaur who appeared oblivious to the misery he was causing to his travelling companion. Back at the ship lay a warm bunk, good food and excellent company. Out here, a soggy evening without any form of repast threatened. Why had the Captain elected to send his best thief on a 'shopping trip' with a lumbering imbecile? It just did not add up.

He resigned himself to the evening and decided that he may at least make the effort and attempt to row before looking about for his oar.

Where was his oar anyhow?

His eyes darted about the small vessel, methodically scanning the deck before resting on a patch of water several meters from the slowly circling vessel. Drifting like some long forgotten wreckage was the object of his quest. Even as he looked on, a small wave caused by the frenzied pulverising of the Minotaur pushed the oar further from the now silently cursing Elf.

Catterick's torch lit city now came into view, its breath-taking beauty lost on the couple of sailors, one cursing his bad luck and the other moaning about how unfair it was having to row all the time.

It would be a long way to Catterick that night.

* * * * * *

In a darkened loft, a small figure lay tossing and turning in restless slumber, a bright light pulsing under the blanket that barely covered him. Ashe suddenly sat bolt upright in bed, shaking his head as if physically shocked at the dreams he had been having. He wiped a stray strand of hair from his eyes and quickly glanced around the room as if scared that someone, somewhere was watching him. Satisfying himself that no uninvited visitors occupied his cramped quarters, not even a stray rat, the Halfling let out a relieved sigh, shattering the silence surrounding him.

"Wow! What a dream." He threw back the blanket and stared at his toes peeking through the holes in his well-darned socks. He wiggled them to be sure that he was awake, then looked down at the ring in his palm, the thought of its untold wealth flashing in his sparkling eyes.

The ring gleamed brightly in the darkness, emitting a sudden ray of light like a lightning bolt streaking across the sky, leaving a visible imprint on Ashe's retina. The Halfling swung his legs from the bunk and dropped lightly to the floor before walking straight through the loft door and out onto the rickety staircase that ran down the outside of the building. His eyes were glazed and his hand outstretched, as if some unseen person was pulling him along by the wrist.

The door swung neglected upon its hinges, the light from the street lanterns outside illuminating a pair of forlorn and forgotten sandals left at the foot of the bed.

Ashe would never wear these sandals again.

* * * * *

Kerian awoke with a start, realising that at some time during his musings exhaustion had overtaken him. He was suddenly aware of the drop in light within the room and the encroaching shadows that had crept silently across the floorboards towards him whilst he slept.

He sat up and ran his hands across his stubble. A shave could wait. Night had fallen and he had a delivery to make. He closed the red leather journal and gazed at the faded gilt cover, his mind flashing back to when his mother had first presented the tome to him for his own personal reflections.

"Oh mother," he began, voicing his sorrows to the non-judgemental room around him. "If only you could see what has become of your son."

He slid from the bed and began a long struggle with his leather-studded armour, slipping his injured arm through the sleeve in a twisting motion that felt stiff and bruised rather than broken. He still did not have full motion but incredibly, the arm felt stronger.

Kerian examined himself in the mirror with a critical eye. With his cloak completing the outfit and helping to obscure his arm the knight felt he could pass the evening without displaying any of the weakness his earlier business had bestowed. You never showed a weakness to the likes of Jerome and his associates; image was everything.

He brought his hand up to finger brush the hairs from his face then paused as he noticed the image in the mirror before him. Cursing, he brought his gaze to his reflected hand and examined his ring finger with disbelief, as if the silvered mirror surface had somehow lied to his ocular senses. The ring finger remained bare, clearly showing a pale smooth band of skin where his birth ring had once rested.

Kerian lowered himself to the floor and examined the warped boards beneath the bed, then began to strip the bed, peeling back the blankets with a care that soon changed into one of resignation. His ring was not there.

The last few days had not gone well.

He collected the sack from the corner of the room, wrinkling his nose at the smell that was now starting to emanate from within and moved to leave the room; his mind replayed the series of events from the previous evening. There was the barmaid, Ferdinand and the … Halfling. There was even the period of his unconsciousness. He could have lost the ring anywhere and at any time. The image of the Halfling returned to his mind, as if suggesting a more likely chain of events.

Kerian smiled slyly to himself. Unless, of course, the ring had been stolen! If the ring was not lost but instead taken without his permission, he had nothing to worry about; the ring would find its own way back to him.

It always did.

* * * * * *

"We are late for an appointment," Kerian informed his magnificent stallion, as he entered the stall in which the horse was resting. Saybier shook his mane and began to prance in excitement, clearly eager for exercise after being left stabled for so long. He turned his white head to regard his owner as Kerian lifted the saddle and tack from the side of the stall and set about buckling them in place before reaching into his pocket and removing an apple by way of apology for keeping his trusted mount in such poor circumstances.

Saybier did not shy away as Kerian fastened the sackcloth covered trophy to the saddle. His horse knew blood throughout its military career and was not troubled. Instead, the stallion champed at the bit as he was led from the stables and out into the street.

Kerian mounted Saybier carefully before digging in his heels and coaxing the stallion into a canter. The route was straight forward, allowing Kerian time to rehearse the coming meeting in his mind, phrasing set portions of dialogue that would give him the upper hand in negotiation. Appearance was everything tonight and he wanted to ensure his performance was flawless. He was so preoccupied that he failed to notice three sets of eyes that observed his departure from a darkened recess opposite, or the slight warning glimmer that arose from his necklace and then flickered out as he moved away.

"I told you I'd found him," hissed a menacing voice. "Not yet!" it snarled, bringing a carbon-streaked hammer down across the stock of a loaded crossbow one of its associates raised in preparation for a killing shot.

"Remember his magical wards!"

The crossbow wielder hissed a frustrated complaint at having its aim disrupted, then reluctantly complied and moved back into the shadows.

* * * * * *

Ashe stood barefoot in the centre of the cobbled street, his face glazed and vacant. As if waiting for an unseen signal the Halfling turned first one way and then the other, scanning one of several junctions that led from the front of his house up into the town of Catterick.

Then, as if a bell had been rung that was only audible to Ashe, he suddenly turned and walked stiff-legged in the direction of the main square in the

Northern, more affluent part of town. This was a place where, by daylight, there lay a vision of grand ornamental flowerbeds and luxurious fountains that created a vivid backdrop to the forecourt of the palace that Ashe had gazed at from the rooftops the previous night.

Unfortunately, in his dazed state, the Halfling missed all the splendour and just plodded vacantly through the area. He passed through the looming shadow cast by the magnificent building, his footsteps unerringly directed straight across the gardens and the exact centre of the horticultural monument that signified the spot upon which the King had met his gruesome and public end at the hand of Isobelle.

Ashe found that he was suddenly shivering; even though his actions were controlled, subconsciously he knew he was moving through a dark place. He placed one foot in front of the other realising something was making him do this, yet he was powerless to do anything but let it happen.

His barefooted advance suddenly stopped as if he had hit some unseen barrier. Ashe stood, glancing one way then another, as if his body was not sure which of the three walkways he should take from this point forward.

In the distance a cloaked rider on a gleaming white stallion galloped across one of the walkways to disappear from sight. The ring in Ashe's hand flared brightly, as if reinforcing its magical claim to the Halfling's mind, and Ashe, unable to voice any complaint, found himself beginning the long trudge up the cobbled pathway towards the cross section the horse and rider had taken.

* * * * * *

The sprawling opulent estate of Couqran was magnificent to behold, its gardens exotic and beautiful, the careful designs bringing order to the disarray that is nature's natural beauty. Evergreens, painstakingly clipped into shapes of geometric symmetry, cast reflections across lightly rippling ornamental pools teaming with fish bred for specific colour and placidity. Kerian found the whole attention to detail artificial but he had never voiced his opinions openly.

He approached the imposing walls enclosing the main house and beheld the stone gargoyles perching there in silent judgement, each detail carved for ferocity and effect. Razor sharp spikes adorned the walls between each stone statue, making scaling the wall an option no intruder would consider lightly. Rumour had it that several slaves had also discovered the futility of that exit and had died slow lingering deaths, hanging impaled for all the other servants to mark well.

Saybier nickered as they slowed before the huge set of iron wrought gates blocking passage into the estate. One of several uniformed guards in attendance stepped forward to intercept their passage, his hand on his sword as he requested formal identification.

"You already know who I am." Kerian snapped coldly at the challenge, giving the guard a look that swiftly informed him to back away or suffer the consequences. He dismounted and retrieved the sackcloth bundle from his saddle without uttering a further word and pushed his way forward through the guards, giving each one the same hard stare.

No one stepped in to intercept him. However, one guard was too slow to step away. Kerian kept up his intimidating role, sweeping past him, deliberately knocking his shoulder with the cloth sack he carried and half-spinning the guard around with the force of the collision. Kerian hid a smile as he came to a stop before the barred gate then raised an eyebrow at the fact it had not yet opened for him. The knight was not irritated at the delay; he just did not want to spend a moment longer here than was necessary.

The guards spoke in low whispers in his wake, arguing as to who should dare delay this visitor further, before one of them lowered his head with a sigh and signalled to a guard on the other side of the gate, allowing it to swing open and permit access. Kerian stepped through before the gate had completed its swing and continued down the carriageway acting to all intent and purpose as if he owned the place.

He was met at the main entrance by a smartly dressed servant who escorted him swiftly through to a private study. The servant cleared his throat and announced the fighter's presence to the man within.

Atticus Couqran was a greasy, thickset man who almost smelt of the misery he had inflicted on others to attain his considerable surplus wealth. Thick gold chains dangled from around his podgy neck and rings of assorted metals beset with precious stones encircled his sausage like fingers.

Sparse hair, worn short and flecked through with poorly disguised grey, parted greasily over and flicked back along the right side of the guild master's sweaty head; dark brown eyes were close set, shrewd and cunning, their depths calculating the weaknesses of those they beheld and the best ways to manipulate and warp those weaknesses to meet his evil desires. His sharply pointed nose, completed the visage of a leering rat holding state, bedecked in gold and voluptuous black silken robes.

Kerian met the man's penetrating gaze straight on. He did not like Atticus. He did not like him at all! If this man had not held the answers to his current problem, he would never have considered accepting the odious work he had carried out these evenings past. Irritation was already beginning to gnaw at Kerian's senses as he observed Atticus returning his attention to sheets of shipping manifests and current market prices of the goods that he traded in. The man even had the audacity to use a spoon to scoop repeatedly at the rich chocolate icing adorning a large gateau at the side of the scribed reports, lifting the doomed chocolate cargo to a swift end in the dank depths of his mouth.

Kerian knew this was all for show, a power game to indicate who was important in the scheme of things but it rankled him all the same. As Kerian looked on, his gaze never wavering, he noticed a tell-tale flicker of concern in one of the merchant's eye movements. It was nothing of note to an unobservant onlooker, but to the knight, the glance made towards him, even though recovered swiftly; informed Kerian that this charade was as uncomfortable for the merchant as it was for his waiting audience. Reassurance can be a powerful ally and with this in mind Kerian allowed his own confidence to silently rise.

A dog of sorts shuffled into the room, its appearance more akin to a scrubbing brush than a canine but its entry temporarily served to move attention away from the power play that silently raged above its shaggy head. It huffed around the desk and collapsed in a heap at Atticus's feet with an audible sigh, as if someone had suddenly deflated the creature, letting out the air from a hidden valve. It was at this moment that Atticus chose to begin his negotiations.

"Well, Styx ..." the guild master opened, his demeanour pleasant and overly friendly. "Why do I find you back before me so soon?" Atticus lent forward and scooped a large morsel of chocolate cake into his open maw then settled back to await Kerian's response.

Kerian watched in barely disguised disgust as saliva-coated pieces of cake fell from one mouth, only to be intercepted, mid-air by the snapping maw of the mongrel at Atticus's feet, showing a turn of speed that belied its plump and scruffy form.

"I have completed the contract," Kerian replied curtly. "Would it be too presumptuous to assume that you now carry out your side of the bargain?" The knight watched attentively as he spoke, hoping against hope for the facial responses and body language of the gluttonous figure before him to display a sign that his goal was now finally within reach. The pause in cake consumption and loss of a sizeable chunk from suddenly twitching nerveless lips told him otherwise. Atticus, like so many men before him, had lied. Kerian felt his hopes die in that twitch, closing his eyes in momentary dismay; an action that was as unfortunate as it was foolish, as in that split second, unobserved, Atticus silently fingered an alarm secreted under his desk.

"I ... I heard you were one of the best," Atticus floundered, his stutter confirming Kerian's earlier diagnosis of the situation. "But, surely, even the great Styx could not have completed the contract and returned as swiftly as you claim to have done. It has been less than a week. Now, please, understand me, it is not that I don't believe you, please do not think that of me. Nevertheless, I have my reputation as a businessman to think about. My contacts are excellent city and country wide; I would have heard of the dispatch of the gentleman you claim to have so swiftly removed. So, I ask of you, as I am sure would you if our roles were reversed, where is your proof?"

"You offered such an attractive bounty on the mark that I felt it pertinent to act swiftly," Kerian responded, not willing to divulge to this slippery man that he had his own reasons that necessitated the fast turnaround. "But, by your actions, it would appear that I was foolish to believe Atticus's word could be anything but empty boasting."

Confident that reinforcements were on the way, the guild master leaned forward, his fingers intertwined before him in an almost laughable travesty of an intellectual who appeared bored trying to fathom the meaning of life, as its mysteries were so far beneath him, much like the man standing before him.

"As I asked before," Atticus replied, his ire clearly rising at the insult Kerian had just delivered, "Where is your proof? I certainly expected something more professional from the likes of you." He risked a quick glance past Kerian towards the only entrance into the room, his eyes telegraphing impatience that Kerian swiftly understood. Atticus had summoned additional muscle.

"Your reputation came out of nowhere in a very short time," Atticus continued. "Let me guess, some coin here, a favour there... Always in the ear of someone I knew, so you would be trusted and come highly recommended to our guild for work. Do you think I am so naïve to believe the word of an old man? I have been in this position a long time and I am not easily fooled."

The sly smile that slid across Atticus's bloated features taunted Kerian with the option of an explosive and violent response but he swiftly discarded such an action as foolhardy. The sound of footsteps at the door behind him and the resulting full-fledged grin appearing on Atticus's features served to confirm that for now this personal restraint was correct. It appeared the hired help had arrived.

"Here's your proof," Kerian stated calmly, lowering the sackcloth bag onto the table in a slow non-threatening manner for the benefit of the figures behind him as well as the treacherous leach sitting before him. He slid the sackcloth bag across the highly polished desk towards the merchant, stifling a grin as it scattered documents and knocked the chocolate confection off the desk to the floor. The departure of the cake appeared to please only one member of the audience who was soon showing his appreciation by wolfing down the dessert whilst wagging his scruffy tail.

Amid the confusion, Kerian's free hand fell lightly upon the hilt of his dagger, while the other, returning from the delivery of the sackcloth, pushed back the edge of his cloak to help gain access to his sword.

Atticus's features turned from confidence to confusion in an instant, before the bag slid to a stop before him, a crimson streak marking its progress across the table's mosaic patterned surface of multicoloured wood. He looked down at the bag as if someone had presented a box filled with the deadliest of vipers and tried to regain his composure by swallowing hard and gesturing at the sackcloth without touching it.

"What's this?" he inquired tentatively.

"What you asked for: Your proof. Go ahead and open it. I assure you, it won't bite... Anymore." Kerian watched as Atticus hesitantly began to untie the drawstring, gingerly pulling out the knot that held it closed, snatching back his hand in case something was indeed alive and venomous within the sack. He glanced back up at Kerian who put on a straight face and motioned for him to continue.

Atticus's barely stifled shriek was worth all the theatrics Kerian had put up with so far. The figures behind Kerian rushed forward to snatch the bag away in fear of their master's life and as they pulled the sack opened further allowing Ferdinand's severed head to flop wetly out of the bag and teeter on the edge of the desk, threatening to drop into the merchant's lap at any moment.

"And I thought this was a private party," Kerian commented, eyeing the four men who were now standing alongside him. He chose to ignore them as they were too busy gawking at the head to be much of a threat and pressed home the element of shock. He looked hard at Atticus's pasty face and fixed him with a cold stare.

"My payment if you please." he extended his hand towards Atticus, ready to accept his bounty. "After all, we both have reputations to think about... You need to show you pay for services when delivered and workers tend to revolt if they are not paid. I'm sure if you were in my place you would ask the same."

Atticus opened a drawer set into the desk and reached in with slow deliberate movements.

"Steady now!" Kerian warned, although just one look at the suddenly over eager man, ferreting in the desk before him confirmed there was no risk of any desperate actions yet. A bag of coins clinked onto the desk and Atticus looked up into the steely gaze of his doom.

"Our deal was for the cure," Kerian stated quietly, the menace evident in his voice. "This," he gestured to the pouch of money, "is not what I had in mind." There was a flash of black and gold as Kerian's dagger embedded itself into the desk's surface, raising splinters and making Atticus jump at the speed of its arrival.

"Now... Where is it?" Kerian snarled.

Hands came forward, firmly restraining Kerian's shoulders whilst the other guards moved around to protect their master. Kerian roughly shrugged his shoulders loosening the confident grip and glared at the guards who had dared to touch him. Swords slid from sheaths and daggers came to ready hands.

Kerian held his breath, allowing the guards a heartbeat to relax before he chose to unnerve them psychologically once more.

"If you touch me again there will be consequences," he threatened.

Atticus looked towards his guards with twitching eyes and gradually relaxed. The old sly persona began to come back to the fore, confident it was he, who now held the upper hand. The guild master began to match his thoughts with actions and slowly drew himself to his full height, pushing the severed head to one side with a napkin in slow deliberate movements that barely contained his disgust, before leaning forwards and bringing his pointed noise mere inches from Kerian's face.

"Nice dagger," he remarked, his voice calmer now, confidence definitely restored, the icy cold demeanour of a true businessman now fully reasserted.

Kerian had to admire how quickly the man had recovered, proving without doubt what personal skills had delivered Atticus to this position of power in the first place.

"You will, of course, be paying for the damage to my desk." He hissed, his eye movements confirming to Kerian that the guild master was drawing silent support from the presence of the guards around him.

"I somehow expected more from you," he continued. "Surely you had to be aware that there could never possibly be a cure for what afflicts you?" He uttered a half-hearted laugh, more for the benefit of the guards looking on than for any emphasis on the facts he was presenting.

"There is no such thing as a cure for old age. Everyone gets old and dies eventually, even me. It is the one thing you can rely on, unless the gods wish otherwise and an accident befalls you. Even the greatest of wizards can only delay its arrival, battling the ravages of time with illusions that come from costly mystical enchantments." He paused as if gathering his thoughts for the finale of his speech.

"Why don't you just live your life now while you still have it," he commented. "After all, it would appear you have only a few years left to run and it would be a shame if an accident stole your few remaining years." He laughed again, looking into the slightly unnerving glare of the man before him, a man who by appearances had lived well in excess of fifty years if he was a day.

"Take the money and go, being grateful that I have deemed you worthy of sparing your life." Atticus reached forward and opened the pouch of coins, removing several from the pile before sealing it up once more. "These I'll take for the table and next time beware of negotiating with a man who has a 'nose' for business. You are simply not in my echelon. Consider yourself dismissed. This guild no longer requires your services."

"I expected as much," Kerian confessed, "...and yet I had hoped that with you it would have been different." He picked up the moneybag, noting how light it felt and how undervalued he had become and something snapped in his mind. This betrayal was not just a slight against him, it was time wasted that Kerian could never recover. The curse aged him a year every month of real time that passed, rushing him towards an early grave. He was thirty-three years old, but an outsider looking at Kerian now would believe him to be rapidly approaching sixty.

The slimy guild master was still smiling in front of him, unaware his empty promise to stop the curse was more devastating to Kerian than his posturing threats. Although only a week had been required to track down the target, in Kerian's reality nearly three months of cursed life had trickled through his hands with nothing to now show for it. Kerian felt a dull ache start behind his eye and a rage welled in his chest.

"I want more chocolate cake." Atticus ordered, licking his lips at the thought of the delicacy, even as he gestured to a servant who stood back away from harm and attentive to his master's every whim. "Oh... and take away this head will you, it's dripping all over the carpet."

The guild master picked up a small pile of papers and pretended to sift through them before looking up at Kerian as if surprised. "Still with us?" he questioned, as if the very thought of it would be absurd.

"You made a deal with me," Kerian stated as calmly as he could. "The head of Ferdinand Kepstin for an ancient artefact that would cure me of the curse that afflicts me; my old age."

"If you want to be surrounded by old artefacts maybe you should become a monk," Atticus joked.

"What did you say?" Kerian was not sure if he was being insulted or if there was a glimmer of something in what the guild master said.

"A monk," Atticus repeated, miming to add emphasis by putting his hands together in mock prayer. "You know, at the monastery of St Fraiser on the hill out of town." He gestured wildly behind him back across the city of Catterick to a building that only knew its place in Atticus's imagination as there was no window through which to view it.

"It is said they have many ancient crumbling artefacts in the monastery and an extensive library. You would be right at home with all the other decaying objects. You could spend your remaining years reading tales of lost lands and when you die you will not have far to go... I hear the graveyard is right next door!"

"I wasn't aware there was a monastery nearby," Kerian confessed, ignoring the insult and suddenly lost in thought. "They just might be the people I need to see..."

"Oh, they don't permit wandering fossils," Atticus submitted in jibe, warming to the topic of conversation. "You have to get an appointment with the Abbot first and that can take months. Even guild members have to wait their turn and your guild membership has been unfortunately rescinded."

"Oh I think he'll see me." Kerian returned. "I can be very determined when I want something."

"Determined? I think you may be mistaken." Atticus replied mockingly. "After all, didn't we just have a conversation about you wanting something... and I don't recall the negotiations ending in your favour."

"You would suppose so," Kerian remarked, "however I don't believe I'm the only one who was mistaken. After all, you told me you had a nose for business." Atticus leaned forwards to offer a suitable rebuttal, not sure what the old man was implying.

Kerian moved so swiftly that Atticus barely had time to scream. The knight threw his head back first; catching one guard in the forehead and stunning the man with a vicious blow above his eye that made him step back and fall over a rug to tumble to the floor. The guard to Kerian's left received an elbow in the stomach and bent over, tumbling backwards as his headbutted colleague grabbed him as he fell.

Atticus felt a flash of pain and something wet flooded down his face to drip across the table, he pulled back in shock only to glimpse Kerian nodding, apparently satisfied at his handiwork, before turning and stepping away across the fallen guards confident the remaining ones would be too busy trying to cope with their squealing guild master.

Kerian took the time to wipe his retrieved dagger on a tapestry and turned one last time to regard the chaos behind him, watching with cold satisfaction as the guards rushed to their master's aid, trying desperately to staunch the wound in the centre of Atticus's face with anything they could get their hands on.

The knight looked down at the lump of flesh still dripping in his hand, then threw it back into the room to the one individual he knew would appreciate it. There was an explosion of fur and the mongrel from beneath the guild masters desk shot forwards, leaping up to intercept the thrown object and devour it before it even hit the floor.

"It appears your dog has a nose for business too," Kerian smiled.

Chapter Six

"I'm telling you this will never work," snapped Scrave, staring up at the towering figure alongside him. "And, for the last time, get that boat off your head!"

Scrave regarded Rauph with barely concealed hatred. This creature had no understanding of the word 'stealth' and certainly no comprehension of 'tact'. Already that evening it had taken them over an hour to get into the harbour, going around and around in circles until they had finally collided with the harbour wall. Rauph had then hoisted the boat single-handedly out of the water and had jogged along the wall with the boat high above his head.

The Elf had personally argued that this was slightly conspicuous to which Rauph had replied that the boat was actually a dinghy, not a *sliteleeconspicuoss* or whatever Scrave said it was. Nevertheless, Scrave did not feel that this disguise as returning fisherman, tired after a long day's work, was working very well. Scrave had not got the heart or patience to explain that an eight-foot tall shaggy monster jogging along the harbour wall with a boat on his head hardly looked tired, or like any fisherman he had ever seen.

"We don't even have any fish!" he had argued.

"So... We had a bad day." Rauph had shot back. "Maybe we can pick some up from a shop?"

Upon securing the dinghy near to one of the docking piers, the shopping trip had truly begun; a time fraught with close calls and the ever-clomping sound of Rauph's immense bulk trying to keep up with his nimble, light-footed associate. Scrave shook his head at the recent memories.

Cats wailing, dogs barking and drunkards who couldn't believe what they were seeing were all present in a montage that consisted of a huge creature sauntering around with an ever growing pile of 'shopping items' on his back and hanging from his arms. Sailcloth, thread, twine, fishing nets, cooking pots and pans, anything left unattended and that was on the shopping list Thomas had supplied to Scrave was liberated for the *El Defensor's* crew.

With growing trepidation, Scrave reviewed the list and noted the candles and incense sticks still required for the ships mage. The shops here all appeared to have barred windows and shutters, with little or no indication of what wares were for sale inside. The evening's nocturnal activities although off to a good start were restricted by time. They only had until the *El Defensor* docked and it appeared the opportunity that remained was shrinking fast. At least the Minotaur was useful for carrying things. There seemed no end to the creature's strength and ability to carry whatever Scrave threw at him. They rounded a shadowy corner and stopped, well Scrave tried to stop and Rauph barrelling into him, pushing the Elf out into the streetlight.

"What is it Scrave?" the Minotaur enquired. Praying no one had seen him; Scrave backpedalled furiously and secreted himself into the safety of the darkened corner.

"Just what we've been looking for." he muttered to himself, sniffing again to confirm the light scent of incense he had caught on the breeze. Scrave quickly scanned the area for guards and other passers-by before slipping out of the shadows and swiftly skirting the area, to come up against a tall stone pillar, covered in intricate carvings.

"What are we looking for?" Rauph asked again, his gravelly voice startlingly loud in the silence of the night as he plodded directly across the courtyard area with no thought for any cover at all.

"Shush!" Scrave returned curtly, alarmed at the lack of stealth shown by his companion. "This is some sort of temple." He gestured to the building that the pillar adorned. "It's more than likely to have the incense sticks we need. And if we are in luck we might be able to secure the biggest prize of all." He looked up at Rauph and swiftly considered his options. "I want you to take all the stuff we have collected and get back to the dinghy. Then wait there at the harbour for the *El Defensor* to arrive. I'll be back as soon as I can."

"You want me to leave you?" Rauph mumbled from behind a pile of worn canvas. "But we haven't finished yet. We don't even have a fish! What are you going to do whilst I go back to the boat? Where are you going to go?"

"I'm going shopping." Scrave grinned and pointed up the pillar.

* * * * * *

"Get your hands off me!" Atticus bubbled, from underneath a scarlet soaked cloth draped across the gaping ruin where his nose had been. He backhanded one servant and sent another sprawling before he threw the cloth away and stood up to glare at his guards. They looked on in horror as bubbles of blood and stringy clots dripped from the open hole in the centre of Atticus's face.

"I want him dead!" he snarled. "I want Styx brought to me and I want to make him pay for what he has done. I want him to die a slow lingering death."

Silence followed his statement, broken by the faint whistling coming from his face as he breathed in and out. He looked towards the guards and arched an eyebrow indicating he expected an answer now.

"Yes master!" responded the quartet in unison before him. They turned to leave, eager to be away from a scene that had left them worrying if they would become unemployed on the morrow.

"Wait a moment!" Atticus wheezed, indicating the last guard. The guard stopped in his tracks and went pale expecting the worst.

"Have you found the dog yet?" Atticus enquired.

"No sir" came the hesitant reply.

"Well do it fast you fool!" Atticus spluttered. "I want my nose back!"

* * * * * *

Scrave scampered lightly up the temple pillar, not taking time to examine the exquisite engraved forms beneath his fingers that portrayed snakes and serpents and people being penitent before them or alternatively eaten alive. Instead he thanked his stars for the foot and hand holds they supplied and soon pulled himself up and over onto the temple roof. Moving swiftly, his footfalls barely making a whisper, he headed off around the outer edge of the roof, sliding from shadow to shadow, ever on the outlook for guards of the building.

Scanning the roof from his vantage point the elf took in the warmer shades in the air around him and noted the tell-tale sign of a guard sleeping on the job. He crept over and delivered a swift smack to the back of the man's slumbering head, putting him into a more permanent form of unconsciousness, before repositioning him with his helmet pulled forward over his eyes.

The next guard was on the opposite side of the roof and more alert than his delinquent colleague. Scrave could not risk a raised alarm and he knew time was against him, so he had no qualms creeping up behind the unfortunate man and slitting his throat in a swift and efficient motion. The guard's body crumpled to the floor and within seconds was positioned in a pose to simulate sleeping beneath a nearby buttress, although for this unfortunate waking up was no longer an option.

Confident there were no more guards Scrave ran across the wide expanse of roof to a raised opening that led directly into the building beneath.

"That's the way in" he muttered to himself, leaning over to confirm that the skylight was positioned directly above the main altar room. The vague shape of a raised dais and an immense ornate altar complete with flickering torches confirmed his guess. The size of the room confirmed Scrave's belief that where there was religion, money and artefacts were often to be found.

The Elf concentrated further on the task, his natural abilities rising to the fore. His eyes scanning the gloom for further signs of guards or worshippers but there were no body warmth signatures visible. Scrave turned his head to listen intently for any movements from below. When this also appeared to be clear, he began to check the surrounding area for traps and alarms. The temple must have realised this skylight was a security risk and an ideal opportunity for a thief but he could find nothing to worry him.

Something still felt off, although he was unsure if this was his excitement at the challenge ahead or the fact resistance had been light up to this stage. One thing was for sure, he worked better in the dark, so the torches had to go.

He looked down at the flickering lights far beneath him and gestured towards them with a gesture of his hand, circling each in turn with an extended index finger that formed an imaginary circle in the air. Then he used his hands to mimic a scooping motion gathering the torches into an imaginary pile in his mind's eye before closing his hands into fists and cutting off the oxygen in his imagination.

The torch flames extinguished far below as effectively as plunging them into water. The small cracking noise at the Elf's ear indicated that one of his gemstone earrings had perished at the use of such arcane power. When he returned his attention to the gloom below, it took his heat sensitive eyes to notice the warm spirals of smoke coming off the torches where previously flames had sprung. Scrave uncoiled a rope from his waist and secured it firmly to a nearby ledge, pulling it tightly several times to check the rope would not fail.

"The things I do to get a bargain!" he joked to himself, thinking back on Rauph's earlier jibes about shopping. Then, confident the rope would hold his weight; he came back to the skylight and swung his legs over the precipice. As he prepared to drop he remembered something Thomas had told him once about the places on his world where he went to go shopping. A smile crossed his face. With a little change, it worked really well.

"Ground floor, menswear and fashions, incense sticks and unguarded religious artefacts... going down!"

With a quick intake of breath, he dropped silently into the still air of the temple and started lowering himself into the darkness.

* * * * * *

Kerian arrived back at the Sunset Spider full of renewed purpose and resolve. His mind racing with probabilities as he had cut across country from the Couqran estate, giving Saybier free reign to find the route the great stallion felt most comfortable pursuing. If there was a great library at the monastery there may just be some information that could point Kerian in the direction his life now desperately needed. He tried to hold his feelings in check; he had suffered dashed hopes on so many previous occasions but something about this felt right.

There was one other thing concerning him. He could not shake the sight of the Halfling he had met days previously from his mind. Even as he had galloped across the open fields, he could have sworn he saw a small figure, remarkably like Ashe Wolfsdale, slipping and sliding through the mud heading towards the Couqran estate he had just left. No, that was ridiculous what would a Halfling be doing in the middle of a field in the dead of night? It had probably been a poacher.

He shook his head trying to shake the cobwebs as Saybier clattered across the cobblestones back into the yard and stables. Clearly, he was more tired than he thought!

He secured Saybier, asking the groom to rub his horse down and water him in preparation for another ride, before striding into the inn and heading towards his lodgings, leaving the groom staring into the glaring teeth of his mischievous stallion.

Kerian felt flush, almost feverish with renewed energy and enthusiasm. He flung his saddlebags onto the bed and swiftly secured his meagre personal belongings. The more he thought about it, the more convinced he was this was the right thread to follow to possible salvation. Could his quest finally be over, if only he could believe it? This time he was sure to find the answer.

He hastily threw a handful of silver crowns on the bed to cover his lodgings and glanced around the room that had been his home for so scant a time. The image in the room's mirror froze him in mid-contemplation. The emerald shard in the silver locket suspended around his neck was glowing with a deep pulsating green.

"What the ..."

The window imploded, showering glass into the room and producing thousands of shards of razor shrapnel. Kerian threw his arm up to protect his face and as he peered beneath, he saw through the ruin of the window frame to a twisted figure emerging from the night. It perched jerkily upon the sill, an ancient arrowhead clearly protruding from the front of its skull and a stench of decay permeating the air around it. Green eyes fixed on the elderly knight, and the creature hissed with satisfied recognition.

Kerian initially stood transfixed with horror at the repugnant sight, then acted in the only way that seemed obvious. He turned and fled for the door. Only to fling it open and come face to face with another barely human form, standing with gruel-white skin mottled by blotches of morbidly blue veins and a neck twisted at an unnatural angle. Of far greater concern, even more so than its horrific appearance, was the loaded crossbow raised in skeletally thin hands that pointed directly at Kerian's nose. Yet again illumination from supernatural emerald green eyes locked their glare with his, adding to the surreal terror of the whole situation.

"Uh oh!" Kerian gasped, slamming the door shut to bar the creature's entrance. The wooden door splintered inwards towards him as the crossbow quarrel pierced through from the other side, stopping a fingernail's breadth from Kerian's face. The knight did not hesitate, grabbing a piece of the destroyed chair that had been stacked beside the door, wedging it firmly under the door handle and securing it with the most desperate of prayers.

Spinning back into the room he turned to face the other undead creature that was still extricating itself from the ruin that had once been the window frame. Crossbow quarrels pounded loudly into the wooden door behind as Kerian lunged across the room to grab the off balance corpse.

Fighting back the bile that rose in his throat, he tried to ignore the cold gelatinous sensation of his fingers sinking into the putrid flesh that clung to these long dead bones and twisted his frame in one fluid motion, lifting the corpse free of its entanglement and throwing it across the room and up against the exit. There was a sickening crunch as the figure slammed directly onto the barbed arrowheads protruding through the ruined door. Green spectral eyes looked down to regard the glinting barbed heads protruding from the corpse's chest before it opened its mouth to laugh insanely.

"That won't stop me," it hissed.

Another quarrel smashed through the wooden door, its point thrusting through the spine of the creature, cleanly severing the bone to send its skull, now without support crashing to the floor. An unearthly dirge howled from long dead lips as the green light pulsing within its sockets faded and then appeared to ooze from the skull as a sickly green mist. The body hanging on the door also began to ooze a fine mist, which ran down its length to pool on the floor below.

Kerian had no time for self-congratulation and turned for the bed, grabbing his saddlebags as the door now received its second form of attack that evening, an axe head clearly visible through the ruined timbers. Only one other exit remained and Kerian took it, heading directly for the shattered window frame. He came up short as a large shadowy figure filled the opening before him. Kerian took in the image and realised instantly how these creatures had found him so quickly. The leather apron stained with soot, a carbon scored hammer and the green glowing eyes highlighting a recently stitched arm confirmed his fears.

"Going somewhere?" the creature taunted.

"By Adden," Kerian swore, "the blacksmith."

"Yes," the creature confirmed, as if reading his thoughts. "How kind of you to recognise me."

"But I thought you could only possess the dead?" Kerian stammered in return.

"Took a blow to the head shoeing a horse," the creature motioned, pointing to a slight dent in the skull as it lifted the blacksmith's hairline to reveal the injury. "I've been the blacksmith for several days now, only problem is the horses don't seem to like me." It uttered a high maniacal laugh. "Who'd have thought you would be delivered right into my arms so soon after our last meeting."

"But," Kerian continued aghast, trying desperately to ignore the fact that the blacksmith was peeling one ruined hand away from the shards of glass that still adorned the remainder of the frame and leaving fleshy strands dangling. "You fixed my arm. You had me defenceless, the perfect opportunity to kill me."

"Now where would have been the sport in that?" the blacksmith grinned. "Besides, that damned nosey inn keeper wouldn't leave me alone with you for one minute. I had no choice but to help you!"

Kerian filed that one away. He would need to be more generous settling the bill if he ever got out of this.

"You don't look so young anymore, how many years have you aged now, twenty or thirty?" The creature continued to mock, stepping carefully down into the room. "Yet you remain hopeful of finding a cure. You should know by now that it is hopeless and ultimately you will die. It was your queen's wishes after all."

The door finally gave in to the relentless pounding it had received from the hallway and flew open. The emaciated figure from the hall staggered fully into the room, axe head gleaming wickedly in its hand, its actual strength no reflection to its withered dead condition.

Kerian exploded into action, using the distraction to run into the blacksmith, using his heavy saddlebags as a shield and pushing directly at the creature with all the force he could muster. The resulting blow caused the grotesque caricature of a man to stagger backwards off balance and Kerian seized the advantage, following through to push the blacksmith back out of the open window high above the cobblestoned street outside.

The creature uttered a disembodied shriek as it realised it was about to fall. Huge hands reached out by reflex, clutching for any lifeline, however thin. It grabbed onto the saddlebags, half dragging Kerian, who was still holding onto his possessions, through the broken window and out into space after the undead blacksmith. Glass shards still embedded in the sill snagged Kerian's cloak, tearing the material as he passed through. His leather armour saved his torso as he tried valiantly to halt his momentum, only to find himself dragged unwillingly across the jagged-edged frame. He tried desperately to free his saddlebags but ended up taking the full weight of both his possessions and the creature that hung from them.

Kerian's face flushed red at the effort; he felt his breath crushing out of his body and his wounded arm screaming in protest as he was dragged over the window ledge. Inch by agonising inch he found himself slowly sliding through the window frame, as the weight outside allied itself with gravity to pull him free. All the time Kerian was terrifyingly aware of the wet footfalls heralding the approach of his second adversary as it slowly shuffled across the room towards him.

"I've got you now." The blacksmith taunted, using his feet to kick out from the side of the building and put even more force on Kerian's battered frame. "It's a long way down!"

Kerian glared down at the blacksmiths green glowing eyes and tried one last futile attempt to pull his saddlebags back into the room and protect his personal treasures but his angle against the window ledge didn't allow him enough leverage. Bright sparks were flashing before his eyes and a red haze was tinging everything as he failed to grab a sufficient intake of breath. With no choice, he mouthed a silent prayer that his belongings would survive the fall and simply let go.

The blacksmith wailed as he fell away into the darkness.

Drawing his sword, Kerian turned back into the room, his seared lungs struggling to regain air as he sought his next target. The violet corona of the enchanted blade created a blurred arc as the steel whistled through the air.

The pale-skinned corpse hesitated for a mere second and then lunged with an open jawed scream, its axe swinging wildly. Kerian jerked backwards as the pitted steel whipped bare inches from his torso, before stepping within the swinging arc. He almost gagged at the putridly overpowering stench of decayed flesh, as he brought his blade up and plunged it deep within the creature's torso.

Foul ichor poured from the rent he made, splashing across the floorboards at his feet and staining his boots but the creature just laughed swinging up its free hand to bat Kerian away across the room. He hit the wall hard, head ringing from the blow. The creature was on him again without giving him time to regain his feet, Kerian's blade still jutting grotesquely from its chest. The axe blade swung both left and right, missing the knight with less and less at each swing as the room for manoeuvrability shrank.

The axe whipped across again, forcing Kerian to duck as a sliced wisp of white hair fluttered down across his vision. He dropped from his knees to the floor and rolled across the floorboards to a temporary area of respite before regaining his feet and staggering unsteadily across the room, his mind racing to think of a weapon that could keep this living nightmare beyond arms reach. His dagger was for close up and considering the strength this creature had, Kerian did not intend to be that close. He tore the thin blanket from his bed, wrapped one end firmly around his arm and lashed out, using the linen as a makeshift whip in an attempt to entangle his axe-wielding foe and stop the path of its whirling hungry steel.

The corpse continued to advance relentlessly, apparently unconcerned at the thrashing material that licked hungrily at its face and arms. One lucky lash took off an ear but the creature did not blink at the loss. It was dead; pain was not an issue here. Whatever Kerian did, wearing it down by injury was not going to work.

Kerian bit his lip at his apparent lack of success and then suddenly had an idea. He lashed out but this time released the end of the blanket he was holding, throwing the entire sheet at the creature's head, the resulting confusion successfully obscuring the monster's vision. He stepped in close, avoiding the flailing axe blade, and jerked his sword free, to the accompaniment of a disgustingly wet squelching sound. By the time the creature had managed to tear the sheet away from its face, Kerian had armed himself once more and his blade was descending to deliver a fatal blow.

The creature's axe appeared to leap up to intercept Kerian's thrust but the feint was so skilful that before the corpse could recover from its mis-timed swing, Kerian had struck twice more. Violet tinged streaks marking his sword's path through the air as he sliced through both the left arm and then the right arm as the creature tried to counter.

The corpse looked on in detached confusion as its arms dropped to the floor severed just below the shoulders. The axe blade tumbled away beneath the bed, useless now, as the creature had no means to hold it.

Kerian took one look at the seemingly helpless creature and grinned, allowing himself time for breath and re-sheathing his sword now the threat was over.

"It would appear..." Kerian gasped, "...that you are now armless." The corpse twisted and gnashed its teeth in anger, unable to use its arms to rend and claw but Kerian was too busy laughing at his bad attempts of humour to notice. He offered a mock salute and turned to leave the room, confident he had one less assailant to face but the creature screamed behind him and lunged, jaw biting at the air as it staggered forwards.

Kerian side stepped allowing the mobile torso to lunge past, then gently pushed it while it was off balance and watched the ragged figure tumble down the stairs with a series of wet snaps as bones splintered within its lifeless body. He ran down the steps after it, jumping over the fleshy remains that lay strewn across the stairwell, oblivious to the green mist that slowly began to form from the corpse and trickle down the stairs after him.

He practically flew into the crowded taproom below, shoving through the crowd of drinkers gathered there as he swiftly made for the door. The emerald shard at his throat flared brightly, indicating the threat was far from over but Kerian was focused on simply clearing a path and getting to his saddlebags as fast as he could, his facial features set in a stony determined scowl as he continued to forge a passage to the street outside.

To their credit, none of the customers tried to stop him.

* * * * * *

The barman looked up from serving those very customers and stared hard at the departing figure, wondering what had caused Styx to leave so swiftly. A fleeting thought wondered if the man had paid his bill but something about what he knew of Styx swiftly quelled this thought of dishonesty. Styx did not seem to be a man who backed out of a promise. This just left the question why the hurried departure? Was he going after someone or leaving something behind?

Exclamations from the stairwell drew his attention. Some of the customers were holding their noses as if from an unpleasant smell and as he looked something rank and liquid dripped down the stairs.

That would be something left behind then...

Even as he watched a patch of eerie green swirling mist also undulated down the stair like a living snake; the movement scaring a couple who had been so intent on making their way to the bedrooms above, they had nearly stepped upon it.

"What's going on here then?" the barman muttered, even as a shriek snapped his head around to the other end of the bar where a second wisp of green mist appeared to be seeping through the ceiling from a room above.

Styx's room if memory served right!

Further shouts of alarm were sounding from outside but the barman was determined to protect his bar first before he worried about others. Quietly excusing himself from the shouted orders of the customers before him, the barman turned and retrieved two large wet glasses from the counter.

"I'll be back in a minute." He nodded to a nearby barmaid, indicating she should replace him behind the scarred oak counter, before he straightened his shoulders, set his jaw and advanced on the threat to his business.

Chapter Seven

Kerian rushed out into the darkened street, darting between the pools of torchlight that illuminated the entrance to the inn and heading for the spot directly beneath what had been the window of his room. Several observers had tentatively approached the figure of the fallen blacksmith and were whispering under their breath at the man's crumpled and broken body.

He pushed the onlookers aside and reached out for his saddlebags but stopped short, when he noticed the green mist lifting from the corpse and writhing around his things. People began to edge away at this strange apparition, even as others who had not noticed the mist voiced the outrage that Kerian would dare to steal the belongings of a man hurt in such a horrific accident.

The mist lazily coiled around on itself, then showing its sentient nature appeared to react to Kerian's approach and started to slide off across the cobblestones, moving away from the threat it faced. Kerian grabbed his saddlebags and slung them across his shoulders glaring at one loud-mouthed onlooker to quell his calls of outrage, before focusing once again on the mist that had dared threaten him. This had gone on long enough; it was time to finish this creature!

Kerian grabbed a burning torch from a sconce on the wall of the inn and set off in pursuit of the ethereal vapour. He could only hope that the look of horror on the onlookers' faces, coupled with the fear of the ghostly apparition-like mist, would ensure no one tried to cause trouble or follow him whilst he undertook this necessary deed.

Swirling like a something made of molten metal rather than moisture, the green mist suddenly gathered into a collective pool before oozing towards a darkened shop front, where it elongated into a long thin tube, appearing to sniff the air before wrapping itself around one of a twin set of pillars that adorned either side of the shop door. Defying gravity, it coiled its way swiftly up the pillar and stopped to gather itself together, high upon a stone-engraved plume carved at the pillars summit.

"Now I'm the one who's got you!" Kerian hissed in anger, thrusting out with the burning torch attempting to see if a naked flame could accomplish damage that his sword had been unable to accomplish. To damage or even destroy the creature whilst in its more vulnerable incorporeal state would give him a confidence he had been sorely lacking when facing these creatures in the past.

The demon mists had attacked five times since he had first seen their like in his queen's ruined castle and each encounter had been more dangerous than the last, with Kerian barely escaping before they oozed away to gather somewhere else and come after him again. They always took over dead bodies and used them to bring deadly force to each encounter. He had never been someone to run away from such danger but these creatures attacked with such ferocity they scared him more than he wanted to admit.

He also had to face the fact that their attacks had been more daring and unexpected at each encounter and he was getting older and slower each time. If he could eradicate one now and discover their weakness he would be more prepared the next time they attacked.

This attempt had been particularly unexpected and Kerian knew his guard had been down. If it had not been for the warning his necklace had given him, he knew his quest would have ended back in his room, with no one to mourn his passing, as his family would never identify him as an old man, especially as he had mislaid his ring.

He had to take steps to end this before these creatures really were the end of him. He waved the torch in a more threatening manner and was rewarded as the mist gathered up to pull out of reach before timing his swings to slip under the lintel and into the shop through a crack in the top of the door. Kerian looked on as a hopeless spectator, powerless to halt the mist's passage as it entered the building fully and disappeared into the darkness.

"Damn!" Kerian cursed, slamming his bare hand against the door in frustration. "I was so damn close!"

He put his saddlebags against the wall and wrestled with the handle, desperate to prevent the creature's escape but to no surprise, he found it locked. He tried to stare through one of the barred windows, yet even with the torch to cast some light he could not make out what lay within. He returned to the door and took a moment to check the street as he contemplated breaking the door down. This creature's life was going to end now! Kerian was resolute in this fact.

A quick body slam against the door confirmed that he was never going to be able to break the door in, so he returned to the window, instantly dismissing the sound broken glass would make and the city watch it would call. Glancing through the window for a clue as to the whereabouts of the luminous mist, he was still unable to see anything.

This was strange. Even with the glare of the torch, he should be able to see something! He angled his hand against the pane and realised that a drape obscured the inside of the window. The shops in town never hid their wares like this! Not unless the goods were valuable, or they were not meant to be seen.

A suspicion began to form in Kerian's mind; a horrible suspicion that quickly grew into terrifying certainty. He quickly stepped away from the shop fighting the instinct to flee as he prayed he was somehow wrong. His eyes rapidly scanned the shop front zeroing in on the faded paintwork, barely discernible in the flickering streetlight. Something indecipherable, a family name of some kind, but the peeling gold paint was curling and obscuring clarity.

The one word he could make out froze him to the spot as he whispered it aloud from a suddenly dry throat, the realisation hitting like a physical blow; '*undertakers*.'

"Oh by Adden, no!" Kerian's breath caught in his throat, the terror turning the blood in his veins to ice. Before he could act the shop front literally exploded before his eyes, sending him tumbling backwards out into the street with pieces of burning debris raining down around him. He regained his feet as quickly as he could and shielded his eyes from the piercing glare.

A gaunt skeletal figure stepped through the ruined storefront, unsteadily moving its withered feet towards him. The animated corpse's robes gleamed new in the firelight, funeral robes decorated with pictograms and runes embroidered around both the hems and sleeves of the expensive silken material. A necklace of precious stones swung from side to side as the figure advanced, the sparkling movement distracting Kerian enough to realise that one stone was missing from its housing.

Greyish skin, withered with age, cracked into a smile as the figure advanced, its empty eye sockets now containing the fluorescent green that signified the demon mist had miraculous returned to physical form. The green eyes flared briefly as they came to rest on the scorched elderly man, before the grin became a snarl of hatred.

"Do you have any conceivable idea of what you have just done!" it screamed. "The blacksmith's body was in perfect condition! It was the most powerful and healthy body I have ever possessed. I had kept that body clean and safe from harm for days, no tell-tale marks apart from the injury where the horse had kicked it. I even tried to use lavender to ward off the smell as it started to rot so that no one was the wiser. The corpse paused, as if gathering breath in its new form was difficult. "And then you had the nerve to drop me out of a window!"

Kerian wanted to slide away from the unsteadily advancing figure but it sensed his disgust and simply moved all the faster as it swiftly became accustomed to its new spindly form.

"Now look at me!" it shrieked, holding up a withered hand that looked as if someone had broken all the fingers. "Look at what I am in!" The creature gestured with its arms flinging the limbs out wide as it motioned towards the current shell it inhabited. It lifted a wrinkled hand to its peeling nose and sniffed deeply. "I'm already a week dead and I smell... awful!"

"All the easier for me to know when you are near..." Kerian shot back, displaying a bravado he did not feel as he purposefully drew his sword.

"I suppose there is one saving... grace," the creature choked as if having problems using a strange tongue, its glance lingering on the sleeves of the garment it now wore. "I appear to be in the body of a mage. Fancy that! A wizard and still wearing his necklace of spell gems. It was the first corpse I came to and it's such an unexpected surprise!"

"I wonder what spells I have locked up in here?" It continued to taunt, tapping the side of its head in a sickening parody of real life, only to find the top of the skull shifting to one side. A seeking hand went into the skull cavity knocking the top off and to the floor. Then after several moments scooping at nothing, it withdrew the hand and laughed. The brain, removed following the mage's death, had been stored elsewhere for further study.

"Maybe not as much as I was expecting." It confessed, its green eyes focusing on Kerian and his violet tinged sword. "I suppose I will just have to settle for the gemstones and choose one at random" A grey white hand reached up to tear a gemstone from its setting, the dead mage's touch setting in motion a sequence of powerful magic probably cast into the stone many months previously when the mage was still alive. The corpse laughed and threw the gem to the cobblestones just in front of its target. It exploded instantly, letting the magical energies within come forth and wreak havoc.

"Now I can *really* make you suffer."

Kerian barely had time to curse as the gemstone hit the ground and disintegrated, the magical power contained within spilling forth to do the pre-enchanted bidding of its former master. Somehow, despite its master being long dead, the power recognised the cold body that held it and leapt to do its pre-arranged bidding as it had been enchanted to do so long before. Red flames tinged with blue roared into existence, racing across the cobblestone street and completely encircling him in a heartbeat. Even as Kerian tried to back away the magical flames licked higher to soar over eight feet in height, cutting off the possibility of leaping over the barrier and bathing him in a sudden searing heat from which he had no escape. Kerian shielded his body with his cloak as he desperately tried to find a way out of his predicament.

Glowing green eyes devoid of warmth looked on satisfied as the focus of its being ran from left to right. Now it was time to have more fun. Almost instinctively, the release of the magical energies around the corpse seemed to spark impossible memories of association that let the creature know if it moved its decaying hands just so...

In immediate response, the circle of flame widened, moving away from its intended target; no, that was not the idea at all! Maybe this way... Bringing its hands together the flame moved again, this time it began to tighten, curling in upon itself, making the heat within more intense for the man struggling to escape. The undead creature looked on as Kerian started to cough from the magical miasma given off. Shrugging indifferently at his discomfort the monster moved its hands again and the circle tightened further.

Kerian fought a losing battle trying to shield his face from the heat, having no choice but to expose it to try and find any signs of weakness in the wall of magic that relentlessly advanced towards him. How did he keep getting himself in messes like this? It was as if the whole world was out to destroy him. He lifted his cloak up trying to offer what limited protection it may give and was rewarded with the harrowing sight of the threads beginning to singe and smoke before his eyes.

Through the flickering wall, he made out the ghoulish figure of the mage jerkily moving around in order to get a better view of its handiwork. Wild insane laughter rose above the roar of the enchanted flames as the creature turned towards him and the flames tightened further.

"You can start begging for mercy now." It informed him in its cold voice. "You won't get it though. I am going to watch you burn inch by inch. I will bathe in your screams as your flesh roasts on your bones."

The creature's eyes blazed through the magical wall of fire, focusing on Kerian wherever he tried to run. "And when I've finished and you lie hoping for death, I may even heal you again just enough that I can start hurting you all over again." Kerian tried to put the words of the undead creature from his mind, nearly dropping his cloak as the fire continued to advance, the heat burning the backs of his hands and raising blisters in mere seconds.

He quickly grabbed the leather gloves at his belt and pulled them on, wincing as the leather scraped across his scorched skin. His eyes were tearing up so he closed them, trying to protect his precious vision from the blistering waves of heat surrounding him. Allowing time for a cloak filtered deep searing breath; the knight reached for the gem-encrusted dagger at his waist and prayed his aim would remain true. Even through the thick protective leather of his glove, he could feel the heat of the exposed metal branding into the fabric.

The reanimated mage's cackling laugh marked where it stood and eyes closed, Kerian turned towards the sound. He paused for an agonising second just to be sure and then threw his dagger as hard and fast as he could in the direction he gauged the creature to be.

"Catch!" he snarled, opening his eyes to slits against the glare in time to see the mage throw its rotting hands up in surprise as the dagger hit true, plunging into the creature, trailing flame and molten metal in its wake from the passage through the magical flaming barrier. Kerian heard an inhuman shriek of frustration, swiftly followed by the blessed salving touch of cool night air, the enchanted barrier dying as the concentration of the creature maintaining it was shattered.

The cobblestones around him visibly steamed in reaction to the cool night air, as Kerian stepped through the spot where roaring flames had been but seconds before, murder now clearly on his mind. He knew giving the creature even a moments respite would be foolhardy and gritted his teeth determined to finish the corpse off and destroy the demonic mist. He swiftly advanced towards the staggering mage who still howled, jerking around arms raised in a spasmodic dance that caused his burial robes to flow about him like a wild shaman involved in a particularly energetic tribal dance. Kerian recognised the need to act in a swift decisive motion and readied his sword.

The mage turned towards him allowing Kerian the opportunity to note the damage his throw had caused. The hilt of his dagger, now almost unrecognisable as the exquisitely carved relic it had once been, protruded from one of the mage's eye sockets, resulting in an unidentified viscous fluid tracing a path down the creature's wrinkled face and cheek.

The monster tried to grab the dagger but the heat retained in the metal scorched its decaying hand. Every time it attempted to extract the blade, its hand slipped along the handle, skin and sinew stripping off in strands like a slow cooked joint of pork slowly pulling apart. Its actions seemed disjointed as if somehow, by Kerian's dagger striking the eye and the mist within, he had managed to cause more serious damage to the creature than he had expected.

One remaining eye socket blazed angrily as the undead creature finally noticed the singed old man before it had somehow survived and a howl of pure fury filled the night. The mage lunged forward without thought or reason, only to meet the violet tinged blade that was Kerian's heritage. A deep gash opened across its chest as Kerian responded to the creature's undisciplined attack with the military training he had never forgotten.

It tottered back on unsteady skeletally thin limbs at the force of the swing, then regained its balance and leapt forwards again in a ferocious and unrelenting attempt to overpower its foe, rotting hands outstretched clawing and scratching, its jaw opened to bite, gnashing with teeth that were brown and rotten.

The speed of its retaliatory strike almost caught Kerian unaware. He parried frantically with his sword, defensive strikes that only served to infuriate the reanimated corpse further. He batted away the clawed hands, the mage's jaw snapping shut inches from his face, sparks raining as his sword finally struck out for a follow through blow. Instead of landing another destructive swipe to the creature's torso the blade edge accidentally tangled with the necklace, knocking another gem from its housing. It tumbled to the floor and shattered upon the stone, magical energy writhing up from the shattered gem, sensing the need of its master, to wrap itself around both of the corpses hands and create huge ethereal claws that made its reach that much greater.

The talons managed to slip through Kerian's guard in a trice, scoring direct hits on his already bruised and battered torso and catching his left eyebrow. He turned his head away instinctively, in time for a second swipe to rend his clothes and smash into his injured arm. The blow felt like someone had hit him with a rod of iron, making his limb instantly numb. The knight yelped out in pain, pulling his arm back and leaving himself open for yet another hit, this time sending sparks up from the studs on his armour.

There was no choice but to lose ground, step back from the ferocity of the attack, intent on getting some breathing space between himself and this hideous apparition. The sound of his singed cloak shredding under the creature's claws only spurned Kerian on and he was soon in a full-fledged stagger, the corpse close behind.

"I remember doing this before." The creature taunted as it began to close the gap, claws slashing through the air.

Kerian allowed himself a sly smile, it would take a spot of luck to pull off what he was thinking of doing but he had nothing to lose. He dropped to the cobblestones spinning on one knee in a direct duplicate action of the move he had carried out all that time ago back in his queen's destroyed castle.

His back protested at the sudden move but he mentally added the injury to the myriad number of other aches and pains he was suffering and threw his full weight behind the swing.

"I remember you doing this too!" Kerian snarled, as his sword completed the arc, whistling through the air and neatly slicing mid-torso through the pursuing monster. The top half of the corpse flew several feet further before slamming into the cobblestones and skidding to a stop in a ruined mass of flopping flesh. The bottom half of the corpse took one further step before collapsing, reverting back into its previous cold, lifeless form.

Kerian pushed the hair back from his face and winced as he felt the tenderness of burnt skin across his forehead. Blood was trickling down his face from his split eyebrow and his clothes and armour were in ruins. He gritted his teeth, trying to put the discomfort behind him and advanced cautiously towards the upper remains of his foe, his exhaustion so severe that he did not have the strength to lift his sword clear from the cobbles. The tip of his enchanted blade raised sparks from the cobblestones as he advanced.

Even from several feet away Kerian could hear a bizarre series of snapping and popping noises and as he watched one arm extended from the sundered corpse but its similarity to the pale white flesh of the cadaver it once belonged to was now lost in the past.

Instead, a stick thin limb, almost fibrous in appearance and covered in thick black hairs began to feel about the cobbles, searching for either a handhold or something that it had dropped. From Kerian's vantage point, he could not be sure, although he was somewhat reluctant to advance further and satisfy his insane curiosity. Long talon like fingers suddenly jerked, stretched to the heavens as if in macabre worship of some dark and sinister god beyond his ken.

The twisted remains of the torso warped as he watched and Kerian finally witnessed his first true glimpse of the demonic hunters that had been after him all this time; the skull stretched impossibly before his eyes, horns sprouting from its scaled forehead. Fangs elongated from the creature's mouth, splitting the already taut skin that had previously been the mage's cheek. The nose began to stretch into an almost wolfen visage and a shrill keening filled the air. The green incorporeal mist was now long gone. This was the creature made real, as if, in its now weakened state, it's most dangerous form now needed to come forth.

It was the stuff of nightmares.

Kerian stood frozen before the unfolding horror before him, his mind screaming at him to turn and run, or plunge his sword into the writhing mass before him in the hope of causing further damage to the monstrosity at his feet. Yet he could no more attack the creature than draw his eyes away from the hypnotic metamorphosis occurring before him. The severed torso stared up at the knight with one baleful eye, the dagger still lodged in its other eye socket and then it jerked towards him, claw like appendages digging into the cobbles, physically wrenching the monster's frame along the ground.

As it jerked up from the cobbles, some deep-seated instinct broke Kerian's paralysis, his eyes widening not at the sudden movement of the creature but at the smoking crystalline remains revealed beneath the body as it convulsed.

The mage's forgotten necklace had broken in the fall; all the gemstones upon it crushed by its violent landing and the jerking that had happened as it changed form.

Kerian turned to flee, just as the combined energies from the shattered gemstones combined. They swirled into the air awaiting a sorcerous command, mixing, merging; and finally with no bodily recognition of the mage who once used them and no will strong enough to control them, ignited in a tremendous fireball that engulfed the demonic mass at its epicentre in an all-consuming, cauterising flame.

The blast roared out across the cobblestones with a speed that reached Kerian before he had barely made a dozen paces. He was lifted like a rag doll, thrown through the air, crashing into the side of a nearby building. He went down hard and stayed there, unconscious and oblivious to the gemstone at his throat that now suddenly gleamed as it recognised the serious danger to its owner. It continued to glow as bright as a star as the flames licked around his still form. The material of his cloak began to twist and smoke and the soles of his leather boots began to smoulder under the intensity of the heat but the flames got no closer; held in check by powers from the magic talisman.

As the magical energies faded, the gemstone silently reverted into the cold glinting, emerald pendant Kerian knew; its darkened facets hiding the secret magic it contained. A loud groan was the first sign that life remained in Kerian's crumpled form, the sound in stark comparison to the shocked silence of the night air and the occasional tinging of unprotected metal cooling after the magical explosion.

It took some time for Kerian to regain his feet, slow agonising movements cataloguing every ache and pain, every bone in his body protesting at the rough treatment it had received. Blood dripped from his split eyebrow and ran into Kerian's vision irritating his already impaired sight. Popped blisters oozed clear fluid that tracked down his exposed skin mixing with the soot and grime already streaked there.

He glanced at his hand and saw that one nail had snapped back, exposing raw flesh beneath and he winced at its rawness, horrified about the nail but unaware of the other ghastly damage his bruised and battered body showed so clearly. His breathing came in ragged almost strangled gasps from heat-seared lungs and his hair was crisp and curly at the ends where they had singed as the blast had passed. His cloak hung in charred tatters from his shoulders and as he took his first tentative step away from the side of the building the sole of his boot came free causing him to hobble painfully.

Advancing cautiously back to the epicentre of the magical inferno he noticed with grim satisfaction that there were no visible remains of the demonic creature that had pursued him. That was one blessing at least! One out of the three was now definitely dead!

He took a moment to gather his thoughts and then retrieve his dropped saddlebags from the ruined remains of the undertaker's shopfront, before turning to stagger back towards the inn. He stopped short as his foot came up against something charred and metallic, almost invisible in the darkness now that the explosion had extinguished all torchlight in the area.

Kerian bent down and plucked the item from the floor staring intently at the heat twisted metal, his scrabbled brain taking a moment to identify what this warped item had once represented. The ruined head of a black dragon stared accusingly at him from one end of the twisted mass, the one visible gouged eye now missing its gemstone. Kerian let the remains of his elegantly crafted dagger fall from his hands and turned towards the inn, determination setting his features into a stony mask of pain.

It took an eternity to stumble back to his temporary home, his mind numb simply trying to place one foot in front of another. Onlookers stopped and stared as they watched the determined charred and bleeding mess walking by.

However, as in all the places he had ever travelled, not a single person offered a hand in friendship, or an arm to lean on.

Kerian almost walked into the door of the *Sunset Spider* by mistake, he was so intent on how difficult walking had become and he staggered in to find the bar almost deserted, which was strange as serving still had several hours to go. The serving lad was sweeping the floor in a premature attempt at tidying up before the early hours of the morning and was attacking the sawdust-covered floor with a relish it had seldom seen in several months.

As Kerian painfully hobbled across the floor to a vacant seat in the far corner, the barman walked in from the kitchen area behind the bar and took in the charred bloody fighter, a concerned look on his face as he recognised his paying guest. He turned his back and began placing items on a tray, taking his time to glance every now and again to check his guest had not collapsed on the spot.

The battered knight sank into a chair with the minimum of winces and closed his eyes as if this simple act of navigating his backside into a seat was akin to having climbed the highest mountain, swam the deepest ocean or held back the hordes of the seven hells with nothing more than a soggy toothpick. His sigh spoke volumes, releasing all of his pains in a mournful gasp as he leaned back basking in a peace that was so alien to this inn but that soothed him with its unexpected comfort.

The calm repast was shattered at the arrival of a tray on the scarred wooden table before him. The barman lowered himself into the seat opposite and regarded his loyal customer with concern still apparent on his face. Kerian cracked an eyelid and took in the look.

"I look that bad huh?" he asked. The barman did not answer, instead taking the time to shuffle the items on the tray before him. A tall, dusty three-sided bottle of liquor sat on the tray along with two pairs of glasses. The two taller glasses were full of a green liquid that appeared to swirl before Kerian's tired eyes, whilst the shorter two remained empty.

The barman uncorked the dusty bottle and poured out a generous measure of the liquor into each of the latter and after pausing to sniff the contents of the glass, he offered Kerian a salute before downing his own drink with the well-practiced action of a man who was used to the consumption of such pleasures.

Kerian took a couple of attempts to grab his glass, raising his split eyebrow in annoyance at his initial inability to complete such a simple task, before he finally sipped at the honey rich amber liquid. He stifled a cough as the liquor burned his tongue and throat before sending waves of warmth through his tortured frame. The knight lowered his drink and gestured to the two remaining glasses.

"I don't like the look of those drinks." He mumbled. "Anything that's still moving is highly suspect in my eye." The green liquid continued to swirl within the glasses as if alive.

"Oh it's not for drinking," the barman replied. "Let's just call it a parting gift to someone that sorely needs a break."

Kerian reached out and touched the glass then recoiled swiftly as two demonic eyes appeared to smash into the side of the glass and glare out at him with undisguised hatred.

"How did you..."

The barman stopped him in mid-sentence putting a finger comically to his lips.

"Didn't they ever tell you never to ask an illusionist how he does his tricks? If you know how it's done the magic is gone."

"But you're not a magician." Kerian stated his confusion apparent.

"How would you know?" came the mysterious reply. "My father always told me you could tell how good a barman was by the weight of one thing and one thing alone."

"And that thing?" Kerian enquired his aches and pains suddenly forgotten.

"The magic they could perform with a glass." He replied offering another salute, finishing his own liquor with a flourish and stepping away from the table to leave Kerian to his own thoughts. He paused in his journey and shouted back across his shoulder from across the bar. "You owe me for the door, the window, cleaning the stairs, the blanket and the drinks! I also suggest you consider a bath and a clean set of clothes. Don't leave town without paying."

Kerian tried to laugh at the smile the barman threw him but it simply hurt too much. He leaned back in his chair, taking in the swirling glasses and the retreating barman with a newfound respect. It was odd that in Catterick of all places there was one kind soul who gave a damn.

He hurt all over; there was no doubt his elderly frame was becoming too fragile for the kind of life he was finding himself leading. Kerian debated looking into a mirror to examine the damage and then looked back at the bottle of liquor and reconsidered. He had all the pain relief he needed right here!

Kerian took the opportunity to review his options. It would be so easy to simply drink himself to oblivion and spend the rest of his shortened life in alcohol induced comfort. Hell he could probably afford to set up a semi-permanent lodging here at the Sunset Spider. The barman was decent enough and the rooms were clean. His room even came well aired! He winced at the pain as a small chuckle escaped his lips. He really, really, should not laugh right now.

Fleeting thoughts of being a failure and of just giving up hovered at the edge of his mind. He could simply accept the increasing pain and inevitable disability that would follow and live the remaining months he had left in relative peace, or he could fight on; day after pain filled day. His quest to find the cure for his ailment had only one thread of hope to pursue and that could easily become just as empty a promise as that Atticus Couqran had offered him. Did he even have the strength to go on, only to dash his fleeting hopes to oblivion? How many more times would he find himself facing a dead end? Why put himself through that turmoil of emotion if it was to be for nothing in the end?

Dejected he reached into his money pouch with a badly grazed and blistered hand to withdraw a single silver crown, both for the payment of the drink but also for something familiar to toy with as his mind began to wrestle with this life changing decision. He paused to examine the silver crown and a sad lonesome smile crossed his lips as he wallowed in his uncharacteristic moment of self-pity. If only he did not hurt so much!

The knight reached for the glass and downed another shot of potent nectar before realising he had to make a decision now whilst he still had the courage, or lack of sense, to do so.

"Shall I rush off again on what could be a fool's errand, suffering all the pain and anguish that could follow? Or do I simply find somewhere comfortable to pass away the little time I have left in what relative comfort and dignity I can find?"

A deeper sigh followed. Cleansing in nature, as if by its action Kerian could somehow steel himself for what was about to become his future path.

"That's not much of a choice," he confessed to himself, still weighing up the seriousness of his situation. Placing the coin on its edge, he began to roll the currency with his fingertips backwards and forwards across the surface of the table, playing with the coin as surely as he was playing with his life.

"Why don't I let fate decide?"

"If it lands heads up I'll continue this mad chase. If it's tails..." He let the thought hang incomplete, already knowing the avenue to which that option would lead.

Looking up, watching others go about their business, oblivious to his own turmoil and the decision he was about to make; Kerian hoped, almost prayed that some distraction would occur stopping his actions before he committed to a decision that held his life so precariously in the balance mere feet from where they stood. He wanted to shout aloud, scream his insecurity to anyone that cared to listen but he had started down this path alone and he had to follow it through the same.

He balanced the coin on his thumb.

"Should I close my eyes?" he entertained, his mind trying to make light of such a serious decision. He steeled himself, downing yet another quaff of liquor, closing his eyes as its warmth spread through his battered frame. He realised his heart was pounding in his chest and when he looked down at the coin, he noticed his blistered hand was trembling.

"To fate," he toasted... and flipped the coin.

Chapter Eight

Rauph gazed up into the heavens as the clouds, swollen with moisture, finally opened to deliver a deluge of large crystal droplets into the Catterick night sky. The rain swiftly caused sheets of water to pour from the shanty shacks that dotted the area near the pier and drummed a staccato beat upon the dinghy in which he sat, saturating all the shopping supplies in seconds. Lightning forked ominously, turning the grey clouds to solid marble before leaving the heavens in darkness. Rumbles of thunder made the hair on the Minotaur's neck stand up in alarm. The gods were not happy tonight.

He looked on in abject fascination as the rain began to drip from the edge of the pier, one drop, defied gravity, swelling to double its size. Eager to examine this dangling diamond more closely, Rauph leaned over and set the dinghy rocking dangerously. The droplet fell into obscurity, lost amongst the dimpling cold seawater below.

Rauph looked up at the sky and tried to figure out where the moon was in relation to the horizon. He was not sure how much time remained before the *El Defensor* docked and Scrave was still out there somewhere shopping.

He snorted loudly, the warm moisture steaming up the gleaming golden ring pierced through his nose. There was something about getting wet which went against all of the Minotaur's instincts. He did not like his red pelt matting to his skin and he did not like that people sniffed and looked at him with distain as he started to smell as he dried.

Grabbing a piece of canvas from the shopping pile, he placed it over his head, hunkering down as the rain came even harder. Scrave should have come back by now. Could something have gone wrong? The Elf had told him to stay in the boat! Rauph felt torn between obeying his partner or going back to the temple and seeing what was keeping him. He would give it a few more minutes and then whether Scrave liked it or not, this Minotaur was coming to save him!

* * * * * *

"Now, correct me if I'm wrong," queried Brother Marcus of the Order of Saint Fraiser. "Your name is Styx and you wish to see Abbot Brialin, the head of our order, at this unsociable hour of the night, to ask his advice about a personal problem you have." He looked sternly at Kerian. "You don't have time to wait until morning, no one else will do and, oh, yes..." his voice took on an autocratic tone, "I almost forgot ... you've been drinking."

The somewhat forlorn-looking figure he addressed stood out in the storm lashed night regarding the holy man with cold, killing eyes that belied his otherwise bedraggled appearance. Rain ran down his aged face, making his grey hair stick to his forehead. His black cloak hung heavy with saturation and his breath steamed in the cold night air, dramatically portraying the wickedness of the elements and adding to his overall appearance of damp and dismal discomfort.

"Just do as I ask," the knight replied impatiently.

Brother Marcus slowly withdrew into the shadows of the monastery, shutting the heavyset doors behind him before sliding steel bolts across to secure the portal. Only then, with the thick oaken barrier closed between himself and the caller, did he dare to utter a sigh of relief.

Glancing through a small diamond shaped pane of stained glass set within the door he could see the old man glowering angrily at the door. The rain began to fall in even greater sheets, if that was at all possible, lashing across the worn surface of the ancient paved path leading up to the monastery's entrance and further soaking the drunkard. Serve him right, Marcus decided, somewhat uncharitably. Perhaps it would help to sober the visitor up. Alternatively, it might encourage him to leave and seek shelter elsewhere.

Lightning flickered and danced across the sky, throwing the nocturnal visitor into silhouette serving to make him appear more intimidating. Risking one last glance the monk turned and headed off down a cold marble corridor that led to the hub of the great building, the sound of his shuffling sandal-clad feet accompanied by a low, less than monk-like muttering regarding the unsociable hours his job entailed.

Monks similarly attired in the blue woven robes of the order acknowledged him as he passed them in the corridor, their long hems whispering across the smooth marble of the floor. Some carried flickering candles, freshly lit to continue periods of study into the early hours, whilst others carried stacks of loose manuscript pages, their destinations as mysterious as the darkness into which they disappeared.

Marcus allowed himself the pleasure of walking at a slow serene pace, his mind already decided on the fate of the fighter at the main gate. He would delay for a short while, he determined and then simply inform the visitor that he would have to come back in the morning.

He did not intend to wake the head of the order on the whim of a drunken old man.

The statue of Saint Fraiser loomed above the monk as he entered the Great Hall. He paused in mid-step, never failing to feel a surge of emotion by the image presented before him.

The engraved features of the saint towered over fifty feet high, the statue capturing the revered figure with an entourage of small animals all around him. A wren perched on his outstretched finger, while a squirrel sat on his robed shoulder frozen in the act of whispering a secret into the balding traveller's ear. Within the folds of his robes, carved field mice played hide and seek and at his feet, a fox stood guard as a baby fowl advanced, all fear absent from its gaze.

Lying open in the saint's remaining hand was a book that all the monks of the order had knowledge of. It was Saint Fraiser's ledger, documenting his travels and wanderings. The first book in the vast collection now housed in the library of knowledge that the monastery protected. Draped across the open volume was a worn rosary; a flaming cross, the symbol of the order of Saint Fraiser, suspended from its end.

Small glowing lights, their carriers masked in shadow, appeared to float in the air around the statue like fireflies. In reality, the lights marked the passage of studious monks, visiting the library shelves on the open tiers that stretched out from this hub like the spokes of a great multi-levelled wheel. A domed glass ceiling high above echoed faintly with the sounds of falling rain, bringing Brother Marcus out from his state of appreciation at the place he was so fortunate to visit daily and back to his current predicament.

He found he was trying to justify to himself his actions regarding the visitor at the door. He was not being malicious; he just liked people to be courteous and respectful to the order he called his home. Abbot Brialin had accepted Marcus into the fold and had sheltered him at his time of need. He deserved respect, working all hours and required his rest like anyone else. No, no matter what the need of the traveller was, Marcus had his own standards and he was not going to make exceptions, even at this time of the night. He could see Abbot Brialin in the morning.

A loud 'boom', from back at the front entrance, shattered the serenity within the hall. All the flickering 'fire-flies' froze in flight and Brother Marcus stopped in mid-stride. What in the world could that be? He turned sharply on his heel momentarily forgetting the dignity he should show in this place of worship and mindful that he should not show agitation within these hallowed halls, gathered up his robes so he could semi-jog back towards the entrance hall. Another boom shattered the silence of the corridor followed swiftly by another. A loud splintering groan turned the monk's jog into a fully-fledged run and he found himself skidding to a stop before the main doors as yet another boom crashed through the night.

The outer doors finally gave way, splintering open with the bolts bent clear of their housings.

In the flickering illumination of the storm, silhouetted like a spectre, was a white monster of a horse, hooves raised ready to deliver yet another crushing blow to the ruined door.

Marcus rushed forward to try to stop further damage to his home in an act that was as brave as it was suicidal. His almost certain death by the stallion's flashing hooves was halted by a flash of light that caught the monk's eye, distracting him enough to change course and rush over to the recognised pane of stained glass vibrating violently within the door frame.

The door shivered to a rest as Brother Marcus rushed forwards and the glass spilt out with an almost audible sigh, caressing the tips of his outstretched fingers as it passed on its doomed journey to the floor below. It exploded into shards of light, instantly ruined beyond any hope of repair and Brother Marcus found himself groaning as he knelt to scoop up the glittering pieces, knowing this was entirely his fault for leaving the stranger out in the rain.

Kerian Denaris strode determinedly past the holy man ignoring the kneeling figure as an arrogant king would his subjects. The raging storm, initially denied entrance by the once-solid doors, accompanied the knight in his sacrilegious entry to the monastery, rushing into the hallowed halls and shrieking with glee as it whistled down the open passages. Parchment flew into the air like tossed autumn leaves, tallow candles winked feebly then died and towers of precariously balanced books tumbled to the floor as the outstretched fingers of the storm assaulted the inner sanctum.

Bathed in the pure wild energy of the untamed tempest, Kerian drew his sword and stood menacingly in the foyer, waiting for just one voice to speak out from the pale faces that now surrounded him. He turned to take in his surroundings and determine the passageway he should take in search of his goal, as more figures gathered from the many corridors and niches around him. He was quick to note that no one was armed.

"I wish to speak with the head of your order!" he roared, daring anyone to defy him in his request.

"Then speak."

The assembled onlookers parted in reverence to let a figure pass through their ranks. Eyes of incredible intensity scrutinised the bedraggled fighter, leaving Kerian feeling strangely naked and vulnerable.

Abbot Brialin approached the humbled figure of Marcus who knelt, like the other monks, upon the floor. A reassuring hand on the shoulder of the penitent man, made Marcus instantly aware that his concerns for the monastery mattered. His scrabbling hands became still from collecting the valuable pieces of stained glass that lay around him.

Silence fell accusingly.

"I'm waiting," the Abbot stated, turning once more to face the desecrator of his monastery.

Under this intense gaze, the warrior once known as Kerian Denaris found himself humbled.

* * * * * *

Scrave had reached the floor of the temple without problem and had begun his slow pillage of goods from the shrine some time ago. As yet, he had not met any resistance and although unusual, had taken full advantage, exploring the main area at his leisure, collecting baubles and trinkets that took his liking from the nooks and shelves that dotted the walls. Extinguished candles and doused incense sticks he stuffed, without ceremony, into a bag carried for just these occasions.

Finally satisfied he had emptied this side of the hall of anything worthwhile, he set his sights on the altar on the far side of the room. He had left this area until last because he felt it was nearer his escape route and also because he had a feeling that the altar held the more valuable items that would have weighed him down if he had collected them earlier. He weighed the bag in his hand and smiled. It was about half full already, with candles and incense sticks clicking around. The list was complete. Anything now was a bonus and Thomas did not need to know about it. Ship's crew percentages be damned!

The hard mosaic floor beneath his feet had a design set into the stone that spiralled lazily outwards from where he stood, with pathways beginning at the altar on the far side of the room and leading to doors that were set into the walls behind him. Large ornate pillars were set between the doors and at regular intervals all around the wall. They held a design that appeared to be massive coils of rope, piled one on the other. The scope of the room and the detail of the floor were lost on the Elf from his present perspective so Scrave promised himself that on the way out he would take the time to look down from his rope and gaze at the room properly from a height.

He paused, listening carefully to double check no one was near at hand and then stepped away from the wall and its concealing shadows, moving out across the swirling mosaic path toward the altar and the open skylight through which he had entered. The rope moved lightly as he approached and Scrave looked up to see a fine sheen of rain was falling. It seemed as if a storm had broken outside.

With the fear of discovery momentarily dispelled the Elf pushed back his cloak to free his shoulders better, then ran his free hand though a mop of scraggy, black, shoulder length hair. His pale face, framed by this unkempt border, gleamed faintly in the pale light, revealing a countenance that was delicate and refined. On his right cheek an ornate diamond shaped tattoo served to add to his exotic appearance, its pattern made more delicate by the dotted glistening beads of rainwater that had fallen across it.

As his black piercing eyes took in the room, a flash of lightning threw his face into stark relief, illuminating the darker left side to reveal an ugly scar that tracked down from his eye socket across his cheekbone, before curling wickedly along the edge of his jawbone.

An Elf should paint a picture of grace and beauty. Scrave's days as a creature of beauty were clearly a thing of the past.

Ornate candlesticks anointed with molten wax stood as silent witnesses to his approach as the Elf advanced towards the altar. Pausing at the bottom of a set of raised steps that led up to the hewn stone block, he swiftly scanned each tile before him, looking for tell-tale differences in the heat signature of the stone to see if any had vastly different colours than the usual cold bluish grey. A lighter colour could indicate a pressure pad, artificially altered to look like the steps surrounding it. One false move and an alarm would be raised or a trap be triggered that could end his night-time shopping trip instantly! You could never be too careful.

Satisfied that there appeared to be no major differentials, Scrave lightly climbed the steps and examined the altar more closely. Its bulk consisted of a single slab of heavily scarred stone, drainage gutters scratched deeply into the upper surface, their edges caked with reddish brown flakes. The candlesticks were brass and not worth the weight to carry.

Lightning flickered through the skylight throwing the temple into a split-second daylight. Scrave froze in mid-step, eyes blinking rapidly as they tried to adjust to the unexpected surge of brilliance. Another jagged flash threw the wall behind the altar into vivid vibrant colour. An immense golden snake, its coils over twenty feet in length, loomed above the Elf, eyes bright and sparkling, fangs dagger sharp.

Scrave threw up his arm instinctively, stepping away from the altar before realisation dawned. The snake was inanimate, its eyes had not traced the thief's movements and the head had remained inert. Barely suppressing a nervous chuckle, he moved closer to examine the massive serpent, marvelling at the intricately carved scales and the amazingly delicate gold leafing that had gone into creating such a life-like structure.

Now that he could examine the statue calmly, the eyes of the serpent were obviously jewels but the slight intruder could no more reach up and pluck them than he could climb the sleek structure. If only Rauph had come along. He could have boosted Scrave in a second. The riches they could have gained! Scrave shrugged: he would never have been able to sell the gems anyway. They never seemed to stay in a port long enough. Thomas was always rushing here and there, vanquishing wrongs and looking for New York wherever that was! If he had a gem the size of one of those eyes, Thomas would just use it to open a portal to the ships graveyard and although the Elf did not intend to go back to that place, he knew this was where they would ultimately return. It made his skin crawl just thinking about it. He could almost taste the rotting smell and visualise the sepia colour of the mists.

Scrave shivered, giving himself a small, exaggerated shake, before turning his attention back to the altar, trying to ignore sub-conscious thoughts in his brain that sneered it was only a matter of time before his worst fears became reality again.

Using his keen eye and his previous experience in desecration and acquisition, he finally noticed what he was looking for. Set into the side of the altar that faced the statue were two doors that he would never have seen if he had not ventured around to examine the golden serpent. He turned his back to the snake and sank gently to his knees, wrapping his bag carefully around his left wrist to leave his right free to examine the doors more closely. Scrave chuckled again: the doors appeared devoid of any lock.

"This is my lucky day," he muttered, resting his left arm on the altar top as he reached out to open the doors and reveal the secrets within. A flash of gold caught the edge of Scrave's vision and he leaned in for a closer look.

Intense pain knifed through his left arm, the force almost crushing his wrist. He felt himself pulled viciously from the cupboard and wrenched violently upwards: his feet reflexively running despite the fact he had left the floor far below. Dangling wildly from his restrained arm Scrave became aware of a terrifying hiss that blotted out his lingering scream of pain. The Elf struggled to move the shopping bag that had fallen across the front of his face so he could see what was happening. Somewhere in the back of his mind, he realised that he had drawn his sword and he came out swinging, his sword clanging loudly off something behind him. If only he could move the damn bag!

He felt himself turning in the air, his left arm feeling pulled from its socket and finally the bag swung away from his eyes. In that split second, Scrave wished he could put the bag back in place. Golden death loomed above him, the snout of the golden snake statue filled his vision, its previously inert eyes now clearly alive and deadly, with Scrave's arm gripped tightly in its venom dripping jaws!

The Elf's sword clattered from his shocked right hand and crashed to the floor far below, as the pressure on his left arm continued increasing to almost unbearable levels. He lashed out with his free hand, his gloved fist bouncing vainly against the serpent's golden scales.

Scrave repeated the action, slamming his hand against the side of the serpent's head, more weakly this time but the snake simply shook him, quelling all resistance in seconds, rattling the Elf's skull and leaving him feeling like a battered mouse, used as a plaything, before it finally met its grisly end. Without warning, he found himself falling back towards the floor, barely having time to register the drop before he hit the top of the altar with a jarring thump, then fell off the far side with the breath forced from his body.

The thief rolled across the cool mosaic floor in agony, his ribs feeling as if they had also been in the grip of the snake's deadly jaws. A shadow fell across him and he instinctively rolled again, as the head of the golden serpent smashed into the mosaic and sent pieces of ceramic spinning across the room from the force of the attack.

In the confusion, Scrave rolled back towards his attacker, moving rapidly across the floor as the snake pulled its head back up into the darkness ready to strike again. The Elf crashed against the cold edge of the altar, putting the solid stone structure between him and his foe.

The enraged hissing of the snake filled the air with menace but Scrave remained where he lay, trying desperately to calm the thudding of his racing heart and the pounding of his pulse in his ears. His eyes flicked to the left and the right, terrified that he would see the snout of the gleaming creature come around the side of the stone slab as it sought him out. He tried to slow his breathing and began to take stock of his injuries.

The cloth bag was still wrapped tightly around his left arm and he pulled it gingerly free. He held his breath as he removed the sodden covering, gazing with concern at the already bruised hand and wrist beneath. The skin was deeply indented and changing colour to a vivid black as he looked on but to his relief the skin did not appear to be punctured. He flexed his wrist and hand experimentally, wincing at the sharp pains he felt. However, his relief at not facing a poison bite easily outbalanced a little pain. Lady luck was still with him!

The flicker of a tongue shot out over the edge of the altar above his head, followed by the underside of the serpent's jaw as it moved directly over him and out into the room. Scrave sucked in his breath and dared not move an inch as the enormous snake, slid off the altar and down onto the floor. Golden scales glinted like a never-ending waterfall of terrible riches as the snake slid out over the thief, passing bare inches from his nose.

Scrave's eyes darted about anxiously for his weapon but his sword was not on this side of the altar. He cursed silently, remembering with disdain that his weapon lay at the base of the statue on the far side of where he lay. Scrave needed a distraction, something big and dumb, more of a mouthful than a spindly Elf.

Where was Rauph when he needed him?

The body of the serpent continued to slide off the altar, coils and coils of the creature piling up on the floor beside him as its head swayed from side to side in search of its elusive prey. The tail finally flickered across the Elf's face; touching Scrave's sweat streaked face for a bare flicker and almost spelling the thief's downfall as he emitted a barely muffled squeak. Yet somehow the snake failed to hear, its attention diverted by the flickering lightning and the rain sheeting in through the skylight.

It slithered across the floor towards the rope displaying a grace that was hypnotic to behold. Nearly twenty-five feet of cold-blooded hunter stretched out as the snake nosed the rope with inquisitiveness, cutting off Scrave's escape route and setting the Elf's teeth on edge as its metallic scales scraped across the mosaic.

Moving as slowly and carefully as he dared, Scrave inched towards the edge of the altar never daring to take his eyes from the back of the swaying death before him. It seemed to take an eternity, moving the bag a small distance, then levering himself up to do the same. Scrave prayed to whatever gods were listening that the snake would not glance back his way. His Elven eyes began to feel like dried fruits that had been left to shrivel in the sun, as he lacked even the courage to blink, in case this tiniest of movements alerted the creature to his presence.

The edge of the altar was finally against the small of his back and Scrave allowed himself the tiniest of tiny mental sighs of relief as he started to put some distance between himself and the gleaming serpent. He slowly raised himself from his prone position and began the painstaking job of crawling backwards, inching his way along the altar edge away from the snake and into the shadows.

The serpent circled the rain soaked mosaic floor, tongue flicking out to taste the air and pick up the smallest of vibrations. It knew its prey was still in the room somewhere it just had to find it.

Instant reassurance poured through Scrave as his hand closed about the hilt of his sword. The odds were only 100 to 1 in favour of the snake eating him now! The fact that he had spectacularly failed to use his sword during his first encounters with the serpent pushed resolutely to the back of his mind!

The forgotten cupboard door swung ajar by his ear.

Scrave peered cautiously over the top of the altar at the circling snake then back down at the cupboard. Something had glinted gold in there… hadn't it? Swiftly calculating the chances of the snake hearing him rummaging, balanced against the fact that a magical serpent this impressive had to be guarding something of worth, the Elf started to explore the contents… quietly!

Inside were more incense sticks, tapers for the candles and yet more candles to spare. Some robes, a book of some indecipherable script, a golden chalice and at the back of the cupboard, a red velvet bag. Scrave did not wait for an invitation. He opened his sack, still sodden from being in the snake's maw and scooped the chalice, some spare tapers and the red velvet bag into it.

A quickly stolen glance confirmed the serpent was still sliding eerily in and out of the shadows under the skylight, circling his rope as if daring him to try to escape. Scrave watched the snake for several moments unsure of a plan to get past the creature. What would Rauph do in a situation like this? Ludicrous images of the hulking Minotaur grabbing both ends of the snake and tying it into a large knot filled his mind's eye and raised a smile, but this action was of course, way beyond the capabilities of the Elf.

Maybe he could get out of one of the doors on the far wall. It meant getting by the snake and heading into uncharted territory but it was a plan… of sorts.

He took a step forwards, trying to get a better view and heard a loud clatter at his feet. He froze in mid-step and looked down in horror at the golden chalice that he had apparently inadvertently kicked and then he looked back up at the liquid gold snake that was suddenly slithering rapidly towards him.

"But..." Scrave was stunned. He was sure he had put that chalice in his sack!

He glanced back down in total confusion just as a candlestick appeared to pass through the base of the bag and fall to the floor, clattering accusingly against its colleague.

"But..." Scrave dropped his hand to where the candlestick had appeared and discovered a gaping hole in the material of the bag amid the snake drool. The serpent's fangs must have split it when it had bitten him! What in the name of the Seven Graces was he going to do now? A loud hiss tore his attention from the bag. The snake was already gathering its coils beneath it in preparation to strike.

It was time to leave!

Scrave feinted left and watched the snake's glittering snout sway with him, mirroring his motion. It was at a moment like this, when everything appeared to move in slow motion, that you could really appreciate how incredible this snake was.

It was huge, magnificent, beautiful... and about to kill him.

He could feel sweat beading on his brow as the snake opened its mouth to reveal a flickering, darkly mesmeric, forked tongue and glittering razor-sharp fangs that dripped clear beads of acidic poison.

Scrave's sword suddenly seemed pitifully small.

The lightning flickered again, turning the magical snake from one of warm gold into cold platinum and it lunged forwards maw open wide and teeth bared. Scrave timed it perfectly diving across the altar towards the serpent just as it attacked, sliding under its gaping jaw, which snapped shut just where he had been standing. The Elf had the dubious pleasure of seeing the snake's underside up close and personal for a second time, before he slipped off the far side of the altar and skidded into a landing.

He came up fast, head bowed arms pumping as he charged for the centre of the temple, not daring to look behind him as the snake swiftly recovered from its attack, its body starting to coil around ready for pursuit. Tell-tale pings and clatters marked the trail of candles and tapers that fell through the hole in his bag as the Elf ran, but losing the odd candle was the last thing on his mind as he tried to set a new land speed record.

He threw himself off the dais, jumping the stairs and almost flying across the open space towards the rope, the mosaic pattern a blur beneath his feet. He made a grab for the dangling rope and found himself sliding past, the rainwater from above turning the already highly polished floor into something akin to ice.

A less than graceful two-footed skid allowed him to remain just about upright, before Scrave was able to turn back towards the rope and his thin chance of salvation.

Gripping the rope securely, he allowed temporary relief to flood through him as he looked back towards the serpent whipping its way across the floor towards him, eyes hard glittering points of obsidian death. Scrave checked his sack, confirming that the bulk of items were still there and that the trip was not a complete loss before staring at the snake with his recovered cocky calmness.

"So near... and yet so far!" he taunted, twisting his hold of the rope and tugging hard with the intention of beginning his climb. The rope felt strangely light in his hand, something cold and damp fell heavily around his shoulders, followed by several wet slapping sounds at his feet.

Scrave stared half-bemused, with a slowly-sinking-in-realisation-and-dread at the limp length of rope in his hand and then in-almost-comic-slow-motion at the rest of the rope coiled lazily across the floor.

This could not be happening! Not now! A low moan escaped his tightly clenched lips, his superior smirk of seconds earlier metamorphosing into a mask of sheer terror. He glanced up into the descending droplets of rain just to check that, by some strange miracle, another length of rope had not appeared, yet even as he blinked his eyes against the descending precipitation he knew he looked in vain. The guard he had earlier knocked unconscious was waving down at him from the open skylight with a smug grin on his face.

Scrave cursed under his breath imagining a thousand violent deaths he could bestow upon the man but before he could act, loud hissing forced him to consider the larger problem at hand. This was it! His nemesis was finally upon him. The serpent's huge jaws opened again, its hiss a funeral dirge for the Elf as its coils tensed for that final lunge that would send razor sharp fangs plunging through Scrave's trembling form.

A high-pitched scream cut through the air, drawing the attention of both snake and Elf to the skylight above. Something fell through the opening, plunging to the floor, arms and legs flailing. Scrave threw himself to one side in desperation but the snake was slower and the rain drenched man crashed down on top of its golden-scaled body.

Just as Scrave was hoping that the snake would have been stunned into submission by the collision, it produced a vicious snapping movement with its back and flipped the fallen figure off. As it did so, a flash of lightning from above revealed the black and gold tabard of the temple guard who had been leering through the skylight. The guard scrabbled to his feet, his face a mask of amazement at surviving the fall, apparently still oblivious to the cause of his salvation, and came up face to face with the Elven thief.

"I thought I was dead..." he stammered looking at his hands and arms with amazement. "I didn't realise how slippery the ledge was up there and I wanted a closer look at seeing you eaten. That is some snake eh?"

"It's beh..." Scrave tried desperately to gesture towards the golden death slowly uncoiling behind the guard but the man assumed his warnings were hostile and had no intention to listen to the strange rain and sweat streaked figure that stood before him. He reached for the sword at his side and struggled to pull it from its sheath.

The serpent's open maw came down upon the guard's head, fangs piercing either side of the skull as if it were paper. Scrave glimpsed his eyes suddenly wide with terror, before the man's face crumpled like a rotten egg.

That was enough for the Elven thief. He took one last look as the snake gorging on the unfortunate guard and then did what any self-respecting Elf would have done in his place.

He ran for it.

His leather boots barely raised a whisper as Scrave ran hysterically across the open area and into the unexplored territory of pillars on the far side of the room, desperate to put as much space between himself and the dining snake as possible. Without pausing to draw breath, he started grabbing door handles and pulling for all he was worth.

Locked, locked, oh for pity's sake... locked!

A wet squelching noise rose from behind and Scrave risked a quick glance from his frantic door checking before instantly wishing he had not. The snake was vomiting up the remains of the guard, his crushed body contorted almost beyond recognition and covered with sticky saliva and slime. Scrave had heard tales that some large snakes did this, incapacitating their prey then leaving them stored to digest later. However, hearing about it and seeing it was an entirely different matter!

Even as the serpent finished the distasteful spectacle, its eyes began to scan the room for the other prey it knew was flitting about in the shadows. Its head turned one way and then the other and then paused to sniff at a dropped candlestick on the floor. Scrave followed its line of sight and realised with resignation that he had left a trail of dropped debris to lead the snake directly to him. He reached down and noticed his bag was much lighter now. He had no idea how many items he had lost on route. He folded up the bag, pushing it inside his shirt and wincing at the unseen sharpened edges and corners that stabbed into his pale flesh. If he did nothing else tonight, he would make sure the snake would not have the means to follow him in such a fashion again!

He took a deep breath, trying to calm his racing heart as he prepared to take flight. However, where to? The skylight was out of the question. The rope lay on the floor, saturated and simply too bulky to contemplate throwing back up towards the skylight, especially with the temple's guardian slithering around down here as well! He had checked every door and found them all locked. He glanced along the wall, noting that only one more door remained. If he was going to find another means of escape that was his only choice but he had to move. Moreover, fast!

The Elf broke cover and ran past the last pillar in the row, crossing into the light before angling back towards the door he had spotted. The scrape of scales informed him his unwanted companion was still close behind and gaining by the second. Scrave pushed the door without hesitation and dove through the opening it offered him.

Spinning around, he was more than relieved to see a sturdy bolt and housing at eye height. His luck was improving by the second! Scrave grasped the bolt and was just about to slide it home when the door smashed into him. Sheer adrenaline allowed the Elf to ignore the pains that now radiated viciously through various door-crumpled parts of his body, and he threw himself desperately back against the protesting woodwork. As he looked up from his frantic pushing he realised his head was mere inches from a large obsidian eye that blinked and stared hungrily at him through the crack. The snake's flickering forked tongue eased around the door edge and wiped across his brow.

Scrave's heart nearly exploded at the horror of the warm moist touch.

"Damn you!" he cursed, trying to find just an ounce more strength from his slight frame to help slam the door. "Why won't you close?" A protesting squeal rose from the bolt at his head and Scrave suddenly realised the enormity of his own stupidity. The bolt, still extended, was wedged up against its housing therefore preventing any possibility of closure at all. Scrave swore at his own folly and wrenched the bolt back, his efforts rewarded by the door slamming square once more. If he could just have a few more seconds... his fingers fumbled with the bolt as he struggled to slam it safely home.

Scrave felt a sledgehammer smash him in the chest and he found himself lying flat on his back as coils and coils of golden snake piled through after him. Temporarily buried in an avalanche of serpent he flailed about frantically, pushing, pulling and kicking rippling bands of muscle that tried to spasm and constrict whenever they felt he was near. The Elf screamed as he threw a massive length of the creature from his leg and managing to wriggle along the passage wall out into safety.

Razor sharp teeth as large as scimitars snapped at his rear as Scrave turned tail again, taking in his surroundings in snippets of landmarks he passed. Hallway, stair, priceless vase, broken priceless vase, smashed table, more stairs, another hallway. Oh where was he going? Scrave realised he did not have a clue. He just kept running with a menacing hiss as his accompanying theme tune.

He took some steps three at a time; his recklessness almost causing him to trip and fall yet, almost impossibly, he kept his feet. Out of breath, he gasped his way onto a landing and turned to survey the status of his situation. The noise had caused people to start waking up and paying attention. Doors were opening ahead and guards were now spilling into the hallway, making it harder and harder to find a route free of obstacle.

This was getting worse by the second! He needed a strategy of some kind ... any kind!

The snake slid around the corner behind him and lunged once more, making Scrave duck as it smashed into the wall above him. Quick as a flash he grabbed an urn from an ornamental niche and threw it for all he was worth. The pottery bounced ineffectually off the serpent's scales and smashed against the wall, scattering fragments of creamy white across the crimson carpet like a mouthful of discarded teeth.

Another flight of stairs, a quick backwards glance and two passageways to take. Scrave found himself all turned around; he did not know where he was or where he was going. He was running out of options. There were no nearby doors to check, no cupboards in which to hide. His indecision was taking too long. This was only going to result in Scrave becoming the main course for his slippery admirer! He turned left, ran for the next flight of stairs barely pausing for breath as he navigated these with the same reckless abandon he had shown for their predecessors, tearing around the last corner to come out into a large foyer and face to face with a massive wooden door adorned with metal studs.

A terrified shove of the door confirmed the worst. His way was blocked. His flight at an end.

Several colourful expletives sprang into the Elf's mind as he repeatedly shook the handle hoping he had somehow made a mistake, no amount of pushing or shoving, shoulder barging or cursing was going to make the door open before him. His mind pictured the time he had remaining in this world trickling away like fine grains of sand through a timer and he found himself displaying his nervous emotions by biting his bottom lip.

With the door locked, and the snake closing, there was no turning back!

He slammed his fist onto the door in frustration and almost wept, yet despite his efforts, the door remained securely firm in its stance to prevent his passing.

"Hello" sounded a familiar voice from the other side of the door. "Can I come in?"

"Rauph... Is that you?" Scrave stammered, unable to believe his accomplice had come back.

"I know you said to stay in the boat but I'm all wet and..." Rauph began.

"Shut up!" Scrave yelled. Loud hissing informed the Elf that his enthusiastic audience of one had arrived to give him the moral support he required to finish the conversation. "Please... just open the door."

An ear-splitting bang snapped the Elf out of his terror as the studded door smashed straight into his face, lifting him up off his feet and out across the foyer back towards the snake. He slid to a stop, only to realise he was looking up directly into the serpent's fanged maw from his now prone position on the floor. It pulled up and then barrelled down in his direction.

Scrave closed his eyes resigned to his fate but Rauph the Minotaur had arrived.

"Scrave, why are you playing with that wormy thing?" A loud voice boomed from the entranceway. "Isn't it so lovely and shiny?" There was a grunt and a loud hissing sound. "That's not nice. What are you doing? Ouch!"

The tell- tale metallic 'schting' of two swords being drawn, followed by the whistling of the air as something razor sharp flew through it, formed pictures in Scrave's mind that no words could do justice to. Several heavy wet sounds followed and the hissing abruptly stopped. The Elf felt Rauph snuffling above him, his nostrils flaring out in concern at his partner lying on the floor in a ball.

"Can you walk?" the Minotaur asked.

"I'm not really sure." Scrave confessed, cracking his eyes and trying to smile in as carefree a way as possible but it came out in a 'wibbly-wobbly' way. He closed his eyes again feeling a little bit sick. Lights were flashing before his eyes.

"What were you doing standing right behind the door?" Rauph quizzed his unfortunate companion. "Don't you know how dangerous that can be, especially when you asked me to open it?" Scrave's head lolled to one side and a forthcoming grunt seemed to agree with the Minotaur's statement.

Rauph lifted Scrave up and threw him over one shoulder, spinning around to let the dizzy Elf take in the scene around him. The first thing he noted from his upside-down viewpoint was the fact that no bolts or locks appeared to be on the side of the door Rauph had come through. The main door had been open all along; it had just required pulling instead of pushing! Scrave's field of vision swung sickeningly to the left and then he found himself looking down at piles of sliced stone snake littering the foyer. The snake clearly reverted into its inert statue form once it was destroyed. One eye lay smashed in gleaming uneven pieces but the other large gem remained intact and clear.

"Get the snake's eye." Scrave mumbled before shutting his eyes and closing his mouth to swallow some particularly bitter bile. "I think I'm going to be sick."

Rauph secured the snake eye in his jerkin and then turned to take in the stream of temple guards piling into the foyer from all directions. They stood back unsure whether to attack at the sight of an eight-foot tall, soggy red haired, sharp horned, Minotaur, with a semi- conscious man slung over his left shoulder and a massive sword in his right hand. Swords, spears and crossbows levelled in his direction and even to the Minotaur, it was obvious they were hopelessly outnumbered.

The door still swung open behind him, exposing the tempest without and the way back to the *El Defensor* and freedom. Rauph considered this for the briefest of moments then looked back into the room at the growing wall of gleaming sharp-edged weapons.

It was just like Scrave to go off on his own and have all this fun without him. He flexed his muscles and whipped his free sword arm through a dazzling set of moves to iron out the kinks.

"Bring it on!" he snorted before stepped forward to meet them.

Chapter Nine

Brother Paul observed the nocturnal visitor walking alongside him with some disdain. The old man was a mess, his cloak was in tatters, his face a mass of scuffed and blistered skin, his leather armour scored heavily and his hands covered in scabbed wounds. To add to this, every step he took his boots squeaked.

"Are those boots new?" he asked, trying to cut the ice. "Because they don't look like they fit very well."

"It's all I could find at this hour of the night." Came back the clipped reply.

The monk looked into the hazel eyes of the visitor and saw winter reflected there.

"What size are you?"

Brother Paul slowed his walk for a bare second taking in the question and the implied threat it delivered. Then he tried to push his robes down further to cover his feet and shuffled along until they arrived at a non-descript door. He ushered the visitor inside and indicated that he took a seat.

"Abbot Brialin will see you soon." The statement was cold and clipped in delivery, Brother Paul backed away and the door clicked shut behind him, swiftly accompanied by the sounds of a bolt being shot, leaving Kerian Denaris effectively a prisoner of the monastery monks outside of the room and a victim of his own thoughts within.

Kerian regarded his prison with a critical eye. A small open fire pit supplied warmth; its heat locked in an unending battle with the chill of the grey stone that comprised the room's walls. Two chairs devoid of any ornamentation stood ready to receive any occupants and a scarred wooden table was set against one wall. In odd comparison on the opposite side of the room stood a small delicate table upon which was running an elaborate water clock, marks upon its surface indicating both meal and prayer times. If accurate, it dictated that dawn was yet several hours distant. In what could only be the east wall, a small grilled window let in a glimpse of the tempest that raged without.

He suppressed a shiver at the rain and the lightning that played to its silent audience by dancing across the night sky and turned to the fire pit in an attempt to rub some warmth back into his tired hands. His cloak dripped steadily from the hem, the material sodden, from his earlier exposure to the elements. The silence of the room appeared to close in on him from all sides and he suddenly found himself moving over to the timepiece in an attempt to divert his mind from the recriminations that threatened to engulf him.

It was ironic how he was attempting to find personal solace in the intricately carved workings of an ornament that marked the passage of time. He reached out, placing his finger directly in the flow of the timepiece, halting its flow and suspending time for a heartbeat within the room, before the water suddenly swelled from the continuous feed and began to flow once more around his half-hearted obstruction.

'Everyone gets old and dies eventually.' The words of Atticus Couqran echoed ghostly in his mind. Kerian shook his head in denial, there had to be a cure somewhere, a reason for continuing, else life itself was worthless and these last few months of killing and the suffering he had inflicted on others would have been for nothing. Even now, he thought of how he had butchered Ferdinand Kepstin, cut him down in cold blood. Where was the knightly conduct he was once so proud to follow? He could have accepted a deal from Ferdinand, especially now with afterthought.

Thinking back, he did not like the Kerian Denaris he had become over the last few months. The selfishness, the lies and the deceit were so far from the man he had always strived to be. He turned from the timepiece and picked up one of the chairs, returning to the flickering fire, where he set the chair firmly before slowly lowering his aching frame into it. He felt so tired, so very, very tired.

The damp weather was playing havoc with his injured arm and his joints. His knees especially. The chill sent dull aches throbbing up and down his body, creating muscular twinges that were like a warped musical accompaniment to the crackle of the fire and the dripping of the water clock. Despite this the room seemed to enforce peace and tranquillity, a sense of order. Kerian felt that just by being here, he had somehow disrupted its sanctity.

He turned his attention to the fire pit, his eyes watching the flickering flames intently as his mind raced, replaying everything that had happened to him since the activation of the fatal curse. Here, finally, there could be an answer to all his hopes and a soothing salve for all his dreams. His entire life hinged on this one Abbot and that worried Kerian as nothing ever could in mortal combat. He hated himself for having this weakness and equally loathed the figurehead who now possibly held such incredible power over him.

Violence would not solve this scenario, threatened or otherwise. He would have to be cautious; diplomacy without the aid of a sword was something which Kerian had very little experience.

Firelight flickered across his creased brow, dancing and flirting with the shadows lying there making the knight look much older than the fifty-six years he was now approaching. He sighed long and hard and then caught himself. He was sighing too much just lately. His eyes turned to regard the wisps of steam spiralling up from his worn leather garments. Evaporating moisture seemed to roll from the material of his cloak in steaming strips whilst the heavier hems of his garments dripped steadily onto the stone floor.

His eyelids slowly drooped with the after-effects of the evening's stresses and the copious alcohol he had consumed prior to setting out to this destination.

* * * * * *

Ashe stood trembling in the shadows, his mind fighting a one-sided battle between what he wanted his legs to do and what they were actually doing. A supernatural force controlled his limbs, disobeying him on a whim. No matter how hard the Halfling tried to order his tired legs to stop moving, or go in a direction he chose, they simply ignored him. His legs simply did not belong to him anymore.

He had been walking around and around in circles for most of the night, plodding reluctantly from one place to another pursuing some hidden agenda that only his legs seemed to have any idea about. It had even occurred to the miserable thief that if he knew the destination, he would have been able to help instead of simply finding himself dragged blindly from spot to spot.

The Halfling's clothes were sopping wet after trudging through the thunderstorm that had almost drowned him on the hills outside of town. His prize yellow feather hung limply before his eyes like a miserable flag of surrender, matted with mud and dripping with water, looking as thoroughly dejected as the Halfling was feeling.

His blistered and torn feet meant each step was an agony to take and to make matters worse, no matter what he tried to do, the little man was unable to release his hold on the golden ring he had found. It stuck to his hand magically, as if by glue.

Looking around with exhausted eyes, he tried to get his bearings as his feet walked persistently onwards. The whole journey so far was a bit of a blur. He had been out in the countryside, walking towards an estate, when a rider had passed him and his feet had decided they wanted to go another way entirely.

He had walked through several hedges and prickly bushes to add to his discomfort, and even found he was a temporary surrogate parent for a birds nest complete with eggs before he had passed close to a small bush where he had been able to put the nest down without any injury to the baby birds inside.

Now he was back in Catterick again, walking down cobbled streets he had already travelled, and he seemed to be heading for the hill where the monastery of St Fraiser lay.

It was a very steep hill!

Gritting his teeth, the Halfling focused his concentration on the roadway ahead. He had to find some way of stopping this! With a fierce determination, his eyes alighted upon a series of ornate iron railings that were coming up on the left-hand side of the path ahead and a gem of an idea, born from desperation, entered his head.

As reluctant footfall followed reluctant footfall, his free hand reached out and grabbed firmly onto one of the railings. His feet clearly on a mission all of their own, kept walking until Ashe was leaning back as far as he could stretch. The railing began to squeak and then scream in protest as unseen forces wrenched the Halfling about. Ashe's free hand gripped tightly, refusing to let go, like a drowning man knowing that if he let go he would sink fast.

He pulled harder, trying to ignore the pains shooting down his bicep and the aches from his shoulder joint as he managed to wrapped his arm around the bar and struggle ferociously against the invisible river of magic that was threatening to continue to drag him along. Inch by inch he managed to claw himself closer and closer to the rest of the railings. When he found himself up against the cold metal, hugging the rain-soaked ornamentation like a long-lost lover, sobs of relief flooded through his little form.

Ashe's left foot twitched constantly. His right answered its partner sympathetically. It was like having some strange nervous disease. The Halfling gritted his teeth even harder, barely recognising the tang of warm salty liquid that was coating his lips.

"No! I won't go any further!" he screamed, sobbing with defiance. "And what's more..." His arms began to tingle as if someone was stabbing them with tiny but very sharp pins and Ashe began to moan.

"Okay!" he sobbed. "I promise I will never ..." The Halfling's little eyes jerked open as he watched his fingers unfurl one by one from the railing about which they were desperately clasped. "...pick up another ring for as long as I live." His hand sprang free from the railing and Ashe could only look on in horror as his small sandal clad feet began their relentless march once more.

"But . . . I promised ..." he sobbed half-heartedly.

* * * * * *

"Excuse me?" the voice questioned, its tone bass deep.

The temple guard kept his eyes closed; trying desperately to play dead, despite the tell-tale shaking that was wracking his form.

"I know you are awake." The voice continued. "How about you look at me if I promise not to hit you again?"

Eyes cracked thinly to squint up at a vision from the guard's deepest, darkest nightmares. A demon towered above him, thick matted chestnut hair dripping and sodden, nostrils flaring, horns razor sharp and curved. It had the body of a man thrown over one shoulder and an enormous sword dripping with blood held in its free hand. Studs gleamed upon its leather armour their reflective light matched only by the excited glitter in the creature's eyes.

"I wonder if you could show me the way out of here?" the demon asked. "You see we were out shopping and I seem to have got slightly turned around in all the excitement."

"Shopping at night?" the guard stammered.

"That's when Scrave said you get the best bargains." The demon replied.

"But...Why would a demon want to go sho..." The guard started to enquire.

"A demon, where?" Rauph spun on his heels, sword whistling through the air, ready to do battle with the demon that had caused the guard to cower in such terror. His sword gouged plaster chunks from the wall of the corridor before sending a shower of splinters flying from an ornate wooden carving hanging on the other side of the empty hall. Of the demon, there was no sign.

Rauph's nostrils flared as he tried to locate even the slightest scent of the elusive creature that was apparently spreading terror throughout the labyrinthine corridors of this accursed temple. This was the seventh guard who had informed him of such a demon. It appeared that everywhere he went, this demon apparently followed!

He stood stock still, listening to the whimpers of the comatose guards littering the corridor behind him, trying to filter out their noise and locate his mysterious foe. Content that no demon was hiding in the shadows nearby, he looked back at the curled up guard at his feet.

The man appeared more relaxed now. In fact, too relaxed. Rauph shook him a few times and realised the man must have fainted. Obviously looking at this demon had simply been too much for him.

Rauph set his jaw firm and sniffed both ways before deciding to head off in a direction he had not been before. The demon was not behind him and he was dying to get a look so he could tell Scrave all about it when he finally woke up.

No way was any demon going to get the better of Rauph Von Kroan.

* * * * * *

Kerian stared bleary eyed at yet another spiral of steam rising from his cloak, then suddenly realised that it was not steam but sulphur tinged smoke parting the air before him. He reached out to pull his cloak away from the flames then froze as he noticed his hand; liver spots covered the back of it, the brown blemishes starkly visible against skin that was paper thin and almost translucent with age.

Veins of mottled greenish blue pulsed through his wrist, his fingers were gnarled and swollen, twisted like deformed claws and as he took in this horrific vision, he became aware of the fact that the water that had been dripping from his cloak had now turned into crimson blood. He knew, without understanding why, that it was his own blood coagulating and hissing on the steps on which he sat. Steps that he had collapsed upon to die. Steps...

A spitting knot of wood snapped Kerian from his trance and he gasped, drawing in a deep cleansing breath through lips that were dry and parched as if exposed to a heat several times more intense than the fire pit that flickered before him. What had just happened? He must have dropped off ... fallen asleep in an unguarded moment. Nevertheless, the imagery had seemed so real!

He shook his head; suddenly realising that the inside of his mouth was feeling dry and there was some slimy deposit on his teeth. He needed a drink but definitely not of the alcoholic type. He could not remember if there was anything to drink in the room. He turned to look around and found the Abbot was standing silently in the doorway.

Kerian spun about in the chair, moving to stand, his free hand reaching reflexively for the dagger at his belt and coming up with nothing but empty air.

"Please." Abbot Brialin motioned with a hand. "Remain seated. After all you've displayed no manners so far this evening, why should I expect a sudden deluge of them now?" The Abbot crossed the room with a grace that would have been more at home had he been a dancer or theatrical performer. He lifted the spare chair from its place beside the table and dropped it across from where Kerian sat, taking the seat and arranging his robes about him.

They stared quietly for a moment, each taking in the countenance and measure of the other, like two strategists facing each other across a playing board. Rubbing his hands, Brialin extended them over the flames for warmth before shuffling in his seat and repositioning his blue robes once.

It was a gambit Brialin liked to play, extending silence to see if the person before him would spill valuable information. Silence was uncomfortable; the weaker man normally always spoke first. As the silence stretched out Brialin realised the old man sitting opposite him was not weak. He was nothing of the sort.

"I believe you have a problem you wish to discuss." he opened.

Kerian paused, searching for a response amid the swirl of emotions that churned within him. He wanted to throttle the man that sat before him, his hands closing around the abbot's windpipe to slowly crush the information he needed so desperately out of him but at the same time he wanted to open his heart to the man as well, throwing himself upon the Abbot's mercy in a bid for absolution.

He examined the man before him, struck by the sense of divine power and peace that seemed to surround Brialin like a suit of unbreakable armour. This was truly the visage of a blessed man, or someone at peace with himself and his life. Kerian was bitterly aware that his own outlook had neither of those things.

"I need information." Kerian began cagily. "I have been informed your archives are extensive and may just hold a solution to the questions I need answering."

"We are not in the habit of sending the needy away." Abbot Brialin smiled. "Whatever way visitors choose to announce their arrival, those who need our help are always welcome within these halls. Your feet are on a path that leads to a destination none of us can pre-determine. Only those who watch us from above know how successful your journey will be. Yet I must consider your request carefully, for information given lightly can have serious repercussions for those who use it indiscriminately. What question is it that lies so heavy on your heart?"

Kerian scrutinised the man before him. Something was not right. He had crashed into the monastery in the middle of the night, caused untold damage and the Abbot was still willing to help him. He looked for signs of deceit, of twitching eyes or obvious tells but Abbot Brialin to all intent appeared sincere. Maybe he had become so used to dealing with the lower echelons of human society that he did not recognise there were genuinely good people out there.

"How did you know to come here?" Brialin enquired.

"An unfortunate business encounter with Atticus Couqran." Kerian confessed.

Brialin's eyebrow twitched as Kerian mentioned the guild masters name but the knight was not interested in how the man knew Atticus, he had more pressing priorities and he simply did not have the time to be side tracked.

Kerian opened his mouth to utter cautious words but instead discovered the truth spurting spasmodically from lips that betrayed their master, yet as the words gushed forth a cathartic relief came over him as his burden was shared for the first time. Finally, his confession completed, Kerian looked up at the Abbot and felt the man's intense stare washing over him, as if weighing him up for a task and finding him wanting. He felt his face begin to flush with heat.

Silence fell over the room; the fire pit had burned down low in the telling, so Kerian added more fuel to the fire in an attempt to calm himself from his earlier lack of control. He shivered in the wake of his spent emotions and huddled closer to the flames, his eyes trying to look at anything but the Abbot who rested in contemplation before him.

The drops of water within the clock appeared to turn into pearls of viscous fluid that clung to the channels and water wheels making up its elaborate construction. The individual droplets seemingly refusing to fall with a stubbornness that was more a product of Kerian's anxiety and lack of patience than any reluctance on the water's part. Time appeared to stretch infinitely, until finally the silence was too much for the exhausted and distraught man to bear.

"I see, regrettably, that you believe I have no right to ask for the information I seek." Kerian blurted out. "Yet I am tormented by the need to reverse the effects of my curse and live once more as a free man. It is like a thirst I cannot quench or an itch I cannot scratch, always just beyond my means." He started to rise from the chair, angry with himself for his open show of weakness, and frustrated that this man ultimately held the power to save or condemn him.

"Just tell me," he blurted out. "Is it possible? Is there a cure? Some way to save my life?" He stared at the Abbot intensely, as if the very power of his gaze could somehow strip down the man before him and expose the secrets he so desperately required. Brialin slowly stood and walked over to Kerian, his grey eyes scanning the anxious man, assessing the degree of urgency and need. He placed a reassuring hand upon the knight's shoulder and noted the slight tremor in the frame beneath.

"In my position I like to think there are always possibilities."

* * * * * *

"Have any of you seen the demon?" asked a curious voice that rumbled like a small avalanche of rocks.

Temple guards turned as one, faces indicating the shock they felt at encountering a creature spawned from the depths of their imagination. Swords flew from scabbards as the guards prepared to take on an enemy that appeared to have already slipped through their defences despite a strangely clumsy and less than well-camouflaged appearance. Resistance was limited and short in length, as guard after guard discovered what folly it was to threaten a Minotaur with a sword.

Rauph was confused. "I only asked you a question," he said in a hurt tone, his sword smacking the skull of a guard who ran at him with a spear. "What's your problem?" Another guard ran off screaming down the corridor leaving Rauph's feelings clearly hurt.

Scrave opened an eyelid and risked looking down at the floor below him. The stench of wet Minotaur hair filled his nostrils and almost made him gag. He had to tell Rauph to put him down, as his head was fit to burst.

A door opened in the corridor back the way Scrave was looking and several more fully armed guards poured out in his direction. Some, clearly more cautious and possessed with greater thoughts of self-preservation paused, waiting to see how their more exuberant, possibly less experienced, colleagues fared.

"Rauph!" Scrave screamed in warning. "Behind you!" The world as Scrave currently knew it seemed to take a sickening slide sideways as Rauph altered his position to face this new threat. The Elf found himself looking quite closely at the floor and fixtures around him before it began to dawn on him that he had seen this corridor before, all be it the other way up. They were right near the temple entrance. What in the world had Rauph been doing?

Blades clashed, the sickening sound of wet crunches indicating Rauph was in full swing. Screams filled the air, all be it temporarily, whilst others shouted out their horror at the sight of the demon that was mincing up their comrades without a care.

Demon? Had Scrave heard that right? He immediately jumped the chasm of understanding that had defeated his colleague. Clearly, Minotaur were rare in this land. To the uninitiated Rauph's very appearance would be demonic to be sure.

Rauph, now heading away from the exit point, continued carving his way through the most recent set of reinforcements with an enthusiasm that seemed endless. He dispatched the last guard with a vicious slap across the man's face, caving in the side of his helmet with his bare hand. The guard slumped to the floor and Rauph found himself facing a terrified figure in red robes who was slowly backing down the hall even as he struggled to unfurl a parchment scroll he held in his hands.

The Minotaur advanced, nostrils flaring and blade whistling through the air, oblivious to Scrave's screams of protest that he was going the wrong way. The priest in red stood shaking in the centre of the carnage and dropped a gemstone at his feet where it began to splutter and hiss. Spidery runes flared as he read his scroll aloud, the impressions disappearing from the parchment as he spoke. The incantation forged the ethereal constructs of his spell from the magical gemstone energy released at the priest's feet.

Rauph continued to advance, intent on dispatching the last remaining irritant from the corridor, when tendrils of magical force shot upwards from the gem on the floor, their angry red coloration mirroring the deadly intent of the spell. Rauph snorted loudly as the crimson energy tried to wrap itself about his head. There was a splutter and a fizzle then the magical lines simply parted, the spell shattering like glass.

The Minotaur reached out and grabbed the priest by the throat in a move that was so fast that the man barely had time to draw a breath, let alone get out of the way. Rauph lifted him so high his feet kicked frantically in the air and then he slammed him hard against the wall.

"Was that magic?" Rauph snarled. "I don't like magic. That was very, very, bad!" He shook the priest for emphasis, rattling him so hard that the teeth vibrated in his head. He went limp signalling an end to the evening's entertainment, so Rauph shook him once more to make sure he was not faking it, then simply dropped him into a dishevelled heap on the floor.

Scrave pummelled hard on Rauph's back signalling to get the Minotaur's attention. Rauph listened reluctantly before turning as instructed and heading for the way out.

"I'm sorry," Scrave shouted back at the dishevelled priest, from his own awkward perch. "It's just that sometimes he gets so over excited!"

Minutes later Rauph stepped out into the cool night air, the earlier tempest now reduced to a persistent drizzle.

"That was fun!" the Minotaur giggled, hitting the cobblestone street at a dead run. Fighting down the urge to vomit, Scrave began desperately hitting his companion on the back and the runaway Minotaur slowly ground to a halt.

"Put me down!" Scrave yelled. Rauph rewarded the vocal Elf by instant complying with the request. Looking up from the wet cobblestones, with the damp seeping in through his jacket, Scrave arched an eyebrow at his hairy companion that spoke volumes.

"Oh! Uh. Sorry." Rauph reached out and grabbed the front of Scrave's tunic, lifting him bodily off the ground and back onto his feet. He stepped back, critically admiring his handiwork, and then hummed as he straightened the Elf's clothes into a position that appeared to please him.

"What happened to keeping a low profile?" Scrave snarled. "Thomas said no one was supposed to know we were here. I think that whole place knows we are present now."

The whistling of arrow flights cut through the disheartening lecture, wooden shafts splintering on the cobblestones around them. Flickering torches began to dot along the temple roof, silhouetting more archers who began gauging the range to improve their aim. Loud shouts arose from the ruined temple doors as guards began to pour out into the street, their associates indicating where the two thieves were standing.

"We don't have time to talk about this anymore," Scrave prompted, grabbing his colleague by the arm and dragging him away down the nearest alleyway. "Come on!"

"I really enjoyed shopping, Scrave." Rauph puffed at his companion. "Can I come with you again next time?"

Scrave's stony silence said it all.

Chapter Ten

Brother Marcus entered the room with care, a stack of dusty ledgers precariously balanced in his arms. He staggered under the weight of his burden before dropping the whole pile upon the room's only table. He was alone in the room with a mad man! Abbot Brialin had summoned him from his quarters, healing his injured hands with gemstone magic before he ordered him to assist with the demands of the insane lunatic who had smashed through the doors of the monastery!

The monk sat down heavily, wiping the sweat from his brow before reaching over and seizing the top volume from the pile. He fumbled within a pocket in his blue robes before withdrawing a pair of reading lenses that he examined critically, wiping them on the hem of his robes before placing them upon the bridge of his nose and opening the book. Marcus was acutely aware of the armed figure sitting across from him but tried to ignore the man and concentrate on the assignment at hand. Even so, his eyes occasionally drifted from the yellowed manuscript pages and their elaborate script to steal a quick glance of the man that had terrified him earlier that night.

"Let's see what we can find," he coughed nervously, his voice trembling despite his best efforts to prevent it from doing so. He began to pick through the books, opening previously marked pages and spreading them out across the table to show them to a man he was not sure could even read.

"So . . . from these ledgers . . . which . . . ah . . . detail ships logs, fables and past recorded mariners' tales there appears to be mention of an island far to the east called Stratholme." He glanced up quickly, sweat dotting his brow and then back down at the page just as fast hoping his actions would not betray the feelings he held inside. The old man's eyes contained a savage hunger that seemed to strip Marcus down to his very soul. "Um . . . it would appear this is where your answer lies. Somewhere on this island lies a magical artefact that grants your heart's desire." Marcus shut the book with a thud. He shuffled upon his chair, moving robes that had become uncomfortable after being in the same place for too long.

"So..." Kerian prompted.

"Well, what I mean is. . ." Marcus flushed becoming flustered and uneasy. "Well, what I'm trying to say is . . ."

"Exactly what?" Kerian growled.

"Well Stratholme isn't exactly close enough to easily confirm its existence. Many say it is just a myth. It requires a ship's voyage of several months." He paused. "If you had the stamina for such a venture you would have to find someone willing to sail right off the known sea charts and there won't be too many captains out there who will be willing to do that... At least, not without a substantial down payment." He looked the old man up and down taking in his dishevelled ragged appearance and raised an eyebrow as if to confirm there was not that much money sitting in front of him.

"There are other forms of encouragement." Kerian let the implication hang menacingly in the air. "Please ... go on. What will we find at Stratholme?"

"Okay." Marcus wiped his hand across his brow, he was feeling uncomfortable now and worried the old man was going to see through him at any second. He took a deep breath and continued.

"There are two other concerns I need to make clear before we continue. Firstly, if you put all your faith in what I am about to tell you I must ask you to consider the fact that this may all just be made up. The mention here ..." he gestured to an open ledger further down the pile, "of a crystal dragon and a temple that magically hovers across a sea of molten lava, or here ... of skeletal guardians and lost love are just the sort of thing bards love. How many free drinks consumed around an open fire, whilst this elaborate tale was spun? How do we know they didn't simply sail across the Lianna Strait, spend time entertaining the local girls, then came back and made this up from the best bits of genuine tales of discovery? Moreover, if we opt for the chance that these tales might be true, how could we verify even one such story? No one who originally penned these tales is alive anymore and people who go looking for Stratholme don't tend to come back..."

"So what you are telling me is that this could all be some kind of elaborate hoax?" Kerian enquired irritation lacing his voice with acid.

"Exactly," Marcus returned. "But, if it were true, if the fables did contain an element of reality, then you may just find the answer to your affliction."

"Then what proof do we have?" Kerian asked leaning forward.

Marcus plunged back into the pile of books pulling out a faded book of fables from the pile and flicking through until finally he placed the open page in front of the knight for inspection. An ink-stained thumbprint served to indicate the preferred passage and Kerian squinted at the neat script with tired eyes. The words stubbornly wiggled and blurred before him. He screwed his eyes up tightly, grabbing the book from the table and holding it slightly away from himself until the words came clear.

'The tragedy of Rosalyine and Strathe'

"It's a tale of a doomed love. Aren't they all?" Marcus chuckled. "Apparently, he loves her someone else loves her, tragedy strikes, he dies and his heart gets turns into a magical object. So, to this day, wracked in grief, she guards her lover's heart, taking the form of a giant crystal dragon so she will never age and can be with him forever."

Kerian's eyes began to water under the strain of trying to read the tight lined script. He squinted anew but to no avail and in frustration slammed the book back down onto the desk making Marcus jump clear from his chair. One thing was for sure the monk was clearly on edge.

"This is a waste of time!" Kerian snapped. "I'm not here to read bedside stories written for little children!" He went to throw the book to one side but Marcus reached up and grabbed the book holding it close to his chest like a mother would her new-born baby.

Marcus surprised himself with his bravery, the old man had threatened his books and that was sacrilege to the monk. Books held a value to him that was beyond compare.

"There are journal entries of the crystal dragon. There is also a similarity with the islands name and one of the protagonists of the story we are following." Marcus pointed out. "I find that coincidences rarely happen."

"Abbot Brialin has collected several documents relating to this tale," He pulled out a small book that looked newer than the others did. "This is the combined works of dozens of scribes from the monastery. It details all the stories of adventurers who went off in search of Stratholme. Many of them set sail but only a handful returned to fill the local taverns with their tales of discovery. I assume the ones who didn't return are likely to now reside somewhere on the ocean's floor, food for the crabs, sharks and sea serpents that patrol the wild seas"

"So, basically..." Kerian picked up the threads of the tale, completed the monk's summing up for him, ". . . I have to travel way off any charted sea route, if I can get a ship to charter, avoiding sharks, sea monsters and other such hazards, before I find an island that may, or may not, exist. I then have to track down a crystalline dragon and ask it if I can see an artefact it guards in the hopes that it will both acknowledge and then grant my deepest desire, all the while praying that this isn't all a flight of fancy from a drunken sailor who has exaggerated this tale in the telling." He paused weighing up the facts and not liking the outcome. "I have no guarantee that any of this is true, and if it is as far away as you say, by the time I'm there it will be too late for me to turn back again. You are proposing a one-way trip."

"That's about it," Marcus confirmed, licking his lips nervously.

"This is a slim lifeline to cling to if it isn't real..." The door opened pausing Kerian in his thoughts.

"Oh ... it exists." Abbot Brialin walked calmly into the room; his serene and calm demeanour cooling Kerian's raising ire in a heartbeat. Kerian noted that beneath the Abbot's arm was a beautifully bound blue leather book. "There are too many tales for it to be totally false. The quest will obviously be long and arduous, even hazardous in nature and therefore I have decided that you shall not go on this quest alone."

"Are you leaving us master?" Marcus enquired shock apparent upon his face. "That would never be permitted; the sanctity of our order would be disrupted. I must protest."

"Leave and pursue my heart's desire?" Brialin paused. "I must confess the idea was an appealing one but no, my place is here. As it has always been."

Kerian's head snapped up from the book he was looking at. His eyes scanned the figure before him, swiftly seeing through the Abbot's cryptic comments.

"No way!" he exclaimed, jumping to his feet and scaring Marcus half to death. "There is no way I am taking him with me."

"Our knowledge is not given freely. Not only that, you owe me for a window and a door. This is my price. There is no room for negotiation." Abbot Brialin's voice was steely and resolute.

"It's too high." Kerian fired back, his hand reaching for the money pouch he had acquired at the guild master's estate earlier that evening. "I'll pay whatever you ask but I always travel alone."

"You will take Brother Marcus with you to Stratholme." Brialin fixed Kerian with an icy stare, his expression allowing no further argument. "He is to travel as my representative from this monastery, both as investigator, chronicler and scribe. Finally, the myth of Stratholme will be laid to rest and another of this world's mysteries solved." Marcus remained seated at the desk, his mouth opened wide, his jaw flapping and, for once, he was unable to give a point of view. Brialin placed a reassuring hand upon the monk's shoulder.

"Those who watch will keep vigil over you." He promised. "Now listen carefully Brother Marcus. I want to present to you this book. I expect both illustrations and accurate record keeping with personal reflection and insight of all aspects of your journey. Upon your return this tome will take pride of place within these walls."

"Isn't it a little large?" Kerian commented looking at the thickness of the volume and imagining all the writing the monk would have to do to fill it up. "I am not expecting to take a scenic route."

Marcus stood up on suddenly, unsteady feet, his mind a whirr and mercifully oblivious to the ranting and ravings coming from the old man behind him. The idea of finally being able to pen his own book was an honour, something that was both real and positive to the young monk but this unexpected trip had not come up in the private discussions he had with the Abbot earlier. He looked at his master with his face a mixture of bewilderment and shock. He could not leave the monastery; the only life he had known!

He also knew the story the Abbot gave about the blue book was a lie.

"You can take the collection of tales with you as well." Brialin offered. "Our order has always been one of learning. Now is your chance young Marcus to go out and experience life to the full. I am indeed envious of the chance that is being offered to you."

"Thank you..." Marcus stammered, holding the blue book to his chest in the same way he had held the earlier smaller tome, this time knowing what was inside was more precious than any written page.

Kerian looked at the young monk gaping like a beached fish, put his head in his hands and groaned.

* * * * * *

"Apparently we're going sailing," Kerian informed his faithful stallion, patting Saybier's flank before swinging himself up into the saddle. Grasping the reins tightly he skilfully turned the horse away from the monastery's gates and began a slow ride back towards Catterick.

"Wait for me!" Marcus yelled.

Kerian turned in the saddle and allowed himself a chuckle. Marcus was hopelessly trying to get into the saddle of a silver haired mule supplied by the monastery for the ride into town. He tried to gain the saddle from first one side and then the other, before throwing dignity to the wind, hitching up his blue robes and unceremoniously hauling himself up onto the startled mule's back. Saybier snorted impatiently, turning to see what all the commotion was.

"That's Marcus," Kerian informed him. "He's unwanted baggage that we seem to have acquired. I want you to bite him at every opportunity." The horse nodded its head as if in silent understanding and began to trot towards the town once more.

Marcus looked up from his saddle and twitched the reins of the mule, digging in his heels in direct mimicry of the old man. The mule reacted instantly: jumping forwards in a startled jolt, it began bouncing its way after Kerian and Saybier. Scant moments later the blue robed monk was bobbing alongside his travelling companion like a cork floating on the sea but with decidedly less buoyant grace.

"Is...it...always...like...this?" Marcus enquired between bounces.

"What?" Kerian replied, trying desperately to keep a straight face.

"Riding..."

"Oh, no. Not always."

Marcus looked across at the elderly man with a questioning look, only to find an evil twinkle in his associate's eye.

"Sometimes it's faster."

Kerian dug in his heels and Saybier responded instantly, leaping forwards into a full-fledged gallop that left the monk and his less salubrious steed swiftly behind. Marcus looked after the rapidly dwindling figure with dismay.

"I...suppose...you...think...that's...funny..." he winced, gritting his teeth at the incessant pounding his holy posterior was being subjected to and resigning himself to the fact that a long and arduous journey lay ahead of him.

* * * * * *

Abbot Brialin watched the two unlikely travellers departing and turned to a young acolyte standing alongside him ready to do his bidding.

"Make sure we include a larger donation to the guild when their payment comes up." He remarked. "Atticus has been true to his word and his unlikely candidate is so blinded by his own needs he will never realise he is doing our work for us."

"Yes Master." The assistant turned and went back into the monastery without another word, anxious to be seen to do as he was requested leaving the Abbot standing alone on the steps. Work had already started behind Brialin to shore up the damaged doors and board up the smashed window. Tomorrow work would begin in earnest to rehang the door correctly and remove any sign of Styx late night entry and the subsequent storm damage that had occurred.

It was important this work completed fast, order and obedience were paramount in this place of worship and study. Anyone breaking such edicts faced severe punishment, all signs of thought outside that decree stamped on and ground out. This was why it was so important Marcus was going on his trip and taking his cargo with him. Nevertheless, he needed a protector and Styx had fit that bill perfectly.

The monastery was set on a high hill above Catterick and Abbot Brialin was able to look out across the sea from the high vantage point to an imaginary point on the horizon.

"We are coming for you Brother Richard." He snarled. "We do not forget. We do not forgive."

* * * * * *

The streets of Catterick were almost silent when the two unlikely travellers arrived before its inner gates. Locked and secure in times of war, they now stood open and unmanned to invite in all the freed lands that wished to trade within the city's walls. At this early hour of the morning, traders were few, most still secure in their warm beds dreaming of the profits they hoped to make that day. Those figures that did wander the streets were the type of traders who dealt in more shadowy merchandise.

The drunks had long since staggered away or fallen into oblivion in shadowed doorways. The ladies of the night had secured their clients seducing them from their money in beds filled with artificial warmth. Even the thieves had long since stolen their nightly prizes and were counting their ill-gotten gains in their respective hideaways or cursing their luck and hoping for better pickings the following night.

The rain was easing up, the slight drizzle that remained petering out and signalling the end of the tempest from the previous evening. Scudding grey clouds filled the sky, moving together like herded sheep heading for an unseen fold. Silver moonlight kissed the rooftops with liquid platinum and the waters of the harbour turned to molten mercury. Without hesitation, Kerian turned his mount towards the sea front, Saybier responding instantly to the subtle tug on the reins and the gentle transfer of his rider's position.

"Are we going much further?" Marcus enquired, almost breathless from his earlier jolting passage through the wilderness. "It's just that... I don't think I was made for riding."

"We're heading back to the inn I'm staying at," Kerian informed his travelling companion. "It's too early to ask on the docks for passage. Most captains will be asleep in their bunks on a miserable night like this one. We'll catch a few hours' sleep and then begin looking for a ship." He looked at the anguish etched on Marcus's face at the thought of further riding and added reassurance as an afterthought, "Don't worry, it's not far now."

Cobblestones gleamed wetly in the illumination from the moon as the two figures entered the main square; the slippery surface making the option of a fast gallop a treacherous and therefore foolhardy one. In response, the two riders slowed their mounts to a walk, allowing both to stare at the majesty of the Crystalline Palace as it towered above them.

Towers and minarets clawed at the velvet sky and torchlight flickered through assorted arrow slits and windows creating the illusion that the structure was ablaze. Kerian remembered Castle Caerlyon and the nightmares it contained then shuddered.

A dozen men, fully armed and bearing torches, entered the square from the west. Most staggered on their feet, helmets at assorted angles, eyes staring blearily ahead: faces clearly displaying their discomfort at being on duty during this miserable night.

Kerian recognised the sight of new recruits pushed to the limit and initiated to night watch; he had done it himself to new recruits in the past. It was better they broke here in safety than out on a battlefield somewhere and Kerian smiled as he noticed the grizzled veteran who led them shaking his head in dismay at the calibre of his recruits.

He caught the commander's eye and a knowing nod passed between them, affirming an instant kinship that went beyond words and into shared experiences where pain and suffering had never been far away.

"It's nice to see we aren't the only ones awake," Kerian commented to Marcus. "Come on, let's get a move on." He dug his heels into Saybier's flanks and eased the horse out of the square towards the *Sunset Spider*, monk and mule clip clopping alongside him.

Saybier suddenly snapped to a halt, almost sending Kerian out of his saddle at the abruptness of the stop. Ears twitching, nostrils flaring, the horse stamped a hoof in warning of an unseen menace within the shadows of a nearby alleyway. Kerian righted himself in the saddle, his curses ignored as he tried to work out what had spooked his horse in this way. He squinted into the shadows making out very little and began to curse anew at his failing vision. His eyes were definitely letting him down.

There it was! A sudden flash of yellow!

"What's wrong with your horse?" Marcus asked. Kerian risked a quick irritated glance at the monk intended to tell him to be quiet. When he turned back to the location of the yellow flash there was nothing there. Whatever it was had gone.

Kerian remained stationary for several moments just in case there was a repeat appearance of the brightly coloured object, his senses strained and his hand hovering by his sword but hearing any sounds of movement was next to impossible due to the commotion caused by the disorganised soldiers marching through the square and the constant shuffling of the monk alongside him. Frustrated, Kerian shook his head in denial and tapped Saybier lightly on the head.

"Getting skittish in your old age, eh?" he joked.

Saybier turned to the knight with piercing red eyes, his lip curled in as close an expression of disdain as was possible for an equine mouth to achieve! Kerian could almost hear his steed's displeasure at being dismissed thus, then Saybier lunged, teeth clicking together inches from where Kerian's outstretched hand had been. Kerian swiftly countered with a playful tap to the horse's nose.

"One day," he mocked. "But not today."

Saybier swung his head away, making low nickering noises of disgust, roles of master and servant clearly established and began to reluctantly trot down the road. Marcus followed close after in uncomfortable bouncing pursuit.

* * * * * *

The patrolling soldiers came to a disorganised halt with a clatter, much to the disgust of their Drill Sergeant.

"What is it this time?" he snapped in irritation.

A small-bedraggled figure emerged from the shadows, walking with a slow, steady pace directly across the troops' path. A sopping wet yellow feather brushed limply backwards and forwards across the Halfling's face as he walked, smearing a mixture of blood and mud across his exhausted features. He looked thoroughly miserable, his eyes darting everywhere pleading for help from any quarter. One of the astonished guards moved forward to assist the pitiful creature before one of his associates held him back.

"What do you think you're doing?" he hissed. "It's mad. Listen! It's arguing with its feet!"

Sure enough, as the figure passed them the soldiers all heard a string of profanities more fit for a drunken sailor than such a small child-like figure. All of which were aimed directly at his muck covered bare feet. As they watched, the little figure disappeared into the shadows along the same path taken by the recently departed riders.

The Drill Sergeant stood there shaking his head at the sorry sight. In all his years, he had never seen the like. It was so sad when people got like this. Obviously, the little figure was beyond all hope. After all, when you started calling your left foot a yellow-bellied cutthroat traitor there clearly was not much sanity left in your future.

* * * * * *

"Do you know something?" Kerian began. "I'm sure someone's coming up behind us." He motioned to Marcus and the two riders reined in their mounts. They sat stationary; heads cocked listening to the sounds of Catterick's night. Somewhere far off a dog howled remorsefully, in an alley to the right several territorially minded cats were apparently ripping each other apart, a stray scream, swiftly silenced, came from the left and as they listened, a low rumbling, like distant thunder, advanced steadily from behind.

Two figures suddenly exploded from a shadowy cross street and tore down the road, swiftly passing between the two wary riders. One of the figures was enormous, the other appeared to be attempting to coerce the larger figure along the street.

"Excuse us," came a muffled voice as the two fleeing figures swiftly disappeared into the shadows ahead.

"Did you see the size of him?" Marcus exclaimed, turning to look at his aged travelling companion with the unmistakable gleam of excitement in his eye. Catterick was full of surprises. Saybier snorted in response and shook his head, eager to get back to the warm stall at the Sunset Spider but Kerian refused to move, staring ahead after the two figures his face deep in thought. After a second, he nudged the horse gently forwards but remained strangely silent.

Loud shouts suddenly arose from behind, making the two riders rein in once more. Marcus turned in the saddle eager to see what Catterick would entertain him with next, only to note a score of burning torches heading his way.

"Move over!" Kerian ordered. "We'll let them pass and then be on our way." Marcus dug his sandals into his mule's side and gently coaxed the creature over to the side of the road.

"There they are!" yelled a voice from amid the flickering torches.

"Wait a minute ..." Kerian yelled, realising instantly what had happened. "There's been a mista ..." The air around the two figures suddenly became thick with stray crossbow bolts whizzing and clattering across the road and ricocheting from the walls.

"I don't believe this! Ride Marcus!" Kerian grabbed his reins firmly and dug in his heels, feeling Saybier respond instantly to his command and launch into a full-fledged gallop. He leaned into the wind and risked a glance over his shoulder to check on the state of pursuit, then cursed loudly. Marcus was still sitting on his stubbornly stationary mule, hands all akimbo as crossbow bolts embedded themselves into the wall beside him.

With a fierce tug on the reins, Kerian wheeled Saybier around. The stallion rolled its eyes and neighed in protest but responded to its master's command instantly, sparks rising from the cobblestones as the warhorse's hooves scrabbled for purchase on the slick surface. Kerian leant as far forward in the saddle as his arm would allow and rested his head lightly against his stallion's finely muscled neck, presenting as small a target as possible for the bolts that were now gaining a greater degree of accuracy.

Marcus looked up at the charging stallion with sheer terror in his eyes, bringing up his arms to ward off an attack as Kerian skidded to a halt alongside him. Saybier turned instantly as Kerian leant forward and grabbed the reluctant mule's reins.

"C'mon you stupid animal!" Kerian snapped, digging in his heels and urging Saybier into a gallop. A crossbow quarrel thwacked into one of Saybier's saddlebags as they charged down the road, terrified monk and braying mule towed unwillingly behind.

Kerian stole another backward glance at the pursuit and satisfied they were temporarily out of sight, wrenched Saybier to the right, guiding horse and cargo into a side street. Marcus leaned dangerously in his saddle, his eyes wide and his hands holding on grimly trying to avoid crashing to the cobblestones that sped below him at an alarming rate.

Gritting his teeth in concentration Kerian tried to picture a map of the streets of Catterick in his mind but the labyrinthine ways looked so different in the dark and it was difficult to gauge exactly where he was. His only hope was to lose their pursuers somewhere in this warren of winding lanes and alleyways.

Saybier cleared the shadows into a wide street and Kerian finally spotted a landmark. A cry of jubilation died in his throat as torch carrying figures appeared in the street ahead. Somehow, in all the confusion, he had managed to get them turned around and had led them right back into the path of their pursuers.

The stallion instinctively skidded to a halt, almost unseating his rider and causing a 12-legged pile up. Kerian looked around frantically for a way out of the noose that was rapidly tightening about them. There! Without hesitation, horse and rider shot forwards once more and slipped into the shadows of another narrow alleyway almost missed in the dark.

Several high-speed turns followed: left, left and then a quick right, until, finally, they arrived at a deserted crossroads. Now, where were they? Saybier turned on the spot, snorting wildly as he responded to Kerian's controlled nudges and tugs on the reins. A glint of reflected silver between the houses gave the knight the bearing he needed. The sea was to the left, the dockyards and taverns all nestled down there at the base of the cove.

Kerian's mind raced. Marcus had to get to safety; he was out of his depth here and slowing Kerian down. That was the priority here. He did not believe that their pursuers were members of the city's watch for an instant, their aim with the crossbow was useless for one and the city watch normally asked questions before shooting at you!

If Marcus could get to the docks, they could regroup there and move on to the *Sunset Spider* once the excitement had died down. Kerian made his decision, losing Marcus would let Saybier and Kerian be free to do what they did best.

He released the mule's reins and slapped the animal hard on the rump, sending the silver haired creature careering off down the road towards the docks.

"Head for the seafront!" he shouted after the rapidly disappearing mule and his rider. "Wait for me there. Don't leave until I come for you!"

Kerian did not wait for a reply but wheeled Saybier around heading back the way they had come. Now Marcus was out of the way, he could lead these lunatics in the opposite direction, using himself as bait and then dispatch them, one by one.

Blazing torches spilled out from one of the passageways ahead and Kerian instantly nudged Saybier back into the mottled shadows cast by an outside staircase. He reached for his sword, and then reconsidered, if he drew the blade its magical glow would give him away instantly. It was better to wait and let his prey get closer.

The first guard slammed into the staircase as he passed, knocking his head as the shadows that contained Kerian reached out and claimed him. His burning torch fell to the floor, but Saybier swiftly kicked the brand away, watching it extinguish in a water-filled gutter, before turning back to Kerian to see what needed doing next. By the time other guards found their unconscious comrade, horse and rider had already slipped silently away to cloak themselves in other shadows. Whispers of concern started almost immediately as the guards vainly tried to locate the source of their associate's accident.

Kerian suppressed a chuckle at the chaos he was causing. He could run rings around these idiots all night. He held his breath as another victim wandered towards him; this was all too easy.

A shout from across the road dictated a sudden change in tactics as the guards began to move down the street towards the harbour in pursuit of Marcus. Kerian had no choice. He had to make himself seen. He reached out towards the nearest guard who had turned fatally towards his colleagues and slid the man's sword from its scabbard.

"Looking for me?" he hissed into the man's ear, smacking him around the face with the pommel of the sword as he turned. The guard managed a loud grunt before he fell to the floor but the effect was still the desired one. The guards turned as one and started charging towards Kerian, swords drawn and blood lust in their eyes. He hesitated just long enough before allowing Saybier free rein to explode into action and cross the road flitting from one patch of shadow to another like a ghost or errant spectre. The horse shot into another side passage leading the crowd away from the docks and Kerian felt his horse relax as training took over and Saybier settled into his stride, weaving an evasive dance in and out of the darkness.

The stallion reached another open area and slowed, allowing the first leading torch to come around the corner, before launching a vicious back kick into the man's midsection and sending him flying back into his associates. Then the horse was off again crossing into another passageway, the guards following in swift pursuit.

"Stop showing off," Kerian hissed.

Saybier responded by galloping into yet another narrow passageway and riding straight through a line of washing that was hanging there, the wet linen slapping Kerian around the face and entangling him within its folds. The knight gasped as cold droplets of water shivered down his neck before he was able to tear much of the clothing from his body.

"I suppose you think that's amusing?" Kerian scolded, through a mouthful of wet skirt. He threw the garment off and struggled to see what lay ahead in the shadows. A thin sliver of moonlight filtered down from above, throwing the rat-infested garbage and mounds of steaming sewage into an eerie perspective.

The houses on each side of the alleyway were so ramshackle that they leant over, almost touching each other, begging for support from their silent neighbours in order to put up with the constant neglect they were all suffering. The alleyway twisted away ahead of him into an even darker patch of shadow.

Something shot out of the darkness faster than Kerian could react, lifting him bodily up into the air, Saybier's saddle slipping out from underneath him. He hung there suspended, feet hanging in space.

"Shall I squash him?" enquired a deep voice.

"Okay... just make it quiet, okay?" came the delayed reply.

Kerian struggled to see who was speaking about him but whatever held him was out of view. He slowly inched his hand towards his sword and prepared for yet another battle, kicking out at the tall figure holding him and for his actions, getting slammed hard into the alley wall.

"Let him down, Rauph. I'll deal with the guard my way."

There was no denying the emphasis placed on the last two words of this sentence. Kerian suddenly found himself dropped painfully to the ground. He reacted swiftly to his newfound freedom, rolling free of his assailant as he landed, putting much needed space between himself and this new threat. The alleyway suddenly illuminated in a pale violet light as he drew his sword.

There was an answering whisper of steel and confident footfalls sounded as two figures closed in. The smaller figure stepped into the violet light to reveal his Elven heritage.

"You're a..." Kerian struggled to find the words. A teasing feint of his opponent's blade causing him to rapidly shelve his amazement and take a hurried step backwards. He swiftly countered the move and lunged in return, watching in silent awe as the figure almost appeared to dance out of the way. Kerian could not believe his eyes; Elves were extinct now, wiped out the last time he had heard! Whoever this was, he was a long way from home.

"I don't like killing people I haven't been introduced to," Kerian stalled, his mind struggling to understand what was going on as a larger figure, presumably the one who grabbed him, walked into the light to offer moral support. It was huge and had horns!

The smaller figure suddenly ran at him, sword blade almost a blur and Kerian reacted more out of instinct than thought, somehow managing to parry the blade with his own. The figure shot past Kerian's feeble attempt at a counter move and literally ran up the wall of the alleyway, flinging himself back across his foe and causing Kerian to duck or risk losing his head. Two distinct sword strikes vibrated along his raised sword before the figure landed lightly on his feet and gave a mock salute with his blade.

"Scrave," the figure introduced himself, without showing the slightest hint of lack of breath. "And you are?"

"Styx," Kerian shot back, circling his blade and trying to move so that both strange characters were in front of him. The response was fast, if not a little faster than Kerian expected, as sword blades touched once, then twice more, this time with the undeniable sparking of magical enchantments clearly audible as metal slid against metal.

Kerian seized the initiative moving forwards in the hope that his six-foot height would act as an advantage to the five-foot elf and slid his blade down Scrave's to temporarily lock hilts.

"And what of your large associate?" Kerian teased, quietly congratulating himself at the ingenuity and speed of his move. He began to push down on his sword, attempting to force the Elf to his knees. Scrave grunted, then dropped to the side, making Kerian fall forwards at the sudden lack of resistance, leaving him with barely enough time to bring his sword up and around to deflect yet another attack from the resourceful elf.

"Rauph Von Kroan," Scrave replied, moving in towards Kerian once again, sword blade held high.

"Enough games," Kerian snarled, meeting the attack head on and temporarily surprising his sparring partner. A fierce string of lunges and feints followed, sword blade sparking against sword blade as their metal edges kissed. He moved to the left, and then swiftly reversed the stroke slicing in from the right with a move expected to slice the Elf clean in two. Incredibly, Scrave leapt up into the air, the blade passing mere inches below his feet before bringing his own blade up and over in a move that would have split Kerian from head to toe if he had not seen it coming and successfully parried the stroke.

Luck appeared to favour Kerian, for as Scrave landed back on the cobblestones his boot slid on some garbage and he fell over onto his back temporarily winded. Kerian stepped forwards intent on finishing the job when the larger figure clomped forward, causing all thoughts of the elegant swordsman at his feet to vanish.

"By Adden," Kerian swore, as Rauph barrelled towards him intent on defending his fallen friend. There was a blur of heavily muscled torso, bulging biceps and a smell like a wet rug, before Kerian found himself on his back again with stars flashing across his vision. A snorted laugh confirmed what Rauph thought of the competition.

"What in the world are you?" Kerian was uncomfortably aware that the Elf was now smiling at his apparent confusion. Scrave re-sheathed his sword and walked closer as his now prone foe took in the bovine head perched upon thickly set shoulders and the gleaming horns that swept out from his forehead to taper to razor sharp points nearly fifteen inches from his skull.

"Styx, meet Rauph," Scrave gestured comically. "Rauph is a minotaur. To some a mythical creature known only in legend, in your case, however ... he's simply bad luck!" Kerian considered backing away from his position but raised voices from the end of the alleyway unexpectedly became his saviour.

"The guards!" Scrave and Kerian both cursed in unison. Scrave turned towards Kerian with confusion on his face.

"As I have been trying to tell you," Kerian mentioned calmly, "I'm no guard. They somehow think that I'm one of you two and have been chasing myself and my companion through just about every street in this accursed city." He paused taking in the size and shape of the two figures before him. "Although I'm not sure exactly which one of you I was supposed to be."

"I think he went down here!" a voice shouted, as the sounds of pursuit grew louder.

"Is there any way out of here?" Kerian asked, indicating the shadows at the end of the alleyway and hoping it was a way out.

"We already checked," Rauph responded, glumly. "It's a dead end and even if we did get out, we've no idea where we are in relation to the sea front."

"Then, we'll just have to fight," Scrave admonished.

Kerian shook his head as Rauph unsheathed two immense swords from his back and Scrave moved to stand alongside him, both facing down the alleyway towards the forces heading in their direction. Kerian briefly considered joining them and then reconsidered. Even with Rauph on his side, they were hopelessly outnumbered and could not hope to survive a full pitched battle within the confines of this alleyway.

"It's no use fighting," he volunteered. "We'll never make it out in one piece. Trust me and we will all get out of this alive. I'll even show you the way down to the sea front once we're clear."

"Why should we trust you?" came Scrave's characteristically negative response.

"Because, right now, I'm your best hope," Kerian replied, his eyes sweeping the alleyway for desperately needed inspiration. His eyes moved up the brickwork of the crumbling buildings.

"Are you thinking of flying us out of here?" Scrave scoffed.

"Not in the slightest, but, maybe ... just maybe there's another way."

Chapter Eleven

The temple guards entered the alleyway slowly and cautiously. Many of their number had already met grisly ends this evening and none wished to be the next victim. They meticulously checked each corner; each scrap of rubbish gingerly overturned with poked swords.

"Where did they go?" asked one voice, nervously. "The horse is here but they aren't."

"Maybe they used magic," hoped another.

"Or maybe they've turned themselves invisible." whispered a third.

"Keep quiet you fool!" snapped the commander of the troop. "If you bring the city watch down upon us, I'll make sure it's your head that's taken first. Do you understand? Now go and secure that horse."

"M... m... me?" A nervous soldier looked over at the ivory stallion who pawed the floor sending up sparks and stared back with eyes like flint.

Kerian watched as the soldiers continued their search, fifteen feet below where he hid. He stood perched on a crumbling ledge, his heels as far back against the brick as he could get them and his top half touching the building on the other side of the alleyway to support and spread the weight. His calf muscles ached like fire and he could not help but notice a wobble in his arms.

To one side of him was the light-footed Elf, Scrave, who seemed to have no problems balancing and gave the impression he would have been able to balance on a knife-edge without breaking a sweat. To the other, the immense frame of Rauph stood on a groaning wooden window ledge, his arms punched into the wall opposite to make him as solid as a statue.

To complete their hiding place, several items of washing strategically hung about their persons, with Rauph looking particularly fetching draped with a large set of frilly pink underwear. All three had a perfect view of the soldiers as they continued their search below and Kerian could not help but grin as he heard the curses and exclamations of the nervous soldier who was even now receiving the less-than-tender ministrations of Saybier's teeth and hooves.

After what seemed to be an eternity, the commander of the troops ordered his men to stop their search and assemble around him. A heated discussion followed wherein they decided that the two men they were searching for had probably slipped away after leading the horse down the alleyway for them to find. A bruised and bitten guard suggested the likely stolen horse, if left where it was, would probably find its own way home.

Kerian was relieved to hear the search was near an end, as his legs were developing an interesting wobble and he was not sure how much longer he would be able to hang on. Saybier had been true to form and would never have let another person ride him; such was the training of the horses in the ranks of the Caerlyon knights.

The guards began to form up into ranks and Kerian risked moving his aching arm under cover of the noise they created. If he could only hang on for a moment longer this would all be over and they would be out of this ridiculous predicament. He held his breath again in silent hope and only then became aware of the muffled chuckles coming from the Minotaur alongside him. He glared at the creature hoping it would get the unspoken message to be quiet and wondered to himself what the creature had found so amusing.

"When are we going to jump out and get them?" Rauph enquired.

With almost military precision, the entire assembly of soldier's heads swung up to take in the view of their missing quarry above them.

"Can't you ever speak quietly?" Scrave snapped back.

"Now is really not a good time for an argument," Kerian tried to point out, as crossbows swung up to bear on the three stationary targets above their heads.

Scrave dropped from his perch with the slightest whisper of sound, his sword lashing out even before his boots had touched the cobblestones of the alleyway below. Streams of crimson life flew into the air as his blade began to wade into the tightly packed guards.

"I love shopping!" Rauph chuckled, dropping after his companion and crushing two unfortunate victims beneath his falling bulk.

Kerian watched the carnage below in a vaguely detached fashion. This could not be happening to him. It all had to be a bad dream. Any minute now, he was going to wake up in the *Sunset Spider* with a bad headache and a girl on each arm. He looked once again at the chaos that was unfolding and then shrugged.

"Well, if you can't beat them ..."

* * * * * *

"Torches are milling about all over the place," Thomas Adams continued to stare long and hard through his telescope at the flashes of light bobbing up and down Catterick's city streets.

"I believe our undercover shopping team are no longer undercover."

"It looks like a load of ants rushing from a disturbed nest," *El Defensor's* first mate Sherman agreed, taking the telescope from his captain and regarding the view for himself. "One thing's for sure; they're definitely looking for something."

"And we can both guess what," Thomas returned, offering a concerned frown to his companion. "Alert the crew and make ready to sail, we need to be ready to leave as soon as they get on board." Sherman turned with a creak of sea-salted leathers and headed off to comply with Thomas's wishes, his wide brimmed hat set at an angle on his head and his left hand scratching his salt and pepper beard. Shouted orders soon filled the air and crewmembers swiftly leapt to obey the commands.

The captain of the *El Defensor* watched his crew come alive around him, marvelling at how well they functioned as a team. He took a moment to absorb the sights and sounds, allowing himself a little nostalgic pride. Who'd have thought, all those years ago when he had first been brought upon the ship bleeding from a traitorous shotgun blast, that he would have ended up here, captain of this magnificent vessel and leader of an excellent crew. Watching them at work nearly made Thomas forget his own personal worries and feel light inside but it was a temporary respite from the heavy responsibilities he had to bear.

Activity on the starboard side of the vessel caught the captain's attention and he looked on as ropes and grappling hooks secured the ship's dinghy that had run alongside. Three identically dressed crewmembers climbed aboard, their quick hand signals informing the captain that their mission at least, had been a success.

Thomas was turning away when he caught sight of a fourth figure bought on-board. The man was dressed in blue robes and holding onto a large dark covered book that he seemed determined not to relinquish. Thomas moved over, gesturing for the crew to fall back and give the man room. Sandal clad feet and a neatly trimmed basin haircut confirmed his fears. This man was a monk!

He turned to the three crewmen and frowned.

The Rinaldo Brothers looked at each other uncomfortably and then Abilene stepped forwards and cleared his throat.

"Well, as you can see, the dinghy was where it was supposed to be and most of the supplies as well but we couldn't find Rauph and Scrave. We did try looking and were dealing with the harbour master just like you told us to, when he saw us." He gestured at the monk who was looking slightly perplexed about it all. "Well we couldn't just knock out a monk, its bad luck to hit a holy man. So, well we... brought him along with us, as it was just easier that way."

Thomas's scowl grew deeper.

"We could always drop him off further along shore tomorrow," Abilene offered, weakly.

"I ordered a covert operation, not a field trip!" Thomas shook his head in dismay. "I'll deal with you all later! Now, man the rigging and help the others trim those sails!"

The three brothers leapt for the ropes, anxious to put as much space between themselves and their captain as possible. Thomas watched the trio of golden and white outfits swiftly ascend into the heavens climbing hand over hand to disappear between the billowing sails, their actions as light-footed and sure, as if they walked on solid ground and not on creaking and groaning rigging.

The captain returned his attention to the shoreline and had to agree with Sherman's opinion, the torches did look like ants: very agitated and angry ants! He silently prayed that Rauph and Scrave would hurry up and get to the docks. This was too much attention. Too much attention indeed.

* * * * * *

Litter and rats scattered in all directions as twenty-five temple guards, one horse, a crazed bloodthirsty Elf, an eight-foot tall mountain of fur with pink knickers on his head and an elderly warrior hacked and slashed at each other in a fifteen by thirty-foot area. Granted Rauph the Minotaur was throwing most of the guards out of the alley and back into the street but more of their pursuers kept arriving by the moment.

Kerian parried a swiftly descending blade and returned in kind, plunging his violet tinged blade into a guard's shoulder. The man slumped to his knees and then screamed anew, as Scrave's blade plunged downwards through his skull and deep into his torso, blood gushing everywhere. Kerian did not have time to comment, as another guard ran in towards him, blade swinging wildly. He drew a crimson etched line across the man's throat and looked on expressionless as the guard dropped gurgling to the alley floor.

This was not a fight. It was a massacre!

Rauph was in his element, seemingly unaware of the severity of his predicament. He reached out and grabbed any guard who strayed too near and cleaved through the defences of anyone who got too careless. Screams of pain mingled with cries of terror, as Rauph playfully despatched his foes. Piles of dead or unconscious guards lay at his feet. Others lay senseless in the far corners of the alleyway or hung suspended from washing lines high above the street where the chuckling Minotaur had thrown them. Throughout the entire episode the pair of resplendent pink knickers stubbornly remained flapping from Rauph's left horn.

"Thank Adden he's on my side!" Kerian thought, as another guard went into Minotaur powered flight.

Scrave was the darkness to Rauph's light. His swordplay was almost too fast for Kerian's eye to follow, at times giving the illusion that the sword was leading Scrave's arm and not the other way around. However, what concerned Kerian more was the way the Elf used sword thrusts to maim and inflict pain before delivering the final killing stroke. As he watched, Scrave took out the eye of his latest foe with a wrist flicking action, gazing down in cold indifference at the screaming, pleading man before he was off again: his blade weaving a glittering trail of destruction that hypnotised and lured yet more victims into joining his macabre dance.

This one needed watching closely... Very closely indeed!

The alleyway was suddenly deathly quiet. The last guard dispatched swiftly by a backhand from Rauph that sent the man pin wheeling into the wall.

"Let's go," Kerian suggested, walking over to Saybier and grabbing the horse's reins before climbing into the saddle and leading his mount out of the alleyway. He paused once he reached the open road checking the way was clear before looking back to motion to the two figures following him.

"The docks are this way." He motioned realising that for now they were a party of three.

* * * * * *

"Our ship is that one," Rauph gestured, pointing down across the harbour to where a twin masted galleon was sitting at dock, its rigging filled with crewmembers setting the sails. Kerian looked at the vessel and although he wasn't a sailor he noted that the ship appeared to be a sound one but it seemed that there ought to have been a third mast to the rear of the vessel and that it was strangely absent. He was about to mention this when he realised that the sails were billowing and then sagging as if something were breathing into its sails but the night was now still following the storm and there was no wind to be felt.

Momentarily confused, he shook his head and rubbed his eyes. He was simply over tired, which had to be the explanation. He looked over at the ship again and it began to dawn on him that this vessel could serve both his and Marcus's needs.

Speaking of Marcus! Where was he?

Kerian cursed under his breath. Here was an ideal opportunity going to waste because the monk was such a bumbling fool. He should have simply taken the books from Marcus once he had left the monastery grounds and gone his own way. Now this ship was going to sail and he was not going to be on it. He had no choice; he was going to have to stick to his original plan and find a ship to charter in the morning.

Flickering torchlight made Kerian pause. Even as he looked back over Scrave's shoulder, more and more torches rushed to fan across the road they had just travelled down and angry shouts arose into the night air once more.

"It would appear that our sparring partners had friends," Kerian observed. "I think this may be the ideal opportunity for us to go our own separate ways."

Rauph turned to look at the approaching mob and grinned, reaching for his two swords but his companion laid a restraining hand on his arm and indicated they should leave.

Saybier tensed beneath his master, chewing at the bit in his mouth and anxious to be off but Kerian remained content to wait as he watched the two strange companions jog towards the departing ship. Tonight had been quite an adventure.

"They're coming along the quayside!" Scrave yelled back. "Hurry or you'll be cut off!"

Kerian looked back and realised the Elf was right but his mind froze with indecision. He could not leave without Marcus and as he scanned the docks over the heads of the advancing mob, he could see no sign of the innocent monk. He stood up in his stirrups to get an even better view over the mass of waving swords and still saw nothing of his missing companion. Where was he?

If he had only taken the monk's book none of this would have mattered! He silently berated himself for his stupidity and turned Saybier on the spot as he tried to locate a possible exit from this mess. There was none unless he counted the exit his newfound colleagues had taken. He watched as a gangplank lowered for the two desperados and swiftly began to reconsider his earlier choice of not using the ship for passage.

Maybe he could secure a lift, get dropped off further along the coast, then return by coastal trail when daylight broke. The air started to hum with stray crossbow bolts and Kerian realised his decision had been made for him. He turned Saybier towards the dockside and dug in his heels, allowing the horse to gallop out onto the wooden decking and head for the only salvation left open to them.

The skeletal masts of derelict ships rocking gently in their berths cast eerie shadows through which Saybier charged without hesitation, his white hide dappling as muscles flexed to the task of carrying his master to safety. Boxes of cargo awaiting loading littered the area, alongside lobster pots and fishing nets hanging to dry or folded in preparation for early fishing trips scarce hours away.

Saybier's hooves clattered across the wooden planking helped to drown out the sounds of pursuit. Kerian risked a quick glance over his shoulder and noted with some amusement that there was a bottleneck behind him as the pursuers struggled to organise themselves. He visibly relaxed, happy that the distance between himself and the guards was widening with each heartbeat.

The stallion inexplicably chose that moment to rear, hooves slipping on the lichen-coated woodwork to tumble both horse and rider to the deck. Kerian relied on instinct throwing himself free from the saddle and narrowly avoiding having his leg crushed. He swiftly regained his feet, hand reaching for his sword before seeing a small huddled figure standing in the path he had been taking. Its eyes were tightly closed, one arm flung over its muddy tear streaked face, its clothes in rags, its feet a bloody mess and a ragged feather hung from a ruin of a hat.

In a flash Kerian realised who it was.

"You!" Kerian snarled. "What in Adden's name do you think you're doing? You could have got us all killed!" He moved to grab the Halfling, intent on throwing the miserable creature off the dock and into the sea, as Saybier struggled to regain his footing and nickered a warning. A crossbow bolt thwacked into the woodwork galvanising Kerian's attention back to the pursuit.

"We will address this later," he promised, climbing back into the saddle, before reaching down to pluck the surprised little Halfling up onto the saddle behind him. "But I guess I can't leave you here now." It appeared that tonight he was destined to collect numerous travelling companions. At this rate, he would have his own legion by dawn!

Kerian dug in his heels, spurring Saybier into movement. Crossbow quarrels hammered into the deck behind him as they picked up speed and Ashe simply held on for dear life. The galleon's sails were beginning to fill as the gangplank was withdrawn, stays and ties creaking as they took up the strain and the ship slowly began to move away from the shore.

"No," Kerian mouthed, seeing his only avenue for escape easing away. "You have to wait!"

The ship continued to move, oblivious to his call. The possibility of the crew hearing his plea was slight against the screaming hordes that pursued him. He leant forwards and urged Saybier to gallop faster. Ashe dared open his eyes and suddenly realised where they were heading.

"No... not a ship... please... I can't swim!" he wailed.

Horse and riders arrived where the gangplank had previously lain at a full-fledged gallop, crossbow quarrels thudding into the wooden plank-work all around them and throwing jagged splinters into the air. The departing vessel was too high from this position. They were never going to manage the leap. He yanked on the reins, tugging Saybier about and glancing further down the jetty. There were stacks of cargo that formed a makeshift stair.

"Go!" Kerian urged, digging in his heels and coaxing every bit of speed he could from his trusty steed. The stallion did not question its master, hooves clattering on the weathered wood before it leapt up onto the first collection of cargo boxes, then jumped higher onto one stacked alongside. They were going to do this, the height would make all the difference, if they timed this just right. Kerian hung on grimly and closed his eyes, willing the horse to leap the gap between the dock and the departing ship.

Saybier launched himself into the air and appeared to be succeeding with ease, when disaster struck. Two crossbow bolts pierced the stallion's flank causing the horse to jerk in reaction to the sudden pain, an inhuman shriek filled the air making Kerian open his eyes in startled horror. The horse hit the deck of the ship hard, legs buckling with a sickening snap that heralded an injury much worse than the earlier scrapes of the first fall.

The knight landed hard, thrown from the saddle for the second time in as many moments and slid across the highly polished decking to slam into one of the main masts. The air rushed out of his body and Kerian lay there struggling to catch his breath. He shook his head, fighting to clear his vision, before noting the approach of a small three-foot high figure that crossed the deck and walked right up to him without so much as an introduction. The small creature wore a scuffed leather apron, tools of all shapes and sizes sticking out from it and a crazy embroidery pattern emblazoned across the front serving to proclaim the figure as 'Barney'.

"Nice to meet you ... Barney," Kerian offered a weak smile. "But, please, excuse me, as I have to see to my horse first."

Barney looked at Kerian with the minimum of expression, reached into his apron for a metallic wrench and hit him soundly about the head with it.

Chapter Twelve

The rat moved slowly at first, crawling from its mould-shrouded hole at the base of the cold damp wall, its taut whiskers twitching as it took in its surroundings. Red eyes cleaved the darkness with rodent inherited clarity as it absorbed the sights and smells of the six-foot square room beyond, nostrils flaring and closing with small hypersensitive movements as it tentatively sniffed the air. Its goal lay along the far back wall, its presence confirmed by another tantalising sniff. A plate of stale bread, excellent faire to a lowly rat!

It cautiously slid forwards onto its stomach, both eyes firmly on its goal as sharp claws scrabbled for holds on the slick stones beneath its grey haired, wiry frame. The rodent's body slid like liquid, in and out of the dips in the stonework, avoiding stagnant puddles that had collected from the dripping darkness above and trailing a long pink sinewy tail behind it. The plate was closer now, the metal rusty from age and neglect: the contents only half-eaten! Succulent crumbs from the bread lay scattered across the floor causing the rat to drool with the anticipation of the feast to come.

A groan froze the rat to the spot as something in the darkness adjusted its position. The rodent stood quivering as its head turned to regard the unwarranted intrusion with hatred blazing in its eyes. The source of the groan lay slumped against the back wall, a strong coppery tang of dried blood lay thick around the figure, quite overpowering to the rat's highly sensitive nostrils. It twitched them again and noted the underlying stale smell of excrement and the clinging scent of despair that accompanied the coppery tang. The rodent noted this miasma and presumed that, in the near future, it would be feasting on more than simply bread.

Satisfied that the threat would not bother it any further, the rat continued its journey, weaving almost silently around the remains of a shredded pair of leather sandals. The smell of a forge confirmed the presence of dark steel bands of confinement that cruelly encircled the limbs within these ragged items of footwear. From above links of chain descended to the floor, clinking softly as the figure moved and severely limiting any notion of escape the prisoner could entertain. The rat moved closer still, red eyes sweeping continually from the plate to the prone figure and back again as it slipped beneath the chains and closed upon its goal.

Rags barely fit as trousers and a crude piece of frayed, torn linen that had once been a tunic completed the prisoner's garb. The tunic had no fastenings, ragged holes betraying where they had been lost some time in the past. Even so, the tunic remained stubbornly around its wearer, accumulated dirt and grime from the cell giving the body a sticky purchase that only a prolonged soak would be able to release. Skin, where visible, was pale and emaciated, rib bones raised to pinch where they showed. A head more akin to a grinning skull than anything alive leaned heavily upon the figure's chest, a pair of sunken eyes barely flickering with the tell-tale movements of life.

Suddenly hesitant, the rat paused, looking up at the man with clear suspicion, noting the figure's position in its attempt to ascertain any further threat.

One arm stretched up above the prisoner's body chained to a shackle that was set deep into the wall. Black rivulets of encrusted blood stood out in stark relief to the white skin across which they ran. The other arm lay motionless against the figure's side, palm up, with fingertips reaching for the sky. A deeply scarred wrist and hand told a story enhanced by the presence of a further shackle, now hanging empty except for slivers of necrotic skin.

Satisfied the prisoner offered no further danger the rat resumed its slow advance. Two feet of black stone floor now separated it from its goal. One foot ... Then it was upon the bread, sharp fangs slicing firmly into the stale substance, muscles tensing as it prepared to spring back towards the safety of its home. It leapt, pushing the plate backwards so that the metal clattered loudly against the stone-flagged floor.

A bony fist shot from the darkness with a speed that defied appearance, snatching the rat in mid-air and causing it to squeal in pain, the bread dropping forgotten from its jaws. Teeth flashed, blood flowed and the darkness almost lit with the intensity of an explosive crack. A dry rasping laugh issued from the darkness as the prisoner regarded his prize.

For the first time in what had seemed an eternity of darkness, the man known as Mathius Blackraven would dine on meat again. He made himself as comfortable as his restraints would allow, then began chuckling quietly as he crunched and chewed through his still warm meal.

* * * * * *

"But your worship," the guard pleaded, "We couldn't continue the chase once they had boarded the ship. We were too busy trying to avoid fighting with the city watch. We would have been sitting ducks if we had continued to run up the jetty after them. We'd have been cut off. We cou ..."

Pelune, head of the *Order of the Serpent* looked on in barely controlled rage. His eyes focused on a thin trickle of blood that was slowly tracing its way through the guard's sweat dampened hair, rolling onwards, down past a battered swollen ear to track slowly along the underside of his jaw and drop to an ornately woven rug below. It originated from far eastern lands. One thing was for sure, the guard would be paying for a replacement.

"You're a pathetic fool." Pelune's ice-cold reply cut off the guard's excuses in mid flow. "The city watch is of no concern to me. You should never have let the thieves reach the docks alive. They should never have even left this temple and for that you will suffer dearly." Pelune started to pace angrily, his mind extremely agitated. The guard winced, as he knew his Master would make good his threat, he had seen it happen to his predecessors but like many men blinded by a higher salary, the sentry thought that somehow he could avoid the same grisly fate.

Silk robes whispered as they brushed the surface of the ornate rugs under Pelune's feet. He was very proud of his rugs. They kept his feet warm. His eye flicked back to the guard's bleeding wound as another crimson drop fell to the floor. The stain was never going to come out!

The guard realised he was following his Master's movements and swiftly averted his eyes to show respect, his eyes widening in horror as he noticed the crimson stain by his feet. His trembling increased noticeably.

Like a stalking predator, the serpent priest slowly approached his prey. He regarded the man before him with barely controlled disgust. This pathetic sentry was supposed to be the best, his proclaimed captain of the guard. After tonight's pitiful performance, Pelune promised himself that the best had better improve immediately! This man would serve as an example to motivate the rest of the guards. No one escaped from the clutches of the *Order of the Serpent* and lived and this so-called captain... Correction, soon to be an ex captain, would have to explain this to them in terms they would understand.

He changed the tone of his voice to a venomous hiss, his interrogation and information gathering continuing to be carried out in as hypnotic a fashion as the creatures the priest worshipped.

"Tell me once again about the type of ship they escaped on? Who was her captain? What was her cargo? Whose house did she sail for? And, more importantly, what was her heading?" Pelune's outstretched finger lightly traced down the unscathed side of the guard's face, an ornate nail tracing a fine red line across his skin.

"W ... we questioned the harbour master as you requested but he saw nothing," the guard stammered in response. "Apparently three men jumped him and tied him up in his cabin earlier that night. So there was no paperwork or logs filled in at all." He risked a quick glance up into Pelune's coldly merciless eyes and then just as quickly redirected his gaze towards the red stain at his feet, which caused him to panic further. Momentary indecision followed as he struggled to ascertain whether to look at his master or look back at the floor and possibly draw attention to the fact he had leaked all over the rug. He needed to placate the high priest and salvage his perilous position. Scenes of the evening's chaotic chase through the streets flashed through his mind in a mad jumble. There had to be something there... anything that might appease his leader.

"Defensor ... the name of the ship was the *El Defensor*," he blurted out with relief. "She went under the name of *El Defensor*."

"El Defensor? Are you sure?" Pelune quizzed, drawing the edge of his nail across the guard's chin. "I have never heard of a ship with this name. Are you absolutely sure?" The terrified guard nodded in mute reply. The High Priest removed his finger from the man's face and examined the bloody smears that now served to highlight the swirls and spirals of his fingerprint with a cold clinical detachment. Then, with a deliberate maliciousness, he slowly wiped his finger across the guard's tunic, pausing to admire his artistic work with a critical eye.

Apparently satisfied, Pelune turned from the guard and returned to his desk, lowering himself into a plush leather chair. The guard, thinking himself forgotten, groaned in relief, his fear induced trembling limbs struggling to support his combat weakened frame.

Pelune ignored the pitiful display of weakness, not even acknowledging it in case the fool thought his High Priest was displaying uncharacteristic mercy. Instead, he brought his hands up before him, arching his fingers and lightly touching the tips together to form steeples akin to those adorning the temple roof above. He needed time to think about the night's unforeseen occurrences and the inherent problems that had ensued from them. The pessimist in him taunted that it was fate but Pelune could scarcely believe in such an unsubstantiated claim. His religion had lived in the shadows too long, its moment of glory was now upon it and he would not allow his careful planning to fail.

The pretence of weakness, a distasteful yet necessary cover, allowed Pelune the required time to nurture his organisation and create his religion from nothing. His religious sapling had now turned into a sturdy oak with strong roots that reached deeply throughout the power structures existing within Catterick's walls. Pockets were lined where necessary, palms were greased when due and fear of the serpent's bite grew with each whispered terrifying tale.

Pelune envisaged his cult's influence would be powerful enough to take on the very seats of Catterick's great churches. Nothing would stand in his way. He would finally have all the power he needed. That was ... until tonight.

He began to crack his fingers one by one as the rage and anger bubbled up within him. Why tonight of all nights? The stars wheeling through the heavens above were celestially slotting into an unholy alignment that he had promised his followers would signal their rise to power. In less than a week, Pelune's status would have been akin to that of a god. Why had a stinking thief chosen now, of all times, to break into the temple and incredibly, bypass all the security and magicks placed around his most treasured of artefacts? Stealing the very instrument required to make Pelune's rise to power complete.

The High Priest's thoughts turned to the unholy object. Did the thief realise what he had taken? It was impossible! He dismissed the idea as paranoid fantasy. Rubbing his nose in frustration, the priest leaned forwards to rest his chin upon a clenched fist. Robes rustled loudly in the stillness of the room as he changed position, but Pelune was too deep in thought to notice how his movement made the guard twitch nervously.

One thing was beyond question, without the magical artefact, Pelune's power would begin to wane, and his dark god would become displeased without its specified tribute. He shuddered, imagining the repercussions of such failure. No! That was not going to happen. He had to retrieve the artefact swiftly, no matter what the personal cost. Nevertheless, the question persisted... how was he to do this?

Pelune's wandering thoughts returned to the guard kneeling before him. What a pitiful mess. Battered armour, blood flowing freely from a severe head wound. The fool did not even seem to realise the severity of his gash. Crimson drops of life still fell from his chin like misplaced tears. Pelune chuckled at the description. Tears of life... he stopped himself. No... tears of respect. Congratulating himself at his own creativeness the priest suddenly realised what he needed to do.

His guards had failed him because they were soldiers, trained and drilled in soldier's ways. If he wanted to catch the man who stole his prize, he would have to send someone after him who knew these shadowy ways and thought like he did. What better way to catch this thief than to set another thief after him?

Pelune gestured at the guard and watched as the man tried to snap to attention. The perceptible tremor in the man's legs brought yet another smirk to the High Priest's lips.

"Bring me the Raven," he ordered.

The wounded guard's eyes went wide in shock. Had he heard his master right; did he just ask for the Raven?

"Now!" Pelune roared, angry at the hesitation the man showed. Nobody had the right to question his orders!

The guard hurried from the room, not even pausing to wipe his blood streaked face, leaving his Master alone with his thoughts. Pelune nodded to himself. Yes, he would use the Raven to track down and slay the desecrator of his temple. The Raven... the very tool Pelune had used to aid his own rise to power. A legendary thief, who could enter any place, no matter how secure and who, with the right motivation, had unwillingly become the bite of the serpent that so many now feared.

However, he would have to be cautious. The Raven had eventually become dangerous and was now a permanent guest of the dungeons beneath the temple in case he had spoken to the wrong people at the wrong time. He would have to take steps to ensure the control of the prisoner and that he would only carry out the task required. He would need Justina's spell craft.

Pelune sat back in his chair and entertained chilling thoughts about the thief who had dared enter his home and place of worship. There was no doubt that whoever it was thought himself safe after successfully making an escape aboard the *El Defensor* last night but he was a fool like so many others who had dared cross the priest. Before he knew it, the far-reaching coils of the serpent would begin to entangle him, ever tightening, as he yet struggled to escape and when the moment was right, the serpent would strike repeatedly, leaving death in its wake.

* * * * * *

The High Priest regarded the figure sprawled across his carpet with abhorrence. It had been a long time since he had been down to the dungeons to taunt Mathius Blackraven. He examined the lice ridden emaciated figure with renewed curiosity. How could this shadow of a man still have the strength left in his bones to resist his demands? Even now, his skeletal head looked up with hatred blazing in his eyes as he recognised whom he knelt before.

Momentary doubt entered the High Priest's mind about the suitability of the man before him for the task he had in mind, then he swiftly disregarded it. After all, the Raven was the perfect killer. Oh, there would be blood and lots of it. The thief who had dared to steal from Pelune would soon be wishing that he had not dared to be so presumptuous.

The smell of confinement rose from the prone figure in waves, offending Pelune's delicate nostrils and making him want to gag. He swiftly placed a lavender scented silken handkerchief over his nose to both conceal his discomfort and attempt to reduce the stench wafting up at him. He gestured hurriedly with his free hand for the prisoner's removal, looking on coldly, as the guards dragged the emaciated figure violently to his feet, leaving streaks of grime across the expensive carpets. Always the carpets had to suffer!

"Make sure the healers see to him," Pelune ordered, "...and make sure he is thoroughly cleaned before you dare to bring him within my presence again!" The guards moved almost as one, anxious to meet their High Priest's commands but also extremely wary of the dangerous 'animal' they were now guarding. They all knew what the Raven was capable of and treated him as such. They led the Raven from the room, unaware of Pelune's barely stifled gasp of horror and disgust: for in the prisoner's gnarled fist hung the remains of a half-chewed rodent.

It was with some relief that Pelune returned to his chair, yet even now, the thought of what the Raven could do filled the High Priest with a perverse shivering dread. With the appropriate enchantments in place, Mathius

Blackraven would perform most adequately. The Raven would soon return with his prize, and Catterick would finally tremble at his name.

Pelune looked across at the soiled carpets adorning his floor and frowned, then smiled as an idea came to the twisted man: When the captain of the guard returned, he would have him lick the carpets clean and then, when he was finished, the priest would take great pleasure in removing his tongue.

* * * * * *

The Raven stood heavily shackled yet openly defiant in the centre of the main temple, the coils of the great golden serpent spiralling out beneath his feet into the ranks of the acolytes and worshippers that chanted all around him. His countenance was now very different from that of the wretched prisoner of a few hours earlier. The magical potions forcefully applied had done their work well.

His fine ochre hair was now gleaming with health and vitality, combed back away from his face and parted at his crown. His face was fuller now and glowing with imbued magicks that accentuated his angled jaw. His nose was sharp and prominent, now devoid of scars and scabs and his dark brown eyes darted everywhere, seeking some clue as to what was about to happen next. Formerly wasted muscle now appeared toned, although not without cost. A muscle spasm suddenly shot up his right leg making him drop to one knee in a rattle of chains. He cursed at the debilitating side effects of swift healing and furiously rubbed the knotted muscle, kneading it with light manipulative fingers until the twinges subsided.

He was dressed in a black linen shirt that hung loosely from his newly lithe form and as the spasm eased his fingers lingered on the material that clothed his legs, the shimmering grey fabric was rare and very expensive. The Raven had only seen it's like once before and recalled that it had been rumoured to turn aside blade thrusts. Pelune wore an undershirt of this. Soft tan leather boots serving to complete his recently supplied outfit and the Raven noted that as he moved they appeared to make his footfalls silent. There was something important going on. Why the expense showered upon him? Maybe he could find some way to use it to his advantage.

Mathius slowly regained his feet and balanced gently upon his right leg, bringing his hand up to brush away a lock of fallen hair and paused, noticing the pale bracelet of scar tissue that still circled his wrist. It appeared that despite the strength of the potions used on him, not all the signs of his cruel confinement were so easily erased. The open skylight called to the man's wandering attention but he swiftly disregarded that escape route. Although known as The Raven, he had no wings to make him fly. Escape would have to come from another avenue.

The chanting rose in volume around him and then, almost as suddenly, stopped, the figures before him parting with a whisper of material to expose a pathway directly to the raised temple altar. The Raven took in the battered appearance of the golden serpent towering above the congregation and raised an eyebrow in question. Either Pelune was not paying attention to the upkeep of the temple or he was falling into disfavour with his god. A cold suspicion began to form in the back of his mind. Was he to be a sacrifice this evening?

Standing before the stone altar stood the pompous figure of Pelune, bedecked in all his serpentine splendour. Black and gold robes hung from his generous frame, glittering with embroidered metallic threads. A live golden serpent coiled around his neck, its tongue testing the air with short sharp thrusts. Pelune looked towards the Raven and smiled, raising his hand in a gesture of apparent friendship to the crowd but to Mathius that grin signified the high priest had left nothing to chance and escape would not be easy.

He would have given all he had to have a few moments free of his chains to wipe that smug grin from Pelune's fat face and throttle the very life from him. The High Priest had taken away everything that had ever mattered to him. He looked at the open hand stretched out towards him and looked away, openly displaying his distain. He knew it was foolish to show such bravado; indeed, he had watched his bride murdered in front of his eyes as punishment for daring to question the priest. This was the price of bravado, the price of bitter betrayal.

Pelune looked across at the Raven's defiance and shrugged, signalling to the guards to yank down hard on his chains and bring him to his knees.

"I see your mind is still sharp after your incarceration," he offered. "Lesser men would have cracked long ago; although you always were stronger than you looked." Satisfied The Raven was secure Pelune walked slowly towards him to stand on the edge of the dais emphasising his height and towering over his captive.

"As you said," Mathius replied, looking up and meeting his gaze, "my mind, as well as my memory." he looked past Pelune at the bare stone altar and a worrying thought crossed his mind. Was he to meet his fate as a sacrifice to the serpent god, now after all this time?

His eyes betrayed his inner turmoil, darting swiftly around the area desperately looking for a way out of the situation before him. Animal-like instincts, relied upon so successfully in the past, felt keen and on edge, desperate to break free and causing a barely susceptible tremble to ripple through his form.

Pelune gestured to a cloaked figure standing off to the side. She moved forwards into the light, embroidered silver catching the flickering candlelight as she threw back her dark hood revealing a pale olive-skinned complexion, framed by a wealth of tumbling red tresses that cascaded around her shoulders and flowed into soft curls at her waist. The most dazzling pair of green eyes scrutinised the prisoner and the Raven found himself gasping at the vision that stood before him. Justina had this effect wherever she went.

"I might have guessed your witch would be somewhere near." Mathius snapped. "Although from what I see I am not sure who the master is between the two of you. Are you here to watch me beg for mercy my lady? Because I assure you I aim to disappoint."

"Shut him up!" Pelune ordered, angry that the prisoner dare address his lover in this way. "Make him show respect." Two guards stepped forward, confident the shackles held their prisoner safely secured, and the largest one smashed a mailed fist into The Raven's jaw. He saw the blow telegraphed long before it landed and rolled with it falling into the other guard at waist level and making the man jump back as he slid down the guard's legs to the floor.

The guards backed away shaken but cocky that they had been able to lay a hand on the prisoner and live to boast of it. The larger one shook his fist claiming it stung, whilst the smaller one just chuckled and tried to show bravado he did not really have. He was unaware that the dagger from his belt was now missing.

Justina continued to concentrate on the ritual at hand. She placed a velvet cushion upon the altar and opened up an ornate box that The Raven recognised immediately. He voiced his opinion regarding its unseen contents even as he slipped the dagger up the sleeve of his shirt.

"I've delivered my last serpent for you Pelune," he stated, seemingly leaving no room for negotiation.

Pelune looked at the box and threw a smile towards the man who had once been the deliverer of the 'serpent's bite'. He had expected just such a response and had already prepared an appropriate reply.

"Oh, I don't want you to deliver another serpent my friend," he hissed. "I need you to do something else for me."

Justina reached into the box and lifted a large golden and red-flecked snake from the box. It reacted instantly trying to bite the hand that seized it but Justina handled many serpents and knew exactly how to prevent injuries occurring. The snake responded by wrapping its tail around her arm but its fight was pointless in her clutches.

"It looks like a serpent to me," the Raven shot back. Knowing all too well he used to deliver such boxes and empty their contents in through cool chimneys, sewers or carelessly open windows to bedrooms and nurseries, killing those within and raising the order's powers by their threat alone. "If you don't want me to deliver a snake then what is it? Am I to be some sacrifice on your altar? Am I to be the latest victim to your sick twisted dagger?

Pelune froze, just for a second but enough for The Raven to know he had hit close to home. The High Priest flushed in anger then stepped closer ensuring the guards holding the chains had the prisoner pulled low to the floor. He gestured to Justina and she stepped down from the altar bringing the secured, writhing snake with her.

Justina walked behind Mathius as Pelune walked up in front of him. The priest leant forward and whispered into his prisoner's ear as a sharp crack sounded behind, signifying a gemstone's destruction and the casting of magic.

"You are not to be sacrificed." Pelune cooed softly. "You are going to get my dagger back and I want you to kill anyone that gets in your way." He looked up past The Raven's head and the prisoner saw the beating jugular in the man's neck. If he tore the priest's throat out he would gain nothing. He had to wait and see how this played out. Wait a minute; did he say he had lost his dagger? The Raven could not help but laugh.

"Oh now I see." He smirked. "You have made a really grave mistake. You..."

Magical energies swirled up into the air to mingle with the soft chanting emanating from the sorceress's delicate lips. The snake in her hand writhed and twisted before it moved forward onto The Raven's head. He stiffened instantly, horrified by the feel of the snake sliding across his scalp, entwining through his hair and moving across his brow. Horror turned to terror but the poisonous bite never came. Instead, the snake turned on itself, its fangs slicing into its own tail as it slowly began to consume its own flesh. The snake continued to jerk spasmodically, the living circlet it was creating starting to crush and constrict as it shrank, digging into his skin and tightening, ever tightening.

Mathius Blackraven screamed shaking his head violently trying to make the snake come loose. He strained against his chains trying to raise his hands high enough to pull the foul thing free but he found himself held securely in place and his struggles were in vain. The pain was all-consuming, debilitating, all The Raven wanted was for it to be over.

"No it was you that made the mistake," Pelune crooned, looking on in fascination as the snake gulped and jerked one last time, its scales slicing into his prisoner's brow and drawing trickles of blood. Justina continued her chanting and the snake metamorphosed from something live into a band of golden jewellery.

"He can't take it off," she assured Pelune. "If he tries it will tighten and kill him. If he tries to avoid your task and make a break for freedom, the same thing will happen. With the band in place we know where he is, we can see what he does and we can bring him home when he is successful."

"I don't want him to be able to talk to others," Pelune demanded. "I don't want anyone trying to take the band off for him."

"I can't stop him talking." Justina confessed, looking down at the whimpering prisoner. "But he will only say what he needs to in order to get the task done."

"It always is a worry that he might betray me again," Pelune muttered. "But I must confess that I feel more at ease knowing what you have done. He cannot be allowed to betray me again... not ever." The Raven's struggles had now turned to silence, his gasps the only thing confirming the pain he was experiencing. Throughout it all Pelune's cold calculating gaze looked on, devoid of any passion or warmth.

"He lives now to retrieve your dagger." Justina confirmed. "Once we let him loose he will do as you have demanded." She walked back to the altar, and Pelune followed like a dog on a leash, eager to see the next part of the ceremony come into play.

"Do you know where to send him?" he asked. Justina gestured to a scrying bowl in which the image of a ship's deck moved gently up and down. Something large and shaggy walked across the view, making Pelune wrench back his head in surprise. "What was that thing?"

"This is one of the creatures that broke into your temple," Justina uttered softly. "I ripped the image from your guard's mind. He was too scared to tell you of the creature less you feared him mad. This is no longer a worry to him." She gestured at an area where cargo limited the view of those around. "This is the place. I will send him there but we do need to do one more thing or The Raven will be seen when he arrives."

Justina stepped away from the bowl and moved to the other side of the altar where a large cleared space awaited her attentions, spaced candles illuminating the circumference of a circular pattern in the floor decorated with spidery runes. Pelune clapped his hands and the five guards restraining the Raven dragged him to his feet by his chains and manoeuvred him to the centre of the circle before moving back a safe distance to draw crossbows, which they then trained on the groaning prisoner. Chains clattered and clinked on the floor.

The Raven staggered slightly but remained standing, blurred eyes struggling to focus on the room around him. What was happening to him? What had he done to deserve this ungodly treatment? Even though the pull of the spell to retrieve Pelune's relic was intoxicating in its grip, Mathius realised that he was still incredibly aware of a profound need to escape. His animal instincts, honed to sharpness in the depths of his cell, appeared to be of some use after all.

He wobbled on unsteady limbs towards the outskirts of the circle and realised that robed figures had closed in from all sides. At this close range, he could also make out the cocked crossbows of the guards within the crowd of spectators and realised that he had no means to escape the terrifying noose in which he found himself.

Another cramp shot through his leg as the potions continued their work, dropping him to the mosaic floor. He rolled onto his side, much to the amusement of the assembled worshippers but this time the pain continued as he rolled across one of the lit candles.

In that instant, with the pain from the candle flame acting as a cleansing catalyst, the whole situation became clear to the prisoner. He stared around with clarity in his eyes but only those closest to the Raven realised something was different from the bumbling figure they had witnessed earlier and they had nowhere to back away to as the press of worshippers from behind hemmed them in.

Pelune's advancing footfalls caught The Raven's attention and he gripped his hands in tight fists, digging the jagged edges of his nails into his hands to maintain the pain that enabled him to focus. The High Priest's mocking smile filled his vision; but this time Mathius knew he held the small advantage, not Pelune. It was just a matter of choosing the right time to act.

The High Priest continued to smile as he dropped a blackened steel dagger onto the floor in front of the prisoner. It clattered across the mosaic floor and slid to a stop, nearby but not near enough!

The Raven stared at the dagger in disbelief! The blade was his, from all those years ago!

The leather wrapped handle, stained from his sweat and smoothed with constant handling. The blackened end of the dagger blade split into two distinctive razor tips that gleamed in the candlelight. Pelune had ordered the constructing of the weapon when some of his delivered serpents had failed to hit their mark. Snakes were strange creatures and could be notoriously fickle. Any wound inflicted by the poison tipped ends of the blade had looked just like the dreaded serpent bite and therefore, if the snake failed to bite The Raven would do its work instead. It was not as dramatic or poetic but the result was as effective.

Silence descended upon the circle as Pelune turned to the crowd addressing them as a father figure would.

"My friends," he began. "I have always been a man of great mercy and understanding, a man who is never afraid of offering second chances." Several faces in the crowd glanced over to the prisoner and thought back over the suffering they had just witnessed as if to make sure he was still there and not a figment of their imagination. "This man," he gestured towards Mathius, "betrayed me a long time ago and he has suffered because of it. He dared to question my judgement and threatened all we have worked towards. Now you see him about to enter my service again, offered a second chance by my merciful and humble self. His success will bring both my forgiveness and his freedom, failure will not be permitted."

Pelune smiled wickedly, leaving no doubt as to the meaning of his words. The Raven simply closed his eyes and tried not to gag as a wave of nausea swept over him.

"Join us in prayer, as we worship the snake." Pelune continued and his followers took up the challenge, chanting rising once more from the crowd. "Join me in thanks for our life, for all the serpent has given us. For all it is yet to give." The crowd roared in appreciation. "For the future when we control Catterick and then the world!" Pelune stood arms raised, his face hot and flushed. There was no doubt his enthusiasm was infectious to the weak minded.

The crowd around the circle held their breath as Justina moved forwards into the light. With great care, she slowly lowered a huge diamond to the floor at her feet, treating the expensive gem like something made of the most fragile glass and then she stood again her eyes now meeting Mathius. She focused her attention on the glowing serpent circlet set above the man's piercing eyes and began to chant archaic, unnatural sounding words. Her chanting speech appeared to become something almost tangible as the words, swept up by the tendrils of magical energy coming from the diamond at her feet, gathered more sound from the chanting crowd. The power grew in intensity falling about The Raven's head like rain.

Even as she looked on, Mathius slowly began to grow transparent and then disappeared altogether. The crowd roared in astonishment and the diamond cracked adding more power to the spell she was casting. All that remained to indicate where the raven stood were five lengths of chain that lay loose on the floor.

Pelune stared on in amazement as his lover wove her spell and The Raven slowly began to dissipate before his eyes, his head, torso, arms and then feet, everything he touched with his bare skin. Finally, there was nothing to show that Mathius had ever stood in the candlelit circle. The High Priest congratulated himself on his own ingenuity. The enchantment cast would ensure that Mathius searched unswervingly for his artefact and the spell cast by Justina would make The Raven invisible for the duration of his search as long as the serpent circlet remained secure upon his brow.

It was perfect!

Now all he had to do was await the return of his unholy artefact and the power he had lost would be his again. He smiled, revelling in the chanting from the crowd, only to have his smile turn sour and then evaporate completely.

A chain fell away knocking a candle from its base, then another fell free and another. The dagger, so casually thrown upon the floor, suddenly rose up from the golden serpent mosaic upon which it lay. The blackened steel weapon 'floating' in the air, before it too slowly disappeared from view. Two final clatters confirmed Pelune's fears.

"He's free!" Pelune yelled, beginning to back away from the circle, arm raised to ward off an attack. What in the seven hells did Justina think she was doing? She had just inadvertently armed the deadliest killer he had ever known! Justina was supposed to transport The Raven and his weapon away, arming him at his destination, not here in the temple!

"Get him out of here!" he screamed, turning in his panic to face the sorceress, "Get him out of here now!" As if in answer, a white flame flared brightly within the rune-etched circle, extinguishing all of the candles in an instant and filling the area with the acrid smell of brimstone. The diamond at Justina's feet imploded as the light rushed back in, all of its magically stored energies now finally exhausted as the guards poured into the circle weapons drawn.

* * * * * *

Mathius had been carefully watching for his chance to escape the clutches of Pelune. When it came, he moved fast. He had not realised what Justina was doing until he saw he was starting to disappear from the waist down. He did not hesitate, tackling the shackles and slipping his hands from the binders with the same method he had practiced repeatedly in his cell.

He lunged for the dagger, snatching up the blade, only to look on in amazement as his weapon disappeared before his eyes. He paused, unsure as to his success, then realised that his invisible hand was definitely holding something. It was incredible! He clearly had the blade firmly within his grasp! Fighting back the pressure of Pelune's enchantment The Raven flipped the blade within his right hand, even as he slipped the guards dagger from his left sleeve, instinct making it unnecessary to see the weapon to carry out the action successfully. He knew right where this guard's dagger was going.

Right between Pelune's serpentine eyes!

The High Priest began to shout and scream, gesturing towards the spot that the Raven had already vacated and for that split second the power that Mathius Blackraven had once known in freedom flooded back. This was justice served up on a platter! He drew his left arm back and prepared to snap his wrist forward to end the tyranny of Pelune forever.

The dagger never left his hand. Instead, something monstrous and dark attacked his mind; spectral serpentine coils crushing the resistance from the assassin as surely as the increased pressure that tore into his flesh as the circlet at his brow tightened to protect its Master. Mathius dropped to his knees in blinding agony as the enchantment rushed forward to take control. No! This could not be happening! Not now! He fought a losing battle; desperate to bring the dagger to bear on his target, before the spell seized complete control dropping a veil over the Raven's mind that was both impregnable and impossible for the prisoner to dispel. The guard's dagger clattered to the floor, the throw hopelessly weak and off target.

A bright flaring light flashed across The Raven's vision and he felt himself ripped apart, as the magical energies of the diamond transported him away.

* * * * * *

Guards rushed into the circle, crossbows and swords sweeping backwards and forwards across the area where the prisoner had stood, just as Justina collapsed in a heap upon the floor utterly exhausted from her casting. Through a veil of scarlet hair, she whispered the words Pelune longed to hear.

"Don't worry, he's long gone."

Pelune sighed with relief and within seconds was clicking his fingers and shouting commands to restore order with his men. One guard arrived from outside and hurried over. Pelune noticed him and walked away from the altar to give space to the new arrival.

"What did the crone predict Villar?" Pelune asked, keeping his voice low, knowing that an all-powerful High Priest would hardly do what he had done. "What did she predict?"

"She ..." He paused and nervously cleared his throat. "She told me she could see nothing but death and disaster in the future."

"Good! Good!" Pelune eagerly rubbed his hands, surprising the gaunt guard with his positive reaction to the terrible news. "Obviously The Raven is going to slaughter everyone on board the ship. This is excellent news indeed. What else did she say?"

"The outcome of your quest remains unclear," Villar continued. "The only definite information she would impart was that your employee's name would be his downfall." Pelune's smile evaporated again as he stepped around the altar to scrutinise the guard's thin face.

"What did you say?" he demanded, examining the guard closely for any possible signs of lying. "His name will be his downfall? What kind of a prophecy is that?" He turned, dismissing the guard with a wave of his hand and headed out of the main temple for the sanity of his own private quarters as worshippers milled about him excited at the display of magic they had just witnessed.

What was Villar on about? It seemed that if you wanted a job doing properly here you had to do it yourself! Pelune was fuming, he had given Villar good money to consult a reputable fortune-teller and he returned with a load of hokum!

Chapter Thirteen

John Hodge was a grizzled old sailor at the best of times, as happy nursing a drink of ale at *The Sloop Inn* as he was mending a fishing net or trimming a mainsail. He had joined the colourful crew of the *El Defensor* several years ago after being lost at sea off the port of St Ives in the Year of Our Lord 1757, during a smuggling operation that had gone sour due to turbulent seas. Ever since, the old sea hand had found himself sharing adventures with his new ship's crew as they sailed worlds beyond his imagination. No matter what world they found themselves in, he was always happy to call the men around him friends.

This morning, as on all others, he rose from his bunk and stretched, hearing his old bones cracking and creaking from sleeping suspended in a hammock, before washing quickly in a small bowl and dressing ready for the day ahead. He stowed his hammock, freeing up valuable space within an area he shared with five other shipmates and steadied himself against the roll of the ship before trimming any stray whiskers that would not comb into place with a cutthroat razor.

Suitably attired in a worn leather jerkin, salt stained from long exposure to the sea, a rough linen shirt and baggy trousers, he headed abaft towards the galley, taking his routine stroll around amidships before he contemplated the ladder up to the main deck and out into the open air. Voices of other crewmembers, rousing with the pre-dawn light or ending their night shifts on watch, rose to his ears as he shuffled along the length of the ship. Some louder exclamations caused him to chuckle as he imagined the more sluggish members of crew turned out of their beds and onto the hard wooden deck below by their ribald colleagues.

He rounded a corner and entered a small open observation area set amidships, the well-greased doors already stood open to the sea, admitting a bracing breeze. A two-man crew were checking the small Roman ballista and medieval crossbow stationed there, ensuring the weapons moved freely and that nothing had corroded in the sea air.

As every morning, John waved to the two sailors, nodding at Ridge, whose bushy black beard masked a near toothless grin, before mock-saluting Cresta who wore his faded blue and white striped cotton shirt as if his life depended on it. The seamen nodded in reply, still half asleep and turned to look out across the waves, on the lookout for potential threats and dangers to the ship. John chuckled to himself; no matter what time he passed this deck Cresta always looked half-asleep!

A loud caw signalled the return of Ridge's pet from its early morning flight. The large ebony feathered bird flew in through the open vantage deck and hopped onto the ballista, strutting up and down before the three crewmen.

Cresta laughed and pulled his beret from his back pocket, his sleepiness suddenly gone, wedging his beret tightly down upon his head. Ridge winked at John who simply smiled, a signal that he was game to a standing wager as he did every morning.

"Let's see you get it this time," Cresta joked, sticking his tongue out at the bird, oblivious to the money changing hands behind him. He slowly circled the ballista, carefully watching the bird, which in turn regarded him with a sparkling eye. Black feathers shone as it suddenly took to wing, flying lazily around the deck before diving straight at Cresta's blue beret. The seaman was so taken back by the speed of the attack that he staggered backwards to avoid the bird's grasping claws. Cresta's boot caught on one of the ballista's outstretched legs and he fell backwards towards the guardrail, arms wind milling uselessly before he hit the side and tumbled shrieking over the edge.

Ridge laughed, watching as the safety line attached to his colleague's waist whipped out over the rail behind him, then he firmly braced himself as the line pulled taut through a metal ring in the deck and snagged tight at his own waist. He winked at John as he started to haul in on the line.

"That's the safety line checked for today then." He joked, as John leant over the open rail to assist retrieving Cresta who dangled below, suspended from the other end of the line. He laughed at the sight of the man, white faced and ashen his face inches from the swell below.

"Are you alright?" John shouted down. "Ridge says you have to lose some weight!"

"Ha, ha! Very funny!" came the weak reply.

They pulled Cresta safely back over the side, John slapping him heartily, checking him over for scrapes and injuries. It was only when he touched the man's head that the real damage was discovered.

"I've lost my beret," Cresta wailed.

Ridge simply handed over some money to John and motioned at his bird strutting up and down the ballista, the unmistakable blue beret hanging from its beak. Cresta recognised it in a flash and swiftly unclipped himself from the lifeline and jumped for the bird, snarling, as it took to the wing and flew off down the corridor, Cresta in hot pursuit.

"Does he ever say thanks?" John Hodge asked his bushy bearded friend.

"He doesn't have to," Ridge replied, clipping the loose end of the line to the guardrail. "I know that one day he will return the favour. I only wish the boy would learn to swim. If we ever, god forbid, floundered in high seas the lad would die and there would be nothing I could do about it."

"One day, Shadow won't win," John teased, pocketing the money he had just won.

"But by then you'll be long gone," Ridge grinned, "And I will have the winning wager." John waved goodbye as he rounded the corner after the bird and crewman and made his way up the wide ladder to the deck above.

Scrave stood hands on hips at the top of the ladders blocking the way. John gently pushed Scrave to one side and then noted that the Elf was trying to block Rauph's progress down to the cabins below. He slipped between them and out onto the main deck wondering what all the commotion was about.

"Come on," he heard Scrave moan. "How did you manage to kill the snake so easily? It's a simple question?" Rauph snorted loudly and picked Scrave up, depositing him to one side of the ladder before ducking his head and walking calmly down towards his cabin. Scrave set off in hot pursuit, his muffled questioning fading as the two characters passed from sight.

John paused in his journey beneath the canvas sails that snapped tautly overhead, allowing himself a moment of luxury by closing his eyes and feeling the cool breeze caress the lines on his face. He turned towards the stern of the ship and stared at the huge billowing creature that was even now powering the ship along. It howled and screamed as it tested the unseen barriers containing it, angry that it had to obey the given commands. The sailor still did not understand magic that well and he felt uneasy seeing the creature powering the ship along by blowing into the sails but the dedication shown from the young novice sorceress who commanded it did impress him. He had heard tales the creature had escaped once before. Without doubt, that had been one of the ship's bad days; an occurrence they seemed to be having more and more of lately.

Shrugging off his unease, the grizzled seaman focused on the job at hand and climbed the ladder leading to the elevated prow of the ship. It was here that John stood watch throughout the daylight hours, his keen sight glimpsing possible rock outcroppings and submerged reefs better than any man who took the crow's nest high above did. Other duties entailed taking depth soundings if they had to thread through shallow reefs and signalling other ships with the twin lanterns fastened to the ship's guardrail. The *El Defensor*, all one hundred and ninety feet of her was a ship to feel at home upon but this particular perch was John Hodge's and his alone.

The sun would be up soon and John loved to be here to welcome its arrival and feel its touch on his weathered skin. This was without doubt an excellent ship on which to sail. He respected and admired the ship's captain, who was always fair and straight with him and on top of this the man had saved his life when all else was lost.

He looked back across the ship, watching the men climbing up into the rigging, trimming the sails to get the maximum advantage of the conjured wind elemental's breath. Others were scrubbing the decks and singing whilst those who had stood the night shift went to their bunks with a light heart and happy soul. This ship did this to people, rescuing them in whatever trouble they were in and then allowing them to set those wrongs right and move on when they were ready to do so.

Truth be told there was a little envy in John's mind too, as had never had the pleasure of running his own vessel. In a way he always regretted the fact that he hadn't taken the chance to do so. However, he also knew he was a little cowardly when it came to moving out of his area of comfort.

He checked the sky for a second and then, confidant he had time to linger, the seaman thought back on the good-natured banter he had witnessed with Rauph and Scrave. It seemed that Scrave liked to goad everyone these days but who would have thought these two would start to hit it off so well after their adventure! He remembered when Rauph had been discovered, marooned on a make shift raft far out to sea. They had dragged him aboard with extreme caution, all the crew concerned about his scary appearance and immense size.

Only Thomas had noticed the huge lump behind the Minotaur's ear, a wound intended to kill that had somehow missed its mark by the narrowest of margins. When Rauph had finally come around he could remember nothing, not even his name and his attitude to life was, dare he say it, always a little 'simple' in nature. Thomas had named the creature Rauph after a spitting cat he had once known at the 'precinct', wherever that was.

John finished his slow meander to the prow and tucked himself in behind the figurehead. He peered over the side and watched the waves crashing against the woodwork. The sky was beginning to turn slightly pink as if embarrassed by the kiss the sun was beginning to bestow upon it.

This was the best part of the day, the time he always loved. Watching the coming dawn. Every morning a different canvas painted by a major artist, no two ever the same. Somehow, the feeling of the first rays of sunlight on his face made the old sailor feel cleansed and young again. Today's sunrise was only moments away; he would have to hurry.

He reached inside his jerkin and retrieved a smooth wooden pipe. The grain of the wood so lovingly polished that it appeared to give off its own Inner Light. This pipe was his oldest and dearest friend and he never saw a dawn in without it. He tapped the bowl against the side of the ship to knock lose any dregs from his previous lighting and then plunged his hand into a pouch at his belt for some tobacco. Seconds later a warm mellow aroma rose from the bowl of the pipe and tickled the old man's nostrils.

John leant his head against the figurehead and relaxed. There was nothing in his opinion quite like smoking a pipe whilst watching the sunrise. This was indeed the life!

A muffled thump broke his concentration and John frowned, turning around to see who would dare to disturb his morning ritual. There was no one there, just a load of boxes that had been haphazardly stacked here upon their rather hurried departure from Catterick.

John turned forwards once more but mentally flagged the fact that he would have to have a word with Thomas about how the items had been stacked. Granted things had been rather hectic recently but the Rinaldo brothers should have stored the extra cargo they had 'borrowed' from the shore safely into the hold by now. From the sound of the thump, the boxes were probably already starting to shift and that could be a danger to the crew. After he had finished his pipe, it would be straight to the captain's cabin to report this problem.

"Where is it?"

He jumped at the unexpected question and dropped his pipe, which slid across the deck towards the figurehead. He looked around; really annoyed but saw no one who could have said anything to him. Someone was playing a practical joke!

John did not like practical jokes! Jokes got people killed.

"Who's there?" he asked, his tone of voice ensuring anyone listening would know he was not impressed.

"Where is it?" The voice came again, louder this time and definitely more determined.

John could not help it, he jumped again and this just made him even angrier. Someone was definitely having a joke at his expense! Well, he would not give them the satisfaction! He turned away, confidant that the joke would soon wear thin if he failed to respond. Now, where was his pipe? He glanced around the deck and spotted his pride and joy sliding about with the movement of the ship. He bent down to retrieve it, hoping that the coal in his tin would be warm enough to re-light the tobacco if it had gone out.

His hand tightened about the pipe just as a heavy, unseen weight pinned both hand and pipe to the deck. The voice repeated the question for a third time, this time right next to his prone ear.

"Where is it?"

John tried to remain calm and collected. He thought logically as he had done all of his life. He had no weapon; he could not fight something he could not see. The next move would have to come from his attacker. Even as he looked on, he observed a red pressure mark appearing across his crushed hand. It was in the unmistakable shape of a boot heel. Whoever, or whatever, had him pinned, was standing on his right hand. He tensed, preparing to grab whatever was above the invisible boot.

Twin scarlet lines streaked across his arm, startling the sailor and making him curse aloud. Blood welled in seconds and began to drip steadily from the wounds, but the edges of the lacerations started to discolour and necrotise before his eyes. John found he had to grit his teeth against the pain. He reached over instinctively to staunch the flow his eyes going wide as he looked around the area desperate for help to appear.

"Where is it?" the voice asked again, anger now clearly audible in its tone.

"I ... I ... I don't know what you are talking about," John pleaded.

Something grabbed the sailor by his hair, pulling his head up and back in a painful grip that brought tears to the man's eyes. He gasped reflexively as two cold pinpoints touched his throat before being savagely drawn across his flesh, ripping and tearing his skin, severing muscle tissue and cartilage. Blood gushed from his exposed throat making the sailor gasp, desperate to draw breath and scream an alarm. The scream died in barely more than a whisper.

John Hodge's corpse slid to the deck, his pipe falling forgotten from his crushed hand. The first rays of the dawn slid over the horizon, deep orange rays tinting the white water crests and painting the ship's woodwork a deep and striking auburn. The clouds above streaked with reds and pinks, mirroring the streaks of blood pooling at the prow of the ship. It was a most glorious sunrise, one that the grizzled sailor would now never see.

The Raven had arrived.

Part Two:- Into the Storm

"A maiden so tempting, it's never a task,
Her colours the clearest that be,
Cool curves of velvet, right there to touch,
An embrace that's so total and free.

So who is this siren? I hear you ask,
And what is her hold over me?
Well where do you go when there's time on your hands?
But down to the edge of the sea."

A Sailor's Lament.

Chapter Fourteen

'I buried my friend today...'

Thomas Adams, Captain of the Spanish Galleon *El Defensor* paused in mid-thought; his quill poised an inch above the page of parchment before him. As he sat contemplating what to write, the quill's black ink began to run to the sharpened tip, collecting to twin the teardrop currently forming in the captain's eye. He tore his blurred vision from the parchment and looked around the cabin, desperate for some form of comforting figure or icon of support but wherever he looked memories of his friend assailed him.

The globe of Minera that doubled as a drinks cabinet, acquired during their earlier years pirating off the coast of Traquair; the Oriental rug that decorated the floor, a relic of bygone days carrying spices upon the Strontio Sea. It seemed John Hodge had been more than just a good friend; he had become adopted family. Thomas wiped his eyes and blotted the nib of the quill before returning to his tragic narrative.

'He was buried at sea this morning by dawn's first light. All crew were present. Somehow I feel he would have wanted it that way.'

He paused again, steeling himself for the next few fated words, as if, by not writing them, he could somehow change the outcome of what had occurred.

'May he rest in peace.'

Thomas sprinkled a fine handful of white sand across the page of the ledger so that the grains could absorb any excess ink before he closed the ship's log. The brown leather cover was faded and scratched with golden archaic script that scrawled across the front bearing the ship's name. Thomas paused to look at the book, imagining all the joys and sadness recorded within before straightening it and squaring the book in the centre of his desk. He leant forwards to flick an imaginary speck of dust from the cover and then turned his attention to his quill meticulously cleaning it before depositing the worn writing implement into a tankard set to the right side of his desk. He allowed a sad smile as he regarded the battered tankard, 'borrowed' as a departed friend had quaintly put it from an old drinking spot in Westport, only then did he turn his attention to the last item upon his desk.

The threat of tears returned as he looked down at the wooden pipe resting forlornly beside the ship's log, the grain of the wood still warm and rosy to the eye with the scent of John Hodge's favourite tobacco still permeating the air around it. The momentary illusion was so strong that Thomas could almost imagine his friend putting his scuffed leather boots up onto the opposite side of the desk and asking for a drink from the globe shaped cabinet in the corner of the room, despite the frowns and raised eyebrow that would have been bound to have resulted. He picked up the pipe and ran his thumb across the grain, his mind wandering far into the past, sharing memories of happiness and poignant sadness, of a life of companionship never easily replaced.

With a sigh, Thomas slid open the top right hand drawer in his desk to reveal an emerald green velvet cloth upon which rested several small objects of personal significance. Each item represented a member of the ship's crew who had moved on to 'sail calmer waters'.

The first item to catch his eye was a cracked silver timepiece, the crystal cut face scratched and battered, the twin hands within frozen at exactly the time the owner had died. A tiny golden ring, so delicate and small that it would only fit a child or a halfling lay beside it. Now she had been a rascal!

An enchanted set of dice, which always knew the number required to win; then stubbornly refused to roll them, unless kissed first. A double-headed coin and a large sapphire that vibrated softly within its green velvet nest lay adjacent to these other treasures. The sapphire repeating enchanted ballads when held to your ear, a recording of the work its bard owner had created in his lifetime, the coin the only way he could make the crowd choose the songs he actually knew. Tails we will sing your song, Heads and we will sing mine!

There was also a small silver tankard, battered and well used but never empty unless willed. Unfortunately, it only gushed forth cold spring water and not the stiff drink Thomas would have liked at this time and even then, it would only work when up against your lips, refusing to empty into any other receptacle.

The other contents of the drawer included a black puzzle box filled with small silver balls that ran in every direction but where he wished them to go. A piece of slate with an engraving of a mouse upon its surface that used to be able to run off the slate and spy for its owner when commanded, although Thomas had never managed to get it to work. A petrified egg supposedly of a phoenix and finally a fist sized golden badge. Thomas gently laid John's pipe amongst these items. There it would stay as a reminder of good times passed by.

He went to shut the drawer then stopped himself, reaching in to retrieve the badge. It still gleamed although the surface of the badge had several ball bearing sized impact points. If you looked closer, the deeper depressions held dark flakes of dried blood where Thomas could not get in to clean it. Of all the items in the drawer, this one did not belong to a past member of the crew. This badge represented a memory of Thomas's life long past, a time he was still desperate to return to. Those corrupt men were still running free and he would hunt them down if he could ever get back home! He shrugged; it was all a dream. Replacing the badge, he slid the walnut drawer shut upon the golden shield, the engraved 3042 numbers catching the light just before the drawer finally slid closed.

"That was a long time ago." He stated aloud, as if by voicing his feelings he could push the meaning of the four numbers to the back of his mind.

He stood to pace and walked from behind the desk, his fingertips tracing along the top of one of several cases that were secured along the cabin walls, intricate models of sailing ships were painstakingly recreated within them. This was his hobby, a retreat from everyday life and the chaos and evil that often went hand in hand with it. Within these cases, everything was perfect and squeaky clean. The patience and steady hand required for the work kept the captain's sanity in line with what the rest of the world demanded from him. He liked puzzles, and assembling sailing ships and slotting the pieces into place was the closest to a puzzle he could attain.

Now he had a puzzle like those he used to face in his old life and it rankled him. How had those packing crates come loose on the foredeck and fallen on John in that manner, crushing his skull like an egg?

He walked past the cases to pause before the cabin door, checking himself over in the mirror mounted on the wall. The reflective circular surface showed a man in his late forties, dark brown eyes, short salt and pepper hair and a square jaw with a day's worth of stubble upon it. His hair was thinning a little on the top now but his eyes still held a sharp gleam of intelligence. He sucked in his abdomen and turned to regard his silhouette.

"You've still got it!" he quipped. Although he recognised he needed to go a little bit more carefully with the pastries the ships chef made! He touched the glass, breaking into a slight grin that showed his misshapen lip more clearly. The upper lip on the left was slightly bigger than the rest of his mouth and malformed from when he had put his teeth through it in a particularly nasty barroom brawl. A large pair of scissors had saved his life that night but the after-effects had lasted a lifetime. He also had numerous other scars including one that ran underneath his bushy eyebrows from when a thug had taken a motorbike chain across his face just before throwing him through a plate glass window. People had often told him he should not look at the age of something but at the mileage it had done. However, some of Thomas's mileage had been very rough indeed!

The mirror was set into the original ship's wheel, the king spoke, the most prominent part of the wheel, pointing straight up at the ceiling, its splintered end signifying straight ahead. Somehow it seemed appropriate that the wheel hung here, sharing the secrets of the captains from both past and present. Thomas hoped it would share the secrets of many more...but not just yet...at least as long as he had anything to do about the matter!

He took one harder look at the now silent image in the mirror, rubbed his eyes and then straightened his leather waistcoat, before his hands reflexively reached to straighten a tie that was not there. Then he ran his fingers through his hair, brushing the stray hairs into place. It was time to take on the role of captain. He had a tragic accident to investigate, three stowaways to deal with and a crew who badly needed his presence amongst them for reassurance and morale.

Allowing himself one more quick visual check, Thomas set his face and snapped a smart salute at the man reflected in the mirror. It was quite ironic! Here he stood a captain! What would the cops back at the 17th precinct have made of that?

* * * * * *

It took Justina several hours to recover from the strain of casting her teleportation and invisibility spells and she awoke from a deep sleep with a throbbing head and shivers racking her frame. She lay upon her black silk sheets and stared at the canopy of the four-poster bed high above her, trying to put her conflicting thoughts in some sort of order so she could face the day.

Pelune was a fool! He had made several revealing errors today. Not only was he using The Raven in a desperate gamble, he had also inadvertently revealed to Justina that his own magical powers were already on the wane. Pelune was normally able to cast his own spells, strangely without the use of gemstones to power them but last night he had asked her to do all of the magic required, something Pelune, with all his pompous gesturing would never normally permit.

It was the clearest sign yet all was not well within the *Order of the Serpent*. Justina knew it would soon be time to act but even now, doubts swirled around her mind. What if Pelune managed to regain his dagger? It was clearly more than just a sacrificial weapon; it was obviously his source of power? The Raven was a legend from her youth and his ability to carry a job to its successful conclusion was as good as set in stone. When she considered the added enchantments she had cast upon the assassin, Justina could not see how he could possibly fail.

If The Raven returned with the relic Pelune would continue his shadowy rise to power, something Justina needed to prevent. She required a contingency plan.

The sorceress slid from the bed and padded bare foot across the rugs that decorated her chamber floor, stepping around a small table and glancing at the fire blazing in the fireplace before coming to a stop in front of a huge mirror that hung against the wall. With a critical eye, she examined her body, scrutinising every curve and dip before she was satisfied that the drain on her body during spell casting had not affected her enchanted disguise in any way.

Satisfied, she leant forwards and touched the wooden frame, stroking her deft fingers across the polished grain, searching for a blemish in the carving. Once located she deftly twisted a small button secreted there and the mirror swung away from the wall revealing a small space behind. Spell books were neatly stacked on assorted shelves set in either side of the alcove, representing several life times of research from mages long since deceased.

Set at the back of the alcove was a glass cabinet, within which sat a collection of potent magical items, rings, wands, broaches, bracelets and assorted gemstones of varying value which all sparkled and gleamed within this dust free environment. She reached past all of these however to pull out a small smoke stained glass jar.

"Hamnet," Justina hissed, holding up the jar to the light and moving her wrist gently sloshing about the contents within. Bobbing about within the confines of the jar was a small twisted skeleton, its overall length a little over eight inches. An enlarged head, swollen and distorted, with ragged clumps of hair regarded the sorceress with slime filled eye sockets. Its body was long devoid of flesh, with two gnarled little hands that extended from spindly arms. The feet of the creature were comically large, in a dark and twisted way; whilst coiled between its legs was the unmistakable bony cartilage of a tail.

Justina placed the jar on a table near the alcove and began to chant softly under her breath, sacrificing a small gemstone from her bracelet as she completed the summoning incantation. A small cloud of mist slowly began to form on the table alongside the jar and as she looked on, a duplicate body of the twisted skeleton began to form from the mist, using the tendrils of opaque moisture as impossible building blocks to form small bones and jelly-like cartilage.

A high-pitched screaming noise rent the air as the creature finally solidified, as if the act of transformation from ethereal state to molecular stability was one of excruciating pain. The small skeletal body fell forwards onto the table top as if unused to the weight of its skull, before scrabbling feet secured their hold, digging splinters out of the table surface with razor sharp claws in an effort to stabilise its diminutive frame.

Slowly the creature's head pulled up to regard the sorceress with red glowing eyes. Hamnet looked at her mistress for a few moments longer before turning her head slowly to take in the room. Her glowing eyes fixed on the inert body in the jar and she mouthed a silent scream before leaping the short distance to the glass vessel, trying desperately to open the lid with claws that could find no purchase. Small, serrated teeth gnashed with frustration before the creature turned once more to the one who summoned her.

"Oh Hamnet," Justina crooned. "You want your body so badly don't you?" The skeletal creature cocked its head listening intently for the promise it knew would come. "You can have it you know ... once you have done a small task for me." The creature stamped a clawed foot in anger sending further splinters up into the air, it had heard this all before.

"Now, now!" Justina scolded. Hamnet turned, ignoring her mistress and began to claw at the jar anew. "Listen to me when I'm talking to you!" shrieked Justina, grabbing the jar from the creature and threatening to throw the whole thing into the crackling fire blazing in the hearth. The creature stiffened visibly, trembling as its glowing eyes regarded the jar with longing. It needed the bones in one piece if it was to be free from Justina and the snarl it voiced showed too clearly that it understood the bargain proposed.

"You know that without this body you can never truly be free," Justina continued to taunt, still holding the jar at arm's length. She moved her arm and felt a slight perverted thrill at the power she held over the creature as its eyes followed the jar with no interest in anything else.

"I'm even willing to give you some of the bones now if you pay attention." Ethereal eyes looked up into Justina's face and listened with fierce intensity.

Now listen very carefully to what I want you to do."

* * * * * *

Rauph looked up from his charts as Thomas entered his cabin. A set of well-worn dividers, looking more like a child's toy in the huge creature's hand than the cumbersome implements they were in reality ceased walking leagues across the illustrated sea lanes and hidden coral reefs. Thomas walked across the room to the Minotaur's side and as he drew closer, Rauph noticed just how tired his captain had become of late.

"Well Rauph," opened Thomas, lightly slapping his hairy friend on the back, "what treats do you have in store for us today?"

Rauph continued to stare at his colleague's haggard appearance before attempting a strained bovine smile, the result of which was closer to a grimace than the friendly countenance Rauph intended. Sensing the ineffectual result, the Minotaur swung his huge horned head back towards the open pile of charts laid out before him.

"Well...I think we are about here." He stated, pointing out an area on the chart before him with the dividers. Thomas moved over for a closer look and was stunned as the Minotaur suddenly whipped the chart out from under his nose before he had actually had a chance to read it.

"Or we could be here." Rauph finished, pointing to a completely different chart and stabbing this one with his dividers. "I'm not really that sure to be honest."

Thomas threw Rauph a questioning look.

"What do you mean... you're not really sure?" He reached for one of the charts held in Rauph's hand and smoothed it out across the table. He examined the chart for a moment then reached for the other selected piece of parchment and examined this illustration with equal intensity.

Both charts displayed landmasses, the first a roughly triangular shape like that of a descending axe blade. The wider, sweeping part of the continent lay to the south, whereas the north part of the landmass trailed off into a string of small islands that curved away in a spur like fashion. The port of Catterick clearly displayed, half way up the continent's right side.

Rauph leaned over as the captain examined the illustration, his huge paw like hand pointing to an area of sea roughly three inches north of the port, his chestnut hair serving to obscure the rest of the illustration. Thomas parted the tufts of red hair and noted that by Rauph's calculations they were now almost level with a port called Alnwick. The captain then projected the course heading they were on and noted that on their present course they would plough straight into the curved spur of islands that formed the north of the continent, much akin to sailing into an outstretched claw.

"I don't think much of this one." Thomas muttered, reaching over his friend and pulling across the second chart. "So what do we have here?" The second chart was not much better; the continent lay out before the captain one of total devastation. It was almost as if someone had physically lifted the landmass illustrated within up from the surface of the chart and then dropped it again, shattering the geography of the picture much akin to shattering a china plate. Catterick was again present, this time it was a port on one of the smaller shattered islands making up the continent's whole. Again, the world devastator known as Rauph moved in obscuring everything as his huge finger pointed to a stretch of sea within a circle of smaller islands.

"If we are on this chart we are about here." He finished triumphantly. Thomas looked at both charts again searching vainly for any possible comparison between the two.

"Rauph these are two entirely different worlds."

"I know," the bovine navigator replied with conviction. "I spent all last night going through every chart we have looking for the port of Catterick and we've got two with the name of Catterick on them."

"Yes..." prompted Thomas. "But which one are we on?"

"I told you I don't know." Rauph replied honestly. "But I kind of like the colours on this one." He said helpfully.

"Have you thought to ask someone?" The captain enquired his hand going up to his forehead in dismay.

"Oh..." Rauph paused before turning his face to his friend. "What chart are we on then?"

Thomas looked at Rauph in total disbelief.

"I thought you were supposed to be our navigator." Thomas tried to point out helpfully, slightly emphasising the point that he was relying on his shaggy companion to show them the way. "I haven't the foggiest which one we are on... however I do know of three people who might just have the answer to our little riddle."

"Three?" Rauph looked up at the captain confused. "Who's that then?"

"Our recent stowaways." Thomas revealed. "I'll be back as soon as I can, until then make your best guess and we had better hope we don't find ourselves turning to port rather quickly in the near future." Thomas turned with a laugh and headed for the door but something slowed his gait and he found his eyes drawn uncomfortably to the far wall of the room.

Shelves filled with crated scrolls and books collected dust in this far corner, the contents untouched and left where they lay. Arcane symbols and astrological charts still covered the walls whilst the wooden floor displayed faded runic characters and summoning circles. Below these items sat the remains of a ruined chair; it was set facing away from the room and therefore obscuring any occupant seated within it. Thomas could not stop himself and found his feet taking him across the room to an encounter that would as always be destructive and distressing in nature.

Behind the captain, Rauph was again in a world of his own, talking to the illustrations on the charts as if they were real people. Even as Thomas advanced steadily on the chair the Minotaur engaged an illustration of an octopus in why only six of its legs were illustrated and what had happened to the other two.

A small porthole set into the wall between two groaning shelves of clutter offered sparse light into the gloomy corner, the feeble dusty rays illuminating the ruined chair ever clearer as the captain advanced.

Magical runes gleamed faintly from where they had been carved into one of the chairs armrests, whilst the other hung free, held in place by a tentative strip of leather that swung in time with the ship's gentle motion. Cream stuffing had exploded from the padded backrest; some of it stained the deepest of blacks.

However, the most horrific sight of all was what greeted the captain as he walked around the chair and stared at the occupant still seated within it.

The decaying senior magic user or arch mage of the *El Defensor* sat staring at the wall of the cabin with horror-filled eyes, the lips of his mouth curled back in pain and accusation. A thick layer of dust had turned the man's hair a premature white, whilst flecks of the substance dangled from his nerveless eyelashes and accentuated the creases and folds in his skin.

Spotless white robes had become both dowdy and grey, drifts of the dust having collected where the material lay gathered in his lap. The corpse's rigor mortised hands still gripped tightly to the weapon that had pinned him so effectively to his final resting place, as if even in death the magic user was terrified to let the weapon go.

Thomas took in the sight for what felt like the one-hundredth time, his eyes absorbing every little detail. This man had died because of an error in judgement; this man had died because of him.

What made this torture infinitely worse was that no one had been able to move the body from the chair, so effectively had the arch mage been pinned by the accursed weapon holding him there.

A spear as black as midnight and etched with indecipherable markings hung in the air before the captain, its very presence daring Thomas to try to draw it out of the pinned mummified corpse. Crackles of magic, barely perceptible at a distance were now clearly visible running up and down the length of the black shaft and Thomas, standing as a silent witness found himself shuddering as he felt the hairs rising on the backs of his hands in response to the magical surges.

Streaks of encrusted blood ran from the spear's blackened shaft down the emaciated arms of the corpse signifying the titanic struggle that had occurred as the spear's wickedly barbed head had struck home, ripping and splintering apart the man's ribcage with the ferocity of a whaler's harpoon. Thomas knew it was futile but his hand still reached out towards the magical weapon. It began to make a howling sound at the unwanted intrusion. Unrepentant, Thomas continued his advance, his hand closing around the shaft of the spear to see if he could remove it and finally let the mage rest.

The weapon responded instantly, wrenching away from his hand, snapping and grinding within the body of the magic user as it struggled to avoid his grasp. An ethereal scream accompanied the movement and for a split second, Thomas saw a ghostly apparition rippling across the surface of the dead arch mage's face. Impossibly the corpse's hands appeared to tighten on the spear as if the sorcerer was still trying to restrain the unholy weapon and prevent it from getting free to kill again.

Thomas shuddered at the image before him and withdrew his hand in resignation. It had been four years since the arch mage had met his end and even now he protected the ship from the evils of the world.

The spear sensing the withdrawal of Thomas's hand stopped moving and the ghostly visage animating the corpse sighed in relief before sinking into the body to disappear without a trace. Sense defeated irrationality; they had another mage on board. If the spear were to be withdrawn, it would seek out the most powerful mage in the area and would slay them instantly. That was what the spear had been enchanted to do and 'Wizard Seeker' was exceptionally thorough at its job.

Thomas turned from the scene and went to walk from the room, only to find the monstrous figure of his friend standing beside him.

"It wasn't your fault you know." Rauph stated. Thomas looked up at his bovine companion's compassion filled eyes and offered a weak smile before mumbling something incoherent and walking from the room leaving his friend standing beside the chair sadly shaking his huge horned head.

* * * * * *

Noise assailed the captain as he stepped through the door at the end of the corridor and out into the bright morning sunlight. A warm breeze tainted with salt spray rustled through his hair blowing the stray wisps back from his eyes as he scanned the bustling main deck before him. Sailors moved in an orderly fashion from ladder flights to either side of where Thomas stood whilst others leapt into the rigging or ran up further steps to the aft castle above and behind Thomas's current vantage point.

The ship stretched out before him, the wooden deck scrubbed smooth with years of scouring and a large dose of loving care. Even now, several sailors were scrubbing the deck with large square blocks of stone, nicknamed holy stones because of their similarity in shape to a church bible. The sails high above snapped and cracked in the wind, the creamy canvas billowing out towards the prow and darting between the sails he noticed the ever-present forms of the Rinaldo brothers hard at work trimming the sails to make the best of the wind offered. He threw a mock salute towards them and they replied in kind, signalling with rapid hand motions that bid him a good day.

Thomas continued his tour of duty, making his way across the deck, wondering again what had initially motivated the three brothers, leading them as one towards their fateful encounter with the ship christened *El Defensor*. What quirk or twist of fate had collaborated with their darkest secrets and led these men into the path of Thomas Adams, his crew of misfits and a ship that by its very name corrected injustices?

For the *El Defensor*, or *Vindicator,* was indeed a 'righter of wrongs' every crewman aboard her was accompanied with a damning secret that hounded him or her until the secret's resolution or the fateful day that the crew member died. Sometimes it was the righting of a terrible injustice that freed the crew from their unwritten contract with the ship, for others it was the facing or understanding of their own individual dark fears.

The ship just knew instinctively where to be when someone needed its help, picking up passengers in strange exotic locales, saving them from certain death and in return, the crew of the ship were strangely compelled to continue sailing aboard the *El Defensor* until their own personal issues were resolved. They either found peace in what was left of their lives or the eternal rest that only death could offer them. It was a ship of the damned, but to Thomas they were the best 'damned' souls he had ever had the privilege to serve beside and this made him a proud man indeed.

A crowd of sailors had gathered amidships and as Thomas approached, their heads moved as one to follow a glinting object that rapidly spun upwards out of sight between the yards of snapping canvas sails. Intrigued the captain walked across the deck towards the gathered men and grinned as he recognised the shape of his first mate's grey hat bobbing above the crowd.

Sherman was a loyal member of the crew and an excellent first mate. He always dressed in grey, whenever and wherever he went, his leathers, non-descript and dull except where the sea had kissed them. The only part of his wardrobe that set him truly apart was the wide brimmed grey hat that sat perched comically upon his head. A large scarlet plume was set into a band and its waving, bobbing motion always made him easy to pick out in a crowd.

The hat defied all weathers with a tenacity that was beyond simple physics. Even in the fiercest of gales, with huge waves breaking across the decks and saturating any crewmember unlucky enough to be in them, the hat stayed firmly in place, with barely a dent to its shape. Rumours amongst the crew even whispered that Sherman slept in his hat as no one had ever seen him without it. Thomas even believed that when it finally came time for Sherman to 'sail calmer waters' he would go hat and all to whatever end awaited him.

Shaking his head to remove such morbid thoughts, Thomas began to push through his fellow crewmembers to get a closer view at the impromptu show. However, his forced smile at the crew's camaraderie turned quickly sour when he realised whom Sherman was challenging. The figure of Scrave, cock-sure and arrogant as always leant against the main mast, arms crossed and head set at a nonchalant angle as if bored by the attempts of the first mate to offer him a suitable challenge. What concerned Thomas most about the situation was the fact that Scrave simply did not like to lose.

Perturbed Thomas watched as Sherman walked into the centre of the cleared desk and looked upwards through the cracking canvas sails to the crow's nest high above. It was impossible for Thomas to see what Sherman was looking at but experience informed the captain that the object of his attention was the warning bell suspended just below the wooden lookout post. As he watched, Sherman flipped a dagger over in his hand and sighted up in preparation of a throw, the look on his face one of sheer determination that he would not fail in his task.

The idea of this contest was simple in nature; all the contestants had to do was ring the bell. The skill was in judging the correct time to throw their blades, avoiding the threat of becoming caught in the billowing sails high above, knocked off course, or over the side and lost at sea.

Although Thomas didn't actively support these tests of skill, or the wagering that always occurred, he did recognise that it brought the crew closer together boosting morale with the highly competitive but nevertheless good-natured competition. However, as Thomas looked on, he realised that the 'good-natured' approach was not Scrave's intention at all.

"I don't have all day." Scrave taunted, trying to distract Sherman just as he prepared to make his throw. "I mean if you can't hit it, simply do yourself a favour and give up." Sherman shrugged at the cocky Elf, displaying his apparent indifference to the jibe as he brought his arm back and sighted once again.

"This time you lose." He grinned, risking a quick glance at Scrave before sending his dagger whipping end over end up into the canvas-filled sky above.

Scrave stepped away from the main mast, watching as the dagger sped towards its goal, somersaulting end over end as it passed the mainsail and continued upwards straight and true. Even with his enhanced Elven vision, Scrave knew that the throw was dead on target and he acted instantly to sabotage Sherman's attempt. Almost faster than the eye could follow, Scrave reached inside his jacket to retrieve something and then sent it spinning after Sherman's throw. To the spectators assembled on deck it appeared that a streak of gold suddenly leapt from the Elf's hand to take up pursuit of Sherman's earlier throw.

"What are you doing?" Sherman snapped in clear irritation, his eyes following the swiftly closing distance of the two objects. "You can't interfere with my throw, it's against the..."

"...Rules." Scrave sneered. "Since when did I ever play by the rules?"

Sherman watched in concern as the two objects closed rapidly, his own dagger now slowing as it spun lazily past the topgallant sail and onwards towards the beckoning bell. He closed his eyes wishing speed into the blade as the blur of gold closed rapidly, pirouetting like a delicate dancer constructed of golden light that performed on a stage with a backdrop of cream canvas.

The peal of the bell rang out across the deck raising a cheer from the assembled spectators and a sigh of relief from Sherman. He had done it! He had finally beaten Scrave! A second peal sounded from high above as he turned to the Elf with a wide smile on his face, only to meet a fierce scowl from his competitor.

"It's not over yet!" Scrave snarled. "You still have to catch it when it comes back down."

"What?" Sherman turned to the Elf in confusion. "Since when has that been part of the game?"

"Since now." Scrave replied, moving over to get under the golden blur that was rapidly descending towards the deck. "Or aren't you man enough?"

Sherman shrugged, turning to scan the heavens for his returning blade and spotting it almost immediately. He swiftly crossed the deck, attempting to gauge both the dagger's descending speed and trajectory and the possibility of his being able to catch it without losing his fingers or worse. There was no way he was going to let Scrave beat him this time!

He prepared to catch the blade and noted a blur of gold from out of the corner of his eye. It angled down at his blade like a hawk descending on an unsuspecting sparrow and there was a resounding clash as the two objects met above his head. Sherman withdrew his extended hand in reflex, pitifully attempting to shield his head from the two falling objects as his mind screamed at his own intense stupidity.

What had he been thinking of?

As he threw up his arms to protect himself he failed to witness the actual collision of the two objects and the subsequent motions of his blade and the golden object Scrave had thrown. Incredibly, both flew backwards from the clash, spinning up and off from the point of impact with Sherman's dagger whirling off into the swirling mass of canvas sails.

Scrave turned his back on the cringing first mate and held out his hand as if comically testing for rain and his thrown missile landed directly in his palm but it did not stay there. Instead in an act of sheer maliciousness the Elf turned in one fluid motion and sent the object straight out again towards his defenceless competitor.

"Catch!" was all the warning he offered.

Thomas Adams launched himself from the crowd as he realised with horror where the golden object was heading and charged across the deck to knock Sherman from his feet in a tackle that would have done him proud if he had been competing in the Super bowl. The first mate and captain crashed to the deck in a tangle of arms and legs as Scrave's throw sliced through the air above them and embedded itself deeply into the main mast. A small thread of red feather fluttered in the breeze pinned by the golden object as securely as a butterfly in a glass collector's case. Scrave turned to the crowd and offered a mock bow, playing to the audience.

"Still the original and the best." He laughed sauntering over to the main mast to retrieve the elegant golden dagger that vibrated softly there. He placed his hand around the delicately engraved serpent that made up the grip and hilt of the weapon and began to ease it gently from the wood.

Thomas and Sherman began to untangle themselves from each other, the captain finally freeing himself from the grumbling first mate and leaping to his feet his face a mask of rage. He charged across the deck towards the Elf and dropped his hand forcefully upon Scrave's effectively stopping the retrieval of the golden blade from the main mast. Scrave scowled at Thomas's interruption as if the captain had no right in preventing him from retrieving his prize.

"What's the problem?" He enquired angrily.

Taken back at the unexpected response, Thomas was initially lost for words, then he noticed Scrave's barely controlled grin and it simply tipped him over the edge.

"What the hell did you think you were doing?" he screamed. "You could have killed someone with your ridiculous antics!"

"It was only a game..." Scrave began to reply, as if that short statement explained away everything.

"And I suppose the losers end up with a dagger sticking out of them?" Thomas snapped back his eyes coming to rest on the golden dagger they both still held. "Speaking of daggers, where did you get this one from?" Scrave's Elven face betrayed no visible emotion but his eyes eventually dropped from the captain's penetrating gaze.

"I asked you a question; you could at least show me the courtesy of offering an answer." Thomas demanded. Scrave reluctantly raised his line of vision, meeting the captain's gaze squarely, but his answer remained unspoken. In response, Thomas slapped down Scrave's hand and wrenched the blade from the mast, the golden serpent hilt immediately feeling uncomfortable in his hand. Ironically the discomfort he felt mirrored his feelings regarding the dishonesty his crewmate had displayed towards him.

"When people refuse to answer my questions it's the same as lying to me." Thomas snapped. "And when people lie to me I get very, very upset!"

"You know the rules of this ship." He continued, lowering his voice, although by lowering his voice it only emphasised his disquiet. "All goods acquired on shore, no matter how trivial, are to be returned to me. The combined profit of these spoils I share by percentage among the crew. The resulting 'lay' is the closest thing to a wage any of this crew is ever likely to see and by giving it, I promote high morale, self-worth and a contented ship. This dagger is worth the lay of at least seven of our crew; you cannot just take it without asking me first. I expect this sort of behaviour from a common thief but not from a member of my crew."

Scrave swallowed hard but his eyes continued to blaze defiance even as his face flushed at the rebuke. He knew he was in the wrong but he had not expected discovery in this stupid, juvenile way.

"What did you think you were doing?" Thomas threw his arms open, encouraging a response. "I expect you to abide by the rules whilst aboard this ship. It's an act that shows respect for the chain of command and you are not above this act." Thomas turned to leave then stopped himself mid-stride turning back and allowing all his anger and distress of the last few days to come to the fore.

"Get that mast sanded down and resealed by noon." He barked, "Then report to me in my cabin. We will discuss your infringement of ship policy at this time and arrange a suitable and just punishment for your indiscretion."

Scrave took the assault tight-lipped and remained standing rigidly at attention. There was no clear way he could respond to his captain's verbal assault. He was at fault and he knew it. The problem was he just did not know what had possessed him to keep the dagger back in the first place. "I don't appreciate dishonesty among my crew." Thomas finished his voice lower now, anger clearly spent. "I will see you at noon. Dismissed."

The Elf snapped an embittered salute, more from habit than respect and walked away, his head slightly bowed. What had he been thinking! Shaking his head in confusion, he started to go below decks to find Commagin the ships Dwarven engineer. Maybe the Dwarf had some time saving invention or hair brained suggestion that would enable Scrave to sand down the mast in record time.

He stopped just short of entering the main body of the ship and turned back to look at the captain, or rather the dagger still clutched in Thomas's hand. Was it his imagination... or did he now feel incomplete in some way, as if he had lost a vital part of himself? He shook his head. That was a ridiculous notion! Somewhat confused, he continued down the ladder towards the lower decks. He had a mast to sand down and seal.

Thomas watched Scrave's departure in silence, waiting until Scrave disappeared from view before turning to assist Sherman from his prone position on the deck. The grizzled seaman stared out from beneath the wide brim of his hat and cracked a smile at the offered hand.

"You're my hero!" He joked, fluttering his eyelashes in a parody of a thankful damsel as he regained his feet. "But I find simply stepping out of the way, is more elegant than being thrown to the deck like a harpooned whale! You didn't even buy me a drink first!"

"So I've made you look a fool eh?" Thomas laughed.

"Nothing I can't deal with," Sherman replied. "And if anyone decides to remind me of our impromptu brief liaison I'll have them keel hauled." He chuckled infectiously, lifting Thomas's spirits for a brief moment at the thought of Sherman terrorising the crew with his threat.

"I'll be off now," the first mate continued, "It's my turn at the helm. Just...Well next time... Don't be so eager to step in. I can look after myself." Thomas threw a pretend punch at his own jaw, pretending to stagger under the blow, as his colleague headed off towards the aft castle laughing.

Thomas watched him go and spared a thought for his own volatile emotions. He should not have snapped at Scrave like that, it was out of character, and normally he never needed to get autocratic to get the best from his crew. The death of John Hodge was affecting him more than it should. He needed to lighten up a little.

A tug on his trouser leg disrupted his thoughts and Thomas looked down to regard a miniature version of his first mate, the figure was complete with both a wide brimmed hat and a mangled feather. Except the feather before him had been bright yellow in some past life and the hat it attached to looked like a huge, hungry sea serpent had swallowed and then regurgitated it after a fierce struggle. Below the hat was a mass of shredded smelly clothes that upon closer examination appeared to contain the correct number of mud and slime streaked limbs to allow a tentative identification of something vaguely humanoid. Thomas looked at the grubby figure before him with only the slightest surprise. It appeared that the smallest stowaway the *El Defensor* had ever picked up had escaped from his quarters yet again.

"Did you see that dagger throw?" remarked Ashe. "It was incredible! Do you think there's a possibility that he will do it again? Could you ask him if he would teach me how to do it too?" Thomas silenced Ashe with a raised finger.

"Follow me." He ordered, leaving no room for argument. Ashe fell into step behind the captain, mimicking his walk with exaggerated Halfling strides.

"This is a very nice ship." Ashe continued, his verbal enthusiasm rekindled now that the captain's finger was no longer hovering above him. "I must say I am so very glad that you allowed us to stay on board when you did. That crowd were rather angry at the docks; they could have really hurt someone."

"Yes, it's a real shame you chose to leave." Thomas commented under his breath.

"Have you seen the size of the sails on this ship?" Ashe continued without missing a beat. "I've noticed that there is always a wind blowing into them, even when there isn't one blowing anywhere else. Well... you know what I mean. It isn't windy out but the sails are always full. Kind of odd that... just like the fact that the other dagger didn't come back down. I also think its clever how that man over there has taught those falcons to fish. Have yo..."

"What did you say?" Thomas asked spinning around suddenly only to catch sight of the Halfling in mid-exaggerated stride, one foot raised high before him.

"Why are you walking like that?" Ashe slowly lowered his outstretched foot to the deck then made a motion of examining his mud stained feet.

"What other way is there?" he asked honestly.

Thomas put his hand to his head. No matter how he tried, this Halfling was constantly throwing him off kilter! He started knowing what he wanted to say and then found himself caught up in the infectious momentum of the little man's actions and became completely lost for words. He took a deep breath to steady and calm himself, his mind taking this opportunity to categorise and file his thoughts into order once more before opening his eyes and blurted out his initial concern. "What was that about a dagger again?"

"Oh...the dagger. What dagger?" Ashe's mud streaked face looked very confused. Thomas stared hard at the diminutive stowaway, so much so that the Halfling could physically feel its intensity. "Oh...that dagger!" Ashe replied lightly, as if he were simply changing the subject at a dinner party. "I was just remarking that after the golden dagger hit the other dagger it came back down but the other dagger didn't." He crossed his eyes as he tried to make sense of his last statement. "At least I think that was what I was going to say."

Thomas stood stock still for a second absorbing this new found information, his head swinging slowly up towards the canvas flapping above his head. Somewhere up there, lodged out of sight, was Sherman's dagger. If it came loose and fell back to the deck without anyone knowing...and if there was someone underneath it...He left the thought hanging.

"Away aloft! Away aloft!" Thomas shouted out across the deck. The effect was like an electric charge jumping from crewman to crewman. Wherever Ashe looked people began to drop what they were doing and leapt for the rigging, stopping a few feet up on the rope ladders to await their captain's orders.

"Now hear this." Thomas yelled. "There's a dagger caught up somewhere in the sails above us. I want it found fast before it comes loose and falls back to the deck. I don't want any more mishaps on this ship." Crew clambered swiftly up the lines with the sureness of monkeys, every one of them eager to serve their captain and totally understanding of his orders. Their actions left no doubt in Thomas's mind that the dagger would be swiftly found.

Now where was that Halfling?

Surprisingly Ashe had remained exactly where Thomas had left him. A relatively amazing feat in itself, achieved purely because the Halfling was too busy staring at the activity in the rigging above with open-mouthed excitement.

"Can I go up there?" Ashe began. There was a sudden flurry of ebony feathers then a scream of horror as Ashe's hands flew up to his head. "Help! Help! I'm being attacked, get it off!" he shrieked. Thomas could not help but laugh as Shadow flew off across the deck cawing loudly in triumph, something black and misshapen in its claws. "My hat!" screamed Ashe, setting off across the deck like a mongoose after a snake.

Thomas watched him go and simply shook his head. Although the little man was clearly annoying and spoke like a runaway mine cart, he did make Thomas laugh. It was only then he realised the Halfling was supposed to be under strict lock and key!

Chapter Fifteen

"Land Ho!"

Thomas turned his head towards the figure of the rapidly gesturing Lubok, who was waving from a position balanced astride the topsail yard high above the wooden deck. The third Rinaldo brother was pointing dead ahead.

The captain quickly ran across the deck towards the stern of his vessel taking the ladder steps to the aft deck two at a time in his hurry to gain height and therefore a better view of the situation. He reached inside his waistcoat as he ran and withdrew a battered old telescope. Within moments, his travels took him to the guardrail on the starboard side of the elevated aft-deck.

In the distance, a thin grey line stood out upon the horizon. Thomas grinned; if anything on this ship could be relied upon, however incredible it may seem; it was Rauph's accuracy with charts. The coastline sprawled across his field of view its grey mass turning the claw on the earlier chart into hard rock biting reality. Thomas turned towards Sherman where he stood at the helm.

"Orders" The first mate enquired.

"Why...turn her to port of course." Thomas replied. "And steady as she goes. I don't want us turning too fast and risk losing the mast and mainsail." Sherman nodded and began to turn the wheel, adjusting the ship's course through the ocean swell.

Thomas returned his attention to his telescope, feeling the ship respond below his feet as it turned into resistance. The landmass through the eyeglass started to slide slowly to the right, so Thomas turned his glass to scan the decks below, his telescope magnifying the crewmembers as they went about their duties. A dishevelled mess moving across the main deck caught his eye and he slowly lowered the telescope from his eye; the Halfling was still determinedly stalking Shadow. Thomas chuckled to himself returning the telescope to his eye and panning it to take in the image of the irritating bird. Shadow still held the little stowaway's hat in its claws, and was toying with him; like a dog desperately vying for its owner's attention.

* * * * * *

Ashe began to congratulate himself. He finally had the damned bird cornered; now all he had to do was advance very, very slowly so that the bird would not startle and fly away. Then when he was sure that he could make it, he would pounce on the blasted animal and he would liberate his hat from the ebony feathered fiend! He moved steadily closer... closer... the hat was now almost in his grasp!

Shadow cocked its head as the Halfling approached, the movement catching the sunlight on its feathers and turning them from black to an impossible white and then back again. The bird looked on as Ashe slid his foot a few inches closer across the deck, feigning disinterest and plunging its beak into the felt material of Ashe's hat before starting to shred the bedraggled feather that was still hanging on to the remnants of the hat.

Ashe bit his lip in frustration. When he got his hat back, he was going to... and then he would... He gritted his teeth determined not to let out a sound and startle the bird, his mind's eye vividly painted scenes of exquisite revenge. Another inch closer and Shadow remained apparently unconcerned, turning its attention to pulling the rim of the hat away from its stitching.

That was the last straw... Ashe prepared to lunge.

"Ha!" he yelled diving towards the bird. "I've got..."

"...You" Thomas grabbed hold of Ashe's shoulder throwing off the Halfling's attack. There was a flutter of black feathers as Shadow took to the wing and Ashe ended up in a pile on the deck empty handed for his efforts. Ashe looked down at his empty hands in disbelief and then at Shadow as the bird strutted up and down the guardrail on the far side of the ship. He looked up into the captain's stern face and smiled.

"Follow me now!" Thomas ordered.

"Okay," Ashe replied. "Where are we..." Thomas turned and began to walk away. "...Going?" Ashe looked after the departing figure and shrugged. "Oh well," he mumbled getting to his feet and dusting himself off, "I'd better do what he says as he looks real mad."

He took a deep breath and launched into another series of exaggerated steps that drew chuckles from the men around him. "Follow me." He mimicked in a gruff parody of the captain. "Eye! Eye! Sir" He saluted to the small audience that watched him before quickly setting off after the captain.

"Fresine!" Thomas roared. A large heavily muscled sailor wearing standard leather hide trousers and a gaudy blue and gold sleeveless waistcoat paused in mid-search of one of the lifeboats fastened on deck. He looked up at his approaching captain and groaned to himself.

Walking just behind the captain was the bedraggled Halfling Fresine was supposed to be guarding. Why had the captain of all people found the little man first?

Fresine dreaded getting into trouble. He stood to attention and awaited the wrath of his approaching captain. The sailor's bald head had started to sweat and trickle down his well-tanned face during his search and his bulging biceps and firmly muscled torso failed to hide the slight tremor his thick bushy black moustache telegraphed at his captain's approach.

Thomas stopped just short of Fresine and gestured at the small figure striding along behind him.

"I thought I told you to lock him in the brig?"

"I...I did!" Exclaimed Fresine.

"Then why is he loose about the deck?" Thomas demanded.

"He... Well..." began the flustered sailor. "He just won't stay there! I lock the door and everything but when I turn my back he's out and the door is hanging open."

Thomas leaned over and whispered into Fresine's ear.

"Listen we can't have this Halfling loose aboard the ship. Before we know it personal items will start to go missing and we will have a riot on our hands."

"What a lovely dagger." Ashe piped up.

Thomas turned swift as lightning to bat the Halfling's grubby hand away from the golden dagger hanging at his belt.

"It's a snake isn't it?" Ashe continued without missing a beat. "Oh, and it's got some kind of rubies for eyes. I bet it's worth a lot." He paused as if considering something very important. "I think I know someone who'll give me a great price for this. I'd be able to buy a new hat and everything."

Thomas turned to look at Fresine. His raised eyebrow and rolled eyes saying it all.

"See?" He left the statement open, the intent clear for the sailor to understand.

"Escort our guest back to his quarters." Thomas commanded.

Fresine swiftly turned to comply but found himself blocked by a large plump woman who squeezed him tightly around his girth. Her laughter rang loud and clear. Fresine flushed beneath his rich tan and carefully untangled himself from the ship's cook before reaching out blindly and grabbing the Halfling's ragged shirt thereby preventing the diminutive thief from wandering off again.

Violetta turned her desirous eyes from the blushing Fresine with a teasing sigh and turned to Thomas, her smile as infectious as ever.

"Master" she began "Something is not right in the kitchens." Thomas stopped her with a raised hand.

"I have never been or ever could be your master Violetta." He smiled. The large chef shrugged with indifference.

"I'm sorry Thomas but you know it's a hard habit to break"

The captain continued to smile but an added sadness tinged his features as he cast his mind back to when Violetta and her daughter Katarina had first come aboard.

Violetta had not been as plump and happy as she looked today. Instead she and her daughter had been clad in rags that barely covered their modesty, their backs beaten raw by their master's riding crop, terror had been clearly apparent in their haunted eyes and the shackles of their forced confinement were still attached around their bleeding ankles when Thomas had granted them sanctuary. They had been on the run from a cotton plantation, trying to escape across the marshlands on a particularly eventful night in 1815 Louisiana when the *El Defensor* had suddenly appeared to find herself sailing in the Mississippi delta.

Thomas had promised safe passage back North but the next safe port of call for the *El Defensor* had not been on the coast of America; in fact, it had not even been on Earth at all! By then Violetta and Katarina did not want to disembark, having secured a spot amongst the crew's hearts as excellent cooks and superb listeners. They politely declined Thomas's offer claiming that the *El Defensor* was their home now and that they had no desire to leave. Overtime Violetta's plump form and jolly attitude also turned her into the ship's surrogate mother: Her billowing white cotton dress and gleaming apron a common and respected sight both above and below decks.

Thomas's reminiscence returned to the present and he motioned that Violetta continue.

"Well Thomas," She bustled." There's some food gone missin' from the stores."

"Don't worry my dear," Thomas smiled. "I believe we have the culprit right here and even as we speak he is about to be escorted to his quarters." Thomas looked across at Fresine as if to say 'go on then' and the expression on his face transformed into a stony frown. Fresine followed the frown down to his hand only to discover that all he was holding was the ragged remains of the Halfling's shirt. Of Ashe, there was no sign.

"Not again." The sailor groaned.

* * * * * *

Sherman's dagger balanced precariously in a gathered crease of canvas atop the spanker sail. The sail stretched out above the aft deck both fore and aft instead of port to starboard like the mainsail and Lubok had spotted the dagger glinting amongst the folds from his position on the topgallant yard sail. Even now, the acrobat started to prepare to swing across and snatch it from its precarious perch before the blade tumbled from sight and headed back towards the deck below.

He took the time to gesture to his other brothers indicating where the dagger was, telegraphing his intentions with rapid hand signals even as he secured a length of rope to the crossbeam beneath him. With the free end looped tightly around his wrist the acrobat dropped from the yardarm and swung out towards the sail. He stretched out his free hand calculating his movements to perfection so that he would end up at the apex of the swing with the dagger securely in his grasp.

The acrobat suddenly noted motion from out of the corner of his eye and swung his head up to notice the form of his brother bearing down on him. Abeline swung in from the other side of the sail and Lubok immediately guessed his sibling's intentions. Abeline wanted to reach the dagger first in an attempt to secure favour with the captain after the other night's fiasco with the monk. The two men collided with the sail instantaneously, arms outstretched for the elusive dagger.

Lubok's line of sight suddenly filled with the confusion of cream canvas and his brother's swinging form. His hand grabbed something hard and so he held on to it tightly, refusing to give up his precious prize.

"Um... Lubok" sounded his brother "Could you let go of my arm?" The two brothers laughed as they untangled themselves from the canvas and straddled the beam supporting the spanker sail.

"Okay, you win." Lubok laughed good-naturedly, "Let me have the dagger anyway and I'll present it to the captain on the behalf of all of us." He held out his hand to receive the weapon only to note the confusion that suddenly appeared on his brother's face.

"I thought you had it."

As one, they looked back along the sail, to the pleats gathered at the end. The dagger that had been disturbed by their mid-air collision slowly slid from its resting-place before their very eyes, to tip outwards into open space and silently fall hilt first towards the deck. Abeline and Lubok followed the dagger's path with their eyes then returned to gaze at each other.

"That's going to hurt" Lubok winced.

"Ouch." Abeline concurred, wondering silently how they would explain this to the captain, before shouting a warning. “Ware below!”

* * * * * *

Today had been 'one of those days' for Sherman. Apart from the earlier embarrassment with Thomas throwing him to the deck in front of the whole crew and wounding his pride as a result, he had also not found his dagger, presumed lost at sea.

He grumbled quietly to himself as he kept up the strain on the wheel, maintaining pressure at the helm so the ship would continue its slow turn to port away from the ever-present risk of rocks that threatened off the mainland ahead. The landmass was now visibly clear of their path but Sherman was ever the cautious type and he wanted to steer wide in case any submerged surprises remained hidden just beneath the shifting cobalt blue ahead.

Setting himself, he spread his legs for balance before closing his eyes and throwing his head back to feel the warm sunlight falling across his face. He was standing there letting his worries wash away when something very hard fell from above and smashed heavily into his left temple.

He fell to the deck senseless, unable to hear the warning shout from above.

The helm began to respond to the sudden release of pressure upon it, slowly turning back to the path of least resistance, the king spoke ascending from the deck towards the vertical position that signified dead ahead. The *El Defensor* began to straighten out of her turn with a barely perceptible creak and started to head unerringly towards the submerged rocks that Sherman had so rightly feared.

* * * * * *

"So his charger has died." Thomas confirmed.

"I'm afraid so," Austen replied, informing the captain of the status of the white war-horse that had boarded the ship several days previously. "I did all I could but the quarrel was coated in some sort of poison. If I hadn't seen that a crossbow quarrel inflicted the damage, I would have believed it had succumbed to some kind of snakebite instead. The horse had no chance. It is tragic, he was a magnificent animal."

"Can I leave you to dispose of the remains?" Thomas requested, quietly relieved that the animal remained out of his sight behind the falcon cages the trainer kept on board. There had been enough death witnessed by the crew recently and he did not need people seeing more, even if it was a horse and not a person. He paused in consideration. "Keep the tack; I feel our stowaway may need it aga..."

Some sixth sense stopped him from continuing. Something was wrong! The movement of the ship was reassuring beneath his feet but he could feel something about the ship's motion that just was not right! He looked down at the deck and noticed the shadow cast by the main mast was beginning to move across the wooden decking faster than it should under normal passage from the sun.

The ship was changing course. For some reason the ship had begun to straighten out!

Thomas glanced towards the mainland, much closer now since his earlier inspection, and noted the sparse undergrowth and trees dotting the landscape. The odd collection of red tiled dwellings also indicated signs of habitation and settlements. He reached inside his waistcoat for his telescope then stopped. He did not need a glass to see that they were cutting very close to the coastline.

That was odd, Sherman was normally so cautious. Had he not considered the possibility of submerged rocks?

"Rocks ahead! Rocks ahead!" The call made Thomas's blood run icy cold, as his fears became reality. "Man down, Man down," screamed a voice from aloft. Thomas spun towards the aft deck scanning the sails for Lubok's shouting figure. The acrobat was pointing frantically at the deck even as his brothers began to slide swiftly down from their lofty stations. For a moment, Thomas could not figure out what the man was pointing at then he realised with horror that the helm was unmanned.

"Oh no!" Thomas launched into a run, charging for the aft castle as fast as he could. He tore across the main deck pushing other crewmembers aside without a glance and rapidly took the steps at the far end arriving at the upper aft deck flushed and out of breath. He continued his run, avoiding an area set in the centre of the raised deck before arriving behind it to find the ship's wheel slowly turning of its own volition, his first mate lying in a heap beside it. Lubok, Abeline and Plano all landed on the deck dropping from the rigging and rushing over to offer aid.

Thomas dropped to his knees before his first mate, wild crazy thoughts rising in his mind. Had Scrave gone crazy after his earlier lecture? Had the Elf taken out his frustration on the man before him? The last thing he needed was infighting amongst the crew on a ship where space was confined. He turned Sherman over, automatically checking for a pulse, his trained eye taking in an egg-sized lump already rising on his colleague's head.

Thankfully, Sherman was still breathing and Thomas found himself torn between caring for his companion and dealing with the more important fact that the ship was currently out of control and heading rapidly for the coast.

"Damn!" he looked around seeing the Rinaldo brothers and snapped out orders as they stood there looking guilty.

"Don't just stand there! I need help here." Thomas lowered his friend's head gently back to the deck and indicated the wheel, "Lubok get Violetta back up here, tell her we have a head injury to deal with. Abeline turn us to port now! Plano tell me what the hell just happened?"

Abeline leapt for the wheel, grabbing it firmly with both hands. He began to force the king spoke over to port but it was like a weedy clown trying to single-handedly arm wrestle a circus strongman. The ship shuddered in response to the man's actions and his brother leapt to assist, both struggling to force the turn in the pitifully small amount of sea that remained between the *El Defensor's* hull and the jagged rocks that awaited her.

"Come on" Thomas cursed, joining in and throwing all of his strength into moving the wheel. The resistance of the ship's current path coupled with the speed the ship was travelling through the waves fought back against their combined strength and Thomas realised he was physically not up to the task.

Another shout of alarm confirmed the rapid approach of the rocks and he dared to snatch a quick look up but was unable to see the plumes of white spray that had to be breaking the surface of the sea ahead. The rocks had to be closer than he thought.

The ship was now tilting dramatically and unsecured items started to slide across the decking, causing a few alarmed shouts from the crew. The mainland drew rapidly closer. To the three men struggling at the helm it was a foregone conclusion that the bottom of the ship was about to be ripped apart. Sherman's dagger rattled across the deck at Thomas's feet and wedged up against the side of the ship.

"We're not going to make it." Thomas cursed; throwing every reserve that he had into the Herculean task, even as he realised that these efforts would not be enough. His personal insecurities as ship's captain returned in a rush. It was his fault the ship was in peril. There was no time to drop the sails, no time to call the alarm and tell crew to brace for impact. No time to ask the mage to halt the magic powering their speed as the rocks beckoned.

His ship needed a miracle but this captain had no miracles left. He closed his eyes and waited for the inevitable sound of splintering timbers and the screams of pain that would surely follow.

A loud grunt sounded besides the captain's ear and something huge and hairy reached past him to grab the wheel. The helm wrenched to the left with such an unexpected force that all three men found themselves thrown unceremoniously to the deck.

The main mast screamed in protest threatening to snap asunder as the billowing sails pulled it one way and the turning ship below pulled it another. Cold sea spray smashed across the deck soaking everyone hanging on for dear life.

Thomas held his breath as he lay upon the deck, expecting to hear the clean crack of timber as it gave in under incredible strain but miraculously the sound never came and the ship began to even out of the turn. Only then did Thomas spare a look at the miracle towering above him 'manning' the wheel.

"Sorry about that," apologised Rauph, his huge Minotaur muscles bulging at the effort of making the turn, "but you looked like you needed a hand."

Thomas staggered unsteadily to his feet, and then turned to assist his other colleagues to theirs. All three stood streaked in lime dust, their clothes damp and sticky with sweat and sea spray. They took one look at each other, before their faces cracked with an infectious grin before they turned to stare at the huge Minotaur in awe.

Rauph took one hand off the wheel to wave at them and then realised his error and caught the wheel again as the ship tried to pull out of the turn. Thomas could not help it; he took one look at his colleagues and then at his own dust streaked form before bursting out with laughter. His laugh was both deep and cleansing, lifting the captain's soul as much as the sight of the coastline moving reluctantly off to starboard.

"Rauph," he grinned, bowing theatrically to his large navigator. "Would you please be kind enough to man the helm?"

"With pleasure." The Minotaur replied turning his attention to the open expanse of clear sea as if nothing had happened.

Thomas returned his attentions to Sherman just as Violetta and her daughter made the deck and came rushing over to assist.

"What happened to him?" he asked turning to face the three brothers who had rushed to his aid. The acrobats suddenly looked anywhere but at their captain. Thomas suddenly remembered the dagger he had seen rolling across the deck and walked over to pick it up.

It did not take a trained homicide detective to figure this one out.

He turned back to the three brothers and found the deck was suddenly empty, the three men having taken the opportunity of Thomas's distraction to disappear back up the rigging out of reach of his wrath. The captain allowed himself a smile, thanking his lucky stars this had not ended on a more serious note before turning to the other matters around him.

Thomas signalled to a nearby sailor and requested that he help Sherman back to his berth after Violetta and Katerina had finished fussing over him, before turning from the helm and allowing his attention to wander to the cleared area of deck before him.

In the past, long before Thomas had come on board, the *El Defensor* had initially had a catapult set in this section of deck. It had been used to hurl balls of burning pitch towards attacking ships with great effect but the dangers of a fire on the ship made its use quite precarious at times. The Captain of the time had then exchanged one peril for an even greater one.

The wooden decking of the raised platform area before Thomas displayed two sets of elaborately illustrated concentric circles painted onto the floor, their ornate borders covered with the swirling designs of arcane symbols.

A maelstrom screamed and wailed in the centre of the larger of the circles, its main body a tall column of cloud like matter that whipped up the air around it, pulling at Thomas's shirt as he moved closer. If you stood and listened carefully the cloud's timber sounded a deep bass note, like wind whistling through a darkened cave system and then in the next second, as high and prominent as a gale shrieking over a mountaintop.

Thomas took in the trapped air elemental with a critical eye. He did not understand magic well and this creature, straight out of a twisted fairy tale, was like a tiger he had once seen pacing in the Central Park zoo. It looked powerful and sleek but there was raw anger behind the creature and it made you glad you were standing on the other side of the bars.

Created from one of the four main elements of life, the air elemental repeatedly slammed into the edge of its containment circle, testing the magical barrier that held it in place, desperately trying to find a weakness so it could break free and get to the slight figure kneeling in the smaller circle before it. Periodically the clouds would stop thrashing enough to reveal red eyes that glared venomously at the young woman just beyond their reach. The frustration and raw anger shown in the elemental's actions clearly emphasised the fate that awaited this person if it ever did manage to break free.

The *El Defensor's* apprentice mage knelt roughly ten feet beyond where the creature wailed and moaned. She was safely contained within the smaller but no less lavishly decorated set of circles and appeared very small and insignificant in comparison to the towering twenty-foot tall tempest she commanded. Thomas wondered anew how her slight form could possibly have the strength to open a portal to another plane of existence. To snatch a creature of such raw power from its home and then order the air elemental to do her bidding by blowing a constant stream of wind into the sails. However she did it, the El Defensor was the fastest ship that ever sailed.

Colette's face was youthful and delicate; nothing like the warrior he felt was required to hold the creature at bay. Her skin was smooth like a porcelain doll and although closed with deep concentration, her eyes, when opened, were the deepest and clearest blue imaginable. Her blonde hair, fastened back into a functional ponytail, had violet braids of material platted throughout the golden tresses, adding additional colour to her slight form.

She was attired in a dusky violet robe that had small symbols embroidered along the hem and was cinched at her waist by a thin leather belt. A small pouch hung from her belt and served as the only other form of decoration on Colette's simple outfit. Her hands sat lightly crossed in her lap, skin lightly tanned and fingernails torn by stressful biting.

The mysterious symbols painstakingly illustrated around the circumference of the circle in which she knelt acted as an additional barrier of magical protection in case the air elemental should ever break free. Each rune in the pattern always meticulously checked before each summoning. Perched on her lap lay the remains of a gemstone that was cracked open like an egg its magical energies drained from the jewel when she had initially commenced her summoning. Alongside her left knee a small incense stick burnt lazily in its holder sending a small spiral of scented smoke up into the air where it mingled with the magical energies she commanded.

Without the aid of the burning taper, the summoning spell would fail to work and Colette would have been unable to bend the creature to her will and make it blow into the sails. Of the drama narrowly avoided, she showed no outward sign of knowledge, so deep was she in concentration battling the creature before her. Commanding an elemental, no matter what its type, air, fire, earth or water was never without risk and not a task to be undertaken lightly.

Thomas did not like this current arrangement but could not see how the *El Defensor* could now fulfil her role without it. For with the power of the elements at the ship's command no one had ever been able to catch her in any flat out sprint across the waves. An important asset when he considered that for some reason, wherever the ship and crew sailed, they always ran into trouble. Indeed, the necessity of having a speedy getaway had become somewhat imperative of late.

Satisfying himself that the sharp turn of the ship had not resulted in any risk of the elemental escaping confinement, Thomas turned from the scene, noting with some concern that time was getting on and that he still had several things to do before his noon appointment with Scrave.

* * * * * *

"Give me back my hat!" Ashe yelled, his little legs pumping hard to keep up with the hopping hat thief that was always managed to stay just out of his reach. Shadow darted about by the entrance to the aft cabins, thoroughly enjoying the chase it had led the diminutive Halfling. The game was far from over yet and as Ashe lunged at the bird for what had to be the twelfth time in the last few moments the bird flew lazily up to rest on the railing above the doorway, clearly eight feet beyond the Halfling's limited reach.

Shadow stared back down at his breathless victim and decided that more teasing was required to recharge the little figure's enthusiasm. It gripped the hat firmly in its claws and began to shred the felt further with its beak.

"No!" screamed Ashe charging from the doorway across the main deck and up the nearest ladder. "Please..." he begged, "not my hat!" Shadow waited until Ashe was almost upon him then squawked loudly at the small thief before flying up into the relative safety of the rigging.

"Now how am I going to get it back?" Ashe threw his arms up in despair "Uh oh!" He ducked as two thickly muscled arms closed in on the space above him, dropping into a forward roll that carried him safely through Fresine's open legs and out onto the clear open deck once more.

The Halfling tore around the aft deck with Fresine in hot pursuit, pausing to wave at Rauph as he passed the helm before practically bouncing up onto the raised section of the deck where Colette sat motionless, unaware of his inquisitive approach.

Ashe slid to a halt wondering what the beautiful young girl was doing before turning around and freezing in his tracks as his eyes took in the swirling column of cloud that made up the captured air elemental. There was only one word in the Halfling's vocabulary that could do the sight justice.

"Wow!"

Upon hearing the exclamation, the twin red eyes in the column of air tore their attention from the young mage and focused on the bedraggled form before them. It reached out with the limited powers it could muster, pleading, begging and finally daring the fascinated Halfling to reach out and touch it, thus breaking the integrity of the magical spell that held it enthralled.

Ashe took very little persuasion and reached out his hand in response, wondering if the fluffy swirling morass before him felt like soft cotton. His hand inched closer and the air elementals eyes began to glow with glee. Then the Halfling giggled as the hairs on the back of his arms began to rise. A flash of black feathers flew across his view snapping Ashe's fascination like an over stretched elastic band.

Shadow did not like anyone else spoiling its game!

Ashe immediately leapt into 'pursuit mode' and shot off after the frustrating bird, leaving the column of air instantly forgotten, screaming in anguish at how close it had come to escaping its prison. Shadow flew over another guardrail and dropped Ashe's hat with a derogatory and defiant caw.

Nobody lost interest in its game unless it wanted them to!

Ashe screamed in open defiance of the bird before vaulting over the guardrail in hot pursuit only to find he had run out of ship! The ocean lay cold and glistening beneath him. There was a lingering scream then a Halfling-sized splash as Ashe got a much-needed bath.

"Man overboard!" shouted the lookout and Fresine did not hesitate, realising in a second who it had to be. He grabbed a coil of rope secured to the side of the ship and threw himself over the guardrail in pursuit of his already floundering charge, ploughing into the ocean like a human cannonball.

Agonising moments later, two sopping wet characters were hoisted back on board, water pouring from their saturated forms. The smaller figure's hand clutched the mangled remains of a black felt hat.

"You..." gasped Fresine looking down at his shivering charge, "are ...coming...with...me."

Ashe shrugged his damp shoulders, trying desperately to prevent his teeth from chattering together and reluctantly followed his captor back down the ladder and into the hold of the ship.

Chapter Sixteen

"Now you stay right there." Fresine swung the heavy oak door shut, turning a large metal key within the lock and finally securing Ashe within his 'quarters'. The sailor removed the key from the lock and looked through the small barred opening in the door to double check that Ashe had not managed to slip out already. He breathed a sigh of relief upon seeing the cell still occupied but felt a lump rise in his throat as he regarded the thoroughly dejected and sorry looking figure of the Halfling within.

Ashe shuffled around the six-foot by four-foot square cell before throwing himself onto the hard bunk that stretched along the back wall. A solitary candle served to illuminate his threadbare clothes and a single tear dribbled down one smudged cheek. Fresine suddenly felt very guilty but orders were orders.

"Do you fancy something to eat?" He offered in an attempt at recompense. Ashe looked up from examining his small hands and solemnly shook his head.

"No I don't think so." He replied. Then a sly grin slid across his face as his inherent mischievous streak kicked in once more. "But I could do with a drink of something. Running all over a ship as large as this is very thirsty work."

If Fresine had ever been around Halfling's before he would have realised that there was more to this timid request than first met the eye but Fresine's guilt was too strong for him to see through the calculating character's ploy. He picked up his lantern from a rickety wooden table by the cell door and turned to leave.

"I'll be back in a minute so just stay there okay."

"Certainly," Ashe replied, determined to play the model prisoner for his audience of one.

Fresine set off up the ladder only pausing to hang the cell key on a hook beside the banister; the glow of the lantern slowly faded away leaving Ashe with his solitary flickering candle to light the small cell.

The Halfling waited a few more seconds before running to the door and standing on tiptoe to glance through the barred opening into the shadows beyond. He looked one way and then the other, checking for the tell-tale flicker of light that would indicate Fresine was still hanging around.

Satisfied that the coast was clear he ran back to the bunk and retrieved the misshapen soggy mass that had once been his majestic hat. Fiddling with the remains of the salt stained headband, he let slip a small gasp of triumph as he located one of his small lock picks.

"Now we're in business," he chuckled, happy that he did not need to spend a moment longer in this cold dank place. For some reason this dark hold gave him the creeps! Seconds later the cell door swung open and the Halfling nimbly skipped through.

Ashe ran up the ladder, following his newfound friend's example. He wanted to try to catch that hat thieving bird and give it a stern talking to. Oh... and there were still several locked cabins he had yet to explore. Maybe he could find some clothes that would fit him and replace his current unfortunate excuse for an outfit! No one could possibly expect him to remain below decks it was dark, scary and well, just boring!

* * * * * *

Fresine returned to the darkened hold moments after Ashe had made good his escape, a wooden platter of precariously balanced bread and cheese carried in one hand and a tankard of ale and a burning lantern juggled in the other.

The open cell door greeted him in silent accusation and he entered the cell with the first swirls of panic beginning to rise in his stomach. Upon finding it empty, he slowly lowered the platter and tankard onto the deserted bunk.

The room was cold and empty. His charge had disappeared yet again.

Fresine groaned loudly putting his hand to his head. The captain was going to kill him! What was he going to do?

Something clattered out in the darkness and Fresine leapt for the door half-expecting Ashe to swing it shut locking him inside as some kind of childish prank. However, when he arrived in the doorway he discovered there was no sign of the little figure. He stepped out of the cell and held the lantern up high to throw sickly yellow light out across the barrels and boxes piled high in the hold.

"Hello?" Fresine offered weakly. A skittering noise arose in reply, its source masked by the shadows that cloaked the back of the hold.

So that was how it was going to be! The little person wanted to play. Fresine breathed a sigh of relief Ashe had not gone very far after all. Not all was lost, at least not yet. All he had to do was re-capture the small thief and lock him up before anyone noticed. Then he would personally guard the door to ensure there was no escape for the Halfling in the future.

"I've brought you a sandwich." He bribed. "Now come out of there."

With no answer forthcoming, Fresine began to thread slowly through the aisles of secured boxes, careful not to trip over any of the thick ropes holding them in place. His lantern produced a circle of protective light that banished the darkness and shadows as he advanced and when the sound came again; further back this time, Fresine moved towards it with unerring accuracy.

The sailor paused for a moment to get his bearings and stared over the tops of the boxes back towards the ladder where faint beams of sunlight filtered down from the decks above, then he gazed forward towards the bow of the ship and the darkness that still gathered thickly there. He swiftly gauged just how far he had come from the light of the ladder and pondered his next move. If the Halfling decided to make a break for it, Fresine was not sure if he would be able to cut the little fellow off before he made the ladder. The ropes securing the cargo would slow him down and make pursuit next to impossible. He knew without doubt that he dared not let the thief gain the deck again in case the captain spotted him out of his cell. He paused in momentary indecision. Catch the Halfling, or spend the next few evenings peeling potatoes for a crew that seemed to exist on the damned things.

Another sound came, louder now and maybe only two rows of boxes back! Fresine was closer to the little man than he had at first thought! He looked back at the ladder and then threw caution to the wind. The Halfling may be extremely agile but if he were to catch him by surprise!

He brought the lantern in closer, trying to reduce the circle of light issuing forth and thereby avoid warning his charge. The light spilled down his tunic glinting off the golden buttons that adorned his waistcoat and then across the faded and scuffed wooden boards at his feet.

The shadows instantly closed in around him, eager to respond to this unexpected invitation and turning the hold into a dark and ominous place. The sailor edged up alongside a barrel and prepared to jump around the corner to surprise the little urchin when something cold and clammy brushed past his ear. Fresine's lantern shot up as he jumped, the pale light briefly illuminating the rear end of a strange looking creature that scrabbled along the edge of a crate near his head only to disappear swiftly into the darkness. He had the impression of clawed feet, pale skin and an enlarged skull before the shock of the image hit him.

"What in the name of the Saracen was that?" Fresine gasped, blinking his eyes rapidly as if the very action would allow him to deny the strange misshapen creature he had just seen.

Was he imagining things? Had he banged his head when he had jumped over the side of the ship to rescue the Halfling? He certainly did not remember doing so.

Something coarse and hairy rubbed against his leg making him jump wildly, his lantern swinging about in such a fashion as to animate the shadows into creatures that lunged for him then retreated when the light threatened their discovery. The startled glimpse of a long pink tail helped to calm the seaman's suddenly jangled nerves. It was only a rat, nothing to worry about at all.

He moved the lantern towards the area where the rat had disappeared and heard a sharp shrill squeal that made him jump. The lantern nearly tumbled from his grasp threatening to leave the sailor in the unforgiving darkness and he swiftly fought to control his growing terror.

It was only a rat for goodness sake! What was wrong with him?

Okay... but he could not ignore the slimy figure that had brushed past his ear and had then scrabbled over the higher crate. What was that then, a bald rat?

Fresine's reasoning was questionable to say the least but somehow the sailor managed to force his fears behind him, even though his train of thought didn't stand up to close scrutiny.

He swung the lantern up towards a gap between the crates and noticed two red eyes glaring back at him from the far side of the boxes. A hissing squeal confirmed that this was an unwanted intrusion and the sailor lowered his lantern before taking a deep breath and turning away.

Was it his imagination or had it suddenly grown much hotter down here? Perspiration dotted his brow and his hand suddenly felt wet and clammy. The lantern light now had a visible tremor to its outline.

This was ridiculous; it was only a rat! He had been down in this cargo hold loads of times in the past, why was now any different? This joke was over!

"Come on out!" he snapped "And stop messing about." A deathly almost audible silence descended and the shadows seemed to sense the sailors fear and began to tighten their grip around his trembling circle of protective light.

"That's it!" Fresine stated to himself. "I'll just have to seal you down here then." He nodded his head for emphasis, deciding that he would return to the ladder and simply pull across the storm shutter at its top and lock it, securing both cargo and Halfling in the darkness until he apologised. "I will not waste my time looking for you a moment longer."

An ear-splitting squeak made him spin on his heels. This squeal was not as close as the last one and came from even further back in the shadows. Fresine grinned; Ashe must have inadvertently stepped on one of these disgusting rodents as he had tried to manoeuvre around the hold and get back past him.

As silently as he could, Fresine moved towards the sound, his earlier fear forgotten as he slipped from the cover of the barrels and boxes into an open space at the furthest end of the cargo bay. From here, the only way onwards was through the fresh water store, the door always locked to avoid possible contamination and permit accurate rationing in times of long sea voyages. He lifted his lantern high and noted that the doorway to the water store was hanging open, inviting the unsuspecting sailor to enter.

"That's odd." Fresine muttered under his breath. The padlock to the door lay just within the circle of his lantern light its casing smashed as if crushed in a vice.

Fresine raised his lantern higher to throw out more light and prepared to step forwards across the wooden decking and then into the room. Ashe had gone too far this time! Running amok and pilfering stores was one thing but breaking ship property and messing with the fresh water supply was simply not on. He could get into serious trouble for this and he was already in more than enough trouble as it was!

He marched towards the door and as he advanced, he began to make out the sound of crunching noises coming from behind the door. What was Ashe doing in there? He closed his free hand around the hilt of his cutlass hanging at his waist and gathered his wits one last time. With a quick deep breath, he stepped through the door lantern held high. The weak yellow light thrown out by the lantern illuminated the whole of the water storage area beyond. Barrels of water were stacked up in rows standing to attention like ranks of soldiers in an invading army, thick lengths of rope criss-crossing backwards and forwards across the area to ensure the barrels remained secure even in high seas. There was no sign of the Halfling and no one else visible in the room.

Fresine swung his lantern this way and that, desperate for a glimpse of the elusive Halfling. Where was he? He had to be in here somewhere! He paused in mid-search the lantern light illuminating something out of place tucked away in the far corner.

He edged closer for another look and spotted an assortment of rags and blankets piled up behind some of the barrels like some bizarre bird's nest. They normally wrapped these blankets around delicate items of cargo and certainly did not leave them piled up like this! Someone had obviously been unwrapping cargo to build this thing. In the centre of the 'nest' lay a scattering of food and the carcass of a half-chewed rat, blood still oozing from the unfortunate creature and indicating that the kill was still fresh.

The sailor froze in mid-examination, the hairs on the back of his neck rising inexplicably as if someone were standing behind him. He spun on the spot drawing his sword to face the unseen observer. The empty cargo area stared back at him then something green and white suddenly fell out of thin air and dropped to the floor. As Fresine looked on in morbid fascination, the object began to roll from side to side with the movement of the ship.

He advanced towards the object with extreme caution trying to identify what this strange item could be and then he laughed aloud. It was an apple! It must have somehow come loose form one of the crates. He reached down to pick up the fruit bringing it into the lanterns light and his laugh died in his throat. The side of the apple displayed a huge bite mark, exposing the white fleshy pulp within.

"What in the worl..." he began. Something sharp suddenly pressed against his throat, the sensation akin to someone putting a thin line of fire against the sailor's skin.

"Where is it?" demanded an incorporeal voice at his ear.

Fresine's eyes darted about in terror, his mind trying desperately to form some sense out of what was happening to him. He tried to stop his rising sense of panic but the sharp edge at his throat was beginning to bite deeper! He needed a distraction of some kind and swiftly. The sailor's eyes darted about the storage area for anything that could help him and then noticed that he was still holding the lantern in his hand. He closed his eyes in swift silent prayer then dropped it to the deck, a tinkle of glass at his feet informing him that the lantern had broken as it fell. There was a second of hushed silence then a 'whoosh' as the oil ignited.

The pressure at Fresine's throat eased and the sailor acted instantly, swinging around and lashing out with his cutlass, the blade whistling through the empty air where the attacker should have been standing, its length appearing to flicker as it passed through the lanterns guttering light.

The sword continued its swing to 'thwack' into one of the ropes fastening the barrels in place and Fresine struggled to pull it free. The small fire at the sailor's feet cast flickering shadows across the ceiling of the storage area. He turned to avoid the flames and found the sharp pain was suddenly across his throat again. This time Fresine acted swiftly and moved to one side, trailing a burning sensation across his neck as the dagger scored into his skin before slipping free. The sailor dropped to his knees in shock his free hand flying up to his throat to check the severity of the wound.

With a resounding 'twang' one of the partially severed ropes parted allowing a barrel of fresh water to crash over, the wooden lid springing free to spill its contents across the deck. As Fresine looked on the water flowed across the wooden planking and then parted to flow around two foot shaped impressions, one of which swiftly filled as the unseen foot lifted and advanced towards its prey.

The sailor staggered to his feet alarmed at the pulsing dampness at his throat and the small splashes of water rising up from the deck before him as his assailant moved in for the kill.

He had to get out and call for help and fast!

Fresine started to run for the cargo hold when the storage area was plunged into freezing darkness, as the water from the upset barrel doused the lantern flames. The resulting hiss made the cargo hold suddenly sound like it was full of angry serpents, intent on plunging their fangs deep into the whimpering sailor and Fresine nearly screamed aloud as his protective circle of light extinguished. He turned back slashing out blindly with his sword praying that his blade would strike something, anything.

However, the gods were not listening.

Something cold and unyielding slipped under his rib cage making the sailor gasp in pain. He dropped his cutlass from the shock, both hands automatically guarding his new wound. A fire seemed to be racing across his skin, not just in the new wound but also along his neck and throat. His breathing was loud in his ears and his heart was racing.

Facing the pitch-blackness alone, Fresine suddenly found he was acutely aware of the sounds emanating from the area around him. He kept seeing unexplained flashes of light in his vision where no light existed and his ears were now ringing as his heart struggled to beat.

The sound of breathing suddenly sounded next to his ear and with a sudden clarity Fresine realised he was going to die.

"Where is it?" his assailant demanded once more.

"I don't know" Fresine was almost weeping in terror now. He took a chance and released his hand from his ribcage shuddering as something warm and wet slid down his side.

His cutlass was here somewhere, if he could just find it.

There was a sudden movement in the air beside him just as his searching hand landed on the hilt of the sword. He barely had time to draw one last breath as the knife blade plunged into the side of his face and he used it the only way he knew how.

He screamed...

* * * * * *

...And screamed and screamed.

Kerian jerked bolt upright, sweat soaked blankets sliding from his bare chest and piling up around his waist as red-hot spasms of agony wracked his shaking form. His lungs gasped loudly, sucking at the musty air as if each breath were his last. For an instant, the knight believed he was back in the Fieldstaff Inn at Kenton fleeing his queen, the cursed scroll delivered by her skeletal raven initiating with its sudden explosion of agonising pain as he held it in his naive hands.

"I'm sorry! I am so sorry! Please forgive me, I beg of you!" he sobbed, reliving the historic scenario as if it were the present and not nearly two years, or twenty-four cursed years, previous. His eyes flew open taking in his alien surroundings, so different from the ones replayed in his mind's eye. An exhausted gasp swiftly followed as Kerian slowly lowered himself back onto the dampened pillow beneath his head. Another month had ended...another year lost!

The curse so foolishly activated by his reading of the scroll those many months before had pushed him closer to death! Desperately trying to focus through the pain that rippled throughout his tired frame Kerian began to mentally tally up the years, using the calculation like a mantra to try to block out the worst spasms of the ageing process. How old was he now? Pins and needles began to race up and down his arms as the years passed through his mind. Fifty-seven, sixty, he could not be sure. It was getting so hard to remember.

A loud knocking shattered his frustrated thoughts.

Kerian groaned as the pounding reverberated around the confines of his skull. This curse was like a damned hangover but without the good times that usually preceded it the night before!

The knocking came again, more urgent this time, followed by the sliding sound of bolts being drawn and the rattle of a key being inserted into the door's lock. Kerian's mental fatigue vanished in an instant. Bolts and keys...He was locked in and therefore somebody's prisoner!

Kerian swiftly glanced around the room for anything that he could use as a weapon. The cabin was roughly six feet square, 'his' bunk stretching the length of one wall. The only door was set into the last few feet of the right hand wall and illumination came from the currently extinguished lantern hanging from the ceiling or a porthole set midway along the left hand wall.

A porthole! That meant he was still on board the ship from the previous night!

His saddlebags lay propped up against the wall, beneath a fold away, ink stained table. It's only companion a battered chair that currently had Kerian's clothes neatly piled upon it. Moreover, if his eyes did not deceive him, washed as well!

His quick scan confirmed his weapons were gone.

The thick oak door swung open and a youthful face peered around the jam. Kerian's initial impression was of the thick mop of jet-black hair that framed the young man's concerned face, a concern that quickly transformed into a cocky grin once the lad realised his personal charge was not in any imminent danger.

"Are you alright?" he asked, a bushy eyebrow rising above his left eye to add emphasis to the question. "I heard screams and..." He left the question hanging, his intent clearly apparent.

"Bad dreams," Kerian tried to indicate indifference with his hand, his wavering voice barely managing to carry the casual air he tried to portray.

"It's good to see you awake at last," the young man remarked; now stepping fully into the cabin from behind the shield the door had become. He offered his hand in warm friendship. "My name is Simons," he smiled warmly, "and you are...?"

"Styx." Kerian's response was swift and closed. He wanted to play his cards close to his chest. It was foolish to reveal too much to someone he barely knew, let alone had reason to trust. Technically speaking although the boy seemed pleasant enough, Kerian was still somebody's prisoner and only a fool gave away information to the enemy.

He started to rise from the bed then realised that he was naked underneath the rough woollen blankets that covered him. He blushed at his own discomfort and turned to regard the young man who stood before him, an embarrassing shrug of his shoulders explaining more than words could.

Simons laughed at the discomfort, his cocky grin infectiously spreading across his freckled face.

"Where am I?" Kerian enquired eager to change the subject.

"On the *El Defensor* of course," Simons returned.

Kerian chewed the name over in his mind. *El Defensor;* she sounded exotic and definitely not a local ship. He took in the lad before him wondering if he was telling the truth or spinning a yarn.

The boy was about five feet tall and wore a white linen shirt that looked several sizes too large for him. Lace cuffs gathered the billowing white linen tightly about his wrists, whilst the rest of the material tucked tightly inside a pair of faded burgundy trousers. A pair of calf-high shiny leather boots completed the 'buccaneer' outfit. An elaborate fencing foil hung from a scabbard at his hip, the hilt of the weapon heavily worn, with some noticeable rust patches, instantly identified by Kerian's military eye.

The youth immediately went down in Kerian's expectations. Any recruit understood that if they did not look after their weapons correctly they should not complain if their weapon did not look after them.

Simons' dark eyes displayed a calculating stare that seemed to be weighing up Kerian in a similar fashion and finding him to be wanting too. Maybe there was more to the youth's innocent demeanour than was openly apparent at first sight.

The sailor broke their gaze first and appeared to be collecting his thoughts;

"You've been unconscious for two days now," he stated.

Kerian's mind spun. Two days! Anything could have happened in that time!

His eyes began to dart around the cabin again; this time frantically collecting clues to his present predicament. The chase with the guards on the docks and his airborne landing on the ship flashed through his mind. Had they set sail? He allowed his body to feel the rolling gait of the deck and confirm his deductive reasoning. The slight up and down motion of the ship was suddenly very noticeable now that he knew what he was looking for. So if he was at sea, what was their heading? He had to get back to Catterick and find Marcus! Any time spent in delay could mean years off his lifetime...literally! There was only one thing for it.

"I...I've got to see the captain of this ship."

"It's funny you should say that," Simons smiled, "the captain wishes to see you too. He was hoping you would be more informative than our other stowaways have been. One of them will not stop talking but rarely about the topic that we want to discuss. The other one refuses to say a word."

"Personally I'm starting to think that the monk is praying or has taken a vow of silence or similar." Simons continued. "Isn't there some kind of order where the monks can go into trances and commune directly with their gods?"

"Does he wear blue robes?" Kerian enquired.

A nod from Simons confirmed the answer. Marcus was here. Kerian instantly hoped the naive monk had not said anything to get them in trouble. He began to swing his legs from the bunk and then remembered his current state of undress. The only item of 'clothing' he had been left with was the silver necklace with the emerald shard, which still hung around his neck and was not nearly big enough to cover his modesty. He looked back at Simons in an open expression of impatience.

Simons laughed at his charge's continued discomfort and turned to leave.

"I'll bring a bowl of water for you to freshen up with and some food to eat before you see the Captain. Don't worry. I'll be back shortly." The young sailor swiftly departed the cabin, the sound of the key turning in the lock confirming Kerian's thoughts on the youth.

It appeared that Simons was not indolent after all!

Kerian rose from his bunk and took a few unsteady steps. He cursed the crippling feeling as the necklace at his neck struggled to adjust to the new ravages of age an extra year had bestowed upon his frame. He hobbled around the cabin, wincing as the blood rushed into his cramping limbs but forcing himself to take the necessary steps.

Limping painfully, he arrived at the porthole. This was his first consideration...a means of escape! He checked the circle of glass for a latch or hinge, but was almost instantly disappointed. He knew a dead light when he saw one!

The porthole construction meant it did not open; instead, its function was purely one of supplying light to the dingy cabin. It confirmed Kerian's fears. With the door barred and locked and this 'dead light' sealed, he was no better than a convict in a cell.

As there was no way out, Kerian decided he might as well make the best of things and try to figure out where exactly he was. He leaned up against the glass of the porthole and tried to make out the view beyond.

The view was as uninspiring as the contents of the room, consisting mainly of the sea rushing by several feet below. He strained his neck, trying to see what lay to either side of the circular window. The roll of the cobalt blue water and the lines of wake radiating to the right appeared to indicate that he was close to the stern of the ship. He moved his head to the other side of the porthole and looked the other way for an equally enthralling panorama.

He found very little inspiration to the left not seen in the mirror image to the right. There was no sign of land on the horizon and the only remarkable feature was the white tipped waves passed him by as the ship ploughed through the water. He studied the play of the water and realised they were certainly moving at a great rate of knots! This was obviously a fast ship!

This keen observation did not ease Kerian's current predicament however; trapped with no idea where he was, or where he headed. Stepping back from the porthole, the knight paused to take in his ghostly reflection in the glass. Squinting with over-tired eyes, he tried to make out the details but the glass surface was too uneven for any real clarity. Frustrated, he turned and made for his saddlebags, noting as he moved that the walk was less painful than his previous movement around the cabin now that he was finally out of his bunk.

Somewhere in his saddlebags he still had his mother's mirror; He slowly began to unpack, laying each personal item upon the ink-stained table. A change of clothes, some battered cooking utensils, his diary and the cursed parchment scroll soon littered the table surface. It was incredible, after all these years and all the efforts he had taken to make something of his life, that everything he owned was able to fit so neatly onto such a small space. He shook his head to dispel such morbid thoughts.

At the bottom of the bag, he discovered the silver engraved mirror. He reached in and lifted out the gilded gift, turning it over to gaze within its depths. The action itself was almost verging on vanity! Kerian chuckled to himself. It was almost a ritual now, gazing at his face after each onset of the curse, trying to spot the extra worry line, the new skin blemish and the slow thinning of his white hair. Then there was the game of trying to look past the ageing features and spot some semblance of the youth so tragically stolen away from him. The good-natured chuckle died on his lips.

The looking glass he held before him reflected back a score of splintered images, its surface smashed into small-disjointed shards of his own reflected face. He lowered the shattered mirror to the desk, shaking his head silently at his loss. He should have realised the mirror would not have survived the fall from his previous lodgings.

The key turned on the other side of the door, snapping him out of his melancholy, and Simons walked in bearing a small bowl of water, some soap, and a sharp blade. He stopped when he saw the smashed mirror on the table.

"Isn't that seven years bad luck." He joked before noting Kerian's downcast face. " What a shame.... I would guess from your expression that it was kind of special eh?" Kerian's silence confirmed the fact.

"Maybe I can get it fixed?" He stated helpfully. "It's not that bad. The frame is still intact; all we need is some mirrored glass..."

"Just leave it." Kerian interceded. "It was simply a memory of the past that I should have discarded long ago." Simons shrugged, recognising the rebuttal for what it was and gestured to the steaming water.

"I'll be back soon to escort you to the captain's cabin. If you want anything, all you have to do is knock loudly on the door." He examined his charge one last time, determined to make Kerian aware of the importance of his next statement.

"I'm going to trust you with the razor okay? Just make sure it is left in plain sight on the table when I return." Kerian nodded in response and waited for the door to close before reaching for the rough tablet of soap. He began to scrub vigorously, hoping that somehow, the very act of washing would leave him with clearer, sharper thoughts.

His hair had grown quite considerably since he was last awake. Kerian felt the long beard and knew that had to go right away! He set to work scraping his skin and clearing the clutter from his mind as he shaved. He felt the moustache that had grown in and figured he could do with a change in look, trimming it by feel before considering the mop of long hair he had.

Simons said he would be back soon. There was no time for something fancy. He gathered it all together, grabbing a lace from his spare clothes, pulling the hair up and back into a rough ponytail that kept it away from his face. Hair still hung down long onto his shoulders and he probably looked like a longboat raider from the Northlands now but that just added more mystery to his identity.

The bandage on his left arm slipped from its position, revealing a faded scar with a small, neat line of catgut sutures criss-crossing above its surface. The stitches were now redundant, unnecessary now the wound had closed. Although it was only a small thing Kerian could not help but grin at the sight, some of his old character returning in a rush.

Healing magic from the reanimated demon blacksmith had repaired his arm the night it had broken. That much was obvious. Kerian still was not sure why the creature's twisted morals had made it do this but he was not going to complain. It was a shame the magic had not helped him recover entirely. Had the role reversed, he would never have been as charitable. In war, it was kill or end up dead. Life was much simpler that way!

However, the blacksmith's magic held no comparison to that of his newly acquired curse. In real terms the wound had occurred three days ago but with the curse considered the scar on Kerian's arm was approximately one year and three days old! He settled back into the chair and reached for the razor with his injured arm, noting that there was no pain from the site of the break or any residual stiffness in the joint. His arm was as good as new!

With a deft flick of the sharpened blade, he severed the sutures, and then gently extracted each individual stitch from his healed arm.

It appeared that this curse had some advantages after all.

Chapter Seventeen

Thomas uttered a gasp as he knelt in the cold, dark water swilling around Fresine's still body. The look of sheer terror set permanently into the dead sailor's features potently reminded the captain of his previous career. He had seen enough homicides in his time to realise that this was no accident.

His eyes began to scour the hold, searching for clues to who the assailant was, even as he looked for something to cover the sailor's body. Thomas's vain search ended with a curse as he swiftly stripped from his own shirt, laying the white cotton garment across the sailor's face to serve as a temporary shroud. With head bowed and eyes closed, the captain began mouthing a silent prayer on behalf of his fallen comrade.

Rauph towered over his kneeling friend, his own head bowed both in respect and in an attempt to avoid his horns from gouging wooden splinters out of the ceiling. He held up a burning brand to light the grisly area, concerned with the possibility that whoever had done this may still be nearby. One of his massive two-handed swords glinted in the torchlight as he hefted it at his side, gaining a comfort and confidence from the inanimate object that only the Minotaur could ever understand.

The pale yellow light from the burning torch gave off little warmth to the dreary surroundings; instead, it seemed to add to the gloom and despair, magnifying it into something almost tangible. It was suddenly very cold down here in the hold, far below the waterline bereft of any sunlight to warm the skin. The accompanying silence added to the bleakness, broken intermittently by the distant squeak of rodents, and the drip, drip, of water from the decimated barrels that littered the deck around them.

A ruined segment of barrel floated past Rauph's foot reminding him of the destruction all about. The fresh water barrels now lay scattered throughout the hold, their wooden frames smashed and splintered following a violent and brutal attack that had no apparent reasoning behind it. No single barrel had remained unscathed; everyone had felt the wrath of this unwarranted violation.

The Minotaur swiftly decided that whoever had carried out this deed was terribly frustrated about something or someone. He continued to look around, searching for a suitable suspect. He swiftly discounted the two figures before him. Thomas...well he was the captain! He would never bring harm to this ship and crew.

Fresine could have smashed the barrels but Rauph figured that smashing all these barrels would not have left the jovial sailor in such a state, after all water barrels did not fight back. This was turning into quite a puzzle indeed! He looked back at Thomas. If anyone could figure out who had committed this horrendous deed the captain would be the one to do so.

Thomas finished his prayer and looked up into his bovine friend's eyes, snapping Rauph out of his impromptu detective work. The Minotaur held out a huge hand and helped him back to his feet. The captain appeared to be oblivious to the rivulets of water that trickled from his soaked trousers and down his leather boots.

The captain looked around the scene of destruction, mentally cataloguing where the body lay and comparing it to the destruction of the barrels. There was something missing from this crime scene. Where was Fresine's sword?

Thomas indicated that Rauph move closer, allowing the torchlight to aid his eyes as he scanned the water gathered around the body and tried to see if the tell-tale glint of metal hid in its shallow depths. His eyes turned hard as his face set in concentration then the captain moved deeper into the mess of ruined barrels, sloshing through the water as he took in the signs of the struggle, checking the ends of the rope that had been severed, the glass shards mixed with rainbow skimmed water that were all that remained of the dropped lantern.

Flickering torchlight showed directional blood spatter on the barrels that remained upright, splintered edges had small fibres from Fresine's gold braid jacket caught on the edges. However, he could not find Fresine's cutlass anywhere in the hold. Did the sick, twisted killer who had done this now have Fresine's sword?

He gestured to Rauph, monitoring where to swing the torch as he continued to scan the area for clues to the killer's identity: His wits raging at the images of the corpse imprinted upon his mind's eye. The wound to Fresine's face had been terrible to behold. Two thin slits had punctured the flesh of his right cheek and had exited through the orbit of his left eye, turning the eyeball within into a mass of useless jelly.

The marks, there was something about the marks.

Then he remembered. John Hodges had similar marks on his arm. Thomas had originally decided it was a burn from either John's pipe, or friction from a rope that must have parted and allowed the boxes to tumble on the crewman's head. Now, seeing this, the wound took on more sinister implications. There was a killer on board the *El Defensor.* A killer who appeared to be working through his crew!

It made no sense! What was the motive? Why Fresine? Why John Hodge?

Thomas had already ordered a thorough check of the *El Defensor's* forward decks following the death of John but perhaps the crew had missed something vital in their initial examination, after all, they had just thought it was an accident. There was no reason to consider foul play. There had to be clues, there were always clues. However, the captain had no access to a CSI team or a lab filled with fancy forensic equipment. He would have to act like the Homicide detective he had once been and do things the old-fashioned way: Search and interrogate.

Following this grim discovery, he would call for a repeat search to cover every square inch of his vessel. He sloshed through the water, his shaggy Minotaur companion following close behind and rechecked the crime scene one last time. With all the water down here, the odds of finding anything as regards to the killer's identity were long indeed.

"Damn it!" Thomas lashed out in frustration, smashing his fist into the side of a ruined barrel and catching Rauph off guard. The Minotaur caught the next blow before it connected and cradled Thomas's split hand in his own. He held it there with a compassion few would have realised he possessed; until Thomas finally realised he had forgotten something even more important.

Their entire fresh water supply was running around their feet. They had no fresh water and saltwater if drunk could turn you crazy. They had to find a port and restock but if they docked, the killer could slip away and avoid capture. Thomas found himself torn again; the pressures and responsibilities of being a captain were never far from his mind. Balancing the needs of the crew against his need to get justice for his fallen comrades was an unfair choice.

However, life was never fair. Thomas was just about to take his first steps from the store, when he suddenly turned and slipped from the Minotaur's protective grasp. With Rauph's flickering torchlight to guide him, he returned to Fresine's corpse and knelt beside his fallen friend. There was a sudden flash of silver in the torchlight, then an answering flash of gold. Apparently finished, Thomas slipped his dagger back into its sheath and returned to his huge companion's side.

"Take us out of here."

Rauph slipped a huge hairy arm around Thomas's shoulders and led him slowly up the ladder. As the two figures ascended, the light from Rauph's torch began to track across the deck to wash across Fresine's fallen body. The light gently caressed the threads of golden braid that decorated Fresine's waistcoat letting them flare as bright as the sun for one last time. Each individual waistcoat button flickered brightly as the torchlight passed it by, then winked into darkness. When the torchlight finally washed across the bottom of the waistcoat, there was no answering flash of gold. Instead, a single naked strand of thread stood exposed, clearly displaying where a golden button once lay.

* * * * * *

Kerian fastened the button of his cuff and brushed an imaginary speck of dust from the shoulder of his cloak. Confident that all was secure, he examined his outfit with a critical eye and a jagged shard of the hand mirror. His calf-high black leather boots shone where he had polished them, the finish a result of his military past, forever learned and impossible to forget. He had folded over the tops of his boots, revealing a strip of grey treated leather that served to mark a clear boundary between boots and trousers.

The hardwearing, black linen trousers disappeared beneath a studded leather tunic that rose from mid-thigh to encase his torso. Each individual stud gleamed, as a bright star set against the backdrop of night. As he re-checked the fastening on his cloak, his free hand dropped to the empty scabbard hanging at his side. It was amazing how naked he felt without the reassuring weight of his sword at his side.

Simons had revealed that the captain deemed it necessary to confiscate the weapons of all passengers on ship as a matter of course to prevent the possibility of any treachery. It was a wise rule to enforce and Kerian wondered how he would measure up to a man who was clearly cautious and intelligent. He made a mental note to address the return of his own weapon as soon as possible.

The now familiar sound of the key turning in the lock made Kerian turn towards the door, his velvet cloak swirling around him. He would show Simons how to dress with style and start to see exactly what he was dealing with here!

The effect was worth it.

"Let's not spend all day catching flies Simons." Kerian grinned, patting his young escort on the back. "We have a captain to visit." He swept past him, the unexpected confidence and bravado catching Simons off guard. Kerian was out into the corridor and picked a direction at random, determined to scope out as much as possible and leaving the stunned youth in his tracks. Simons quickly recovered his wits and followed the departing warrior, shouting after him as he hurried to catch up.

"Hang on... You're going the wrong way!"

* * * * * *

"So, tell me," Kerian began as he stepped out onto the main deck, breathing in the freshest air he had tasted in days. "What is the name of your captain?"

"Thomas Adams." Simons responded. "And Rik Kavaliare before him... But..."

"I must compliment him on his vessel." Kerian interrupted, pretending to ignore the blustering youth, thereby keeping him off balance. "She is a fine ship."

"The best I've ever served upon." Simons replied. "Now..."

Kerian suddenly stopped, allowing Simons to catch his breath and pointed up towards the main sail where three yellow lions roared defiantly in a painstakingly detailed design of embroidery that stretched across the crimson canvas.

"That wasn't there when I boarded," Kerian stated. "Indeed, If I remember correctly the main sail was quite plain. I have never seen a crest like it. With what navy do you serve?"

"Oh, the sail," Simons laughed. "We sort of acquire those from ships we pass. As I understand it that one tried to board us, although it was well before my time. Captain Adams seems to have taken a shine to it. He is a stickler for tradition and says that as we are on a crusade we might as well look the part. I am not sure what he means by that but he chuckles a lot whenever he mentions it. "

Kerian nodded his head as if he were interested but his eyes continued to scan the deck and take in his surroundings.

"Come to think of it Captain Adams does have a strange sense of humour, he often comes out with things none of us understand but which he seems to find very amusing."

"So the captain fancies himself to be a lion, does he?" Kerian broke in. "I must confess I've never seen the like. A man who sails under lions and has the heart of a lion to boot I have no doubt."

"We also have another sail in the stores with a huge white cross emblazoned across it, but it was damaged in a storm and requires extensive repairs before it can be used again. I am not sure where that one came from. Oh what am I doing?" Simons caught himself. "I don't know how to say this but the Captain's cabin is back by yours. You headed off in this direction before I could tell you otherwise and you haven't let me catch my breath, let alone tell you that we'd gone wrong." Kerian pretended to scowl at the apparent lack of communication and the time wasted by the impromptu tour.

"Then lead on Simons," he gestured, "lead on."

Simons set off back the way they had come with Kerian following willingly from behind. As soon as he knew the youth was not looking, he allowed a huge grin to illuminate his features. He now knew the general layout of the ship, the identity of the captain and if his geography was correct, they were just sailing around the Cape of Fareham. The unmistakable silhouette of the Haneck mountain range was slowly sliding by to his right. His over enthusiastic approach had worked just the way he had wanted it to.

The two men soon arrived outside Thomas's cabin. Simons stopped and offered his hand once more.

"Well, I must say I did enjoy taking the scenic route with you," he laughed, "but it is here that we must part our ways. I am sure I will see you around. Maybe we can talk some more then?"

"You can count on it." Kerian replied jovially, his demeanour successfully masking the double meaning concealed within his response. He would almost certainly be talking to Simons again. The youth was a veritable font of untapped information.

"Anyhow," Simons continued, "Captain Adams doesn't like to be kept waiting and your friends should already be in there by now." He waved goodbye and set off down the corridor, back to the main deck.

"Friends?" Kerian questioned, "Did you say friends? I thought he wanted to speak to me alone?" He turned to the door, grasping the handle and pausing only to take a deep breath before stepping through into the captain's cabin beyond. There could be a lot at stake in this meeting if he was going to convince the captain to take them to Stratholme; and if he was going to impress the captain and secure passage, he needed to make a good impression. He just hoped his 'friends' hadn't ruined that possibility before he'd even started.

Kerian's first impression was how lavishly decorated the cabin was, apparently as befitted a ship's captain. Works of art hung in gilded frames and intricate models of sailing ships stood displayed within small glass cases secured along the walls. His eyes lingered as he appreciated the attention to detail, before moving on to a small bookcase that held several assorted volumes with authors names Kerian did not recognise.

A large set of windows hung open in the centre of the far wall, allowing sunlight to stream across the huge desk standing before it. Three gilded chairs blocked Kerian's full view of the desk and the high ornate backs of the chairs were too exaggerated and extravagant in size for him to see if anyone sat in them. The glare of the sunlight made it equally impossible for him to examine the shadows below for any tell-tale feet.

Kerian took all of this in from where he stood in the doorway, before noticing the mirror hanging just inside the door. He swiftly took stock of his latest appearance and was satisfied with the outcome.

"Come in," ordered a voice.

Kerian focused on the matter at hand and began to walk across the cabin towards his host. Captain Adams sat impatiently on the far side of the desk, the look in the man's eye seeming to imply that he had far more important things to do with his time than wait whilst Kerian examined himself in the mirror! Kerian took this look in his stride. Let the man wait. He did not want to show any weakness unless he knew how the cards lay.

The captain gestured to a chair on the right and Kerian decided he would lose nothing by obliging, so he walked towards it, taking the opportunity to examine a faded globe that sat partially obscured by the desk as he had approached. The map displayed on its surface did not look familiar at all! A standard he had never heard of and now a world he had never seen. Just what kind of a ship was this?

A small pendulum movement caught his eye as he prepared to take the offered seat. Now that he was closer to the table, it had become easier to distinguish movement in the shadows below the chairs. Under the middle chair, two small feet were clearly visible, swinging backwards and forwards; nearly fifteen inches clear of the ground. There was something very familiar about those feet.

Kerian extended his hand to the captain for courtesy's sake prior to sitting and couldn't help but notice how Thomas's hand started to respond in reflex but was then swiftly pulled back out of sight again beneath the rim of the foreboding desk. Kerian noticed the freshly bandaged hand and considered the meaning. Was this an attempt to put him ill at ease? Alternatively, did this rebuff mean something else?

"My name is Thomas Adams," his host opened, gesturing with his remaining uninjured hand towards the vacant seat. Kerian complied without further prompting, settling himself into the chair and allowing Thomas to continue.

"I'm captain of the ship *El Defensor,* on which you currently sail… and you are?"

"Styx," Kerian replied in what he hoped was a nonchalant manner.

"I believe…" Thomas motioned to the other seats, "that you have already met Ashe Wolfsdale and Brother Marcus. Ashe informs me that you and he are friends but for some reason Marcus currently refuses to speak to any members of my crew, no matter what their religion."

Kerian swept his eyes across the tight-lipped visage of Marcus, taking in his nervous eye movements and taut body language, before moving down further to rest upon the small child-like face of Ashe.

"Oh he's still here then?" Kerian shrugged his shoulders, as if to show how little the Halfling meant to him. Even though somewhere he realised he was actually starting to like the fellow.

"Hello Sticks." Ashe grinned warmly. "I must say that I'm pleased to see you. The people on this ship are so cold towards me. One minute I'm minding my own business and then I'm locked up in a cell, fall overboard and get locked up in a cell again…" Ashe's enthusiastic response to Kerian's arrival suddenly stopped, his grin turning into a look of concern as his left hand began to shake uncontrollably.

He stared at his hand in horror and lunged for it with his remaining limb trying desperately to pin his rogue hand before it did anything stupid. His attempt came just too late, the hand with a mind of its own delved into a battered pouch hanging at the Halfling's waist. Ashe's face turned scarlet, as he appeared to struggle against this action. It appeared that he both wanted to and then did not want to show the assembled onlookers what he held in his hand.

Finally, the rogue hand came free of the pouch and something golden flew up in the air. Ashe's face was now a vivid purple, with small pulsing veins standing out on his forehead and his hand, now open, showed a white circular imprint in the centre of his palm, a clear indication of how tightly the diminutive thief had been holding on to the object that had just come free.

"Oh give me a break!" Ashe pleaded with thin air.

The ring fell with a clatter onto the desk. It rolled across the table towards its astonished owner, picking up speed even though the table was perfectly level.

A silver tankard containing a forlorn quill stood directly in the ring's path. In answer, the ring flashed, as if it had caught the sunlight for the briefest of instants, before it rolled into a small arc, skirting the edge of the drinking implement before resuming its journey towards Kerian unhindered.

It began to slow, trundling past the huge ledger that sat in the centre of the desk, before coming to a stop directly in front of Kerian's chair where it began to spin on the spot, rotating faster and faster until the movement was almost a blur. The golden metal flashed at each rotation, as if celebrating its 'homecoming' in a display of vibrant light.

"So it was you who had it then?" Kerian raised a stern eyebrow as he looked at the Halfling.

"I was going to return it, honest," Ashe blurted, flexing his fingers as all feeling and control suddenly returned to them. "You see, you dropped it in that fight and I've been trying to bring it back ever since."

Kerian was not so sure! A thief with a conscience! Especially this one. He did not think so! Their paths had crossed on the jetty that night in Catterick and no ring had been forthcoming at that moment or at any moment previously.

An important cough made him turn back to Captain Adams, his diminutive larcenous friend forgotten. Thomas leant forwards and spoke quietly and firmly.

"Why are you on my ship?"

Ashe responded first.

"Well I was returning the ring to Sticks." He blurted out.

"That business is now completed." Thomas confirmed, watching as Kerian placed the ring firmly back upon his finger. "And you?" he questioned his other guest. Marcus still refused to respond. Finally, he turned to Kerian.

"And what about you?"

"Surely your two crewmen can answer that one." Kerian replied sharply, taking the captain's interrogation as a challenge and instantly feeling the need to verbally fence back. "After all, they were the ones who got myself and Brother Marcus into this mess in the first place."

"Who is the fourth member of your party?" Thomas Adams face flushed and his look was of barely restrained rage. Silent alarm bells began to ring in Kerian's mind. The Captain was clearly angry about something that much was certain. His mind retraced their conversation so far. He had not mentioned anything out of turn, or that exposed why he and Marcus were on the ship. In addition, as far as he knew, they had caused no harm to come to the vessel or had hurt the captain or crew in any way. Moreover, what did he mean by a fourth member?

There was obviously something else going on with this ship; separate from the three of them and probably also to do with the injury the man had sustained to his hand. This Captain was not going to be in a negotiating mood. Something told Kerian that he was not going to like the way this was going to turn out.

"I will ask you again." Thomas demanded his tone of voice leaving very little room for argument. "Why are you here and who else came on board with you in Catterick?"

Silence was his only reply. Ashe clearly wasn't paying attention as he was too busy rubbing his hand, Marcus sat bolt upright with a face that looked as if he had a really bad case of loose bowels and Kerian... Well he simply was not sure how to answer the question!

"As none of you are being forthcoming with the truth I will expect you all to be confined to your quarters until we arrive at our next safe port. There you will be escorted from my ship and your weapons returned to you." Thomas raised himself up from his chair and walked over to the open window, turning his back purposely on the three unlikely comrades.

This meeting was at an end.

Ashe slid quietly from his seat and headed for the door, taking the most meandering route possible as he attempted to examine every glass case and model ship along the way. Kerian stood more slowly and walked over to Marcus, who had stubbornly refused to move or utter a sound throughout the entire conversation. The click of the cabin door shutting behind them indicated that Ashe had already departed the cabin and would stretch the terms of confined to quarters as much as he could, before being corralled again.

"Come on." Kerian motioned, guiding the monk to his feet and walking him towards the door. "What have you told them?" he whispered into his ear.

"Nothing." Marcus mumbled, "Nothing at all. I haven't said a word because I have been waiting for you to wake up! They have been watching me like a hawk ever since I arrived and have kept me well away from the Halfling or yourself. But now you are awake we need to be sailing for Stratholme and we are currently heading in the wrong direction." The monk paused double-taking in his glance at Kerian's face.

"How come your hair is so much longer?"

"I eat my vegetables," Kerian grinned reassuringly. "Just keep everything quiet for the moment. I will figure out something to get us on another ship when we dock at the port the captain mentioned. Don't worry all is not lost. I never give up easily." He opened the cabin door and Marcus obligingly stepped through but something made Kerian hesitate to follow.

Thomas expected him to disembark at the next port anyway, so what better opportunity would he have for a parting jibe. He silently closed the door and walked back across the cabin staring at the captain's presented back and wondering what the best choice of words would be to inflict the most venom.

"When someone lies to me I get extremely upset." Captain Adams opened, steeling Kerian of his thunder. "Why hasn't Kerian Denaris followed his stowaway friends?"

"How do you know my name?" Kerian stated coldly, his manner instantly on the defensive as he realised he had never revealed his name to anyone on board.

"Why the charade?" Thomas questioned, turning from the window and fixing Kerian with an interrogatory eye. "I asked you straight out to tell me who you were and why you were on my ship. Yet the very first words from your mouth, something as simple as your name... are a lie. Tell me why the mystery? What game are you playing?"

"I asked you how you knew my name." Kerian repeated; his tone and ire rising at the challenge.

"Why is it...?" Thomas continued straight on, "...that someone living under the identity of an assumed name would be stupid enough to carry a diary with the title of his family clearly written across the cover and his real name on the main title page?"

"How dare you." Kerian snapped. "That diary and its contents are personal."

"Oh don't worry." Thomas reassured, watching Kerian's face intently for further signs of deceit "Your secret identity is safe with me. I only read the first few pages, as I like to think I respect other people's privacy, unless of course you put my ship and crew at risk by those secrets. Yet you hardly fulfil my expectations of a hero who needs a secret identity. You look too old to be a Clark Kent or Peter Parker."

Thomas allowed himself a sly smile at the joke, thinking back to the comic book heroes of his childhood, then realised that his attempts at humour had gone straight over the elderly man's head and simply resulted in Kerian looking confused.

"So I ask again...Why the masquerade? What are you trying to prove? Why are you on my ship?" He powered on with his questions, trying to keep his stowaway off balance but also reminding himself to be more careful with his improvisation.

Kerian struggled to compile a response to the man's rapid questions. What did he mean by Clarke...who was it again? This was insane! He was leaving the ship anyway! He might as well leave the cabin and go and pack, his silence would serve as a suitable reply. He turned to leave but something made him stop short of actually carrying out his plan. Sensing his hesitation Thomas continued with his verbal accusations.

"Kerian Denaris, your diary describes a man with a great burden upon his shoulders, but also someone who tries to do the right thing with honourable values. Nevertheless, your double identity makes me question both your sincerity and your honesty. It may be true you do not know who the fourth stowaway is but I have observed the way you walk and act and how hot headed you quickly become. This is not the actions of an old man. Certainly not someone who has matured and suffered the harsh lessons we gain by living. Something is very wrong here and this troubles me immensely."

"I am simply a traveller who has lost his way in the darkness." Kerian responded. "Much like your strange ship and crew seem to have lost yours." Thomas's face twitched with discomfort and Kerian realised he had guessed close to the mark. The ship had indeed travelled from afar. "My colleagues and I know nothing of a fourth stowaway, I have been out of action since I arrived here and I know you have kept watch on Marcus and Ashe so whatever is causing your anger, we are not the cause."

"I am what you see, a retired adventurer who has been hired by the monastery of St Fraiser to travel the ways of the world and protect the monk that was in here before. Brother Marcus is doing some dangerous research for the monastery and as you can see he is so innocent to the ways of the world that it would have been inhumane for them to simply send him out on his holy quest without some form of esc..."

"If you believe you are lost and travelling in shadows, I should remind you that it also appears your judgement has become as impaired as your sense of direction." Thomas warned. "Why don't you simply tell me the truth? I despise liars. All my life people have lied to me. I have seen through the best and frankly, you don't even come close. I also dislike secrets on my ship and your eyes tell me you have more than a few of those to spare."

"It would be my guess that you are solely responsible for your ship being lost." Kerian shot back, determined to fight back against the unease he was feeling from Thomas's statements. "Why don't you tell me some of your secrets too? You know, share the burden so to speak."

"I'm not ready to share mine" Thomas responded with exasperation. "And many are not mine to share. Your secrets can remain your own." He paused to gather his breath and try to cool his annoyance at the stubbornness of the man before him. "Let me just say that as captain of this ship, I have offered you the opportunity to unburden your soul and be honest with me. In my experience the darkest of secrets have ways of getting out and sometimes they can destroy the person who carries them."

Kerian turned for the cabin door. He was not going to win here. He needed to leave but as always, his youthful mind refused to leave without a parting salvo of vitriol.

"If I wish to unburden my soul, I'll talk to Marcus, not you!" he snapped.

"That is indeed your prerogative," Thomas agreed, now trying to adopt a calmer approach. "Just remember, the sea we sail upon is very much like a mirror. Whilst you sail upon its surface you will find plenty of time to reflect."

"Leave your philosophy to your crew," Kerian snapped, throwing open the door and stepping through, to leave Thomas standing by the window staring thoughtfully after him.

The captain could not help but wonder if Kerian's anger directly attacked him as the captain, or showed Kerian's frustration at himself. Did the old man feel that vulnerable, or was he simply embarrassed at the ease of his discovery? Maybe there was something else going on.

Suddenly Thomas wanted to know more about Kerian Denaris and wished he had pushed his guilt aside and read the whole diary instead of the first few pages.

"I think he'll be back." He promised himself.

* * * * * *

Kerian was furious with himself! He had not expected to lose his verbal fencing match so easily against Thomas Adams and his thoughts were in turmoil! He marched swiftly around the corner, risking a quick glance back as he did so. Whom was he kidding! What did he expect to see? The Captain rushing out after him offering some sort of apology. Do not be ridiculous! Even in his angry state, he knew the man had no need to apologise! If anyone needed to apologise for his behaviour it was himself and this made him angrier still!

Occupied with his thoughts, he did not see the other person in the corridor until it was too late. In the ships close confines, a collision was unavoidable. There was a gasp as the two figures knocked into each other, the slighter form falling to the floor in an undignified heap, her violet robes splayed all about her and sheets of parchment flying in all directions.

Kerian started to voice his outrage, his ire still ready for a suitable victim. However, as he moved to do so, their gazes met and Kerian found himself instantly disarmed by blue eyes that left him flushing crimson with embarrassment. He swiftly knelt to help the young woman to her feet, as she angrily brushed aside his helping hand.

"I can help myself thank you!" she snapped. "Why don't you just look where you are going?" She stood, shaking her mussed blond hair from her face and Kerian suddenly found a burning urge to want to look at the floor and pick up her parchment sheets, mumbling apologies as he did so.

He swiftly gathered what he could and then stuffed them unceremoniously into her hands before setting off for the main deck muttering a further apology as he went.

Did not want his help… The cheek! If she did not want his help, he was not going to waste his time any further. For that matter, to the seven hells with the captain's orders! He was not going to stay in his cabin. He was going to find Marcus and discuss their plans for continuing his quest. Time was a luxury he did not possess and there was no way he was spending any more time in that dreary old cabin!

Colette watched the elderly knight stomp off down the corridor muttering to himself, a bemused look upon her face. The crew on this ship got stranger every day.

Chapter Eighteen

"Our three stowaways are not involved." Thomas stated to his select assembly of crewmembers. "One's been unconscious for days, another seems to have a severe case of laryngitis since coming aboard and the last one is too busy annoying the hell out of everyone to have ever had the time to kill anything!" Thomas paused to catch his breath, shook his head and then continued.

"None of them knew of the fourth stowaway, or what we have discovered. That obviously leaves one other unaccounted person who came aboard this ship at Catterick who seems to have taken it upon himself or herself to destroy the sanctity of this ship and murder members of the crew. I want whoever it is found and brought before me."

His eyes looked like winter as his gaze swept across the figures standing before his desk. Rauph stood alongside Simons, Colette and Sherman whilst standing away from the others Scrave continued to sulk. Thomas wanted to grab the Elf and shake him but there simply was not time. Why could Scrave not see he had done wrong? His punishment was fair, now he needed to get over it!

"Needless to say," Thomas continued, pushing his annoyance to the back of his mind. "I want you to search every inch of this ship until we find John and Fresine's killer. Nowhere is to go unsearched. Whoever it is, they must be hiding somewhere and they are to be considered armed and exceptionally dangerous."

"If they don't come quietly you have my permission to use force."

Rauph leaned forward, hand raised to say something.

"Do we have to search all the storage spaces?"

Thomas immediately second-guessed the Minotaur's concern but he could not pamper his crew in this grim situation.

"Yes Rauph, I do mean everywhere." Thomas clarified. Rauph's eyes bulged at the implications. "And ask the crew if they have seen or heard anything out of the ordinary. The smallest clue could hold the difference to us finding this murderer."

"Even in the dark places? But what if they have..." Thomas cut him short with a wave of his hand.

"There are only a few more hours until sundown. I want the killer routed out and found by then. I suggest that for your own safety you search in pairs. Simons and Sherman take the main deck, Colette, find Austen and take him with you to search the hold. I don't suppose you could try some magic to locate him could you?"

Colette looked at Thomas with concern.

"I'll try but I've never done anything like this before. I'll see if the Master's spell books have anything in them about methods of detection."

"All I ask is that you do your best." Thomas smiled warmly. He turned his attention to Rauph and Scrave. "You two search the mid-deck. I want every inch examined. We'll all meet back here in two hours."

He dismissed the crew, shaking his head as he overheard the departing Rauph telling Scrave that he was scared of certain things that hid in the dark places on board the ship. The Minotaur slept with a decaying arch mage sitting in the corner of his cabin for goodness sake! Some things in life simply did not make sense!

Thomas also worried about Scrave's attitude; the Elf seemed to hold a grudge as if everything was personal long after others had forgotten about it and moved on. He would see how Scrave handled himself with the search and if he failed to lighten up, they would have to sit and have another uncomfortable talk.

He settled back in his chair, finally alone with his own thoughts, and opened his logbook in readiness to document his meeting with the three stowaways and his decision to search the ship. He reached across the desk towards his tankard and stopped in surprise.

His quill was gone!

Thomas swung back in his chair to look under the desk, then tilted the chair back onto its four legs and lifted his logbook bodily from the desk to see if the quill was underneath but there was no sign of the elusive feather.

What was going on with this place? Now his pens were going missing! This place got more like the precinct office every day! Although normally it was doughnuts and parking spaces that ended up disappearing.

Cursing under his breath, Thomas got out of his chair and down onto his hands and knees, preparing to search the shadowy area beneath the desk in more detail. Although the quill was a downy brown colour, it had several vivid orange stripes across the plumage, which should have made it easy to locate against the deep red carpet on the cabin floor.

An area of darkness flitted across the carpet as Shadow flew through the open window; 'cawing' loudly to announce its landing as it sailed down onto the desk, bobbing it's huge, pitch-black head up and down and tilting its head to see what the captain was up to.

Thomas tried to dismiss the skittering of Shadow's talons on the highly polished wood of his desk but the tapping disrupted his thoughts as easily as it interfered with his search. Angry at the lack of attention shown, the bird had begun to strut up and down the desk, clacking its appendages even louder on the polished surface.

Gritting his teeth in frustration, he turned towards the huge bird, intent on throwing something at the annoying creature. Then he paused...

He needed a quill, didn't he?

"Come here boy." Thomas beckoned slyly.

* * * * * *

Kerian stood alone upon the fore deck, his turbulent thoughts allowing no peace. In his hands, he held the bridle and trappings of Saybier. His horse had died and he had not been there when his steed needed him.

Simons and another sailor called Sherman had been very sympathetic and assured him his horse had not suffered. They had been carrying out a search around him but had given him a wide berth showing a respect for his privacy that was surprising to the hardened fighter.

A sombre sailor called Austen had given the tack to Kerian shortly after he had left his unsatisfactory audience with Thomas, catching him off guard as he had set off across the deck to find Marcus.

Marcus had swiftly moved down the priority list as Kerian had taken in the news, hardly believing the hand that life was currently dealing him. Atticus's contract had been a lie, people had been out to kill him left right and centre and he was day nursing a monk on a strange ship. Now this quest had cost him the life of his horse!

He was on his own now and life just kept on kicking him whilst he was down.

The beautiful young lady he had collided with in the corridor had called Austen away and had looked at him with pity as Austen had politely excused himself and then left Kerian alone with his memories of the magnificent charger.

Kerian did not want pity from anyone. He just wanted his horse back.

The sky had started to turn deep orange as Kerian looked up from the tack in his hands and realised with surprise just how much time had passed. He watched the sun set in a daze as it transformed into a glowing ball of fire, the vivid sight of the fiery orb plunging into the sea wasted on the fighter, his mind and thoughts flitting elsewhere, going through his memories and reliving more and more painful ones of horse and rider saving each other's lives. As the sun finally extinguished its glow into the ocean, a rosy red smear lit across the sky, a portent of things that were yet to come.

"Red sky at night soldier take fright!" Kerian remembered.

He gripped the carved wood of the guardrail and glanced over the side of the ship, watching the white wave heads rushing by. Then he reached out and over as far as he could, tack held at arm's length above the moving water.

His eyes teared before he found the courage to cast the bridle into the wind, watching as the leather straps fell into the sea's embrace, a white crest briefly forming on the surface as the cold waters swallowed it whole.

Kerian knew he would never have used this tack on another horse anyway. It just would not have seemed right.

Maybe it was his tear-blurred vision but Kerian was sure that the resulting foam, if only briefly, formed into the shape of a small galloping stallion, charging across the deep blue backdrop of the swirling sea.

* * * * * *

"Yup!" Rauph confirmed. "There's definitely something moving in there."

Rauph and Scrave were below decks, digging through some storage space. The area was cramped and dark, seldom used due to its location being so near the engineer's compartment and therefore at constant risk of things going bang, scalding clouds of steam, noxious vapours and other weird happenings. As a result, no one would ever consider sleeping quarters here. Instead, it had become a small scrap heap; full of bits and pieces that they used to repair the ship.

Assorted cogs, wheels, bits of copper wire and other indescribable junk lay in this area and the Minotaur's current area of search was a huge pile of metal sheets and coils staked against the wall so they would not come free in a storm.

"So what does it look like?" Scrave asked, clearly unconvinced at his associate's supposed 'vision' of some creature.

"Well," Rauph replied, pulling a large piece of machinery from the hole he had excavated, "It's small, kind of like a rat but it's bigger and uglier. Ooh... Maybe it's a cat that got lost or something. I have always wanted a cat. Maybe the captain would let me keep it."

"So it's either a cat or a very large rat then?" Scrave leant back against the wall and put his hands behind his head after mocking a bored yawn. "Have you ever considered that a cat, or for that matter a large rat, would be unable to kill Fresine or John Hodge? We are looking for a dagger wielding psychopath, not a rabid pile of fur with pointy teeth!"

"Well, why don't you look?" Rauph asked, plunging his head into the hole once more.

"I am." Scrave replied, lifting a small piece of metal with the toe of his boot. "Of course I am."

Rauph continued to push his way further into the pile of rubbish.

"I can just reach it," he gasped, his hand outstretched as far as he could.

"Just grab it and let's get it over with," Scrave commented, leaning even further back against the bulkhead and looking up at the ceiling trying to stretch a kink out of his shoulders.

An earth shattering 'moo' jerked Scrave to alertness, causing him to smack his head against the doorframe. His hand reached out for a handy steel bar balanced on top of a nearby pile of refuse and he prepared to take on the unseen assailant.

"What is it? What is it?" He asked, looking down at the writhing chestnut haired figure trying desperately to back out of the sheeting, he had squeezed behind. "Has it bitten you?"

Rauph continued to moo and snort hysterically, then staggered to his full height to send discarded rubbish falling all around him in a shower of hard metal, spilled cogs and wooden planks. Scrave threw his arms up and dodged several launched missiles, only daring to peer through his hands once he was sure no more falling objects were heading his way.

With a deafening howl, the now disentangled Minotaur ran pell-mell for the ladder leading to the main deck.

Scrave raced after his screaming companion, desperate to slow his colleague down and discover what had caused this sudden pandemonium. Every now and then, he had to duck and swerve as pieces of rubbish continued to fall from Rauph's lumbering form and ricochet in his direction.

He tried to pass the terrified Minotaur in the close confines of the corridor. He found himself brushed back each time, until finally, he was able to leap past on the ladder, and bring his colleague to a stop.

"Stop Rauph!" he screamed. "Just stop!"

Rauph, eyes rolling in terror bowled his friend over. The collision was like an avalanche, metal fragments that had stuck stubbornly to Rauph's fur flying off in all directions. Scrave bounced painfully across the wooden deck before entangling himself, yet again, in the charging Minotaur's legs. The charging behemoth crashed down on him in a tumble of hairy arms and legs.

Scrave swiftly disentangled himself from the mountain of fur that was his friend and turned the hysterical Minotaur over, his hands grabbing for each of the Minotaur's flailing limbs and desperately examining them for bites or gouges. However, he could find no injuries on his friend.

"Where are you hurt Rauph?" Scrave shouted, "I can't see anything wrong!"

"N...N... Not my hands. My...H...H... Horn." Rauph stammered, gesturing frantically with a shaking hand.

Scrave followed the gesture upward to see a small spider dangling from Rauph's left horn. It still swung backwards and forwards hanging on stubbornly throughout the Minotaur and Elf high-speed collision.

"It's going to bite me!" Rauph wailed. "I can see it in its twenty eyes! K...K...Kill it Scrave."

Scrave reached up and snatched the tiny spider from its precarious position, letting it run across his hand and around the side into his palm, before bringing both of his hands together and squashing it where it crawled.

"There, see!" Scrave motioned, showing the sludgy mess that now dangled from his hand. "It's dead."

Rauph's eyes rolled up into his head, leaving Scrave with an eight-foot-tall unconscious Minotaur to watch over.

* * * * * *

"So that's all you managed to find?"

Thomas looked down at the remains of a half-chewed rat, some partially eaten food, a collection of hats and hair ties and finally a blood-streaked cutlass.

"That's the lot of it." Sherman confirmed stepping back to join his fellow colleagues.

Thomas looked up into the faces of his surrounding companions, questioning what lay before him. Obviously the hats and ties were the result of Shadow's favourite pastime but the half-eaten rodent; the scraps of food and Fresine's cutlass were obviously of a more sinister origin.

"We found the food and the cutlass in one of the lifeboats on deck." Simons offered. "But there was no stowaway with them."

Rauph was frantically dusting his horns free of imaginary cobwebs, as Thomas's eyes alighted on him. He paused meekly in mid-polish.

"I only found big spiders. They scared me."

"I know that Rauph." Thomas agreed. "However, there are other important issues we need to worry about. Have you had time to consider where we can dock to replenish our water supplies?" Rauph shook his head.

"I'll get on it next." He growled, trying to sound like the gruff tough Minotaur they all knew.

"I can't detect what is causing these deaths with any magic that I know," Colette interrupted, drawing Thomas's attention mercifully away from the Minotaur. "I'm afraid I never practiced scrying and now I have no one to teach me, I have to rely on the master's books for reference. His handwriting was never easy to read. It's much harder than I thought it would be."

"Everything is much harder than you thought it would be. Can't scry, can't get us home." Scrave muttered under his breath.

Thomas bit his tongue, ignoring Scrave's negative comments and turned to Sherman who shook his head, signalling similar failure at his end of the ship.

"We found nothing more but the night watch did report hearing a strange sound on the aft-castle."

"That would be Colette's brain finding things hard." Scrave sniped with a sarcastic grin.

"Well," Thomas questioned, turning on the antagonistic Elf. "What ideas does the mighty Scrave have? Do you actually have any ideas? Or are you just content to deride your colleagues?"

Scrave's sarcastic grin turned to a scowl in a snap.

"I still think the three stowaways know more than they are letting on." Scrave shot back. "You tell us they are not guilty but we didn't start having people killed until we took them on board in Catterick. Give me a few moments with them, I will soon get them to confess to the killings and we can all go on with our lives and return to the task of making our way home. We have one gemstone now that can force a way back to the ship's graveyard, thanks to me, we only need one more to open a portal from there to wherever we want to go."

"Don't be preposterous!" Thomas shot back. "You know I don't run that kind of a ship! These people are innocent of any wrong doing against us, so we will treat them as guests, all be it ones with restricted rights, until we dock. It's my ship, it's my decision how things are run around here."

"And we know where that has got us all." Scrave attacked. "You haven't even managed to get us home yet. Ever since our only real mage died, we have been dead in the water and you know it. Let's just face it we are never going to get home with you in command."

"As far as I was aware Rauph got the snake's eye gem in Catterick not you." Sherman spoke up in defence and you are the only person that has been acting strangely since Catterick, no one else. So shall we start questioning you?"

"I'd like to see you try." Scrave snarled.

The cabin erupted into sound, accusations flying at Scrave's outburst as the crew leapt to their captain's defence.

"Stop it! All of you!" Thomas shouted, silencing everyone within the room in a heartbeat, his face a mask of unprecedented fury. "Until we find this killer I want an around the clock watch. Whoever it is, they can't hide forever and when they move...we will be waiting."

He then turned to face the mutinous Elf. "Scrave, as far as your absurd outburst is concerned, I can only say that I will treat it with the disdain it deserves. You know as well as I that none of the stowaways or the crew could have carried out these killings. They have no motive or reason to do so and I will not stand for such a blatant attempt to spread discord amongst my ship's company. Seeing, as you are still so sore at how I run my ship, a fact evident by your latest outburst, you and Rauph will have the honour of first watch this evening. I hope that it will give you the time you need to think over your recent actions and behaviour. If you don't like how I run this ship you are welcome to disembark with our three stowaways at our next port of call."

"Everyone to your stations!"

He waved his hand curtly ushering everyone from the room and watched as they began to drift from the cabin, Rauph loudly voicing complaints that he had not done anything wrong, so why did he get the first watch? Moreover, what was it they were supposed to be watching anyway?

Thomas let the door close behind his crew and only then let out a huge sigh. Was he really starting to lose his control over the ship and the crew?

Doubts swiftly grew in his mind. Things were moving too fast. He needed time to pause and gather his thoughts before Scrave's caustic attitude started to permeate amongst the men. Maybe it already had. Maybe he was not good enough to do his job. Was any of this grief worth it? Was mutiny the likely conclusion? What happened in Catterick to make things turn so bad so quickly? What had caused the Elf's attitude to change so dramatically since his fateful return from the port town?

Wait a minute...Of course!

Thomas reached down into his drawer and retrieved the golden serpent dagger. Could this be the reason behind Scrave's uncharacteristic outburst? Surely, greed was not enough of a motivator for Scrave to lose it the way he had been recently.

He looked down at the dagger and shuddered. Simply holding the weapon made him feel uneasy but there seemed no outward sign that this blade would cause Scrave to act so recklessly. He turned it first one way and then the other but nothing seemed amiss. A little voice in Thomas's mind shouted at him to trust his instincts. To listen to his gut and act on it!

Thomas felt cold, suddenly certain that this dagger was the cause of Scrave's continuing problems. He held it up to the fading light, staring at it in morbid fascination, looking for some kind of sign that would serve to prove his theory. The ruby eyes set into the golden serpent's head appeared to glow within the heat of his hand and the golden scales rippled in the light of the cabin as if the serpent was alive.

His theory was almost too ridiculous to be true. It was unbelievable that Scrave could act so bitterly over the simple confiscation of this silly dagger! Maybe it had some kind of mystical effect on the Elf. Maybe Scrave was experiencing some kind of magical dagger withdrawal. Maybe it was a cursed dagger!

"Yes of course..." he voiced aloud, "And I suppose this dagger is why we have a killer running around on board too!" Thomas shook his head. That was thin. Still, there was something unsettling about the weapon. He just could not place a finger on why.

He flipped the blade in his hand, then stood up and walked over to the open window. The sky had darkened now and the breeze was very chill in the shadows at the stern of the ship. He stood there poised to close the windows for the night when a thought came to him.

There was a simple solution to his problem, he could drop the blade overboard and then no one would have it. Sure, Scrave would be ill tempered for a couple of days but with luck he would soon return to the swashbuckling figure of old. Cranky to be sure but at least he would be back to being loyal to the ship... That is, if it was indeed something to do with Scrave being near the blade.

It would be worth losing the fortune this dagger may represent if it was!

The grey foam wake trailing the *El Defensor* had a marked contrast to the ever-darkening sea around. The earlier warm cobalt blue had now dissipated into a liquid shadow of deepest black as the day surrendered to night.

Thomas shuddered again. He hated the sea at night. During the day, you could see the fish that swam in its depths, be forewarned of monstrous attacks but at night, the sea held its secrets close. There could be anything down there, lurking just below the surface. Maybe watching him right now and he would be none the wiser for it.

The captain was so lost in his thoughts that he failed to notice how the dagger in his hand continued to glint and catch the light, even in this shadowy area of the ship. Light slid across scale after individual scale, as if the dagger was somehow moving in his grasp, the serpent somehow sensing the threat to its existence and preparing to slide through his hand to safety.

He held his arm out over the lapping waves below the window and prepared to drop the dagger into the depths below, pausing only to look at it one last time. All he had to do was open his hand...

* * * * * *

Thomas blinked and looked at the desk before him. Wasn't he about to do something important? He looked about the desk for clues. His logbook lay open before him and items of food still littered the far side of his desk.

That was it!

He had to document the search in his log! He brought out a small bottle of ink and reached for the battered tankard before him, a solitary jet-black quill standing quietly to attention within.

The captain picked up his quill and began to write, oblivious to the now locked and bolted window behind him. The golden serpent dagger lay temporarily forgotten alongside the open logbook, its ruby red eyes appearing to glint even brighter.

* * * * * *

"What's going on with you Scrave?" Rauph questioned, having completed his current circuit of the upper deck and finding nothing interesting to watch.

"It's just you've been acting kind of funny just recently. Is it something I have done? You know I did not mean to kill your worm back in the temple. It just, sort of, happened."

Scrave looked up at his bovine friend, wanting to rant and shout but instead began to smile. No matter how angry he felt and how unorthodox their initial outing together had been, the Elf had to admit that he was starting to like having his huge companion around. He cracked another grin finding he just could not help it when Rauph was about. Being angry with this 'gentle' Minotaur was simply impossible.

"It's nothing you've done Rauph." Scrave finally replied. "I did something stupid, that's all and the thought of it is still rattling me. I know I was in the wrong and I confess that I'm also a little angry with myself. But what is really concerning me is that I am starting to see threats in everything people say and before I know it, I'm lashing out."

"Just like you did in the captain's cabin." Rauph stated.

"I didn't need to be reminded." Scrave replied shaking his head in remorse. "I don't know why it happened. I just felt strange in Thomas's cabin and I cannot explain my actions. You know the longer I think about it the sillier it gets."

Scrave set off along the edge of the starboard side of the main deck, his hand tracing along the top of the guardrail that ran all around the deck and gave sailors something to tie off to in rough seas. Rauph swiftly fell into an uneven step alongside him, before they reached the ladder leading up to the fore deck and began to climb.

Rauph stood looking up at the steps and raised a finger.

"I need to ask something Scrave." The Elf paused mid-climb expecting to have a meaningful discussion with his colleague.

"Why is it these steps, which look awfully like stairs and are to all-purpose stairs, are called a ladder on this ship? I've often wondered and John Hodge said he would tell me but now..." He left the sentence hanging as Scrave waved him up.

"I'm not completely sure." Scrave shrugged his shoulders. "I have heard they are called stairs on a ship that has passengers."

"And are we not passengers?" Rauph suggested.

"I don't think so." Scrave replied. "I think we are classed as crew."

At the top of the steps, they both turned to look back across the ship and noticed a figure disengage themselves from the shadows of the aft-castle to head swiftly down towards the main cabins.

"Hang on... isn't he a passenger?" Rauph began; his hand easing from his sword when he recognised it was the old man from the alleyway in Catterick. "I wonder where he's going."

"To bed if he has any sense," Scrave replied, crossing the foredeck and walking up to the rail so he could stare out across the sea. The waves lapped quietly against the hull and the only break in the mood of the moment was the sound of Rauph's approaching footsteps and the occasional creak of the anchor chain.

It was a beautifully calm night, if a little chill and Thomas had ordered that they drop anchor whilst daylight was absent from the sky. Following the earlier near miss, it had been decided that navigation of these waters during the night was simply too risky to contemplate at the speeds they sailed. Colette had also needed a much-earned rest from her extended magical use and the time to research possible solutions to their current problems.

"So in effect," Rauph continued. "What you are saying is when we use the steps they are ladders and when he uses the steps they are stairs."

"No I think it's down to the ship you are on." Scrave replied looking down over the side at the ocean below.

"But that doesn't make sense." Rauph shook his head trying to figure it all out. "So if I'm on another ship it's a stair and if I'm here it's a ladder? Or is it the other way arou..." Scrave stopped the Minotaur with a wave of his hand and motioned down to where he was staring intently at the velvet surface of the sea.

"Did you see that?" he motioned, pointing at the smooth silky blackness below. "There's something down there." Rauph scrunched up his eyes, trying to see what his friend was raving about. The only thing he could see was the reflection of the moon floating in the night sky above.

"That's funny Scrave," Rauph laughed, throwing back his head to look directly at the moon above. "There's only the moon out there silly." He punched Scrave playfully in the arm and sent the Elf reeling across the deck with the force of the blow. The Minotaur lent over the side and looked back down at the sea, watching a cloud slowly cover the moon and then appear to float on by and reveal it again.

"And there it is again." He chuckled, blissfully unaware that his friend was now struggling to regain his feet from where he had landed on the deck.

Scrave came cautiously back to the guardrail rubbing his arm and looked back over the side to the glassy smooth surface of the sea. He swiftly checked his bearings and position then glanced at the sea once again. Without a doubt, he was staring exactly at the same place he had been looking at earlier. This time however there was no sign of the ghostly reflection that had initially stared back up at him. He shook his head: he could have sworn he had seen a grinning skull down there!

A small wave split up the image of the moon, creating two incomplete images. That must have been it; a trick of the light, coupled with the swell of the sea. He definitely was not feeling right!

"So come on, what did you do wrong?" Rauph intruded. Scrave turned to his friend and began to continue the circuit of the foredeck, the mysterious ghostly shape shortly forgotten.

"Wouldn't you like to know?" He teased. "Now as we were saying about those ladders... Let's just say, you don't want to get me started on companionways."

Chapter Nineteen

Thomas paused in mid-flow as a knock came from his cabin door. He shook his head before looking up in frustration. It seemed every time he tried to write in his log someone was going to interrupt him.

"Come in," he answered.

The door swung open to reveal Styx...No, Thomas reminded himself, Kerian Denaris. The old man's face was drawn and haggard, a clear sign that his thoughts were troubled.

"I wondered if I might have a moment of your time." Kerian began.

"So," Thomas laid his quill carefully alongside the golden dagger, careful not to cause any more ink spills. "What can I do for you?"

He risked a quick glance at the dark night sky through the closed window behind him then returned his gaze to the elderly fighter and grinned. "Do you always have this unusual habit of doing things nocturnally?"

"You did say anytime." Kerian retorted with a smile, starting to warm to Thomas's strange sense of humour. "After all, I don't appear to have woken you." He gestured to the open logbook.

Thomas nodded; he could not fault the fighter on that statement. He motioned for Kerian to pull up a chair and stood and walked over to the globe, sliding the top to one side to reveal crystal decanters inside.

"Care for a drink?" Kerian nodded his head and got more comfortable in the chair as Thomas returned with two glasses containing generous measures of smoky liquor.

"I'm afraid I don't have any ice." He apologised. "Now...what is it that you wish to talk about?"

"Ice?" Kerian remarked. "Whatever would you want ice for?"

* * * * * *

"I stole a dagger," Scrave blurted out.

Rauph checked his own dagger then looked back at Scrave with a strange look on his face before snorting. "Who's?"

"Nobody's..." Scrave grinned, finally starting to feel at home confessing to his shaggy confidant. "At least nobody we know. I picked it up in the temple we visited but I didn't tell Thomas about it when we returned, you know how strict he can be? Taking every spoil and then splitting it amongst the crew. Well, as you can imagine, he was not exactly impressed when he saw how much the dagger was worth and the fact that I had 'forgotten' to inform him of its 'liberation.' So now he's taken the dagger away from me and has stated quite clearly that even when the spoils are distributed at the next port, I will not receive one iota of what the dagger was worth in my share."

"Serves you right," Rauph laughed, "You know rules are there to be followed."

Their walk had taken them to the prow of the ship and they paused to stare out into the darkness.

"You of all people know, I don't play by the rules." Scrave chuckled. "I just wish I could have kept this one thing though." He sighed as he remembered the exquisite detail of the piece and the hairs rose at the base of his neck in the recall.

"You've never seen a dagger like it Rauph." He began to gesture with his hands, as if to emphasise the beauty of the blade even as he formed its shape in the air. "It was solid gold. It had to have been but unlike any gold I have ever seen, as it kept its edge. I am telling you the gold was hard not soft! The hilt and grip were carved like the body of a swirling snake." He passed his hand through the air again to show how the snake curled around.

"Instead of one edged blade it had two, side by side like snake fangs and its eyes were made of the finest rubies I have ever seen." He sighed. "If they caught the light just right you could almost imagine that the snake was alive, such was the craftsmanship of the piece. It was truly magnificent."

"Where is it?"

"How should I know?" Scrave and Rauph replied together.

They both stopped and stared at each other. The front of Scrave's tunic sliced open before he could even draw a breath. Reflexively he threw himself to one side, falling to the deck, his hands instantly feeling for the severity of the wound, confirming it was just his garment, and luckily, not himself injured. Rauph just stood there looking down at his friend in amazement.

"Scrave stop messing about," he chuckled. "Come on. Get up off the floor."

"Someone's here!" hissed Scrave, his Elven eyes scanning the deck.

"Who is?" asked Rauph, turning swiftly to face the open deck behind them and throwing his huge arms about comically.

"Come on...There's no one here."

Something unseen connected with the Minotaur's arm and fell heavily to the deck with a crunch. There was a flickering in the air, much like a desert mirage and for a second a figure in dark clothes was plain to see sprawled on the floor. Rauph unfortunately failed to notice, intent on walking back over to his fallen colleague with the closest thing to a smile a bovine face could muster.

"Very funny." He giggled holding out his arm to Scrave. "But I don't like magic stuff. So don't do that to me again..."

Scrave lay eyes wide, staring past the Minotaur as the figure that had attacked him slowly regained his feet and with a strange shimmer disappeared from view.

"You've torn your clothes." Rauph remarked.

"No..." Scrave remarked seriously gesturing to the deck behind the Minotaur, "He did." His Elven eyes flickered as they adjusted and began to scan the deck looking for signs of body heat.

"There's nobody there." Rauph whirled around again seeing just an empty deck. "Are you making fun of me?" He asked suspiciously.

Scrave ignored his lumbering companion and watched intently as a glowing humanoid shape defined quite clearly by its own heat began to stalk slowly towards them. It took a wide circular route across the deck, allowing time to assess them and plan an attack.

The Elf's mind raced. They needed to sound an alarm but Scrave also needed to keep up the ruse that he was unable to see the man drawing closer to them.

The nearest alarm bell hung on the deck below, on the wall between the flights of ladders they had been discussing earlier. His eyes stole a quick glance towards the rail that ran between the ladders. He could see the rest of the ship beyond it and knew if he could just get to that rail and reach over; the bell would be within his grasp!

There was a lot of open foredeck between himself and that guardrail!

"Are you fooling me or is someone really here?" Rauph asked, waving his arms about and stepping forwards into Scrave's line of sight.

"Move, you idiot!" Scrave snapped. "He's right behind you!" Rauph swiftly obliged, stepping back to reveal the suddenly stationary warm silhouette of the killer.

As Scrave watched, the figure stalking them turned and then appeared to zero in on the prone Elf, advancing swiftly across the deck, each footfall barely a whisper as the gap closed between them.

"So much for the element of surprise!" Scrave muttered to himself, suddenly realising his error in revealing he could see his approaching assailant. The Elf regained his feet and drew his sword, keeping the blade low and turning side on to give his attacker the smallest area to strike.

The image before him lacked definition and appeared blurred as it moved but Scrave was quick enough to notice the colder colour of a metal dagger that stood out sharply silhouetted against his attacker's body heat. As the dagger was in the person's left hand and down low, he moved his own sword in preparation to parry, only to watch his opponent note this and toss their dagger into their other hand so they could strike from above.

Scrave flicked his wrist, his sword responding with a dexterity and speed that would have left most attackers cold, whipping up the blade to intercept the new attack, only to watch the approaching dagger drop out of sight again and the blurred figure pivot before him. In a flash Scrave recognised his folly and tried to block as the dagger now came in at him at waist height straight at his unguarded abdomen.

With more luck than skill, he managed to jerk his arm down, bringing the hilt of his sword back as the two blades finally met, the force of the blow sending stunning vibrations up into Scrave's sword hand as the assailant's dagger turned aside. He counterattacked instantly, sending out two lightning fast strikes with his sword, first high then low, the steel sparking at each interception and parry from his invisible foe.

Rauph suddenly filled his vision, slamming into their attacker, nostrils flaring as he used scent to locate their foe. The assailant's outline flickered, revealing a man taller than the Elf, dressed in black, long hair loose, insane piercing eyes, as the Minotaur grabbed their adversary around the chest and attempted to crush the air from his frame. The attacker lashed out with blinding speed, smashing his head back several times into Rauph's snout making the Minotaur yelp in pain and release his grip as his hand moved to guard his assaulted nose.

Crimson drops of blood began to well between his fingertips, as their attacker disappeared from view.

"That's it!" Rauph snarled, "Now I'm angry!"

Rauph's sword practically whistled as he drew it, carving the air around him in a futile attempt to hit the invisible target he faced.

Scrave took this opportunity to assist, already knowing where their assailant lay and he moved purposefully to force the glowing figure towards his deadly friend. Unfortunately, it was not as easy as he first thought. Despite numerous feints and slashes, Scrave noticed the figure's skill was incredible!

Red heat trails blurred all around between them as their combatant dodged and lunged, stepping aside and ducking below the lumbering slashes from Rauph and the Elf's own highly accurate stabs and cuts. Despite Scrave's own combat skills, he failed to get a clean hit or inflict a wound, despite coming close several times. Unfortunately, close was not good enough!

Rauph blundered into a particularly vicious attack and suddenly found his left horn yanked down towards the deck as his assailant leapt up to grab him, swinging his whole weight from the horn. The Minotaur bellowed in pain as his head crashed to the deck.

The sound jarred Scrave like hearing fingernails dragged down a slate board. It was so alien to hear the Minotaur in pain. His actions were suddenly galvanised, this had gone on long enough. He watched as the heat signature straightened up over Rauph and prepared to deliver a killing blow. Scrave rapped his sword hard on the decking, grabbing the killer's attention before he could deliver the final thrust and delivered a salute with his blade, making it perfectly clear he was the target his foe needed to concentrate on before launching into a lightning fast series of attacks.

Left, right, across from high to low, followed by a deft lunge. Sparks flew at each parry then finally a grunt of pain from his adversary as Scrave's blade shot high and caught him on the side of the head. The heat signature stepped back and a small drop of crimson life hit the deck.

"Have I got your attention now?" Scrave goaded, noting his friend still lay groaning in pain holding his head on the floor. He needed to keep this person focused on himself to give Rauph time to recover. "Let's fight as we are meant to... one on one."

For the first time in any combat situation the Elf could remember he suddenly realised his bravado was all for show. He tried to swallow but his throat was suddenly parched. He had no doubts of his own skill with a blade and if things were desperate he could use the innate magic in his sword to fight faster but this option had limitations and would not last long.

He needed to see his target clearer and use his bravado to intimidate and build insecurities in his opponent. Fighting a faceless figure was disconcerting, he could not tell what this person was feeling and the way the heat trails blurred it was hard to score a true hit.

In answer, his opponent lunged low, forcing Scrave to jump up and flip backwards out of the way. He landed on the guardrail, arms pin wheeling to maintain his balance as he temporarily found himself on the high ground and the advantage this perspective gave. In a flash he realised the railing was a raised pathway right around the deck to the alarm bell.

His attacker slashed out with the dagger again, causing Scrave to side step. He stamped down as the blade passed, trying to pin the weapon against the rail but his foe was simply too fast. The dagger whipped back again and as Scrave moved he suddenly realised it was another feint and he had stepped exactly where the killer wanted him to be.

The shoulder barge to his legs was unexpected; causing Scrave's feet to shoot from the rail beneath him, out over the sea. His top half fell forwards over his attacker but his reflexes kicked in, using this unexpected momentum to his advantage. He emphasised the fall to lean over and grab his assailant's legs, adding force to the resulting flip and turning his fall into a tumble that snapped his own legs out of where they were held.

He ran full pelt for the alarm bell, acutely aware his foe was close behind and vaulted over Rauph as the Minotaur was getting to his knees, pushing him back down to the deck again.

"Keep him busy!" Scrave screamed, throwing himself into a spectacular slide across the deck, ending with the Elf coming to a stop at the railing situated directly above where the alarm was located. He looked over the salt stained wood and saw the highly polished bell below him. No other crewmember was in sight. Scrave just hoped reinforcements would arrive in time.

Grunting with the effort, he leant over and attempted to stretch across the distance between himself and salvation. Several coloured curses followed as he realised even on tiptoe and teetering off balance his fingers could not quite reach the bell. He threw himself forwards, both feet leaving the security of the deck and was rewarded with the tantalising sensation of his fingers brushing the cold metal but he could not gain sufficient traction.

With another colourful expletive he landed back on his feet, steadied himself then practically attempted to dive over the barrier, one hand outstretched, the other grasped firmly to the guardrail to slow his fall to the mid-deck below. His fingers brushed the edge of the bell then felt the rim edge.

He was going to end this now! He had i...

Something grabbed him around the legs and physically dragged him back over the guardrail, clipping his chin on the rail and leaving the Elf seeing stars. His head bounced violently on the deck leaving Scrave unaware if the bell had rung due to the sound of the vibration travelling through his skull.

The bell gave a gentle low dong and then settled back to silence again. No crewmember of the *El Defensor* reacted to its call. The sound simply was not urgent enough. A dead weight came down on Scrave's chest, pushing the air from his lungs.

"Where is it?" snarled the disembodied voice.

"How should I know?" Scrave gasped. "I'm not your mother and I don't clear up after you!" The Elf realised he needed to regain the advantage swiftly and held up his hand palm up directly in front of the red blur that indicated where his assailant's face was.

"*Komorabi*" he chanted, instigating a simple trick he had learnt when first studying magic. A small gemstone cracked in the setting of his earring, a ball of flame appearing in his palm, before shooting upwards straight into his foes face.

Scrave heard a curse as his attacker turned away from the flame, slapping at the magical light and lifting some weight from the Elf's chest. Scrave gasped in some air and allowed himself a small congratulation at the ruse. The magic was harmless, it did not generate any heat and simply served as a basic illusion to supplement sleight of hand in stage presentations but his assailant did not know that.

His relief was short lived as the weight returned and his attacker plunged his dagger straight at Scrave's head. He threw up both hands to intercept the attack, grabbing his assailant's wrist with his hands, stopping the dagger inches from his face.

With a grunt, the weight of his enemy shifted, inching the dagger closer. Scrave was surprised to see that up close the blade appeared to have two distinct prongs, much akin to the fangs of a snake. A snake! Was this a new fashion? Why did everything have to be like a serpent recently?

He snarled back into his attacker's face, spittle on his lips as he tried to push up against the weight bearing down on him. Oh, where was Rauph when he needed him? He tried to push the wrists to the left or the right, hoping to plunge the blade into the deck and escape but his enemy was resolute and the blade inched ever closer.

Scrave turned his head, exposing his right cheek to the oncoming blade but also giving himself valuable inches of space to work with. His face became flush with the effort, sweat breaking out on his brow. His heart pounded with an expeditious beat as his mind raced and he willed himself to somehow sink through the deck and escape his current predicament.

Something wet dripped from one of the fangs of the blade and landed wetly on his exposed cheek. There was an ominous sizzle, then the stench of burning flesh. Scrave realised with horror that it was his own. He screamed, wriggling vainly to escape, his boots squeaking with the futile attempts he was making to find purchase with the deck as the caustic drip slowly tracked across his diamond tattoo towards his right eye.

Panic threatened to paralyse him, sheer terror to make him lose all control. He tried to kick out again but the pressure from the blade remained constant as it bore down towards his cheek. He needed another spell. Something stronger than a party trick! His mind raced, but gathering his thoughts was hard when faced with the pain from his burning cheek and the imminent danger he faced!

Maybe he could shrink himself? He had done that before. However, he would have to time it right and hope that he could lunge to the side as he decreased in size. He kicked again then mouthed the words through gritted teeth, fighting back the pain as he prepared to move.

Nothing happened.

There was no crackle from either of his gemstone earrings and the deck got no closer. He tried to repeat the words, the muscles in his arms wobbling at the constant pressure being put on them. His mind raced to understand what had gone wrong. Had he mispronounced the words? It was so hard to focus through the pain as his skin continued to smoke.

Then he realised the problem: he had used both of his gemstone earrings! One back in Catterick to extinguish the torches in the temple and the other just now with his illusion. He had no magical energies left to cast his spell! He hadn't replaced the gems since they had left port. He was powerless and out of time.

This was nothing like Scrave's usual sword fights, where he could kill from a distance of an arm's length. This was up close and personal, dirty and terrifying and he was losing!

His boots left another sole mark across the deck as he struggled to gain purchase and flip his attacker away but the Elf was tiring now and his attempt was weaker than his previous ones and equally as futile. Tears of frustration, mixed with an element of resignation welled in his eyes as he mentally debated the morbid thought of letting go, allowing the dagger to plunge home, through his cheek and into his brain, killing him quickly and cleanly.

The dagger's twin blades touched his cheek. He pushed back as hard as he could, physically jumping at the contact and regained a couple of millimetres of dwindling life.

Scrave's tears began to run more freely. He could not speak from the weight on his chest, could not form words, all he could do was mouth a breathless scream. Then the caustic drops finally finished sizzling across his cheek and slid into his eye where the tears had collected and Scrave found a completely new meaning of pain.

The vision in his right eye sizzled to black.

Scrave released his grip on the dagger in shock, his hands reflexively reaching for his injured eye. His mind screamed out his error but it was too late to grab his assailant's wrist again.

All he could do was wait for the blade to slide into his flesh and stop his suffering forever.

Chapter Twenty

Abbot Brialin signed yet another work edict and looked at the pile of manuscripts still awaiting his attention on his worn teak desk. There were reports on the daily running of the monastery. Provisions, planting schedules, orders for seed and tools, stocktaking, repairs... There was always something to repair. Then there was the second pile, reports from monks who kept Brialin appraised of any threats or conflicts that went against his Orders interests.

There was always something to do.

He signed a writ authorising purchase of timber for the front door and this action made him consider how Marcus was getting on. He had not heard from the monk since he had left Catterick and it was nearly a week now. The fire crackled in the hearth behind him throwing comforting warmth onto his cooler worries.

Marcus was naïve in the ways of the outside world and often looked very innocent but like others within the order, he had a darker side. He was perfect for the task of a bearer. He was unquestioning with following orders and was fiercely loyal to the faith.

A knock at the door disturbed the Abbot.

With a shout to enter, Brialin looked up to see the figure of Brother Anthony, an older monk than many in the cloisters, who was tactical in thinking and used his initiative well. The man would never disturb him without reason.

"I have a message that has just come for you." Brother Anthony offered the manuscript and placed it on the desk on top of all of the other paperwork. "It's important." Without prompting, he took a step to the side waiting silently in case the Abbot wished to send a reply.

The message was from Justina. Brialin quickly scanned it and noted it was an update on how Pelune's attempt at recovering his religious artefact was going. So far, the priest had not been successful.

Abbot Brialin smiled to himself, this was better news than he expected. He continued to scan the page, and then stopped short. It appeared The Raven was after the relic and it was currently located on a ship called the *El Defensor* several nautical miles out to sea.

There were two issues to consider here.

Firstly, the name of the ship: The El Defensor. Abbot Brialin bit his bottom lip as he thought. The ship's name was not recognised and the church knew all the ships that came and went into harbour. He would need to find out more about this vessel and the port from which she originated.

Secondly, The Raven. Pelune had to be desperate. Last Brialin had heard The Raven was a shell of a man locked in the dungeons beneath the temple. If he remembered rightly, placed there for betraying his master. If The Raven had returned, he would need to have words with his fellow monks to ensure they double-checked all windows and doors at night to prevent future nocturnal visits.

His eyes continued to scan the report. Justina reported several deaths had already occurred on the ship as The Raven was closing in on the artefact. This was not such good news. Pelune and his pet assassin could not regain their religious icon.

Justina had recognised this and put a contingency plan in place guaranteed to send the ship to the bottom of the sea. Therefore, both threats, The Raven and Pelune's religious icon would trouble him no more. He was impressed with Justina; she was thorough in her work.

He turned to throw the parchment into the flames of the fire, not happy for the brothers to scour such an incriminating document for reuse, as they often did for other parchments. As he turned to do so, his eyes raced along the bottom line of the message and he froze in the act. Even though this was a letter, the hurt tone in the message was unmistakeable.

'Do you doubt my ability to solve this task for you? I cannot understand why you have also sent a St Fraiser monk as a passenger on the ship. I told you I would deal with the problem. I cannot assure his safety when the ship goes down and the icon is destroyed.'

Abbot Brialin sat bolt upright in shock.

Of all that was holy! She could only mean Marcus. What was Marcus doing as a passenger on the same ship as The Raven? He could not possibly be there!

There was another knock on the study door and without asking, Brother Ivan walked in, only to find himself under the intensely wrathful stare of his master. He gulped and stammered his news.

"Atticus Couqran is at the door. He is quite vocal that he needs to see you immediately. He is demanding to know where the *El Defensor* is sailing and believes we know. Apparently, there is a passenger on board he wishes to kill over the matter of a nose. He tells me that you will need to find someone else to escort your *bearer*."

Abbot Brialin almost turned as scarlet as the claret on the desk before him.

Brother Anthony and Brother Ivan instantly found themselves wishing they had any other duty than the one they had that night!

* * * * * *

Scrave's screams of pain wrenched Rauph from his own feelings of wounded distress. He saw his Elven companion lying on the floor apparently fighting with himself and swiftly, for Rauph that is, realised it was an unlikely action for his friend to be doing at this time.

"Don't worry Scrave; I'm coming to save you." He snorted, staggering to his feet and clomping as stealthily as possible for an eight-foot-tall Minotaur, back across the deck towards his screaming, grunting friend. As he got close, he saw the ruin that was Scrave's face and how the diamond tattoo on his right cheek was sinking in as if something was pressing against it. As he looked on, blood started to well from the Elf's cheek. Then Scrave's hands flew up to his eye and his thrashing increased.

Rauph reacted instantly, realising their enemy was on top of his friend, so instead of delivering an overhand strike with his sword that could have resulted in hurting Scrave further, he swung his two handed sword side on to bat Scrave's assailant aside with the flat of his blade. There was a resounding 'thwack' as the sword connected and the weight appeared to lift from Scrave's chest but the Elf did not leap up as Rauph had hoped but instead remained lying on the floor whimpering in pain.

The railing physically splintered as something invisible crashed into it, signifying the resting place of their foe but Rauph was more concerned about his friend.

Scrave started rocking where he lay, his hands clutching his ruined face, guarding the scarred burnt skin and his right eye.

"Not again," the Elf moaned. "Not my face."

"Umm, Scrave," Rauph shook his friend gently. "I think he's coming back!"

Scrave remained inconsolable, writhing and sobbing where he lay on the deck.

"Why doesn't someone sound the alarm Scrave?" Rauph asked. Then he paused considering his own question. That was right! Why didn't someone sound the alarm? In fact, why didn't he sound the alarm himself?

"Stay there," he warned Scrave. "And don't worry, I'll protect you." The Minotaur turned to face back along the length of the ship, making sure he was standing protectively in front of his wounded friend. Satisfied no one could slip past him he reached up and unsheathed his second two-handed sword before settling himself, feet slightly apart with a sword firmly grasped in each hand. No one was going to hurt Scrave again, not if Rauph had anything to do about it!

The Minotaur struggled to put Scrave's cries of pain from his mind, attempting instead to focus on the immediate area before him. He slowly turned his head from side to side taking in his current predicament with a seriousness that was quite out of character for the large hairy creature.

The prow of the ship was now at his back, the rest of the fore deck stretched out before him. The waist-high guardrail running around the edge of the deck now clearly defined his field of battle, with the path to safety taking the form of the two flights of ladders, (or was it stairs?) one to the left and one to the right. At the bottom of those steps, lay reinforcements and much needed medical aid. Rauph calculated the risk of running for it, but there was a lot of smoothed oak deck between himself and the relative safety of those ladders!

Scrave groaned from his place on the floor, swiftly dismissing that idea for the Minotaur. If he were to carry Scrave to the safety of the mid-deck he would face being cut to ribbons before he had taken five paces and there was no way he was going to leave his friend to face this foe alone. That left Rauph only one alternative; he had to stand and fight, defending his friend from the invisible threat until reinforcements arrived.

Rauph swallowed hard, his throat suddenly dry. Bovine nostrils flared and sensitive ears twitched as the Minotaur attempted to catch every amplified and possibly portentous sound. A chill wind blew across the deck, making the rigging creak and groan from high above. Small waves lapped gently against the aged wooden hull of the ship, the white crests pushed to certain destruction by the sudden breeze.

Rich chestnut brown hair rippled as nature passed cool, reassuring fingers across the Minotaur's brow. All Rauph had to do was sound the alarm and keep his friend safe until that help arrived.

He risked a quick concerned look back at his friend. Scrave lay curled in a bloodied mess, his body shivering despite the warmth of the tepid night. His mumbling had changed now but it was repetitive and scared Rauph.

"I can't see... I can't see..."

"Where is it!" the now familiar disembodied voice screamed.

Rauph spun towards the sound, his two swords flying together in a blur, the lengths of gleaming steel forming a defensive cross by instinct. Sparks showered from his sword edge as his weapon connected with unseen metal. The twin blades that began to move almost akin to a physical extension of Rauph's mighty frame, his actions with the swords based on instinctive reactions the likes of which no man could ever hope to duplicate.

As his ears detected a slight movement of air to the left, his sensitive nostrils flared to confirm that his attacker had moved to the side and one of the Minotaur's two-handed blades swept through the space, sparks flying as it connected yet again.

Rauph paused, nostrils flaring as he tried to sense his assailant's location again. A raw strength born from the combined emotions of anger and fear began to send adrenaline coursing through his body, the nervous burst of energy making him quiver.

Where was his foe now?

The chill touch of an unseen dagger made Rauph yelp in pain, his skin parting on his forearm at its cold caress. He lashed out in fear, his two blades sweeping both high and low. There was a gasp of pain and his left blade came away dripping red.

Rauph lifted the sword up to his face, sniffing at the crimson smear to confirm his strike. The reddish glint reflected back into the Minotaur's eye turning his normally gentle expression into something almost demonic in nature.

A small drop of scarlet suddenly appeared on the deck, slightly to the right of the Minotaur's current position. Rauph calmly noted the position of the drops but made sure his head did not move to give away this new advantage. Another drop followed the crimson marker, this time slightly over to the left.

The Minotaur took the initiative, lunging towards the spot where he believed the next drop would fall. His blades flashed through the air repeatedly, sparks raining upon the deck as the unseen fighter successfully parried his attacks.

Rauph piled on the pressure, stepping in towards his unseen attacker at each cut and sweep of his blades, pushing his foe backwards and away from Scrave's vulnerable form. The sword thrusts began to merge into one continuous blur as he reacted faster and faster, sweat starting to appear as patches of white froth across his hairy coat. The Minotaur had never fought like this in his life before. It was an attack that he dared not let up on for an instant, for failure meant his attacker could slip past him and if he allowed that Scrave could get hurt again.

His breath started to gasp from between his lips but Rauph refused to back down, pushing his unseen assailant gradually across the fore deck until the combatants arrived at the top of the left-hand ladder. Incredibly Rauph managed to keep his two swords slashing through the air before him, maintaining the punishing pace and the astonishing rate of attacks by adrenaline rush alone but it was unmistakable to the Minotaur that he was beginning to tire. His breath was coming in gulps now and his wounds were bleeding afresh, he was obviously more drained than he had realised!

Sherman chose this moment to come out onto the mid-deck from below, customary hat and feather bobbing. He took one look at Rauph fighting with apparently thin air and shouted up to him.

"Rauph! What in the world are you doing?"

The Minotaur hesitated in mid-swing and the momentary distraction cost him dearly. The air moved before him and something cold and unforgiving slid upwards into his chest. The Minotaur bellowed with pain his swords dropping from spasm-wracked hands. He crashed to his knees gasping as the hilt of a dagger slowly began to materialise in the centre of his thick leather armour.

An evil laugh hung mocking in the air.

Sherman ran up the ladder towards the Minotaur as Rauph threw a mighty punch in open defiance of the wound he had received. There was an audible smack and then something fell away over the rail running up the side of the ladder to smash into the alarm. The bell peeled out, loud and clear. Whatever hit it fell to the deck below and there was an explosive crack followed by a haunted scream of pain.

Sherman reached the top of the ladder only to find Rauph's eyes glazing over and rolling back into his head as the huge creature started to fall in his direction. Before the sailor could react, Rauph crashed down the ladder and into the sailor's outstretched arms.

"I've got you," Sherman gasped as Rauph's huge weight initially flopped down on top of him. "...Then again I could be mistaken." There was a yelp from Sherman then both sailor and Minotaur tumbled down the ladder in a flailing pile of arms and legs.

The first mate landed hard, swiftly followed by the bulk of Rauph who collapsed on top of him in an undignified crumpled heap. If anyone had been around to observe the finale of the fall they would have remarked at how interesting it was that even under the crush of the unconscious Minotaur, Sherman's hat remained firmly on his head.

* * * * * *

"So what does this do?" Ashe quizzed, holding up an elaborate tool with wires, hooks and long probing bits sticking out all over it. He stood impatiently before a scarred worktop in the engineer's lab, his eyes gleaming with barely contained excitement as he took in the towering construction of hissing and whooshing glassware before him. When no answer was forthcoming, he repeated his query.

The target for Ashe's questions paused in his work, his brow furling with the irritation of being disturbed for the twentieth time in the last five minutes. He wandered along the far side of the workbench until he found a relatively uncluttered section between the spiralling tubes of glass and stared through at the inquisitive Halfling wondering what item Ashe had found to fiddle with now.

Commagin pushed aside his bushy white beard and fumbled in his shirt pocket before withdrawing a pair of bent spectacles. He perched the thick lenses on the end of his bulbous red veined nose and adjusted them in vain as he tried to bring his interrogator and the tool he held into bleary focus. It never failed! Why did people always interrupt him just when things were going so well!

"Let me see that." He muttered impatiently; his smeared glasses unable to make out what the Halfling held. Ashe moved closer to the workbench and responded to the Dwarf's gesturing by standing on tiptoe to bring the tool level with the engineer's bulbous nose.

"Ah!" Commagin sighed after several long moments. "I wondered where that one had got to."

The Dwarf chuckled then returned to his work, forgetting the question as he turned a small tap and slowly filling a thin glass tube with a clear amber liquid. He allowed himself the luxury of a sniff and shook his head as his eyes watered from the concentrated vapour.

Oh, this was going to be the best batch yet!

"But what does it do?" Ashe interrupted, tapping his foot with clear impatience.

"What does what do?" Commagin reluctantly raised his head from the swirling amber liquid and squinted at the little figure before him with barely disguised contempt. "Are you still here?" Ashe's hurt look stopped the dwarf in his tracks.

"Oh hang on a moment!" he snapped in frustration, lowering his glass tube with almost saintly reverence into a holder before disappearing from view. There was a loud 'thump' as he jumped down from the bench he was standing on, followed by several loud exclamations as he crashed heavily to the floor. Brief glimpses of white whispery hair indicated the engineer's progress as his head bobbed up and down behind the tubes and beakers as he made his way around.

Ashe found himself distracted; the Dwarf's progress forgotten as he followed a drop of amber liquid racing along the thin lengths of glass spirals at one end of the worktop only to drop unceremoniously into a large glass reservoir at the other. This room was great!

Commagin uttered a few muffled curses as he tripped over a pile of unseen scientific debris that leapt out and ambushed him as he made his way around the workbench. He struggled to catch himself, his outstretched arm catching a teetering pile of parchment, only to observe its metamorphosis into a paper waterfall that instantly drowned the partially sighted Dwarven engineer in a deluge of long forgotten scientific formulae. Finally, with much spluttering and cursing, the Dwarf completed his hazardous journey and arrived to stand before the chuckling Halfling who was following yet another amber drop complete its assault course on the way to join its colleagues in the beaker below.

The engineer held out a thickly callused hand and gestured for the tool. Ashe looked reluctantly at the delicate item, then shrugged and returned it to the engineer's care. As the Dwarf began to launch into a tiresome explanation of the recently re-claimed tool, Ashe found his eyes wandering and he instinctively began to filter out the drone of the technical lecture, replacing it with the fascinating visual stimuli of the lab around him. The Halfling had been in some places in his time but he had never seen such a 'mish-mash' of unusual items in one room before!

Coils of copper wire shared boxes with gleaming metal sheets; multi-coloured wooden blocks negotiated space with nails, screws, paper and string. Lengths of twisting twine wrapped about an intricate gilded birdcage (minus bird), whilst brown bottles (actually there were rather a lot of bottles!) jostled with boxes, bags and tools of all description, size, shape and form. Moreover, this was just the stuff on the floor!

Bookshelves lined the walls, groaning under the weight of mechanical models, thick dusty engineering manuals, pots of strange smelling solutions and the odd forgotten long mouldy sandwich. Ashe just did not know where to look next unless he missed something!

A gleam of white caught his roving eye and he set off across the lab to investigate, stepping over large interesting piles of debris that he briefly catalogued in his mind's eye on the promise that he would examine them more closely on his return. Commagin droned on behind him, explaining how the tool improved torque, oblivious to his now wandering audience.

The flash of white turned out to be a suit of padded armour, the likes of which Ashe had never seen before. The arms and legs were thickly padded and adorned with multi-coloured patches that displayed stars and a weird yellow triangular shape in a circle. As Ashe got closer, he was delighted to notice that a pair of thick chunky boots accompanied the suit; well actually, now he looked closer, they appeared attached to the suit.

The Halfling reached out to touch the armour and squeezed the white surface astonished to find he was holding a pliable material. It was not metal! This was a bizarre suit of armour! He looked up at the helmet and could not help but laugh. It was no wonder that these suits had never caught on. The helmet fascia was some kind of tinted glass. A good swing from a sword would smash it to pieces in seconds! He went to move away then noticed some strange writing on the suit. The armour was personalised. Who was the knight who owned this suit?

N... A... S...

"What are you doing?" Commagin demanded, dragging Ashe bodily away from the suit. "You mustn't touch anything in here!"

"Why?" Ashe asked in open-eyed innocence.

"Things around here tend to explode if not treated properly." Commagin flushed slightly in embarrassment.

"Wow!" This place was becoming more Halfling friendly by the second!

Commagin recognised the mischievous glint in Ashe's eye and hurriedly guided the little thief back to the workbench where amber liquid continued to race through the glass labyrinth assembled upon its surface.

"What is this stuff?" Ashe asked, slightly annoyed at his exploration ending prematurely but determined to make the most of the situation.

"It's a fine malted wh... paint remover." Commagin coughed, recovering quickly at his verbal slip. He nervously stroked the side of his nose with the returned tool he still held, trying to act as if nothing was wrong whilst watching the Halfling carefully from the corner of his eye.

Ashe seemed unaware of the slip up; his eyes already off on another visual safari of the room around him.

"Now over here," the engineer continued, deciding to act confident and bluff his way along. "We have..." The Dwarf turned to move towards the safer end of the laboratory, hoping the Halfling would follow him. Ancient eyes smeared with the milky white of cataracts, searched for something Ashe could do that would not cause Commagin's angina to start up again.

"...Paint stripper, huh?" Commagin slowly turned around expecting to face another inquisition only to find Ashe was up on his bench, twiddling with taps and flicking the glass tubes to make the liquid move faster.

"Don't touch!" the Dwarf screamed, running around the back of the bench and slipping on the loose sheets of parchment he had toppled all over the floor. Ashe looked at the Dwarf wide-eyed as Commagin ploughed uncontrollably into the side of the worktop and ended up flat on his back.

"This is a great invention." Ashe offered, hoping that by showering praise he would not face summary eviction from the room. "We don't have paint stripper where I come from. We simply paint over the top or scour the walls to get the old paint off first. An invention like this is simply wonderful."

Commagin pulled himself to his feet using the workbench for support, his mind initially intent on slaughtering the Halfling but hearing Ashe's comment he paused. Was that a compliment? His chest began to swell with pride.

"It's more wonderful than you can possibly know." He flushed, patting the hip flask at his belt.

Ashe suddenly leaned forwards and stared at the dwarf hard and then he began to laugh.

"What?" Commagin demanded, angry that his praise had so swiftly turned to ridicule.

"Your nose." Ashe chuckled. "The tool's stuck up your nose!"

The dwarf brought his hand swiftly up to his nose and confirmed the Halfling's observation. Somehow, during the fall, the tool had managed to lodge firmly up his left nostril. He tugged hard, bringing tears instantly to his eyes but the tool stubbornly held fast.

Ashe observed the unfolding scenario for a few moments before jumping at the chance to help. He dropped lightly from the bench and firmly grasping the tool handle, jerked the tool viciously to the left and the right and then did it again for good measure.

Commagin grabbed Ashe's little hands in panic, trying to stop the blinding pain the Halfling was causing but Ashe misinterpreted this action and simply tugged all the harder. Red throbbing blood vessels started to stand out in sharp contrast to the engineer's pale, sweaty forehead but other than that, the tool showed no visible signs of movement.

"I think it's really wrapped up in your bushy nasal hairs." Ashe added unhelpfully. "They sure are dense up there." He wrenched the tool backwards and forwards one more time then paused. This clearly was not working!

The Dwarven engineer held his head in relief, vainly trying to fight back the throbbing headache that was swiftly growing between his eyes. Ashe stepped back and rested his hand under his chin in an attempt to look deep in thought. His left foot began to tap in frustration.

"Hum!" he mumbled. "What would Kerian do in a situation like this?" After a momentary pause, he clicked his fingers. "I know, he'd draw his trusty sword, beat up a few people, throw the damsel over his left shoulder and then eat, drink and be merry."

Commagin's eyes widened in concern at the thought of assault and then finding himself thrown over the Halfling's left shoulder but Ashe shook his head, swiftly discounting the 'hero' approach, returning instead to tugging at the tool, much to Commagin's continued distress.

The door to the laboratory swung open and Barney, the engineer's Gnomish apprentice ambled his way inside. In his arms, he held a large box from which trailed yards and yards of canvas piping. The piping looked patched, secured all over with small pink pieces of material and looked as if it had seen better days. Barney waved as he passed the two struggling figures and placed the box near the large white suit of armour Ashe had examined earlier.

The Gnome turned from his task and smiled, ready and eager to accept the next chore his master would no doubt have in mind. It seemed that Commagin always had jobs for Barney to do. He took in the struggling of the two other occupants of the room and very slowly his keen apprentice mind began to realise something was not quite right. He wandered over to have a closer look.

"Why have you got that tool hanging from your nose?" he queried, his voice carefully measured to avoid insulting his master.

"Its duk ub by dose, you idiot." Commagin replied, swinging Ashe off his feet as he moved his head to answer. Barney's tools clanked loudly as he positioned himself to gaze thoughtfully up the Dwarf's nostril.

"Umm!" He remarked, in the tone that all workers strive to perfect during their apprenticeships. "Oh dear..." he continued, followed at exactly the right moments by several expensive sounding 'tuts'. Commagin strained to see what his apprentice was doing. Barney appeared to be rummaging through his brown leather apron, pulling out spanners and pairs of pliers, staring at them hard, shaking his head and then putting them away again.

'That is it lad,' he thought, 'even if you haven't got a clue always look like you know what you are doing.' By golly, he had taught this lad well!

There was a striking noise and a 'whoosh' followed swiftly by the unmistakable smell of singed hair. A high piercing scream of pain swiftly followed as the tool fell to the floor. Commagin hopped around the cabin, his hands clutched to his still smoking nose. Barney ignored his master's discomfort and blew out the lit candle he was now holding with a practised 'puff'. He efficiently dropped the extinguished candle back into his bottomless apron pocket. Ashe meanwhile had moved to stand by the door trying to stifle his giggles but he set off again when he saw that Commagin's nostril hair was visibly vacant and smoking where the tool had come away.

Barney returned his attention to his pouch, bringing out a dog-eared pad. He reached behind one of his ears and retrieved a small piece of lead, examining the end with a critical eye. Then after licking the end and leaving his tongue slightly protruding, he began to make out a bill for his services.

Commagin paused in his agonising hopping and watched as Barney struggled to sign his signature. By golly, the Dwarf reiterated to himself, he had taught this lad well! Loud shouts and cries suddenly sounded outside the cabin door, snapping the engineer back to his senses. He swiftly walked to the open door and listened intently.

"Someone's sounding the alarm," he muttered to himself. The Dwarf paused for the briefest of moments then turned to his colleagues.

"We appear to be required on deck," he stated, walking with purpose towards one of the groaning shelves behind his workbench. "I think we might need the services of the '*Lady Janet*'." Commagin reached up and lifted down a roll of cloth, blowing a fine film of dust from its surface and patting it with affection.

Ashe watched in confusion as Commagin tucked the roll of material under his arm and walked out through the door. Who exactly was this Lady Janet? He had not seen anyone from the aristocracy present amongst the crew. His little mind suddenly conjured up an image of a lady in waiting, holding off diabolical threats with her embroidery cross-stitch needle!

Now this was something he could not miss!

Chapter Twenty-One

Initially there was nothing but blinding pain. The suffocating fog of magical enchantment shredded like a sharp blade through fine silk, freeing the man's conscious thought and awareness in a heartbeat. His first thought was for his ankle. It felt like it was on fire! The Raven reached out instinctively to examine his limb then paused in horror. He could not even see his hand let alone the severity of the wound! He reached out again with gently exploring and probing fingers then winced when he felt the unmistakable wetness of blood and the odd angle his ankle now lay. He groaned in momentary despair, his ankle was broken! How in the seven hells did that happen? He staggered to pull himself back to his feet and barely managed to stifle a cry as searing agony coursed up his leg.

It took several moments before he caught his breath and only then, balanced on one foot and acutely aware of the dragging sensation where his ruined foot hung useless beneath him, did he try to take a tentative step forwards. Fresh pain assailed him as his fracture grated in protest. He tried to shift the balance more firmly onto his good leg but the ruined foot still crunched stubbornly beneath him. A small puddle of fresh blood began to ooze across the deck at his feet.

The deck! He was on a ship! The last he could remember was the temple in Catterick!

Raised voices shouting in anger forcing him to take in his surroundings. Members of the ship's crew were cautiously advancing towards his position swords drawn and fury clearly visible on their faces. Behind them, slumped at the bottom of a flight of steps was a huge chestnut coloured creature with the biggest horns he had ever seen. More incredibly, there appeared to be a conflict in the biological makeup of the creature as there was definitely a human arm sticking out from beneath it.

'Did I do that?' he questioned, his mind racing at high speed to try to piece together the jigsaw puzzle around him. What exactly was going on? The mocking face of Pelune returned vividly to his mind. He had been under some kind of enchantment. It all suddenly flooded back like some warped and twisted nightmare from which there had been no awakening. He lifted a hand reflexively to his head and felt the unmistakable shape of the serpent headpiece; its scale covered exterior still warm to the touch and horrifically pulsating as if still breathing.

What had they done to him? Moreover, what had he done to these people?

His vision suddenly began to grow indistinct and blur as the dark shadows of enchantment began creeping forwards to take control once more. The Raven gritted his teeth, realising instantly what assailed him, smashing his foot back down onto the deck as hard as he could. The spasms of excruciating pain that lanced up his leg threatened to make the assassin black out but also refreshingly cleansed his mind and vision of the tendrils of dark magic.

He did not know what was going on and he had no idea as to the intricacies of the spells that Pelune and his witch had placed upon him but he was damned if he would be killed without being in control of his own body!

His eyes returned to the assembled crewmen advancing across the deck towards him, their hands shuffling nervously, weapons still at their sides as if they were unsure what they faced. Despite this, they began to organise themselves, clearly well trained, forming a roughly circular pattern with the Raven at the epicentre of their gathering.

A sharp exclamation to his left made the assassin note the reaction of two crewmen who were gesturing to their companions and pointing to the deck at his feet. He looked down and noted the tell-tale spots of blood that were dripping onto the sanded timbers. He realised his precarious predicament in seconds. Although they could not see him, they almost certainly knew where he was!

He reached for his dagger, normally sheathed at his belt and came up empty. It was a strange disembodied feeling of panic that swept through him, made more so by the fact that a visual inspection of where the weapon should be turned up nothing but empty air!

This was getting worse by the second. A broken ankle, no weapon and no way of knowing what he had been doing aboard this vessel.

He noticed the grim visages of the closing crew members and decided that he had solved at least this part of the enigma. By the looks of these newfound admirers, he realised that whatever he had been up to it could not have been much good!

His first concern was to get a replacement weapon. Whatever the cost!

He quickly scanned the tightening noose of men about him, his eyes locating each of the weapons they carried and discarding the possibility of their use in seconds because of either the owner, the position of the weapon, or the ease of getting to them. His calculating gaze came to rest upon three men who all dressed similarly, their appearance much akin to the carnival performers that used to frequent the night-time markets of Catterick.

One of the men looked less sure than his colleagues, his eyes darting nervously about and his hand flexing repeatedly on the hilt of his sword. This man was uncomfortable with the thought of killing. He would hesitate to land that final blow and was the obvious weakness in the circle.

The Raven smiled for he had no such compunctions about ending someone's life. At the man's belt was a sheathed dagger. The Raven chose this weapon to take.

Taking a deep breath and gritting his teeth anew, he moved silently forwards towards his target, slipping between the man and his similarly dressed associate like a wraith, the slight waft of air the only clue to mark his passing. The pain in the Raven's ankle was intense but he ensured that the wounded limb touched the deck for the barest of moments therefore leaving only the slightest of traces of blood, easily missed in the shadows moving across the deck.

Now free of the tightening circle, he circled behind the blissfully unaware sailor and set himself, mentally preparing for the killing that was about to come. In one fluid and graceful move, his left hand slipped below the sailor's corresponding arm to slip the dagger free from its scabbard. Instead of risking the blade catching the oblivious sailor's arm he instead chose to flip the blade up into the air before the astonished man's eyes.

His left arm continued to rise even as the blade left his hand, pushing up the sailor's arm as he pulled the man into a cold-blooded embrace from which there was to be no escape. The sailor's chin raised with the motion, cutting off his shout of alarm, whilst permitting the bizarre experience of watching his own dagger fall back towards the deck and halt in mid-air, caught by The Raven's invisible right hand. The assassin slid the blade surgically across the sailor's now clearly exposed and taut windpipe without hesitation.

"Thank you." He whispered coldly, as arterial blood sprayed across the deck.

The Raven allowed himself no remorse as the sailor's body dropped, spasmodic twitches racing throughout the man's crumpled frame as his fellow crew stepped away in horror. This was what The Raven excelled at, causing chaos and despair and it was here in this role that he felt most at home. Let these fools try to catch him if they could.

The dagger slowly disappeared as the enchantment of the circlet moved to obscure it from the visible world and The Raven wasted no time, acting on the stunned reaction of the crew to sow further discord. He lashed out to the right and the left with sickening speed and accuracy, one man's face erupting in a spray of crimson whilst another sank to the deck clutching a deep slash to his chest. It would take valuable time to follow his trail now, with all the fresh blood spilt across the deck, so he would use this opportunity to make his escape!

Chaos erupted all about as screams of hatred; cries of horror and wails of ultimate loss filled the air. The three crewmen were no longer a concern, surgically excised from the fight with the speed and cold efficiency of a fishmonger filleting a fish. Even as the other crew members began to lash out blindly with their weapons, jumping and slashing at shadows, The Raven was moving once again, struggling to put as much distance between himself and the collapsing circle as was possible. He ended up with his back against the main mast, his body gasping unaccustomedly for breath and his vision edged with a red haze from the pain of walking on his shattered ankle.

He took this opportunity to turn and observe the chaos he had spawned. Several of the sailors were still blindly slashing the air about them in an attempt to locate their unseen foe and avenge their fallen colleagues but other more battle-hardened members of the group chose to stand still and scan the decks looking for the crimson trail they had witnessed earlier. In another time and place, The Raven would have found this display of ingenuity entertaining and almost certainly a challenge to his skills but for now he had several more important issues to consider.

Having armed himself he needed to find a way to get off the ship. There was a lifeboat in the centre of the deck. If he could get to that and somehow get it overboard, he would have a chance at rowing to shore.

Crew were now spilling onto the mid-deck from all directions. The assassin prepared to move, determined to put as much space as possible between himself and the enraged crewmen when a sound from above froze him in his tracks. He looked up to observe a sailor swinging across the ship on a line that carried him from the aft castle down onto the mid-deck in mere seconds compared to the time it was taking his colleagues to make the same journey on foot. The sailor let go of the rope and dropped lightly to the floor ready to rush forwards and join his colleagues, cutting off the assassin's path to the boat.

When the sailor regained his feet, The Raven and his unforgiving blade were waiting.

* * * * * *

Commagin marched up onto the mid-deck, with his two small companions behind him and entered a scene of utter carnage. People lay wounded and dying all around him. Even as he took in the scene, a sailor charged across the ship in front of him, shouting to his colleagues as he moved to defend another man who was holding his head after a scalp wound. The Dwarf stared grimly, noting another sailor who had just dropped from the rigging and was now up on his toes, stab wounds appearing across his chest, inflicted by nothing but thin air! Blood sprayed across the painted white hull of the lifeboat in the middle of the deck, leaving the engineer in no doubt the crew needed his services.

More crew surged forwards, pursuing crimson trails across the deck, swinging their blades left and right in the hope of hitting their target. Whatever they chased had been heading towards the lifeboat but now seemed to be heading away again. There was too much noise out here to think carefully. The lifeboat seemed a logical base to work.

"That will do for me." He mumbled to himself walking over to the deserted vessel with his roll of material firmly tucked under one arm. Ashe and Barney staggered after the Dwarf, the two diminutive figures dragging a large canvas sack between them. The bulk of the item was such that they barely managed to clear the deck as they struggled to keep up.

"What's in this thing?" Ashe gasped, his little legs straining to carry the weight of the object. Barney looked across the wobbling sack and shouted a reply drowned out by the chaotic sounds of battle about them.

"An indie-red what?" Ashe shouted back expecting some form of confirmation and explanation from the Gnome.

"That's right." Barney shouted back, leaving Ashe no clearer of the subject matter in question. The Gnome gritted his teeth and attempted to pick up speed, almost dragging the poor Halfling along behind him as they headed unerringly towards the lifeboat and the Dwarven engineer.

Barney suddenly dropped the sack with a gasp, causing Ashe to crash to the deck as all the weight of the item transferred to him. As the Halfling struggled to get to his feet, the world around him suddenly went black, leaving him with no clue as to what had just happened or more importantly, where he now was. It was Ashe's turn to gasp as a small flame suddenly flickered to life before him revealing that the three diminutive associates were now under the upturned lifeboat.

The engineer and apprentice launched into action, squatting on the deck as they utilised one of the upturned seats as a crude worktop. As Ashe watched, Barney removed yet another wax candle from his apron pocket and lit it from the one in Commagin's hand, placing the candle on the 'table' in a manner as calm as if they did this sort of thing every day. Ashe was not sure if this was a display of total sincere confidence or that his friends had slid down the slippery slope to shrieking insanity and he hoped he would not have to find out anytime soon.

The Halfling shuffled over to get a closer look as Commagin set his glasses firmly on the bridge of his nose and settled down to work. The Dwarf unrolled the material he had been carrying with great reverence to reveal several disassembled pieces of a gleaming crossbow.

The stock appeared cast from solid silver, painstakingly engraved in the most delicate and breath-taking design Ashe had ever seen. The hunt displayed so vividly before him detailed flowers, trees, prancing stags and huntsmen all engaged in their deadly game of 'hunter and prey'. Clearly engraved on one side of the stock glittered the words '*Lady Janet*'.

Ignoring the gasps of delight that filled the underside of the lifeboat Commagin began to set to work, slowly snapping the pieces of the weapon together as the candlelight reflected from the surface of his glasses.

* * * * * *

The Raven struck; plunging his dagger into an unguarded back and twisting the blade through the unfortunate sailor's still beating heart, ribs snapping as the width of the blade forced the bones reluctantly apart.

The Raven cursed as the corpse fell lifeless to the deck at his feet. This was insane! He was moving further and further away from the lifeboat. Why couldn't they have just let him get the boat overboard? Now he had to find some other way of getting off the ship and there were crew pouring from every available hole on this god-forsaken deck! It was like watching rats trying to escape a sinking ship but instead of escaping they were hunting and he was the prey.

He shuffled painfully along the deck, finding himself heading towards the stern of the ship. Perhaps he would find another lifeboat there, one a little less exposed and then he would be able to cast off from this ship, make his way back to Catterick and the sweet revenge awaiting him there. If escape was not possible or indeed practical, then maybe he could find somewhere to hide; a place of sanctuary to rest and recuperate in until all this chaos had abated: that was if people did not keep getting in his way!

A trapdoor swung upwards at his feet revealing yet another handful of idiotic sailors. They were like all the others he had slain so far, mindless lambs heading obliviously for slaughter. The Raven stepped smartly to one side, noting how many people were below and swiftly finalised a plan as the first sailor ran up the ladder, eyes wide with the excitement of going into battle.

The Raven noted the elaborately jewelled fencing foil sheathed at the young lad's hip and simply reached out as the youth ran past, drawing the blade from its scabbard with such speed and precision that the surprised young sailor found himself spun around by the force of the action.

The man initially believed he had caught his sword belt on an unguarded nail but when he realised his sword was missing from its scabbard he returned to the top of the ladder, effectively halting the passage of his colleagues from below.

"Oh come on!" he exclaimed, looking back down the hatch at his associates. "Give me back my sword!"

"You must mean this one?" The Raven stated at his ear, sliding the now invisible blade through the centre of the sailor's back and lifting him up on tip toe as a rose of blood suddenly blossomed from the centre of his chest.

The Raven pushed the impaled sailor back down onto his now screaming shipmates, kicking the trapdoor shut, temporarily blocking off any pursuit from below as the sailors tried to help the critically wounded youth who had fallen on them. The assassin turned his attention back towards the stern of the ship, his ruined ankle trailing painfully behind him, smearing yet another drop of blood across the deck to mark his trail.

* * * * * *

"But why Styx?" Thomas enquired, taking another sip of the amber liquid in his glass.

"I suppose because of the association the name has with death," Kerian replied. "When you encounter Styx death is not far behind... or something like that."

"If you wanted to be associated with death, why not change your first name to Carrion?" Thomas laughed, drawing a stony scowl from the elderly fighter seated before him.

"It was a joke." He offered, holding his hands up to reassure Kerian that he intended no insult. "But seriously, have you realised that your pseudonym is actually an accurate description of your turbulent life. You have named yourself after a fabled river from my world that flows into the realms of the dead and at your age you are travelling that river ever faster, to a destination from which no man has ever returned."

Kerian looked across at Thomas and debated internally whether he should tell the captain just how accurate his insight had been. Thomas was a lot closer to the truth than he could ever realise. Kerian was indeed racing on towards death due to his accelerated ageing and yet it was ironic that he himself had never made this logical leap regarding his namesake. It sent shivers up his spine at the very thought of the subconscious label he had adopted.

"There is something that I need... no... have to tell yo..." he began.

Thomas Adams suddenly lifted his hand stopping Kerian in mid-confession He sat listening to something beyond the silence of the cabin then stood up sharply his chair sliding back from his desk.

"What's all that noise?" he muttered, pushing open one window in the wall behind him and putting his head on one side. Thomas stiffened, then strode swiftly past Kerian's seat and out through the cabin door. Their conversation appeared to be over.

Kerian watched the captain leave in astonishment. Here he was trying to explain his actions to the man, all be it not entirely truthful in content and Thomas had simply stood up and left him. He shrugged to himself; maybe the captain of the *El Defensor* had realised just how many holes his story had held within its elaborate retelling. It was a fact that to be a good liar you had to have a good memory and Kerian had to admit he was not entirely sure that all his 'edits and amendments' were entirely consistent with the overall fictitious plot he had described.

"And what was that about a noise?" He asked aloud, oblivious to the fact that he no longer had an audience. He cocked his head to listen. There was not any noise! Could it be his hearing was beginning to fail him? He listened again but all he could hear was an annoying background buzz.

Kerian slowly got to his feet admitting the fact that his audience with the captain was obviously at an end. He sauntered towards the door of the cabin, taking his time to pause and examine the models of the ships within the glass cases as he passed. A noise! Now that was an original way to end an annoying conversation. He wondered if it would work with Ashe?

Lying forgotten on the desk behind him, the golden serpent dagger winked ominously in the lantern light.

* * * * * *

The aft castle was much closer now but The Raven reluctantly found himself having to admit to the fact that he was rapidly beginning to tire. He cursed in renewed frustration at the length of time it was taking him to cross such a ludicrously short distance of vessel and winced anew as his ruined ankle grazed the wooden surface below him. He could not continue for much longer and he desperately needed a place to rest and gather his thoughts.

The deck was crawling with sailors now; they rushed out from access hatches all over the deck only to end up jumping at the shadows flickering across the deck as torches milled about. Sailors slashed out, causing more risk to themselves and fellow crewmembers than to the invisible assassin. However, there was an increasingly slim chance that one of them could run into him in their enthusiasm, and land a 'lucky' hit. In The Raven's weakening state, he realised that it was simply too dangerous to continue his travels upon the deck. The only option was to find a vacant cabin or darkened corner somewhere below decks where he could hole up for a while.

He changed his direction of travel aiming for the single doorway that led to the cabins directly below the aft castle. There was bound to be an empty room somewhere under there, then with luck he would be able to find something to bind up his ankle and allow himself a much-needed opportunity to catch his breath.

The door suddenly swung open before him, framing the silhouette of a concerned man attired in a dark blue shirt and leather waistcoat. Faded brown trousers disappeared into tan leather boots polished to a high sheen and from his waist hung a well-used cutlass. The man's hair was dark brown, his eyes a sparkling green and his face went from an expression of confusion to a look of horror as he took in the vision of carnage that littered the deck before him. Pain visibly swept across his face as he visually identified each fallen crewmember and The Raven realised instantly from the reactions displayed, that this could only be the ship's captain.

The captain's eyes dropped suddenly to the deck and his face went from a look of horror to a picture of bewilderment in a heartbeat.

The Raven glanced down and cursed under his breath. A scarlet smear marked the outline of his boot upon the decking and a quick glance over his shoulder confirmed that a track of similar red smears clearly telegraphed his movements straight across the main deck to his current location.

He cursed again; realising instantly that the blood loss from his ankle was worsening and that if one man could easily spot his trail others would swiftly follow. His imminent discovery was now only a matter of time. As he watched another crimson drop splashed down to join with the rest of the incriminating evidence pooling there.

Shouts arose from amid decks confirming The Raven's worst fears; someone else had now spotted his trail. This scenario was all going so terribly wrong. He risked a quick glance behind and observed the reaction of the crew.

Sailors were pointing and bringing torches, they would be on him in a matter of minutes and with the trail of carnage he had left in his wake, they would not be too fussy about taking prisoners!

He glanced back towards the captain and gritted his teeth anew, a fresh surge of adrenaline temporarily numbing the pain as he began to slide across the deck in the man's general direction. Escape was now out of the question. What he needed now was a hostage and what better hostage to take than the very man no crewmember would wish to see come to harm.

Chapter Twenty-Two

"Don't move." A voice hissed next to the captain's ear. Thomas reflexively started to raise his hands and pull away from the sound, his head turning in the direction of the spoken order. "I said don't move!" Something slammed into the side of his temple bringing stars to Thomas's eyes.

"Okay!" He affirmed, his voice responding automatically to ingrained training, dropping both in pitch and slowing to sound less threatening to his unseen captor. "Who are you and what do you want?" In answer, the air appeared to shimmer inches before his eyes and then the captain felt the unmistakable cold edge of sharpened steel at his throat.

"Don't say anything!" the voice snapped. "And start backing up real slow."

"I wasn't very good with small talk anyway." Thomas quipped and instantly regretted it as the cold steel pinched uncomfortably across his throat. His right hand twitched in response to his mind's contemplation regarding the possibility of his reaching for his cutlass. He mentally tallied up the risk and decided that it was next to suicidal to contemplate the move. His throat would end up slit from ear to ear before he could even half draw his weapon from his belt.

The ever-present pressure of the blade edge at his throat momentarily lessened as if his captor were also considering the possibility that Thomas would carry out this brash move but then it returned confirming to Thomas that the threat he represented had been considered less than worthy of consideration.

That was fine; he did not want to upset this man and did not want to make him feel threatened in any way. He knew hostage negotiation training. Until he had an opportunity to take this man down, his captor was always right!

His eyes darted across the open deck before him, searching for someone or something that could aid him in his dangerous predicament. Crewmembers were heading towards him from all over the ship and one by one, they stopped as they noted the wide-eyed look their captain was giving them. His crew knew him so well that his look was all it took for them to weigh up the horrific scenario now unfolding before them and almost as one they stepped back to give him room to manoeuvre.

Thomas tried a strained smile to help calm the situation but by the looks of his crew, he knew he had failed miserably. The looks on their faces did little to put his own mind at rest; all looked pensive whilst some looked determined to try to rush his assailant, a course of action that was very foolhardy and instantly fatal.

He waved gently with his hands, wiggling his fingers against the sides of his trousers in the hope the crew would see his hand motions and ease off. The captain's feeble attempt at sign language failed miserably, leaving the crew simply standing there with swords and daggers drawn waiting for the one signal that would allow them to strike as one and save the man that meant so much to them.

"What do you want?" Thomas asked, following his training and attempting communication.

"Tell your men to step back!" The voice screamed at his ear. "Or I will have no choice but to kill you."

Thomas realised there was no need to repeat his assailant's comments as all the gathered crew had clearly heard the grim statement. Instead of compliance however, one of the crew, Harris by name, stepped forwards offering himself in place of his captain. It was a selfless and noble sacrifice and Thomas realised seconds too late that Harris had given him his best and only chance of escape that he squandered due to its unexpectedness.

The invisible edge of steel at Thomas's throat suddenly moved and Harris went down, a dagger appearing to sprout absurdly from the centre of his forehead like a cheap street magician's conjured flower. Harris dropped heavily to the deck, dead before he even hit the floor but the swiftness of this cold-blooded action and Harris's faithful sacrifice were too quick and shocking for Thomas to register a response. Before he could react, he felt his own cutlass slide from the scabbard at his waist and watched it disappear before his eyes only to feel it adopt the vacated space at his exposed throat.

"It would be ironic if I were to kill you with your own sword." The voice taunted in his ear. "Now back up before someone else dies."

"Of course," Thomas replied calmly, "You are absolutely right."

He shrugged in resignation; his options sorely depleted and reluctantly began to comply with the cold-hearted killer that whispered into his ear. He was in a classic textbook hostage scenario but at present, there was no way out of it. As long as no one else got hurt, he would play it out for now, using his senses to spot any openings that presented themselves.

At each tentative backward step, he heard the unmistakable sound of a sharp intake of breath at his ear. He already knew this killer had been wounded in the earlier skirmishes on deck prior to his own arrival on the scene, the trail of blood confirmed it. Could this be the 'chink' in his 'armour' Thomas could exploit?

"You appear to be hurt." He began.

"I told you not to talk." The voice at his ear snapped back. Thomas reluctantly continued to back up; well aware that even in his wounded and weakened state the assassin was managing to maintain the pressure of the blade against Thomas's throat.

A sudden roar caused Thomas to pause in mid-stride, resulting in an unavoidable wince as the blade cut deeper into his throat. The upturned lifeboat lying forgotten at the centre of the main deck suddenly rose up from the wooden floor and crashed over, revealing a sight that filled Thomas with dread, his blood turning to ice in his veins.

Commagin stood yelling a battle challenge across the deck towards them, at his feet lay the unmistakable form of the *'Lady Janet'*. Thomas raised his eyes up to the heavens and mouthed a silent prayer. It appeared that no matter how bad a situation could be it always had the potential to get worse!

The crew surrounding the captain's position took one look at the Dwarf and his elaborate crossbow and dived for cover leaving the captain swiftly abandoned and framed beautifully in the open doorway to the cabins. Several splashes sounded to the left and the right as men threw themselves overboard in sheer panic leaving Commagin with an unimpeded view of the hostage situation.

The *El Defensor* suddenly became a ghost ship. Thomas could not help but think that if this were a western movie a tumbleweed would have blown across the deck before them. Those crew that remained peered cautiously out from behind any available barrels and masts, none of them daring to move and all holding their breath as one. Even the night wind suddenly dropped in sympathy as all awaited the explosive action that would come from the firing of Commagin's favourite weapon.

Thomas's mind briefly flew back to what little he knew of the weapon forged by the Engineer. This was without doubt Commagin's greatest creation; however, the terror regarding its use lay not in the fact that the weapon was unreliable in any way but that Commagin was as blind as a bat when it came to aiming the thing!

"Don't shoot!" Thomas yelled, bringing his hands up in terror. Thomas's captor went silent, the pressure of the blade at the captain's throat the only sign that he was still standing behind him.

"Don't worry!" Commagin shouted back. "I've made some adjustments since the last time. I have fitted an indie-red sight. It's impossible to miss!"

"What the hell's an Indie-red sight?" Thomas worried aloud.

"I have no idea." The voice at his shoulder muttered in reply.

"I have a suggestion," Thomas whispered, the unfolding situation causing the most unlikely allies. "Can we back up a bit faster?"

Commagin, apparently oblivious to everyone's reaction, reached down to firmly grasp the weapon at his feet. Strapped across the top of the silver crossbow was a barrel shaped object over three times the size of the glorious weapon beneath it. Wires, tubes, whirring cogs and flashing lights covered every inch of the sight and Commagin grunted loudly as he tried vainly to lift the weapon complete with its new attachment up from the deck. The Lady Janet, displaying her prerogative as a lady, stubbornly remained where she lay.

Sensing the Dwarf's unexpected difficulty Thomas breathed a sigh of relief.

Commagin turned the sigh into a barely stifled scream as the Dwarf finally managed to lug the crossbow up from the deck with a huge grunt. As the weapon came level with his shoulder he sighted through his elaborate site, pulled back on the trigger and made the air fill with deadly crossbow quarrels.

The first two quarrels from the weapon flew directly towards Thomas, buzzing angrily through the air like enraged hornets, the shafts of the quarrels spinning erratically due to the poorly constructed feather fletching Commagin had glued on to each shaft.

One quarrel whizzed by Thomas's ear missing the captain and his assailant by mere inches, the second was closer still and by sheer 'luck' only grazed Thomas's shoulder before slicing on to hit home in the assassin behind him. There was a wet 'thwack' and a scream and Thomas found himself coursing backwards as the wounded man who held on tenaciously behind him dragged him through the cabin doorway and onto the floor. They landed with a crash, Thomas momentarily on top of his assailant; the cutlass at the captain's throat mercifully, yet mysteriously, flying away as jagged splinters of doorframe showered down to litter the carpet around them.

There was a grunt from behind Thomas's ear then a winded demand.

"Get up." The disembodied voice snarled, obviously in great pain.

Thomas struggled to comply; grimly aware that if he hesitated for even the slightest moment the killer could stab him with yet another unseen weapon. He did not intend to give the man that opportunity and he swiftly regained his feet, turning back towards the open doorway they had both crashed through only to have the mystery of the cutlass removal fully explained.

His cutlass was still quivering where it remained wedged in the wooden doorframe. The doorway was only three feet wide; Thomas's cutlass was closer to four. When they found themselves thrown back through the opening, the blade had been unable to follow and had wedged into the woodwork.

Thomas mercifully thanked his lucky stars. If the door had been wider there would have been nothing to prevent the force of the killer's backward motion and he would have been about a foot shorter! He gulped to check his throat was still working but his hesitation cost him dearly. The cutlass suddenly disappeared before his eyes; its exit from the doorframe showering even more splinters to the floor as the unseen killer rearmed himself.

"Keep backing away." Demanded the disembodied voice, an audible edge to his voice as if he spat the order through clenched teeth. Thomas moved to comply, realising that the man's angry tone left no room for negotiation, a deep-seated terror beginning to rise in Thomas's gut. Where was the invisible killer now! He could be anywhere!

A sharp prick at the side of his neck made him jump to comply but it answered his most urgent enquiry as his assailant herded him towards his cabin. Thomas knew that this time the killer would think twice about leaving himself exposed and he would be more diligent using the captain's body as a shield. He also noted that from the force of the prick angling up into the flesh at the side of his neck the killer had now decided to angle the blade so that there would be no further obstructions from any stationary doorframes!

As Thomas stepped backwards, he spared a quick glance at the loyal crew he was leaving behind. The momentary opening offered for escape flashed through his mind, taunting him with the opportunity to retake those fatal steps in his mind's eye until he succeeded in getting free and saving Harris's life instead of squandering it. He closed his eyes, tears blurring his vision as he realised the hopelessness of it all.

The wounded hostage taker was both angry and exhausted, his thoughts becoming increasingly paranoid. Thomas realised, with a grim finality, that in all likelihood he was walking to his death. The weight of this realisation hit him hard and Thomas's body visibly sagged at the notion of what awaited him at the end of the corridor.

As he moved around the corner of the passageway, he noted the track of crossbow quarrels tracing from the doorway back across the deck towards Commagin's stocky form. The arc of the dispersal pattern showed quite clearly that the engineer had continued to fire his weapon even as the weight of the cumbersome crossbow had dragged it back down towards the ships deck.

As the sight of the deck receded, the captain noted the carpet beneath him and the copious streaks of blood that had collected there. That was a lot of blood! Somehow, by some miracle Commagin had made his one accurate shot out of twenty count!

* * * * * *

Commagin looked across the deck to the cabin opening, his eyes squinting to see through his thick glasses, a huge grin visible across his face.

"Gottim!" the Dwarf remarked, clenching his fist in apparent victory at the successful field trial of his finest invention. Nobody would ever doubt that the '*Lady Janet*' was now an excellent weapon to use in future combat situations.

Ashe and Barney clapped their hands loudly, encouraging the Dwarf to take a bow and adding further fuel to the huge grin Commagin now wore as proudly as any medal. The engineer started to turn to show his appreciation to the enthusiastic audience of two then realised that he could not move his lower half. He turned back in frustration his bleary eyes tracking the crossbow quarrels that had embedded into the wall by the cabin door and the further sporadic pattern of quarrels that raced back across the deck towards him.

"Humm!" Commagin stated in a matter-of-fact manner.

Sticking straight through his leather boot and into the deck below was the final quarrel the crossbow had managed to fire before her brief escape from gravity had ended. With his weather beaten hand barely shaking, Commagin reached for the flask hanging from his belt and took several deep 'chugs'. Moments later, he turned to his two still clapping friends unaware that several drops of the amber liquid were dripping from the end of his beard.

"I need it for the pain." Commagin explained before collapsing to the deck in a dead faint.

Ashe stood in deep thought, his claps slowing as he realised that the performer he was congratulating was no longer hearing his ovation. He reflected on what fun he was having since coming aboard this ship. He had never heard of 'paint-stripper' before coming aboard and now the Dwarven engineer had informed him that it was an active pain-relieving agent too!

* * * * * *

Kerian had paused in his examination of a particularly intricate model ship after hearing the disturbance in the passageway. Through the doorway, he heard Thomas talking with someone and saw the Captain was slowly backing towards him. From his posture and the fact Thomas was talking to himself, it was clear that something was very wrong!

His warrior instinct made him reach for his sword, then he cursed Thomas's stupidity when he realised it was not at his side. The Captain had confiscated Kerian's sword and his dagger was a pile of molten scrap lying in some alleyway back in Catterick. Thomas had damned himself with his fanatical adherence to 'ship's rules'.

Keeping his eyes firmly on the captain's approaching back, Kerian ducked behind the cabin door, careful not to knock against anything and give away his position. He peered through the thin gap between the door and the frame and blinked twice, disbelieving, as a drop of blood appeared to form in the air just behind Thomas and drop to the carpet below. It was as if someone, or possibly something, unseen, was slowly herding the captain back this way.

His thoughts whirled in his mind; he would need a weapon if he were to be of any use to the man he had now decided was the answer to his current predicament. He took one last glimpse at the shape of Thomas approaching and knew whatever he did he would have to do it quickly. Kerian's eyes darted swiftly around the Captain's cabin, sizing up the items he could use. There were always the chairs. One good smack over the head with one of these monstrosities would silence in an instant whoever or whatever was heading this way.

He quietly moved over to the nearest one and tried to lift the gilded item of furniture from the plush red carpet. The result was instantly laughable; the legs of the chair barely rising a foot before Kerian needed to lower it back down to the deck. There was no way he would be able to get one of these chairs up over someone's head, at least not without risking serious injury to himself!

Kerian turned towards the desk exasperated at his failure and noted the golden dagger lying to the right of the captain's ledger. This was just what he needed! He picked up the ornate blade and instantly regretted it.

The dagger in Kerian's grip suddenly felt hot and uncomfortable, almost as if the strange weapon were somehow alive and not made of gold. He tried to tighten his grip on the hilt, but the pulsing sensation he felt in his hand when he applied pressure made his hold unsure and equally unreliable. He swapped hands, wiping his now empty hand against his trousers as if to remove some unseen taints that the blade had left on his skin, unaware his necklace was glowing green in warning.

He had no time to find another weapon; it was this fancy object or nothing!

Kerian tried to justify his sweating palm as simply pre-combat nerves, pulling a handkerchief from his pocket and wrapping the hilt securely before daring to grip the dagger tightly. With his pulse hammering in his ears, he eased back behind the safety of the door, just as Thomas started backing through it.

The sound of shuffling feet behind the door, confirmed there was someone other than Thomas in the hallway, so Kerian took a slow breath in and prepared to act. He tightened his grip on the slippery dagger, trying to ignore how it seemed to be wriggling in his grasp and tensed as Thomas moved past him.

He noted with admiration how professional the captain was, registering his hiding place with the barest flicker of an eye, so as not to give Kerian's location away. He tightened his grip on the strange dagger, preparing to strike and then stopped himself, suddenly at a loss. Where should he aim, what if he missed his target? He let the doubts hang unanswered knowing how dire the consequences could be if he failed.

Thomas recognised his hesitation and started to talk to the air before him in an attempt to distract their foe.

"Why are you doing this to us?" he coaxed in a low non-threatening voice, "what have we ever done to you? Why don't we sit and talk about this? You are safe in this cabin: we can bolt the door, tend to your injuries. There is still time to make this right."

"Be quiet," The unseen figure snapped back, rage and pain thick in his voice. "I can't think straight! Can't focus on what is happening. It is so hard to... Where is it?" The change in voice and timbre was dramatic making Thomas flinch away.

Kerian had used those brief seconds to study the captain's retreating form. Thomas's head was leaning over to the left and a raw line ran across his throat on the right, so it made sense that his assailant was standing more over to his right side. With a deep breath, he stepped out from his hiding place and plunged the dagger forwards hoping it would connect with something solid before it sank into Thomas's unprotected right flank.

The dagger jumped in his grasp, the ornate hilt elongating and wrapping around his hand before leaping forwards, dragging Kerian's arm physically along with it. The twin blades met slight resistance, before plunging into soft yielding flesh. Faster than Kerian could respond, the dagger withdrew then lunged forwards again, two more strikes in rapid succession, raising a scream of anguish from the air between where Thomas and Kerian stood.

"Kerian please stop!" Thomas warned, raising his arms up as much in reflex to ward off the flashing dagger as it was to try to calm the rapidly escalating situation. His unseen assailant had sounded tired and exhausted before his voice had changed. Maybe his strength was flagging and they could catch him alive and find out why he had chosen to attack the crew. As he watched fresh blood dripped from the air before him, exactly where the golden blade had struck.

Several things happened in quick succession.

The sentient dagger went to move again, this time selecting another target and lunging for Thomas but Kerian recognised the signs and reacted faster, snapping his hand backwards against the door in revulsion at the horror in his hand. A loud frustrated hissing filling the air as the blade, jolted by the collision with the door, loosened from Kerian's grip and uncoiled, falling limply to the floor.

There was a clang of steel as the captain's cutlass suddenly appeared in mid-air and dropped from Thomas's neck, catching the wall as it fell.

Something unseen crashed into Kerian's chest and what the fighter felt was possibly an elbow, caught him across the jaw, sending him spinning across the room.

Taking advantage of the distraction, Thomas darted forwards to try to grapple with their invisible foe. Instead, he discovered the fist at the end of the invisible elbow, which delivered him a serious numbing blow to his right temple.

Kerian's spin across the room ended with him falling head first into a large glass display case; the miniature galleon within suddenly coming into vivid close up detail, seconds before his head obliterated it. He struggled to pull himself free, his hand painfully crunching down upon several miniature wooden beans and carved crew, as he ripped a paper mast and tangled rigging from his hair and tossed it to one side.

He stepped back; off balance, realising he was unarmed again and turned to throw another punch at where he thought their unseen foe was. His hand was caught mid-swing and wrenched painfully to the side, making him stagger forwards and collide into the very man he was trying to save.

Kerian crashed into Thomas and winced as the Captain's head hit the wall with an audible crack. They tangled together and fell to the floor, Kerian trying desperately to regain his feet, his hands splaying on the carpet next to the dropped golden dagger. The serpent blade, sensing his presence, lunged for his flattened hand; the pommel opening its fanged mouth and snapping shut inches from his finger, its ruby eyes flashing in anger.

Staggering to his feet, he kicked out at the weapon in a desperate attempt to send it spinning away from Thomas's prone form. As he did so he heard the unmistakeable sound of the enchanted blade hissing in frustration at the quarry it had just missed.

The cabin door slammed shut behind him, the bolt sliding into its housing, moved by an unseen hand. An audible crunch followed, sounding much closer, as some ragged and torn miniature rigging crumpled beneath an invisible foot. Kerian ducked reflexively, rolling to the side, only to cry out as something wrenched his hair, pulling his head painfully around.

His eyes teared with the physical pain as he pulled his head away from the attack. Suddenly free, he backpedalled swiftly across the floor on his hands and knees. A fistful of white hair tinged with crimson fell discarded to the floor. Whatever this unseen creature was, it was undeniably fast!

There was a flutter of wings from behind the captain's desk and Kerian turned instinctively towards the sound, cursing as he realised it was only the damned bird that tenaciously pursued anyone who dared to wear a hat on deck. Shadow flew through the open window and perched on the back of Thomas's chair, cocking its head to one side and settling down to watch the scene unfolding before its mischievous midnight eyes. Kerian turned back to the room, cursing his own lack of attention. His assailant was somewhere in here and he had no idea where!

Thomas groaned, struggling to rise from the floor. In response, a glass case on the far side of the room suddenly lifted into the air, appearing to hover for a second, the bottom edge of the case starting to turn semi-transparent, before the whole thing crashed down on the captain's unguarded back. He sank back to the floor, his resistance gone.

Using the chaos as a distraction Kerian scurried across the glass showered carpet and threw himself into the last hiding place left in the cabin where he could hope to avoid detection: under the captain's huge desk.

A stray sliver of glass lanced into Kerian's hand but he barely noticed the additional discomfort, his eyes frantically scanning the room for a new weapon to use, or any inspiration on how to get out of the mess he had found himself in. The cutlass was lying redundant near the bolted cabin door and clearly too close to his invisible foe, therefore unusable. He shuddered at the thought of attempting to use the golden dagger once again but when he looked for the blade, it was not where it had fallen. He wasted several valuable moments scanning the debris-strewn carpet before he noticed the weapon impossibly sliding across the floor away from him, its form now completely transformed into a venomous golden snake!

Kerian briefly contemplated making a suicidal dash for the door, hoping he might get lucky and catch his invisible foe off guard, then reconsidered. Trying to get across the room was exceptionally foolhardy and he would need to unfold himself painfully from the well of the desk before he could move! He was going to have to find some other means to get out of this. Smashed glass embedded into his knees as he backed further under the desk and started to emerge from the other side.

He tried to calm his winded breathing. His eyes and ears were his only weapons now and he had already realised how limited they could be. He glanced over at the still form of Thomas lying senseless near the door, his weapon alongside him. The discarded cutlass called to Kerian but the big question remained... How was he to get across to it and the possible salvation it offered?

Gnawing his lip in frustration, he tried to calculate the variables and plan his moves, discarding them all and coming up empty. What was he going to do? He could not stay hidden under this desk forever! A thin line of blood trickled down the side of his face making his skin twitch uncomfortably.

'Why doesn't he tread on something?' his mind screamed silently. 'Come on! Give me a sign as to where you are!'

The only sound in the cabin was the tap-tap-tap of Shadow's talons as it marched backwards and forwards on the desk surface above, its beady eyes checking over the fragments of the galleon that littered the desk, just in case any of the parts turned out to be edible.

Kerian swore if he ever got out of this, he was personally going to stuff that damned bird!

There was nothing for it! He could not stay here and risk discovery! It was time to move! He slid slowly out from the shadows that cloaked the underside of the desk and began to shuffle backwards past the captain's chair, putting the heavy item of furniture between himself and the door. At least, his mind suggested, he would have some element of protection between himself and the invisible assailant somewhere within the cabin.

He continued backing towards the open window when another thought occurred to him. If the bird could fly in through the window, then maybe he could climb out. Then, after climbing up the outside of a wet and slippery ship, he would lure the killer out after him, dispatch him in front of the crew and be a real hero; saving the captain and making the ship eager to take him where he pleased.

In addition, while he was at it... oh who was he fooling? He had to face it that he was making this up as he went!

Kerian continued to back up not daring to take his eyes from the room beyond the desk and sighed with relief when his searching hand finally located the cool wood of the window ledge behind him. Shadow stopped its examination of the debris on the desk, snapping its large grey beak before turning to look at the battered and bleeding man before him. Up close, Kerian had to confess that Shadow was surprisingly ugly, although, in his current predicament the fighter was hardly an oil painting himself!

He went to move backwards and then became worried at not being able to see where he was going. To get out of the window he really did need to turn around and see what he was doing or risk falling overboard but if he did turn, he would leave himself open to a strike by the killer still somewhere in the room. He froze with indecision. Should he risk it and simply throw himself out through the window in the hope that he could grab something to stop his fall?

The bird squawked loudly making Kerian jump.

"I suppose you think that's funny!" Kerian snapped, thinking the bird had aimed its outburst at him due to his insecurity to commit to action. He reached back with his other hand and grabbed tightly to the ledge. It was now or never!

Something wet dropped onto his hand.

Kerian reacted instantly, knowing anything else would result in his death and threw himself physically forward across the captain's desk, sending Shadow squawking up into the air as the tankard, ledger and fighter crashed to the floor on the far side of the desk in an undignified heap. Loud frustrated squawks split the air as Kerian brought himself frantically to his knees, swivelling his body in a panic to face the window even as his hands and knees propelled him painfully back across the glass strewn carpet towards the far cabin door.

As he moved, Kerian witnessed the bizarre spectacle of Shadow flapping its wings rapidly in mid-air whilst lashing out with its talons as if to grab something. A wide pool of crimson had collected on the windowsill below the thrashing bird. His eyes went wide as he fought back the chill sensation that sent trembles up and down his spine. He had almost backed right on to the killer!

There was a shrill squawk of triumph and Shadow rose into the air a golden circlet clutched tightly in its talons. As the bird lifted the circlet away from its wearer, the gold headpiece flashed within its claws and the legs of the bird started to disappear as magic started to take hold. Beneath the bird the air appeared to shimmer, as if Kerian were looking at a mirage and then a blood soaked figure materialised, vividly framed against the open window.

The man's right arm hung useless at his side, twin spots of blood oozing from wounds made by the golden dagger. Embedded deeply into the man's shoulder was a crossbow quarrel that appeared to have passed right through the bone of his shattered shoulder blade. Blood seeped freely from around it, soaking the man's tunic down to his waist. His gait also appeared shaky and Kerian noted the bloody shattered remains of the man's ankle through the well of the captain's desk and noted the way the figure held it gingerly off the floor. It was incredible that this ruin of a man had been able to move at all, let alone walk and fight.

The man's left hand shot out with incredible speed to snatch at the swiftly disappearing Shadow, knocking the golden headband from its claws and causing the bird to appear solid once more. Shadow caught itself before it fell and in a flap of ebony wings, wheeled across the cabin to perch on the drinks globe. The circlet bounced once on the surface of the desk before falling to the carpet just a few feet away from where Kerian was sprawled. As Kerian's eye followed its path, he noticed a golden flash out of the corner of his eye. The dagger slowly slithered from the shadows, crossing the floor towards the item of jewellery and making Kerian's skin crawl.

The now visible killer's eyes also focused on the two gleaming items, his face becoming frozen, almost hypnotised, as if in in-decision. He dropped to the floor where he stood and was shortly lost from sight behind the desk, a low moan issuing from his mouth.

Thomas groaned groggily as he came around on the floor, the loud squawking of Shadow having roused him from his dazed state. Kerian ignored him, his eyes not daring to move from the captain's desk and the figure he knew was somewhere behind it. His hand blindly patted the carpet behind him, until his seeking hand fell on the one thing he was looking for.

Another lamentable wail arose from beyond the desk, as the nightmare image of the crazed bleeding figure moved back into sight, now on all fours, his eyes wide, blood smearing everything he touched as he attempted to crawl forward through the well in the desk to claim his golden prize. Kerian winced, hearing bones crack as the crossbow quarrel caught painfully on the edge of the tight space, before it crunched free and allowed the man to pass through.

The figure was crying now, clearly distressed and in unbelievable pain, reaching out his shaking hand toward the golden dagger, which instantly coiled up about his arm, nestling there contented. There was no horror shown on the man's face at the behaviour of the weapon and no disgust at the feel of the object being alive. Instead, his face showed unexpected relief at the blade's recovery. Satisfied it was secure he turned his attention to the golden circlet his focus total and absolute on the object before him.

Kerian took this opportunity to launch bodily back into the fray. He hefted the discarded cutlass from the floor, instantly noting the perfect balance and lightness of the blade, before swiftly moving back towards the desk intent on finishing this madness.

The kneeling man looked up at Kerian's approach and in a sudden rush of clarity realised his dire predicament. He reached out with his other hand, securing his hold on the circlet. There was a flash as the magic in the headband reactivated and the man's ruined body began to turn invisible.

Kerian continued his charge determined there would be no magical advantage gained and no time to hide before they collided. The assailant seemed to realise this at the same instant and looked up, his eyes meeting Kerian's and reflecting back the conflict raging within him.

"Help Me," he pleaded, unexpectedly.

"With pleasure." Kerian snarled swinging the cutlass in low, the entire force of his body behind the devastating blow.

"No!" Thomas screamed from his prone position on the carpet, his hand extended towards them as if he could somehow stop the inevitable.

The battered and bloodied killer looked at the swinging steel descending towards him and brought the circlet up as a pitiful flimsy protection against his incoming glittering death. The cutlass sliced straight through the metal guard like a knife through butter, the cleaved pieces of the headband flying off in separate directions to land somewhere in the shadows. The blade continued its swing lifting the killer physically from the floor, slicing through skin and bone before coming to a jarring stop half embedded in the captain's desk.

There was a sickening crunch and then silence.

Kerian let the cutlass go, leaving the hilt quivering with the force of the blow, the attacker suspended from the weapon, head hanging forward. The serpent dagger, initially wrapped around the killer's wrist now fell inert to the floor and slowly resumed its normal eerie shape.

He paused for a moment to catch his breath and examined the pinned figure with his experienced eye. Incredibly, the man still breathed, all be it raggedly and with a shallowness that confirmed the seriousness of the landed blow. The fight was over; this man no longer posed a threat.

Thomas staggered to his feet his features set in a mask of horror at the coldness of his demonic saviour.

"I wanted him alive!" He snapped.

"He still is." Kerian gasped coldly. "But not for much longer. If you have any questions, ask them quickly. Oh, by the way... the pleasure was all mine!"

Thomas pushed past Kerian and moved grim faced towards his desk and the figure pinned upon it. He did not utter another word in the elderly fighter's direction, horrified at the brutality he had just witnessed.

Kerian looked at the captain's turned back and shrugged indifferently. What was it with these people? He tried to do the right thing, rescue a man in clear need of rescuing and this was all the thanks he got. It seemed that whatever he did, it was always wrong. Thomas should have been thanking him that he was still in the land of the living. For a moment, he had almost thought they were starting to get along!

He headed for the door, noting as he approached that a loud frantic knocking was coming from the corridor outside. He reached up to free the bolt and then hesitated, taking the opportunity to glance at himself in the captain's mirror.

A face covered with fresh blood from numerous cuts and scrapes stared back at him, a patch of hair noticeably missing from the side of his head, a blackened rosary of haemorrhage blossoming under the skin of his eye. He lifted a hand to brush his hair in such a way as to hide the bald spot and only succeeded in streaking his white hair with a fresh stripe of scarlet from the blood on his hands.

There was no doubt about it! He was getting too old for this!

Chapter Twenty-Three

"We were so close!" Justina mimicked. "So close..." throwing back her auburn tresses with a practiced flick of her head the wizardess regarded her reflected image in the bedroom mirror before her.

Her mouth curled into a mischievous grin as she wiped the last few sweat soaked hairs from her forehead, noting how the black silk sheets were sliding from her bare form and piling up erotically about her, creating an image that just cried for capture on canvas. To one side of her a pale exposed piece of flesh raised another giggle as she turned to regard the cold extremity that was Pelune's foot.

The Raven had even been in the same room! All he had to do was pick up the headpiece long enough to be teleported back and he could not even do that! She tugged her sheet harder pulling the linen from beneath the snoring priest who had come to her demanding comfort after his plans had turned to ashes before his eyes in her scrying bowl.

She slid up close to him, her heavily scented body still tingling with the delight at what she had done scarcely half an hour before, her finger tracing up his leg and onwards across his stomach and up over his chin, where she leant close to brush his purplish lips with a sensual and lingering kiss of farewell. Justina did not love Pelune, she did not even find him attractive but the heady rush she felt when she used her sensuality to control and manipulate the priest was an intoxicating experience. She also knew her time for revenge would be soon.

Pelune was weakening visibly now. His pallor and health suffering, his abilities pirouetting away like freefalling leaves descending from a tree in autumn. With the loss of the blade and the brutal demise of The Raven, the final vestiges of his power were slipping through his fingers like fine sand, leaving him finally helpless and vulnerable.

Eight years of planning was finally ending.

She slid from the bed, hardly feeling the cool air on her naked skin as she walked across the cold tiled room to her wardrobe and selected a silken robe that she slipped into, cinching it at the waist with a thin belt that pulled the material tightly to her curves.

Was it really that long ago?

She thought back to when Pelune's cult had first come into her life, orchestrating an attempt to put pressure on her father to support the cult's actions by introducing her to the fatal bite of the serpent.

Strangely, the attempt on her life had failed: they found the snake dead at the foot of her bed. The more she thought about the Raven's success rate the more Justina had realised this was down to the power struggle between Pelune and his assassin, rather than blind luck. Not one to dismiss this as an act of fate her father had acted swiftly in protecting his daughter, carrying her away under cover of darkness and placing her under the care of the Order of St Fraiser.

Her father had been killed mere days later for his failure to comprehend the benefits of the serpent regime, leaving Justina fostered under Abbot Brialin's care where he raised her, nurtured her and fed her need for revenge.

She looked back at Pelune's still form and imagined a dagger plunged into his chest, stopping those breaths and finally freeing her. It would be soon. She could almost taste it! However, she was not there yet. So much still hung in the balance. The dagger was still out there and the threat of the evil that the artefact represented was still a tangible and very real horror. If the wrong person found the dagger and succumbed to its promises of power, the evil could perceptibly arise again and this risk Justina would not allow.

Hamnet still had her work to do and would be as reliable as always. Justina briefly considered recalling the enchanted creature but the dagger's continued existence threw that line of reasoning into doubt. No, it was better that Hamnet completed her mission and sent the *El Defensor* to the bottom of the sea where the artefact would pose no further risk to mankind.

She walked from her bedroom into her study chamber, savouring the feeling of the fur upon her bare feet from the plush rugs that lay piled there. Reflections from the water within her ornate scrying bowl flickered up the walls of her sanctuary as if illuminated from beneath and as Justina leant forwards over the simmering liquid, the image of a ship greeted her, sailing across sun drenched cobalt blue waters. The image as always was silent; the ship as doomed as the cold priest that now lay ironically just as quietly behind her, both destroyed by the venomous vengeance that was Justina.

* * * * * *

The innkeeper of the *Sunset Spider* looked up at the loud crash from behind the bar and wrinkled his brows in frustration. At this rate, he was never going to finish his accounting!

He walked over to the bar and looked down at the new serving maid his wife had asked him to hire. Some distant cousin, in need of a job, from her side of the family, clumsy, ugly and impossible to fire without risking his wife's wrath.

"What have you broken now?" he sighed, watching her sweeping up jagged shards of glass.

She paused in her work of sweeping the stone floor and flushed a vivid crimson about her ears and along the line of her tied back blond hair.

"I...I had an accident," she stammered. "I...I was dusting your shelves like I always do and the glass fell to the floor and shattered. I will get another from the kitchens straight away... I'm so dreadfully sorry, please forgive my clumsiness. I thank the Saint's that it was nothing of value..." She paused in mid-apology noting with concern the expression on the Innkeeper's face as his eyes scanned the shelves and identified from where the glass had fallen.

"Where are the contents of the glass?" he asked breathlessly.

"I didn't drink it. I swear I didn't!" she replied in sudden terror, realising that the one thing her aunt's family connections wouldn't save her from was an accusation of theft or being inebriated on the job. "It was just some kind of smoke! Most of it went down there." She gestured to the small drain in the floor, placed to catch accidental spills and save serving staff from going home with wet footwear.

"Most of it?" the innkeeper asked, his hand reaching slowly for the dagger at his belt.

"Well, some sank into the cracks in the stonework...but there were thankfully no stains for me to remove, just shards of the glass."

The innkeeper paused in his movements, allowing himself a sigh of relief.

"Take a break," he ordered, dismissing the serving girl with a look that he hoped masked the turmoil of emotions he felt within.

He watched the kitchen door swing closed then bent down to pick up a missed jagged fragment of glass. He turned it over in his hand and considered how such a fragile material had managed to imprison the forces of darkness for so long. He turned to gaze up towards the window set high on the far wall, his thoughts and fears turning to the departed man Styx.

"How much of a lead do you have?" he muttered aloud, knowing deep inside that no matter what lead had been secured, from these creatures it would never be enough.

* * * * * *

"This voyage has been a costly one I fear.'

Thomas Adams re-dipped his black quill and continued his morbid log entry. As was his duty as captain of this seemingly cursed vessel.

'Our passage through these troubled and turbulent waters paid with the lives of comrades whom I had always felt would remain on this ship long after I had sailed on.

The stench of death lies heavy about us even though I have ordered the decks scrubbed until the crushed white lime had obliterated any trace of the violence our crewmen have suffered, portholes have been thrown wide open to air the ship and the carpets stained with our life-blood are to be changed at our next port of call. It must be soon as we have little water and our spirits need a lift that only shore leave can bring. Even so, I fear it will not be enough to remove the taint that stubbornly remains upon my soul.

We have lost so many crew in such a short time; John Hodge, Fresine, Simons, Harris, Atlebarr, Jules, Scott, Mayes, and Lubok. So many names with such vivid and vibrant lives that have now come down to the simple ink marks on this parchment and the single memento that I have collected from each. In return, I feel the weight of each death in the form of a deep despair that descends upon me, nudging the already immense weight of responsibility that it may move over and allow yet another crushing weight to join it. How many more souls can I knowingly lead to their doom? Simons was barely twenty, his whole life before him. How can I not take his death personally?

At times like these, I would gladly hand over the mantle of being captain of this ship. The weight of this position now lies so heavily upon me that I feel crushed by the burden of this responsibility and the continued one-sidedness of its demands. I give and give to this ship and yet it has never once returned the favour. Never a hand to rest comfortably upon my shoulder, never a congratulatory comment to say that I have done well or that I am a credit to the men that I serve in more ways than they can ever believe.

Why am I here? Moreover, where am I going?

How many times have I tried to answer those very questions for my colleagues and crew, aiding them with complete conviction as to where they wished their future to lead them? However, when I find myself alone with only this logbook for company the questions remain largely elusive and frustratingly evasive to the one person who sorely needs them answered.

In some twisted way I blame myself for the hardships faced by this crew and I repeatedly find myself searching high and low for some clear cut sign as to where I went wrong, where mistakes were made and what bad commands did I issue that have resulted in these repeated tragic episodes that have befallen us.

Today I find that I am still no closer to finding an adequate explanation for the carnage that has swept across the decks of this magnificent vessel. Our assailant is unable to explain his actions, leaving me confused as to why we have encountered such wrath and we remain effectively marooned in these waters until we can find some way of opening a passage onwards that is safe for all on board.

I can lay none of the blame on Colette. She tries hard to study and learn the spells left behind by her master but they are taxing incantations and she has not the experience nor the mentor to help her cast them. Until she feels confident to control the powers required we must flounder as a fish caught on dry land unsure of which helping hand to trust in case they throw us literally into the frying pan instead of back into the water to swim free.

The wounded are almost too numerous to count and add further fuel to my feelings of intense failure. If it were not for the tender administrations of Marcus, Colette, Violetta and Austen, I believe the final death toll would have been so much higher.

Scrave's face is a mess despite our greatest attempts to heal him; Abilene and Plano grieve for their lost brother Lubok, ironically the one brother I felt would never find death in a fight, as he was so reluctant to get into one. Commagin bears his first war wound quite stoically even if it was self-inflicted. Rauph...my dear Rauph, what am I to do with you? It appears he is not yet ready to sail calmer waters and his passage with the El Defensor is gladly far, far from over.

Thomas topped up his quill again. He needed to mention the heroes of the piece, but felt it difficult to do so, especially when one hero caused such a conflict of feelings for him.

Shadow saved us all. Who would have thought a Raven could be such an asset to this crew! Then there is Kerian Denaris... now here is an enigma indeed, a man brought to us by accident, like a head on collision at a crossroads. The man unsettles me. He has no tact; he does not think before he acts. If I did not know better, I would think these were the actions of a youth, not an old man. He is not intentionally evil but his actions are sometimes close to the murky waters that surround it.

I have already informed him that he is to disembark at our next port of call and yet I owe him my life. I shudder to think what would have happened if he had not been there when I had needed him.

What am I to do?

Thomas stopped his narrative with a deep sigh and as before, he went through the ritual of cleaning his quill and squaring his desk. The wrecked cabin lay untouched around him.

Somehow, he did not feel like cleaning it up.

* * * * * *

"Well that's about it then," Kerian commented, securing the last of his possessions within his saddlebags and pulling the straps tight. "Are you both ready?" He turned towards the figures of Ashe and Marcus sitting across from him on his bunk and watched as they both nodded in reply, their own meagre belongings packed alongside them.

"Let's go then." He motioned, turning to leave then spinning back again to smack Ashe's hand away from the straps he had just fastened. "Hand's off!"

Ashe looked at his elderly friend with a face dominated by a look of intense indignation.

"I was only checking the straps were fastened correctly." He offered in a huff. He reached up and straightened his new khaki hat that had somehow come into his possession. Where he had found a *bycocket* hat on the *El Defensor* was a mystery. Not so much a mystery was the brown and orange-flecked feather tucked along the edge. It looked suspiciously as if it was a quill at some point in the past!

The cabin door flew open before Kerian could continue his argument and Rauph's shaggy form blundered through the opening to join the three companions in what was already a tightly cramped setting. The Minotaur looked even shaggier than normal with bandages wrapped all about him and tufts of chestnut hair poking through the strips of rough linen where the medical administrations of Marcus and Colette had slipped. Rauph managed to crack a strained smile for the assembled onlookers but it was clear to everyone that the usually jovial creature was in a sombre mood.

Kerian looked down at his bandaged hands, still wincing at the discomfort of slapping Ashe's hand away, then back at the darkened patch of linen in the centre of the Minotaur's chest. Somehow, his discomfort paled in comparison to what this majestic and noble creature had suffered.

"I've come to escort you above," Rauph gestured, his huge hands reaching out to grab Kerian's saddlebags. "And to thank you for saving the captain's life. I know he won't tell you, so I'm going to do it for him."

Before anyone could yell out or advise Rauph otherwise, the Minotaur lifted the baggage from its resting place and turned to go back out through the door and up the corridor. Marcus caught the saddlebags just under his unsuspecting chin and flew back onto Kerian's bunk, cracking his head against the wall. Ashe dropped flat to the deck, narrowly missing the bags that passed through his hair as he fell and Kerian found himself wedged up against the wall, the buckles from his bags sliding painfully across his mid-section and reminding him that he should really be taking more care of himself.

Was he really putting on that much weight?

Rauph, oblivious to the chaos he had left in his wake, bashed his way out of the room and out of sight, although not quite out of earshot. Several raised exclamations and curses echoed back towards the three colleagues, as fellow crew encountered the tidal wave known as Rauph, and were either swept along with his enthusiasm, or crushed under the saddlebags he carried.

Kerian looked around the room for one last time. For a while there, he could have almost believed that this was where his future lay. Ashe tugged on his arm impatiently.

"Come on or we will miss the ship sailing into port."

Kerian smiled and gestured theatrically that the small thief left the cabin first. He paused, patting himself down and making sure that everything was still in place as Ashe meandered his way up the passageway. Then he lifted his hand and sighed deeply.

His ring was missing!

* * * * * *

The *El Defensor* slid quietly into port with no visual celebration or fanfare. Her masts were trimmed and the pennants hung at half-mast as a sign of respect for the recently departed crew. Thomas Adams stood silently beside the helm, closely watching the skilled administrations of the harbour master who had rowed out to meet them and was now guiding the ship gently into the dock that was Perenord.

Thomas hated docking in a civilized port. Although he was relatively positive that the man standing beside him was more than capable of doing his job, the ship, after all, was physically out of Thomas's control and he felt uneasy at the prospect of putting both his ship and his very livelihood in the hands of a man whom he had only met mere minutes before.

This was worse than being in a patrol cruiser and letting the rookie drive! Thomas remembered vividly when he used to pump non-existent brakes on his side of the vehicle when they had driven recklessly in car chases throughout the darkened city streets.

He hated not being in control!

Desperate to take his attention from the unsettling harbourmaster, Thomas turned his focus towards the white and cream single story houses spilling down the hillside towards the jetties lining the artificial bay. Hanging gardens filled with flowers of deep vibrant colours cascaded from flat rooftops and window baskets, turning the port into one of warmth and friendship.

He cast his eyes higher and frowned. High on the hillside was a dark fortress with flags flying proud. Someone was at home and obviously in charge of this out of the way port of call. Thomas had the feeling palms would need greasing quite liberally if they were to get all the supplies and repairs they needed within the allotted time span he required.

Looking back down into the port, Thomas noticed the seagulls taking to air as they moved closer to land, the birds arguing loudly with each other and jostling to see who would be closest to a potential new food source. A pennant hoisted at the end of one of the deeper berths highlighted where the *El Defensor* would recuperate for the next few days. It wasn't as near the harbour mouth as the captain would have liked but he wasn't piloting his ship and had little say in the matter if they were to continue his ruse as a trading ship coming into port on genuine business instead of a snatch and grab mission like they had done in Catterick.

The harbourmaster skilfully piloted the *El Defensor* within the tight confines of the harbour walls, before letting the ship wallow in its own momentum, utilising the resulting wake to wash the ship gently backwards alongside the jetty. She nudged none too gently into dock, her lines thrown from the crew to the dockhands alongside. Within moments, they had tied off and secured the ship. Once the movement of the vessel had subsided, Thomas turned to the harbourmaster and looked him firmly in the eye.

"If the paint is scratched it's coming out of the docking fee." He growled.

"Then I will have to raise the fee accordingly." The harbourmaster responded without breaking his stride, used to the over protectiveness of ships captains that he encountered on an almost daily basis. Thomas watched the man disappear down the gangplank and hurled imaginary daggers at his exposed back, before making his own way down from the aft castle to the main deck and the three people that were waiting there for him.

Rauph suddenly appeared at his side his presence instantly reassuring. Commagin, Sherman and Scrave accompanied him. Abilene and Plano also dropped lightly from the rigging above to see this unlikely trio off.

Thomas cast his eye over his proud crew and winced. The six of them looked like absurd relics from a back street museum exhibit, rejects from an Egyptian dig that the archaeologists were too embarrassed to confess they had discovered.

Sherman looked like a panda bear, his face mottled with bruises from his encounter with a large hairy crewmember. Abilene and Scrave had bandages and gauze on their respective faces. Plano and Rauph had bandages about their midsections and Commagin...well Commagin stole the show. The Dwarven engineer staggered around limping with huge exaggerated strides as he showed off the huge ball of bandage that now engulfed his foot and most of his leg. Every now and then he took a long pull from a hip flask at his belt and gasped with pleasure.

Thomas raised his eyes at this behaviour. Commagin would never drink from a flask unless it contained something a great deal stronger than water. Where did the contents of that flask come from? There was no liquor allowed on ship other than that administered by the captain from his private stores to improve ship morale! Even as he watched Plano asked to taste some of the drink and the Dwarf swiftly rebuffed him, confirming in an instant that something alcoholic was swishing around inside both flask and engineer!

A shadow fell across him and Thomas reluctantly tore his gaze from Commagin to focus on the matter at hand. Kerian Denaris stood there, a spectre of darkness silhouetted against the backdrop of the sun.

Thomas shook his head; bringing his hand up to shade his eyes and noticed the elderly fighter's hand outstretched in an offer of friendship. Thomas swallowed, attempting to hide his momentary fluster and shook Kerian's hand warmly finding it difficult to dislike such a rare display of warmth from the man.

He held up his hand to prevent any emotional farewell and turned to Plano, offering the key from his jerkin and signalling that the man head to the armoury and retrieve Kerian's enchanted blade. The acrobat presently returned and offered up the weapon with a particularly artistic flourish. As Kerian took the blade back into his possession, the crew around him started to applaud.

It appeared that the stowaway was a hero in the eyes of the men on this ship. Why was it that Thomas could not feel the same way?

"Thank you." Kerian offered sincerely, before turning to face Thomas. "It has been an education sailing with you."

"Well at least it wasn't boring." Thomas laughed, attempting to make his comment light hearted and nothing at all like he felt inside. There was a pregnant pause where Thomas knew he should now gesture for the man to leave yet something deep within him still felt there was going to be more to this turbulent relationship.

Ashe interrupted by pushing up alongside the elderly fighter and offering his hand to the captain in direct imitation of Kerian. Thomas went to reach out his hand in response and then paused. The Halfling was dressed in a Robin Hood style hat! Where had he ever found one of those? Then he noticed his quill proudly presented on the brim. So that was where it went!

"It appears I owe you a debt." Thomas stated, returning his attention to the elderly figure before him.

"That is unnecessary." Kerian replied, taken back at his own uncharacteristic show of charity. He motioned with his hand that no gifts or gratitude were expected. Thomas ignored the gesture, reaching instead into his waistcoat and withdrawing the golden serpent dagger.

Kerian's blood ran cold at the sight of it, his mind flashing back to the terrifying metamorphosis that had occurred to the malevolent blade in the captain's cabin the night before.

"This is the least I can do." Thomas continued unaware of the discomfort caused to his temporary guest. "I noticed that you had lost your own weapon and this seems as good a replacement. At least take it as a temporarily replacement until you find another one more suited. You could even sell this dagger to pay for one more suitable if you wish, although I'm not sure what its current value would be."

"Approximately 5000 gold crowns for the blade, 500 silver florins for the rubies and maybe an extra bonus for an elaborate tale regarding its origin." Ashe piped up. "I know an excellent contact who would cash that in for you no questions asked." He winked at both men and tapped the side of his nose for emphasis.

Intent on refusing the weapon, Kerian tried to come up with a good reason why he did not intend to let this blade come within miles of himself. Didn't the captain realise what it was that he held in his hand? Did he not remember what this monstrous dagger could do? Of course! Thomas could not know because he had been unconscious on the floor of the cabin when it had been slithering about!

He looked down at Ashe for inspiration and noted the Halfling looking at the blade with a mesmerised glaze in his eyes and transparent dreams of avarice plainly readable in his tight-lipped smile. Kerian took one look, hesitating only for a moment, before he leant forward and accepted the weapon, attempting to hide the fact that he was handling the gift as if someone had just handed him a recently dissected frog or tail arching venomous scorpion. Using his cloak to avoid directly handling the weapon, he dropped it into one of the smaller pockets of his saddlebag and securely buckled the pouch down.

Kerian swept Ashe along with his free arm, trying to end the farewell meeting without insulting Thomas's feelings and trying to keep the Halfling quiet at the same time. Ashe was like an unexploded, unstable bomb in situations like this, liable to open his mouth and say exactly what was on Kerian's mind at just the wrong moment without any consideration for the consequences; but there was something else too.

The elderly fighter suddenly recognised that by accepting the blade and taking it with him, he could ensure it was not free to hurt anyone else on board the ship. This uncharacteristic act of concern surprised even him. Maybe being on the *El Defensor* had changed him in ways he had not realised.

"I simply don't know what to say." He stated, turning back to Thomas as he continued to manoeuvre Ashe towards the gangplank and shrugging, whilst secretly knowing his choice of words had an accuracy way beyond what Thomas would ever comprehend.

Thomas nodded in acknowledgement and then turned to Sherman, switching focus and asking his first mate to arrange the restock of ship supplies and the availability of local carpenters with minimal delay. Kerian marvelled how the captain could move from one task to the next and prioritise so seamlessly. He looked over at his other travelling companion and wondered how the captain would manage him.

Marcus tapped his foot impatiently on the deck, eager to move off and book passage to their future destination and something about his impatience rankled Kerian. Yes, they were in a hurry; none more so than himself but it did not feel right leaving like this. Something remained unsaid and required fixing before he left the ship and crew behind.

"Ahoy on board." A voice raised from below. Thomas hung his head at the sound, even though there was no way he could have known the source of the hail. "I wonder if you are looking for any fresh hands."

Thomas looked over at Kerian and waved his hand for him to wait for a moment before he disembarked and Kerian was happy to do so, curious to see what this turn of events meant to the crew. Marcus huffed in impatience but Ashe was already half way down the gangplank anxious to explore Perenord. His eyes kept wandering to the foreboding castle that loomed over the town. Storm clouds seemed to hover around its turrets, like iron filings to a magnet and thunder rumbled ominously whilst lightning danced across the clouds. What treasures would he find up there?

He paused halfway down the gangplank and jumped to one side as the source of the cry came up from the dock, gently edged past him and stopped just short of the deck he had left.

"Weyn Valdeze requesting permission to come aboard."

Thomas looked up at the man before him and took in his attire with a critical eye. Valdeze wore a chain mail shirt and leather leggings his mail glinting brightly in the sunlight reflecting the care each link had lovingly received. Strapped to the man's back was an unstrung longbow and at his waist instead of a sword hung a quiver of arrows and a hunting dagger. Valdeze's face was a mass of old pocked scar tissue but his eyes were honest, meeting the captain's gaze square on. Flaming red hair completed the man's appearance and Thomas found he instantly liked the man.

"You may have lost something!" Thomas pointed out. Indicating where Ashe stood on the gangplank examining one of Weyn's long wooden arrows, looking down the shaft and running his finger along the flights before touching the shining barbed hunting head to see if it was sharp.

"Oh they are perfectly safe from little hands." He replied gruffly, noting the vacancy in his quiver that normally held a dozen such shafts.

"Give it back Ashe!" Kerian shouted. Ashe true to form placed the arrow swiftly behind his back and tried to look innocent.

"Who me?" he asked with the sweetest smile he could muster. The crewmen started laughing at the act only to laugh harder when Ashe's face became a mask of confusion and he brought his hands back around looking at them in surprise, the arrow now nowhere to be seen.

Weyn patted his quiver and smiled, the twelfth shaft now safely returned at his side.

Thomas noticed the return of the arrow with his keen eye and chuckled quietly to himself, even as he worried what dark secret Weyn Valdeze had yet to share. He looked up expecting more voices to ask for passage and was surprised when no further calls arose.

This was odd. Somehow people were drawn to his ship when deaths occurred, there was never a need to advertise, they just arrived on the dock; Lost souls who suddenly found themselves with a need to sign up and face an adventure that could offer only one end.

He mentally did the arithmetic. Nine crewmembers were dead. One new man was here. That left a deficit of eight. There were three others on deck and another below, but as far as Thomas could see, it was unlikely that these three would be sailing any further with him. That meant he was still down seven.

"Kerian," he motioned the old man to come over. "Why don't you stick around a bit longer? No ship is going to sail before the morning tide. At least stay with us this evening and join us on shore. I'll buy the first round."

Kerian looked across in confusion, firstly at the offer to stay, especially as he needed to refuse for both his and Marcus's sake and to the strange turn of phrase he just heard. What indeed was a round? He moved to apologise and refuse.

Colette walked out onto the deck, slightly flustered as if she had run, her cheeks flushed red her eyes bright and vibrant. She was a vision in violet and gold.

"Oh thank goodness." She remarked, breathlessly "You haven't left yet. I didn't want you to leave without saying goodbye and I wanted to thank you for saving our captain's life." She walked up to Kerian, stood on tiptoe and planted a kiss on his cheek.

Colette stole his breath. His will no longer his own. Kerian felt the flush in his face and tried to hide it but simply knew that by thinking this way it would only get worse. He closed his eyes, breathed in her fragrance and was smitten.

"A round it is." He croaked, actually having no idea what he was agreeing to and temporarily not caring.

"Come on!" Ashe shouted impatiently from down the gangplank, now eager to set off, explore Perenord and start finding glorious treasures that did not belong to him.

His impatient eagerness turning into a sour frown as he realised his two friends were not following him.

"What's up?" he asked as if to confirm his observations.

"We have decided to stay a little longer." Sticks replied. "At least until tomorrow morning."

"We have?" Marcus appeared stunned and a little put out by this unexpected development.

Ashe stood slightly perplexed at the answer. The castle continued to beckon but the Halfling had to admit that Sticks and Marcus had been kind of fun to travel with. He looked at the men standing at the other end of the gangplank and stroked his chin thoughtfully. He could stay here and continue adventuring with Sticks and Marcus or he could set off and explore the interesting castle on the hill. Decisions...decisions.

"Just until tomorrow morning?" Ashe double-checked, mentally calculating the time it would take to explore the castle and then get back on board the *El Defensor*.

"That's the idea." Kerian replied.

"Okay!" Ashe announced, turning at once and setting off down the gangplank to the dock and the bustling town beyond. "Just make sure you don't leave without me!"

"As if we could?" Kerian remarked, watching the little figure slip into the crowd and onwards into trouble.

Thomas looked at Kerian and smiled innocently, knowing what the elderly man was thinking. Then he turned to his newest crewmember.

"Please follow Abeline below, he will get you quartered and give you the guided tour. Say any goodbyes you need to your loved ones, as we sail promptly as soon as repairs are completed."

"Have you seen some action then?" Weyn asked suddenly interested.

"Too much," Thomas replied sombrely. He looked down at the empty dock and did the mental arithmetic one more time.

"There's no one else." He muttered to himself.

Plano, overhearing the question looked over the side of the ship and shook his head, leaving Thomas with some large questions to answer.

Chapter Twenty-Four

Scrave tried to centre himself, calm his breathing and smother the tempest that churned within him. He drew his sword in his right hand, testing the weight by feel alone then spread his feet shoulder width apart, closed his eyes and began to work through his exercises.

He moved into a two handed stance, then reclaimed the blade in his right hand moving it back behind himself, then arching the blade back over his head and whipping it down by his right side, before grasping the blade two handed again, his left leg now in front of his right.

What had Thomas thought he was doing? He had no right to give away something that was not even his in the first place! He glowered silently as his mind replayed the image of the two men shaking hands on the deck that afternoon.

His sword arm came up again, whipping the blade in the path of a figure eight backwards and forwards in front of him, slowly picking up speed and making the path of the blade closer and closer to his body.

Why did Thomas hate him so? In addition, what right had Styx to his golden dagger?

The blade shot out, stabbing an imaginary foe, slicing to the left and the right to disembowel others as his feet moved lightly through a dance practiced time and again. He sank to one knee bringing his sword around horizontally before angling it down his back to parry an imaginary attack.

Thomas not only had the audacity to give away his dagger but had also decreed that Scrave stay behind this evening and watch over the ship whilst they carried out repairs and had stores replenished! It was outrageous that they expected him to do these demeaning tasks! Even if he was injured and his cheek continued to smart every time he tried to move his jaw, he certainly did not need time to rest and recuperate! Rauph's wounds were much worse than his were, yet they granted the Minotaur's shore leave without hesitation.

Life simply was not fair!

An imaginary Styx felt the keen edge of his blade as he continued to work out the kinks of tension in his muscles and sweat started to break out on his brow. He bounced the blade off the deck and flipped over backwards, slashing out left and right again before using both hands to spear his sword forwards and up in a move he had used to disembowel a sand ogre many years past.

He scrunched up his face, gritting his teeth and felt the sutures pull tight in his wound. Five ugly stitches, administered by the monk Marcus, travelling companion of Styx and thereby guilty by association of conspiring with an enemy! Moreover, this was something else that confused him. Violetta normally did the healing on board and if she had administered to him, he may not have required any stitches. Where was she anyway?

Opening his eyes, heart beating ever faster, Scrave threw his sword up in the air, spinning around in preparation to catch his blade in a manoeuvre he had practiced repeatedly. He reached out, missing the hilt by a wide margin and watched his weapon bounce across the deck. Oh, this was great! Somehow, he had discovered a great way to disarm himself in the heat of a battle!

The Elf walked over closing one eye and then the other. Left eye the ship appeared cloaked in thick fog; right eye vibrant colour; Left eye tones of black and white; right eye warm yellow lanterns and vivid pennants snapping in the breeze.

Scrave bent to pick up his sword and winced at the pain above his right eye. Colette had cast some magic charm that had improved his scarred vision. At least he could see now! She promised it would improve in time but it was distressing him more than he would admit.

The Elf bent to pick up his sword and closed his hand inches short of the blade. Great! His depth perception was off as well! He gritted his teeth again, feeling the sutures pull with tension. Everything had gone wrong since Styx had arrived.

Moving back into the centre of the mid deck he repeated his spin and catch routine, grimacing repeatedly as his hand missed the blade again and again and again. Finally, in disgust he picked up the sword and slid it into the sheath at his side.

The sooner Styx and his companions left the *El Defensor* the happier Scrave would be!

Practice was over! He needed a drink and he knew just where to find one.

* * * * * *

"There was three of them." Commagin boasted, swinging his recently replenished tankard up to his lips.

"Three?" Weyn stared hard at the Dwarf trying to take the measure of the bandaged engineer. This Dwarf was either exaggerating or simply too drunk to tell the truth, nevertheless he wanted to hear the rest of this heroic tale.

Commagin heavily replaced the tankard on the bar its metal 'clunk' informing the new crewman that his drinking vessel was empty. The Dwarf fixed him with one blurred eye before turning his gaze once again to the empty tankard and then back at the scout. Weyn took the obvious hint and signalled to the barman bringing a smile to the corners of Commagin's mouth.

"As I was saying," the dwarf continued, "the four of them had me surrounded but was I scared? Not Commagin the mighty I can tell y..."

"I'm sorry," Weyn butted in, "but didn't you say there were three of them a minute ago?"

"Don't interrupt when I'm spinnin' me yarn boy!" Commagin snapped making his listener flinch. "Now as I was sayin..."

Thomas grinned broadly, as he overheard Commagin retell his tale about Lady Janet's last stand. Anyone else overhearing would have believed that it was the Dwarf and not the captain who had been battered and bruised at the hand of the invisible assassin... correction, as Commagin told it, assassins.

The Dwarven engineer always occupied a bar stool when he had shore leave. Whether this was because he liked the extra height the stool gave his four-foot high frame, or that he was worried his drink would have a chance to evaporate if he sat further from the bar was unclear. However, it was refreshing to see something normal after so much recent upheaval.

As Thomas watched, Commagin gestured for yet another drink, precariously perched on his high stool, the request drawing a therapeutic smile to Thomas's face and a predictable wince from Weyn, who would discover that the Dwarf could stretch out a story for as long as the drinks continued to flow.

Thomas tore himself from the epic tale of swords and sorcery and leant back in the chair he occupied, feeling relaxed and comfortably full for the first time in as long as he could remember. With his seat set just right to monitor his surroundings the captain allowed his gaze to wander around the tavern the crew had decided to call a 'home away from home' for the evening.

The 'Swashbuckling Dandy' was rather a sophisticated establishment in comparison to the usual dockside dives the crew normally frequented. Indeed, the only reason they had managed to get in through the door was due to Rauph asking the man so nicely. That was if you viewed bouncing someone's head off the doorjamb asking nicely.

The captain risked a quick glance over at the owner, still receiving nursing care from one of the barmaids. Although he was still groaning at opportune moments to favour affection from his staff, the complaint was not too sincere, as money had exchanged hands freely since their arrival.

Rauph had decided to sit sentinel behind the main door of the tavern, making sure that if the door opened no one would notice him and feel intimidated into not coming in. Despite trying hard to appear friendly, his appearance was still drawing guarded glances from other customers in the room. It appeared eight-foot-tall Minotaur were not common in Perenord any more than they were in Catterick. It did not help that Rauph had decided to arm wrestle Sherman, Abeline and Plano all at the same time. A painful grunt confirmed that none of them stood a chance against the hulking Minotaur and Thomas turned away, eager to continue his visual tour.

A scattering of tables draped in creamy white lace, ornate napkins, gleaming tableware and small wicker baskets of freshly baked rolls, occupied various viewpoints in the large well-lit room. Wooden beams criss-crossed the ceiling in what Thomas had been told was the traditional style of the area and they added warmth to a room whose walls were hung with watercolours and oils of knights on horseback rescuing damsels in distress from serpents that were supposed to be true artistic representations of dragons. Thomas knew otherwise.

Dragons were much bigger, dirtier, and had more stabbing teeth and slashing claws!

A charred stick, apparently some fabled lance from one such illustrated combat hung above the bar, more to promote discussion than to make a statement of the barman's prowess with a weapon. The bar itself was spotlessly clean. No one had as yet carved their initials into the bar top, although watching Commagin bash the polished surface with his tankard it was only a matter of time before the crew of the *El Defensor* had made their 'mark' to show they had passed this way.

He stared down at the china plate that had been set before him and reminisced fondly at the gravy-streaked plate that was all that remained of his beef and ale stew and spiced potatoes that had only recently departed to what Thomas knew to be an excellent home. He stroked his stomach in silent satisfaction and tried to justify ordering another plateful.

Thomas felt Violetta's culinary repertoire deserved the recipe for this: so he decided to ask for a copy from the waitress, knowing in his heart that this was a meal to enjoy. There was only so much fish and gumbo a man could take!

The captain searched the tavern for the remaining waitress, only to discover that she was making eyes at a waiter who sat alone from the group nursing a glass of water. Although her brunette eyelashes fluttered alluringly over the solitary man with a force that could bring many to their knees, the youth was like most of the male population Thomas knew, self-absorbed and oblivious to her flirtatious advances.

Thomas examined the waiter closer. Short well cut hair, clean shaven, broad of chest and shoulders, with biceps that showed he kept himself in shape. As a middle-aged man, Thomas always felt a little self-conscious when considering the younger and fitter people around him. He sucked in his stomach and regarded the waitress again. Given time, she would soon tire of the waiter's lack of response and then Thomas would risk her deadly eyelashes to secure the secret to this excellent recipe.

It was a hard job, but somebody had to do it for the good of the ship and crew!

Chuckling quietly to himself, he slid his chair as far back from the table as the wall behind him would allow. He stretched out the toes within his boots in rapturous contentment; his meal and comfort only temporarily marred by the brief flicker of sadness for the members of the crew that had not been lucky enough to see this night. He sighed before shrugging away his guilt. He and all of his crew deserved this, they had paid dearly for their recent mistakes and this was a way to unwind and finally relax. Guilt be damned! He was going to enjoy this!

Now where was the sweet trolley?

A raucous laugh from the left dragged Thomas's gaze across to the rest of his crew who had dragged a load of tables together in one corner and were laughing and joking now that their own meals had ended.

Colette had discarded her violet robes for a pale cream blouse and a practical yet figure hugging pair of fawn leather trousers and knee height soft brown leather boots. She wore her hair platted up high upon her head, in a simple yet eye catching demure style. Interlaced throughout the blonde tresses was her trademark violet silk ribbons.

Kerian gazed across at Colette from over the top of a half filled wine glass, his face clearly displaying an attraction that he felt for the girl. The old man was still dressed in his black uniform, the darkness broken by the studs in his armour and the silver embroidery on his cloak. Thomas was starting to wonder if Kerian ever wore anything but dark colours. Dressing this way all the time was sure to be depressing!

Beside him, barely containing his impatience sat Marcus, who was looking backwards and forwards between the pair, clearly the unwanted third member of the party, itching to be moving on to whatever it was they had planned in the near future.

Colette laughed again, moving in closer to whisper something in Kerian's ear and Thomas suddenly noticed the occupant of the table behind them. He seemed quite tall at first glance, olive complexion, dark hair and a small well-trimmed beard, set beneath intelligent eyes that were taking in the measure of others around the room. His clothes looked exotic, possibly a merchant from far lands, he wore a keffiyeh headscarf that was down and laid loosely around his neck and where his cloak was open, Thomas could see a tunic, trousers and a thick belt through which numerous daggers were thrust. The man was nursing a drink and more worryingly looking directly at him!

Well two could play at that game!

Thomas propped his arms on the table and brought his hands together so he could rest his chin upon them and stare right back. The man smiled at the challenge and started to stand up.

Movement at Thomas's side broke his chain of thought. The waiter he had noticed earlier, having miraculously pulled himself away from the waitress with the devastatingly fluttering eyelashes was clearing his plate and utensils away.

"Did you enjoy your meal?" he asked politely.

"It was excellent," Thomas replied. "Please give my complements to your chef."

"I am glad you enjoyed it sir. I shall certainly pass on your praise." Balancing the plate, utensils and glass in one hand, the waiter flicked the tablecloth of imaginary crumbs to restore its pristine appearance then turned to walk away.

"Thank you and who is it that has served me so well this evening?" Thomas addressed his turned back.

The waiter paused, clearly surprised at the request. He turned face slightly flushed.

"I am Aradol of Deane, sir. I am glad you are enjoying your evening with us."

"Aradol of Deane. That's rather a grand name for a waiter?"

"I take work where I find it." Came Aradol's wounded reply, before he turned and headed towards the kitchens.

Thomas followed the departed waiter with his eye. There was obviously a story there just waiting for discovery.

A throat cleared beside him.

"Is this seat taken?"

Thomas looked up, slightly surprised at being caught off guard, and stared into the eyes of the man he had been examining earlier.

"May I sit?" the stranger asked, still awaiting the reply to his earlier request.

"Umm, oh of course, sorry where are my manners?" Thomas gestured to the empty seat before him. "Can I get you a drink?"

"I don't drink with a man until I have been introduced," came the jovial reply. "My name is Ives Mantoso." He struggled for a moment to adjust the crescent sword at his waist, exposing the cream engraved hilt to Thomas as he sat. Thomas immediately took notice of the unusual weapon.

"That's an elaborate blade." He remarked. "Oh and my name is Thomas Adams captain of the ship *El Defensor*. How can I help you?"

"I'm hoping I can help you." Came the reply Thomas was dreading. "I am looking for new opportunities and outlooks in life. I have seen your crew..." He gestured to the men seated about them. "...Heard your tales and feel this is something I wish to be a part of."

"Many men have said those very words." Thomas replied cryptically. "And just as many have regretted them. What makes you feel you would be different?"

The blinding white smile that served as a reply immediately made Thomas realise he had a character before him. Ives leant over the table and whispered into his ear.

"We are both men of the world," he stated. Thomas raised his eyebrows. If only the man knew, he was not a man of this world, or countless others he had visited.

"We are both well versed in the riches such a world can bring, the adventures it may hold." Ives continued, "Unfortunately my father is trying to arrange my seventh marriage to my cousin Yasmin as a business arrangement but she has the face of an ox and the body of a hairy goat. I wish to look on the faces of women who stir my loins and make my heart feel fit to burst. I am sure if I remain here and am forced against my will into this passionless marriage, I shall wither away and die."

"Seventh wife?" Thomas shook his head at the thought. "What happened to the other six?"

"Ah," Ives threw his arms up in the air as if it was of little concern. "Questions. Always it is questions with you! It is lucky we are not to be married, you would nag me to death within a week!"

"Are you going to introduce us to your friend?" Thomas looked up to see Kerian and Colette standing there. Before he could answer, they grabbed two more chairs and sat down to join the conversation. Ives looked at Colette and rolled his eyes back at Thomas.

"You see," He stated. "I am with you but mere moments and beauty has come into my life." Thomas noticed Colette's flush and Kerian's glare and chuckled to himself.

The door to the tavern swung open, silencing the atmosphere within the bar, as if it had suddenly rushed to join the cold air outside. Four heavily armoured men walked into the room their dusty black and silver armour, adorned with the carved representations of silver screaming dragonheads, stained by the dust of the road.

Thomas could not help but notice the similarity in appearance to Kerian's slightly simplified and scaled down colour scheme. He also noted the fact that Kerian's body language had stiffened as the men had entered and he was now toying with the half empty wine glass before him as his eyes flicked over then back at his glass several times in short order. Kerian's other hand had dropped below the level of the table and the captain did not need x-ray vision to realise that the hilt of his rune-etched sword would not be far away. Something about these men upset Kerian. Their very demeanour and swagger signalling trouble.

The captain was not the only one to notice the new arrivals. Rauph had paused in mid-arm wrestle, oblivious to the straining faces of the three men opposite him who were still determined to pin his arm to the table. Aradol had also returned from the kitchen but had paused in mid stride, the door swinging into him as he stood, unsure whether to continue into the room to serve tables or hang back in expectation of trouble.

The soldiers removed their helmets as they reached the bar, placing them on the smooth wooden surface and depositing dust and sweat upon the highly polished wood with little or no concern. The barman swiftly took in their orders and hurried to comply, his twitching eyebrow the only sign at his displeasure at the soldiers' arrival.

Commagin took another long draft of his drink and realised to his horror that his tankard was empty. He turned to Weyn to pursue the possibility of yet another refill and noted the man was no longer focusing on him and was instead looking towards the new arrivals at the bar. The Dwarf hated his audience, especially a paying audience, to desert him and so he turned to take in the rivals to his performance, considering all be it briefly that these men may also pay to hear his heroic saga.

The Dwarf prepared to introduce them to the rudiments of his tale and opened his mouth to speak only to find the soldiers turning their backs on the merry engineer, dashing any hopes of further liquid refreshment. Commagin was flabbergasted! How dare they turn their backs on him!

"Now that's not very polite." The Dwarf snarled placing his hand on the nearest soldier's shoulder. The man turned to regard the engineer, his gaze lingering on the hand that had dared to touch him as if it were some disgusting deposit from a passing bird.

"Remove your hand before I remove it for you."

Commagin flushed and pulled at his beard in frustration.

"Why... That's no way to speak to your seniors"

Before the Dwarf could react, the soldier lashed out with his boot, kicking the stool out from beneath Commagin's perched form. The engineer dropped like a stone, yelping in pain as his bandaged foot dropped onto the floorboards. The soldiers burst into laughter at his misfortune. Weyn bent over to assist the spluttering Dwarf but he found his offer of assistance briskly shoved aside by his new shipmate.

"I can stand up myself." Commagin snapped bringing himself upright and dusting himself off. He scowled intently and walked determinedly back to the man who had accosted him, his nose barely level with the man's breastplate.

"Just who do you think you are?" He demanded pushing out his chest defiantly.

Thomas cringed from the sanctuary of his seat as he took in the display. Commagin had drunk too much as usual and in the Dwarf's bid to massage his over-inflated ego their evening was going to end as most shore leaves did... with a fight.

The other soldiers had taken notice now and Thomas realised that the potential for explosive violence was rising dramatically. He dropped his hand beneath the table and winked good-naturedly at Kerian as if they both shared a joke. Kerian's stony gaze stopped the captain in mid-motion, the elderly fighter indicating with the intensity of his look that these men would not be as easy a push over as the captain may have believed.

"I am clearly your better." The soldier replied loudly, addressing the Dwarf as he also played to the audience before him.

"And on behalf of my colleagues may I thank you for the courtesy you have shown me by offering your seat to me, it has been a long ride and my feet are weary." The soldier slowly and deliberately lowered himself onto the stool he had just kicked out from under Commagin before deliberately turning his back on the Dwarf, much to the appreciation and amusement of his colleagues.

Commagin started to go a deep scarlet colour as if he were about to explode: ferociously tugging at his beard and making his eyes water. However, before the engineer could launch a retaliation the door to the tavern flew open and Ashe rushed in out of breath, his eyes darting frantically around the room before he noticed the captain and his companions sitting at the far table.

"Sticks!" he yelled. "We've all got to get out of here and fast! Caerlyon knights control this town they have skeletal birds and everything! I went up to the castle on the hill, you know the one with all the lightning and stuff and there's a whole battalion of knights stationed up there." He rushed across the room and tugged on the elderly fighter's arm as if by some miracle his urgency could propel Kerian's muscular form from his seat.

Kerian turned a wintery gaze on the Halfling and remained seated despite Ashe's feverish attempts to move him.

"Come on Sticks... We all have to get out of here. These men are killers; believe me I have seen what they can do. We've got to get out of here before they..."

A gauntleted hand fell on the Halfling's shoulder stopping Ashe in mid-sentence.

"Before they what?" the soldier towering above the little thief asked.

"Before they find us...oh mouldy acorns!" Ashe gazed up into the face of the soldier his youthful face betraying the horror he felt at his discovery by one of the very men he had tried to warn his friends about. He turned his head towards Sticks in expectation of aid and noted with sudden realisation that the elderly fighter was not leaping to his aid and showed no intentions of doing so.

"Sticks?" Ashe mouthed in disbelief.

The officer restraining Ashe paused in surprise as he realised the words the Halfling had used to address the elderly fighter sitting beside him.

"What did you call him?" He stepped back, tilting his head to get a better view of the man seated before him and his eyes widened with recognition. "Denaris? Kerian Denaris?" he questioned incredulously.

Kerian realised it was foolish to maintain his charade any longer. He knew the man would guess who he was regardless, so he lifted his head high and fixed the soldier with his cold hazel eyes.

"My queen it is you!" the soldier hissed. He gestured to his three companions. "Come over here... You will never guess who this is! Its Lieutenant Styx, old death or glory from the academy." The three men responded to the soldier's command and sauntered over, armour creaking ominously as they moved to see what all the fuss was about. Commagin stood in their wake, stunned that his 'fight' had up and walked away.

"The years have not been kind to you." The soldier laughed, his hand reaching out to touch Kerian's white hair. Kerian snatched his head away from the outstretched hand, drawing a snigger from one of the other soldiers, whilst allowing the main antagonist to look around at the other occupants of the table, visibly pausing when he noticed Colette sitting over to one side.

"Well, well, well. It is good to see that at least your taste in the ladies remains consistent." continued the armoured figure without missing a beat and drawing more jeers from his colleagues. "Impressive, she is almost as beautiful as your last. Does she like sharing you with others too?"

The Caerlyon knight moved around the table towards Colette's chair, motioning as he did so for his colleagues to take up guarded positions around the elderly fighter who had once served in their ranks. Under the table, Thomas began to inch his sword from its scabbard.

Kerian began to rise from his chair as the men closed in, his hand starting to draw his sword.

"No you don't." The solider stated coldly, a wicked smile on his face. A cold edged dagger appeared against Colette's delicate throat stopping Kerian more surely than any verbal order could. A look of defeat swiftly crossed his features and he slowly resumed his seat cursing silently as the remaining men moved in closer.

"Leave the lady alone." Ordered a clear voice from across the tavern.

Thomas tore his attention from the drama before him and looked up to notice the waiter walking determinedly across the room towards them. What was the idiot doing? He did not even have a weapon in his hand. This was clearly not a wise way for Aradol to introduce himself!

The door to the tavern opened and a dozen more knights rowdily made their way into the bar but these had swords drawn and they were out of breath as if running.

"He came in here." The first stated. "I swear he did."

There he is." gasped another, gesturing at the cringing Halfling. "He stole our silver mascot!"

"Who me?" Ashe asked innocently from under the table next to where Kerian was pinned, thereby confirming his guilt to all that knew him beyond any reasonable doubt.

Thomas looked across the rapidly crowding bar and noted with concern that Rauph had swiftly pinned his three colleagues and now appeared to be rubbing his hands in glee at what was transpiring!

This was going to get messy!

The conversation at the table was heating up before him and Thomas suddenly wished that he had stayed on board the *El Defensor* and had a quiet night in!

Aradol had now arrived at the table and the fighters before him had swiftly weighed up his unarmed status and sniggered derisively at the display of heroic stupidity they saw before them.

"I told you to let the lady go." Aradol demanded. "If you wish to pick a fight with someone at least pick a fight with someone who can fight you back. Let's step outside and settle this dispute, leaving these people at peace with their drinks." Glowering faces responded to Aradol's display of chivalry, none more vehement than Colette's, her face flushing at the indignity of the waiter's implied helpless female comment.

Kerian stared up at the young man who had foolishly decided to attempt suicide and tried to warn Aradol off with exaggerated but silent expressions. Aradol refused to acknowledge the warning, his face clearly displaying he had no intention of complying, whilst over his shoulder the twelve new arrivals had stopped in their pursuit of Ashe to observe the fight they clearly saw coming.

"I told you to let the lady go." He warned one last time.

"Or what?" mocked the soldier.

Aradol lashed out with his hand in a blur of speed, snatching the dagger from Colette's throat in one lightning swift movement, before anyone had a chance to react he had firmly grabbed the front of the soldier's tunic and dropped himself bodily to the floor, pulling the surprised soldier with him. The soldier gasped in surprise before Aradol's weight dragged his head straight down onto the hard wooden table. There was a crunch and two teeth spun out across the white linen trailing spots of blood.

"I warned you to let the lady go." Aradol stated coldly, regaining his feet from his position beneath the table. The other soldiers remained motionless, surprised at a waiter bringing one of their own down so quickly. Aradol lifted their colleague's head from the table to reveal the bloody mess that was now his face and then took it one step too far.

"Now do me the honour of apologising to the lady."

The reaction was instant. The three remaining soldiers suddenly recovered their wits and piled on top of Aradol, fists flying. All four crashed to the floor in an undignified brawling heap.

Kerian grinned as the restraining hands that had been upon him suddenly withdrew. It was what he had been waiting for. He swiftly stood, drawing his sword to trace a violet line of light through the air of the tavern. The nearest Caerlyon knight threw his head back instinctively as the blade passed mere inches from his face.

"You mis..." Aradol's punch took the soldier by surprise and he staggered back stunned. The other Caerlyon knight pounced on the already battered form of Aradol and inserted his knee into a place that brought water to the waiter's eyes.

Aradol kicked back hard pushing the knight against the table and slamming it backwards, squashing Thomas painfully across his stomach and pinning him against the wall as effectively as an insect in amber, his sword still only half drawn.

Kerian's unimpeded sword swing ploughed into the embroidered hanging that decorated the wall, sending thread and gold braid stitching flying everywhere. To Kerian's distain and Thomas's relief, the sword then promptly refused to budge, caught in the decoration bare inches from the captain's flushed face.

"Are you some kind of idiot swinging a sword in here?" Thomas yelled, struggling to push the table clear. "Be a bit more careful, you're supposed to be on my side remember?"

"I get the job done don't I?"

"Need I remind you I am not 'the job'?" Thomas returned caustically.

The knight whom Aradol had kindly introduced to the table top now decided to raise his head, uttering a bestial growl. He shook himself, splattering more blood droplets across the table linen as he recognised the man responsible for his injuries still struggling on the floor. Unimpeded, the soldier drew his sword and moved to stand over the wrestling men, preparing to swing his blade down onto the lowly peasant who had dared to attack him. His rage was so great that it was obvious to all watching that this time no quarter would be given and there would be no concern over any 'friendly casualties' that could be inflicted on the way to this soldier's bloody retribution.

Kerian tugged at his sword with increased urgency but the blade still stubbornly refused to budge. He turned to Thomas for assistance but the captain was still pinned by the table and Colette seemed to be content just to hold on to the lit candle on the table in case anyone knocked it over! He was on his own. He tugged again and could only wince as he saw the soldier's sword swing up in preparation for the fatal blow to follow.

A bar stool crashed across the soldier's back dropping him senseless to the floor and making all the occupants at the table jump at its unexpected arrival. Kerian, Thomas and Colette found themselves gazing upon Aradol's saviour. Commagin tottered up behind where the soldier had stood a satisfied smile on his lips.

"I thought you wanted my seat!" The Dwarf screamed at the senseless soldier. "Instead when I finally give it over, you wander off showing me nothing but disrespect for my sacrifice! Well I always pride myself in giving someone what they ask for and believe me you asked for this!" He kicked the man for good measure then stood over the inert figure as if waiting for something.

"Well aren't you going to say thanks?" the stubborn engineer demanded to his now unconscious target.

Satisfied that there would be no reply, Commagin stared past the downed soldier at the three other figures still wrestling under the table. He rubbed his hands together, taking time only to decide where he wanted to start first, before throwing himself into the pile, pushing the table further back into the alcove and crushing Thomas even further.

There was a stifled scream followed by a louder more piercing one as one soldier suddenly grabbed hold of the table edge in front of Thomas as if it were the side of a boat at sea and he was struggling to pull himself from the water. The captain looked on, powerless, as the man screamed again, his body tugged viciously back down under the table as the Dwarf bit deeply into his exposed calf.

"You're going to need a bigger table." Thomas deliberately misquoted; sharing a moment of humour with himself as he paraphrased a famous Stephen Spielberg movie about a killer shark from many years ago.

The other soldier paused in pummelling Aradol, wondering what all the renewed screams of pain were. He lifted his head and came level with Colette's knee. He looked up into her sweet innocent face and flashed her a look that suggested he would enjoy dealing with her after polishing off the struggling man beneath him. Colette smiled back and opened her hand inches before the stunned soldier's face to reveal the naked candle flame dancing in thin air within her palm. She smiled again before bringing her face closer to the flame and blowing the man a sensuous kiss.

The soldier's smile turned to terror in an instant as the flame leapt from her hand and licked hungrily across his face and clothes, igniting them in seconds. Colette remained seated, continuing to look at the burning man before her with a coldness that stunned everyone at her table.

"I can look after myself." She commented under her breath. "Helpless female indeed!"

The fighter sprang to his feet running blindly about the tavern, his head consumed by rapidly spreading fire and giving the macabre image that he had become in essence a 'human candle' with his hair crisping away instead of wax. He careered about the packed tavern frantically flapping at his head and face in an attempt to extinguish the magical flames, his screams getting louder and louder as he ran. Small fires sprang up in his wake as the fire hungrily snatched at curtains and tablecloths along his terror-crazed path.

Aradol rose from the floor with his eye swelling shut and his face a mask of shock that matched both of the stunned expressions worn on Thomas and Kerian's faces. Colette looked at them all and shrugged indifferently.

"What? He drew the knife on me. I had every right to defend myself." She blew gently on the palm of her hand as if to extinguish any flame that remained, then winked flirtatiously and rose to her feet. "Didn't you realise I was hot stuff? Now what does a girl need to do to get a drink around here?"

As Colette stood, the three men looked past her at the other end of the tavern and the chaos ensuing there. An explosion of several brawls and skirmishes had turned the civilised end of the tavern into a whirling morass of pounding flesh and spilt blood. The rest of the *El Defensor's* crew had taken the visual cues from the altercation at Thomas's table to launch themselves at the twelve knights that had unfortunately run into the tavern after Ashe and now found to their horror that the tiny Halfling had friends.

Ives and Weyn fought side by side, Weyn dispatching foes with a wicked looking dagger and Ives with his thin white curved sword. Ashe had even gained the courage to creep out from the table he had been hiding beneath and was now up on the bar, 'whacking' a soldier ferociously over the head with a serving tray.

Rauph took in the chaos about him, ensuring that all of his friends had took the opportunity to enjoy part of the fight before he slowly stood up from the table where he had patiently sat and with cool deliberation slid the bolts across on the tavern door.

He had shared with his friends nicely, waited for everyone to have a go, now it was his turn, and Rauph hated interruptions when he played.

Chapter Twenty-Five

Scrave leant back in the captain's chair; his feet perched upon the desk, a glass of Thomas's smoky liquor in his hand. He watched the artisans and carpenters hurry about him, replacing the ruined carpet and tidying up the destruction that had been the captain's cabin. The Elf took this rare opportunity to caress the arms of the monstrous piece of furniture from where Thomas ruled. He closed his eyes and fantasised about being captain of the *El Defensor,* his hands gripping the arms of the chair as if they were made of solid gold and a prize to be widely coveted. In his imagination, Thomas ran to do his bidding and all was right with the world.

The door slammed shut, snapping Scrave back to the present and he realised with astonishment that he had fallen asleep in the chair as the work had gone on around him. He was obviously more exhausted than he would have liked to admit; although this self-inspired revelation was one that he did not intend to share with anyone. His eyes scanned the room for imperfections in Thomas's orders, the Elf subconsciously scared that another verbal berating would be due if something was missed.

They had repaired the glass cases, panes of the expensive luxury still marked with the fingerprints of the now departed craftsmen. The front of the desk, now sanded and polished to a high sheen, formed a perfect resting place for Scrave's scuffed boots. The sight where Thomas's blade had embedded in the wood now a topic for after dinner conversation, rather than the splintered eyesore it had been when the Elf had first sat down in his chair.

Had he really slept through all of that?

The replaced carpet was a dark maroon pile, adding a further opulence to the room and serving to increase Scrave's already raised ire.

So these were the benefits of being a captain!

If anyone deserved a reward, it was Scrave! He moved from the seat and pushed against the top axis of the globe, reaching inside for the decanter and another refill, before returning to the chair and swinging it up on its hind legs.

He took large swallows of the sickly sweet alcohol and gasped as fire raced down his gullet to warm him pleasantly inside, relishing the buzz and light-headedness that the alcohol swiftly brought to his system. Perched this way, he noticed a box of debris left standing near the door. No matter how highly praised craftsmen were, you always had to clean up after them! He got back to his feet noticing with mild amusement that his legs appeared to belong to someone else! They felt rubbery and numb as if made of some strange and pliable material that had a will of its own. He wandered over, via a slightly meandering course and looked inside to view the shattered remains of several model ships that had been Thomas's pride and joy.

Scrave found himself chuckling at the box of shattered dreams and then he looked blankly at the glass in his hand and noted that only a small amount of the smoky liquor still clung stubbornly to the sides of the glass. He swallowed it in seconds sighing loudly as the sweetness infused his being. What in the world was this stuff?

He looked back down at the ruined galleon, smashed into tiny pieces. Why had Thomas asked to save all this junk? There was no way he would be able to put these models back together! He reached in, grabbed a tangled mess of thread and wood, and lifted it up to his face before dropping it back into the box. Talk about a waste of time!

The glimmer of gold caught Scrave's eye as he was about to turn from the box and he paused, swinging his head back over the container in an attempt to catch a repeated flash of yellow and confirm his findings. He plunged his hand back into the detritus of the galleon and pulled up a semicircle of gold etched with the most intricate and realistic carving of scales he had ever seen. What part of the galleon was this supposed to be?

His alcohol-induced brain failed to come up with a suitable answer but his calculating eye swiftly realised that this was something that was worth money. Maybe this babysitting session was going to be worthwhile after all. He examined the ends of the golden semi-circle he held and noted the sheared ends with mild bemusement before ascertaining that this was a part of something infinitely larger than the piece he held in his hand. He looked back at the box of refuse, a sly smile sliding across his face.

* * * * * *

The wooden frame of The Swashbuckling Dandy was the last part of the building to succumb to the roaring hunger of the flames engulfing the inn. The crew of the *El Defensor* stood out in the street watching the building's demise, the flames of the inn as symbolic as they were real, cleansing and cauterising them all and lifting their spirits high, with no room for guilt or regret.

Rauph stood snorting with mirth and others were clapping their colleagues on their backs whilst sharing the warmth from the fire as the evening's robust entertainment drew to a suitably theatrical close.

Ives walked over to Thomas sharing the infectious mirth that was so impossible to ignore.

"You certainly know how to throw a good party." He gestured, jumping as another timber crashed into the ruins that were part of the tavern's smoking shell.

"Haven't you ever heard of the reputation us sailors get?" Thomas returned. "I have to ask, you seemed very comfortable with your sword. It is a strange colour. What metal is it made of?"

"You see, again it is questions!" Ives laughed. "It is not metal..." he winked and leaned closer to be heard over the crackling flames. "It's a tooth. Now am I in or not?"

"In," Thomas agreed nodding his head. "I just hope you don't regret it."

"How could I regret it when you show me a good time like this?" Ives laughed, heading over to slap Weyn on the back, cementing their new-shared comradery.

A large sack clanged loudly on the ground by Thomas's feet and he looked over to see the waiter Aradol, covered in soot, blood and many, many contusions.

"I hope the contents of that sack haven't been looted?" Thomas asked.

"I have never taken something that isn't rightfully mine." Aradol shot back insulted. "My waiter job and this sack are all I have in the world and now it appears I just have the sack!" Thomas tried not to laugh at the irony of the waiter's statement and looked up past Aradol's wounded face before frowning. Lines of torches were trailing down from the mountain, heading in their direction.

"If you need a job I have need of hands such as yours." Thomas gritted his teeth as soon as he had said the words, realising his error but Aradol's face indicated his delight at the unexpected offer. "We can discuss wage and terms later but for now I believe we have outstayed our welcome. Come on... It is time to go. We may have to run for it."

"A gentleman never runs." Aradol lectured.

"He does if he wants his job to last longer than the last one." Thomas shot back, heading off towards the harbour in pursuit of his departing crew.

* * * * * *

Barney finished sweeping up the laboratory floor and examined the results of his endeavours with a critical eye. That was quite a pile of rubbish he had collected! He sighed as he thought of all the trips it would take to transfer the pile of rubbish down here into a pile of rubbish far up on deck so it could be disposed of in Perenord. That would be many trips.

One day he would have his own apprentice and all this menial work would be a thing of the past! Apparently, the first rule of his engineering apprenticeship that he had learned was that an engineer, especially one called Commagin, never did anything his apprentice could do for him. This fine example of theory, once put into practice, had taken the little Gnome just over an hour! This was ridiculous; it would take another hour just to move all this stuff! Unless...unless.

The Gnome turned his head rapidly about the room before alighting on a heavily upholstered chair that stood forlorn and forgotten in the far corner. With rapid determination and a practiced flick of the brush, the pile of rubbish swiftly slid across the floor and Barney lifted the ornate fringe of the chair in preparation of his forthcoming deposit.

Piles of old refuse stared back at him, swiftly putting pay to that idea! He cursed, his critical eye scanning the cabin for yet another suitable hiding place, before noticing the burnt rug that stood before the main workbench.

Yet again, a dazzling display of brushwork followed ending with the ceremonial replacement of the rug on top of the rubbish. A few quick stomps and the pile had flattened sufficiently that the centre of the rug was no longer quite level with the height of the worktop and Barney rubbed his hands together in satisfaction at a job well done. The broom flew onto a nearby shelf with a skill that defied logic and the Gnome was swiftly out of the door, his head full of real engineering problems. Engineering textbooks beckoned and needed to be considered as he carried out his apprentice studies. Barney extinguished the lights and shut the door before retiring to his quarters and the texts awaiting him there.

Scrave watched the departing Gnome from the shadows, staying patiently in his hiding place until long after the apprentice had left. Satisfied that he would not be at risk of being disturbed he slipped from his place of concealment and approached the lab benches.

It took several moments before Scrave found what he desired, then a small spark lit the darkness and a flame roared to life. The illumination flickered across the Elf's ruined face without any concern for flattery but it mattered little, for there were no witnesses to gaze upon Scrave's unusual actions, just the silent yet stern textbooks and stuffy scientific paraphernalia that made up Commagin's lab.

* * * * * *

By the time the rag tag crew of the *El Defensor* reached the dock, there were shouts of alarm ringing clearly from behind.

"Do you always leave ports this way?" Kerian enquired as he escorted Colette politely up the gangplank.

"I did tell you we had a reputation didn't I?" Thomas replied, even as his hands signalled for the crew to assume their stations. "Have you any idea how hard it is to keep that reputation up?"

"I have an idea." Kerian smiled, grabbing Ashe's hand as the ship began to come alive behind him. Commagin swiftly hopped up the gangplank and threw himself across the gap as they slipped the mooring lines. Thomas looked towards Sherman who nodded to confirm they had accounted for everyone safely on board.

A howling wind suddenly rose from the aft deck and the sails snapped above the crew's heads, filling with the enchanted breeze Colette had summoned. The *El Defensor* creaked and groaned as she rapidly picked up speed and headed for the harbour entrance. The tide was against them now but the El Defensor rarely waited for the tide with an air elemental filling her sails.

Thomas sighed as he felt the cool breeze upon his face, there was nothing like being out on the surface of the sea. This was undeniably his home now, as captain of this magnificent vessel. He listened intently to Sherman's watch report. The supplies had been stored below, the carpets in place, repairs carried out to his cabin and Sherman was sure there was a rat loose on the aft deck. Nothing to worry about! This was the life! Kerian remained at his side looking slightly embarrassed.

"We were supposed to be getting off at this port." He reminded Thomas.

"And miss all this?" Thomas shot back.

"Well your adventures do seem to be somewhat... eventful." Kerian smiled. "If somewhat predictable."

"Predictable! Me? You know you could always stay on..." Thomas suggested with an infectious grin. "I could do with another fighter, Colette and Austen could do with another healer and Commagin is always looking for another assistant since he blew up the last one." Kerian stood silently for a moment considering the offer.

"The problem is..." Kerian began. "I have a need to be somewhere else." He shook his head, unsure what to say next. "What are your plans for future travel?"

"To be honest I have very few ideas." Thomas confessed with a grin, hoping that his carefree demeanour helped to hide the deeper concerns he actually held. "We are, as I am sure you have heard from the crew, currently... stuck here and unfortunately we do not have the resources or the power to move on."

"What resources do you mean?" Kerian replied. "I have many contacts... If I can help in any way?"

"I think you have helped enough already." Thomas replied, aware that his response was possibly brusquer than he had intended it to be. "We need gemstones of a value and purity that your contacts would never be able to acquire. A veritable 'king's ransom' as it were."

Kerian leant on the railing and appeared to be in deep thought, watching the waves rushing by below him and then he leaned forward and took a deep breath.

"I may just know a way of finding you this 'king's ransom'" He offered. "You see I have in my possession this map..."

* * * * * *

Scrave appeared at the entrance from below decks and looked where he could move to assist, then paused as he noticed Styx was still aboard the ship. His eyes scanned the elderly fighter from afar and a prickle of agitation ran up the Elf's spine.

What was he still doing here? He was supposed to have disembarked in Perenord! His eyes scanned Styx belt, looking for the absent dagger that was rightfully his. So, Styx did not even consider the blade good enough to wear!

Scrave made a silent promise to himself there and then. He was going to get that dagger back, no matter what and use it, as it had been intended.

* * * * * *

Kerian moved up onto the forecastle and noted Ashe sitting silently in the shadows by himself.

"What did you take from those soldiers?" he asked.

Ashe reached into his satchel and removed a small silver dragon statuette, one claw extended before it. Kerian laughed as he saw it, recognising the mascot and realising how humiliating it would be to his old unit to have had such a treasure stolen away by such a small individual.

"You know we are going to be together for a long time now." He remarked. "Thomas has asked if we will remain as crewmen on this ship." Kerian paused, gathering his thoughts. "You need to know that stealing people's belongings are wrong and it could get you into serious trouble on a ship like this. You need to stop now. Thomas will be paying you wages and you now have a place to live. So there is no need to continue."

"I suppose you are right," Ashe looked at Kerian with his wide eyes and nodded his head in agreement. "I'll try to stop now and make a fresh start."

"Then you can start right now." Kerian smiled, holding out his hand. "Where's my ring?"

* * * * * *

The knock at the door startled Violetta and her daughter from their sleep causing the large chef to slip from her covers and pad softly to the door, her voluminous nightdress billowing out behind her. She paused only to slip the meat cleaver she kept by her bed firmly into her hand, before motioning back across the room to her daughter and telling her to remain in bed, only then did she turn to address her nocturnal visitor.

"Who is it?" she whispered through the door.

"It's me." came the cryptic reply.

Violetta threw the bolt and opened the door swiftly, letting her mysterious visitor slip silently into the room. Attentive as always, she closed and bolted the door behind her guest before speaking any further.

"I thought you would never come." She hissed. "It has not been easy to keep this secret of yours from the crew."

"How is he?" The shadowy figure enquired. "Will he live?"

"Follow me." Violetta motioned guiding her guest by holding gently to his arm. She took the cloaked figure to one of the store cupboards set on the back wall of the galley and carefully moved the items of food aside to reveal a small recess. There was a spark, bright and blinding in the darkness and then a small candle softly illuminated the opening beyond. Small figures of saints surrounded by offerings of fruits and food first greeted the visitor's gaze and lying beneath these on a stained pallet was a man, his breathing ragged and forced.

"He doesn't sound too good." Violetta's guest commented.

"He still remains in the land of the living don't he?" came her caustic reply. "I don't like hiding this from the crew."

"You owe me." came the response, the figure suddenly turning into the light. Thomas Adams gazed down at the bloody wheezing figure lying before him then back at Violetta. "You must keep him alive. I need to know why he was here and more importantly, who was behind him. I don't like surprises and certainly don't wish for anymore." The chef nodded her head in reply and extinguished the candle plunging the store cupboard back into darkness.

"Not a word you hear?" Thomas ordered, before turning his back on Violetta and making his way from the cabin.

"Not a word." Violetta mimicked, re-bolting her cabin door and slipping under her covers once more. She tucked her meat cleaver under her pillow, ensuring that she remained firmly holding on to the handle. This was the problem when you 'owed' someone your life; they always came to collect on the favour.

* * * * * *

The three dolphins leapt as one from the clear azure surface of the sea, their sleek grey bodies trailing droplets of glistening gem-like water in their wake. Their brief escape from gravity ended as spectacularly as it began, in explosive plumes of white foam that flew up to soak the figurehead of the *El Defensor* where it sliced through the swell mere seconds behind them.

Water splashed up from the dolphins' path soaking Ashe in cool salty beads and raising a gasp from the startled Halfling. His laughter rang rich and pure as he looked down at his rolled up leggings, totally saturated from the spray and regarded his pale white knees. His little feet dangled through the netting and out over the water and he wiggled his toes in delight.

Ashe giggled as the dolphins repeated their performance, rising and falling from the sea in perfect formation and sending water splashing down to soak him afresh. He hung scarcely five feet above the crystal clear depths, safely suspended in a net that had been tied to the tip of the bowsprit and then taken back to be secured to the anchor chain ports set at either side of the ship's bow. Directly above the laughing Halfling, the figurehead, carved into the image of a stern yet beautiful auburn haired woman pointed ahead into uncharted waters, her sword held high and her facial features devoid of any fear.

This was fun!

"Watch out for the sharks." came a teasing voice from above.

Ashe looked up to behold the windswept features of Colette and could not help but smile, waving his arm and inviting her to come down alongside him. Colette glanced at the sails high above her and shrugged, the wind had been up all day and the elemental was not required, leaving her temporarily unemployed. She slipped over the side with a nimble and sure-footed action that left the Halfling nodding in appreciation and she was soon sitting alongside the diminutive thief, her petite feet and slender tanned legs wiggling alongside his own.

"Do you think sharks would really come and get us?" Ashe quizzed, his eyes nervously scanning the swell of the clear sea below him. "I've heard tales but I never really thought any would jump out of the water to eat a Halfling."

Colette laughed as a dolphin broke the surface of the sea and turned to reply to her little colleague. "Only if they were really hungry." she teased. "But I think we are perfectly safe with these fellows here to protect us." She gestured towards the acrobatic mammals. "It's only when the dolphins disappear that we would have cause to worry."

"Why?" asked Ashe, his curiosity piqued?

"Because if the dolphins leave us it's probably because something that's nasty, more agile and decidedly bigger than them is prowling around in the area and to be honest with you I certainly wouldn't want to encounter something like that."

Ashe gazed at the sea again with his face afresh with worry.

"Oh don't worry." Colette laughed. "After all I'm here to protect you."

The Halfling flushed at this remark, realising that Colette was probably right after her actions of the previous evening when she had turned her aggressor into a human candle. An uncomfortable silence descended upon the jovial thief, broken only when Colette nudged him hard in the ribs and laughed at his embarrassment. She leaned back in the netting, resting her head on her arm and closing her eyes to the warm sun, allowing stray blonde hairs to tickle the skin of her face.

"Tell me about yourself Ashe?"

Ashe leant back alongside the ship's mage, swaying the netting slightly before finally getting comfortable and relaxed in the safety of the makeshift hammock.

"What is it that you want to know?"

"Oh anything..." Colette replied. "Where you were born? What it is that you do? Spin me tales about the loves of your life, the trials, the tribulations... and almost certainly the disappointments. What successes have you had and what are your dreams for the future... You know... something that won't take too long."

Colette laughed anew, easing Ashe's initial belief that Colette was mocking him and her infectious laughter soon had the Halfling joining in too.

"Where do I start..." he paused as if collecting his thoughts, his mind a whirr as he tried to decide what aspects of his pitiful existence should be omitted and what elements could be enhanced for Colette's entertainment.

"Just tell me what you are comfortable with." Colette prompted as if reading his thoughts.

Ashe began his shaky narrative seconds later, spinning tales of his life on the streets and how he had struggled day to day to etch out a meagre existence that kept the rain from his head and scraps of food in his stomach. Colette teased out the more difficult parts with light probing that the Halfling found irresistible to deny. Within minutes, he had put the shaky narrative of the past behind him and a more confident tale began to emerge as Ashe decided to change tact.

Under the watchful gaze of the morning sunshine, Ashe told of liberated fabulous treasures, deadly traps sidestepped and monsters slain, causing Colette to smile to herself as the little thief continued to paint his elaborate masterpiece on an imaginary canvas. The tales become taller by the second, chronicling a hero who needed to be both suave, debonair, adorned with rippling muscles and seven feet tall to accomplish all the things he could do.

As Ashe continued his tale, Colette leaned across him and looked him sternly in the eye.

"I'm amazed you have managed to find the time to travel with us boring people." She teased. "Why don't you tell me how you are settling in here on the *El Defensor* instead?"

Ashe glanced across at Colette's smiling face and sighed deeply inside.

"Well work in the lab is boring. All I seem to be doing is carrying one lot of stuff from here to there and then from there to here." Ashe began to moan. "They never let me do anything interesting. Commagin is working on a white suit of armour that he believes will go under water but it keeps springing leaks! I have to mop and sweep the floor and save Barney from drowning!"

Colette laughed but encouraged Ashe to continue.

"I do have something exciting happening soon." Ashe continued. "Austen and Ridge tell me the falcons on board have hatched some eggs and I can have one of the baby birds to train. There is a little egg in the clutch smaller than the others that is not brown and white but black and white instead. Ridge said I could call the bird Sinders when it hatches. It sounds all mean and nasty doesn't it?"

Colette stifled a giggle at the joke her crewmates were playing on the Halfling. Cinders and Ash... She struggled to keep a straight face.

"But you will have to feed it if it is small." Colette smiled.

"How do I do that?" Ashe asked innocently.

"Well parent birds normally chew up the food, fish guts, worms and the like and then regurgitate it straight into their baby bird's mouths."

"Doesn't regurgitate mean be sick?" Ashe asked, turning slightly green. "I don't even like worms."

"Why don't you tell me about your friends?" Colette requested, trying to hide her smile behind her hand as she finally bought Ashe's torture to a close. "Tell me about Marcus and Kerian. How did you three get together? You seem such an odd group of companions that I'm sure there's a great tale in their somewhere."

"Kerian. There is that name again. Who is this Kerian?" Ashe turned towards Colette with a bemused look on his face.

"You know." Colette laughed pulling a comical face. "Mr old, cold, and sombre looking. No sense of humour, wears black a lot."

"Oh." Ashe beamed, clicking his fingers in sudden recognition. "You mean Sticks...Kerian indeed!" He crinkled his brow in thought. "Why do you call him Kerian? All of his close friends like me call him Sticks."

Colette motioned for him to carry on and Ashe started to retell his more recent adventures; explaining how he had saved Sticks from almost certain death in the back alleys of Catterick. He went on to tell her of his quest to return the ring Sticks had dropped in the fight and how he had battled through storms, riots and tempestuous seas to return the precious item at great risk to his own personal safety.

The mage listened attentively to it all, politely refraining from interruption or correction even though she knew the Halfling was obviously embellishing the story to enlarge his role. Even so, it was a thrilling tale of murder and swashbuckling excitement and Colette found that she was gasping at the knife-edge escapes and daring deeds Ashe had made before the fateful night they had come aboard.

Ashe paused in his tale at this point and looked across at his beautiful companion. She looked so peaceful and at ease with his retelling, the sunlight reflected from the sea below sending spangles of light across her features. Colette suddenly opened her eyes and stared at Ashe and was instantly aware that she was being scrutinised.

"Now tell me," she smiled, aware of Ashe's discomfort at discovery. "Just how much of that tale is actually true? Especially the part about the magical ring?"

"All of it." Ashe replied without a moment's hesitation. He watched Colette's frown for a moment before reaching up and retrieving his satchel from where he had looped it around the bowsprit. He dropped his hand inside and withdrew a piece of velvet cloth, which he gently unwrapped to reveal the crystal prism he had borrowed from the jeweller's shop at the start of his adventure. He offered the prism to Colette for examination and she gasped as the light refracted within it and cast a dazzling rainbow across her arm and blouse.

"To think." Ashe continued. "If I hadn't decided to liberate this prism from the evil Warlord's heavily guarded fortress, freed the slaves, fought the hell hound pack and kissed the delectable Helen of Worchester, Sticks and I would have never met. The thing is that as a reward it appears to be next to useless. I have tried to find a use for it but nothing seems to happen apart from this colour-splitting thing. It doesn't even appear to be magical."

"Oh yes it is." Colette murmured mysteriously. "What else have you got in there?"

Ashe dropped his hand absent-mindedly to his satchel and lifted out Kerian's gilt mirror, now fully repaired. He had not told Kerian he had spent most of the day in Perenord getting it repaired as a token of thanks for saving him and bringing him on board the *El Defensor* instead of leaving him on the jetty back in Catterick.

"What's this?" Colette asked. "It's beautiful."

"Oh it belongs to Sticks." Ashe piped up. "He gave it to me to look after. You have no idea how absent-minded he is. I mean last night I gave him his ring back and now just look..." He fished his hand into his pocket and plucked out a golden ring. "It's right back in my pocket again. How clumsy can he get?"

"May I look?" Colette asked, holding out her hands for the precious item.

"Only very quickly," Ashe replied looking about nervously. "If Sticks finds it missing again he may get upset. Oh... And don't hold it too long in your hand; it makes you do the most unprofitable acts!"

Colette took the ring and held it up angling the light, the writing within igniting her inquisitive nature instantly. She thought about what she had seen, and what it could mean as she handed the ring back into Ashe's keeping. She remembered hazel eyes looking at her across a glass of wine, actions and responses that had no place in the actions of an old man.

"I don't suppose you would like a trade, seeing as I can't get the prism to work?" Ashe offered, prompting her back to the present. "Although the trade would have to be pretty high for a magical item, I don't just give them away you know."

Colette looked down at the prism in her lap and then slipped one hand to her neck, catching a chain with her finger and pulling out a pendant that had hung hidden within her blouse. The sheen of the ancient gold, fashioned into a thin, delicate droplet of swirls was set with diamonds and pearls and instantly caught the Halfling's attention like a moth to a candle flame. In the centre of the droplet was suspended a gemstone that was as pure white as the pearls surrounding it but Ashe's professional eye knew this was no pearl he had ever come across.

Colette appeared to reconsider before drawing in a deep breath and handing over the one thing that was obviously very special to her.

"It was my great grandmother's." she added as if in afterthought.

"It's very pretty." Ashe replied. "But what does it do exactly?"

Colette clutched the prism tightly to her as if looking for some reassurance from the item she was trading.

"The pendant will show you any one you care deeply about, no matter where they are, however far away or inaccessible. All you have to do is look into the centre stone and think of them as the sun rises in the sky."

This time it was Ashe's turn to look at Colette with disbelief. He lifted the pendant to his eye and noted the hairline crack across the white gem in the centre.

"It's broken isn't it?" Ashe looked across at Colette again, his eyebrow arching at the obvious delay in her reply that confirmed his thoughts in seconds. Then he examined the necklace again. The setting was nice and he could probably get some worth from it. He surprised himself by nodding and accepting the deal.

Colette paused, then leaned across and gave the surprised Halfling a small kiss on the end of his nose. Ashe flushed bright red and was stunned, suddenly speechless.

"Just remember, for it to work you must really, really believe" She grinned before swiftly making her escape above, the prism held close to her breast.

It took Ashe a while to collect his thoughts but before he dared to show his head back on deck, he took a moment to examine the pendant before him. It was obvious she had just duped him... hadn't she?

He looked closely at the pearl encrusted jewellery before slipping it securely within his satchel and quickly climbing up onto the deck of the ship. He walked across the smooth decking barefoot, following in the wet imprints of Colette's earlier passage until the moisture trail faded, then he meandered off to terrorise other unsuspecting members of the crew.

Someone up here had to know what time the sun was due to rise tomorrow and Ashe was not going to miss it for the world.

Chapter Twenty-Six

"Marcus stop being an ass and let me show Thomas the damn map."

"You know I can't." Marcus replied indignantly. "Thomas is not of my order and therefore not deemed worthy of examining its pages. You of all people know that knowledge can be dangerous in the wrong hands. I've told you the heading that should be enough!"

Kerian frowned at the monk before turning in frustration to take in the surroundings of their cabin, his eyes sweeping over the two extra hammocks now squeezed into the room and the fold down ink stained table upon which the large blue bound book in question rested.

"If you won't let me show him the book you will leave me with no alternative but to take it from you anyway." He stated, determined that Marcus would let him have his way whether the monk liked it or not. He turned to the book and lifted it from the desk.

"Please don't do that." Marcus warned.

There was a yelp; a brief flash and the scent of singed hair filled the room. The blue book dropped heavily back onto the desk and Kerian found himself blowing at the ashen remains of the hairs on the back of his hands.

"I told you no one is allowed to pick up the book but me." Marcus lectured. "The contents of the journal are for my eyes only and my observations within are private and personal. Abbot Brialin knows I am not a fighting man so he has protected the book the only other way he could, with enchantments. Since you feel so determined to ignore my wishes, you leave me with no choice but to refuse you access as well. I thought you would respect me better than that."

"Come on Marcus, you know I can be reasonable. Why can't you at least meet me half way? We both want to go in the same direction. Why can't we use the book to show them the way? I heard Brialin telling you it contained all the maps, so I know there's one in there." Kerian threw his arms wide in exasperation, trying desperately not to give in to his internal rage and pound the monk's face into a bloody mess.

"Although we ultimately want the same things Kerian, there are still things I will not stoop to in order to achieve them." The monk replied self-righteously shaking his head and making Kerian almost choke on the anger rising within him. "I will not let anyone view what is inside this book unless they are permitted to do so."

"Well at least open the book and let me copy the page."

"You could never do the illustrations in this book justice. It takes years of training to reach the level where we can illustrate just one letter. What makes you think you could copy one of our maps after a preliminary glance?"

"Right..." Kerian snapped. "There's more than one way to do this." He turned and headed for the door, leaving the indignant monk flushed from the verbal conflict he had just experienced.

"But...but where are you going." He enquired.

"To get some parchment and some ink." Kerian snapped back. "These people have never seen the charts you hold. They do not know what is right or what is wrong. Therefore, I will make up my own chart. At least it will get them going in the right direction. We are bound to hit the island at some time or another."

"But that's deceitful!" Marcus wailed.

"Then let me see the book."

Marcus turned and picked up the thick blue leather bound book and held it tightly to his chest.

"Certainly not!" he shook his head to reinforce his decision.

"Then on your own head be it." Kerian snapped back, "I guess I am better off not relying on anyone but myself to get this thing done." He slammed the door shut behind him leaving Marcus alone with his thoughts.

* * * * * *

"So this is where we will find a 'king's ransom' eh?" Thomas asked, leaning over the desk in his office and examining the ink spotted map before him. "It's kind of rough and surprisingly still wet for an ancient treasure map."

"What's that?" Rauph asked. Towering over everybody and pointing at a strange mark in the bottom left hand corner. "Some kind of coral reef?"

Kerian leaned forwards to look and flushed.

"Isn't it obvious?" he remarked. "It's a sea serpent. I thought all sea charts had one."

"Looks more like a worm to me." Rauph stated helpfully. "What scale is it? How many nautical miles to an inch?" Kerian stared at the hulking Minotaur with bewilderment, firstly at the idea of scales and more importantly, at how intelligent the usually dopey creature was with maps and all of their uses. It was like two distinct personalities were inside the same creature and he found it vaguely unsettling. Had the creature seen right through his ploy? He returned his attention back to the map and tried to ignore the glances directed his way by Thomas and Sherman.

"So where's the original?" Thomas enquired his expression still very much suspicious.

"The original map is..." Kerian stalled, desperately searching his mind for inspiration.

The only images that flashed through his head were of Marcus, Ashe and his own backpack. It was infuriating that Ashe had moved in to their cabin and had taken the only serviceable bunk bed. Kerian had to hide his backpack all the time from the Halfling's light fingers, why the other day he almost got hold of the cursed scroll that had first started him on this damned fool's crusade. The scroll... of course!

"...On a scroll that is in my cabin. The scroll is so delicate... and so personal that I could not risk it being damaged, so I have just copied it and brought the copy straight here. I must have omitted the scale and the island's location in my hurry. I'll come back with these details as soon as I can." He glanced at the men around him with an expression he hoped looked sincere.

"Okay." Rauph stated, happy with the answer to his questions.

Sherman moved closer to the map, examining the still glistening terrain.

"Just look at this place." He motioned. "It looks like hell on earth. There is thick monster infested swamps, vast deserts, volcanic mountain ranges, ruined castles, dense jungles and even a glacier. It looks just like something a child would make up. If I didn't know the source was genuine I'd have sworn this was pure fabrication."

"Oh... it's real all right." Kerian reassured them, licking his lips nervously. Well it was real in his imagination!

"What's this bit?" Thomas asked, pointing at Kerian's crude drawing once again. "There's a duck or something here with steam coming out of its beak. Is that an inn or something?"

"Actually it's meant to be a dragon." Kerian confessed, stunned at the severity of his inquisition.

"So where's this king's ransom?" Thomas continued.

"Right under the steaming duck." Kerian shot back sarcastically.

"Are you sure a king's ransom lies here?" Sherman interrupted. "I mean I've heard dragons are very large, mean and dangerous and they have sharp claws, teeth and stuff."

"They also have treasure hoards." piped up a voice from beneath the chart. The assembled members of the crew looked under the captain's desk and into Ashe's sweetly smiling face.

"How did you get in here?" Thomas demanded, gesturing to Kerian as he did so. "Get him out of here." Kerian swiftly grabbed Ashe and dragged him from the room, secretly praising whoever was watching over him for the unexpected but much appreciated interruption.

"Are you sure the treasure is here?" Thomas asked again, catching Kerian mere seconds from the freedom of the outside corridor.

"I'd wager my life on it." Kerian replied, the irony of the statement not lost to the elderly fighter.

"Would you bet my crews lives on it too?"

Kerian paled at the question, his mind fighting both a sense of guilt at his act of betrayal and the thought of all the lives he could be endangering by setting them off on this quest of his. No! He had as much right as any man to life, no matter what the cost. If there was a chance at ending this curse, he was going to take it and no one had the moral right to stop him.

"Just keep to the heading I have told you." Kerian shot back. "With the incredible speed this ship goes we should hit our destination in just over ten days or so."

"In that case we have nothing to lose," Thomas acknowledged. "We will set sail on this new course as soon as possible. Rauph please plot a suitable heading based on Kerian's calculations and notify Sherman as soon as you are ready for us to alter course."

The cabin door closed behind Kerian's departing form and Thomas turned to his fellow crewmen an undisguised look of joy about his features.

"Who would have thought it?" He laughed. "The very stowaways we wanted to throw off the ship had the answer to our prayers with them all this time."

"Incredible indeed." Sherman nodded, although personally he was far from convinced.

"If the riches in this dragon's hoard are indeed as vast as Kerian states we should have no problems finding a gemstone able to hold sufficient power to open the second gate." Thomas slapped Rauph enthusiastically on the arm and looked across at Sherman's unconvinced face.

"What?" Thomas demanded.

"You seem to be forgetting one small thing." Sherman admitted.

"Yes?"

"The dragon..."

"I'm not scared of any dragon." Thomas laughed again, clapping his friend on the back. "After all I have Rauph here to protect me and with you as my first mate, I just know you will have thought of a way around the creature by the time we arrive. You always have to put a downer on things. Live a little." Thomas turned from the two crew and left the cabin whistling to himself. Sherman looked across at Rauph and shrugged.

"What is it?" Rauph enquired.

"Well..." The seaman replied, slightly embarrassed at his own self-doubts. "It's just that I find it strange that there should be a king's ransom hidden on an island with no villages or cities anywhere for the king's ransom to come from."

"Ahh..." Rauph responded mysteriously. "Maybe that's because the dragon has devoured them all."

"Is that supposed to make me feel any better?" The first mate questioned.

* * * * * *

'Thwack!'

The arrow embedded deeply into the straw boss at the far end of the main deck.

"Dead on target!" Sherman exclaimed watching in fascination as Weyn Valdeze lowered his bow.

"I know." The archer commented without looking. "If your aim is correct, posture straight, action unhurried... you simply cannot miss. Become the arrow; know where it is going to strike before you lose the string. To miss then becomes an impossibility. Come on... have a go."

Sherman reluctantly stepped forward and took the bow from the hunter.

"Are you right or left handed?" Valdeze enquired.

"Right." Sherman replied.

"Okay, turn so you are side on to the target, your left side facing where you wish the arrow to go."

"I said I was right handed." Sherman piped up; trying to make a light handed comment about his positioning and manhandling by the hunter.

Intrigued by the action on the deck far below, Plano and Abilene suddenly swung down from the rigging and stood to one side, grinning at Sherman's obvious discomfort like two cats that were watching a cornered mouse.

"Go on Sherman, you can show him." teased Abilene.

Sherman squared his shoulders, purposefully erecting an imaginary shield between himself and his shipmates and turned back to Valdeze ignoring the jibes from behind him.

"Okay. Show me."

Valdeze plucked an arrow from the quiver at his side and spun it, tip down in the palm of his hand; the feather fletches whizzing softly as they spun through the air. The tip of the hunting arrow skated across the palm of his hand like a blade across ice, the rest of the arrow shaft remaining vertical throughout the entire process.

"You do this to check the shaft of the arrow is straight." Valdeze continued. "It's important to check an arrow before you shoot it because if it is not straight it will not fly true... and sometimes you need all the help you can get." He looked up at the red feather bobbing alongside the edge of Sherman's hat, taking in the grinning men behind his student and tried not to laugh at the serious expression on Sherman's face.

He handed the arrow over and Sherman examined it intently.

"It's so light." He exclaimed looking down at the deadly piece of wood he held in his hand. To his surprise, he noted that upon closer examination the shaft was actually fashioned from two lengths of wood carefully cut and interlocked into each other.

The hunting tip had wicked barbs down both sides, allowing the arrow to pass seamlessly through an object, but making it practically impossible to withdraw without inflicting tremendous injury to its target. What damage could an arrow like this do to a man? He looked over at Weyn's quiver and noted the other eleven identical arrows that waited there. What could all twelve do to a man?

He suppressed a shiver and looked up again only to note that several other crew had gathered around to watch the display. This was not good. Sherman hated making a fool of himself and he did not intend to do so in front of all these men. He gritted his teeth and turned to Valdeze, determined to get this not only over and done with but with a modicum of skill. At a nod from the archer, he pulled the fletched end of the arrow onto the bowstring feeling the initial resistance before the arrow nock clicked around the string.

At least Sherman had no worries about dropping the arrow now; it hung suspended from the bow as if it could hang there all day! Confident the arrow would remain put; he gripped the string with his hand and started to pull.

"No, no, no!" Valdeze scolded, drawing several titters from the onlookers. The archer moved forwards and repositioned the first mate's fingers, the first finger above the arrow and the second two below. He held his thumb and little finger away from the string, encouraged to shape his hand so they touched each other.

"Don't make me look stupid." Sherman muttered under his breath.

"I have no intentions of doing so." Valdeze returned. "Trust me." Sherman looked down at his fingers again and nodded silently, the tone of his tutor's voice confirming this was no tease.

"Now bring your left arm up and hold it steady, allowing for a slight bend in your arm." He nodded reassuringly as Sherman carried out his instructions. "Pull the string back and bring your hand up under your chin in one smooth motion. You will find that you will be able to 'kiss the string' when it is back far enough."

This comment brought yet another titter.

Sherman felt himself flush but stubbornly refused to back down. He pulled back on the string determined to show the onlookers he knew what he was doing and discovered that he could hardly pull the string back at all! Instead, he found to his acute embarrassment that his upper half was leaning towards the bow, with his lips puckered as he vainly tried to make the twisted lengths of twine reach his 'kiss'. The effect was comedic to all around him and several more laughs ensued.

"Take it down again." Valdeze directed. "Then, when you are ready, bring the bow back up and pull the string back in one smooth motion. You can do this."

Sherman lowered the bow accordingly, took a deep breath and then swung the bow back up to vertical drawing the string back as instructed. The bow bent under the applied pressure and incredibly after only a minor struggle, the string was at his face and his hand was beneath his chin.

"You will find that you can now hold the bow at full draw in relative comfort." Valdeze continued. "Take your time, sight along the notches in the upper part of the bow stock and when you are satisfied release the string."

Sherman grunted at the ongoing drone of Valdeze. Why couldn't the man shut up and let him get on with it? Surprisingly, he noted that the archer was correct about the bow being easier to hold at full stretch and there was very little pressure or strain apart from across his fingertips now the string was back. Now where was the target? What had Valdeze said about sighting?

He squinted his eyes and tried to see exactly where the archer had been talking about. What notches? Why was everyone suddenly laughing? All he could see was a light grey colour before his eyes, no stock and certainly no target!

The laughter continued and suddenly Sherman realised what it was they were all laughing at. His hat! The string of the bow had bent his hat brim down when he had pulled it back effectively blinding him to both the target and the ship about him. His eyes widened in horror! He was bending his hat!

In a panic, Sherman let go of the bowstring, his fingers snatching away and causing the bow to react, jerking wildly from his movements. The arrow leapt from the bow, snapping forwards into the unknown as the string retracted, launching off somewhere beyond the brim of Sherman's hat. Valdeze watched as the arrow shot down the length of the ship missing the straw target completely before ricocheting off the railing at the far end and flying harmlessly out to sea.

Sherman meanwhile had dropped the bow to the deck and frantically grabbed for the edge of his hat, his eyes swiftly scanning the grey felt and checking for any damage, mindless of the bellows of laughter about him. Only when he was satisfied that there was no lasting damage did he turn back to Valdeze.

"Where is it?" he enquired, looking intently at the target set at the far end of the deck as if he expected the shaft of his spent arrow to be quivering at its centre. Valdeze turned the sailor slightly and pointed along Sherman's newly directed line of sight.

"Somewhere over there, heading back to the coastline as we speak." He laughed. "You were not one with your arrow."

Sherman shrugged his shoulders.

"Another time then." The sailor replied sheepishly. "Next time though I'll choose the sport. Have you ever thrown a dagger?"

"Once or twice." Valdeze confessed before offering his hand. "I'll look forward to it." Abilene stepped forwards and slapped Sherman soundly on the back.

"Most impressive." He grinned, stalling Valdeze departure with a knowing look. "But you won't have to wait that long before getting your own back on our archer friend here."

"Oh no?" Sherman and Valdeze asked together, curiosity apparent in both of their voices.

"Cards tonight in the captain's cabin. Be sure to bring all your money." Abilene laughed theatrically. "You will need it."

"Why not?" Valdeze replied. "I'm game if you are."

"Certainly." Sherman answered. "Wouldn't miss it for the world."

"Great." Abilene exclaimed enthusiastically. "Spread the word then. Now all I have to do is convince the captain to let us have his cabin and then I have to find a pack of cards.

Thomas threw the last pack overboard during our last game because he lost so badly and we left port rather faster than I expected to allow me to buy another deck. I wonder if Violetta has a deck we can use." The man wandered off in search of a venue for the evening's entertainment leaving the other two men standing side by side.

"I'm sorry about your arrow." Sherman apologised.

"Not a worry." Valdeze replied, patting the quiver at his side as the twelfth arrow reappeared.

Chapter Twenty-Seven

"The game gentlemen," Abilene smiled, "is Lords and Ladies."

The acrobat opened a pine box set on the table before him and reached in to retrieve a deck of cards wrapped up in a silken scarf. He unwrapped the elaborately inscribed deck within and fanned the cards out across the surface of the captain's desk before gathering them up again in one smooth practiced motion.

"Aren't they Violetta's fortune telling deck?" Thomas asked, curious as to how the cook's precious deck had arrived before him.

"Yes they are." Abilene grinned. "And I have been made to promise that I will return the deck in the same condition in which they left her. Otherwise it's the evil eye for me and potato peeling for the next six weeks!"

"I would never have believed she would have let that deck out of her sight." Scrave muttered, knowing Violetta's explosive nature all too well.

"I know," Abilene agreed, "I guess I still have the way with the ladies. One flutter of my eyelashes and they can't help but run to do as I ask."

"Run away from you more like." jibed Scrave.

"Well she did want me out of the galley as fast as possible. Maybe she's cooking up a surprise for us?"

"Maybe you should just stay away from her." Thomas warned. Everyone paused and turned to look at the captain for some kind of explanation to his comment.

"Well..." he paused, trying desperately to think of an appropriate response. "Haven't you seen how dangerous she can be with that cleaver of hers?"

The room erupted into laughter and Thomas sank back into his chair instantly relieved that he had successfully sidestepped his slip of the tongue. Abilene tapped the deck of cards hard against the table's surface to square them and continued with his theatrical introduction.

"Welcome to the Cartoman deck," he stated cutting the cards and beginning to shuffle. The crew around the table leaned forwards for a closer look only to find that the speed with which Abilene was shuffling made it impossible for them to make out any particular card or as to whether the acrobat was stripping and stacking the deck in his favour.

Thomas watched the unfolding proceedings with horror, wondering how he had ever managed to been talked into this. Okay he knew it was important that the crew have some rest and relaxation whilst at sea but why did it always have to be cards? Thomas had an almost legendary status when it came to card playing. At least when it came to losing that is. In fact, Thomas had never won a game of cards in his life!

He looked across the desk at the smiling faces of Scrave, Rauph and Sherman and silently balked. All three of them knew Thomas's form when it came to card playing and as he watched they were rapidly mounting up piles of coins before them in preparation for the bloodless but excruciatingly painful slaughter that was to come.

Kerian sat silently to Thomas's left watching the men seated around the table with a calculating gaze. He knew how to play cards all right, although he had never played with a Cartoman deck before. Even so, he felt that some people in the room obviously felt they had the advantage over him already. How else could he explain the idiotic grins on the faces of the three men facing him? Was he about to become penniless in some kind of inane crew initiative test? Well... not if he could help it! He grinned back across at them trying to unnerve the opposition. The expressions on the three men remained stubbornly consistent.

Kerian looked to his right and watched Abilene continue to shuffle. If the cards went his way, his chances of winning could be quite high. Kerian was a tactical player and had learnt his game playing with hired mercenary fighters during the Ivilene Peninsular campaign. Oh yes, Kerian could cheat with the best of them.

Abilene continued to explain the deck of cards before him as if the players had never held a card in their life before.

"This deck of cards is split up into four suits. Arrows, swords, crowns and gems. Each Suit consists of thirteen cards numbered accordingly. The first card in each suit can be either the highest value card, or the lowest depending on the set rules of the game. For tonight's purposes, the card will be of face value only. Somertai rules do not apply during this game. I will not allow Dukant flushes; however, for the purposes of ascertaining who will be dealer the first card of each suit will hold highest value during the draw. In case of a tie the swords suit holder will win by default.

Abilene flashed a card at the group illustrating a king holding his head in his hands, piles of gold surrounding him. This was the highest card in the Crowns suit for the dealership, but the lowest in point value for the game.

He slid the card back into the deck with a professionalism honed from his years working the sideshows of the circus and looked around at the faces before him, sizing up the varying piles of money before each crewmember.

"Shall we decide who deals?" He asked, flicking a card towards each of the men sitting around the table. "Let's start the bidding at one silver florin and to set the evening off to a good start lets bet on who deals first, and see where we go from there. May Lady Luck shine on us all and me in particular!"

Thomas watched his card gracefully slide across the table towards him and stop the prescribed few inches from his hand as if halted by some unseen spectral being. He leant forward and slowly slid the card towards the edge of the desk, determined not to let any other member of the crew see it. He summarised the rules in his head as swiftly as he could as his other hand slid forwards, depositing the coin for his opening stake.

The deck consisted of fifty-two cards much like the traditional deck of cards from home. There were even four suits, although the names were not the same. As it was a fortune telling deck, the traditional card face held a unique picture but in the top right corner, the symbol and value of the card were illustrated.

The card in his hand showed a graphic illustration of a street urchin robbing a wealthy merchant in an alleyway. The gem on the card was just visible in the handful of ill-gotten gains the urchin had acquired. Thomas could not help but worry if this card signified what the evening had in store for him.

He looked at the top corner of the card and blinked in disbelief. He had the highest card of the suit! This was incredible. Thomas swallowed quickly, trying to compose himself, knowing that if he did not his face would give away the 'treasure' he held in his hand.

The captain risked a quick glance to his left at the quietly composed elderly fighter whose arrival had signalled such a dramatic change in his life. Kerian's face was calm but a twitch above his right eye appeared to indicate he was not particularly sure of what he held. Thomas swiftly surmised that the fighter did not have much.

Abilene was unreadable, Valdeze looked decidedly dejected, Scrave and Sherman appeared indifferent with what they held and Rauph... well Rauph was still smiling, or at least trying to. The only problem was in interpreting whether the Minotaur was smiling because he had a good card, or because he liked the picture painted on it. No clues there then.

As Thomas looked, Rauph showed his card to Ashe who was standing on tiptoe at his side and desperate to see onto the surface of the table and take in the sight of everyone's available stakes. The Halfling had decided not to get involved with the game and had instead spent the majority of the evening chatting with Colette and Commagin.

Colette sat off to one side silently observing the table and nodding at appropriate times to Commagin who was in the middle of his latest swashbuckling yarn.

The Dwarf toasted loudly, drawing Thomas's attention to the fact that somehow, he had managed to open the globe drinking cabinet without Thomas noticing and he was even now pouring out drinks for all the crew seated at the table. Thomas noted the generous measures poured, none more so generous than the glass that finally made it to Commagin's lips. Did the engineer realise just how expensive that stuff was to buy? Judging by the speed with which the liquor was disappearing the captain did not need extra sensory powers to figure that one out.

Still, even if the liquor cabinet was taking a beating tonight, Thomas was not going to be. He had the One of Gems!

Abilene decided to break the almost palpable tension first. His card showed the picture of a coat of arms made up of nine swords set out in a fan shape.

Thomas noted the wince from Scrave and the shuffling from the seat to his left. The Nine of Swords was quite a high card, the equivalent of the Nine of Spades to Thomas, but tonight compared against what Thomas held in his hand, it was not high enough!

Valdeze dejectedly laid his card revealing the picture of an Archer standing in the woods sighting on a startled deer. Five arrows sunk into the ground at his side. Not a hope Thomas chuckled to himself seeing the equivalent to a Five of Clubs instead of the Arrows suit it represented. He risked a quick glance back at his own card just to assure himself it was still there. The face of the street urchin winked back reassuringly at him.

Scrave laid the Eight of Crowns, depicting a royal tomb set in a glade. So near and yet so far from the Eight of Hearts Thomas knew it as. Thomas held his breath. He was so close. Soon those seven silver pieces glinting at the centre of the table would be his.

Kerian laid the Seven of Crowns showing a King holding state and talking to his loyal subjects, and Sherman revealed a knight choosing from three offered swords at a tournament. Then it was Thomas's turn.

He beamed at everyone, relishing the actions and looks of the men around him as he carefully revealed his card.

"Behold your crushing defeat." He crowed.

Scrave's mouth dropped open, displaying more articulately than anyone else in the room, exactly how all the crew felt. Thomas had just laid the highest card. The Elf had to be dreaming!

"I believe these are mine." Thomas continued to swagger leaning forwards across the desk to sweep up the silver coins before him.

"Don't I get a turn?" Rauph mumbled, delaying Thomas's victory celebration.

Thomas looked up at his navigator, annoyed at the interruption during his finest hour. "Well go on then and lay your card. I want to gather my winnings in. What have you got anyway?"

"Just a picture of Kerian's sword." the Minotaur replied, lowering the One of Swords on top of the pile. The rune etched, violet tinged blade appeared to glow within its pictorial representation, held by a sword maiden for all to see.

Thomas groaned at the Minotaur's revelation. Rauph had the highest card in the deck, destroying his personal moment of triumph more effectively than plunging a burning torch into a waterfall. He buried his head in his hands unaware of the fact that Kerian was staring at the card as if in shock.

Kerian took his eyes slowly from the card and lifted his head to find the rest of the crew roaring with laughter at Thomas's downfall. The fighter took one more glimpse at the picture as if to confirm his initial findings, before determining to himself that he would ask the owner of the deck what she knew about the One of Swords at the first opportunity. He joined in with the laughter around him, all be it half-heartedly.

Thomas reached over to the globe and grabbed the nearest decanter, pulling it out whilst the laughter fell on his 'deaf ears', a task that was easier said than done. He smiled weakly at the men sitting across from him, trying desperately to avoid looking at Rauph as the Minotaur scooped up the coins littering the table top, even though he did not have a clue how he had just won them.

"Are you sure these are mine?" he asked Ashe. The Halfling nodded enthusiastically rubbing his hands in glee, taking time to ensure that Rauph's original card, the Two of Crowns stayed firmly hidden up his sleeve.

Thomas lifted his decanter to his glass, watching closely as Ashe continued his discussion with Rauph. There was something funny going on here he just knew it. The absence of weight to his glass, accompanied by the lack of liquid sounds from within the decanter confirmed that something strange had been going on with the liquor cabinet as well. He looked down at the cut crystal and confirmed with a quick glance that the contents were drained dry.

A loud rhythmic snoring began to rise from the floor behind him and Thomas turned in his chair to find the answer to his sudden alcohol shortage. One very robust, comatose Dwarf was lying asleep on his new carpet, nostrils flaring at each expelling of air from his lungs and a large contented smile plastered liberally across his face.

It was going to be a very painful night indeed.

* * * * * *

Ridge stood silently at his position on the aft castle taking in the solitude and peace of the night that was slowly passing around him. The night had always been his favourite time to stand up here on watch. There were always so many distractions during the day. More importantly, these hours, from dusk to midnight, were his time. Quality time with no interruptions, when he could unwind and analyse, reflecting on what had happened during his day.

He chewed on his lip absent-mindedly and fiddled with his thick bushy beard, a sign that he was deeply agitated. This voyage had been one long lingering nightmare from the start. His friend Cresta had died terribly at the hands of an assassin that had somehow managed to board the ship unseen. It made him shudder to think about the recent losses this ship had taken and the fact that somehow he had managed to avoid becoming one of the casualties. He had to wonder when it would be his time to 'sail on'.

The ballista on the mid-deck, his normal haunt during the daylight hours, had remained unmanned since the massacre. Ridge could not bear to be down there operating his station alone, justifying his actions by claiming it was a mark of respect for his departed colleagues but he knew in his heart of hearts that one day he would have to take up his post again. What concerned him the most was that it would fall to one of the new crewmembers taken aboard during their last port of call to staff the post with him and from what he had seen; none of them would really fill the void left by his hapless friend.

His eyes swept the open deck and the glittering sky above, the twinkling stars resplendent against the velvety backdrop of the ebony night. It was funny but away from the cities on the mainland the stars appeared to increase in their brightness and clarity, as if they knew the sailors crossing the seas far below needed to see them that tiny bit clearer than the landlocked travellers tucked up safely in their beds.

The canvas sails flapped high above, their presence somehow reassuring in this climate of recent change. The creak and groan of the rigging sang a lullaby that would have lulled the seaman to sleep if he had not taken his duty as seriously as he did. He paused in mid-contemplation as a shadow suddenly detached itself from one of the access hatches in the main deck and headed up onto the fore deck. He squinted his eyes to confirm that his vision was not playing tricks on him, which only served to confirm his suspicions. Someone was definitely moving around down there.

He adjusted his position ever so slightly to improve his line of vision and watched as the new crewman known as Aradol positioned himself in a clear section of the deck. His sack, which appeared to accompany the youth wherever he went, dropped to the decking beside his feet, resulting in a loud clanking that seemed incredibly invasive to the watching seaman.

Ridge shuffled a fraction closer, cautious not to let the young man see him watching from his vantage point. What was Aradol doing out here at this time of night? Everyone else was playing cards so why wasn't he with them? As he continued to watch, Aradol suddenly stripped from his shirt and reached into the clanking sack that he appeared to guard so closely and would let no one near.

The sword he withdrew from the sack was of such beauty that even though he stood clear on the other side of the deck, the radiance of the weapon took Ridge's breath away. It was an antique design and looked incredibly heavy but the blade gleamed, displaying how well it was sanded, oiled and cared for.

Aradol began to run through a series of routines with the blade, parrying and attacking unseen foes with a grace that defied explanation and a speed that would have put even Scrave to shame. The youth pushed his body to its limits, sweat soon streaking his finely muscled form. Every now and again a telling groan escaped the youth's lips as muscles pulled at the increasing strain.

Ridge suddenly realised he was staring and he flushed with embarrassment. Aradol was definitely something more than just a simple waiter but the grizzled seaman knew better than to continue intruding on this private moment. It was not his place to pry into this young man's business and he respected the youth's need for space and solitude, a necessity they both appeared to require. He reluctantly turned away, although he made a note to watch out for the boy on future occasions.

The seaman turned his attention up towards the rigging, aware that Plano was sitting a silent vigil up in the crow's nest his eyes scanning the seas that lay around for any hidden threats that would put the ship and crew at undue risk. Ridge shrugged, knowing that Plano did not sit up there alone, instead the acrobat shared his post with the cruellest and most patient of foes. Despair.

Although Abilene had gone to the card game this evening, his brother had remained aloft, unwilling to share his feelings following the loss of his brother. Most of the crew had not noticed the deep change that had fallen over the man but Ridge had not lived to this stage of his life without being observant. If he knew the brothers as well as he thought he did, he would not be surprised if the two of them were to elect to leave ship if they discovered a passage back to known waters. That was, if they could ever arrange a passage to home again.

He shrugged off the chill touch of the cold evening air and decided that it would be for the best if he started to walk about the deck and get the blood circulating through his limbs. Ridge headed from his resting place near the ladders and decided to do a circuit of the aft deck, pausing only to lift a shuttered storm lantern from the barrel beside him so he could light his way. He walked past a secured crate, noticing a tall, dark and decidedly sinister figure detaching itself from the darkened area of deck near Colette's summoning circle and heading stealthily into the central inscribed area of decking.

Ridge swiftly followed, his curiosity aroused sufficiently to investigate the behaviour of this unsuspecting 'stranger'. As he rounded the corner, the huge figure suddenly dropped to the deck at the edge of the inscribed circle and there was a scuffle followed by a high-pitched squeal and a grunt of pain. Scampering sounds of small feet echoed across the wooden deck and something small shot off into the shadows.

"What's going on over there?" Ridge challenged, raising his storm lantern and flooding the area with light.

Ives Mantoso got unsteadily to his feet masking his eyes against the sudden glare of the light and waving the man away. Ridge ignored the unspoken command and advanced, determined to find out what this man was doing on this sensitive area of the deck.

He slowly lowered his arm as Ridge approached and the light from the lantern angled away from his face, before lifting his other hand into the light and examining a fresh wound that dripped blood to the deck below.

"You're hurt." Ridge exclaimed moving closer to assist. “What were you doing up here? Thomas doesn’t like people near this area.”

"It appears your ship has an unusual class of rodent." Ives replied, his trademark carefree grin, absent from his features. “If I had known I would have brought a cat on board with me.” He turned to walk away, leaving the guard standing stunned.

"Now wait just a minute!" Ridge demanded, moving to pursue. "I asked what were you doing up there?"

"As I said," the merchant’s voice replied, "I was hunting rats." He leant forwards, shuttering the lantern and plunging them both into darkness.

It took Ridge a few moments to wrestle open the shutter again, flooding the area with light. Ives was nowhere around. He began to follow the man's departure from the aft deck when his foot kicked something and sent it skittering across the deck. The sailor swung his lantern left and right and then found the cause of the sound. A small jagged piece of metal lay on the deck where he had kicked it, completely out of place in this area of the ship. He picked it up, turning it first one way then the other. Its edge appeared scratched and worked with, the tip blunted as if worn repeatedly by constant use.

He wasted several more moments rechecking the area to see if anything else was amiss, before reluctantly giving up his search. Standing exposed here on this raised area of decking with magical symbols all about him made the suspicious seaman uneasy. He swiftly decided that he would sweep the deck in the morning before Colette arrived and summoned up the wind elemental for the following day's travel. He did not want her to kneel on any other pieces of debris and hurt herself at a critical time!

As Ridge's footsteps faded away, two small red eyes suddenly blinked open in the darkness. A small sniffing noise followed an angry chattering of teeth before the small skeletal form of Hamnet emerged from the darkness and swiftly scurried across the wooden surface of the raised decking.

It scampered to a halt at the edge of one of the huge inscribed containment circles and paused, sniffing the air and checking that there were no crew around this time to disturb its work.

The man who had just jumped on her had surprised her quite badly, making the little creature now incredibly skittish in her actions. If it had not been for her sharp claws and razor teeth, her work for her mistress would have been incomplete, preventing Hamnet from meeting her contract and freeing her remains from Justina.

The creature's deformed skull swivelled first one way and then the other, allowing for further checking of the area, then when it was quite satisfied that there were no more guards around she lifted one of her elongated claws from the deck. Testing the edge of its claw and finding it suitably sharp, the creature turned its attentions back to the pattern on the floor and continued with its task of scoring tiny thin lines through all of the arcane symbols depicted there. It had been much easier using the tool she had just lost but Hamnet always found ways of completing what she was asked to do.

* * * * * *

Kerian smiled as they tidied the cards away before him. It had been an entertaining evening; Thomas had lost the most in a series of hands that were more a heist than a game of cards, holding the worst cards possible five times in a row. Sherman had doubled his takings and Rauph and Ashe had teamed up to present the most unlikely cardsharps the elderly fighter had ever seen.

"Better luck next time." Weyn Valdeze laughed from across the table, lifting his glass to his lips in a toast to their gallant loser. "May your luck at cards always remain consistent... especially when I'm at the table!"

Thomas nodded in acknowledgement, flushing red in embarrassment but good-natured enough to return the toast with the last of the drink he had in his glass.

"And to our winners..." Weyn continued, gesturing to the two grinning figures sitting to his other side. Rauph and Ashe waved back, hastily sweeping coins off the table and into a sack that had somehow appeared during the game.

Kerian could not believe the gall of the two conspirators, it was as brazen as their grins. Didn't anyone realise that the two had been cheating everyone out of their money all evening? At one point, Ashe had even approached Kerian and suggested which cards he should play, despite the fact that the Halfling should not have been able to see the cards let alone know what was in his hand! Even when he had turned his chair away from the diminutive thief Ashe had continued to frown and nod his approval from the other side of the table at each lay of the cards.

What had finally convinced Kerian that something less than honest was going on was when he had purposefully palmed a card, keeping it hidden from the main deck and playing it in the next hand much to Ashe's horror and Rauph's anger. What had followed was a comical chase involving the Minotaur pursuing the Halfling around the table until both had collapsed to the floor, one in a fit of giggles and the other holding his head in an attempt to stop the room from turning round.

Kerian looked at the assembled crew, desperate to say something and then realising that no one would have cared if he had anyway. These people were like an extended family towards each other, sharing something within the confines of this cabin that went far beyond simple monetary gain. He shrugged; here he was ever the loner, amidst a group of people that would welcome him warmly if he just let them.

Colette stood up from her stool and slowly walked over to the table, coming closer to Abilene and the fortune telling deck that he was desperately trying to collect. She leant over his shoulder, eyes sparkling from the intoxicating effects of Thomas's liquor cabinet and scooped up the cards flicking through them one at a time, pausing every now and again when an illustration caught her eye.

"Please," Abeline gestured. "I need to return these now."

"Why don't we all go?" Colette asked. "I haven't seen Violetta in a while and it would be nice to say hello."

Thomas snapped up in his chair instantly alert.

"I'm sure there's no need for that." He suggested. "Let me take the cards back for you."

"And risk them going missing and I face a month of potato peelings!" Abeline scoffed. "Fat chance."

"Okay, we'll all go." Thomas replied gruffly, getting to his feet and feeling the sudden rush of blood to his head that always came after investing time in his liquor cabinet. He stubbornly centred himself and collected the crewmembers, ushering them out of his cabin and back to the main deck so they could descend the ladders that led towards the galley.

Abeline lit a storm lantern as they navigated their way below decks, stepping over places where brass cannons once resided and pointing out trip hazards to Colette as he acted the gallant gentleman. He did not care one bit that she already knew the deck better than most of the gathered crew, or the fact that Kerian appeared disgruntled with how she responded to his flirtation.

The acrobat smiled up at her, fluttering his eyelashes comically and paused near the hammocks that marked the berth where the brothers normally resided. In the alcove old faded posters curled from the walls, their lettering proclaiming the death defying stunts the Rinaldo brothers had been famous for in the circus days of old.

He pulled a blanket from his hammock and wrapped it around his head, forming a hood about his face, from within which he continuing with his artistic performance, pulling faces and opening his eyes wide as if amazed by things he saw before him. Clearly, Abeline had also taken one too many drinks from the cabinet.

"Please, Madam of the Winds," he gestured theatrically. "Would you be kind enough to tell me my fortune? After all I already have the cards here."

"Why sir, I don't do fortunes for free." Colette laughed back. "Everyone knows my palm must first be crossed with silver."

"Oh yes please!" Ashe dodged through the group, reaching into the bag of winnings and offering a silver piece as requested. Colette looked up surprised. She had not really expected anyone to agree and did not really know how to read fortune telling cards anyway.

"But I must know..." Abilene continued huskily. "Is there love written in the cards for me this night?"

"Okay." She laughed. "I'm game. Let us see what the cards hold for us all."

Before they knew it, they had forgotten the journey to the galley, as Sherman and Rauph started pulling over barrels for seating and everyone perched around Colette as Abeline lifted the silken scarf that had contained the cards from out of the fortune-telling box. He wrapped the shimmering material around her head, skilfully tucking the ends of the scarf into her hair and transformed the mage into the conventional image of a fortune-teller.

Colette eased herself down onto an upturned barrel and placed the cards on the larger barrel before her. She paused for a moment toying with the card deck before gazing into the eyes of every member of the room and smiling wickedly, laughter dancing in her eyes.

"Do you really think you should be doing this?" Kerian warned, suddenly feeling uneasy and quite claustrophobic in the confines of the sleeping area.

"What harm could it do?" Thomas joked, looking over at Kerian's serious visage and shaking his head. "Come on, it's only a bit of fun."

"I need vun silver piece for everyone." Colette chuckled, adopting the cliché accent of a wandering gypsy. Thomas acknowledged the request, turning in one swift motion and grabbing Ashe by the collar as he started to step away.

"That's another six silver pieces please," He requested. Ashe looked up at the captain of the *El Defensor* in horror at the thought of parting with his 'night's earnings' but one look into Thomas's steely grey eyes confirmed to the Halfling that the captain had his suspicions about the little hustler. He reluctantly slid the extra six pieces of silver onto the table and Colette took up the cards, falling fully into her make-believe role.

"Sank you, sank you." She began, trying hard not to laugh and spoil the atmosphere. "Let us zee now, vhat do zee cards old for our intrepid adventurers?" She shuffled the cards, closing her eyes slightly and mumbling under her breath. Kerian moved closer, still unsure what was making him feel uneasy and was rewarded by a flirtatious wink from Colette that surprised him and left him feeling as if someone had just smacked him around the head.

"Scrave, the cards call for you first." Colette beckoned the Elf forward and let him shuffle the deck before handing it to her. "Think about your future and zee cards will tell all."

The cards appeared to blur under Colette's control then suddenly a card flew from the deck in her hand and slid across the top of the barrel to land before Scrave's startled features. He flipped it over to reveal the illustration of a young novice wizard travelling a long and dusty road, the road split before him, presenting a choice of an open road of bright sunlight that ascended to a peak ahead, or a dark dismal road where thunderheads beckoned. In the young man's hand were three small gemstones, his only power source for the difficult choices ahead.

"You stand at a fork in the road of life," Colette suddenly stated, startling everyone around the table as her voice became deeper and more mysterious. "The choices before you, number but two. The road that is clear, reveals the way through, although it is a steeper and harder to follow, the second path leads you only to sorrow."

Scrave sat back from the card as if stung but the others missed his reaction as another card shot from the deck, sliding unerringly to stop before Thomas. He turned over the card to reveal the picture of a puppet dressed like a clown, its sad painted face staring out from beneath a heavy crown adorned with seven gems.

Strings attached to every limb led up out of the card to an unseen hand that made the figure respond to its every move, a mirror reflected a darker, more evil version of the clown, but the marionette appeared more concerned about the strings above it than the evil the reflection portrayed.

Before anyone could comment, Colette started to talk again.

"Someone controls you and leads you a dance; but the error you make is in how you then prance. For the foolish one only watches what's near, instead of looking ahead and then facing his fear."

Thomas looked up from his card, mouth opened wide in question but another card was already drawing the eyes of everyone towards Abilene. The sailor looked down at his card to see a warrior in the desert, bowed under the weight of his pack and down on his knees before a glowing angel.

"This angel speaks of pain, both historic and sad, right now it is great and your tidings are bad. Soon your dark path will clear you'll see, your burden will lift, your soul will fly free."

Abilene's eyes began to tear as Colette's prediction filled his ears but again the crew were unaware as another card slid silently from the deck towards its unsuspecting recipient. Rauph looked down at the card to see a child hiding under a bed sheet as something dark and terrifying moved near. On the floor by the bed, a book of bedtime stories lay forgotten in the child's terror, the title of the book read *'The Labyris Knight'*.

"There are times in your life you feel small and are scared, but your size is so great you are one to be fear'd. A ruler of lands you are destined to be. Your future your past, as soon you will see."

Rauph simply looked across at Colette and shrugged, unsure as to what the worded message meant.

Another card was on its way stopping this time before Weyn Valdeze. The archer looked at the card and then paused to judge the stunned expressions of those who had already seen their cards. Something strange was going on here beyond the simple play-acting intended.

Illustrated on the card was a hooded figure, an archer lost in a maze, wandering towards a spiked trap that waited his fall.

"This trap looms bare, danger stalks too, of strangers beware, as one will betray you. The dead still walk, don't succumb to the call and ware all that's been said least you find that you fall."

The dead still walk. What was this girl going on about?

It was too late to ask, another card was falling lightly upon the table, its contents arrowing unerringly towards Ashe. He found himself staring at the representation of a leather bound book, with four golden crowns resplendent at each corner.

"This book," Colette intoned, "lies unopened, heaped sorrows within, its locks should be closed else chaos begins. Your nature is foolish, your actions are sound and your friends will betray you as secrets are found."

Ashe looked across at Colette, questions on his lips. Again, there was no time for response, instead the sixth card slid to a stop before Sherman. He turned it over to see a storm and a man struggling against the wind and the rain.

"Your future holds trouble, gusts of wind, pours with rain, despite all your struggles, you'll find nothing but pain. Beware of the tempest, your doom lies within. Face at your peril, survival is slim."

Kerian moved forward, knowing it was his turn and not wanting to face it. His card flipped over and he stared into the face of death. The ghostly figure of the skeletal cloaked rider, complete with scythe said more than any words could have done.

"Hah! Hah! Very funny." Kerian snapped throwing the card back across the table and snapping Colette out of her trance before any ominous commentary could follow. "Enough is enough."

Colette blinked repeatedly, looking up at the elderly knight as if she were temporarily confused to time and place. She looked down at the cards still held tightly in her hands and gasped, dropping them to the table.

"What just happened?"

Kerian walked purposefully around the barrel pausing to pick up each dealt card from before the assembled crew, the evening's 'entertainment' as far as he was concerned was at an end.

He stopped before Colette and held out his hand for the deck, nodding as the ship's mage handed the cards over, looking bemused, then he placed the collected cards firmly at the bottom of the deck and shuffled them again.

"What are you doing?" Colette asked, clearly unsure as to what had just transpired.

"I didn't like the future you just dealt me." Kerian confessed. "So I am now going to deal myself another." He turned over the top card and stared at it intently. The knight gestured for the empty box that Abilene had left on the table and gently deposited the cards within before dropping the lid and sealing the fortune telling deck away. Once completed Kerian turned to the people around him looking at them all one by one.

"Thank you all for a lovely evening." He nodded to everyone and slipped silently from the group, off into the darkness.

Colette slowly removed the scarf from her head, her eyes searching the other crew for some clue as to what had transpired. With no answers forthcoming, she removed the lid of the box and lifted the cards out onto the table, placing them in the centre of the square of silk and preparing to wrap them properly.

She knew she had no right but something told her she should look at Kerian's card. It was a bizarre unexplainable feeling that was impossible to resist so she leant forwards and lifted the top card from the deck, flipping it over onto the wooden surface with a practiced hand.

As the card hit the desk, Colette shrieked, bringing her hand to her mouth in shock.

The skeletal horseman stared knowingly back at her.

Chapter Twenty-Eight

"The luxury of sleep never comes easy to one plagued with a mind of guilt." Kerian muttered as he struggled to extricate himself from the tangled ruin of blankets that served as his make shift hammock. He raised his aged form with difficulty, finally sitting up and looking around in exhaustion, aware that one overzealous move could result in the hammock tipping and him falling to the floor in an undignified heap.

The darkened cabin that had initially served as his place of solitude now resounded in snores that had kept him tossing and turning throughout a restless and exhausting night. Faint grey illumination through the deadlight indicated the future coming of dawn and a particularly loud snore from below made Kerian's mind up for him. It was definitely time to get up.

He shook his head in an attempt to clear away the compounded feelings of lethargy that assailed him and began to collect his thoughts. The *El Defensor* was now well into her voyage of exploration, the last 'known' seas fully five days in her wake.

Luckily, the seas had remained calm and clear, parting in reverence before her bow as she sliced a path through 'virgin' uncharted waters.

Kerian had attempted to converse with Rauph each day, enthusiastically exclaiming that they were still sailing straight and true, although there were no landmarks as such to confirm or deny they were heading in the right direction, just an old compass the Minotaur had to hit several times to make the needle move around. Nevertheless, two weeks had now passed since they had altered course, they were four days overdue for landfall and the island was still nowhere on the horizon.

Even the gullible Rauph was going to become suspicious at some time! How long could he expect to stall the crew when for all he knew there could be nothing out here anyway? In addition, if the island was real and they were just one nautical degree off course they could have sailed right past Stratholme and none of the crew would have been any the wiser.

He shook his head at the futility of it all and then dropped to the gently rolling deck where he began to dress quietly, settling for a plain white linen shirt and tan breeches that fastened at the knee. Then he ran his wrinkled hands through his long white hair, teasing out most of the knots before tying it back from his face with practiced fingers.

Kerian was feeling his age today and unmistakable small dark splodges were starting to appear on his hands as his skin became slightly transparent with his advancing cursed years. It was ironic that his thinning skin was becoming much akin to the façade he was attempting to maintain. Eventually someone would see through it. Kerian tore his eyes away from his hands and shuddered to himself.

What would happen if they had somehow missed Stratholme?

What if his only chance at salvation now waited behind them somewhere and he was now on a fool's errand, doomed to spend the remainder of his days sailing around in circles looking for something he would never find?

Some questions were not worth contemplating, let alone answering! He could go mad thinking about this and he suddenly realised that the air in the cabin was stale and stifling and he needed the fresh air of the deck above.

He turned to leave the cabin, snores still vibrating loudly about the tiny room, then paused and turned back to take in the image of one of the snoring members of the *El Defensor's* crew. The innocent, almost angelic features of Ashe poked out from the blankets of the only proper bunk in the room. How Ashe had come to get the bunk and he the treacherous hammock was just one of those unsolved enigmas of life? Ashe had claimed that because of his small stature he was unable to get up to Kerian's hammock, even though he could scamper up and down buildings in Catterick without any apparent difficulty.

To make it even more infuriating, when Kerian had strung up a lower hammock to accommodate his smaller companion Marcus had promptly entered the room and tripped over it, making that idea impractical too. Therefore, Ashe got the bunk whilst Kerian and Marcus swung from the ceiling like a couple of overstuffed bags of onions. Life simply was not fair at times!

The elderly fighter watched Ashe's nostrils flare as another roaring snore issued from the little man. How could someone so small make so much noise? A wicked smile suddenly slid over Kerian's face and he silently tiptoed across the room to the other slumbering figure in the room.

Marcus's hammock swung gently in time with the ship, the netting wobbling with the monk's equally deafening cacophony of snores. If these two should ever snore together, the combined racket would turn the dead light into a fully functioning porthole!

Beneath Marcus, draped across the chair were a pair of the monk's smelly socks. Marcus always washed his socks in the morning, being too tired to do so before bed and when Kerian saw these, he knew just where he could put the socks with good effect. Gingerly, with extreme caution, the fighter lifted the socks from the chair, cringing when he realised that they had conformed to the edge of the chair and now remained bent stiffly no matter which way up Kerian turned them. This was disgusting!

He crept back across the room and gently draped the socks over Ashe's face, making a tent over the Halfling's nose with the bend in the material. Then he stood back trying desperately to hold in his chuckles, before making his way above decks.

* * * * * *

The sky was a startling scarlet, shot through with wisps of bruised purple cloud. The sickly light washed across the deck like sticky congealing blood, turning the pale sanded decking a deep cerise and the embroidered lions flapping across the sail above to an ominous black. The sea was cold and dark, the tips of the waves frothing crimson from the dawn instead of pure white; the air tinged with the electrical scent of brimstone. It was as if the ship had silently sailed overnight into one of the hells depicted so often in folk tales.

Kerian took in the breath-taking panorama from his position on the main deck, staring out across the railing and allowing his imagination to run riot. You could almost imagine the ship was sailing across molten lava, or traversing down the fabled river he had elected as his pseudonym, being drawn ever onwards towards the realms of the damned.

In the vivid light, he noted the solitary figure of Ridge standing watch at the helm and waved to him, grateful for the sight of another human being to share the incredible spectacle alongside. He headed across the deck and mounted the stairs before joining the bushy bearded sailor at his post beside the wheel.

"Good morning." Kerian volunteered.

"Morning it is." Ridge replied. "But there's nothing good about it." The sailor gestured ahead pointing towards the brilliant red horizon. "There's a storm brewing, mark my words." Ridge paused, as if thinking over what he was about to say, his beard moving up and down as he chewed on some unseen breakfast morsel. "I felt it in my bones this morning that something was up. Confirmed it too when my arm started hurting." Ridge rolled up his sleeve and pointed at his elbow joint. A deep twisting white scar tracked across the joint.

"A lover's kiss from my only brush with a great Kraken." He reminisced.

"Every time there's going to be a change in the weather it hurts like a demon, as if the squid still had hold of my arm, even though I know for sure that the fish is now long dead. And I can tell you it hurts good and proper right now." He looked across at the elderly fighter, pausing whilst he continued to chew what was in his mouth, before gesturing to the fiery streaked horizon ahead.

"And just look at those clouds." He pointed. "Mother Nature gives colours to all things for a reason. That way, we know what is good to eat and what may just be hiding a sting in its tail. Red always means there's a danger of some kind, from a face that's flushed red with liquor induced anger to a red striped Segaran coral snake that's brimming over with poisonous venom." He chuckled to himself as he continued to philosophise. "Even the Kraken that grabbed my arm had red eyes."

Kerian's puzzled expression halted the sailor in mid-telling.

"Oh, so you didn't know the giant squid had red eyes." Ridge teased. "That's cause you've probably only seen a dead one, with the fight long gone out of it.

Probably looked into those dead grey eyes and wondered what all the fuss was about? Am I right? Well let me tell you, when you are up close with one of those things and its tentacles are crushing the life out of you and its stinking bird like beak is cawing for your flesh you get to see things with an entirely different perspective. When you are about to meet your maker, wrapped tightly in its grasp you will see its eyes go red all right, flushed with the blood lust of the kill. Those eyes go as red as a virgin bride on her wedding night you mark my words." Ridge laughed at his choice of simile.

He gestured back at the scarlet horizon. "Now what you have there is an angry sky with turbulent seas tumbling beneath it. That will be a storm and a half when it hits."

"When will that be?" Kerian asked with concern. He had never been out on the open sea in a storm and did not wish to add that experience to his life skills just yet.

"The trick is to make sure it never will." Ridge smiled. "We are on a sturdy ship, one with its own wind supply and an eager crew. We will just set the sails and go around the squall. Surely you didn't think we'd be foolish enough to sail right through the thing now did you?" The sailor's eyes sparkled as he continued to jibe the inexperienced man. "We don't have trees to cower under or caves to hide ourselves in and shiver whilst the storm passes by overhead out here. Oh no, we aren't stupid, we just make sure we aren't caught in the thing when it heads our way."

* * * * * *

Thomas gazed with concern through the smeary porthole in Rauph's cabin and regarded the massing clouds on the horizon with clear disdain. Every now and then a flash would light the clouds from somewhere deep within the ominous mass and the unmistakable rumble of thunder vibrated through the thick glass. There was a storm coming in their direction all right! Nevertheless, if any ship could outrun it, Thomas reassuringly believed it would be his.

Sherman had delivered the news of the storm in his usual deadpan manner at the morning report, his face the only clue as to the underlying concern the sailor truly held. True enough, the clouds steadily gathered pace throughout the morning, creeping across the horizon like a dense winter fog, unrelenting and unforgiving in their advance.

Initially Thomas was unsure about how to handle this problem. He had no wish to change course with the promise of Kerian's island leading him on like a 'holy grail' he did not intend to give up. Nevertheless, his motivation appeared to be evaporating into unsubstantiated mist day by day, with no sign of landfall and rising frustration, Thomas confessed to himself that even he was starting to show consideration of turning the ship around and heading back towards charted waters.

Sherman had added another worrying revelation, several days ago Ridge had brought it to his attention that he believed they had gained a shadow. It made no sense, they were the fastest ship he knew, yet a mysterious frigate kept dropping in and out of sight on the horizon behind them, disappearing as they sailed during the day and catching up again over the passage of night: shadowing the ship with a persistence that made no sense.

Who was following them and more importantly what did they want with the *El Defensor* and her crew? Thomas had tried to make light of the situation by asking if it could possibly be the 'Dread Pirate Roberts' and that they would likely 'all be killed on the morrow' but none of the crew recognised his quote from William Goldman's work and his attempt at humour fell as flat as he felt inside.

Questions needed answering swiftly but the one person who may have been able to cast light on the matter was far from able to respond to an interrogation as yet.

He had briefly thought about 'turning about' and boarding the pursuing craft but had swiftly ruled it out. The strengths and complement of the craft pursuing them were currently unknown. That left evasion and a course alteration to avoid the impending storm. Both requirements could solve the immediate problems they faced. This meant turning to the ship's navigator for the answers he needed.

Thomas returned his attention to where Rauph was pouring over the canvas and parchment charts that completed the Minotaur's collection. Even as he moved across the room, Rauph was furiously walking his dividers backwards and forwards over the charts, mumbling calculations and probabilities to himself.

"Can we outrun it?" Thomas asked.

Rauph looked up from his charts and shrugged.

"Maybe. If Colette's creature blows really hard."

"What about making landfall. Where are we on our largest chart?"

Rauph looked up at Thomas and scowled, lifting his dividers and plunging them into the table top.

"Right about here." He stated calmly.

Thomas looked down at the dividers where they had plunged into the wooden desk. The chart was five inches away, the position of the dividers indicating that the *El Defensor* had sailed well beyond the position Kerian's island was supposed to be. Rauph's look of frustration confirmed Thomas's worst fears.

"I don't know where we can go. I have no idea of whether a port is near."

"So Kerian's map is a lie?" Even now, the captain found himself reluctant to believe the elderly fighter would betray him in this way.

"It must be." Rauph nodded. "I think we would have felt something if we had sailed over a dragon in the night."

"So..." Thomas summarised. "We have no idea where we are, an unknown vessel is snapping at our heels and we have nowhere to hide from the ugliest storm I have ever seen in all my years at sea. I don't know about you, but I think it's time we saw the original chart for ourselves."

Rauph nodded in agreement and followed his friend out of the door, the forgotten dividers vibrating softly in the desktop behind him.

* * * * * *

"That's absolutely perfect." Justina crooned, as she leant across her bed and focused on the small image of her favourite pet. "So, the ship is doomed and you want to come home now." Hamnet nodded eagerly, her eyes wide, her hands held palm up expectant on the magical summons that would pull her back to her mistress's arms.

"I'm afraid that's not possible." Justina stated coldly, her expression turning glacial. "You will not come back to me until I am sure the ship has gone down and all aboard her are lost."

Hamnet's eyes narrowed in anger and she stamped a clawed foot in frustration.

"There's no need to be so angry." Justina replied, switching swiftly back to her calm demeanour. "Just make sure it is done and then your bones are all yours."

* * * * * *

The wooden stairs creaked, signalling the arrival of another crewmember and Kerian caught his breath as Colette came into view. She was radiant, there was no other word for it and she lifted the gloom of the day as she passed.

Kerian bid Ridge good day and walked across the deck to meet her, flushing slightly as he overheard the crude chuckle that rose from behind him. Kerian turned to scowl at the sailor but found that Ridge was now suspiciously looking up into the sails above and was even attempting to whistle a tune. Convicted and found guilty without a trial the fighter thought, shrugging and returning his attention to the ship's mage.

Colette's long blonde hair was still damp to the touch from washing and her cheeks flushed from the exertion of climbing the stairs. The magnificent backdrop of the fiery red sky complimented her image surrounding her with a glowing halo-like effect that made Kerian suddenly wish he could freeze the image to remember it for all eternity. Crystal blue eyes took in Kerian's appearance and her smile warmed him through as she approached.

"Good morning." She smiled, walking past the elderly fighter as if she were a traveller passing him by on a busy trail. "I like your breeches."

"What do you mean?" he laughed, reversing his direction and moving lightly to catch up with her on the walk to the summoning deck. "I kind of like them."

Colette brushed away a stray wisp of hair from her face and turned to regard him.

"I must confess to finding them better than the black you keep wearing." She joked. "It's so solemn and nondescript, like you have to attend a funeral every day. The crime of it is that when someone gets to know you, you're nothing like that at all." She moved to the centre of the smaller inscribed circle and dropped to her knees, unrolling a bundle of cloth she carried with her and revealing all the items required to summon the elemental.

"What am I like then?" Kerian dared to ask, suddenly excited. "And do you really like my breeches?"

"Well, you're funny and sincere, a little too serious at times." Colette got back to her feet and began to walk around the circle, her eyes darting to the floor throughout the conversation, so she could check the inscriptions for signs of weakness or wear. She paused, bending over to look at the pattern more closely before looking back up at Kerian who stood like a page from the magic school she attended on Balsathar, hanging on her every word as if she were the greatest mage that ever lived. "Where was I?" she questioned, trying hard not to laugh at his appearance.

Kerian gestured down at his breeches, putting his hands into the pockets and making the image in Colette's mind unmistakable.

"Oh yes." Colette laughed lightly. "The breeches... Well they are a bit young for you."

Kerian winced at the remark, his features turning sullen and sombre in an instant. The remark although not intended to be delivered with malice, ripping into him with all the cruelty of a barbed hook. Colette noticed the change in demeanour instantly and realised she was staring at a fallen man.

"Oh... I didn't mean anything by it." She gasped, reflecting on what she had just said. "I just meant that they are such a change from your usual wardrobe." She moved over to the fighter, her examination of the magical circles forgotten as she laid a reassuring hand on his sleeve. "I'm sorry if I caused offence."

Kerian looked down into Colette's piercing eyes, wide with concern and genuine apology and lifted his hand, lightly stroking the side of her face. He could not fail to notice the contrast between her unblemished creamy flesh and his own wrinkled and aged complexion. The comparison left him cold.

"Thank you for telling me the truth." He sighed. "I realise I was a fool to believe anything otherwise." He turned and walked away without another word, leaving Colette with her hand outstretched towards him.

* * * * * *

Ridge nodded to himself as the sun disappeared behind the clouds, as if the very act confirmed his suspicions regarding what was to come later that day. The rosy colours of the ship appeared to drain away before his eyes as if the vessel was sucked dry by some unseen vampire. A sickly greenish yellow, much akin to fresh clay, replaced the vanishing redness with the colour of a fresh corpse, further adding to the sailor's dread. This was going to be a storm and a half!

He looped a noose of rope around the king spoke, keeping the ship sailing on a straight course, then debated heading off to find Sherman and tell him the news that the weather was closing in faster than expected. Footsteps fell behind him and he turned to watch Styx walking away from the summoning deck, his face much akin to the storm on the horizon. Ridge was sure that eggs were eggs; there went a sign of trouble in paradise! He chuckled to himself and returned his thoughts to the task at hand, considering how to phrase his report to the first mate.

Sherman would also need to know their shadow was back, the ship having come back into sight as the sun had started rising. It was better asking Sherman to tell the captain rather than risk putting Thomas in a bad mood himself. He looked over towards the captain's cabin and was surprised as the door to the senior cabins opened. Rauph and Thomas walked out, Thomas scowling as strongly as Styx had been.

Yes, taking in that view... his news was definitely a job for the first mate! He would just stand here and try to look busy!

Little footsteps pounded up the stairs, making Ridge raise his head again. A small headless figure rushed out onto the main deck and launched into a flurry of activity; suddenly growing arms that slipped through the tunic top thrown over its head.

A shaggy mop of hair followed, sprouting out of the collar like a fast-growing weed. As Ridge looked on Ashe finally sorted himself out, straightening his tunic and pulling his bycocket hat down hard upon his head before looking around the deck wildly.

"Did I miss it? Did I miss it?" Ashe enquired, his expression turning into a frown when he realised that the sun had indeed risen.

"Missed what?" Ridge replied.

"It doesn't matter." Ashe returned, dejected at his repeated failure to catch the sun's rays. He wandered off across the deck mumbling incoherently under his breath, a small necklace clutched tightly in his hand.

Ridge followed the Halfling's passage for a short while and then shook his head. That was the problem with the youth of today. They took things far too seriously.

* * * * * *

"Open up!" Thomas ordered, banging his fist loudly on Kerian's cabin door. "If you don't open up now, I'll let Rauph open the door for us and you won't even have the privacy of a door to hide behind."

There was a mumble from within and then a bleary-eyed Marcus opened the door, hopping on one foot and looking around the floor as if he had lost something.

"Where's Kerian." Thomas demanded.

"I don't know." Marcus replied honestly. "He isn't in here. Maybe he is above decks? Can I help at all?"

"Just tell him I want to see him now!" Thomas's face was like thunder and Marcus swiftly realised what was going on. The ruse was up; they were after the map, a map that Kerian did not have.

"My ship and crew are in danger, there's a storm rapidly approaching and I need to find us some shelter, sanctuary or haven." Thomas stated. "I need him to bring me the map now. Every second we waste puts my ship and crew at further risk."

Marcus paled at the anger before him. Thomas was clearly worried about his crew and this was to the man's credit and a clear explanation for his ire but Abbot Brialin had directed he never show maps or documents to anyone else, ever! Just in case anyone viewing them decided to go on an independent quest, seeking the legendary treasure for themselves. The church needed to get to Stratholme for more than mere treasure. This was Marcus's charge and he was going to keep it.

"As I said, he's not here." The monk replied. "But I'll be sure to let him know you need him straight away."

"Make sure you do." Thomas snarled. "Because I swear if Kerian has lied to me..." he left the threat hanging, leaving Marcus staring at a shrugging Minotaur standing in the shadows behind him.

* * * * * *

Colette rubbed her arms, trying to warm the 'goose bumps' rising on her skin in the suddenly chill morning air. She knelt within the circumference of the smaller arcane circle inscribed on the aft deck and tried to settle herself comfortably on her kneeling cushion in preparation for the summoning of the wind elemental. However, no matter how she tried to settle herself she still felt ill at ease. It appeared that Kerian's uncharacteristic response to her innocent comments earlier that morning had upset her more than she cared to admit. His distraught face and cryptic response played on her mind, as if there was something deeper to these reactions and that there was somehow another important piece of the mysterious puzzle of the man called Styx, or was it Kerian Denaris, that she was missing.

She thought back to the warriors in the inn that had called him that name, the ring Ashe had shown her bearing the birth date of a much younger man and now this out of proportion reaction to her earlier comments. She chuckled to herself, admitting that he did have her attention if nothing else!

She rubbed her arms again, attempting to clear her mind of the pleasant distraction, before turning to the task at hand. Thomas had instructed that she summon the elemental swiftly, ordering it to fill the ship's sails so that they might outrun the storm on the open sea whilst he worked on finding a place of safety to seek refuge. The captain intended to steer a course that just skirted the tempestuous seas ahead, allowing the *El Defensor* to slip smoothly in behind the storm and continue on their current course, safe in the storm's wake.

"Get our cloudy friend up and blowing." Thomas had winked to her. "I want that creature to blow so hard that he coughs up a lung!"

With these orders clearly in mind, Colette prepared to summon the elemental and take on the constant mental battle that came with trying to make an angry storm with a bad attitude do as she commanded.

Colette reached for the roll of cloth that she had laid down earlier and sorted through her magical paraphernalia. She removed a stub of candle from the collection of items and using a small pinch of gem dust ignited the candle with a sharp click of her fingers.

Drops of molten wax fell upon the decking until a small mound formed there. Next, she removed an incense holder from the roll and secured this firmly to the desk by pushing it down hard into the pliable candle wax. Colette did not want anything slipping about on the deck if they skirted a little too close to the storm!

She gently placed one of the 'acquired' incense sticks from Catterick within the holder and ignited it with the candle stub. Soon a small spiral of scented smoke began to rise from the incense stick, gently filling her nostrils with the delicate essence of rosewood.

Colette breathed deeply cleansing her thoughts before withdrawing a multi-facetted sapphire as big as her thumb. She lifted the gemstone in her hand, concerned at the value of the gem and the fact that the ship's treasury did not hold many more of this high quality. The mage briefly considered what would happen if they were to run out of gemstones adrift at sea with steadily dwindling supplies, then shrugged, concentrating on the 'here and now'. What Thomas asked for he got!

The sapphire winked alluringly in the small amount of light remaining about the ship making Colette smile as she paused to regard the beauty of the object. It was such a waste! Taking one final cleansing breath, she uttered a swift mantra of protection before placing the gemstone on the front edge of her kneeling mat and acknowledging to herself that she was ready to begin the summoning.

"Aurion I call thee from your home. Come to your mistress and do as I command, without question, demand or hesitation." She paused, taking another breath as the gemstone before her began to hiss, signalling the release of the magical energies contained within its glittering heart.

"Aurion hear my second call. I command thee to come forth and do my bidding!" The magical components from within the gemstone slowly spiralled up into the air before her, thousands of tiny sparkling shards of light flowing like a waterfall in reverse. The spiral rose higher and higher above Colette's head before gathering like a miniature sun, hovering ten feet above the deck.

"Aurion my third call binds you to this material plane pulling you from your place of rest. To resist my summons is futile and pointless. You are my servant and you will come at my call." The combined might of the sapphires released energy suddenly fell to the deck landing right in the centre of the larger inscribed circle. Glittering points of light rippled and waved across the deck, giving the appearance that the wood was no longer something solid but instead becoming something ethereal, detached from the ship itself.

The floor rippled like water, the impossibility of such an action just adding to the overall eeriness of the summoning. Sickly grey and yellow cracks began to appear across the transforming surface, flashing brightly only to disappear again, as if the area within the circle was now pulsating with some life force yet unknown. With a loud crack, much akin to an egg hatching the deck disappeared completely, revealing a perfectly spherical hole that stretched down into nothingness where the cabins below decks should have been.

Colette paused in her chanting and opened her eyes to regard the open gateway in the deck. This part of the summoning she hated: It was what scared her the most. She knew instinctively that the elemental was waiting just below the surface of the deck daring her to finish the spell. She tried to hide her fear and called the creature's name aloud.

"Aurion, come to me now." There was no shouting or emphasis of the order, yet the words sent trembles up and down Colette's back, raising more goose bumps on her arms but this time she dared not rub her arms or take her eyes away from the hole that loomed ominously before her. That was what the creature wanted... to catch her off guard.

Whistling, much akin to the sound of the wind whipping across chimney pots, shrieked around her, then something huge and very, very angry crashed into the barrier bare inches from Colette's kneeling figure. Sparks rose giving a vague impression and outline to the creature trapped within the summoning circle as it threw itself repeatedly at the barrier holding it in place.

The magical runes of protection flared brightly along the edges of the confinement area as the elemental tested its strength to the limits but they performed perfectly, holding the creature back exactly as the magical artist who created them intended and Colette moved swiftly onto the next part of her spell: The binding.

She lifted the incense stick from its holder and cupped it in her hand, gathering the smoke and pooling it before drawing in a breath and blowing hard. The tendrils of smoke flickered out from her hand as if somehow mentally directed towards their goal and passed through the protective barrier surrounding the kneeling mage, raising small sparks of resistance as it crossed the magical field. The smoke continued without hesitation, the grey fingers of scented matter raising more sparks as it passed through the second barrier encircling the enraged elemental. The smoke shot forwards after it breached this second barrier, sucked in to integrate throughout the airy form of the summoned elemental giving it colour and shape as Colette continued to chant.

"With this smoke I give you form that I may behold you. With this smoke, I bind you to this ship so that you will do as I command. With this smoke I control your actions and with this smoke I will return you from whence you came." Colette stared at the elemental with her emotions closely in check, observing how the smoke writhed across the creature's immense rippling musculature coating the elemental as effectively as if someone had dipped it in a bucket of whitewash. The marbled effect served several purposes, not just the fact that it allowed Colette to see the practically invisible creature.

The mage had total control over the rosewood smoke that had been an integral component of the spell. With a thought, she could engulf the elementals head in the thickly scented material and blind it, suffocate it or more importantly order it to do what she wished. The impurities of the smoke also bound the creature to the ship, its integration with the creature making it impossible for the elemental to return through the hole from which it had arrived unless Colette ordered the smoke to withdraw. Twin red eyes blazed fury towards her small form as the monstrous force tried to escape back through the gateway to its home. A loud howl of pain and frustration filled the air as the creature recognised the futility of its actions. The elemental turned its anger towards the one who held it there against its will with an enraged shriek.

Now the battle of wills truly began.

Colette coldly ignored the hissing and snarling from the constantly moving marble streaked cloud and instead demanded that it blow into the sails. The scented rosewood smoke moved up the creature's body until small pieces eased in towards the elemental's brain. The tempest reacted violently as always, lashing out with limbs assembled from swirling cloud matter raising more sparks as it encountered the invisible barrier containing it.

The creature continued to assault the barrier until it had battered every square inch of the containment field, testing Colette's limits as she fought to enforce her will through the smoke conduit whilst also struggling to reinforce the magical barrier holding the creature at bay.

Her head began to throb with the strain as her mind fought against the stresses the elemental was placing upon her. What was going on? The creature was normally much easier to control than this. Panic began to rise within the pit of her stomach as she determinedly hung on and sent another demand out towards the swirling cloud mass. The runes set within the outer aspect of the circle flared brightly as the magic contained within threatened to break free.

"Blow into the sails damn you!" She screamed, teeth gritted, as her full will slammed into the monster's brain. There was a frightful silence as if the elemental was considering what to do, then it turned away from the mage and began to do her bidding. A low whistle arose, transforming into a full-fledged roar, answered with the usual groans from the main masts and the accompanying snapping of canvas as the sails took the strain and began to fill to their limits.

The *El Defensor*, oblivious to the struggle that had just occurred on her decks began to pick up speed, her keel slicing through the water like a warm knife through butter. Ridge adjusted his position at the helm, turning the wheel so that the ship headed onwards at a sharp angle to the dark green and black flecked cloudbank bearing down on them.

Chapter Twenty-Nine

Kerian was in a bad mood. He had purposefully taken the long route back to his cabin, mumbling and muttering to himself as he tried to review Colette's earlier comments and see if there was any way he could have misunderstood them. He arrived back at his cabin and threw open the door to find Marcus sitting with the smaller notebook he had been given at the monastery, the book lying open in his hands, flicking through the pages and adding notes in his own scratchy handwriting.

"What are you doing?" Kerian snapped without thinking.

"Recording our travels," Marcus shot back, before pausing as if caught in a lie. "Thomas is looking for you and he's really angry." He replaced the cork in the top of his inkpot and started to gather his things, eyeing Kerian from the corner of his eye and flushing red.

Kerian looked on, too worked up in his own thoughts to notice the out of character actions.

"Why is he angry?" Kerian asked. "I haven't done anything to upset him. Has Ashe stolen something again? He can't keep blaming me for that little character's action all the time."

"He wants the map." Marcus said finally, stopping Kerian as swiftly as he closed the book, he had been writing in.

"Oh." Kerian paused, lost for words. He turned his attention fully on Marcus and glared. "So now what are we going to do?"

"You started this lie. You finish it." Marcus snapped back, sidestepping around Kerian's scowling face to leave him standing alone in the cabin. Kerian slammed his hand into the cabin door causing Marcus to jump.

"I wouldn't be in this damned mess if you had given me the map when I asked." Kerian moved to slam the door in Marcus's face but Marcus snapped back pushing the door back against him. The door protested at the treatment and a loud crack split the air. The door fell from its hinge and crashed to the floor. Kerian looked down at the door then back up at Marcus and resumed his verbal attack.

"If we don't show Thomas the map, everything we have worked towards is in tatters, our quest is lost and this ship will be turned about, all because you were too damned proud to share that stupid map with me."

"Everything we have worked towards?" Marcus reflected. "If I remember rightly the only person who has tried to coerce this crew through lies and subterfuge is you. I certainly had no part in it. As for everything being in tatters it would appear you are the sum cause of that as well." He gestured at the ruins of the door as if to emphasise his point.

"I wasn't the only one that wanted to go to this island." Kerian snapped back. "You have as much a vested interest in this destination as I do."

"That is undeniable." Marcus acknowledged. "My faith has instructed me to go to the island but my actions are open for all to see, not corrupted with the selfish reasoning that powers your own."

"Why exactly are you coming then?" Kerian barked. "I would hardly call this the ideal vacation and it is far removed from a quiet trip to one of your dusty libraries."

"It was in one such dusty library that your hopes were re-kindled." Marcus reminded the elderly fighter, pointedly ignoring the question. "And I would remind you that books can transport you anywhere if you are willing enough to take the time and digest the knowledge transcribed within." He moved forwards suddenly propelling Kerian backwards towards the deadlight.

"Look out the window." He snarled grabbing Kerian roughly by the front of his tunic and shoving him up against the dead light, pushing his face up hard against the glass.

"See that mass of clouds out there? It's one of the biggest and nastiest storms Thomas has ever seen and by the looks on his face when he came to me earlier it has got him scared."

Kerian struggled in the grasp of the monk, surprised by the treatment he was receiving at Marcus's hands. He kicked out, connecting with something and hearing it crash but Marcus stepped out of the way and swiftly resumed the pressure.

"How is my making a fake map responsible for that?" Kerian spat, squirming his way free, and slapping Marcus's hands away. "I don't even know where we are going. That's all down to you..." Kerian suddenly reversed positions, slamming Marcus painfully against the wall causing more furniture to fall. "...and the fact you wouldn't let even me look at your stupid book!"

"Let go of me." Marcus warned, as the thin book he had been writing in earlier fell to the floor and spilled open revealing pages of maps and diagrams.

"Or what?" Kerian snapped, his eyes darting down quickly to look at the book before gazing at his roommate again.

"Or I will be forced to kill you where you stand." The monk stated calmly, something about the edge in his voice bringing Kerian up fast. He let go of the monk's clothes releasing him from his position up against the dead light and laughed, trying to make light of the situation and clear the uncomfortable tension in the air.

"You know you are going to have to stop hanging around with me." He quipped, as Marcus bent to collect the book from the floor. "Where is that quiet little Marcus I once knew? Next thing we know you'll be wielding a long sword and rescuing damsels in distress and that would never do."

Marcus ignored the comments, dusting himself down before walking slowly out the open doorway. Kerian looked after him, then at the broken door and the wreck of the room about him. Somehow as they had tussled the bed linen had fallen all over the floor, the table had broken, and his own belongings were strewn about as if a storm had been in the cabin and not just threatening outside.

He did not feel like shouting out after the monk. He did not care about making amends. His life just appeared to be going to pieces.

Kerian went to retrieve his saddlebags and started scooping his belongings back inside. Something flashed within the avalanche of items he had collected. He caught the item before it slid back into his pack, the cool metal of the vanity mirror suddenly comforting in his moment of need. He turned over the mirror and froze as the reflective surface showed an elderly haggard knight with red-rimmed eyes staring straight back at him but instead of showing a multitude of fractured images the mirror's surface was unbelievably intact! The residue of several small, smudged fingerprints marred the edge of the vision. What was…?

"Ashe…"

Then it hit him. Marcus had been writing in the smaller book, the one that supposedly had the tales in, not the large blue one. The smaller book did not contain stories! It was this volume, not the large one, which contained the maps and charts. He had seen it with his own eyes when the book had fallen onto the floor in their scuffle. Just what in the world was going on?

Moreover, where was Marcus's big blue book?

* * * * * *

Thomas and Rauph arrived on the bustling mid-deck and swiftly made their way over to Sherman who was trying to explain to Ives Mantoso how to tie a sheepshank knot. The seaman looked up at their approach and took in Thomas's serious face, then swiftly told the new man to keep practicing and moved over to Thomas's side. Seconds later, after a nod for the captain, the first mate began to shout for attention, assembling the crew above decks who instantly gathered around to hear their captain's carefully selected words.

The captain took a moment to regard all the anxious faces gathered around him, wondering how he could inform his crew of his error in trusting a complete stranger and that their captain had been following a fool and his dreams for the last two weeks. Dreams that had inexplicably turned into a very real and terrifying possibility of a nightmare. The crew sensed his reluctance to begin and exchanged worried glances with each other while they waited for the silence to be broken.

A crack of thunder turned heads towards the tempest that was undeniably sweeping down towards them and when the crew turned back to look at their captain, they faced a man with grim determination clearly etched on his features. Just one look was all many of the crew needed, Thomas's look of resolve instantly bolstering their flagging morale and making them realise to the man that they would see this through to the bitter end no matter what the cost.

"Listen up." Thomas began, initially unsure as to how to continue. "I'm sure it has come to all of your attentions that a light shower is heading our way."

He smiled at the nervous laugh raised by the crew and decided to continue with his unrehearsed, light-hearted approach, even though his insides felt like someone was tying them quite successfully into the sheepshank knots Mantoso was trying so hard to master.

"Aside from the suggestion that we may all need to change into our waterproof leathers... Oh, apart from you Jenkins," He pointed to one of the men whose jerkin was damp with sweat and grime from the effort of scrubbing the decks. "I have had requests that you strip off entirely in preparation for your yearly wash which I know has come slightly earlier than expected this year." The ship erupted into laughter at the sailor's expense and another crew member threw across a dirty rag suggesting that Jenkins could use it to get even cleaner. Thomas waited for the hilarity to die down before resuming.

"The *El Defensor* is the fastest ship I have ever had the pleasure of serving on." He continued. "Colette has our mutual friend whistling into the sails and I am sure we will be able to skirt this storm with the minimum of fuss. But I do need to ask you all to ready the ship just in case things decide to get a little bumpy."

The crew sobered almost to the man, strained smiles on their faces. They knew that the storm they faced was a large one but they also trusted their captain and knew he would use his skills to avoid it if he could. To a man, they recognised the signs that the storm was getting closer, the swell on the sea was starting to get larger and the ship was perceptively moving up and down as she cut her way through the waves.

"Plano and Abeline go aloft please and trim the sails. I want our elemental able to utilise every square inch of canvas to its full advantage." The two athletes threw mock salutes and swung up into the sails as Thomas turned his attention to Rauph.

"Rauph. If you will excuse the pun and no insult intended, please 'man' the wheel. As for the rest of you, I want all the cargo securely stored below, the hatches battened down and the whole ship so ready for this storm that not a single piece of crockery slips free and breaks. If anything does break it comes out of your pay packets and not mine, understood?" The crew nodded in agreement and weak laughter filtered to Thomas's ears.

"Well what are you all standing around for?" Sherman butted in. "You heard the captain. Move those lazy good for nothing backsides and get the job done."

The crew dispersed like water droplets off oil, each man knowing his role and rushing to fulfil it like an orchestrated dance rehearsed and committed to memory. Thomas nodded his head in appreciation for the crew's response even though there was no one to see him do so. He risked a quick glance towards the ominous cloudbank that was still rolling across the sea towards him and shuddered. The storm was closing faster than he expected. This was going to be close.

He turned towards the helm, putting the storm firmly at his back and watched as Rauph finally reached the huge wheel, he nodded to Ridge, who even at this distance seemed relieved at being asked to step down. The Minotaur then reached down to retrieve something from a small cubbyhole beneath the helm and began to slip it over his head. Thomas did not need to get any closer to realise what Rauph was slipping into. The leather harness swiftly took on shape as the ship's navigator set about tightening the straps across his chest and about his arms before he leaned forwards and secured four thick bands that hung from the harness about the base of the ship's wheel. With a grunt, Rauph stood straight once more, the harness secure, wheel and navigator now one. No storm known to man would separate this navigator from his helm!

Confident that all was going according to plan, Thomas turned from the sight of his huge friend and turned back towards the cloudbank. Even this far away the storm was leeching what little light remained from the ship, plunging the *El Defensor* into a world of perpetual twilight. Another crack of thunder echoed ominously from across the waves followed by flashes of angry lightning that flickered within the dark green clouds.

"Okay... okay." Thomas snapped as if he were arguing with the storm. "I know you're coming to get me." He scanned the deck, ensuring all was well, before turning back towards the storm once more.

"Run, run as fast as you can." He muttered. "But you won't catch me..." he resolved. "I'm the gingerbread man."

* * * * * *

Sherman stood at the rail staring out and up at the huge mass of clouds that now hung over the *El Defensor* like a tsunami at breaking point, the summit of the clouds threatening to drop down and bury them all without a trace. His eyes traced down the wall of thick cloud and back across the waves towards the ship, noting the line of shadow that slowly crept across the surface of the sea, turning the waters into an inky impenetrable darkness that made him shudder. If they did not get a move on this ship was going to be under the clouds and sailing on those formidable waters soon and the superstitious crewman did not like the idea of that at all!

He reached into his pocket and withdrew a gold coin he had been saving this coin to celebrate his birthday at his next shore leave and he stared at the gleaming metal in silent contemplation, oblivious to the shouts of the crew running about securing the ship behind him.

Sherman looked back across the deck to make sure no one was watching, his gaze lingering on the figure of Thomas shouting orders to the crew, before looking back to the coin in his hand. He owed Thomas a lot. The man had always looked out for him. Ridge had once told him that sailors of old threw coins overboard before sailing into a storm to appease the gods whose waters they sailed through thereby granting them safe passage.

He looked back at the coin and shrugged. Ridge was sleeping in his cabin, or at least trying to, especially with all the noise going on above decks, so he would not be performing this ritual. Thomas would not even entertain doing something as 'ridiculous' as this, so that left Sherman as the one to do it. He flipped the coin and watched as it spun end over end to drop into the olive-green waters rushing alongside: then he closed his eyes and mouthed his silent request for aid.

The ship appeared to lift from the water, then slammed back hard into the surf jarring everyone on board and nearly knocking Sherman from his feet. He tilted his hat to look at Rauph who was shrugging his shoulders at the rude gestures sent his way as if the crew felt the navigator was to blame. A barely audible sorry echoed across the decks then the ship smashed down into the surf again, falling from one swell to the other and raising fresh calls of frustration.

Taking this as his key to set off and talk to the enthusiastic 'pilot' Sherman headed unsteadily across the rolling deck and made it to the stairs mere seconds before the ship slammed into the surf again. The sea was getting rougher by the second!

A quick glance back at the storm clouds showed that they were now starting to enter the shadows beneath the towering cloudbank and Sherman found himself holding his breath as they passed through the barely discernible barrier marking the boundary between the darkness and the light. He shivered, then continued his climb, coming up alongside Rauph and grinning with a humour he did not feel.

"Can you make it a little less bumpy?" He joked.

Rauph shrugged as if he had little to do with it and set himself firmer as the helm shuddered under his huge hands. The cold shadow slid agonisingly across the rest of the deck plunging the vessel fully into the cloud's domain and as one, all of them paused in whatever they were doing and looked up at the towering clouds. Sherman wanted to believe it was a trick of the light but as each man looked skyward, his face appeared to go deathly pale.

The ship crashed down heavily, jarring the sailor and Sherman looked at the Minotaur with an expression that spoke volumes.

"I know," he acknowledged to the huge helmsman before he could utter a word. "You're sorry." Rauph chuckled his strange bovine laugh and shook his head joining in the momentary joviality then paused as his eyes noticed Thomas staggering in their direction looking decidedly green.

"Can we pull away just a little bit more?" the captain asked as he came up alongside. "The sea swells are slightly larger over here under the cloud cover and I don't want to see my lunch twice in one day." Rauph chuckled as Thomas gulped a huge mouthful of air, trying to quell the rising gorge he felt within.

"Have you ever seen the like?" Sherman gestured at the clouds looming above them, shivering slightly despite himself.

"No." Thomas confessed. "And if I have my way, I'll never see the like again."

"There's someone coming to see you." Rauph interrupted, pointing his finger at the robed figure of Marcus who was wobbling his way in their direction.

"What does he want?" Thomas asked.

"Have you made your peace with your god?" Sherman teased.

"I'm not quite ready for that yet." Thomas conceded, smiling despite his discomfort.

Marcus staggered up seconds later, his cassock billowing in the wind, revealing his hairy legs beneath. He reached the helm gasping for breath and held out some sheets of parchment in his hand.

"What are these?" Thomas enquired, regarding the crumpled parchment with as much contempt as he would view one of the street merchants handing out free flyers advertising short lived gimmicks and get rich quick schemes that never quite delivered back home.

Marcus paused to catch his breath, his facial expression showing he was wrestling with a conflict within him and then he looked up at the three people as if carefully considering what he wanted to say.

"I have your map." He opened, handing over one of the sheets to the stunned captain.

"I think Rauph and I have had our fill of your maps." Thomas growled menacingly.

"See for yourself." Marcus replied, opening the parchment to reveal a sea chart that clearly portrayed the waters upon which they sailed. All the correct longitude and latitude markers were present and the position of the island they were searching for was clearly marked, if the detail of the island was indistinguishable, it was because the map was a shipping route document and not a close up of the island in question.

"But..." Thomas stammered. "Is this real?"

"Of course it is." Marcus snapped. "I'm giving this to you against my better judgement. Against my Abbot's orders. I am breaking his trust in giving this to you; do not make me regret it." He reached over with the precious parchment, just as the ship ploughed into another trough. The parchment jarred out of Marcus's hand and flew up into the air, missing all three sets of hands that leapt to intercept it.

"Get that map!" Thomas screamed, drawing the attention of everyone in earshot that was still standing following the latest jolt. He watched as the parchment flew up into the back draft from the sails and whipped back down towards the small gathering of crew. There was a rip and then the map stopped in mid-free fall, wrapping itself firmly around one of Rauph's huge horns, the centre of the map caught up on the razor-sharp tip.

Sherman laughed in relief and Thomas found himself smiling in despite of himself. He looked up at the Minotaur with a stern eye.

"Well what are you waiting for?" He snapped. "Bend down here this instant!"

* * * * * *

Where was it? It had to be in here somewhere!

Kerian paused in his search, stepping away from Ashe's bunk and the pile of items strewn across it and looked around the small compact cabin one more time. It had to be here; Marcus would never let the book go far from his side! He shook his head angrily.

Why hadn't he seen that there was something bizarre about the monk's attitude when it had come to sharing the information within the blue bound volume? He had been quick enough to share from their collection within the library, why was now different?

The book obviously contained something Marcus did not want him to know, something other than the maps Kerian had wished to see! Nevertheless, the question remained, what exactly did the book contain and why was it so important and secretive that Marcus had gone to such lengths to hide it from him?

He could not believe it! Marcus of all people lying to him!

Kerian dropped to his knees and stared under the bunk at the empty space he already knew lay beneath, as if by repeating the action, some previously hidden artefact would suddenly appear from the nothing that lay there and become solid reality. Several orphaned dust balls rolling with the movement of the ship kept silent, moody company with a ragged and currently vacated spider's web. The bare boards beneath the bed still showed the scuffmarks from his and Marcus's altercation, but other than that, there were no signs that anything or for that matter anyone had ever disturbed the sanctity of the dust-choked world under the bed. Of the blue bound book, there was no sign.

He looked up at the remains of Marcus's bed linen stretched out across the bunk assured that he had searched there already, then over to the empty hammock still hanging from the wall and the sleeping roll now lying across the table on the far side of the cabin. He knew none of these places contained the book but it had to be here somewhere.

Kerian regained his feet, only to feel the whole ship suddenly drop beneath him, sending him back down onto one knee. What in the world was going on? He moved unsteadily across the floor of the cabin, checking his footing at each step, just in case the floor should suddenly betray him again, before arriving at the dead light. He moved his head up against the smeary glass anxious to see what was going on outside.

Huge dark green waves moved menacingly outside of the circular glass like a shoal of circling sharks around fresh prey. The ship suddenly slammed down, then again in sharp succession smacking the fighter's forehead off the glass with the suddenness of the motion. Kerian rubbed his bruised temple and gingerly looked outside, noting the dark menacing sky and the peaks and troughs of the turbulent sea. The storm had descended upon them with a speed that was frightening.

Although the light had been steadily darkening as Kerian's search had continued, there had been no major warning to the fighter of the storm's arrival below decks until now. No little waves turning slowly into medium and then bigger waves; no serious motion of the deck beneath him. It just seemed that they were suddenly sailing through increasingly exaggerated swells with each passing moment.

This went against everything Kerian had heard about storms at sea, making him realise that the yarns he had taken as gospel on his travels were tales of fantasy with no basis in fact at all! Then again, his narrators had probably never considered that their listener would ever be able to find out how inaccurate their inventions actually were! Kerian allowed himself a chuckle at his own naivety and vowed to return to his storytellers when this was all over and explain to them their mistaken ways!

Another tooth-jarring drop from the ship made Kerian seek the sanctuary of the wall and he paused there to collect his breath. Who was piloting the ship in these terrible conditions? Didn't they have an experienced sailor on board who could take them through this with a few less bumps? Flakes of powdered lime gently cascaded down from the planking above, lightly dusting him like a piece of expensive confectionery and he paused to brush the material of his jacket before turning his gaze up to the source of his irritation.

One plank was slightly out of line far above his head, the resulting gap allowing accumulated eroded lime powder and sawdust to shower him where he stood. Kerian instantly recognised the source from the heavy stones used to scrub the main deck. Obviously, with increased application, the flakes of lime from the holy stones flaked through the planking and collected in the space between the underside of the main deck and his ceiling but this did not explain the sudden unexpected shower.

No! Marcus could not have, could he?

Would the monk have been that devious as to secret the book away from Kerian and Ashe in the ceiling? He thought again, about how absurd the question was. Of course! Marcus would be that devious! He had hardly been a paragon of virtue so far on this voyage! What was more there was nowhere else within the cabin that the book could be and from examining the detritus scattered about the cabin the knight knew his search had been nothing if not thorough.

Kerian swiftly looked around the cabin for something to stand on, mentally kicking himself for breaking the table earlier before moving over to the hammock and trying to swing himself up into it. This action was normally much easier in calm seas and it took several false starts before he managed to fall into the net and swing precariously backwards and forwards. As he moved, the ambient light appeared to leach from the room, plunging the cabin into semidarkness and stopping the elderly man in his tracks.

"Who turned out the lights?" he muttered, whilst trying to get up on all fours within the swinging hammock. Several curses followed before Kerian felt steady enough to resume his quest with a growing sense of irritation.

He was constantly aware that Marcus could return at any time and any delay now might give the monk warning that something was amiss, allowing him to hide the book somewhere where Kerian would never find it.

The ship dropped away once more, making Kerian fall face-first into the hammock. This was ridiculous! With the ship movement so unpredictable, climbing this relatively small distance was becoming hazardous indeed! All he needed was to take a tumble from the hammock and he could easily find himself with a broken leg, fractured hip or much worse and this time there would be no honourable mist monsters to repair the damage!

With great trepidation Kerian levered himself back up onto all fours, his mind teasing him with the thought that Colette could walk in at just that moment and catch him looking totally ridiculous. Colette... What was he going to do about that? He had feelings for her, there was no denying it but she was blinded to the 'real' Kerian and saw him as all the others did, as a tired cynical old man.

He shook his head angrily, annoyed at the distraction and focused on the hammock beneath him, lifting his upper half on ever-wobbly arms, his knees splayed uncomfortably to try to maintain his balance. His knees cracked as he straightened and Kerian winced as a swift warning pain shot up his legs. His knees were getting worse! He was going to have to watch that when he got old!

Reaching out slowly, he was finally able to get his hands on the wall, stabilising himself to the degree he could walk his hands up the wood towards the ceiling. This was better! The deck tilted alarmingly, sending all the wrecked cabin debris sliding across the floor. Kerian found himself with his head squashed against the wood, his perspiration marking the surface and clearly showing where his shaking hands and forehead had touched. This was ridiculous! He just had to grab the bit by the teeth and get it over with!

He ran his hands up the wall in one swift moment, teetering as a momentary episode of vertigo assailed him, making the cabin appear to spin and lose solidity for the briefest of instants.

Spreading his stance further, he finally found the courage to look up at the loose plank above and after a few false starts, due to the violent motions of the ship, he was able to take his hands from the wall and free the board from its position. A fresh shower of lime cascaded down as he reached inside the hole and drew forth a large canvas wrapped object. At last! This was what he had been looking for!

With shaking hands, Kerian unwrapped one corner of the parcel to reveal the spine of the blue bound volume he had so desperately sought. With a grunt of satisfaction, he uncovered the rest of the book and let it drop into his hands. Sparks immediately shot from the book causing Kerian to cry out in pain. The book fell from his nerveless fingers and painfully bounced off his toe before coming to a stop in the hammock between his splayed legs. Kerian reached for his injured foot by reflex, leaving himself unbalanced and very vulnerable to motion.

As if it were patiently waiting for just such an occasion the ship lurched again and with a cry of horror Kerian felt the hammock give way beneath him, dropping him onto the bunk below with such force that the wooden rails across it snapped.

He found himself lying with his face inches from the dust balls he had seen earlier. The cobweb appeared occupied now, with a mean looking spider that looked much bigger from this perspective. He took a moment to check himself over and sighed. That was a close one! Just a few bumps, bruises and lost dignity. Nothing he could not handle.

Marcus's book chose that moment to finally slide free from the folds in the hammock above and made Kerian seriously reconsider his thoughts.

* * * * * *

Colette gritted her teeth as the wind elemental challenged her hold over it, the red eyes glaring defiantly from amidst the marble smoke streaked creature's body. What was with this thing today? She had never known the elemental to put up such a fight!

Footsteps reached her from across the raised deck and Sherman walked out onto the platform, giving the whirling pillar of wind a respectable berth as he made his way over towards her. She looked up at his approach, taking in the red bobbing feather whipping about upon his hat and smiled, wiping a sweat streaked lock of hair from her forehead and dropping her guard, allowing the elemental free reign to crash about and scream within the magical confines of the protective circle. It did not disappoint her, lashing out at its prison walls in open angry defiance at its capture. The runes painted across the decking flared brightly as the creature continued to test the magical wards to their limit.

"Hi." Sherman nodded. "How's it going here?"

Colette looked the sailor up and down and scowled.

"What no drink?" she joked.

Sherman dropped down to the deck alongside her and pointed back towards the helm.

"Thomas wants us to change course. Give us all a second to set the tack of the sails and when we say, get that thing to blow like it has never blown before."

Colette shivered and looked up, noticing the green-flecked clouds for the first time.

"How long have we been under those?" she asked, jumping as a crack of lightning split the sky overhead. Her sailing companion initially thought she was joking with him but one look at Colette's strained face told Sherman that she had been too wrapped up in her spell casting to notice the change in weather or Rauph's none too gentle sailing.

"Not too long now." Sherman confessed, casting his nervous gaze back over the rest of the ship and checking on the progress of the rest of the crew. "The thing is we don't want to stay under here either." The ship smashed down heavily into another trough, jarring the young mage and the sailor sitting alongside her.

"Goodness." She gasped as the incense stick fell from its holder and rolled about on the deck. "I hope Rauph is going to treat us a bit more gently than this!" Sherman looked back across at Thomas and nodded an acknowledgement to a signalled order.

"We are ready for you now." He informed her. "When you can please."

"I aim to please." Colette replied huskily, laughing at herself in the process. She closed her eyes and sent out the tendrils of smoke to order the elemental to do her bidding. The sheer ferocity of the elemental's reaction to her initial order set Colette back on her heels as if physically struck a blow. The monster screamed, wind blowing about the raised area of deck in no set direction and causing Sherman to hold on to his hat or risk losing it for the first time in ages.

Determined, Colette furrowed her brow and sent forth another, more urgent command. The elemental went berserk! Runes flared and sparked as the creature thrashed about the containment circle desperate to escape its bindings and wreck revenge against all those who had enslaved it. Talons grew from the marble streaked smoke and scratched wide red-hot trails of promised destruction across the inside of the invisible shield it's shrieks of frustration from rising to new heights.

Sherman staggered to his feet, sensing something was wrong and drew his sword, spreading his feet to maintain balance on the tilting deck. He looked up at the towering creature writhing bare feet from him and then back at his cutlass. Somehow, the weapon seemed wholly inadequate for facing a creature like this. He tensed expecting the worst but the creature surprised him and suddenly quietened.

The sailor shrugged to himself, sliding his sword back into its scabbard with a nervous laugh. Everything would be all right now; Colette appeared to have the creature back under control. He doffed his hat to her in a theatrical gesture and smiled just as spots of rain began to drop sporadically from above, splattering the deck with patches of damp as the ship slid further and further beneath the immense storm canopy.

Sherman turned from the kneeling mage and headed back across the deck towards Thomas and Rauph, only to come up short as he came parallel to the swirling mass of cloud. Thomas and Rauph were gesturing up at the sails and waving their arms about.

Whatever was wrong with them both?

"Come on!" Thomas shouted. Sherman looked at his captain bemused. What was the man going on about?

"Tell Colette to make the elemental blow." Thomas shouted back, pointing at the sails again for emphasis.

Everything suddenly appeared to move in slow motion.

Sherman looked up at the sails, which hung strangely, the canvas not filling out in the direction they wished to travel; then he looked back over at the kneeling mage he had just left. Colette was still kneeling safely within her circle but she was holding her hands to her head and appeared to be screaming, although it was difficult to tell with the rasping sound coming from beside his ear.

A loud explosive crack, like fragile glass shattering, made the sailor jump and the rasping sound suddenly became much clearer as if someone had taken their hand away from their mouth.

Sherman swung his head, moving from Colette's screaming form to follow the deck, tracking his eyes along the floor to the edge of the containment circle, which had held the elemental secure. Horror etched his face as he watched the magical runes char and warp before his eyes. Small hairline cracks etched directly through the pattern, flared brightly then darkened as the magic died within them changing the protective pattern into something that was next to useless.

His head continued to trace on into the circle, the rasping sound getting steadily louder by his ear, only to discover that the swirling elemental was no longer standing where it should have been. Sherman's first thought was that the creature must have been dispelled, sent back to where it came. That was an odd thing for Colette to do. Didn't she realise the storm was bearing down on them and they needed to get out of here?

He analysed all these stimuli in a matter of seconds, even though the events when viewed retrospectively would have appeared to take a lifetime. Then he turned to the last annoying part of the puzzle and attempted to ascertain what the loud rasping was beside his ear. He looked up at the swirling nightmare hanging before him and initially could not comprehend what he was seeing. Wasn't the elemental supposed to be standing in the containment circle? Hadn't Colette banished it? What was it doing out on the deck?

His mouth opened in astonishment just as his mind filled in all the blanks and Sherman went for his sword as the world around him exploded into flesh raking claws and those terrible, terrible red eyes bored right down into his soul.

Chapter Thirty

"No!"

Thomas cried out in horror as the air before his friend filled with a fine blood red mist, the talons of the air elemental ripping through his associate's form as if his salt streaked leather jerkin were paper. Sherman screamed, his shriek cutting through the howling wind and rain to fall on Thomas's ears like the accusing tones of a jury who were already convinced he was guilty. Sherman's sword was still in its scabbard, the speed and ferocity of the attack being such that the sailor had no time to attempt a defence. As the captain looked, the creature threw Sherman's crumpled body the length of the aft deck, flying out over the centre of the ship to slam into the base of the main mast with a sickening thump. He fought to avert his eyes from the grisly sight as his friend began sliding down the mast, leaving a crimson trail to mark where he had collided with the sanded wood.

"Marcus get to Sherman, see what you can do for him." Reacting on some subconscious level Thomas turned to his stunned colleagues and swiftly barked orders, snapping them out of their horrified states. He looked across at the ruined form of his friend, knowing instantly that any aid the monk could supply would probably come too late anyway and then turned to Rauph who was struggling to extricate himself from the harness that he wore.

"Rauph, I want you to stay here. I cannot have the ship going out of control in these waters. We have enough to deal with here." he looked the Minotaur firmly in the eye. "No matter what happens you stay at this post."

He did not wait for a response, heading off across the deck as the alarm raised about him. The elemental had already turned from where it had ripped apart Sherman and was now bearing down on Colette's kneeling figure. As the captain made his way across the deck towards her, he could not help noticing how small and helpless she looked against the sheer menace and horror of the creature towering above her. Smoke filled claws lashed out at her cowering figure, raising sparks from the protective barrier that saved her life several times in rapid succession.

Thomas ran across the blood-splattered deck, vainly trying to put out of his mind the fact that it was his friend's blood upon which he ran. He looked at the expanse of deck between himself and Colette, stunned that it appeared to be stretching into infinity; he was never going to reach her in time! As he ran, a blurred figure passed by overhead, running along the crossbeam with a grace that identified him immediately, it was something only an Elf could muster in the unpredictability of a storm such as this. Thomas hit the ladders and started to climb, just as Scrave dropped lightly from the rigging to land way ahead of him and bare inches behind the swirling mass of cloud.

"Excuse me." Scrave opened, drawing his sword. "But I thought I had the pleasure of the first dance."

The elemental spun around so rapidly it almost took Scrave's smile clean from his face. It towered over him, the menace it projected almost paralysing in intensity. Red, hate filled eyes, bored down on the Elven fighter and outstretched claws made of spiralling smoke, whirling grit and debris flexed in anticipation of another kill. The intimidation made the swordsman take a faltering step backwards.

"However, because you asked nicely..." Scrave commented, displaying a bluster he did not feel, before lashing out with his blade, sending the gleaming steel flashing in and out of the elemental's form almost faster than the eye could follow. At each thrust small wisps of smoke escaped from the tangible form that shaped the creature, raising snarls of pain that indicated the attacks were more of an irritation to the monster than a serious wound.

The Elf swiftly realised he couldn't fight with his grip loose about the hilt as he normally favoured in a sword fight, as each strike he landed threatened to rip the blade clean from his hand as the winds within its swirling body fought to snatch the weapon away.

Talons sliced through the air, barely missing the nimble Elf as he darted and weaved his way around the huge creature. He ducked as another attack passed harmlessly overhead slicing through some taut rigging and sending the severed lines flying up into the air like missiles to shred holes in the taut canvas sails above. Scrave took the opening as an opportunity to lash out again, plunging his sword under where the whirling column of wind appeared to have an armpit, inflicting what would have been a mortal blow on a human target. Instead, all the Elf got for his effort was a small puff of smoke that blew in his direction and obscured his vision.

The wind roared around him, its sound louder than anything the Elf had ever experienced. He waved the smoke away and realised his loss of vision had been costly. The elemental had elongated its body, totally encircling the fighter with its swirling marbled torso. The creature touched the deck as it spun, lifting more debris and dust to add further friction to its shrieking body mass. There was no escape for Scrave, he was trapped, as neatly as a butterfly in a jar.

"Never was much of a dancer anyway." The Elf snarled, settling his body and preparing for the devastating attack to come.

* * * * * *

Marcus hit the main deck at a run, sandals flapping noisily, his robe stretching out behind him, breath coming in ragged gasps at the sudden burst of activity. He arrived at Sherman's ruined body seconds before anyone else and was aghast at what he saw. The sailor lay in a lifeless heap, his eyes glazed over, hair matted across his face. One arm lay twisted beneath him and a bone poked from the ruin that remained of his left leg. Worst of all, his chest had been ripped apart, pieces of pulverised bony matter and raw bloody flesh turning the ragged remains of his jerkin black with his lifeblood. It was as if someone had dragged the poor man for miles behind a runaway horse.

The monk turned his head, fighting back the urge to vomit and gasped large gulps of cleansing air before turning back to the downed sailor. What was he to do? Where was he to start? The pungent smell from Sherman's body cavity began to overpower the monk and he gritted his teeth determinedly trying to put it to the back of his mind as he set to his grisly task.

"Oh, dear god!"

Marcus looked up to see that another sailor had arrived at his side and was taking in the awful sight. He turned to the man, anxious to share the terrible burden of responsibility, swiftly taking in the fact that the sailor was middle aged with blond hair and a scraggy beard framed by a red headscarf. A large gold earring hung from his pierced ear, a look ridiculous in any other time or setting but somehow right at home amongst the carnival that made up the crew aboard this ship. The man's green eyes reflected the horror he saw, yet he had an air of solemn maturity that Marcus instantly respected.

"What's your name?" the monk asked.

"Bernard." Came the trembling reply.

"Bernard, I need some sheets to wrap around Sherman's wounds. We need to make him as comfortable as possible."

"Okay." The dazed crew member replied. "Oh hell, what's that?"

Marcus turned to the ruined body and shook his head in disbelief. The body appeared to have taken on a greenish mist like tinge before his eyes.

Was he starting to become faint? He could not faint now! This man's very life depended on him! The monk wracked his brain for another answer. Was it an electrical discharge from the storm raging about them? Possibly St Elmo's fire? He drew his hands away, wiping them against his robes, inadvertently smearing his habit with Sherman's blood.

Huge raindrops splattered heavily across the deck and Marcus threw his head back to the heavens letting the water cleanse his face and wash the horror from his eyes before he turned his attention back to his charge, this time finding the ruined body had no signs of the eerie green glow about it that he had witnessed earlier.

His hands gently wiped the water from Sherman's face, as he thought what a pathetic action this was in the scheme of things. There was so much blood everywhere. What in St Fraiser's name was he supposed to do? He leaned forward, trying vainly to arrange the sailor's clothes to cover the most grievous wounds but the shredded material of the jerkin could only achieve a token job.

Tears began to well in the monk's eyes at the futility of it all. Where was Bernard and those blankets anyway?

Marcus gently removed Sherman's grey felt hat and lowered the sailor's head softly to the deck, ignorant of the fact that he was now seeing something none of the crew had ever seen before. Marcus took in the bald patch on the sailor's head without a second thought, unaware that Sherman had taken such pains to hide this affliction from the rest of the crew with the trademark hat that had made him so infamous.

The rain increased in tempo dropping engorged, saturating drops from the very depths of the dark green clouds, swiftly saturating the kneeling monk and his deathly still patient. Marcus put his own petty discomfort from his mind, torturing himself as he continued to wipe Sherman's face with the edge of the grey felt hat. Would this have happened if he had handed over the map sooner? Why had he been so stubborn? He had found himself in an impossible situation.

He could not show Kerian what was truly in the blue book he guarded due to the nature of his mission. It would have gone against the orders of the Abbot. Maybe there had been another way of releasing the information to the captain, but Marcus had no idea how he could have done so without raising suspicions and difficult questions he was not at liberty to answer. He kept wiping Sherman's unresponsive face, unsure now if it was the rain he was wiping away or his own regret-filled tears.

* * * * * *

"By Adden!"

Kerian swore as more electrical sparks leapt from the book, arcing along his searching hands and up his wrists. This was insane! No matter how hard he tried, he could not open the damned book! He looked about the floor for the canvas sheeting that had originally protected the tome and found it lying forgotten under the table. Crawling on his hands and knees Kerian retrieved the material and prepared to do battle.

The blue leather clad book lay staring up at him accusingly from the floor, its cover now dusted with lime from its fall. The book was quite large; the scuffed cover about eighteen inches from top to bottom and twelve inches in width. The leather grain had a marble-like texture that extended across the whole cover making it incredibly appealing to the eye. Two golden clasps encircled the book, protecting its secrets securely and making it nigh but impossible for even the slightest glimpse of the pages without opening the locks on the clasps. Engravings of holy knights stood to attention along these golden metal strips and near to the twin locks, two knights bowed their heads in reverence, as if bestowing the holder of the appropriate keys great honour. Kerian instantly hated the representation of the knights as they all had Marcus's stupid haircut!

Carefully wrapping his hands in the canvas, he hoisted the book over to examine the reverse side, wincing expectantly for shocks that never came, due to the insulating properties of his makeshift glove. He cautiously examined the rear of the book checking for any signs of weakness, knowing intuitively that there would not be any found. As he turned the book back over, he noticed another engraving that he had previously missed. It lay where the clasps passed over the gilded pages, and it drew Kerian's attention immediately. A monk, engraved within the gold, carried a book almost identical in appearance to the one the elderly fighter now held in his hands. This monk looked more like Marcus than ever. Now what was that supposed to signify?

Kerian returned his attention back to the locks, knowing that the way into the book was through these two frustrating obstacles. He knew he was missing the keys to open them, so the question remained, what was he going to do? Kerian did not know how to pick locks and he did not have anything thin enough on him to attempt it. However, this was not the worst of his concerns. With the canvas sheet wrapped around his hands, dexterity was now impossible! His fingers had taken on the uncomfortable sensation of not belonging to him anymore. Everything he touched appeared to be spongy and indistinct! He tried to position the canvas between two fingers whilst attempting to grab one of the clasps in a pincer-like movement, but the material stubbornly slipped through his fingers and he ended up holding nothing but thin air.

Irritated at his initial failure, he attempted the manoeuvre again, with the same result. This was never going to work! Kerian looked over towards the ruined door, worried about the amount of time this relatively simple exercise had taken. Marcus could return at any moment and if he were to see him kneeling on the floor trying to force open the book, there would be no way the knight would be able to talk his way out of it. Time was definitely of the essence.

Maybe he could force the book open by bending the clasps apart. Kerian shook his head. How exactly was he going to do that: With his teeth? The damage would also be too obvious. There had to be another way.

He took another quick look at the open doorway then reached down into his saddlebags for the cursed serpent dagger. He lifted the weapon gingerly, by the top of the hilt, expecting it to writhe and wriggle at any moment but the blade remained firm and lifeless.

The tip of the golden blade looked small enough to pick the locks in the clasp but Kerian was still wary about using the sentient weapon and prepared to dash it to the floor if it as much as glinted at him.

He placed the book back on the floor and prepared to insert the dagger, wrapping his hand in the canvas, to avoid any shocks that might arc along the blade and up his arm. He rechecked the keyhole, preparing to line up the lock and blade perfectly. This had to be done carefully to make sure no damage was done that would indicate the locks had been tampered with. Then he stopped himself. What if the weapon was simply lulling him into a false sense of security? What if it was waiting for a moment like this; ready to go crazy on him at any moment? He would just have to risk it and be careful.

"What have you done to the door?"

Kerian's hand slipped, the blade glancing off the clasp and leaving a clear incriminating scratch.

"Ashe, what are you doing down here?" he snapped in frustration, before grimacing at the clearly visible mark. How was he going to explain that away?

"It's my room too you know." Ashe stated boldly. "Mouldy acorns look at the state of this place. Did Rauph come down here and sneeze or something? And what are you doing with Marcus's book?"

A large thump from above shook through the timbers, making Kerian steady himself as another shower of lime dust rained down on his head. Marcus's book slid from his grasp towards where the Halfling stood in the doorway. Footsteps moved rapidly back and forth on the main deck above and a sound like rolling thunder appeared centred directly above their cabin. The adverse weather must have torn free some cargo and it was obviously rolling around up there. Kerian returned his attention back to the immediate concern of how to deal with his accuser.

"Well Ashe, you see, it's like this..."

* * * * * *

"Colette?"

Thomas dropped swiftly to his knees alongside the mage's kneeling figure and reached out to reassure her that he was there to help.

"Don't touch me!" she screamed, making Thomas draw back his hand as if he had been stung. "Just don't touch me!"

Colette lifted her head from her hands presenting the captain of the *El Defensor* with a horrifying glimpse into the trauma that this young woman had just experienced. Her eyes were haunted windows set within a pale ghost-like face, one wide and staring, the other shot through with blood as if she had just been a victim of a terrible assault. Crimson also trickled from her swollen lip adding to the overall picture of violence, even though Thomas realised she must have bitten herself as the elemental had broken free.

"You could at least smarten yourself up when the captain comes to see you." He teased gently; his sarcastic comment rewarded with a strained smile from the beautiful young woman he had grown to consider as part of his own family. He quickly glanced over his shoulder at the rampaging elemental and noted Scrave was leading the creature a merry dance. Galvanised into action he reached out to gather Colette into his arms.

"I said don't touch me!" she screamed again. Thomas stared at the mage as if betrayed.

"What do you mean?" he demanded. "We have to get you out of here."

"If any one of us reaches across this." She tapped the circle of blazing runes set into the wooden floor, "the circle of protection will fail and the elemental will be able to destroy the one person on this ship who may just be able to send it away again."

Thomas sat back on his haunches in thought. That was awkward.

"But whilst you stay within the circle, you're safe?" he enquired.

"As long as the magic holds." She confirmed. Thomas's face fell as he realised the implications of what Colette had just revealed.

"So we have to take this thing down." He muttered to himself, his mind already horrified at the implication of what that meant. How in the world could you kill the wind?

"No, just give me time to reset the spell and I may be able to send it back from where it came."

"Hang in there." Thomas grinned feebly, setting his jaw. He slowly got to his feet and turned stoically to head off across the deck towards the swirling maelstrom, determined to stall the creature for as long as Colette needed. "I'll be right back."

"I know you will." Colette whispered after him.

******

Scrave gritted his teeth and lunged with his sword, determined to inflict as much pain as possible to the creature that had so successfully trapped him and was even now preparing for the coup de grace. This had seemed such a good idea at the time, a way of returning the lost favour of the captain by dealing with his minor escaped elemental problem. Instead, he now found himself fighting for his life against a creature that was anything but a minor problem.

The elemental shrieked as the Elf's blade sliced a wicked gash along its side drawing out yet more of the fleeting smoke that bound it to this plane of existence, but it was not enough to save Scrave this time. The creature's eyes glared hungrily and a mouth started to form within its swirling body, opening impossibly wide, ready to swallow the annoying fighter whole.

Scrave knew there was no way he could stop the speed and ferocity of this attack. To parry those teeth was impossible, to dodge to one side equally beyond question as he hardly had any space left to manoeuvre in. Facing his fate, he dropped to his knees, head bowed for protection and brought his hands together in front of him, his sword blade snapping vertically upright to impale the creature as it descended. If this creature was to be the death of him, he was determined to return the favour!

The air filled with whistling sounds and Scrave looked up in astonishment as arrow after arrow ripped through the elementals descending body, the wounds making the creature roar out in pain. One glanced off its right eye and the creature went berserk, forgetting the crouched Elf in favour of facing the new threat, as the whistling shafts drilled small holes straight through its head and mouth.

Scrave used the distraction to land two more gashes up the elemental's flanks. His mock bow and flourish after the manoeuvre was finished, instantly cut short by the howling elemental as its fist smashed into the deck inches from him, causing Scrave to dive out of the way as the fight resumed.

Buzzing filled the air as more arrows pierced the elemental's frame and Scrave noticed a gap in the creature's encircling body as it pulled away from the pain. He rolled repeatedly across the deck, determined to put as much space as possible between himself and the creature. Wooden splinters of deck dogged his every step as the elemental hurled pieces of shattered wood after the annoying creature that had caused it so much irritation. Whole planks ripped from the ship and flew up into the air. Scrave ran for the railing at the edge of the deck and leapt up onto it, running along the beam with a confidence that would have been more apt if the wood had been fifteen inches across instead of the five inches of rain soaked slippery oak it actually was.

The elemental closed swiftly in pursuit but Scrave ignored the creature's wails, intent only on putting as much distance as possible between himself and the furious tornado pursuing him. He risked a quick glance down at the main deck and the alarm bell he had been unable to ring in his battle against the invisible assassin and quickly judged the drop knowing it was easily manageable before turned to taunt the elemental.

Another flight of arrows shot overhead to plunge through the enraged monster, drawing Scrave's attention to the position of his would-be saviour. He threw a mock salute as he recognised the figure of Weyn Valdeze standing across the ship on the fore deck. He had to admit with the pitch and yaw of the deck and the distance involved, the man's skill with a bow was very impressive for a human.

A snarl of fury brought Scrave back to the more pressing concern of the approaching elemental and he prepared to leap to safety. He knew his actions would have brought the extra time Thomas needed to free Colette so all he had to do now was fall back and wait for the others on the ship to do their bit. This could reaffirm his status with the captain by these actions and his standing would be rock solid amongst the crew.

Let Kerian Denaris beat that!

He risked a quick look over towards the captain and noticed in horror that Colette was still kneeling within her circle and that incredibly Thomas was even now walking towards the elemental sword in hand. What was the idiot doing? Didn't he recognise a diversion when he saw one?

The answers to these questions remained unanswered, for at that moment, a sweep of the elemental's claws took out the railings beneath the precariously perched Elf and he fell from his point of vantage with a surprised yelp. He noted with some disgust, that this time it was relatively easy for him to strike the alarm, as his backside clanged loudly off it as he plummeted towards the main deck.

* * * * * *

Weyn Valdeze fitted another arrow to his bow, drew in a smooth fluid motion and let the shaft fly towards the target at the far end of the ship. The archer did not pause to examine where the arrow had landed, or even if he had scored a hit before retrieving another arrow and sending it straight out after its predecessor. The elemental's enraged roar confirmed a hit to the archer more accurately than his eyesight ever could, considering the poor light and the distance involved.

Valdeze's hand returned to the quiver at his side and came up empty, causing the archer to halt his attack from the foredeck. He grinned to himself as he considered what he had achieved. He had managed to shoot a dozen shafts before even one arrow had magically returned to his side! He was getting faster. Maybe he could commission for more arrows. He waited patiently for the enchanted shafts to return relishing the cool raindrops landing on his back, easing the strain in his shoulders with a feather light cool massage.

A tingling near his fingertips signalled the first arrows return and Valdeze swiftly withdrew the shaft with two fingers eager to send it out.

He swiftly raised the bow and sent his arrow streaking out across the open deck after the others, leaving the archer waiting for the tell-tale scream that heralded a direct hit on the rampaging monster chasing Scrave. His hand instinctively dropped for the next arrow that was materialising in his quiver but even as he grabbed the shaft, he realised that this time no scream had been forthcoming. Instead, the haunting peal of a bell rang out across the deck causing the archer to pause in his sustained attack and stare across the ship for the reason why his marksmanship had inexplicably failed.

The first thing he noted was the sprawled figure of Scrave lying on the main deck below the smashed and shattered railings on the aft deck and his blood ran cold in his veins. Had he inadvertently shot the Elf by mistake? His mind raced, replaying the shot, as his eyes tried to make out Scrave's body on the wooden deck but the rain that had originally been at his back was now stubbornly in his eyes making the task more difficult.

Valdeze blinked the rain away rapidly but more rain was driving directly into his eyes as if the ship had somehow turned around or the wind had changed direction. A low whistling sound was the first warning the archer got that all was not well but with the annoyance of the rain in his eyes and the worry that he may have caused harm to a fellow crewmate foremost in his mind the importance of the sound was lost on him. His right hand absentmindedly touched the arrows in his quiver and came up with only two shafts instead of the dozen that should have now returned, yet even then, the ominous absence failed to register in the concerned archer's mind.

The arrows ripped into their unexpected owner with a force that lifted the man from his vantage point and threw him physically across the deck towards the prow of the ship, barbed hunting heads slicing through leather armour and greaves, punching holes through cloak and jerkin and ripping through muscle and sinew with no mercy offered or given.

* * * * * *

The elemental turned back from the direction of the archer and his distracting arrows, the breath funnelling from its mouth dropping in intensity as it noted with satisfaction that the 'annoyance' had successfully fallen foul of his own weapon, his arrows blown back at him with over ten times the force that they had left the archer's bow. The storm billowing across the *El Defensor*, recognised the sudden lack of opposing force from the elemental, and began to blow the rain back across the ship in sheets from prow to stern, as if nothing had challenged its might bare seconds before.

Scanning the deck for its original prey the elemental spotted the female mage exactly where it had last seen her, kneeling within the safety of her magical circle. Raising itself to its full height it ignored the storm raging about it and the staccato raindrops hammering indiscriminately across the deck, concentrating instead on destroying the one thing that had kept it prisoner here.

Planks and cargo flew up into the air as the creature smashed its way across the deck, cloud swirling limbs scouring holes into the very fabric of the ship that had been its cage for these many years. Lethally splintered wooden missiles flew everywhere, sweeping all before it as the creature set itself to remove the mage from her place of safety.

One small puny man stood between the creature and its goal. One small insignificant figure that even now, between the gusts of wind, the tilting deck and the howling storm, was raising his sword in open defiance of the approaching elemental. The monster raised an arm allowing the cloud-like material within to pour into the shape of five razor sharp spinning claws. It stepped forwards intent on removing the nuisance before it.

Ives Mantoso chose that moment to strike, having circled the elemental warily, his gleaming white sword leading the charge of several crewmen, who were brave enough to risk their own lives to save their captain from his current plight. He signalled to someone high above the whirling elemental and in response, a large piece of canvas sail came loose from its lines and fell across the whirling nightmare, the bulky weight of the material dropping the stunned creature to the deck. Lines filled the air as the crew threw hawsers across the thrashing mass, attempting to secure the elemental firmly in place and stop it from doing any more damage.

Thomas could only look on in amazement as his men ran forward towards the canvas edges, grabbing lines to secure the sail tightly and pull the writhing, rippling material as taut as they dared to prevent the struggling elemental from freeing itself. Mantoso leapt up onto the sail, swinging his sword high as he mounted the undulating surface, before plunging his blade straight through the canvas into the creature beneath. The scream that issued from the elemental confirmed that his one attack had hurt the creature greater than any other had managed to do so. He withdrew his gleaming white blade preparing to stab at the monster again and noticed that his actions had inspired the other crew who took his lead and plunged their weapons into the trapped elemental.

The captain looked on in horror as he realised what the men were doing. By cutting the canvas, they were inadvertently weakening the trap. Tearing canvas sounded all around as hundreds of pieces of whirling, slicing debris ripped up through the stretched taut material slicing the sail to ribbons and making the figure of Ives Mantoso dance back out of the way. The crew collectively stepped back as the canvas settled then exploded upwards again.

Crew scattered like ants as the elemental roared, rearing up to its full height. Funnels of wind swirled left and right, the debris they contained slicing into those sailors who were simply too slow or stunned at their cruel twist of fate to escape its deadly reach. The elemental snatched one man and threw him to the floor making the deck splinter and crack beneath the doomed sailor. Incredibly, the creature did not turn to finish the task; instead, it left the man groaning in pain, sending other sailors flying senseless, this way and that, as it cleared a path towards the mage who had dared to summon it.

Suspended high up in the rigging the two remaining Rinaldo brothers looked despondently down at the torn and destroyed sail they had dropped, knowing in their hearts that their best and only chance of restraining the elemental had just been shrugged away.

Sailors ran for their lives and were smashed to the floor in a world that seemed far removed from the rain slick beams upon which the brothers struggled to maintain a hold. All they could do was hang on grimly with white knuckles as the rain fell about them, watching the terrifying scenario unfolding, feeling every sword thrust and wishing it were their own.

Chapter Thirty-One

Thunderheads clashed together in the sky above, the loud booms and the answering forks of lightning causing Marcus to jump despite himself. The monk vainly tried to stop his hand from shaking as he continued to wipe Sherman's brow but the pallor of the sailor's skin and the bluish tinge to the man's thin lips spoke more about the futility of the task than the monk dare admitted. He raised his head blinking out the raindrops falling with renewed ferocity and tried to spot Bernard through the gloom. Where was the man? Although the monk knew it had been but moments since he had sent the sailor off on his errand, his personal period of solitude spent mopping Sherman's brow as the sailor's life slowly seeped away made Marcus feel that Bernard had been absent for so much longer.

He tried to put the screams of the other crew members out of his mind, to ignore the plunging of the ship beneath him as it hit swell after swell and to deny the shrieking column of terror that stalked the decks, threatening to rip the *El Defensor* apart. His life had come a long way since leaving the peace and security of the monastery back in Catterick. How desperately he yearned to be back there.

Marcus glanced down at Sherman's grievous wounds and faced a fresh assault from his own personal feelings of inadequacy and helplessness. What could he possibly do for this man? None of the lectures about human anatomy and biology he had endured back at the monastery had ever accounted for anything like this!

He tried to locate a pulse on the sailor's wrist but the extremity was cold and clammy indicating that peripheral circulation was beginning to shut down due to the sailor's trauma. Marcus tried to feel for a pulse at the sailor's neck but whether it was due to the rolling of the ship, his own revulsion to the bodily fluids smeared all over his hands, or the chill blood-soaked body of Sherman, it was impossible to ascertain if his patient was still clinging to life or was already dead.

Bernard suddenly appeared from amid ships, dragging a roll of material that flapped angrily in the wind, threatening to blow away from his grip at any time and fly out across the boiling sea. He threw himself down on the deck and gestured breathlessly to what he carried.

"It's a tarpaulin." He gasped. "It's the only thing I could find. Maybe we could fashion it into a stretcher and get him to somewhere of safety."

Marcus nodded in agreement and helped to hold down the trailing edge of the cloth before both men gingerly lifted Sherman from the deck and carefully moved him over onto the sheet.

The monk was painfully aware of the coils of exposed intestine that dragged across the deck as the sailor was moved, stunned that they looked like some gigantic earthworm that had been exposed by digging and was desperately trying to plunge back into the darkness that was its home. His stomach threatened to rebel and he closed his eyes to collect his thoughts.

"Is h... ali...?" Bernard asked, causing Marcus to open his eyes again and try to catch what the sailor was trying to relay. The wind had grown so fierce that it was snatching the words from their very mouths.

"Where can we take him?" the monk screamed.

Bernard tried to respond but after several failed efforts simply gestured at the deck beneath their feet. They had to get him under cover and below decks was as good a start.

Nodding in response Marcus stood at one end of the canvas and gestured for Bernard to stand at the other. Grabbing the opposing edges of the sheet, they both lifted Sherman's body from the deck and began to carry him in their makeshift stretcher towards one of the hatches that led below. Both men were oblivious to the thin trails of green mist that slithered along the slick deck behind them or the fact that Sherman's battered felt hat lay forlorn and forgotten in their wake.

They staggered unsteadily across the slippery deck, desperate to reach safety with the heavy load they carried. The nearest hatchway, although only a matter of feet away, seemed impossible to attain as the ship rolled and bucked beneath them. Screams and wails of terror echoed around as crew ran through the darkness, caught up in a vivid nightmare from which they could not awake. Haunted visages faced innate fears only to find themselves sorely wanting. Marcus looked on helpless, wanting to offer moral support but unable to tear himself from his own grim task.

A wave crashed across the deck threatening to sweep both men from their feet, the icy cold water making them gasp as it passed chill fingers across their flesh and threatened to drop them to the deck. Somehow, the need of their fallen colleague bolstered them both, enabling the men to withstand the cold as it leeched the warmth from their bones. Bernard lowered his end of the canvas to the deck and Marcus looked up stunned to find that they had indeed reached their impossible goal. Bernard struggled with the hatch before throwing it wide and revealing access to the swaying ladder steps beneath.

Seawater surged across the deck, foaming hungrily up against the raised storm-sill surrounding the open hatchway before flooding over and splashing into the darkness below. Bernard ignored the flooding water and gestured anxiously to Marcus, intent that the monk snapped out of his thoughts and helped him get Sherman under cover as fast as possible.

Marcus took his end of the stretcher and headed over to the hatch, staring down into the darkness with a worried expression before stepping into the hole, his sandaled feet struggling to find purchase on the slick steps. As he manoeuvred Sherman's body into the hole after him, he realised that the storm-sill was going to be more of a hindrance than a blessing. Sherman's dead weight was catching on the wood from this angle, making the monk struggle to pull the man in after him and turning his already precarious footing into something that was inviting disaster.

Bernard realised the problem and strained to lift Sherman higher, threatening to slide the man out of the make-shift stretcher and down onto Marcus's head. The monk shouted out warning as another wave poured over the sill and drenched them, making Marcus gasp out as the cold threatened to make him loose his grip on the stretcher all together.

Another freezing cold wave crashed across the deck, cascading through the open access with such force that it threw Sherman through the hatchway ahead of it. The sheer weight of the water pushed Marcus physically down the last remaining steps, the make-shift stretcher crashing in after him. Suddenly darkness rushed in upon the monk, stealing his orientation from him and sealing him in silence as effectively as a corpse within its wrappings.

Bernard's gasp of shock appeared so loud in the darkness that despite himself Marcus found himself jumping. It was only then that Marcus realised he had been holding his breath. His own sigh of relief was so loud it scared him. It took some moments before he dared to voice a shaky laugh.

"You know," commented Bernard from the darkness, "for a second there I didn't think we were going to make it."

"Neither did I." The monk whispered back. "Neither did I."

* * * * * *

"So exactly what are you doing Sticks?" Ashe enquired with his usual directness, taking in the image of the aged fighter down on his knees and streaked in powdered lime all in his stride.

Kerian did not know whether to laugh or cry at the absurdity of the situation. Initial terror at his discovery had evaporated like water after a desert storm, yet even as he knelt there, his mind was turning the situation to his advantage. He had wished for a miracle to help him open the book and the very miracle he had asked for had just walked through the door. A plan swiftly began to take shape and a sly smile slid across his lips.

"Can you keep a secret?" He asked, capturing the Halfling's attention more securely than a fly wrapped in the silken strands of a spider's web.

"Of course." Ashe replied, his expression displaying the fact that it was a personal insult to suggest he was below such a challenge.

"Marcus lent me his book," Kerian continued deceitfully. "And I've gone and lost the key. The trouble is he needs the book open because there is a map in here that will tell Thomas where he needs to sail this ship and avoid the storm."

"But Thomas already has the map." Ashe replied, stopping Kerian cold and leaving him exposed as the fraud he truly was. The elderly fighter realised his mouth was open in surprise and closed it with a snap.

"How? What?" It did not make sense! What map had Marcus given over? Kerian was starting to get a headache. He began to feel himself squirming inside but tried to make his face look like he was simply aware of the Halfling's statement rather than embarrassed at the fact.

"You drew it after all." Ashe continued, "You know, the one with pictures of dragons and sea monsters. Although between you and me your dragon looks more like a duck."

Kerian's internal sigh of relief mirrored the idiotic grin that now slid across his face as he remembered he had removed Ashe from the captain's cabin when he had originally revealed the fraudulent and mythical map he had drawn. His mind swiftly caught up with the Halfling's and the lies began to flow anew.

"Ah! Of course, that map. Well you see in my haste to copy the map I made some errors, several important figures are missing, namely the longitude and latitude of the island we are travelling to and a few important landmarks. Marcus gave me the key to open the book and copy them down and when the ship rolled just now the key flew from my hand and is somewhere here on the floor."

"Oh," Ashe replied, relieved that the task in hand did not warrant too much input from himself. "So, you need me to help you find the key." He dropped to his knees and looked around the ruined cabin taking in the bedclothes scattered all about and the contents of Kerian's backpack dumped unceremoniously across the bed. "That must have been some bump you had in here."

As if to reinforce Kerian's statement the ship dropped, jarring the fighter's head and neck. He crawled forwards and scooped up Marcus's book using the canvas as a shield for his hands.

"Oh, is that the book?" Ashe asked, reaching out to examine it more closely.

"Don't touch!" Kerian snapped more sharply than he intended.

Ashe looked wounded at the rebuttal, causing Kerian to consider taking back his harsh words.

"The book is trapped you see." He lightly touched the book, snatching his finger back at the warning crackle. "It gives off quite a shock."

Ashe nodded in understanding, then set off across the floor on his knees, moving blankets and bedding to one side.

"What are you doing?" Kerian asked. Ashe turned to look at the knight as if he had gone slightly insane. What was the old man on about?

"I'm looking for the key of course."

"We don't have time." Kerian replied as the ship slammed into another wave sending vibrations through the deck beneath their feet. "The storm is upon us; we have to act quickly." A loud splintering sound appeared to give sudden urgency to his request. "We have to open this book now."

Kerian looked towards the Halfling expectantly, even as he tried to imagine what was causing the turmoil above decks. Well whatever it was, he owed it a great debt of gratitude! With noise like that rampaging above, Ashe had to agree that the situation was of great urgency.

"Do you think that roof is going to hold?" Ashe asked, looked at the ceiling above, his eyes wide.

"If we hurry..." Kerian prompted, shaking the book in emphasis. One look at Ashe's face, now crunched up in concentration told the elderly fighter that the Halfling was now putty in his hands. "If only we had someone who was good at opening locks on board, they would have this book open in a second."

"I just so happen to know someone who could help you." Ashe replied, puffing up with importance.

"Who?" Kerian asked, playing the role of an innocent for once.

"You understand that this person would only do something like this because of the circumstances involved don't you? And that they never normally do this sort of thing."

"Oh of course." Kerian replied, looking at Ashe's stern face and trying not to laugh. "And I promise I will never speak of them doing such a thing either."

"That's okay then." Ashe paused. "As long as it's just this once understand. I wouldn't like to get a reputation for doing this sort of thing."

"Just this once." Kerian reiterated. Ashe responded by digging into a small pouch hanging at his belt and pulling out his trusty, if slightly rusty lock picks.

"This will take just a second." He winked.

Kerian looked down at the Halfling as he bent intently over Marcus's book and refused to give in to the guilty feelings that threatened to overwhelm him.

He had no right to lie to Ashe but something told the knight that what was inside this book was important to the quest at large and if the quest failed then so would his chance at life. If he had to tell the odd fabrication to ensure he lived through this, then so be it.

Several mumbles and 'tuts' came from the corner of Ashe's mouth as he wiggled his pick first one way and then the other, his hand using the canvas cover for insulation to prevent shocks racing along his pick. The lock buzzed angrily at his attentions like an enraged hornet but Ashe simply scowled at it, before discarding his first pick for a slightly 'wobblier' one. He looked up at Kerian and grinned, twisting the pick with a flourish and an audible 'click'.

"Piece of cake." He gestured.

"And the other one?" Kerian teased.

"I was getting to that." Ashe threw the knight an annoying frown and bent to the task. Seconds later another faint click signalled similar success.

"Now let's see what we have in her...." Ashe suddenly found himself lifted bodily from the floor and heading towards the door even though he knew he did not intend to do so.

"Thank you so much." Kerian smiled, depositing the ruffled thief outside in the corridor. "And I promise I won't say a word to anyone."

"Now look here Sticks." Ashe stamped his foot in frustration, "I picked the locks, and I should at least get the opportunity to see what's inside."

"You know you can't read." Kerian shot back, "But thanks for your time." Kerian picked up the ruined cabin door and wedged it into the opening blocking Ashe's view and leaving the Halfling standing irritated in the hallway with no further opportunity for argument.

The diminutive thief went to knock loudly on the door in protest then stopped in mid-knock. Sticks did have a point he really could not read. He frowned hard unsure what to do next then rapped hard on the door anyway.

"Can I at least look at the pictures?"

* * * * * *

The ship ploughed through another wave, jarring the whole vessel and bringing Colette sharply back to her senses. Another bone-jarring thump followed and a spray of freezing cold seawater doused her body making the ship's mage gasp. Her barrier of protection may have served to keep magical creatures at bay but it did nothing to stop the rain and water that comprised the storm.

She struggled to maintain her position on the slippery deck, her eyes darting around the battlefield the main deck had become. Crewmen were holding on to bleeding limbs, others holding dear friends close, trying to protect them from the ravages of the storm and hide from the terrifying creature that rampaged among them.

The waves in the path of the *El Defensor* had now reached sufficient size to repeatedly crash over the sides of the ship adding additional peril to the struggling sailors. As she watched, one sailor found himself knocked from his feet and slid to the rail as the water sluiced from the deck.

Rauph stood stoically behind her, piloting the ship well, despite his obvious frustrations at not being able to assist his crewmates. *The El Defensor* turned head on, under his command, meeting the tall black walls of water before plunging straight through, with no apparent concern for what lay on the other side.

Looking above the waves the sky was simply a mass of growling green and black clouds, stretching as far as the eye could see. The creamy canvas of the sails appearing bleached and bone white in stark contrast to the stormy backdrop. The leading edge of the storm was now a long distant memory to those who could recall it.

The wind howled in her ears, blotting out any other noise and making the panorama she viewed seem surreal in nature, as if she had fallen into a storybook illustrated with black and white plates; the scene illuminated with sporadic flashes of lightning, making all the participants in this tragic tale appear monochrome.

Colette winced at the ferocity and sheer bestiality of the attacks the wind elemental was inflicting, turning sharply away as the air elemental's jaws crunched down hard on a sailor's head. She mouthed a silent prayer, for her fallen colleague, eyes closed tight as she listened for the harsh whistling breath of the creature that wanted for nothing better than to inflict similar damage on her.

She needed to take control but her head hurt so much! People were dying around her and they needed her to take responsibility and become the ship's mage, instead of the apprentice that she was. She had to tether the air elemental, pull it back and leash it like the wild animal it was. Colette looked down at her incense stick and noted it had extinguished in the storm. The sodden sorry taper was beyond lighting, split and hanging limp. It would need a replacement. She glanced up to see where the wind elemental was and watched another sailor meet a grisly end.

As if aware of the scrutiny, the monster paused in its attack and looked up to regard her with hate-filled eyes. They seemed to bore through her, making Colette shudder as the creature started to stalk towards where she knelt.

She took a deep breath, then with numbed fingers, retrieved her last remaining incense stick from the small bundle of things she had managed to tuck within her skirts. With a mere thought, the jewel in one of her earrings disintegrated, releasing arcane power into the air for her to shape at will. The stick sputtered to life as she imagined the air about the stick raising friction to combustible levels.

"Come on!" she snarled, angry at her own limitations. Small tendrils of smoke began to curl from the end of the stick and she bit her lip in concentration urging the smoke to ignite into flame.

A wave slapped across her lap dousing everything in freezing water and making her gasp at the shock, the incense stick falling from her hand to roll to the very edge of her protective circle. Colette blinked her eyes clear, not just of seawater but also tears of frustration and tried to focus on the task before her.

"Don't you dare!" Colette cursed, leaning over as far as she could, gritting her teeth, praying that just this once luck would finally be on her side. The ship suddenly dropped away to one side, sending her sliding forwards towards the edge of the circle and scrabbling for a way to prevent herself from falling through the thin layer of protection it represented. Her fingers closed around her precious goal just as the ship hit another massive swell. The whole deck slanted up and then plunged back down again, the motion causing Colette to look up to find the wind elemental was now towering high above her.

'By the Saints.' she prayed, looking on as the swirling column of smoke extended small tendrils of smoke from its central column that became thickly muscled arms and then claws that she had seen used with such devastating effect on the crew and the ship.

Colette refused to close her eyes in the face of such a terrifying spectacle, in truth she was slightly mesmerized by the majesty of the creature she had been able to summon with the strength of her magic. The creature had a beauty, which until now had viewed behind the shimmering magical barriers she had to erect to stay safe. Now she could see the elemental's rich swirling colours, interlaced with subtle tones and textures, astounding her with its magnificence. She had conjured this creature by herself, many, many times! Contained so much raw power by skilled magical manipulation. She would have had great potential as a ship's mage.

She angrily berated herself. This approach served no one and only delayed the inevitable! She was a member of the *El Defensor's* crew and she was a great mage! A gemstone set in her ring crumbled to dust at a thought, producing more swirling magical energies for Colette to force to her will.

She took in another steadying breath, willing heat back into the incense stick. It fizzed and spluttered, struggling to ignite after its dousing in cold unforgiving seawater.

"Come on damn you." Colette cursed; forcing her will into the swirling magical energies that swarmed about the end of the stick, determined that this time she would succeed.

Whether it was the direness of her situation that served as a catalyst or a simple fluke of luck, the incense sticks finally flared to life, sending pungent smelling smoke into the air. The deck continued to tilt slowly beneath her but Colette was now focused on her task and oblivious to the small collection of magical paraphernalia that slowly rattled and rolled across the deck.

The thin spiral of hope rose lazily in front of her, before it puffed out as the tempest caught it up. This was what Colette needed; her leash was now in her hands! With a nod of her head, she took control of the scented vapour, condensing the incense even as she continued chanting her spell. The smoke spiralled and coiled, then with a gesture, Colette sent the spiral of smoke out over the edge of the protective circle.

Like some bizarre fishing line, the swirling incense smoke moved first one way and then the other. It's bobbing motion like the trough and eddy of a particularly turbulent river. Then it slid out impossibly across the deck, resisting the wind and rain to coil towards the elemental. Fighting the apprehension that she felt, Colette looked on as the thin thread of aromatic smoke curled about before suddenly streaking straight and true towards its intended target.

The reaction was instant. The air elemental shrieked as it realised she had reactivated the magical tie. There was a roar of anger as it found itself tentatively touched by the smoke before the spiralling incense plunged deep inside the swirling creature's form, snagging hard on something within and snaring the elemental like a wriggling fish on a hook.

"I have you now Aurion." Colette snarled, a sharp gesture from her hand starting to reel in the smoke, snapping the ethereal tether and snatching the elemental's base out from under it.

"It's time you came to heel!"

Chapter Thirty-Two

Lightning crackled angrily above, splitting the night sky with brilliance as the ship suddenly listed starboard, dropping into a trough between waves. A sudden lull in the wind brought a snatch of a scream to Thomas's ears. He turned towards the source of the sound, trying to piece together what was happening and how the *El Defensor* had come to be in this position.

The aft deck looked ripped to shreds. Pieces of deck literally thrown everywhere, sails torn asunder, rigging hanging in ragged tatters, swinging backwards and forwards in a parody of slow motion. The larger summoning circle stood destroyed; the intricate patterns etched into the wooden surface a thing of the past. Only the bare bones of the support beams remained, the rest of the deck now scoured away by the raging elemental.

Another lightning flash sliced through the darkness, throwing the deck into bas-relief and exposing a sight that chilled Thomas to his soul. He caught a haunting glimpse of the elemental lashing out, concentrating its frustration on Colette's small protective circle.

Sparks rained down as the monster pounded on the mage's protective barrier, yet somehow the magical field refused to yield. Colette was furiously working her magic trying to control the smoke trailing from her incense stick, safe for now but the question remained for how long? As if hearing Thomas's unspoken thoughts, the elemental, recognising its failure, ceased its futile attack and instead began ripping the deck around the edge of her circle intent on weakening the very floor beneath her. The sight of such destruction galvanising Thomas into action.

He hefted his sword as if to reassure himself, noting freshly flowing blood on his hand that he had no idea he had injured. He filed it away with the rest of the minor irritations he had to deal with. His priority was to his ship; all else would have to wait. The *El Defensor* was in pain; the lives of his crew threatened. He did not have time to bleed!

Thomas moved across the deck towards the snarling creature, hatred rising in his chest, a force so powerful he felt he would burst. It was time for this creature to die. His sword slid across the elemental's turned back, drawing a thin surgical incision that initially led the captain to believe he had missed. However, as the creature reared up above him, its attack on the deck forgotten, he realised he had inflicted an injury that could not be ignored. In that split second, as red eyes bore down on him, he knew real fear. The captain plunged his sword into his foe repeatedly; smoke escaping from the creature's skin like steam from a boiling kettle.

The creature's screams of pain washed over him as he fought, the roaring of the storm whistled about his ears, yet despite this Thomas realised there was a new sound washing over the decks of the ship. It took the captain several moments to realise that the sound was the cheering of his own men at watching their captain face this beast with such courage; the sound lifted his spirit and set his resolve, even as it bolstered the very men resigned to facing their end and they rushed to aid him.

"Get..." Thomas screamed with rage as his blade scored yet another gash across the creature's body.

"Off..." A fellow crewman fell to the deck alongside him, his body torn to bloody ribbons. As the elemental passed over the body, its smoky body tinged with pink as it ripped the man to shreds with the efficiency of a food processor set on purée. Thomas turned his head in horror, afraid to glimpse what remained of the crewman and continued his attack, red rage filtering his vision so that he was unsure if the glaze before his eyes was blood running into his eyes or his own internal anger threatening to overwhelm him.

"My..." His sword slid deep within the creature, all his hatred and frustration venting in that final action. "Ship..."

Thomas's actions exhausted him; his final thrust delivered with arms that felt full of lead. He looked up at the creature daring it to retaliate and the elemental moved to lash out with both arms, its claws seeking the soft yielding flesh of its foe with no intention of surrendering its position of power.

Colette yanked on her smoke leash, pulling the elemental's arms back from delivering the killing blow mere inches from the captain's head.

Thomas grinned as he realised the game had changed in their favour, only to have it wiped from his face as a dark wall of freezing water suddenly smashed into him and knocked him from his feet. The imminent danger of the elemental was swiftly forgotten as the captain found himself struggling against yet another deadly foe, his arms flailing as he tried to catch a desperate breath and secure a tentative handhold before he found himself swept overboard into the unforgiving tempestuous seas.

He stumbled and rolled, tumbling backwards through a broken rail to fall to the main deck below. Thomas tried to tuck with the fall, bracing himself for the impact, only to discover in amazement that his landing was cushioned and not half as bad as he thought it would be. He pulled himself unsteadily to his feet, gasping for breath before searching for his salvation and recognising the unlikely battered source.

"Thanks, Scrave." He offered apologetically, nodding to the crumpled Elf and swiftly stepping away, just in case another attack happened to come his way. An enraged elemental was one thing but a volatile squashed Elf was something else!

Thomas looked back up at the aft deck ladder with dread. In the height of the storm, the usually short ascent to the deck was now on par with climbing a small mountain, only without the oxygen, Sherpa guides or the energy chocolate bars. To top it all the vista before him was also totally uninspiring or worthy of a Kodak moment. His ruined ship, the raging storm, bodies of his men lying everywhere, discarded like so many rag dolls. If there was a hell for Thomas in this life, he was living it right now. For the barest of seconds, he considered not making the climb then mentally kicked himself. He was the captain! It was time to take control, even if he felt it was impossible.

A very bedraggled Ives Mantoso gained the deck alongside him, water sluicing from his shredded clothes, his gleaming albino bone sword clenched tightly in his hand. His hair hung in a bedraggled state and a wicked wound gleamed wetly across his forehead, the edges puckering and turning white from exposure to the cold waters. Despite this, the trader's infectious grin lit him up.

"You know the water isn't that bad once you get in." he quipped through chattering teeth. He took one look around at the chaos and gestured towards a figure dragging a body towards the shelter where they shivered. Thomas shrugged his shoulders having no witty response to offer and quickly moved with Scrave to assist, as Aradol's features became clear out of the rain dragging the fallen form of Weyn Valdeze to safety.

They hoisted him bodily, carrying the archer towards the entrance to steerage. The archer looked pale and drawn, his jerkin stained heavily with blood, yet there seemed no cause to the puncture wounds that marked his body. With a rattled cough, the archer opened his eyes and stared at the four men as if he had problems focusing.

"Are you all dead too?" He muttered matter-of-factly before grinning in his annoying way and closing his eyes with a groan. "At least I won't be lonely here."

"We are not dead yet." Ives quipped in relief. "At least not if my mother has anything to say about it." He looked over at Thomas and shrugged. "I haven't given her any fine young grandchildren yet and she would never let me live it down if I didn't."

"The pickings here are kind of slim." Thomas grinned back, the humour of his colleague becoming more infectious by the second, despite the fact it was ludicrous considering the circumstances.

"Oh, I don't know." Ives shot back. "I think you or Aradol would look quite fetching in a dress." He blew a mock kiss in the captain's direction. Thomas playfully slugged the trader in the arm before turning back to Weyn's battered and blooded form.

"What the hell happened to you? Can you move?" he enquired.

"You could say I got the point," the archer groaned back, before furrowing his brow in thought. "Well several of them actually." He looked up at his four 'saviours' with mild confusion, as if only just comprehending what the men had been talking about earlier. "Look, if you lovebirds want some space for yourselves just leave me here to die in peace okay!"

"You're not dead yet." Thomas grunted as they swung him through the doorway into the corridor and relative calm.

"Are you sure?" Weyn enquired, wincing at each movement, his full quiver of arrows slapping against his legs.

"Can you feel this?" Ives asked with a mischievous grin, squeezing the archer's ear and giving it a wicked twist just for good measure.

"Get off!" Weyn shrieked, slapping futilely as they swung him along between them. "That really hurts. Oww! Be careful. Oh, mind the step."

"He never knows when to stop complaining." Thomas chuckled, gripping Weyn tighter to a chorus of further painful groans.

"Undoubtedly he is a true professional. Like my third wife. Oh, the ear bashing she could give me." Ives agreed as they finally lowered Weyn to the floor.

"Why are you leaving me here?" Weyn moaned, as they painfully sat him up against the wall. "Can't I at least have a bed?"

"We don't have time. We have a ship to save." Thomas replied, checking Weyn over quickly and satisfying himself that he was able to leave him safely. "I bet you never knew that sailing the high seas could be so stimulating. Are you regretting signing on as a crewman now?"

"You know Weyn's mother never taught him to write." Ives laughed as the four shipmates turned and headed back towards danger, leaving the archer propped up against the wall.

"I knew it all had to be a big mistake." Weyn wailed comically to their backs. "I thought it was a day trip tour of the islands. You know see some seals, buy some keepsakes, that kind of thing..."

* * * * * *

"So, what are you hiding?" Kerian asked aloud. The blue leather tome was non-committal with a reply, relying on the stern visage of the crusading holy knights engraved across the clasps to show its lack of appreciation for the comment. Kerian lifted the first one locking bar with trembling hands and then the other, noting how stiff the clasps were and pausing only to look at the monk to which all the others were paying homage. The carrier of the book remained resilient to the last, close lipped and silent with accusation.

He shook his head and chuckled, finding it hard to get over how much the illustration looked like Marcus. Well whatever secret Marcus had been carrying it was about to be found out, for better or for worse. Using an edge of the folded canvas to prevent any further shocks Kerian took a deep breath and opened the first page.

The illustration that greeted him was so incredible, so vibrantly alive, that it took Kerian's breath away. The whole page focused on the image before him, no words were inscribed or wide borders illustrated to detract the reader's attention from what lay before them.

The darkened room portrayed in Kerian's lap had all the appearance of a large windowless cell. The illustrator had cunningly made it appear that the damp stone of the walls nearest to the edge of the page were brighter than towards the centre, deeper part of the room. The mossy growth on the stone slabs gleamed as if alive, the colours as vivid and believable as any natural hue displayed in real life.

Torchlight flickered from flaming sconces set along the cell walls, revealing a room roughly twenty feet square, filled from floor to ceiling with stone bunks. Most of the beds appeared occupied with nondescript human shaped figures, lying silently in the shadows, apparently sleeping. The attention to detail was beyond anything Kerian had ever seen. Personal items were lying by each bed, never the same in any one place.

Swords, shields, armour, saddlebags, a forgotten sandal, open books, parchment and ink and even an unfinished game of Bishops and Pawns led the eye of the beholder from one bed to another, the detritus of each occupant revealing subtle clues to the individual identities of all the figures illustrated within. In all, a dozen such beds were laid out for the knight to examine at his leisure.

Kerian silently took in the image, amazed at what he beheld, even as his canvas wrapped fingers toyed with trying to turn to the next page. Frustratingly, although the paper content within the book seemed to be several pages thick the knight found he was unable to lift the edge of the parchment and complete this simple operation. Before he could investigate the matter further, his eye captured a figure on the far side of the page who appeared to be kneeling in prayer.

Again, the level of detail stunned the knight. The man's undergarments looked stained from perspiration and sweat as if he had worn his clothes for a long period without change. His face stubble was rough and uneven as if he had shaved without the aid of a mirror and Kerian noted that the figure had apparently nicked his face, as a spot of crimson gleamed on his chin. Smoothly polished Prayer beads wrapped twice around the kneeling figure's hand, before dropping away to hang in the air, the dangling beads incredibly appearing to swing in time with the *El Defensor's* turbulent movements.

A small wedge of mould-streaked cheese and a hardened loaf rested on a clay platter upon the praying man's bed alongside a suit of armour and a gleaming sword. Kerian grinned at the presentation; the cheese looked so festered and rotten that he could almost smell it! He uttered a small laugh at the ludicrous thought and looked on mystified, as the praying figure appeared to stiffen under his gaze.

Mesmerised, he continued to watch as the illustrated warrior cautiously opened one cobalt blue eye and impossibly turned his head to gaze in Kerian's direction. What kind of enchanted storybook was this? The figure slowly got to his feet, his prayer beads falling with his hand to hang at his side, his face splitting into a relieved grin.

This was incredible the man was looking out of the book, reacting as if he could see Kerian regarding him, even squinting as if the light from the cabin was somehow blinding to those portrayed within the darkness of the cell. Shading his eyes, as he got closer to his observer, the illustrated character did the last thing Kerian expected.

"Is it time brother?" he enquired. Kerian delivered his response to the question with his usual eloquent style. He slammed the book shut and dropped it in shock.

* * * * * *

Staggering through the shadows below decks Marcus almost believed he had entered a world of purgatory. Haunted faces loomed out of the darkness, eyes wide with fear and trepidation, their faces turned upwards as if awaiting judgement from some unseen all-powerful figure. Others prayed by swaying bunks or hid in whatever places of sanctuary they could find, their shaking forms anticipating torment and suffering beyond anything the monk could ever save them from.

Moving from one weak pool of lantern light to another Bernard and Marcus continued to weave their way onwards through the eerie and somehow alien bowels of the ship. Their steps fell slightly faster when they found themselves between light sources as if the impenetrable patches of resulting ebony held other unseen terrors that crouched in wait, ready to pounce and claim their souls as they passed.

The ceiling was much lower down here and although Marcus was not a particularly tall man, he found himself ducking frequently to avoid knocking himself out on the stout beams that criss-crossed the ceiling. Water dripped noisily from above, a fitting tempo to the wails and mumbled psalms of the crew so deeply submerged in their own misery that they failed to notice their passing audience of two.

Sherman's body swung silently between them, the canvas stretcher moving in time with the swells that rocked the ship, its weight threatening to overbalance the two men and plunge them even deeper into the shadows and much further away from the imaginary safety of the lantern light. The monk gritted his teeth determinedly and staggered on, eager to reach his goal before his wavering courage failed him completely.

The door to the galley swung open at the first knock, revealing Violetta in all her glory, a wicked gleam of silver indicating that the ship's cook had her meat cleaver close to hand and was ready to defend her kitchen with her life. At the sight of the two men and the burden they carried, her Amazon-type demeanour melted into the caring woman both men needed.

She ushered them in without a sound, her facial expression offering tenderness and sanctuary. Bolts slid into place behind Marcus as he lowered Sherman's ravaged body to the deck, only then did he slump against the wall, sliding to the floor sodden and exhausted.

"What have we here then?" Violetta bustled to herself, moving swiftly around the makeshift stretcher and throwing the edges wide. Lantern light flooded across the body within, revealing the terrible intensity of the patient's wounds, the entire trauma, all the blood, bright red and gory. The cook leant forwards examining the damage with a critical eye unaware that the hem of her dress trailed in the sticky ichor that now ran unchecked across the floor. She reached forward to check the sailor's pulse and only then became aware of who her patient was.

"Oh no!" she wailed. "Oh Sherman, my dear Sherman, who has done this to you?" Another horrific gasp came from behind Violetta and she turned to see her daughter staring in shock, a lantern held shakily in her hands. Despite her own shock, the cook removed the fire risk from her daughter and started snapping off orders for fresh water, lint bandages, ointments and thread for sewing.

Violetta was aware of the brusqueness of her demands but it was intentional, snapping her daughter out of her stunned state and into action with more success than she could have ever motivated the two exhausted men who had carried Sherman this far.

Marcus looked on from his spot on the wall, unable to assist the procedure going on before him, amazed and angry that his own limbs had turned against him in this way. His arms felt like they were made of lead, his legs as if they belonged to someone else and were simply on loan for the day. He looked across as Violetta worked and took it all in, as if the scene before him were somehow detached from reality.

Blood soaked rags tenderly washed the wounds that oozed and needles flashed in the overhead light as stitches normally used to hold together prepared joints of uncooked meat now pulled the edges of wounds painfully closed. Violetta's hands turned red as they dipped repeatedly to their tasks, applying cream and salves to the more minor wounds and fresh lint dressings to the more violently damaged areas. Violetta's daughter delivered fresh bowls of water, complete with a silver coin at the bottom and sprinkled with a handful of mint. This basic preparation allowed the cook to rinse her hands between each dressing, remove any foul-smelling bodily fluids from her hands and reduce the risk of carrying infection from one wound to another.

Sherman lay silently throughout it all, staring up at the ceiling, his chest stubbornly refusing to rise and fall, his skin, where it was clean, showing the colour of fresh clay. Violetta paused in her work and moaned softly to herself. She was losing him that much was obvious just in the pallor of the man's skin and the amount of blood all over the floor.

Something more was required, if she were to save his life. She turned to Marcus, expecting to ask him to watch over Sherman while she searched for what she needed only to find that the monk was staring hypnotically at an onion that had come loose and was rolling backwards and forwards across the floor in time with the ship. Disgusted, she turned to her daughter and beckoned her over; pointing out which wounds concerned her most, and where to apply pressure to stop the more severe bleeds.

Confident her daughter would obey her, she strode to the back room and headed for the cupboard. Colette was not the only one who could cast magic on this ship! The cupboard door swung ajar with the movement of the ship, kitchen implements swaying where they hung on the walls and plates creaking ominously together in their racks. She threw the door wide and stared into the shadows examining each shelf intently for the item she sought.

Finally, she recognised the small wax saint figurine she was after and reached out for it with slick bloodied hands. The ship dropped rattling everything around her and the precious saint slipped from her grasp, tumbling from the shelf into the darkness and raising a shriek of frustration from the cook. Her wax figurine was so delicate that a fall from this height could destroy it and all the magic it held would be lost!

She dropped to her knees and began to search frantically for the saint, only to come up short and gasp again, this time in horror as a pale grinning face loomed out of the darkness. Her hand flew instantly to a knife hanging on the door, snatching the blade with a speed that would have taken many assailants by surprise.

Instead, she found her knife hand pinned tightly to one side, as her attacker brought his other hand up as a fist and sent it straight at her face. She closed her eyes and waited for the violence she so abhorred, holding her breath for the explosion of pain she expected to feel. Instead, after an extended moment of apprehension she realised that inexplicably, the attack had not materialised. Violetta slowly opened her eyes to take in the grinning face that would haunt her dreams for many nights to come. As she watched, the pale fist hovering inches from her face slowly opened, revealing the small wax saint nestled gently within.

"I think you dropped this." The Raven hissed.

Part Three:- The Ship's Graveyard

Out at sea, sailor's fears are the same as all men,
Violent storms, pirate hoards, kraken's claws, siren's ken.
When faced with these things, men shake and they shiver,
But there's worse waiting here, made to send them a quiver.
When night skies split light, as bright as the day,
Green mists will seek out, so the old women say.
Neath decayed mustard cloud, through the portals of Sages,
Piles the carcass of ships, reaching up through the ages.
Here are gateways to worlds, stood impossibly high,
And a graveyard of ship's, there to see when you die.
Among rusting hulks, Scintarns hunt those who stray,
And the ghosts of lost men, scream aloud as they pray.
A sailor's warning

Chapter Thirty-Three

A feeling of vertigo assailed Kerian without warning. He closed his eyes, willing the hammock to stop swinging beneath him and the room to stop tilting from side to side. His stomach protested as the ship pitched and rolled as if alive. He slowly cracked his eyes open and tried to put the feelings of nausea out of his mind. He needed to replace Marcus's book before the monk realised it had been tampered with and the rising anxiety at being discovered was only helping to heighten his uneasiness. The timbers of the wall shuddered under his fingertips and large wet slapping sounds reverberated off the dead light. The ceiling above was vibrating louder, something heavy thundering backwards and forwards and getting louder all the time. Amid all this noise and chaos Ashe was still incessantly knocking at the door pleading to come back in.

"Will you just shut up!" Kerian screamed, his anger directed at everything and everyone, but regarded with equal lack of respect by all. What did a man have to do to get some peace and quiet down here? He carefully looked up at the loose plank and took in the wobbling ceiling, squinting to keep the cascading lime flakes from blinding him as he hoisted up the canvas covered book and prepared to reinsert it into its earlier hiding place. If Marcus found the book right where he had left it there would be fewer uncomfortable questions asked and as regards Ashe, well he could be easily placated when it came to keeping secrets. The threat of pain can be a great motivator!

He slid the book up the wall, using it to brace his own wobbling frame and started to insert it back into the hole. There was a flare of emerald and the necklace at his chest started to pulse brightly, warning of imminent danger.

A cacophonic crashing and wrenching sound made Kerian jump, despite his precarious balance and he pulled the book away with a start, just as the corner of the ceiling ripped clean away before his eyes. Lime dust exploded everywhere, covering the elderly fighter from head to foot and making him look like a refugee from an explosion in a flour mill. Large splintered beams crashed to the floor, bouncing off the walls and slamming against the door and the roar of the storm raging without now whistled mercilessly through the hole in the ceiling and tore about the room unchecked.

Kerian dropped flat into the hammock and felt his world tilt as the bed flipped over and deposited him abruptly back onto the floor for the second time that day. He landed hard, the breath whooshing out of him, his saddlebags, previously left on the floor, digging jarringly into his spine. The canvas-covered book he held in his arms thumped up hard under his chin, making his teeth clack painfully together. With an undignified grunt, he rolled across the floor, trying to drag all of his belongings with him as more debris rained down from above, thumping onto the hammocks and smashing the lantern that hung by the door.

The wind roared through the enlarged hole in the ceiling, inviting raindrops to share in the invasion; obliterating Kerian's earlier tell-tale finger-marks in seconds. Ashe was shouting out in the corridor, complaining about the noise from inside the cabin, stating huffily that Kerian didn't need to lose his temper and that a simple 'no' would have been good enough.

Fuel from the shattered lantern ran down the wall before suddenly flaring into hot tongues of flame that cast flickering shadows across the room. Okay, so first things first. The cabin was on fire!

Kerian moved to tackle the blaze, not sure what he could actually do but determined to try anyway. He briefly considered trying to smother the flames with Marcus's book but as he waved the book gamely in the fire's direction, the flames just seemed to get higher. A menacing howl reached his ears. He instinctively stared up at the hole in the ceiling and stared in shock as several large marble-like swirling columns of debris plunged down into the cabin and began ripping an even larger piece of ceiling away.

With horror, he realised these were the claws of some creature. As the appendages slowly ripped free, taking yet more of the ship with them, two baleful red eyes stared through the opening, chilling the elderly fighter where he stood. This was not good. Kerian edged further towards the door, his steps slow and measured, trying to remain as small and unthreatening as possible. He needed to get out into the corridor and the freedom that lay beyond it but the flames from the spilt lantern fuel was making his choice a warm and uncomfortable one.

Black smoke was now beginning to fill the room, the highly varnished wood blistering and popping as the fire took hold. Dry coughs assaulted Kerian's form and his eyes began to tear as he tried to get close enough to the door to get out. Conflicting emotions ran through him as he considered whether to stay and fight the fire, risking encountering the owner of those red eyes again, or simply get out in the corridor, find a place to hide and let the ship's crew deal with the blaze.

Before he could choose, a huge deluge of freezing water poured through the hole in the ceiling, soaking him and extinguishing the flames spreading hungrily along the wall in one foul swoop. Kerian gasped at the cold unexpected shower, coughing and spluttering at the indignity of it all whilst trying desperately to protect the canvas wrapped book from the worst of the freezing wave. He glanced back at the hole in the ceiling and noted in alarm that the red eyes had returned to regard him through the opening. In seconds the whirling grinding winds funnelled back into the cabin, ripping into the door through which he was trying to exit. The cabin door shot into the air, missing Kerian's head by inches, banging and clattering its way across the ruined ceiling before exiting through the hole where something swiftly snatched it away.

Kerian turned to look through the open doorway and saw Ashe standing in the corridor his little mouth opened in shock.

"Sizzling Sausages, Sticks!" he exclaimed at his travelling companion, sensing that using sizzling sausages was the only way he could sum up the destruction the old man had wrought on the room beyond. His eyes took in the fire damage, the water sloshing around the floor, shredded bedding, gouges in the ceiling and the white streaked man before him. "Thomas is going to go nuts when he sees what you have done to our cabin!"

Another wave crashed through the ventilated ceiling, allowing Kerian temporary respite from Ashe's recriminations and pushing him out into the corridor to knock the Halfling from his feet.

"Now come on Sticks!" Ashe yelled over the shrieking wind, as he struggled to get back to his feet and balance against the violently rocking ship. "What have I ever done to you?"

Before Kerian could answer, the tempestuous sea sent another freezing wave their way, soaking Kerian and Ashe where they stood and knocking them both to the floor as the water swirled around them. Gasping and spluttering, Kerian raised a hand to his face and wiped his eyes, blinking rapidly to clear his vision from the gritty after-effects of the seawater. The two companions flopped and slipped like beached fish, struggling to extricate themselves from one another in the cramped space of the tilting corridor.

"We have got to stop meeting like this." Ashe commented pulling his boot out from under Kerian's backside and roughly tugging it back onto his foot with a squelch. "You know on a ship as small as this people will start to talk and I do have my standing as a dashing swashbuckler to think about." The Halfling moved off into the darkness and bent to pick up something that had clattered to the floor in all the confusion.

Kerian growled a response, his sense of humour an early casualty in the night's activities and began rising to his feet, only to find himself slammed roughly against the wall as the ship plunged through yet another heavy wave. He staggered over to recover his saddlebags from the floor, flinging them over one shoulder and tucked Marcus's book closer to his chest. Could it have been the wind elemental that he had just glimpsed destroying the cabin? That was impossible. Colette had it contained in her summoning circle. He shook his head; this was a problem for later. He needed to prioritise. Hide the monk's book first, get Ashe to safety and then consider helping the others. He turned around to collect the Halfling and stopped in his tracks.

Ashe stood alone in the darkness, a nightmare image, frozen in Kerian's mind, staring down at the serpent dagger, the golden scales of the hilt glinting, making the Halfling's eyes evil and threatening, even in the dim light of the corridor. Ashe was sighing heavily, the weapon whispering empty promises into his mind. Fantasies of a life he could lead, if he only had this blade!

"I'll take that." Kerian stated, shattering Ashe's momentary delusions of living a life of luxury with a tone that left no room for argument. The little thief barely had time to voice a protest as his elderly companion whipped the dagger from his grubby hands and went to secure it safely away from the Halfling's roaming fingers. Ashe managed to throw a hurt look before noticing how Sticks was struggling to hold the book and the dagger and open his saddlebag all at the same time.

"Well at least I can help with this." He began, reaching over to grab Marcus's book and scooping it up into his arms. "Now I can look at the pictures inside."

Sticks' stern stare quashed any idea the book was now his to examine. With no choice, Ashe stood, biting his lip in frustration, until the elderly fighter had secured the golden dagger. Then he reluctantly handed back the canvas wrapped book, his little eyes looking on in sad longing.

"I was always told if you don't ask you don't get." He stated indignantly determined to get the last word.

"Well you're still not getting it." Kerian replied with stoic resolve, struggling to balance the saddlebags and the canvas wrapped book.

Ashe paused in mid-argument, realising there was no way he was going to win against his stubborn companion. Instead, he turned his attentions past the scowling man and gaped at the ruined cabin beyond.

"Thomas is definitely going to kill you!" he muttered, shaking his head solemnly as he stepped past Sticks and into the cabin beyond, narrowly missing his companions grasping outstretched hand as Kerian moved to stop him. A loud scream wailed down from the hole in the ceiling, freezing Ashe's advance in its tracks. He glanced back at Sticks, still standing safely within the corridor but the old man would not follow him into the wrecked area, instead he kept looking up, a worried expression on his face.

"Please come out of there. I don't think it's really safe." The old man warned. "Please come out here with me."

Ashe took in the tone of Sticks' voice and allowed his resolve to harden. Sticks may be his friend but he certainly was not going to tell Ashe Wolfsdale what to do! There was no way he wasn't going to examine this room thoroughly, mentally cataloguing the damage so he wouldn't be blamed when Thomas asked who had caused such devastation.

"You know Thomas may not kill you," He commented after taking in all the devastation. "He may just throw you overboard when he sees what you've done with the place. He better not lay the blame on me for any of this stuff."

A loud thump resonated from above sending a fine mist of lime flakes cascading down through the air of the room. Something very large, and exceptionally fast, passed by overhead before a terrible rending noise lifted the hairs on the Halfling's neck. He swung his head up towards the hole and paused, his nerves jangling, suddenly unsure of just how much of the action above he actually wished to see. He looked back at Sticks for reassurance and noted that the fighter still wore his worried look, only now more pronounced and his necklace was interestingly glowing green around his neck.

"What?" Ashe enquired sharply, shrugging his shoulders at his crewmate as if it was perfectly natural to hear noises like this through the hole in the ceiling of a ruined cabin... in the middle of the ocean... miles from anywhere. Oh dear!

With a resounding crash, the entire ceiling collapsed, depositing what debris remained; planking, dust and seawater, straight into the cabin. Ashe shrieked in alarm and turned for the doorway, decorum be damned, finishing his exit from the room by Kerian physically dragging him clear. The cabin wall shook as something heavy smashed against it. Swirling clouds screamed down into the cabin, ripping and shredding anything not bolted down. Ashe took in two red intense eyes and shivers ran down his spine. He had seen those eyes before.

"Next time listen to me!" Kerian snapped. "It's time to go!" He set off down the corridor half dragging the Halfling behind him, determined to put as much space as possible between himself and the destroyed cabin. The corridors wall exploded behind them, debris flying along the narrow confines to whip viciously past the two fleeing companions.

Kerian risked a quick backward glance through the billowing cloud of dusty lime, his mind racing as he took in the destruction. He needed to go and help the crew but Ashe was so stupid he would just stumble right into the path of whatever was causing the problem and Marcus's book needed to be hidden... and quickly! Through the ragged remains of the wall, swirling claws continued to gouge away the structure of the ship. Kerian stole one more glance, before bundling Ashe around the corner, ignoring the Halfling's comments about how he now wished to stay and see what was happening.

The ship shook violently at that very moment, as if it were a toy in the hands of a particularly boisterous child. The corridor appeared to twist beneath Kerian's feet, making the juggling of both Halfling and book a near impossibility. Another stomach-churning lurch threw them up against the wall, smashing the breath from Ashe's small form and causing Kerian to bite his tongue in surprise. Enough was enough! He slid further along the corridor wall to one of the cabin doors and recognising where he was, threw it open and shoved Ashe roughly inside.

That was one problem out of the way, now all he had to do was find somewhere to hide the book!

* * * * * *

Ashe stood all alone in the darkness, momentarily stunned. What was Sticks playing at putting him in here without so much as a by your leave? He placed his hands on his hips indignantly and was about to open the door and demand an apology when the door unexpectedly swung open again. A very angry looking Sticks standing in the doorway, his hand outstretched.

"I knew it all had to be a mistake." Ashe stated jovially. "I knew you wouldn't entertain leaving me down here with a monster running about and wrecking the place. What's the plan now Sticks?"

His elderly colleague continued to hold out his hand, a stony look across his face.

"I will give you till the count of three." He stated coldly.

Ashe looked up at the thunderous face before him and suddenly decided that now was not really the best time to play games.

"Okay." He confessed, reaching into his pocket and drawing out the worn golden ring. "But you have to admit I'm getting better and better at taking it."

Sticks took the ring without a word and slid it roughly back onto his finger.

"So," Ashe continued without missing a beat. "Where are we off to now?"

Sticks took a long hard look at the thief, then slammed the door securely in place, leaving Ashe alone in the darkness. A loud thump from the corridor signified Sticks was doing something to the door latch.

"Well I never." Spluttered the thief, stepping forwards to try the door only to confirm it was now securely jammed from the outside. He struggled with the door for a few moments longer before shrugging his shoulders and resignedly admitting to himself that it would be futile to try to escape. Locks he could deal with but there was no way he could free the door if it was wedged from the other side. Especially if the wedge was a particularly ill-tempered man with no sense of humour!

Trying to put a bright perspective on things, the Halfling turned away from the door and tried to fathom out exactly where it was Sticks had put him. Maybe there was something in here that he could use to placate his companion; maybe even a long-forgotten sword or a discarded dagger that Ashe could use to take on the monster down the corridor, save the day and earn Thomas's undying respect. If Sticks then tried to pin the wrecked cabin on him, he would find it tough to prove with the judge firmly in Ashe's pocket!

He slowly took in his surroundings as his eyes adjusted to the inky darkness. Shelves filled with dark, shadowy and interesting shapes lined the walls but Ashe fought down the temptation to explore these just yet, moving slowly out into the centre of the room, his earlier near brush with death swiftly forgotten at the prospect of exploring somewhere new.

It was here that he discovered a huge table bolted securely to the floor. He stood on tiptoe, just managing to get his eyes above the lip of the table, only to discover that the whole surface was covered in maps and charts secured by clips or heavy paperweights. There was nothing interesting, or within his grubby reach on this side of the table, so he dropped down and moved around to the far side, lifting himself up to check if there was anything more interesting on this side.

His eyes widened with delight as they settled on a large measuring divider embedded into the tabletop. Suddenly everything became clear; he knew where he was... this was Rauph's cabin!

Ashe dropped back to the floor and began to look around the room with greater interest. In all his time on board he had never managed to be alone in Rauph's cabin as it was either normally occupied or the threat of possible Minotaur violence had been too great a risk for the Halfling to take.

He did not really mind missing this room in his travels because there were so many other fascinating places on board the *El Defensor* for him to explore and Ashe also liked to wake up in the morning and find his legs were firmly where he left them the night before!

Of course, none of this changed Ashe's current situation in the slightest. He was now in Rauph's cabin and he was alone! If Rauph found him here... well, it was not his fault he was locked in here! Sticks had put him here! Obviously, if he was stuck in here for a while, he needed to find something to pass the time! He thought again about the gleaming navigation tool on the desk and the fun he could have walking the divider across one of Rauph's maps.

He, Ashe the cartographer, would become ship's navigator; skirting perilous reefs, stopping off at islands filled with cannibals, short lusty females and many forgotten treasure hoards. To Ashe would come the onerous task of finding the only navigable course through impassable perilous seas. It was a terrible job but someone had to do it!

Ashe chuckled to himself. He would only play at this for a little while; no one would be the wiser. After all what could possibly go wrong? His mind made up; the Halfling moved closer to the table and tried to jump up high enough to reach the dividers. Frustratingly for Ashe the instrument stayed tantalisingly, just beyond his reach. He dropped back to the floor and stood for a moment in deep thought. Being short was such a nuisance at times! If only he had magical powers to levitate the divider from the tabletop and down to him on the floor but then he supposed he would also have to levitate down all the maps, paperweights and other nautical paraphernalia. That could take all afternoon!

Okay, so he needed to find something to stand on. His eyes scanned the room for a suitable means to access the table surface, quickly disregarding the enormous bunk on which Rauph slept and the equally huge chest that stood at its base. Well, not totally disregarding... he could come back and explore the chest later if there was time. It was Stick's fault he was in here after all!

He was about to give up his plans for circumnavigating the globe and sailing his armies in conquest of the nine seas, when he finally noted a chair in the far corner of the room. The chair was strangely turned in towards the cabin wall, which was probably why he had missed the item of furniture in his first hurried reconnaissance. He started forward into the deeper shadows and was surprised to find that the temperature over here was slightly colder than the rest of the cabin.

The hairs began to stand up on the backs of his arms causing shivers to run up and down his tiny frame and a slight nagging doubt began to creep into the Halfling's brain. Maybe he should just leave the dividers and maps well alone? He paused in contemplation then angrily shook his head. What was he so worried about? Rauph would never know! He only had to move the chair. He was not going to break anything!

He stepped closer, the argument raging silently in his head as his feet became heavier and heavier with each reluctant step. There was definitely something not right about this chair, something that made the Halfling wish he had the navigation tool from the chart table in his hand right now! Not as a navigation tool he was surprised to acknowledge but as a weapon!

Ashe moved slowly up to the chair, the stubborn part of his mind that always got him into trouble refusing to back down and be scared, the other more sensible part wishing that he were outside in the corridor once more taking his chances with the rampaging monster. Ashe could not deny that he found the whole thing really exciting and spooky at the same time! Why, oh why, had he waited so long to come in here and poke around?

The little thief inched closer, then realised with shock that there was someone sitting in the chair and that he or she appeared to be sleeping. This revelation brought him up fast and he stood there unsure what to do. He could not afford discovery here! If it was Rauph in the chair and he woke up, what would he think to find Ashe in his room? Ashe felt attached to his body's limbs and did not wish to find any of them missing!

He nervously cleared his throat, his mind made up that it was better to wake Rauph and explain his predicament, rather than have the Minotaur discover his presence and be angry with him.

"Err. Hum. Excuse me?" He started meekly, before realising that the figure in the shadows had no horns. His tact changed in a heartbeat and a new question sprang to mind. "Have you been locked in here too?" The figure in the chair remained silent, a response that Ashe found to be most impolite, especially after building up the courage to talk in this way and be friendly.

"I said excuse me!" Ashe stated louder, thinking this person was ignoring him, or could be deaf. He moved closer and reached out his hand to give the person a shake then stopped as the hairs stood up on his hand. A thought suddenly occurred to him. Maybe it would be better if he simply went back to the door and tried to see if he could get it to open and then leave.

The image of Sticks standing behind the cabin door suddenly entered his mind. Of course, with old grumpy out in the corridor somewhere, he could not just slip out undetected and that was only if he could un-jam the door. Oh, this was ridiculous! Ashe stamped his foot in frustration.

Okay, so if he could not get out maybe he could get this person to help him open the door and deal with his elderly friend for him. If he ever found himself locked in a room with someone, he knew he would most certainly help them deal with any problems they might have!

With that issue firmly resolved, Ashe stepped around the front of the chair to announce himself and gazed up into a nightmarish image that took all the Halfling's courage not to scream aloud. There was a dead man sitting in the chair! A dead man in Rauph's room! What was wrong with the people on this ship? They had not even had the decency to bury the poor chap! He skittered backwards, getting himself a safe distance from the corpse, before taking in the sight with less terrified eyes.

A troubling thought suddenly occurred to him. Why was there a dead man in Rauph's cabin? More importantly, who had killed the poor chap and hidden him in here? Rauph would be so angry when he found out.

Ashe could feel himself getting all flushed as he considered the implications of such a discovery. He had to report this outrage to Rauph immediately. He turned for the door then stopped himself, remembering in his excitement that the door was out of bounds for the moment and he was not going anywhere. He sighed and turned back to regard the figure in the chair. There was something else about the corpse bothering him.

His eyes widened with horror as he took in the layers of thick dust that filled the creases of the corpse's clothes and skin. This body had been in this room for a long time, Rauph must have known about it. Why hadn't the Minotaur told anyone?

"Oh my..." Ashe's hand flew to his mouth as he realised where all the clues were heading. Had Rauph killed this man and then stuffed him in the chair in the corner of his room to hide him? Was this some deep dark secret of the Minotaur's that had somehow been kept quiet all this time? He moved closer. If Rauph had carried out this deed, how had he murdered the poor chap?

The black ebony spear stared back at Ashe making him tut loudly at himself.

"Okay, so that was a stupid question." He was aware that he had spoken the statement aloud; a sure sign of his increasing nerves. He moved closer, his eyes taking in the image from a fresh perspective. Congealed blackened blood around the wound where the spear jutted from the poor man's chest, thick layers of dust liberally covering the corpse. To think he almost believed this man could have been alive and of assistance to him!

"Rauph could have at least had the decency to pull the spear out." Ashe continued to mumble to himself. He reached forwards to grasp the black-shafted weapon. "You must have really upset Rauph, what exactly was it you did?" His little hand got within an inch of the spear and stopped just short of touching it. "You didn't play with his charts and dividers without asking, did you?" He gasped as he realised what he had just said and looked over the ruined chair arm at the table where the navigation items lay. That was just what he had been about to do! He looked back up at the corpse's face as his hand closed around the spear shaft and prepared to pull it free.

The corpse suddenly moved, its brittle hands snapping tightly closed around the spear that Ashe was starting to slide free. Soulless eyes ripped open with a sound like the skin sliding off a raw onion and gazed down at the diminutive thief literally freezing him to the spot with the intensity of their gaze. Billows of dust flew everywhere shattering the moment by making Ashe sneeze loudly and repeatedly. When the Halfling finally blinked the dust away, he found himself less than an inch from the decayed face of the figure before him. Its mouth split open like an over ripe fruit allowing a musty dead air to escape into the freezing cabin air.

"Get... Out!" It hissed.

Ashe jumped almost clear out of his sandals and screamed, back-pedalling rapidly away from the chair in abject terror. He bumped hard into the cabin wall; somehow managing to get himself turned around in the confusion and continued his rapid retreat until something hard clipped him on the head. He spun around once more, gasping for breath, horrified at the thought that somehow the corpse had moved from the chair and had managed to get around behind him and walked headfirst into the chart table.

Stars spun before his eyes and he sank to his knees dazed. His double vision realised the door to the cabin was now broken and as he strained to focus, two eerie yellow lights bobbed through the top half of the door and started wobbling across the floor towards him.

Every limb in the Halfling's frame was shaking, his teeth chattered, his legs wobbled and he felt hot and cold all at once. He tried to stand on protesting legs; eager to get away from whatever the bobbing horrors were that headed his way, bashing his head hard against the underside of the table and seeing stars again.

Ashe closed his eyes tightly trying to fight off the urge to vomit, gulped in one large breath and literally began screaming his head off.

* * * * * *

"Are you going to kill me?" Violetta asked, barely controlling the nervous waver to her voice.

"The fact that you are still around to ask me should answer that." The Raven replied, his intense gaze roving across Violetta's terrified features like a skilled interrogator who missed nothing. A smug smile slid across his lips as he noticed the slight tremor about the woman's frame, recognising how terrified his presence made her feel. "You need not worry. I was always told that only mad dogs bite the hand that feeds them."

"What do you mean?" the cook remarked, determined to meet her patient's gaze dead on. She had promised herself all those years before that she would never bow her head in servitude to a man again but something about this man's intensity made her memories of her time on the slave plantation flood back. Even the thought of blinking terrified her in the face of such a volatile, unpredictable danger.

"Come now. You are an intelligent woman with training in the healing arts. Those skills require intellect and wisdom, not simple mimicry. You have a brain; please do me the privilege of using it and save me the annoyance of having to respond to stupid questions."

The Raven paused, watching intently for signs his nurse might start acting irrationally and lash out but she seemed to be holding her emotions in check. Confident she would remain calm he asked questions of his own. "Would you do me the honour of explaining what is going on outside. Is it a storm that I feel moving this ship, or is an idiot manning the helm?"

Violetta's eyes widened, both at the abrupt closure of her questions and the sharp interrogation in response. The man's manner reminded her of her former slave master, clinically cold, precise and fearless towards her. The chef staggered backwards to regain her feet. The Raven followed swiftly, the knife he had earlier removed so deftly, appearing to jump up into his hand, flip across his palm and then dance back into his waiting grasp, the steel gleaming wickedly every twist of the way.

"I thought you weren't going to kill me?" Violetta jibed, motioning uneasily towards the blade.

"I also told you I wasn't a stupid man." The Raven snapped, "Now let's take things slow shall we and you can introduce me to your friends." He motioned out of the small cupboard space and back into the main galley, urging Violetta to comply with his wishes or face the most unpleasant of consequences.

Marcus suddenly snapped out of his exhaustion, realising something was wrong! Violetta had been in a rush to grab something when she left the kitchen but there had been no sounds of chaotic searching, no clatter of pots, rattle of pans, or drawers opened or shut, just a noticeable silence from the area beyond where he sat. It was almost imperceptible to begin with but the feeling grew undeniably strong! He rose lightly to his feet and headed across the room in the direction Violetta had departed.

Movement from within the next room made him pause and swiftly duck behind the open door, snatching Violetta's meat cleaver from the side where she had discarded it during her attendance of Sherman. His action was so fast and fluid that Violetta's daughter was left second-guessing if she had seen right.

"What are you doing?" Katarina hissed her eyes wide in concern. Marcus silenced her with a raised finger, just as Violetta walked through the door into the galley, a ragged man stepping closely behind her. Katarina let out a gasp as she realised who was walking behind her mother followed by a wail of anguish when she saw the knife in his hand.

"Mother, no!" she wailed. "Please sir, leave my mother alone. She's done nothing to you."

"Yet another waste of time." The Raven shrugged coldly. "I can see the family resemblance." He stepped fully into the room, his back an open target for the hidden monk.

Without any compunction, Marcus raised the cleaver with the barest whisper of robes, intent on putting the blade to full devastating effect.

"Do you make it a habit to hide behind doors?" The Raven commented, not turning around, yet making it perfectly clear that he was not addressing Violetta, her daughter or Bernard. Violetta glanced over her shoulder to see what was going on and gasped as she saw the monk and what he intended to do.

"Habit." The Raven sighed. "An interesting choice of words... wouldn't you say brother."

Katarina's eyes flew to the hidden monk, expecting to see Marcus display the same terror she felt toward the man that her mother had worked so hard to save. Instead, she saw a man about to carry out the act of cold-blooded murder. His eyes briefly met hers, registering her horror, her look enough for him to hesitate.

"What's the matter?" The Raven continued. "Haven't you got the guts to use the weapon you hold? Believe me if I were in your place, I wouldn't be thinking about it."

Marcus paused at the implied threat, delivered so succinctly, with a calm voice that caused a shiver of unease. 'Finish the job' his mind screamed. 'Do it now!' However, the seed of doubt was sown in his mind and now starting to fester there.

"No," The Raven decided, shaking his head. "You aren't fast enough... You could never be fast enough. Put the weapon down now before I do something that we both regret."

'I can't win.' Marcus realised with a final dread; his innocent mind defeated before the battle had even begun. The monk began to lower the cleaver in his hand.

"Ever so slowly now." came The Raven's warning, his eyes wary as he slowly turned to face the monk fully. His piercing eyes locked on Marcus's like a steel trap, freezing the monk in place and destroying any further resistance in a heartbeat. Even as the monk tried to form words to defend his cowardly actions, he felt the firm, unyielding hand of the ragged man close about his own and forcibly remove the cleaver.

"A cleaver..." the Raven laughed. "Hardly a warrior's weapon... or for that matter a monk's. You are from The Order of St. Fraiser if I am not mistaken. Is Brialin still running the place? I assure you he would have had no compunction to kill me if he had been in your position. Now..." He paused, as if for dramatic effect or for emphasis on what was to come. "...What is a brother of St. Fraiser doing so far from home?" Marcus stood stony faced, refusing to reply, despite the fact the eyes of the man before him were becoming harder by the second.

"Do I take it Brialin recruits mutes as brothers these days?" The Raven continued to taunt, the blade in his hand continuing to flash hypnotically before Marcus's eyes.

"I only talk when there is something of value to say." Marcus replied. "Our teachers always told us to listen and learn, rather than waste time in idle comment."

"It's a shame you seem to have forgotten that!" The Raven responded, sliding the naked edge of the cleaver up against Marcus's throat drawing a sliver of skin with it. He expected a wince or some acknowledgement of pain but the monk refused to reward him with any reaction at all, despite the welling of crimson beads of blood gathering on the wound. The lack of response unsettled the ragged man, the balance of power was wrong here, the monk was holding something back. This was something The Raven had not seen in a long time.

Marcus met The Raven's gaze with one of his own. The monk swallowed hard and then something within his calm demeanour snapped.

"Remove the knife from my throat." He stated quietly, the intensity of the delivery making it clear there would be no room for argument.

"Now why would I do that?" The Raven replied, angling the cleaver's blade ever so slightly, to reflect the figures shuffling nervously in the cabin behind him. The monk was becoming confident but a swift glance in the blade assured him no help was coming to the monk from that direction.

"Because if you don't I will do it for you." Marcus replied. "And you don't want me to do that."

The Raven stood shocked, initially unsure that he had heard right. That this humble academic had the gall to threaten him.

"Marcus, no!" Violetta exclaimed. "You don't know what this man is capable of."

"I would say the same of *Me*." the monk replied, his eyes never wavering from the man before him, the tension between them almost making the air crackle.

"Listen to your friend." The Raven gestured with his head. "She knows all too well what The Raven can do."

"But not..." Marcus smiled, "what Brother Marcus is capable of." He brought up his right hand with lightning speed, sweeping it between his own body and the assassin's hand, then swept it down again, using the back of his hand to strike across his foe's outstretched wrist and force the cleaver away from his throat. The edge of the chef's blade lightly creased his chest as it descended but the angle meant it did no serious harm. As Marcus completed the move with his right hand, his left palm came up to snap The Raven's hand out to the side, pushing the lowered cleaver well away from his body.

The Raven reacted by instinct, recognising the moves for the blocks and sweeps they were. He counteracted, steeling himself for the palm strike, allowing the cleaver to move out, offering minimal resistance from the blow, before whipping the blade in again. Intent on scoring a hit at the monk's chest, his eyes followed the move only for Marcus to step back, clearly anticipating the action, dropping to the floor, to leave the astonished assassin holding the cleaver up against nothing but thin air. Movement was now purely instinct, The Raven leaping up from the deck, just as Marcus's left leg swept out, swift as a striking snake to try to snap his foe's fibula or tibia.

The monk's leg almost whistled through the empty space where his target had stood mere seconds before but The Raven was already responding to the move, angling his descending feet to crush the monk's now vulnerable extended leg. Marcus showed he was not to be underestimated, snapping his leg back in with millimetres to spare, allowing The Raven's attack to injure nothing but the galley floor.

The Raven threw himself backwards, across the room, his head brushing the kitchen utensils hanging from the beams in the enclosed space. Pans knocked against each other, clanging like bells calling worshippers to service. Judging the space sufficient he regained his feet and threw back his head, laughing aloud before incredibly bowing to the monk, acknowledging his error in underestimating the skills of his foe.

"From one master to another." He remarked; his voice edged with admiration and respect.

"You are no master." Marcus replied, getting slowly to his feet. "You work only in the shadows, whereas I embrace the light."

"Oh my..." The Raven gasped, his mind suddenly connecting the pieces of the puzzle that had been so confusing to him. "You're a bearer." He paused, taking in the monk with a closer, more scrutinised gaze. "But where are the twelve? And why would Brialin send a bearer out here in the middle of nowhere?"

Chapter Thirty-Four

Kerian staggered along the passageway to Thomas's cabin on legs that did not seem to belong to him. The unpredictable movement of the ship bouncing him physically from wall to wall, raising bruises in places the elderly fighter did not want to think about and reducing his knees to jelly. He needed to hide Marcus's book quickly and had suddenly realised he knew just the place to put it.

Spluttering lanterns swung wildly from the ceiling, threatening to extinguish at any moment and casting erratic shadows that caused him to shy and jump. Although the distance he travelled measured in mere feet, it felt that he had traversed several miles of particularly rough road before he finally arrived at Thomas's cabin door.

The door swung open at his touch, the view within showing little resemblance to the plush cabin Kerian had visited so many times before. A forgotten tankard was sliding around the floor, a model ship swayed and plunging in direct unison with the sea outside, feathered quills discarded, strewn across the carpet as if a fearsome predator had taken a stray bird in mid-flight.

Kerian timed the rise and fall of the ship to lunge across the distance to the first chair, slamming into it and winding himself as the deck lifted again. He looked up from recovering his breath and gazed upon a harrowing sight.

Beyond the indigo stained carpet where the inkwell had overturned and the cork had fallen free, past the lighter patch of woodwork on the ledge beyond the desk that had so nearly marked his own resting place, he saw the full force of the storm framed in the delicate borders of the rattling window.

Ebony black sky swirled against an impossibly darker sea, the raw power and physical presence of the waves clashing for supremacy over the air above, rising higher than the window could show, blotting out everything but the inky blackness that roared unchecked around the ship. All that stopped this tempest from crashing into the captain's cabin were several delicate panes of vibrating glass.

Faced with such a daunting spectacle, Kerian suddenly realised just how small the *El Defensor*, his current home, really was and real stirrings of fear rose within his chest. The waves slapped heavily against the glass, causing the panes to groan and shiver, making Kerian jump with the noise and snapping him out of his morose reflection. He had come here for a reason and there was no time to spend worrying about the seaworthiness of this vessel.

He hefted Marcus's canvas wrapped book up in his arms and located the hiding place he had been considering, the one place he felt Marcus would never find it. Thomas's literary associates Eales, Gaiman and Williams, looked down from a shelf on the wall, their well-thumbed pages and creased spines silent witness to the secret actions of the elderly warrior. They, and the previous ship's logs they stood beside could look after the strange volume from now on, at least until Marcus had a long talk with Kerian to explain his actions. He slid the book in amongst the others in Thomas's collection and stepped back to admire his intuitive hiding place. It was perfect; Marcus would never think to look there.

Turning his back to the disrupted cabin, Kerian caught himself staring back into the looking glass behind the door. He took in the soaked grey figure that stared back at him and in a moment of vanity paused to stretch his skin where a new crease had decided to form. He sighed resolutely; other people on board may not have noticed what was going on but Kerian knew without a doubt that the one-man race he was leading against old age had suffered yet another setback. How much time did he truly have left now? He had no real idea and he had to ask himself did he really want to know?

A loud crash from further down the corridor reminded the fighter that he had fulfilled his role and now he could turn his mind to helping the others against whatever was ripping the *El Defensor* apart. He slid his sword from its scabbard before glancing back at his reflection.

"I'll see you later," he winked at his reflection, as the violet glow from his sword accentuated his pale features. "Wait right there and don't do anything I wouldn't do."

"I know... I know..." he muttered to himself, "that leaves me fairly free."

* * * * * *

Thomas looked at his men with pride, noting the dark blood oozing from many of their wounds, their saturated forms and obvious weariness, yet despite all of their ills there was an overwhelming sense of purpose and camaraderie tying the four of them together with more cohesion than the greatest of fighting teams.

"Our ship is under attack from a monster that has yet to understand the finer points in ship etiquette," Thomas stated. "It's time we removed our gate crasher. We have tried to be nice. Now it's time to not be nice." He smiled as he recalled the words of a cooler played by Patrick Swayze in a 1980's film he had loved.

"Our what?" Aradol asked, totally bemused by the captain's comments. "Which gate has been broken?"

"Let's ready our weapons." Ives butted in, surmising that Thomas may have hit his head in all the excitement. "Scrave, Thomas and I have our swords." He turned to Aradol, barely missing a beat. "And Aradol has his trusty... What exactly do you have Aradol?"

Aradol looked down at his hands and meekly brought up the only item he had been able to find not swept overboard. The battered wooden pail was splintered and chipped and dripped suspiciously from beneath.

"And Aradol has his trusty bucket." Ives continued, not missing a beat, stating the facts as if they were nothing out of the ordinary. "Let's face it gentlemen, with such deadly arms we are unstoppable and cannot possibly lose."

A wall of water crashed across the deck threatening to sweep all of the sailors from their feet but as one, they clung to each other, the strengths of some supporting the weaknesses in others as they shouted a challenge to the elements around them to do their worst.

"Let's go and rescue our damsel in distress." Thomas stated coldly, just as a scream cut through the air with crystal clarity making several of the men jump and causing others to grip their weapons more tightly.

"Never misses a cue, does she?" Scrave muttered as they started skilfully negotiating their way across the remains of the aft deck, jumping precariously from one rain slicked exposed beam to another. Thomas was horrified at the damage the elemental had caused to his mighty ship. Even now, it appeared oblivious to their approach, concentrating on enlarging the hole it had smashed into the deck, its actions reminiscent to a cat worrying a mouse hole.

The Captain of the *El Defensor* jumped across to another beam in order to get a clearer view of the deck beyond and the kneeling figure of the ship's mage. Colette was magnificent, yanking on her smoke leash and infuriating the elemental as she struggled to cast her final spell to banish the monster back to its home.

The elemental shook off the weight of another crashing wave, viewing the dark swirling waters that parted around its billowing form as another minor annoyance preventing it from carrying out its task. As the water sluiced from the deck and into the depths of the ship, the creature turned its head to scan the ruined timbers for anyone foolish enough to attack it. Satisfied no threat was within striking distance, it started ripping out a main support beam. Part of the deck started to sag with a protesting groan.

Colette yanked the smoke leash hard, pulling the creature up before it could compound the damage it had caused and commenced weaving her spell to open the portal and send the elemental back to where it came. A relatively simple task if the creature in question wanted to leave but Colette knew this monster had no such ideas and was not intent on leaving quietly. As she drew on the power necessary to complete her task, her foe, recognising that delay meant a risk of imprisonment or banishment, decided to take matters into its own hands.

Spiked claws slid from various places about its marble like form. It leapt straight up, elongating its shape as far into the sky as possible, towering above Colette's kneeling form. With a shriek of triumph, it slammed down hard onto the front of the slanting deck she knelt upon, bringing its considerable weight to bear on the splintered decking. There was an explosion of timber as a larger hole formed. Colette gritted her teeth in frustration and tried to steady herself as the deck moved beneath her and her initial casting fizzled out with her loss of concentration. She flicked her hair back with a frustrated sigh, before reaching back into her pouch for another gemstone and prepared to begin casting again.

Thomas looked up from his treacherous foothold and squinted through the sheeting rain. Scrave was moving up on the left, Ives and Aradol on the right. Colette's current situation appeared to become more tenuous by the second. She clearly was not aware that she now knelt on the smallest portion of deck, the rest of the aft castle stripped from around and beneath her by the elemental's razor-sharp claws. The raw exposed beams supporting her precarious perch bent dangerously beneath her, threatening to send the mage tumbling into the very depths of the ship if the carpentry should fail. Thomas recognised that if this were to happen, she would fall through her enchanted circle and death would certainly follow as her magical protection failed.

They had to distract the creature and give her the time to cast her spell. He took a deep breath and mentally prepared to face the monster again: the demands and self-inflicted morals of being a captain overwhelming his apparently failing of common sense. His shipmates had hardly fared well against the creature, nevertheless Colette needed the time and that was what they would give. As he watched, the elemental swung up a claw sending a piece of splintered deck whistling across the ship, missing Scrave by inches and snatching the captin from his morose musing.

He bellowed a challenge, covered the rest of the deck as fast as opportunity and his balancing skills allowed, intent on inflicting a wound that would count! He swung his cutlass with all his strength, screaming in rage as the gleaming blade whistled through the air to slice clean through the creature's back. Scented smoke billowed out into the air, as the elemental literally split in half, its scream of rage roaring out defiantly as a grim smile of satisfaction flickered across Thomas's taut features.

The unexpected blinding flash and explosion that followed staggered Thomas, hitting his back and propelling him right to the edge of the hole in the deck the creature had ripped out. He frantically grabbed for a handhold, stopping himself short of tipping into the ruined cabins below. Colette threw up her arm to shade her face from the flash, as the air filled with the smell of brimstone and super-heated pieces of wood from the main mast scythed through the air. Ives gritted his teeth as electrical discharge from the lightning strike set his teeth on edge, and Rauph doubled in size as all the hairs on his body suddenly stood up.

Thomas shook his head, looking back behind him and noticed in horror that the base of the main mast was shattered. Several small fires had sprung up on the main deck and as he watched, the entire mast groaned and started to tumble towards the deck. Sodden canvas, mast and rigging crashing down in a deadly cascade of destruction.

The ruined mast crashed upon the deck, crushing everything unlucky enough to be beneath it, before it began a torturous slide towards the edge of the ship, dragging rigging and sail reluctantly along with it. With an audible groan, the mast slid over the side, its dead weight combined with all the canvas acting as a drag in the water. It swiftly sank under the surface of the churning sea, the braces and stays still attached to the mast pulling taut against their anchorage on the starboard side of the deck. With a tortuous creaking, the *El Defensor* began to shift at the new weight displacement, the whole ship settling over on her port side as the weight of the mast dragged the deck of the ship down towards the swirling waters.

Rauph roared his disapproval from the helm but could do little as the ship started to list. Crew slid across the slanted deck, some falling overboard and swallowed by the unforgiving seas, whilst others came within feet of the voracious waves lapping at the side of the battered vessel. Some arrested their tumbles by grabbing onto the tangled mass of taut lines making up the remains of the rigging. The cold swirling waters seemed to sigh as the sea met the edge of the main deck, before surging up and breaching over the side of the *El Defensor*, seeking gaps in the ruined portholes and breaches in the deck through which to pour with malicious glee, dragging the ship further over onto her side.

Thomas found his worries about dropping through to the open cabins suddenly inconsequential, as the whole deck moved beneath him, threatening to tip him overboard. He hung on grimly, as Colette chose this ill-judged moment to complete her spell.

The image of the smashed rooms below blurred and warped before the captain's eyes. The air suddenly obscured by glittering points of light that rippled and waved as the cabins became ethereal then disappeared, as the portal began to form. Sickly grey and yellow cracks appeared pulsed across the transforming surface, with a throbbing intensity Thomas had seen many times before.

However, the deafening crack of magic that signified the opening of the portal sounded nothing like previous times, its intensity very unnatural to the captain's ear. The rippling area darkened then split apart, like an enormous jigsaw puzzle that had been shattered. The space beneath became a hole into another shadowy world. Two planes of existence now connected by magical means, the pathway to returning the air elemental now open for Colette to use. Unfortunately, in her haste to cast the spell, the ship's mage had failed to consider that she normally opened the gateway within a magically shielded circle. With the shielding present, any unequal pressure between the planes was localised within the area of containment but this time there was no such shield.

The spherical hole yawned wide, stretching down into nothingness, air rushing into the portal with a hair-raising shriek as the gateway began to suck in everything around it, nature trying to equalize a condition that would normally never exist.

Scrave crashed down alongside Thomas grabbing him firmly and screaming in his ear.

"What is she doing? There's no protection, nothing to stop other creatures coming out, nothing to stop this world going in."

Thomas tried to focus on what his companion was saying, tried to grasp what he meant, as the suction coming from the hole snatched and grabbed at him with a ferocity that was breath taking. This had never happened before. He watched dazed, as debris started to roll against the slant of the deck, moving uphill and picking up speed, before falling through the hole in the deck to wherever the elemental had come from.

"Don't you understand?" Scrave continued screaming. "There's no shield."

"Aurion, I banish you!" Colette's voice wailed, rising through the sounds of the storm and sounding pitifully frail. Thomas looked up, past Scrave's terror filled face into the angry horror of the wind elemental, searching for salvation, hoping that this time something would go their way, that the elemental would simply be sucked into the portal and be gone. The creature had no real facial features, yet Thomas realised with a sinking heart that if it had, it would have been smirking with distain. The monster had no intention of leaving.

Thomas looked past the creature, trying to absorb everything that was happening around him. The water crashing over the side of the ship, the listing of the vessel, dropping it further and further towards the waves and the incredible shrieking hole, sucking in everything not bolted down. Then he looked back to the terrified Elf before him, who had continued shouting despite Thomas hearing none of it.

"She's doomed us all!" Scrave screamed.

"We're all going to die!"

* * * * * *

"You ask too many questions…."

The explosion from above shook everyone within the cabin, pausing Marcus in mid-speech.

"What was that?" he demanded rhetorically, already aware that no one in the room could answer his question. The resounding crash that reverberated through the bowels of the ship had the monk subconsciously backing up against the wall for protection, his eyes reflecting the questioning look of the others alongside him.

The agonising groan of the ship was almost deafening in the confines of the galley, as the deck began to tilt ever so slightly beneath them. A roll of lint lying against Sherman's still form started to slowly unwind before their eyes as if an invisible nurse were about to attend to a procedure, then an apple bounced from a work surface to the left, tumbling away across the floor and into the shadows.

Marcus spread his legs to maintain his balance, hoping the disturbance was simply a large swell but his hopes dashed as the deck continued to tilt inexplicably. Everyone appeared frozen in place as the chaotic scenario continued unravelling around them, heads moving as one to focus on individual objects that suddenly appeared to gain lives of their own as they began to move haphazardly across the floor. As the list increased the groans from within the ship intensified, drowning out any possible attempts at communication and making the closer crashes within the galley appear almost muted in comparison.

Katarina and Violetta held onto each other tightly, their eyes wide and terrified. Bernard simply stood stunned, unbelieving that his luck could get any worse than it already was. However, the tension between Marcus and Mathius Blackraven continued to grow perceptively as they stared, glancing from the falling objects around them and then back at each other, as if expecting to launch into another series of attacks despite the worsening of the situation unravelling about them.

A large cauldron came free and clanged loudly across the galley floor glancing off Sherman's prone form with a dull clang, before ending up against the far wall, snatching Violetta out of her thoughts.

"Oh Sherman." She wailed aloud, pulling away from her terrified daughter and moving to the injured sailor, her quick professional glance confirming that the sailor's condition had anything but improved. She tried to lift her patient out of the way of the falling debris but the slant of the deck and the constant barrage of falling detritus made the manoeuvre impossible to carry out by herself. In desperation she looked across at the two protagonists, her eyes informing them both that their individual quarrels should wait for another time.

Marcus shook his head angrily and moved to assist, his calling preventing him from displaying any more bravado at the expense of another living soul. However, as he moved to assist, the creaking sounds of the ship muted. He realised that his breathing was suddenly loud in his ears and all other sounds had ceased. The deck remained tilted beneath his feet, objects still lazily wobbling and cascading across the deck but everything had taken on an almost unreal quality, the everyday paraphernalia appearing bizarre in context, somehow fake, as if he had entered into a dream like trance.

"Well that was scary wasn't it?" The Raven joked, his outburst cleaving the tension more skilfully than any blade he could have wielded, his joviality surprising not just the people around him but also the assassin himself.

"What's going on?" Bernard began, slowly moving himself up the slanting deck towards the door. Marcus watched the crewman go, expecting the ragged man to intercept him on route, only to find himself surprised again, as he simply let him walk by, apparently intent on some other private concern.

"Shush!" The Raven motioned frantically with his hands, tilting his head to one side as he struggled to listen to a low mumbling sound that originated somewhere in the distance, indistinct and difficult to identify. Everyone stopped moving as the sound became more pronounced, a high-pitched shriek and beneath it a deep roaring, the sounds becoming louder and louder the closer they approached. Marcus looked towards the galley door with growing trepidation.

"What is that noise?" Bernard enquired, reaching the galley door and staring through, oblivious to the fact that Marcus and The Raven had separated and were adopting their individual fighting stances.

A stream of rats exploded into the galley, causing Violetta and Katarina to scream at the sudden rush of vermin; wiry haired and almost slimy in the way they moved as one, falling over each other in the rush to escape from some unseen pursuer.

Bernard backpedalled frantically from the rush of bodies, kicking his legs out and brushing the writhing bodies from his leggings as they struggled to gain high ground. Violetta instantly swung into action, determined to defend her galley, diving for a mop she had secured behind the door. A flood of tools cascaded across the deck as she opened the small storage space and reached in for her trusty weapon but she ignored the mess, turning in a blaze of fury, swatting the rats away from her charge.

Marcus moved to protect Katarina, angling in front of the rodent stream to launch snap kicks at any of the creatures that came too near, the sounds of small bones snapping like kindling confirming attacks the naked eye could barely follow. Bernard continued to stamp angrily at the swirl of rats beneath his feet and reached out to snatch one of the creatures from his back, only to wrench his hand away in agony as sharp teeth embedded deeply into the fleshy flap of skin between the thumb and finger, tearing tissue and spilling blood.

The Raven coolly stood his ground, his feet whipping out to flip the approaching rodents up into the air where the glittering death of the cleaver blade sliced them apart and ended their short lives. The rats were oblivious to their losses and continued to pile into the room, desperate to escape the unseen menace that pursued them.

Seawater surged through the doorway in a wall of white bubbling foam, plumes of spray sweeping everything before it into the galley. Rats and people alike found themselves lifted by the flood and thrown physically across the room by the unrelenting freezing torrent.

Marcus found himself slammed into the far wall as Bernard lost his feet and went under the water scrabbling for purchase on the tilting deck, his arms thrashing about in the swirling morass of rats and ship wide flotsam. He came up moments later spluttering for air and disorientated. Violetta screamed in fury, her attention torn between the unconscious sailor before her and Katarina who was hanging on for her life by a hook at the door. Family loyalty clashed with responsibility, until the chef weighed up the options and started to wade through the water towards her daughter.

"Help me shut the door." The Raven screamed. "We have to stop the water coming in!"

The assassin was already moving, fighting against the pull of the freezing water that was even now swirling up about his knees. He arrived at the open doorway and reached through, fighting the incredible force of the water as he tried to grab the edge of the door and pull it through the torrent of water rushing towards him. However, the slant of the ship was against him, giving the door an incredible, unmoveable weight as the water forced it back against the wall. Veins stood out on his forehead as he tried desperately to pull the door towards him but the task was next to impossible due to the sheer weight of water crashing through the opening.

"Are you going to stand there all day Brother?" he snapped in exasperation.

Marcus did not waste energy replying and angled sideways through the water to join the man who seconds before had been his enemy and now ironically had become an ally against a deadlier foe. Groaning aloud they pulled as one against the water level that was now up to their waists and still climbing rapidly. The door inched reluctantly through the water despite their best efforts to move it faster before catching in the stream and suddenly slamming shut, nearly catching both of their fingers in the crush.

The crash of the door against the frame was so loud that Katarina screamed in fright. As Marcus and The Raven turned to congratulate each other, something large slammed into the far side of the door. The Raven stood breathless and shivering in the waist high water, staring across at Marcus as they both fought to catch their breath.

"Well that was fun." He joked, before looking around the room with a more critical expression.

"That's some strength you have there." Marcus admitted, pushing back against the door testing the wood, half-heartedly attempting to open it again and finding unsurprisingly that it was stuck fast. "I hope we can still get out."

"When the initial rush of water settles, we should be able to open the door without too much difficulty." The Raven confirmed, apparently unconcerned at the turn of events.

"Maybe not as easy as you think." Marcus pointed out, moving aside a sodden apron hanging on the back of the door to indicate a large splintered dent protruding from the wood. "Was that there before?"

Violetta looked over, her eyes registering the protruding wood with alarm.

"Does that mean what I think it does?" She enquired, barely containing the waver in her voice as she struggled to hold her skirts up out of the flood.

Marcus and the Raven both turned and slammed against the door, expecting the wood to give, at least a little but the door stubbornly refused to budge.

"I think something is wedged up against the door." Marcus stated.

"Thanks for stating the obvious." The Raven shot back, suddenly pausing as he realised something was wrong with the scene. "Where's your patient?"

"By the Saints." Violetta wailed, staring down at the bubbling water around her as she suddenly remembered her charge.

Bernard instantly dove under the surface at the far end of the cabin, coming up again seconds later, gasping for breath at the shock of the cold liquid swirling around him. Marcus dived in after him searching the cloudy seawater through stinging eyes, dimly aware of the flickering pale circles of light that existed in the other world above. Incredibly, another form joined him in the dark, cold water and gestured towards a large bundle of darkness in the far corner and as one the two rescuers swam down towards it.

Marcus broke the surface moments later, the cold dead weight of Sherman clutched between his arms and as he blinked his eyes clear of water he suddenly realised that his assistant was not Bernard but instead the lean muscular form of the ragged man. Hiding his continuing shock at such a change of character, Marcus wrestled his burden over to the galley table where Violetta and Katarina joined the struggle to place the sailor's body up out of the water.

"There's no point." The Raven stated in his matter of fact manner. "He's already dead."

"No he's not." Violetta angrily rebuked, lashing out at the thought of failing her charge.

Marcus looked down at the pale body laid out on the table, resigned to the fact that his colleague's assessment was probably correct and that they should face the facts that Sherman had passed on, when he saw the sailor impossibly take a ragged breath.

"That's impossible." He muttered under his breath, blinking his eyes just in case he had imagined the whole thing but unbelievably Sherman continued to take ragged fluttering breaths.

The Raven moved up alongside to assist in positioning their charge and saw the inexplicable rising and falling of the sailor's ragged chest. His speech failed him at the sight.

"Brother Marcus." He questioned breathlessly. "How can this be?"

"I have no idea." Marcus confessed. "Help me get the others up onto the table and then let's figure out some way to get out of here."

"Tell me that we have a way out of this place that doesn't involve going back through that door." The Raven groaned.

Violetta's shaking head told them all what they feared the most.

"Well it's lucky we can all swim then," he continued, staring at the rising water swirling about him and trying not to show that the water levels mirrored his own hidden feelings of growing unease.

Chapter Thirty-Five

Kerian advanced down the corridor, the soft violet light of his sword helping him to find the exit out onto the main deck. He turned a corner and saw the new crew member Weyn Valdeze propped up against the wall, water sloshing around the man's legs as the ship continued to list. He paused to check Weyn was still breathing and out of danger, then struggled towards the night beyond, noting with some concern that the ship was listing further to the left with every step he took.

He shuffled along, trying to push himself away from the wall of the corridor and finding it harder and harder to do so. As he exited onto the main deck, the storm slapped him around the face, causing him to gasp at how cold it felt. He squinted his eyes against the deluge of rain and sea spray hammering into his form and struggled to make sense of the devastation. The smoking mast, the twisted rigging and the increasing list of the ship. Did the monster that had wrecked his cabin do all of this? Was it still free? How many people had it hurt?

A wave smashed across the ship, white water crashing over the deck, knocking crew into the sea as they struggled to free the ruined mast. Kerian threw up his arm to protect his face from the worst of the freezing water then paused, suddenly feeling an unshakeable need to turn his attention from the chaos before him and focus his thoughts towards the aft deck.

Colette... What about Colette.

Damn, he had been so preoccupied with Marcus's stupid book! He should have been out here helping where he could. He headed for the ladder leading up to the aft deck and gingerly climbed, ensuring each handhold was secure before daring to move his hand to the next rung.

As his head cleared the deck, a haunting vista opened up before him. Framed by splintered pieces of wood, the unfolding scene showed Colette kneeling on a jagged remnant of deck looking small and defenceless up against the cloud swirling creature of nightmare that attacked her protective circle. The breath caught in Kerian's throat as he took in her bedraggled frame, long wisps of golden hair whipped up into a frenzy by the elements that raged about her. The saturated material of her robes clinging to her figure like a second skin, revealing curves and lines that left Kerian powerless at her beauty.

Colette's clenched fist held a thin line of smoke that writhed and wriggled in her hand and as he watched, she yanked hard and the elemental whipping through the air above her slammed down towards the ruined deck. Her refusal to give in was a cause for inspiration, her appearance as addictive to the fighter as a drug. If there was ever reason for him to continue his quest, a catalyst energising him onwards in seeking a cure for his ailment, he realised she was it. She made him feel young and vibrant again, an effect he found unsettling and invigorating all at the same time. He drank in her image like a man who had never tasted water as pure and dared to dream whilst the storm raged around him.

The elemental was shrieking in defiance, hooking its claws into the deck and halting its passage back through the portal. Inch by inch the creature started to draw itself up, even as the small figures of men leapt to attack it. Kerian tried to focus through the rain and picked out the figures of Scrave, Thomas, Ives and Aradol engaging the swirling monster. He screwed up his eyes and squinted further.

Was Aradol fighting with a bucket?

* * * * * *

Thomas suddenly found his world turning upside down. He hit the deck at an angle, bounced heavily and fell into a roll. Shrieks and curses from his colleagues indicated that they too were having problems as the wind elemental lashed out left and right.

Sliding to a stop on his back, Thomas took a second to orientate himself with his surroundings then rolled rapidly to the side as a swirling mass crashed into the deck inches from his head. Rolling twice more the captain found himself caught up against the railing, the sea crashing dangerously close below him. From this undignified position, he somehow managed to haul himself to his feet, wiping a hand across his face, before lifting his sword and charging back into the fray again.

Colette's perch was becoming more dangerous. The suction from the portal was physically pulling her circle of deck down towards it, magic crackling in the air as items bounced from her shield and then slipped into the abyss below. She still displayed a steely determination to draw the air elemental in towards her, despite the precariousness of her position and the tether whipped and snapped in her hand as she struggled to rein in the creature responsible for all of the carnage.

Ives Mantoso struggled to attack the creature with his sword but he was not as agile as the others were and his flapping robes made it harder for him to stand as the portal sucked them away from his form.

Aradol swung his bucket in a valiant attempt to distract the elemental and watched as the handle came away in his hand, the bucket bouncing tantalisingly out of reach across the deck towards the far corner of the ship. The side of the young man's face was puffed up and swollen where the elemental had grazed him but his resilience was such that he took off after his trusty weapon without a seconds thought.

Scrave moved with the ship, his actions as fluid and graceful as always, his sword a deadly extension of his being. Air elemental smoke billowed into the air, coupled with snarls and screams of pain as the Elf repeatedly attacked his foe, with no quarter given. The elemental to its credit tried to ignore the wounds, concentrating instead on crushing the mage that had it tethered but Scrave was having none of it, darting in and out like an annoying insect, delivering bites more devastating than any bee sting.

"I believe we never finished our dance." He jibed, skidding to a halt on the slanting deck right in front of his foe. The air elemental snarled at the outrage, lifting an arm bristling with claws determined to wipe out the threat this Elf offered for the last time. Scrave turned to face it, unaware that the creature had elongated a similar construct at the other end of its body. The unseen spiked appendage crashed into Scrave with all the force of a stampeding stallion, lifting the Elf from his feet to send him tumbling across the deck. He landed heavily, his Elven dexterity no use against the unexpected blow.

* * * * * *

Ives dropped to the deck, to gather in his robes and secure them with his belt. Satisfied he was more in control, he slid down the slanting ship towards where the monster waited. He opened his hand to prevent his knuckles getting squashed painfully between his sword and the deck and looked on in horror as the discarded blade, once a monstrous tooth in a previous life, flipped up and bounced across the ship with a life of its own as the suction from the portal acquired it. The ivory blade flipped over twice more before embedding deeply into a cross beam above the mouth of the opening. Then ever so slowly, it started to bend out of the wood towards the portal below.

The merchant cried out in frustration at being disarmed so easily. His father would have turned in his grave if he could have seen how his son had lost his grip on the family heirloom. How was he going to get his sword back? All his good intentions and sense of duty evaporated in an instant as he realised the only way he could secure his blade was if he let go of the deck and slid straight into the elemental. That was not much of an option!

He drew in a mouthful of air to voice a particularly colourful curse and found himself knocked from his feet by another wave of freezing seawater. The elemental towered above him, as he bounced across the deck towards his doom. Ives closed his eyes and threw himself forwards preparing for the worst.

Something slammed into his chest, blasting the air from his body but he hung on to whatever had hit him, refusing to let go, imagining himself shredded into tiny pieces by the monster he fought. Cold rain continued to pound his body but no brutal death or limb removal followed, so he cracked open an eye to find himself clinging resolutely to the aforementioned exposed crossbeam, his face mere inches from his sword. However, before the merchant could count his blessings, he found the beam starting to shiver beneath his body and firecracker snaps jolting his perch as the wood started to snap under the strain.

* * * * * *

Thomas did not know where to run to first! Scrave appeared to be unconscious to one side, the shrieking draw of the portal initially tugging the hair on the Elf's brow, before it started to tug more firmly at the sailor's tunic. Ives was undeniably starting to slide to his doom but was hanging on with his eyes closed tightly, as if the very act of ignoring the problem would make it go away. Colette was struggling to stay upright, the tilt of her perch now so pronounced, that it was a matter of not if but when she would slip outside of her circle.

There was only so much one man could do. He whispered a silent prayer for a sign to show him where he should go. Incredibly, from out of the darkness, someone appeared to hear Thomas's call for help. As he watched, a lone figure stepped out in front of the elemental, placing himself firmly between the monster and the ship's mage. Thomas blinked twice before he realised it was Aradol that stood there and another blink before he realised the youth was still armed with nothing but his trusty bucket, all be it now a bucket without a handle.

As he looked, Aradol threw the bucket for all he was worth. It ricocheted off the deck, flew up in the air and smashed through the elemental, plucking one of its eyes out as it passed. The bucket shot up, then caught in the suction of the portal to fly back down, hitting the cabin wall, pirouetting off a cross beam and skipping through the open portal to disappear forever. The elemental went berserk, lashing out with renewed wrath.

"That's just great." Thomas sighed, watching Aradol standing before the elemental armed with nothing but his bare hands and his sense of morals. "Now he doesn't even have a bucket!"

Colette's perch snapped, adding a fourth impossible choice of destination to the captain and sending the mage tumbling forwards, her magical items rolling across the circle and out over the edge. The mage slid across the magical threshold with a scream, passing through the barrier of protection which shattered with a clean crack audible even over the howling of the storm. She reached out, desperately grabbing onto a splintered piece of the deck, swinging defenceless above the roaring portal, unable to lift herself free.

The elemental stopped its thrashing, sensing the fall of the shield and turned towards its enemy, it's one remaining eye displaying a hate that bored into the terrified mage, leaving her in no doubt as to what fate was about to befall her.

* * * * * *

Marcus sloshed through the water, the cold unforgiving liquid now up to his chest. A carrot floated by, followed by a wooden spoon and a serving bowl, spinning silently on a journey to nowhere. The ragged man was moving around the room, looking for possible ways out of the galley they could access, his calm, meticulous demeanour rubbing the monk up the wrong way.

The man attempted to open a porthole, causing the others to hold their breath in alarm at the thought of more water swamping the room; however, Marcus knew from the darkness through the glass that the pressure of the water outside would make it impossible for the ragged man to open. Sure enough, within a short while, the man gave up and moved towards the stove, looking at the flue with a critical eye.

Ripples of current still surged from the doorway, indicating that even though the door was closed water was still slipping inside. Marcus turned his attention fully onto the door problem and tried to calm the growing panic he felt. He had never considered death by drowning a possibility but he knew if they did not find a solution to their current predicament the likelihood of such a demise became more likely by the second.

Bubbles rose from the deck beneath his feet, showing that the breached water was also making its way below, so there was no point considering the floor as a possible way out. The amount of seawater draining away was also considerably less than that coming through the door, so the sea level was not going to subside any time soon.

He looked at the dent in the woodwork with a critical eye and tried to imagine what could have smashed so heavily against the door to trap them inside. Obviously, the door would not open if there were something wedged against it but what if he could somehow weaken the door around it. Remove some planks and once the pressure equalised, they could get free, swim through the ship and get above decks to relative safety.

His mind thought back to the whirling column of cloud that had attacked the crew above. Relative safety took on a completely new meaning when he considered what awaited them above decks.

Marcus tried to calm his breathing, focused and prepared to attack the door. His hand shot out, the heel of his palm striking the wood with a dull thump and a mighty splash. He drew his hand back again, disappointed at his lack of power, realising that the rushing water was taking some of the force of his strike away. He centred again, breathing out, before his hand lashed forwards, to bounce harmlessly off the heavily grained surface again.

In the back of his mind, Marcus became aware that the others were watching him but he did not want them to distract his concentration and humbly bowed his head, trying to focus on the now and the problem he faced.

Katarina whispered to her mother, pointing out the few rats that remained alive, now frantically swimming around their table. Water was lapping over the edge of the work surface, soaking Sherman and sloshing around the knees of the mother and daughter. The rats seemed to be circling, paddling frantically, slick black shapes that were seeking out areas where they could pull themselves from the swirling seawater.

Marcus slammed his hand into the wood again and felt a slight crack beneath his hand. He struck again at the same spot, trying to make the weakened wood splinter further. It pushed in slightly but refused to give completely. The monk stepped back, focusing on the damaged section of door and lifted his foot almost clear of the water, striking out and withdrawing his foot so fast that the others were not sure what they had seen. The wood snapped cleanly and more water started pouring through into the galley.

"I don't want to dampen your enthusiasm," The Raven commented, "...but we already had enough water in here." He indicated the stove he had been closely examining and gestured that Marcus come over. "Why don't you help me with the flue, if we can weaken the wood maybe we can squeeze out there and up through the floor to the deck above?"

Marcus examined the hole he had made; trying to get his arm through the door to feel for the size of the obstruction but all he initially got for his troubles was a jet of freezing cold water hitting him in the face. He gritted his teeth and tried to angle his body, his searching hand feeling the object that was wedged with cold numbed fingers. His heart sank when he realised it was a lot bigger than he expected, possibly a cupboard of some kind and not something they could push to one side in the time they needed.

His shoulders sank in defeat as he removed his arm from the hole. He turned dejected and watched the stream of water he had created begin to jet into the room in a torrent as the list of the ship worsened. It whipped a floating apple around and sent it shooting across the galley at speed. The rats started to get more frantic, sensing the water level was still climbing and headed for the table in a bid to climb to higher ground.

Violetta lashed out with her mop, catching one of the more courageous rodents and snapping its back. It flew across the room and slapped wetly against the wall before tumbling into the bread bin on a shelf on the far wall.

"Try not to be too despondent," The Raven joked, gesturing at Marcus to come and help him. "As long as we can keep our heads above water we have a chance and Violetta is already starting to make us sandwiches for the trip. Although between you and me, I wouldn't count on the lettuce and tomato component and the meat may be slightly tough."

Katarina burst out in a nervous laugh and Marcus could not help but smile at the ragged man's attempts at humour. He sloshed over in his sodden restricting robes to where the man stood and both of them looked up at the flue as the water surged around their chests. Marcus noted that the water appeared much deeper on this side of the cabin but he moved to position himself on the far side of the main stove and tried to move the flue. It bonged with a hollow ring but refused to budge.

"Come on Marcus," the ragged man jibed. "I'm sure between us we can do better than that."

"That's easy for you to say," Marcus snapped back, "I don't even know what your name is."

"Mathius Blackraven at your service," he gestured. "Forgive me if I don't bow. Now push cloister boy!"

They braced themselves and pushed, hearing the metal creaking and groaning in protest as they struggled to free it from its mountings. Behind them, Bernard and Violetta continued defending the high ground from the rats as the waters continued to rise and the rodents started to become bolder in their forays for a dry refuge.

Marcus felt as if his head would explode, pushing against the chimney for all he was worth with Mathius snarling alongside him, when suddenly the whole chimney buckled and tore from its housing, sending the monk off balance with the sudden lack of resistance and making him slip under the water. He rose, choking and coughing but happy they had managed to free the stubborn thing. His eyes cleared to see Mathius still standing but looking less than impressed at what they had wrought.

A pale circle of light filtered down through the hole in the ceiling where the chimney had come away. One glance confirmed the opening was too small for an adult to pass through and the structure of the ceiling beams meant that without some serious sawing there was no way they would be able to fit.

Marcus watched Mathius consider this but then the man did something unexpected. He turned to Katarina with a smile on his face and without dropping a smile tried to act all gallant towards the young girl.

"I believe its ladies first!" he remarked, moving over to Violetta's daughter and lifting her from alongside her mother, boosting her up towards the hole. Marcus moved to assist, allowing Katarina to stand on his shoulder as she looked doubtfully at the small opening.

"Now listen carefully," Mathius stated calmly. "It only looks really small. You can make it but you have to control your breathing as you fit through."

"Are you sure?" Katarina asked.

"Of course he is," Violetta encouraged, suddenly realising what was going on. "You go through first and into the dry and we will follow shortly after."

"What are you talking about?" Bernard snapped. "We will never..."

Violetta's mop swished around and swept Bernard from his feet, making him disappear beneath the churning water.

"Go on up darling." She smiled, a tear forming at the side of her eye.

Katarina started to wiggle through the small hole, her slight frame passing through as she passed first one arm and then the other up.

"I think I'm stuck." She panicked as her ribs tried to pass, her breathing actually working against her. "It hurts. I need to come back."

"Stop talking." Mathius stated sternly. "Take very small shallow breaths. You can do this, now when I say, I want you to breathe in as far as you can and we will push you up okay."

"Okay" came her timid scared reply.

"On three now..." Marcus warned. "One, Two, Three!" Mathius and Marcus shoved as hard as they could, drawing a shriek of pain from Katarina, then she popped through the hole safely into the cabin above.

There was some stumbling around above them as Katarina gathered herself together. Violetta moved up to Marcus and Mathius and put her hand on both of their shoulders.

"I will never forget this." She whispered. The three of them shared a look that spoke volumes without words. Then they looked up to see Katarina's anxious eyes looking down through the hole.

"Who's coming up next?" she asked in innocence. It took a moment for her to notice no one was moving to try. "Come on mother." She smiled. "Get Marcus and Mathius to boost you up."

"I can't fit darling." The words caught dryly in Violetta's throat. "None of us can."

"What do you mean?" there was a pause, and then her little hands came back through the hole, trying vainly to make the opening bigger. "No, no, no, no!" her cries became desperate.

Bernard struggled back over to everyone, fixing Violetta with a stony frown before looking up at the opening he knew they could never pass through.

"So that's it then?" he asked. "Are we just going to sit here and drown?"

"Do you have any other bright ideas?" Mathius snapped.

"Please don't argue." Marcus interceded. "It doesn't become any of us." He tried to close his ears to the cries coming from Katarina and the vision of her little hand stretched out to her mother who struggled to hold onto it and not lose balance, offering coos and reassuring sounds to calm her hysterical daughter.

"Maybe we can stop the water coming in the door?" Bernard whined. "Why doesn't someone try?"

"That's an excellent idea." Mathius replied icily. "But if you look the door is now under water."

Bernard glanced over and sighed.

"Well that's just great." He snapped.

"Why don't you run off now?" Violetta cried, stroking her daughter's hand. "Go find Thomas, tell him where we are. Then he can get help."

"Go find Thomas, ask for help." Katarina repeated it like a mantra, as she reluctantly let go of her mother's hand, her footsteps heard running across the ceiling above them.

"What can Thomas do?" Bernard moaned. "It will be too late by then."

"She sent her away so her daughter doesn't see her drown, you idiot." Marcus stated in a voice much calmer than he actually felt.

He pulled himself over to the table and helped Mathius and Bernard up alongside the sobbing chef. They struggled to lift Sherman and keep his head above the water as the table shifted precariously beneath them, threatening to send everyone back into the freezing seawater filling the room.

A candle fizzed out as the seawater doused it, followed by several more. The darkness closed in and all the primal fears the flickering light had kept at bay came flooding in too. Bernard started to cry. Marcus mouthed silent words of prayer, whilst Mathius stared silently at the rising water like a fighter trying and failing to stare down his enemy, in the knowledge the battle was now lost.

"I'm getting cold." Violetta confessed. "Please hold me. I don't want to die alone."

Marcus fought his own feelings of impropriety and tried to offer a comforting hug but still felt uncomfortable, despite the seriousness of their situation. Sherman's head barely kept above the water between them and as the level rose, their grip on him became all the more tenuous. Violetta's shakes from the cold water appeared to become contagious and soon they were all shaking as the cold seawater leached away the remainder of their body heat.

Bernard started to panic first, his movements becoming more violent and panicked as he tried to make the small hole above their heads wider for him to fit through. His efforts were to no avail and he started to make low whining noises in the base of his throat as he struggled to push the others away from the valuable breathing space so he would have the area to himself. There was a loud splash as Mathius pushed him away from the opening, leaving it clear with his muffled tones that any further attempt to be selfish would be a serious error to make. With the sailor removed, cool air came down through the hole from above but every one of them perched on the kitchen table knew it was a matter of moments before they slipped under and were lost.

Marcus tried to fight back the feelings of terror racing through his trembling frame. All the sights and smells within the small dark space they shared heightened in intensity. Heavy breathing from Violetta as she struggled to control her fear, a high-pitched explosive squeak as a swimming rodent got too close for Mathius's liking, the ridiculous golden earring in Bernard's right ear blinking and reflecting three bobbing points of light.

Bobbing points of light?

The monk tried to lift his hand to rub his eyes clear but his habit made it hard moving through the water and his body felt so heavy and cold. Everything was such an effort. His teeth were clattering like castanets and it was so hard to think. What was he trying to do again?

"They are down here!" came a small-excited voice from above the floundering group.

Bright light seared down through the hole and a very unexpected face appeared above them.

"Hello," said Ashe. "Whatever are you doing down there?" His light wobbled and threatened to fall off, but the Halfling swiftly grabbed it and pulled the miner's hat back firmly on his head, his infectious grin beaming down at everyone as if this was something the little man saw every day.

Another beam of light appeared at the edge of the hole and the stern face of Commagin appeared, he tutted loudly and held his hand under his chin as if in thought, then he turned to the third hat-wearing member of the group and a loud clattering started out of sight of the paddling crew below.

Katarina poked her head over the hole too.

"I couldn't find Thomas." She apologised down to her mother. "But I found Commagin and Barney, they were pulling Ashe out of Rauph's cabin and they said they could get you out."

Violetta laughed and then spluttered as seawater passed into her mouth, causing a coughing spasm that failed to crush the lightness she now felt in her soul.

"It's always the way." Mathius stated, squinting up at the lights and the group of excited faces above him. "You find somewhere nice and private for a swim and then someone always tells a friend and suddenly everyone wants to join the party."

A loud rasping sound started to the left of the hole and something started to bite deeply into the floorboards, swiftly followed by a colourful curse as a metallic snap echoed down through the hole.

"It's too thick, you dolt! Commagin muttered, clearly dressing someone down. "You need something stronger, like this!"

"Cover your eyes," Ashe warned, glancing over at something out of sight. "Commagin will have you out in a second. I must warn you it will be a bit loud!"

There was a deep cough, a rasping choke, then a mighty roar, accompanied by the smell of something burning in the air, the ceiling above them began to shake and then sawdust started falling through the flue opening like confetti. It drifted softly down covering the four bedraggled crew with a warm light brown dust that coated their heads and eyebrows in seconds.

A large part of the ceiling fell in with a crash; causing a wave within the galley that swamped those awaiting rescue, threatening to throw them from their table and back into the water. As they gasped in unison, the sawdust in the air set them coughing again.

"I told you it was loud." Ashe shouted down through the enlarged hole, his miner's helmet had now disappeared, his head looking ridiculous with hair sticking out everywhere and an oversized set of goggles perched on his nose; his grin, as always, wide and enthusiastic.

Heavily muscled arms reached down and hoisted the shivering group out of the freezing water and up onto the floor of the cabin. Bernard found himself beaming in the light from the three miner's lamps; his grin infectious to all around as they hugged each other and congratulated themselves at escaping what had been almost certain death.

"Well that's the last of that then." Commagin looked at the tool in his hand and sighed as the whirling toothed blade spluttered, whined and finally died. "Without petroleum it is useless, just so much waste." The roar in the room faded, leaving the groups ears still vibrating softly. "It was a good chainsaw too." He continued to himself. "Not a patch on the classic Mark III experimental *Shredder* from Sol 237, 400 gas cartridge rounds a second, with saw-tooth bayonet attachment but as a chainsaw this one's never let me down until now."

Mathius, overhearing, looked at Ashe totally bemused. The Halfling shrugged his shoulders in response.

"I have no idea what he's on about either!" he shouted, still slightly deaf from the noise. "But you have to admit it's a lot of fun being on this ship!" He pulled the goggles away, and pushed them up into his sawdust coloured hair, leaving his face looking like a strange racoon with large red rings around his eyes.

Barney walked over with a stern face and slapped a piece of paper into Marcus's hand, then he turned and set about collecting the heavy cutting tool from Commagin as the Dwarven engineer stood reminiscing. He lowered it into a heavy bag on the floor and motioned to Ashe as he hoisted his end and started tapping his foot impatiently until Ashe took the hint and picked up the other end.

"Have to go now." Ashe grinned enthusiastically. "We have more people to rescue. Apparently it's all part of the job description." With a quick check in Commagin's direction, the three comical characters set off through the open cabin door leaving Violetta, Marcus, Mathius and Bernard thanking their lucky stars they were still alive.

Violetta swiftly resumed command, indicating that Sherman be put to bed in any dry cabin they could find. Bernard swiftly helped lift Sherman with the chef's help and they exited through the door with Katarina fussing behind.

Marcus stared at the paper in his hand with bemusement then started to laugh at the absurdity of what he held. Mathius walked over and slapped him wetly on the shoulder.

"What's so funny?" he enquired, gesturing at the piece of paper that Marcus was finding so entertaining. "What did he give you?"

"Well you won't believe this unless you see it with your own eyes." Marcus continued to chuckle. He handed the wet paper over and watched Mathius begin to read it.

The fighter's intense gaze and stern visage cracked almost instantly. Then he started to laugh, something he recognised had not happened in as long as he could remember.

"I think we may have to ask the captain for a loan." Marcus continued to laugh. "I don't have any money for this kind of thing."

Mathius tried to wipe a tear from his eye and simply smudged sawdust in there instead. The pain was instant but for once, the fighter did not care. He was alive, he was free, and he was apparently in debt to the engineering department of the *El Defensor* to the tune of 30 silver florins. The paper invoice in his hand was most specific.

Payment clearly requested for 'Wun Prufeshunol Rescew'.

"Maybe we can split the bill five ways?" Mathius howled, sending Marcus into further spasms of laughter.

Chapter Thirty-Six

Colette could feel her fingers slipping.

She hung suspended over the deck, her hands slick, stubbornly refusing to find purchase on the slippery portion of deck she struggled to hold onto. She could hear the roar of the elemental gathering itself mere inches below her feet and could feel the portal screaming and sucking at her from below. Terror coursed through her slight frame at the sounds of the snarling creature preparing to rip her apart when she fell. The thought of freefalling through the portal below into the unknown, made her throat dry and her tongue feel like it was made of sandpaper.

As she looked up, struggling to focus through the red haze blurring the edge of her vision, she noticed the thin burning taper she had earlier been using to control the monster slowly start to slip over the edge of the deck towards her. The fragile spiral of smoke that had been acting as a magical leash spluttered at its exposure to the elements. She tried to focus harder, fighting to pull herself up, because she knew if the taper went out the elemental's leash would be broken and it would be free to wreak havoc within the ship.

The rain soaked timber she held started to slice into her hand, drawing blood and making her grip even more precarious. Colette looked on powerless as the taper tipped further out into the void. She tried to hold her breath, as if by not breathing she could prevent the impossible but the pain in her hand made her breathing come in stuttering gasps whether she liked it or not.

The elemental swirled lazily beneath her feet, its elongated form sprouting claws to anchor itself firmly around the edge of the portal. It knew that finally its tormentor was powerless and was relishing the thought of the kill to come. Its eye swirled to the centre of its mass below where the terrified mage hung and it set about forming a mouth from its cloudlike structure ready to catch her when she fell.

Colette's heart sank as she realised no one could save her and this was how she would meet her end. She closed her eyes and prepared for the agony to come as her hand finally slipped free.

"Got you!" grunted a voice from above, as a pair of firm hands snared her wrists as she fell.

Colette looked up into the eyes of her unlikely saviour just as he took her full weight. Kerian's smile turned to one of shock as her downward momentum pulled him off his knees to smack his chin comically into the deck. He shook his head to clear the stars dancing across his vision and flashed another roguish grin. With a distinctly inelegant grunt, he tried to shift himself out of the obvious discomfort at taking her weight and tried to pull her back up. However, as he did so, his arm brushed the balanced taper, sending it spiralling past Colette, to tumble through the portal.

The elemental roared as the magical tether failed. Its teeth snapped together in anticipation as it slowly gathered its form beneath it, ready to push itself up and engulf its prize.

"Don't worry," Kerian gasped breathlessly, struggling to secure his tenuous grip on Colette's slippery blood slicked hands. "I've got you and I won't let you fall." The deck below him cracked ominously threatening to make the old man's statement a lie, yet Colette realised he was determined to keep her safe and at that moment if he had told her she could fly she would have believed him.

Another loud crack sounded and Kerian's look of reassurance turned to one of concern as he found himself starting to slide over the edge after his charge. His feet struggled to find something to hang on to, some way to get to his knees and gain leverage to aid his rescue but there was nothing within reach to prevent his own body painfully slipping over the precipice after her. This had seemed a great idea at the time but his failure to whisk the mage to safety was slightly disheartening. If only he was young again and had more strength in his arms!

He gritted his teeth and tried to will his body to have the texture of rough sandpaper rather than the wet slippery outfit he wore. A button snagged painfully then pinged off into the air and his body continued to slide. This was getting worse by the second. The elemental's teeth snapped together, catching Colette's heel of her boot and setting her swinging wildly in Kerian's hands. She looked so slight but somehow weighed so much!

"Please try and stay still!" He grunted, hands slipping as he tried to arrest his slide, eyes sweeping the deck below desperate for someone to notice his situation and come to a speedy assistance.

Figures darted around the deck below him, He could make out Scrave, Thomas and Aradol running about trying to knock the elemental from its perch above the portal but the creature just made new limbs and swatted them aside like flies. Bits of debris slid, rolled and crashed towards the portal, caught up in the suction, gone from this world and never seen again. As he watched, a large barrel bounced towards Aradol and almost clipped the young man on its one-way trip to oblivion.

Something moved at Kerian's hip, snapping his attention back to his predicament. He glanced alarmingly at his scabbard, only to watch his precious sword start to slide free as gravity took hold.

"Oh come on!" he shouted aloud. "What do I have to do to get a break around here?" His hands started to slip from the mage's wrists.

"Don't you drop me Kerian Denaris! You hear me?" Colette shouted up at him from her precarious position.

"I can hear you just fine." Kerian grunted in reply. "But I really need you to be quiet right no..."

A loud snarl from below tore Kerian away from his concerns about both Colette and his sword, presenting him with a third problem.

The elemental had now gathered itself below Colette's swinging form, its nebulous swirling shape pressing right up close against the rippling surface of the portal. With another triumphant roar it rushed straight upwards, mouth wide open. Kerian could only look on in horror as the open maw moved up and around Colette's middle preparing to snap shut and slice her in two.

Thomas recognised the threat, yelling aloud as he hacked ferociously at one of the elemental's claws. Scrave, noticing his concern, resumed hacking at another. Ives swung his blade one handed at the creature's elongated torso, his white blade slicing effortlessly into the monster. Despite the weakness of his swing, it threw the merchant off balance. He dropped back to his knees and wrapped himself tightly around the exposed wooden beam, squeezing his eyes tightly shut whilst he waited for the world around him to stop spinning. He had done his part now and just hoped it would all soon be over.

A cry of anguish rose form the monster as smoke gushed from its inflicted wounds and the elemental dropped sharply back down towards the swirling portal as its body rushed to create new limbs to arrest its fall. Its teeth snapped shut as it fell; coming together just below Colette's feet.

A section of elemental whipped out, knocking Thomas from his feet and sending him tumbling towards the edge of the magical gateway. His leg slid over the edge, his boot rippling in the suction. The Elemental continued to struggle, with two limbs severed its outstretched new replacements flailed as they tried to grip, leaving it off balance at one end and at the mercy of the pull of the portal below. Its body started to sink through the magical opening, its upper limbs scrabbling and clawing at the edges of the hole, desperate to pull itself free and back into the world of the *El Defensor* and her crew.

"Just focus on me." Kerian ordered, as one of her hands slipped from his grasp and flailed in the air. Colette's eyes widened with fear, her terror clear to see as he gave another determined try to pull her up again but he had no way of gaining leverage and instead found himself sliding further over the edge. Out of the corner of his eye, he noticed the heavy hilt of his sword was sliding farther from its scabbard.

The world appeared to move in slow motion as conflicting emotions raced through Kerian's head. If he let go of Colette to save his sword, she was dead. She would fall to her doom. If he dropped his sword, it would suffer a similar fate; lost forever. He grunted again, veins standing out prominently on his forehead, his breath coming in laboured gasps as he willed with every part of his body to find some way of resolving his situation. He had to find some way of saving the two important things he had left in his life. He had already lost Saybier on this fool quest. He refused to lose anything else.

With a lurch, he slid further over the edge.

An ironic thought suddenly occurred to him. If he did not find some way to stop his own slide forward none of this was going to matter. He would end up suffering the same fate as both his sword and his charge, either ripped apart by the monster that was even now gathering itself again, or a one-way trip to another world where he would find himself at the mercy of a whole race of these terrifying creatures.

If he survived the fall, that was!

The exposed edge of the deck beneath him started to splinter loudly, making Kerian freeze in place. Then with agonising slowness, his perch peeled away below him. He slid forward another foot, dropping Colette even closer to the swirling death awaiting her. This was it, he was going over and there was no way to prevent it happening.

Something grabbed his leg with a crushing force, bringing him up sharp. The sudden stop serving to launch his sword fully from its scabbard. Kerian acted instinctively, sacrificing his two handed grip on Colette's wrist and using his freed left hand to lash out and try to deflect the path of the blade and save it. The uneven weight distribution pulled him even further over, eliciting a shriek of dismay from the mage as she dropped further. Whatever had hold of his leg had his eternal blessing but he did not have time to look and see who or what it was.

* * * * * *

Thomas joined Scrave hacking at the nearest of the elemental's claws in sheer desperation, trying to make it lose what balance remained and drop it further into the portal. Yet despite all their ferocity, the creature stubbornly held on, gathering its form and preparing to lunge upwards and claim the life of the person responsible for enslaving it.

"We need to strike together!" Thomas screamed through the gale. Scrave nodded in agreement as the rain and sea spray lashed them. The Elf was struggling to focus, finding it hard to gather himself. He had a terrible headache and his vision was all blurred. Strike together; he tried not to laugh aloud at the request. He barely had the strength left in his arms to lift his blade let alone hit anything!

* * * * * *

Kerian's sword arced length over length as it fell.

Watching his sword fall in slow motion, Kerian willed with all his soul that it would somehow deflect from its path and not plummet through the rippling portal but it was certain that its path of descent could end only one way. His sword was lost. There was no way he could save it. Colette slipped in his hand, making him focus back on her tear streaked face. He struggled to pull her up so he could hold her securely for the limited time they had remaining but it felt like he was tearing his right arm from his shoulder!

Aradol came out of nowhere, extending his arm, hand open wide as he raced across the deck and physically threw himself over the rippling portal, diving between the sucking gateway and the monster rampaging mere feet above it. Thomas stood open mouthed as he watched the youth disappear beneath the swirling elemental before coming out the far side to snatch Kerian's tumbling sword inches from oblivion. The momentum of his jump was just enough to clear the far edge of the portal and skid across the deck on the far side, landing in an undignified heap.

Brilliant white light flared, turning night into day as the runes on Kerian's blade lit up at the young man's touch. The rain falling around him appeared to turn as bright as snow as the sword's eerie light gave each drop a brief burst of its blaze. Kerian closed his eyes at the unexpected glare, his mind racing even as his arms continued to scream at the punishment they were taking. How could his sword flare white? It had always been violet in his hands. It did not make sense!

Aradol did not hesitate or allow surprise to register at this startling development, wielding the sword like an extension to his arm, slashing into the elemental left and right as it turned all of its attention towards him and the deadly threat he represented.

* * * * * *

Thomas looked up at the youth suddenly blazing with light; he looked like a vision of a holy paladin, a stalwart foe of darkness, cleaving the demons away before him. It took mere seconds for the awe to pass before Thomas realised that with Aradol now armed, this opportunity needed acting on immediately. He signalled frantically towards Scrave, who appeared to squint and look clueless, before recognition finally swept across his Elven features. With a nod, they commenced their own furious assault in time with Aradol's unexpected but extremely welcome intervention.

Two claws severed with a ghostly howl from the elemental, dropping its rear half back down through the portal's sucking surface. The elemental's grip on the other side of the portal started to slip free, the claws gouging deep scars into the deck as the creature slipped further through. Aradol swung Kerian's sword again, severing tendrils that were shooting out from the elemental's body as it struggled to keep in place. All the young fighter could do was grit his teeth and keep swinging and that was exactly what he intended to do!

* * * * * *

Kerian opened his eyes, blinking furiously to clear the glare that Aradol had seared into his retinas, little red images of the waiter danced across his vision as

Colette slipped again. He tried to catch her but his fingers were now numb with the strain.

"I'm sorry!" he gasped, "but I can't hold you anymore." His hands slipped on her skin bruising her wrists as she slowly slipped through. His hands finally closed together on nothing and Kerian's heart broke as she fell.

Colette screamed as she dropped, her arms flailing, robes billowing. There was only a split second left for her to dispel the magic she had created. Everyone who had struggled so hard to save her held collective breaths as she plummeted towards the ruined deck. She had no choice, whether the elemental was gone or not, she had to say the words to close the doorway.

The portal shimmered, rippled and then bulged upwards obscenely as the elemental tried to launch itself back through, the force of the attempt deflecting Colette off to the side and away from the ruined area below Kerian's perch. She took a deep breath and shouted the word to end her spell. The portal rapidly shrunk to a small dot and then disappeared with a loud crackle just as Colette hit the deck. The elemental, half in this world and half in the next imploded with a loud pop as the portal sheared it clear in two like a horizontal guillotine, the last pieces of scented smoke making up its body in their world dissipating and scattering in the storm.

Kerian sighed with relief as he saw Colette tumble onto the solid deck but before he could congratulate himself on a successful rescue, the deck finally gave way beneath him, he slipped forwards, arms wind milling and clothes askew but instead of falling, he felt himself impossibly lifted into the air. He swung around desperately trying to see what had hold of him and came face to face with an enthusiastic but slightly damp smelling bovine face.

"Oh Rauph." Kerian sighed from his undignified inverted position. "If you weren't so ugly I could kiss you!"

"No thanks." Rauph replied. "I don't think that would be proper and you are really not my type." He held a straight face as long as he could, before breaking into his wrinkly misshapen attempt at a smile.

"Could you perhaps put me down now?" Kerian asked meekly.

Thomas ran across the ruined deck and helped lift Colette to her feet. She brushed her hair from her eyes and smiled despite the terror she had just experienced.

"That was close." She sighed.

Thomas pointed down at her right boot drawing her attention to the fact that the toe end had been sheared clean away as the gate closed exposing her little pink toes to the air.

"I think it was closer than you thought."

"Oh damn!" Colette moaned looking down at her toe and wiggling it. "I loved those boots!"

The whole ship slammed to the side as another swell hit. Thomas staggered trying to support Colette and himself as the ship's list increased dramatically. He looked back up at Rauph and realised instantly that the Minotaur had abandoned his post.

"What are you doing!" he yelled, as the ship started to turn sideways beneath them, exposing the *El Defensor's* flank to the rise and fall of the waves. "I told you to man the helm!" That damned Minotaur had the brains of an ox sometimes! "Tell me you left someone in your place!" Rauph's suddenly meek body language spoke volumes.

Scrave ran over with Aradol and came to a stop alongside Thomas, swaying slightly as the ship came about. The captain swiftly indicated what was going on to his colleagues, even as his mind raced at what to do next to ensure the ships survival. There was a piece of grit in his mind's eye slowly turning into a pearl of an idea but it was insane to consider such a scheme.

"I thought the ship was running smoother." Scrave quipped. "Now that Rauph has stopped steering that is!"

"Get back to the helm!" Thomas yelled gesturing at his bovine navigator. Rauph shrugged slightly hurt and moved to respond to the captain's orders, taking several steps before he realised he still had someone in his hand. He dropped Kerian unceremoniously to the deck and headed back to his station without a word, stung at the captain's anger towards him.

The ship continued to list steadily to port. Thomas mentally calculated the fact that if the ship slanted more than forty degrees the galleon would be unrecoverable. They needed calm seas and fast.

The captain knew where those seas lay but he was likely to be swapping one danger for another. His eyes scanned the remaining sails on the only functioning mast left on the ship. The topsail and mainsail were already secure, reefed in by the brothers, the spars naked and skeletal against the sky, like a deciduous tree in winter months. Lightning forked, dancing across the cloud backdrop and using it like a stage to display its power.

Kerian finally made his way down to the deck and ran to Colette sweeping her from her feet and hugging her tightly with relief.

Thomas turned away, feeling uncomfortable in witnessing their closeness from the ordeal. He wiped the rain from his face, taking in the remnants of his ship. The ruined deck, the splintered main mast, the torn sails and tangled rigging that was threatening to take his ship to the bottom of this unforgiving cruel sea.

As other crewmen rushed up to congratulate them, Thomas finally completed his assessment, tucking his hands under his arms to try and get some warmth back into them as he continued to mentally chew over the options available. Waves continued to crash across the ship and with each breach more water flooded the inside of the ship increasing the list further.

They had no choice. There was only one place to go.

What about the Scintarn hounds and the master that used them. Could he allow his crew, in the state they were and with the ship this unseaworthy, even near such a terrifying creature? A mistake now could kill them all. This decision had to be the right one for the sake of the ship and crew but he was not sure what to do. The image of multiple fans in the darkness flittered chillingly in his mind.

He turned back towards the helm in an attempt to remove his doubts, looking at Rauph wrestling with the wheel, then beyond him to the tempestuous seas. Then he paused and looked again, his eyes taking in the wall of darkness he could see barrelling towards them. What was that? A lightning flash threw the image into clarity, the dark green surging wave towering high above his ship made his blood run cold.

The decision was no longer his to make.

Thomas threw his fellow crew into confusion, his look of horror in complete contrast to the glee they all felt. He started snapping orders, shouting and making them jump at his sharpness. He grabbed Abeline, gestured wildly and sent the man off to retrieve what would be required.

He turned to Kerian and Colette and pushed them apart. Kerian turned angry at the fleeting moment now lost and the apparent rudeness in Thomas's actions but the Captain had no time to care. He grabbed Colette by the shoulders and looked into her eyes with a steel gaze that urged she take notice.

"You need to open the gate!"

"Are you insane" Scrave hobbled over not believing what he heard. Thomas had finally lost his mind. "We have no gems to complete the passage. We would be stuck midway, at the mercy of..."

Thomas hesitated for a second as his mind raced to consider options. He shook his head. There was none. However, what if...

"Colette can you keep the gateway open if we have one gem with enough power?" He shouted over the storm.

"I don't know." Colette replied wearily, "I'm so tired. If I have to keep the spell going, I would be unable to do anything else. I would not be able to help if anything went wrong. If something breaks my concentration the gate will close and we will be trapped."

"I will make sure you are guarded." He promised. "Nothing will happen to you..." His hesitation was accidental, not meant to show how scared he was of his own choices but his racing mind was acting on instinct. He glanced back over his shoulder towards the wall of water rushing towards them but for the moment, the threat was out of sight, masked by the other waves surging over the side. Out of sight, but its menace was still there racing icy fingers up the Captain's spine.

Abeline ran up gasping, a bag clutched tightly in his hand. Thomas was already leading Colette over to a sheltered part of the deck that was still intact despite the destruction around it. The area once contained barrels of supplies and had a small lean-to over the top, keeping the worst of the rain away. The barrels had now gone, sucked into the swirling portal but the empty deck was perfect for what they needed.

Colette gathered herself and sat cross-legged on the floor before she tipped the bag out revealing the snake eye gem from the temple in Catterick. It was the largest and most energy filled gem they had but it was not enough to travel through the ships graveyard and out the other side. It would only have the power to open one gate but that was all Thomas needed.

"There is plenty of power here." Colette confirmed weighing the gem in her hands, "but you need to keep me safe. If my concentration breaks it's over."

"Please just hurry." Thomas snapped. "We don't have time to second guess this"

"Are you sure?" Her voice wavered, apprehension clear in her tone at what they were about to do.

Thomas's grim look confirmed he was set to take this course and the risks it entailed.

"You can't do this Thomas." Scrave interjected, waving his arms in agitation. "We could all die. Remember what happened last time."

"Do you think I don't" the Captain snapped. "But I have no choice." He grabbed Scrave roughly by the arm and spun him around gesturing off past the guardrail and out across the sea at the approaching danger.

Scrave squinted into the darkness trying to see what the captain was gesturing towards but his Elven vision was still recovering from his fight with the invisible assassin.

Thomas turned from him and focused on Colette.

"I need you to do it now!" he ordered. "Open the gate."

"By the Gods." Scrave cursed behind him as the danger came into view.

"Do it now or we all die!" Thomas reinforced his command.

The ship groaned beneath them, in time with a mighty roar, which snatched Thomas's attention over towards the helm. Rauph had now spotted the danger rushing towards them and was trying to turn the ship into the wave but the drag from the sails and rigging and the heavy flooding was making steering the ship practically impossible. A sinking brick would have responded better to his valiant efforts.

With a grunt Rauph fell to the deck, the ship shuddered beneath them and slowly reverted to its side-on wallow. Thomas watched as Rauph regained his feet and spun the now useless helm. The rudder had snapped; the ship now free to move as it wished. They were dead in the water.

Other crewmen continued to hack at the ruined sails, trying to cut free the tangle and at least bring the ship upright but the *El Defensor* continued to swing about like a piece of driftwood. The spars from the downed sail dragging into the sea and causing further resistance.

Kerian stood back from everyone else, holding onto the guardrail as he watched the crew move urgently about. His thoughts lingered on the fleeting moment of intimacy he had shared with Colette. He wished it could have gone on for much longer.

Aradol arrived, shattering his romantic notions by offering him back his sword: He bowed with a flourish and offered the blade hilt first across his arm. As Kerian took it back, the weapon's magical runes lit up once more but this time with the normal violet nimbus he knew, leaving the warrior with questions he had no way to answer. Why had the blade gleamed white with Aradol but not with him?

Shouts started to rise from the crew as they realised all was not well.

Colette struggled to put them from her mind and concentrated on the spell they required, even as the whole ship started to move ominously towards the threat bearing down on them. She started to chant and took time to wink mischievously in Kerian's direction but he looked lost in a world of his own and to her disappointment failed to notice.

The ship started to slant upwards on the right, bringing the ship back to an even keel, before it agonisingly started to list the other way as the galleon started to encounter the base of the rogue wave coming towards them.

"Is that a tsunami?" Ives asked Thomas, his curiosity peeking in an attempt to forget his recent near brush with death and his less-than-heroic need for rescue from his earlier perch.

"No," Thomas replied, using the question to calm his own jitters. "That's a common misconception. That is a rogue or killer wave. Tsunamis are rarely felt this far out at sea, they only get big close to shore. This is something else, so we need to leave.

"This is a very good idea." Ives nodded enthusiastically and then looked around the ship at the undulating sea about them. "But Thomas, I don't see where we will be leaving to."

"Just hold on tight." Thomas warned. "The speed that thing is bearing down on us we may arrive more quickly than usual."

Ives took a glance at the now visible wave, its tip curling with white spume vivid against the dark green sky. A roaring was filling his ears above the crashing sounds of the storm.

"I would like us to arrive faster if possible." He conferred but Thomas had already left shouting warnings to the crew to grab on tightly.

Colette finished the last chant and the jewel in her lap beginning to shimmer as the spell took form. Over to port, the sky suddenly split asunder. A piercing beam of light slammed down from nowhere into the sea as if someone had just opened a crack in the sky.

Massive glowing pictograms shrieked across the vertical beam of light as if drawn by a large invisible hand. Symbols with meaning only comprehended by the ships young mage, overlaid the initial patterns, then the beam of light slowly started to widen, impossibly splitting apart to let the sea around them rush through.

Kerian shaded his eyes in shock at the brightness, what in the name of Adden was happening now? He looked on as the bright light faded and a sickly offensive smell of something rotting started to waft across the ship. As his eyes adjusted, he was aware there was something beyond the light and he narrowed his eyes to try to glean as much information as he could regarding their destination.

There was a pallid yellow green sky and an island of some kind in the distance that made the hairs on his arms stand up. Past the island and its unusual geography of sharp lines and un-natural valleys and mountains, the misty horizon appeared to consist of never ending archways as far as the eye could see, towering into the sky, impossibly high, structurally unsound but with the impression they had been there for a very, very long time.

Whatever that place was, he suddenly realised he did not want to go there. His instincts screamed this place was somewhere he should not be. They should take their risks with the rogue wave thundering towards them rather than face this.

The *El Defensor* continued to list but the drag of the sails in the ocean now started to act in their favour, taking the lead in a musical waltz that only the galleon could hear as it turned the ship around so the prow now faced the supernatural gateway before them.

Scrave ran up alongside Thomas.

"Are you sure we are doing the right thing?" He screamed above the roar of the wave. "Will you really take us back to that hell?"

"Just hold on." Thomas snapped. "And pray this isn't a one way ride." He looked back across the ship, thinking about all the people on board that now looked to him to give them a fighting chance to live.

"Brace! Brace! Brace!" The call was taken up all over the ship as crewmen bowed their heads and uttered silent prayers to their gods for what they knew was to come. Only the newer crew, such as Aradol and Kerian dared to watch as the wave finally slammed into the *El Defensor* and flung her forwards towards the opening Colette had created.

Rauph let out his own ear-splitting roar of defiance as the wave crashed down upon them pushing the weary galleon through the gateway with the speed of a bullet. Kerian had a chance for one big breath and then felt himself hit with the force of a hundred sledgehammers.

It was all he could do to hold on and wait for the inevitable.

Chapter Thirty-Seven

Even though Thomas had travelled through the ship's graveyard many times as Captain of the *El Defensor*, it still made his skin crawl being here.

The sky was a weak mustard green that drained the colour from everything over which it surveyed. The air had a taste to it that coated the back of the throat and lingered like something rotting in a musty tomb. The seawater was brackish and filled with massive mats of seaweed festooned with red and blue crawling crustaceans that Thomas did not intend to get close enough to identify but the most noticeable difference here to the open sea was that there was no breeze, not even a whisper. Everything was still and becalmed, as if the entire place was holding its breath ready to scream.

He used his eyeglass to examine the breach they had sailed through and allowed himself the briefest of congratulations of avoiding the tempest beyond. The ancient stone archway they had entered stretched up to the sky, towering over 100 feet above them. The pitted stonework, festooned with algae, sported gaps where the masonry had tumbled free in the past. The structure acted as a frame, allowing the captain to view the storm beyond as if through a window. The grey black sky still lit with occasional lightning forks and errant waves crashed through the opening into their unlikely sanctuary with explosions of yellow spray, making the mats of seaweed bob up and down like living carpets that caused the crab like creatures to scurry back and forth in agitation.

To either side of the opening, other crumbling archways of the same design stood like silent sentries, their shoulders touching further arches that stretched away to port and starboard as far as the eye could see. It was only through experience that Thomas knew the archways continued in a wide circle before finally joining again. Hundreds of gateways leading to lost worlds that he had no way of charting. It would have been easier if the landmarks around him stayed still so they could map the gateways but each time a portal opened water rushed in and slowly turned the mass of debris at the centre of the hub, making it impossible to plot with accuracy.

Thomas looked at all the closest dormant archways and the grey mist swirling beyond them. He could see the water surging under them, but as soon as the seawater hit the mist it became indistinct and visibility swiftly reduced to nothing. He had tried to row through an arch several years before, his dinghy attached to a rope so the crew could pull him back if he got lost and even though he had been sure that he was rowing in a straight line, within moments he had come out of the mist right back where he started. It had been a confusing experience to be sure.

It was clear that you only ever left the ships graveyard through an open portal. Otherwise, you were doomed to stay here forever... If you lived that long.

He swung the eyeglass around to take in the sorry state of his ship. Every exposed beam and splintered spar an open wound he needed to tend; each piece of tangled rigging or torn sail a gash on his psyche. He lingered for a moment on Colette, still kneeling in a magical induced trance, the gemstone still shimmering in her lap, a trace of magic swirling through the air and back over to the gateway they had passed through. Kerian stood guard alongside the roughshod shelter they had created for her, keeping her shaded from any rogue elements, a self-appointed guardian, with his heart worn on his sleeve. At least she did not have to worry about sunburn. There was no sun here to be of concern, just a sickly light and a terrifying darkness.

Continuing with his observations from the aft deck, Thomas shifted his attention to the prow of the ship. It looked far removed from the ship he knew. The speed with which they crashed through the gateway had caused the *El Defensor* to plough deep into the seaweed mats they normally took great pains to avoid when they journeyed this way. The ship had collected great strands of weed during its turbulent passage, piling up vegetation that had pulled taut across the ship tangling what rigging remained with lengths and lengths of clinging, thick slimy seaweed. His trapped ship was like an errant fly in a spider's web.

Thomas spared a thought for his crew. He had come so close to sinking his ship, miles from any land. At least here he had temporarily saved them but he knew they were still in a fix and that their future remained uncertain. He shivered, imagining the eyes of the creature he knew to be somewhere on the shadowy mass before him. Cold dead eyes, like those of a swaying cobra about to strike haunted his thoughts, the clicking of fans taunting Thomas on his current state of helplessness.

They really were helpless. Indeed, due to the incredible speed of their arrival, the ship had actually half ridden up onto the seaweed mats, suspending the ship above the waves. At least she was not sinking anymore. He supposed he should be thankful for small mercies at least!

However, Thomas's main concern with the weed was that he already knew a small handful of people could effectively cross the water on the matting. He had done it himself in the past, when he first decided to explore the centre of the hub. The problem was, if he could cross that way, something bigger and nastier could easily cross in reverse towards the *El Defensor*.

He dared not contemplate that nightmare.

His eye caught sight of the little animated figure of Ashe running around bashing red and blue scuttling creatures with clear disgust and horror on his face. Of course, when you had the weed, its occupants often came along free of charge.

Looking past the prow of the ship, he swung the telescope up to take in a massive corroded steel wall covered in barnacles which formed part of the hull of the vessel *Rubicon.* She was a large but now ominously derelict cargo ship. Peeling paint showed that she had hailed from Venezuela. The sheer size of the vessel dwarfed his own small ship and cast a large part of the surrounding sea into shadow.

The crew had stared in awe when they had first seen such a massive structure, especially something that large that actually floated but then they noticed the wreckage stretching out to either side of her and suddenly something as otherworldly as the *Rubicon* became quite mundane.

As far as the eye could see, there were shipwrecks: frigates, cargo ships, schooners, steamers, yachts, freighters, and brigantines, even some classifications Thomas had never seen before and had no hope of identifying. The whole melange piled together like the dropped contents of a giant box of toys; some vessels having crashed at speed, some impaled on one another, skeletal masts reaching to the sky, as if pleading for rescue from their terrible fates. Funnels of iron plate stood corroded, paint peeling, gaping holes clearly showing where the metal cancer of rust was slowly eating them away.

As the sea continued to flow unabated through the gateway behind him, the ships occasionally groaned at random times; a sound that sent shivers up Thomas's spine. He knew it was the sound of the shipwrecks as they slowly spiralled further and further into each other, grinding and shredding themselves painfully to pieces, like grains crushed on a miller's stone. Long forgotten ships from different times, places and worlds, all destined to die in agony within the ship's graveyard.

The *El Defensor* was once like these doomed vessels; trapped in the ships graveyard after being lost at sea along with two of her sister ships in the year 1750 off the coast of Georgia near the port of Savannah. She had once been part of a much larger Spanish fleet, her hold filled with treasure destined for the King of Spain, her name, now lost to history.

Thomas closed his eyeglass and ran his hand nervously through his dark hair. It was difficult to judge time in this place, but he knew when it became dark they would need to be as far away from the other ships as possible. He knew what came out at night, and he knew what they hungered for.

It was time to summon the crew.

* * * * * *

Thomas gathered the crew amidships, and listened as they described the ships status. It made grim telling. Her rudder was snapped, and required replacing, a repair which would take time and a possible visit to a dry dock. The main mast now lay across the deck, temporarily secured, with the possibility they could rig a temporary replacement with what remained serviceable. However, the rigging and sails remained a tangled and torn mess that would never see practical use again, the whole assembly required a complete rebuild.

Supplies of food were also low but fortunately they had enough fresh water for now. The beached ship, although a more accurate description was matted ship, required all the seaweed swamping it cutting away from the prow of the ship and where it lay under the hull. The galleon also needed re-floating and a channel carved out of the floating mats so they could manoeuvre her back out towards the archways and through the open portal once the storm beyond had abated. The longer they took to get seaworthy, the further away the gateway would become, as the movement of the hub slowly spiralled them away from their only means of escape. Speed would be of the essence.

The deck of the ship was declared a hazard to all, cabins had been destroyed, decking torn apart, splintered and in some places was entirely missing. A lot of timber was required to patch these holes, so after heated discussions with Commagin and Ridge they decided that a series of walkways be fashioned with planks from less travelled areas so the crew could move up and down the deck without jumping across the tops of the crossbeams and risking further injury.

Their current location also dictated the need for guards set around the clock, monitoring the skyline and the reed beds for any signs of movement or danger. Another guard rotation was required for Colette, because Thomas was all too aware that she was unable to defend herself whilst holding the gateway open.

He lay out his tasks to the crew, assigning teams to set to work on various problems they faced. Commagin's team would free the ship from the vines. Others would work on patching the ship. Thomas thought about the rudder and the lack of resources and then looked over at the ominous graveyard wreckage as it slowly turned and took them with it. Somewhere in that wreckage...

How ironic... The place he feared the most held the very things he needed.

Thomas looked up and stared at his colleagues. This was going to be a hard one to sell. Slowly with measured words displaying as little emotion as possible, he started to lay out his plan.

The less than enthusiastic response was as expected.

"Are you seriously kidding me?" Scrave erupted. "You want us to actually go into that mess and find the sister ships of the *El Defensor* and cannibalise them for spares!"

"It makes common sense," Thomas replied. "The parts will be compatible. You set up a relay system where the two dinghies can row back and forth and take the parts they need. But we need someone to find the ships and then guard them so our people can work safe."

Scrave looked at him with eyes that displayed nothing but disbelief, as if he was looking at a manic impersonation of the captain and that the real one would return shortly.

"What about him." He hissed loudly. "What if he comes and finds us. You know what he can do and what his hounds are capable of. You are expecting us to go into his lair!"

"You know as well as I do he only hunts at night. I suggest you stop moaning about it and get on with the task. Find the galleons, send one person back with the dinghy and then start stripping those ships as quickly and as quietly as you can."

"I'm taking Rauph." Scrave shot back. Thomas raised an eyebrow and allowed himself an inner smile. Someone needed to keep Scrave grounded and Rauph seemed to do that quite well.

"Talk to Commagin and get a shopping list, try and get as much as you can."

Rauph's head shot up from where he was playing with a torn stitch in his leather armour plate.

"Did someone say we could go shopping again?" he beamed eyes suddenly bright with an enthusiasm only Rauph could show. "I hope we have as much fun as we did last time."

"I pray to all that's holy we don't!" muttered Scrave as he led his companion away and headed towards the prow of the ship. Commagin also turned to leave, taking his small constantly chattering companions with him and waving his arms as part of an extremely animated discussion with his partners in crime.

* * * * * *

With a loud clatter of pipes and chinking of tools carried in large sacks, The *Commagin Underwater Diving Team* signalled to the whole crew they were about to be in business. Ashe was practically hopping about in excitement. All of these pipes and accessories; painstakingly designed especially for a job like this and he could not wait to see it all in action. He lowered his end of the large sack he carried and narrowly missed crushing Commagin's toe. The Dwarven engineer shot Ashe a stare that would have melted ore but the Halfling was so excited he barely noticed.

Barney came up behind them carrying the large white suit of armour with the strange golden visor. He placed it carefully on the deck, causing Ashe to stop looking at the mass of seaweed coating the front of the ship and turn to ask Commagin for what seemed like the hundredth time if he could be the one to wear the suit and go under water.

"Nope." Came Commagin's cool reply. "That's my apprentice's job."

"Yes." Barney butted in to reinforce the engineer's comments. "It is the apprentice's job." The little man suddenly paused as if realising what he had just said and who, in fact, the apprentice was.

"It takes years of training." Commagin continued. Barney tapped him meekly on the shoulder.

"What if the apprentice doesn't want to..."

"But I carried loads of tools and helped you rescue people below decks!" Ashe exclaimed.

"Only after we rescued you first." Commagin pointed out. "Anyhow Barney is the best person for the job."

"Maybe we haven't looked hard enough," Barney offered meekly.

"Anyhow Ashe, we need you to clear the side of the ship, free the weed away and then cut a hole in the seaweed mat so Barney can go below and free the ship. It's a dangerous job, not any Halfling can do it." Commagin smacked Ashe on the shoulder in a poor attempt to get the deflated thief to feel more positive.

A frayed harness came out of the main bag of tools, its webbing covered in oil and brownish red smudges. Ashe looked at it and swallowed hard. He was sure the stains looked like dried blood. Then Commagin reached into the sack again and hefted out a large pair of sharp shears with a loop on one handle for securing to the user's wrist, to prevent accidentally dropping it whilst in use.

The Halfling went to the guardrail and looked down at the mounds of seaweed tangled there and sighed loudly. This was not exciting at all. It looked like a massive, dirty, and smelly job. What was more, it would take ages to complete.

Something skittered across the rail near his hand causing Ashe to jump back. A now familiar looking red and blue crustacean glared at him with its beady black eyes and waved a claw threateningly towards him. The claw clacked ominously. There were hundreds of these things in the weed.

"Yuck!" Ashe remarked, taking in the knobbly shell and multi-segmented tail that clicked and clattered with every move.

"Oh collect some of those crabby creatures." Violetta shouted across the deck towards Ashe. He raised his eyebrows in surprise at the request.

"Why?"

"So we can make gumbo to feed the crew." Violetta shouted back. "These things will cook up fine."

Ashe looked at the monstrous creature before him, its feelers twitching in the air, its beady eyes watching his every move, and its claw clacking angrily in his direction.

"What if it decides to make gumbo out of me first?"

* * * * * *

Rauph positioned himself comfortably in the rowboat and swung the oars about in practice strokes that sent some of the less fortunate crawling crustaceans around them into near orbit. He watched as Scrave turned to prepare for his descent into the dinghy and paused at the handrail. The Elf looked at Thomas with searching eyes, still clearly uncomfortable about the task.

"Are you sure you want me to do this?" he asked.

"Would you rather we sit and do nothing and wait until darkness falls and what scares you comes to visit us instead?" Thomas replied, his eyes betraying nothing of the anxiety he really felt inside. "I know if anyone can do this it is you Scrave. I know you won't let me down." He paused debating whether to say anything further but then against his own better judgement he continued to speak.

"If you feel unable to do the task there are plenty of others here willing to go." Thomas was unaware his colleagues were now looking anywhere but in the direction of the Captain and his Elven crewmate. "I am sure you can nail a few planks of wood back into place or man the pumps to empty the ship. Commagin can even use you to cut away the slime and weed around the prow. If you think those tasks are more to your liking just let me know."

Scrave's venomous look made Thomas pause in mid threat but the captain was resolute. He needed to make a point here. He took a breath and then sealed the deal. "I could even ask Kerian Denaris to go if you prefer."

This barbed mental spur finally goaded Scrave into action. His face went white with rage, his lips tight, his fists clenched by his side. Thomas was not a fool, he knew there was something going on between the two of them and right now he was not too proud a man to exploit it.

"If an old man is considered good help Thomas, you must be truly desperate." Scrave looked at all the crewmembers that were currently examining their shoe leather or a particularly interesting piece of mustard cloud sky and then cursed softly, before sliding down the ladder to land lightly on the boat below.

"Remember Kavaliare's log states there are two galleons you can use for parts, *La Hechicera* or *El Conquistador*. Any spare lumber in good condition that we can use to fix the ship is a bonus, get as much as you can and set up the relay so we can get repairs done quickly. If you get into any trouble be sure to make a lot of noise."

Rauph caught a crab, giving a completely new meaning to the rowing term and sent another blue and red, clawed creature skipping across the weed mats before he fell flat on his back in the base of the boat, setting it all rocking wildly.

"Oh don't worry." Scrave shot back, trying to get his balance as the dinghy wobbled beneath him. "We will."

Thomas watched them skip across the seaweed for some time before his mind told him it was his time to leave too. He went to turn from the guardrail then paused.

"May your gods watch over you." He whispered after them.

* * * * * *

"I wish to be called Mathius from now on."

Marcus looked up from checking the wreckage of his cabin and stared into the face of the man he had now come to respect and even admire from their shared brush with death in the submerging galley. The frustration on the monk's face was clear to see.

"Have you lost something?" the assassin asked.

"Just a book." Marcus replied, lifting another ruined piece of ceiling and peering underneath just in case his precious tome remained buried beneath, immersed in the stagnant water collecting there. He lowered the splintered timbers with a sigh, he lost book was not there.

"I guess it's an important book to you." Mathius commented, maybe we can buy you a replacement when we next find a port."

"It's not that kind of a book." Marcus replied. "It's something I was supposed to protect." He shut his lips tight realising what he had carelessly said.

Mathius hit himself on the forehead with the palm of his hand.

"How could I be so stupid?" He muttered. "You are a bearer. You've lost *the* book." He threw his head back and laughed. "I guess you're fired then! The Abbot doesn't take well to bearers that lose their books."

Marcus's look of total dejection made Mathius pause and rethink his comments.

"Maybe we will find it as we clear up?" he offered, knowing the chances of such a discovery were slim indeed. He reached down into the cabin through the hole in the roof and offered a hand.

The monk looked at the offered hand then shrugged it away with a shake of his head and then he ran at the cabin wall. He pushed back lightly with his leading foot, placing his other foot higher on the other wall so he could deftly flip himself up through the opening. Marcus landed on his thigh, perched on the side of the hole as if he were sitting on a park bench, a weary grin on his face.

"Show off." Mathius laughed, before continuing with his original conversation. "I want to leave The Raven behind me."

"I can't see how you can do that." Marcus offered.

The assassin indicated a stack of wooden beams piled up and all ready to form the makeshift walkways. Shaking the heavy hammer that he held in his hand, he indicated they had work to do.

Marcus studied the pile of wood carefully then flipped one up with his foot and checked the sawn end.

"I love working with wood." He commented, positioning the wooden plank into position.

Mathius spun the hammer and slammed it down; embedding a nail into the wood at exactly the right angle, dropping it flush to its head with the one blow. Marcus reached for another length of wood, checking it for size, before wincing as his companion delivered another solitary strike, another nail perfectly seated.

"You shouldn't be asking if you can leave The Raven behind." Marcus added, reaching for another length of wood, "What you should be asking is if The Raven will leave you. Are you sure that you can keep such a killer in check? Do you have that kind of control? How can you forgive yourself for all the deaths you were responsible for?"

"Don't you believe in second chances?" Mathius replied. "After all, none of the crew ever saw me properly. Thomas has stated to the crew that I asked him if I could join the ship at our last port of call and no one ever doubts your captain. To everyone in my past life, I'm actually dead. I really can start again." He lined up another hammer shot. "And I'm always in control." He slammed the hammer down and the nail bent over to the side, causing Mathius to scowl.

"In control eh?" Marcus jibed, raising an eyebrow in question as he held the nail up for his companion to inspect.

The haunting shriek stopped them in their tracks. Heads turned as an archway about a quarter of a nautical mile to port flashed and crackled before opening to reveal another storm lit sky. Something flew through the now active archway trailing smoke and flames in its wake, wings holed and the whole contraption shaking.

Thomas took in the distressed scene from the aft deck and instantly recognised the flaming machine for a Cessna, possibly a Stationair. He had flown in one on a vacation in Canada another lifetime ago, wanting the opportunity to see the mountains from a unique, once in a lifetime, vantage point. He watched the plane splutter and cough as it struggled to gain altitude and remain in the sky.

"Aww Hell!" Thomas groaned as the plane passed overhead, clearly in trouble and by the sounds of the engine now out of control. It passed away into the distance losing altitude all the time, before disappearing out of sight behind the towering shape of the *Rubicon*. There was a loud crash and a plume of dark smoke rose into the sky.

"What's that?" Marcus asked.

Thomas looked at the rising smoke with concern but before he could reply, the monk grabbed his arm and gestured off to the side. The captain turned to see four parachutes popping open and gently gliding the passengers from the doomed plane out over the mass of shipwrecks.

"Mantoso, Aradol, Kerian, you're with me." He snapped.

"What do you need me for?" Kerian asked, torn between the captain's request and guarding Colette.

"A rescue party." came the ominous response.

Chapter Thirty-Eight

Grappling hooks and lines whistled up from the ballista on the *El Defensor's* deck to sail over the heads of the swiftly assembled rescue party, past the railing of the *Rubicon* to clang loudly out of sight. After taking up the slack, Thomas determined it was safe to attempt the climb up the almost vertical side of the gargantuan vessel.

Kerian found the whole thing hard going. The initial balancing act of walking carefully across the seaweed mats, trying not to put a foot wrong and plunge into the sea below was akin to climbing the rigging of the *El Defensor,* whilst not permitted to use his hands. The crustaceans snapping at his boots as he passed did not help with the fighter's confidence but when he looked at the over hand climb before him he seriously considered asking to go back to the ship. He was not twenty-one anymore!

His feet slipped on the algae coated metal surface several times and flakes of paint and rust snowed down on his head from Thomas's ascent above. The debris constantly threatened to irritate his eyes, clog his nose or slip into his mouth. It seemed an eternity before someone slipped their hands under his arms and pulled him onto the deck, where he lay for too short a time, gasping for breath and realising how out of shape he had become.

"Mantoso and Aradol wait here for a second." Thomas ordered, "Keep watch over the rest of the ship for signs of movement. If you see anything moving, hide."

"Where are you going?" Aradol asked. Thomas pointed up to the top of the *Rubicon* where the ship's bridge lay at a jaunty angle.

"I want to get up high so we can see where the parachutes came down." Thomas replied, squeezing Kerian by the shoulder and indicating a seemingly endless flight of steps running up the side of the vessel.

"Come on old man." Thomas jibed. "I'll race you to the top." Kerian groaned and got to his feet, his arms and legs already feeling like rubber and looked at the task ahead of him. It was clear Thomas was trying to make a point and all he could do was grit his teeth and go along with it.

The climb seemed endless, Kerian's booted feet falling heavier on each step taken, Ives Mantoso and Aradol becoming smaller with each turn as he ascended. He felt his heart would burst in his chest, his breath coming in ragged gasps before Thomas stopped and allowed him to catch up.

They had finally arrived at a gangway that ran around the side of the enormous structure. Thomas headed unerringly towards the front of the ship and examined the door to the bridge with a critical eye. Someone had tried to brace the door closed but by the amount of old blood stains splashed across the narrow opening and the ragged bullet holes he saw they had not been very successful.

"Let's see what the *Rubicon* can tell us." He remarked aloud, before shoulder barging the door.

Kerian was looking out along the deck of the ship, amazed at the sheer size of her and the multi-coloured huge box like objects that were scattered along her length adding to the *Rubicon's* lopsided state. It was like a box of wooden bricks after a child's tantrum, tumbled and piled upon each other, huge stacks collapsed, some with staved in sides, others crushed flat.

"What are you looking at?" Thomas asked, turning to see why he was not getting any assistance in his forced attempt to open the door.

"Those blocks all over the ship. What are they?"

Thomas looked over Kerian's shoulder.

"Oh those are cargo containers."

"Cargo?" Kerian looked bemused, "Why would anyone want to trade those?"

"It's not what they look like." Thomas offered, turning his attention back to the door. "Help me with this will you." He bent to force the door and Kerian joined him, grunting as he put his back into it. "As I was saying, it's not the containers but what is inside them."

"Could any of it be of use to us or the ship?" Kerian asked hopefully, his guard not completely down at the fact Thomas had purposefully taken him off away from anyone else.

"You're out of shape." Thomas jibed, as he noticed sweat starting to appear across Kerian's brow. "I guess our life at sea is agreeing with you too much. I'll have to tell Violetta to cut back on your portions."

"I'm not fat." Kerian snapped, wounded at the suggestion. "Well rounded maybe. Which helps when it is cold out at sea. Definitely getting older… Every single day! But not fat."

Thomas laughed at the response, just as the door finally squealed open. A swarm of flies flew out to greet them, accompanied with a stench that boded ill for anyone still in the room beyond.

Corpses littered the floor. Kerian took it in and winced, despite his past military experiences. These people had not died in battle; their bodies torn apart by something with sharp claws, the slash marks across their torsos all too evident. One outstretched hand had several puncture marks across the ravaged skin. Teeth and claws. Animals must have done this.

There was dried blood everywhere. This had not happened recently. Thomas struggled with the windows, desperate to open them and allow slightly fresher air to enter the bridge. His eyes flicked over the consoles and the scene around him.

"They holed up here." He remarked, taking in the empty tins of food and bottled water scattered around the floor. Thomas bent to pick up an empty brass casing on the floor and held it up to the light. "And they tried to make a stand. For all the good it did them."

Kerian was taking in the huge paw prints across the floor.

"What kind of an animal did this?"

"Scintarn hounds." Thomas replied, "Hunting for their master." He walked over to the helm and the captain's chair. Slumped on the floor beneath the console was the man himself: or what was left of him. Part of his skull was missing. Brain matter sprayed across the console and charts before him. Thomas did not need any crime scene training to determine this was a self-inflicted wound.

He leant down, now all business. Searching the man for anything of use. Cigarettes, nope gave them up when he came to this land, he did not want to get on that old horse again. ID, Alvereze, Santiago. St Christopher medal, equally ignored, as it did not appear to have given this traveller any luck. He moved the body to one side and took in the gunmetal blue finish of the Smith and Wesson Model 14 revolver on the floor beneath him. Its six-inch barrel and wood grip were unmistakable.

Thomas had seen this model before back at the precinct. The K-38 handgun, favoured by the Los Angeles police department in the 1960s and early 1970s, often turned up in 211's, robbery, or 245's, assault with a deadly weapon. Most handed in as curiosity pieces in arms amnesties, as the automatic pistol increasingly became the weapon of choice on the streets.

Kerian walked over a brass casing in his hand.

"What is this?" He asked. "They seem to be all over the floor. Is it some kind of currency?"

"It's not currency," Thomas replied. "Although people do use them to gain things they want."

"Bartering?" Kerian suggested.

"Violence." came Thomas's reply. There was a soft click, as he swung the barrel free and started examining the .38 special cartridges within the spindle. Three spent shells had the tell-tale impact markings where the gun's firing pin had hit home but three others appeared live. He snapped the barrel back with a well-practiced flick of the wrist and stared at the man at his feet with sudden distain.

"You were a coward, Alvereze." He remarked. "If you feel the need to go this way you save yourself the last bullet. Until then there are always possibilities."

He turned towards Kerian who was looking at faded photos on the wall.

"How do they paint these so realistic? Did they use magic?" he was asking himself.

"Why are you with us?" Thomas asked him. Kerian paused in his open-eyed exploration of the wonders around him and slowly turned back towards the captain. "What are you really after? The map you gave me was a lie. How long do you think you could have kept the pretence up before I noticed, another week... maybe two? Why is it that everyone in my life has to lie to me?" the last question was not aimed at Kerian but the fighter felt the barbs just as keenly.

He considered a reply, his mouth suddenly dry but one look at Thomas's scowling face told him he would have more luck trying to drink dry the ocean on which they sailed.

"Let me explain..."

"I don't want to hear any more tales." Thomas cut him short. "Do you realise the mess you have got us into? The dangers we face simply being here?" He gestured to the dead lying about them. "This is nothing. If he finds us here, if he tracks us down. You will wish you were one of these people rather than the horror you will face."

"But Marcus is the problem. He wouldn't let me..."

"Do you fear discovery so much that you would try to condemn another crewman for your actions?" Thomas questioned. He had located the ship's log and started flicking through the pages, noting the ship's headings and activities.

"It is not me you need to fear." Kerian replied. "Marcus has a darker secret than both of us."

"I find that doubtful," Thomas shot back, his mind trying to imagine Marcus in any sinister light at all. He stopped at the last journal entry and confirmed his suspicions. The ship's destination listed as Bermuda, their final heading taking them right through the Sargasso Sea. Apparently, fine weather and calm seas lay ahead. If only Captain Alvereze had known.

A howl rose from outside, answered by another. Thomas cursed at the interruption and pulled the eyeglass from his waistcoat, placing it to his eye. He had forgotten the reason they were up here. The parachutes!

"This discussion isn't over." He warned.

"It is for me." Kerian shot back, heading for the open door and the stairs to the deck below.

Thomas mentally kicked himself; he needed to sort this out. He needed to find out what angle Kerian was playing. He needed to fix his ship, needed to get away from this place. It was putting him on edge, making him jittery.

He moved to the open window, finding the height of his position gave an incredible vista over the shattered and ruined vessels laid before him. There was smoke off to starboard, clearly marking where the doomed Cessna had fallen from the sky.

No, the parachutes were not over near the plane. He swung the eyeglass swiftly over the panorama of shipwrecks, taking in ragged sails, corroded hulks, a sad steamer ship on her side, lengths of seaweed dangling from her stern like a set of vivid green curtains, drawn to protect her modesty.

Movement caught his eye; he swung the eyeglass to bear, noting the ancient naval vessel from which it had originated. Someone was desperately trying to free themselves from their parachute but it had caught up on the foremast, wrapped around the main royal staysail and they were swinging wildly trying to grab the yard and stop spinning. He strained to focus more clearly and noticed that below where the man swung a colleague was trying vainly to reach him.

Another howl echoed through the open window. Thomas swiftly panned his eyeglass away and noted the black canine shapes of the Scintarn hounds he knew would be there, pairing off then re-joining again as they leapt from ship to ship closing in on their prey. The pair were oblivious to the fate closing in around them. He had to warn them; had to try to save them.

He swung the eyeglass again, scanning rapidly for any other chutes as there were still two unaccounted for. There! He stared hard at the figure through the glass; this passenger was much smaller in height compared to the other people he had seen. The harness disengaged, dropping the passenger to the deck. Clearly, this person was quite animated. A hat thrown angrily to the deck revealed a head of short-cropped hair, hands placed on hips to draw the captain's attention to clothes fashioned more to accentuate a figure than functionally cover it. Dark thigh high boots and aviator glasses completed the picture. Could this be the pilot?

Thomas lowered the glass from his eye now this was interesting. He replaced the eyeglass and noticed the final chute; further back and tangled in the decaying mast and rigging of a tall ship. The man underneath was struggling to free himself as the canopy tangled and tore, before he dropped from sight between two ships. If he was lucky he had hit the water but how long he remained lucky was yet to be determined.

He had seen enough. Thomas secured his eyeglass and made for the cabin door, slipping the Smith and Wesson revolver into his waistband as he went. He raced down the stairs, taking them several at a time and causing his companions to look up at the loud noise he was making. Kerian turned in alarm, reaching for his sword before he realised that the man flying down the steps towards him had no intention of harm but rather was intent on talking to his crew and acting with all matter of urgency.

"Mantoso, Aradol!" Thomas shouted, "Two people in that direction. Go!" He indicated a mass of dark corroded vessels set at angles to each other and listing badly on the horizon. The algae coated hulks streaked with terracotta rust, showed signs of abandonment for some considerable time. From this low vantage point, the only sign of the chutes was the tall mast from which ragged remains of one chute still hung limply.

"One fell from the tall ship, possibly into the sea, the other looks like a pilot." Thomas shouted after them as they set off without question. "The hounds don't seem to have located them yet. Get to them fast and save them, if daylight fades find somewhere to hide and don't come out until dawn... or what counts for dawn around here."

Ives waved acknowledgement with his white sword, signalling he understood and set off in the direction indicated. Aradol followed slightly behind him as they jogged across the *Rubicon's* huge deck towards the tall ship in the distance.

Kerian looked expectantly at Thomas waiting for the captain to continue with his earlier discussion but a swift shake of the Captain's head indicated they had bigger problems to sort out. He simply pointed to the other side of the *Rubicon* and ran past gesturing that Kerian follow.

The two teams split up, heading off in their separate directions, Thomas and Kerian towards the hounds and the greater danger, Aradol and Ives towards the other parachutists in a bid to bring them to safety.

"How do we know when it is getting dark?" Aradol asked, running lightly up alongside his shipmate. "There's no sun here."

"Oh that's easy." Ives replied. "When it is night I am normally in a beautiful woman's company, her body wrapped tightly about me." He raised a grin as he jumped over an old coil of rope on the deck. "I find it helps me sleep so well."

"So that's why I hear you snoring so loudly at night then." Aradol replied, grinning at the closeness they shared. "But I have a secret to tell you. Commagin is not a girl."

"But those silky whiskers are just like my first wife's" Ives joked, vaulting the rail and sliding down the deck of a wooden schooner.

"I can't wait to hear about your second." Came Aradol's reply.

* * * * * *

The oars dropped into the sea, scooting the little dinghy across the water like a pebble tossed from a hand. Rauph appeared to be really enjoying himself, settling into the strokes and pulling back so hard the rowlocks groaned at each row.

Scrave looked around scanning for threats but his search was not an exhaustive one. From this far out, in the channel free of weed near to the archways there was not many things to be worried about. Even so, he kept a keen eye on the shipwrecks, looking out for the sleek black shapes he had sworn to remain as far away from as possible.

"Clyde, Saha Bank, Wildcat, Parta Noce..."

"What are you talking about?" Scrave asked. "You are making no sense."

"Sandra, Doris Hamlin. Vreeland." Rauph continued, happily speaking aloud words that made no logical sense.

Scrave allowed himself to look where his large navigator friend was and then smiled.

"*Pioneer*," they both mouthed together, looking at the rusted remains of a steamship and reading off the faded name on the stern.

There was a hard bump, as if the little rowboat had collided with something and Scrave found himself face down in the bottom of the vessel as it ground across something and plopped down the other side. He got to his knees and glared at Rauph who he swiftly noted was equally as surprised as he was.

"What was that?" Scrave asked. "What did you hit?"

"Nothing." Rauph exclaimed holding his hands up as if to show he had nothing in them so there was nothing to blame him for. The dinghy slowly skimmed to a halt, settling down in the water with a soft hiss.

Scrave got to his feet and looked over the side. There was a flash of silver and the image of something long and streamlined moving at speed under the surface, swiftly joined by several other long serpent-like creatures that showed no interest in the boat bobbing along above them.

I wonder where they are going in such a hurry." Scrave mouthed to himself, suddenly feeling a little vulnerable on a small wooden boat far from the relative safety of the ships nearby.

"Can I make a suggestion?" he asked, suddenly quite nervous "Let's stick a bit closer to the boats, okay."

"That makes sense." Rauph replied. "Look." He gestured over to a gap in the shipwrecks, a small channel down which the unmistakable skeletal remains of a Spanish Galleon leaned. "It's the *La Hechicera*."

* * * * * *

"This will never work." Barney complained looking down at himself in dismay. "The suit is simply too big."

Ashe, hanging from the side of the ship, pricked up his ears at the statement. Maybe he would have a chance of getting to try on the suit after all, especially if Barney had decided he did not want to go. He started to work his way back up to the main deck, winching the pulley system to raise himself up to where he could look over the side.

Barney looked forlorn and a tad worried. He stood in the white suit of armour a long patched pipe coming out of the back of it like a man made umbilical tube, lengths and lengths of it coiled up awaiting use. However, Barney was not worried about the tube; instead, it was the suit itself. Fitted for a man at least six feet tall, it gathered around him hanging loose and saggy below his waist, threatening to trip him if he tried to take a step. He held out an arm to show his concern but even with his arm outstretched, the suit, from elbow to glove dangled empty on the deck floor.

He raised a questioning eyebrow towards Commagin, who stomped over and shook him by the shoulders.

"Don't worry I have it all in hand." He pulled a cord that ran from the groin of the suit down one leg, under one boot and then up again to Barney's hip. With a sharp pull the whole leg of the suit, concertinaed making his leg look like a segmented caterpillar. Three more quick successful applications of Commagin's suit adjuster device and Barney finally stood in a suit that almost fit. Unfortunately, the Dwarven engineer could not shrink the gloves meaning Barney could only operate three fingers on each hand.

Ashe tried to stop himself laughing but could not help it, causing several other crew to stop their repairs and look at the strange sight.

"He looks like he has been squashed in a vice." Ashe spluttered.

Commagin looked over, realised Ashe was watching and gestured him over.

"Help me with the helmet will you." Commagin motioned, lifting the huge visor into place and clicking it down securely. Barney offered a fretful smile from inside the suit as the visor sealed tightly. He used the thumb of one glove to activate a button on his other sleeve by stabbing it repeatedly until a small light came on.

Barney was much clearer now inside the helmet but he looked slightly hot. He seemed to be gesturing frantically about something but the suit flapped around without making much sense.

"He is sweating quite a bit." Ashe remarked, shading the visor with his hands to get a better view. "He seems to be turning blue."

"The light is yellow." Commagin snapped, "Anyone can see that." He clomped over, moving Ashe to one side so he could see what was going on. The inside of the mask was starting to fog up. This seemed to confuse Commagin for a second. He pulled Barney forward and started to examine the tubing coming out of the back of the suit, following it along until he found the far end where a large set of bellows were on the deck.

"Start pumping." he gestured at Abeline, who had slid down from above to get a closer look.

The acrobat, eager to perform, started to pump the bellows with all the effort he could muster. The tubing jumped from the deck, going from flat to round and plump in seconds, then with a pop the visor flew open leaving Barney gasping in the air.

"That's too hard." Commagin twisted his beard in frustration and then waved his finger warning Abeline to slow down, before stomping back over to the suit, slamming the visor down again before Barney could offer another complaint.

"Is that better." Commagin smiled. "Give me a thumb up if you can breathe."

Barney looked confused, then after a slight wiggle, his left arm came free and flopped to the deck. Commagin picked it up wondering where his companion's limb had gone, when he saw a thumb pop up inside the helmet.

"That's great then." He gestured to Ashe to help him move Barney over to a winch and pulley system situated on the side of the deck. They positioned the apprehensive apprentice out onto the creaking platform, becoming aware that as they did so that the number of spectators grew around them.

"Ashe will you man the winch." Commagin requested, puffing his chest out in pride. "I want you to slowly lower him into the water. Abeline, please continue to pump the bellows."

Ashe slowly turned the squeaking winch, alarmed at the protesting sounds it was making.

"What is he going to cut the weeds away with?" he whispered in Commagin's direction.

"Oh... yes." Commagin reached for a sack of heavy tools and dragged them over to where Barney was slowly descending towards the water. He looked down at his apprentice with pride in his heart, smiling warmly as he watched the little figure use his concertinaed hands to steady himself against the side of the ship as he set out on his epic quest. "Catch this lad."

He dropped the tools into Barney's open arms and watched as the weight made the apprentice sag. With a loud crack, the winch snapped, ropes flew everywhere, long lengths of pink tubing started whooshing across the deck and over the side as Barney, complete with suit and tools plummeted to the water below. There was a horrendous splash, bubbles and then silence.

"I have one question." Ashe asked, holding the broken winch handle up. "Did you really expect he would sink that fast?"

* * * * * *

Thomas raised his head and looked carefully over the side of his hiding place at the grey ship below. Things were not going well for the two men who had been unlucky enough to choose the *Atlanta* as their landing platform.

The Scintarn hounds were everywhere, growling and spitting, lips curled back to expose cruel ivory fangs ready to rend flesh and inflict harm. The two passengers from the plane appeared corralled like sheep, completely penned in by the Scintarns and looking worse for wear. Both bled from several places where the hounds had established who was in charge with a swift slash of their claws, or sharp nip of teeth. Kerian arrived, dropping to his knees, his head sagging forward, breathing coming in ragged gasps.

"Please breathe a little quieter." Thomas hushed. "We don't want to end up joining them." He gestured over the barrier so Kerian could look and see what he thought of the situation and returned to his own observations. How was he going to rescue these poor people?

Several more hounds appeared, herding another man who was bleeding heavily from his head, his arm hung limp and useless at his side and he appeared vague and confused, often staggering from one canine to another and suffering for his error in judgement with more injuries sustained by the circling creatures.

This had to be the man who fell from the tall mast! Thomas tried to shift his position so he could see more of the deck. Where was the female pilot? In addition, where were Aradol and Ives? They needed to form some kind of plan.

"What do you think?" He asked his heavy breathing companion. The lack of reply raised prickles along Thomas's neck and he turned to take in Kerian's appearance more carefully. The old man was rubbing his left arm and his breathing was ragged.

"What's wrong with you?" Thomas hissed through clenched teeth. He took in Kerian's pasty colour and the ragged breathing and realised with a sinking feeling that this was serious.

"Oh hell Kerian you cannot do this to me. Not right now." Kerian looked at him vaguely, rubbing his arm and trying to control his staggered breathing.

"Something's wrong..." he gasped. "Maybe... I ate something... bad."

Thomas's scowl turned to one of concern. He tried to smile, despite the fact he knew he was looking at a man suffering cardiac problems.

"Maybe Violetta overdid it with the spice in her last stew." He offered trying to loosen Kerian's clothing at the neck and allow him to get comfortable and breathe.

He risked a quick glance back over the railing at the circling hounds. Then felt a sudden chill as the hounds raised their heads and howled to the sky. He knew what that howl meant. Darkness was falling they were signalling their master that it was time to wake and that fresh food had been found. He looked back over at Kerian who was gasping like a beached fish, all sweaty, clammy and unresponsive to anything around him.

This was bad. This was very bad indeed!

* * * * * *

Ives and Aradol had noticed the sky was starting to darken. The process was slow at first, barely perceptible but as the time passed and they continued to search for the two people who fell from the flying object they had to admit it was getting harder to see clearly. They had discovered a fresh streak of red down the side of a high ship and the remains of a ragged parachute tangled in the rigging above, which did not bode especially well for the man that must have hung there but of the other person, they had no sign at all. What they had seen repeatedly, were a multitude of huge paw prints but thankfully no sign of their owners.

They had now reached the end of the section of the hub they were investigating. There was one more piece of wreckage to explore and then they would have no choice but to double back. It appeared their search was going to come up empty but neither of them would give up and risk disappointing Thomas.

"What manner of ship is this?" Ives asked looking down through the oval open door at his feet. He banged on the surface with his bow, his ears taking in the clang as his eyes ran the length of the vessel and took in the strange tall metal sail pointing up to the sky.

"It's definitely metal of some kind." Aradol replied, feeling the smoothness of the opening but not like anything, I have ever seen. He thrust his lit torch down into the opening and saw two distinct archways leading off.

"Well we won't find out just talking about it." Ives replied, pushing his colleague out of the way and lowering himself down. "We know one of them must have come this way because the only other choice is to walk out across the seaweed mats and no one in their right mind would dare do that in this poor light. It was bad enough during the day."

The vessel creaked ominously as he landed and a slight feeling of claustrophobia started to creep in now he was inside. There was a doorway immediately to his left. However, the door it contained appeared very heavy and plain with a small glass dot set near one end. What was more, the door hung in the middle of the wall, far from the floor, as if whoever used it hurdled inside. He tried the handle and realised it was locked tight. The whole machine wobbled as he took another step, this time towards the right, where a path of clear panels led off in a straight line along the floor.

"This isn't very steady," he remarked to himself.

Aradol stepped across the open hatchway and continued walking along the outside of the ship, noting the glass windows at his feet, clearly designed to supply light from above to the people inside as she sailed. This was a most peculiar vessel. Beneath his feet, the windows started to light up one at a time marking Ives progress within.

He reached the tall sail and examined the damage to its ragged edge. This whole thing was metal, even the sail. How then, could it possibly move? He noted the far edge and saw the sail tapered and appeared to be on levers so it could move, beyond this was a huge egg shaped device secured to the underside of the sail, its inner workings of thin metal sheets radiated out from its centre like really thin wagon spokes, indicating that the whole internal surface turned somehow. An ornate engraving showed two interlocking R's. Maybe this was some kind of propulsion device?

He turned and started to head back to the open doorway, aware of the hounds howling in the distance. Aradol could not help but shudder, it was getting progressively darker and the mustard sky had turned a dark mouldy green as warmth leached from the world around him. All the shipwrecks started to look dark and more foreboding than ever, if that was even possible. It was getting cold too. Maybe they needed to hold up for the night as Thomas had suggested, keep safe until the sky returned to its usual rotting hue. He tapped his foot on the glass, slowing Ives in his exploration.

"Wait for me." He gestured, indicating he was heading back for the open door.

Ives mistook the gesture and set off towards the front of the ship, his light flickering from the ceiling windows as he went. Aradol laughed and ran lightly along the top of the vessel, arriving at the opening just as his colleague did.

"I'm coming down." Aradol explained, dropping to the deck and slipping his legs inside the hole. "It's getting too dark to see and we need a safe place to rest. This place has a door and it is dry. So why not?" he lowered himself to the floor and felt the cylinder wobble under him.

"Oh it's dry alright." Ives volunteered as Aradol steadied himself. "But it's the most bizarre ship I've ever been on." He gestured to the left, allowing Aradol to look at the rows of seats attached to the wall in front of him that stretched back into the rest of the vessel. "I think it's on its side. But there still appears to be no way to sail her."

Bags lay scattered over the floor and bright coloured books with vivid impossible painted pictures lay discarded everywhere. "Maybe we will understand more looking at these?" Aradol gestured.

"Well I do have some time to kill." Ives grunted as he closed the door above them, latching it firmly into place. "Just wait until you see what I have found down here. Little bottles of liquid but the glass is not hard, it's soft and crunches when you squeeze it."

"Let me see!" Aradol followed his associate, wide-eyed with wonder, as they walked further into the ship, unaware that they were both being watched carefully every step of the way.

* * * * * *

Rauph pushed open another rotting wooden door, popping the lock with a mighty thrust of his arm and turning his head as pieces of wood exploded in the air around him. Scrave stepped forwards, his heat sensitive eyes scanning quickly from left to right, checking for blurry red figures with his eyes before stepping back to allow Rauph in to secure the room.

"It's clear" he confirmed, as Rauph rumbled into the room a burning torch held high burning cobwebs on the ceiling into fine ash. Scrave took a moment to watch his bovine friend at work, lifting bunks with one hand and waving his torch beneath. All without an ounce of concern or worry. Indeed, despite the lingering fears of what existed somewhere out in the hub, Scrave had to admit he was starting to relax too. If only the damned headache would go away. He rubbed the cold metal circlet on his forehead as if it would somehow ease the tension he felt there but to no avail.

They moved out of the room and headed further down the corridor of the *La Hechicera*. It was quite a bizarre sensation to be searching a ship that to all intents and purposes was a duplicate of the one he had been a crewmember for all these years. The differences were obvious, mould, mildew, fungus growing in the corners, dripping watermarks, seaweed, warped wood and crabs: Many crabs. However, if he closed his eyes slightly he could be back on the other side of the hub and at home with his friends and shipmates.

The corridor ahead slanted down with the tilt of the ship, the end slipping below the waterline. The bobbled carpet running the length of the corridor grew dotted mushrooms that glowed faintly in the torchlight and its maroon weave turned to a fetching slime green under the waterline as it disappeared into the darkness.

"Well that's that then." Scrave confirmed. The *Enchantress* is no good to us. She is sinking and the water damage is too severe for us to salvage much at all. That leaves us with the *Conqueror*."

The ship creaked and groaned as Rauph walked past Scrave to see for himself, sparks of flame jumping to light every time his torch encountered something combustible. Scrave's eyes blinked rapidly at the glare and soon switched to normal vision, dancing torchlight leaving after images across his sight.

"It's flooded." Scrave shouted after him.

"I'm just making sure." Rauph replied, kicking away an over inquisitive crab with blood red claws. He waded into the dank water up to his shins, nostrils flaring.

"There's something not right here." He mumbled. "I don't like it in here."

"I'm not too keen either." Scrave replied. "Let's cut our losses and go."

Rauph turned and sloshed from the water, each footfall causing the deck beneath him to groan in further protest.

"Rauph!" Scrave scolded in jest. "What are you doing? I just had this carpet cleaned!" They laughed aloud, the sound echoing eerily in the enclosed space as they turned the corner and left the partially submerged passageway in darkness.

Something sleek and black slid free from the water and crawled up the carpet in their wake, claws ripping the fabric with each step as it commenced stalking its prey.

* * * * * *

Marcus listened to the howling in the distance and felt the hairs rise up on his arms. There was something about nature, its rawness and savage cruelty that thrilled him and at the same time scared him. He admired the way such creatures banded together for survival, working as a team and solving problems together, forming bonds and identities where they were stronger as a whole.

Much like how he felt being part of the monastery. However, all this remained in jeopardy due to him losing the book. He sighed deeply, unaware of how the guards around him were shuffling uncomfortably peering out into the darkness straining their eyes looking for the dangers they knew were out there from bitter experience.

The monk's innocence and current deep thoughts of failure isolated him from the fear washing through the crew. He started to walk along the newly laid paths across the top of the ship, taking in the sights and sounds around him as the darkness descended, wrapping the *El Defensor* in the shadows of night. The green and red navigation lights showing starboard and port to oncoming vessels glowed softly from within their stained glass lanterns, making the illumination across the ruined deck slightly surreal.

On the aft deck, a soft warm glow highlighted Colette's face where she sat in her magical trance. A thin sparkling trace of energy snaked out over the side of the boat and off across the seaweed mats to the open archway they had travelled through. Although the storm was still audible in the distance, it was no longer visible from the *El Defensor* due to the slow rotation of the hub.

Was he losing his faith? The thought stopped him cold. Marcus had looked vainly for the leather-bound tome throughout the day, his last glimmer of hope fading with the light. The book was either lost through the portal of the wind elemental or washed overboard in the turbulent seas. Returning to the monastery was out of the question: His time with the Order now over. Maybe he should just retire to his cabin and try to get some sleep? Then, with a blow, he realised that he did not have a cabin to go back to.

Marcus pondered his situation. Did he have a right to feel so self-centred? Surrounded by all these wonders, the incredible sights he had seen, he felt there had to be room for miracles if he just looked hard enough. Indeed, he had witnessed a miracle the other day when Sherman had breathed, despite his horrendous wounds. He suddenly wondered how the man was doing. This would be a fine distraction. Lift his low spirits by seeing another soul on the mend. He smiled at the thought and set off in the direction of the cabin where Sherman recuperated.

The monk knocked gently, but there was no need for quiet as the hole in the floor was allowing clattering and clashing from the galley below as Violetta and her daughter continued an epic clean-up operation whilst rustling up some crab containing stew from the crustaceans that had been collected from all over the ship. Fragrant steam wafted up through the hole, the brightness from below making it hard to see what was in the darkened cabin above. It took a while for

Marcus's eyes to adjust to the dimness of the room. He walked over to the bed determined to sit and talk gently to a man who by all intentions should have been dead and offer him comfort throughout the twilight hours.

To his surprise, Marcus found himself discovering the greatest miracle of all.

The bunk was empty.

Chapter Thirty-Nine

Thomas raised his head over the railing and watched as the Scintarn hounds started to herd the three men away with cruel bites and growls. He looked back over at Kerian still gasping beside him and realised they needed to get undercover before Kerian's loud struggles for breath gave away their position. As if on cue, one hound's head shot up, ears twisting this way and that, nose scenting the air, the armour like ridges along its back rippling in response to something it had detected.

With a slow, almost machine-like motion, it turned its head, focusing hard in the direction of Thomas's vantage point. Then with a whine, it was off across the deck towards them, leaping debris, crates and other hounds with a single-minded purpose that had but one end.

"Aww shit!" Thomas cursed, "It's time to go old friend." He moved to pull Kerian to his feet, knowing that the creature would be there in seconds and that their time for escape was diminishing but Kerian was in no shape to travel. Thomas tried to get behind his fallen comrade, slipping his arms around the old man's chest, attempting to hoist him to his feet but Kerian was totally limp, unable to bear his own weight and he slipped through Thomas's grasp and fell back to the floor. The term dead weight took on a vivid new meaning.

Thomas got down on his knees, his mind racing, what did he need to do in a heart attack situation? Umm... pulse. He pushed his fingers under Kerian's jaw and felt for signs of life. Was that a faint pulse under his fingers? Okay, next step, breathing, or was it airway? Damn he should have taken more attention in those annual training sessions. ABCD! Airway, breathing, coffee, doughnuts? No that was not right. Was C for circulation?

The thump on the deck beside him made Thomas jump, dropping Kerian's head onto the floor. He jerked to his feet falling back several steps as he scrambled to move clear of the growling horror before him.

The Scintarn was eight feet long from flared nose to swaying tail; its barbed end twitching excitedly from side to side. A bony frill travelled from the creature's tail up along its back all along its muscular length, running down between its ears to its pointed nose. The frill gleamed like black flint, catching what little light remained and accentuating every terrifying move the hound made. Short black fur allowed hackles to stand proud as it lowered its head and snarled.

When Thomas had first seen a Scintarn, he thought that it was some kind of panther, because its paws looked like those of a great cat. He had seen the claws produce an agility that canines simply did not have, allowing the creature to climb to places a hound never could. However, when you viewed these animals up close, there was a pointed muzzle and an angular head, rather than the rounded skull cats had. Ears were upright and angular, like a cross between a Doberman and a German shepherd dog, which twitched constantly for sounds and instructions. Further gleaming armour points ran above both of the creature's eyes, but instead of the slit pupils of a cat, these pupils were round, deep and terrifying. A pulled back lip allowed saliva to drip to the deck and exposed gleaming teeth.

However, Thomas had teeth of his own. His sword leapt into his hand, he could deal with this, the odds were still favourable.

Thump.

Another hound landed behind him, snarls now coming in stereo.

'I'm still in control.' Thomas thought to himself. 'I'm in complete control..." Another hound powered around the deck towards him, making it three against one. 'It's just the situation that's a little out of hand."

* * * * * *

"Bad doggy!" Rauph smashed his hand down onto the head of the hound near him, making its jaws clack loudly together and its eyes roll back into its skull. Another hound threw itself at the Minotaur, jumping from the roof with no thought for its own safety. Rauph spun and caught it in mid-air, flipping the creature over the side of the *La Hechicera* and down to the seaweed below.

Scrave leapt across the gap towards where the hound came from, his sword flashing left and right, making the hounds closing around him back off with yelps and barks.

"There's more coming!" he shouted. "We need to get off this ship!"

Rauph turned to where they had tied up the dinghy but three hounds stood on the deck before him and slowly moved towards the navigator. Others came in from the left and right, and then something bit him on the back of the leg. The Minotaur did what any creature would do in these circumstances. He turned towards the new threat, leaving his back exposed to the pack that were trying to bring him down. The hounds came in as one, claws slashing, teeth biting.

Rauph let them come.

They piled on, snarling, growling and covering the Minotaur like an animated oil slick. Biting, scratching, determined to bring down the mighty creature they attacked. Rauph was not having any of it. He lashed out with his horns, goring two of the hounds and tossing one limp body aside with a flick of his head. As he lifted himself, another Scintarn leapt up from the floor determined to get its teeth into his exposed throat, only to find Rauph was there first, grabbing the open jaws and snapping them wider still, leaving the monster dead in his hands.

He proceeded to use the carcass on the creatures around him, pounding some flat, sweeping others off their feet and making them all rue the day they took on the navigator of the *El Defensor*.

Five hounds remained, circling warily, regarding Rauph with more respect now he had shown them he was not a Minotaur to trifle with. Hackles raised, bodies low to the deck, they moved cautiously searching for an opening to take advantage of.

"Will you stop playing with them and finish them off." Scrave shouted down from his vantage point. "There are more on the way and I for one don't want to be here when they arrive."

Rauph shrugged his shoulders and threw his makeshift cudgel at one hound with such power it blasted the creature clear off its paws through the rotting guardrail and over the side of the ship. With a snort and a flaring of his nostrils, he reached behind his back and drew his swords.

The hounds attacked as one, leaping from all sides, straight into the whirling blades of their foe. Heads flew from bodies, carcasses dropped wetly to the deck and Rauph threw his head back to roar his anger and pain to the world.

"Anytime now." Scrave yelled, plunging his own sword into a hound that had started to climb the side of the ship in search of him. "We have to go."

Rauph whipped his swords around spraying droplets of blood in arcs across the deck and then winced as he felt a pain in his side. He reached down and pulled a wicked curved claw free from his abdomen, grunting at the discomfort before glancing at the claw and throwing it away to bounce off the deck.

"I've found the *El Conquistador*," Scrave beamed. He gestured over his shoulder into the darkness. "It's about six ships over and it looks in much better condition than its sister."

"Then let's go." Rauph huffed, pulling himself up onto the roof and staring into the darkness to where the Elf pointed.

"After you," Scrave mocked a bow, before slashing out with his sword, just as a hound leapt from the shadows behind Rauph, to impale itself on the Elf's flashing blade.

They set off together, leaping gaps between the shipwrecks, hearing the sea breaking below as if a feeding frenzy was going on just beneath the surface. Rauph skidded across algae coated decks, as Scrave ran lightly across spars and rigging above him, shouting down when the Minotaur needed to turn right or left to avoid the hazards ahead.

Scintarn hounds exploded from the night, their howls rich with the excitement of the hunt, lunging out from the left and the right but Rauph swatted them aside with his huge bulk, or brought them down with a mighty swing of a sword.

He crashed through a rotting sail and skidded to a halt at the edge of a crumbling bulkhead just as Scrave dropped lightly down from the mast above; almost earning himself a punch from Rauph's blood-soaked fist.

They looked out together across an open patch of sea and took in the sight of the Spanish galleon. No sight had ever looked more beautiful.

"She's upright and doesn't appear to have taken on much water." Rauph reported. "Let's go and get her."

"I think you are forgetting something." Scrave pointed down at the open sea between the vessels and the way the seaweed rippled as if something were below it. As he pointed, a massive silver eel's head reared from the water, only for another one to come up from below it, teeth snapping as the two intertwined, knotted around each other in a slimy twisted embrace. Tails lashed the water into a frenzy as other eels joined them, creating a mass of squirming, snapping, flesh eating serpents of the sea.

"It appears there is something of an obstacle in our way."

* * * * * *

"I don't think this is water at all," Ives laughed, falling flat on his face as he tried to throw another empty bottle into one of the opened compartments on the floor. "In fact I would go as far to say this is some sort of alcoholic beverage."

Aradol stopped flicking through the glossy magazine in his lap and regarded the merchant struggling to get himself back onto his knees. A broad smile cracked his face as Ives staggered over towards the cupboard that contained these amazing miniatures.

"Do you want...?" Ives squinted his eyes and looked at the two latest bottles he had selected. "...Jack or Gordon?"

"No... no more for me." Aradol held up his hand in protest. "These books make no sense already; I dare not think what they would be like if I drank more." He flicked through the magazine again. "It's just full of pictures of bottles, beaches, people with hardly any clothes on and some sort of food stuff but there seems no story to follow."

"No clothes." Ives raised an eyebrow and wobbled over to his companion before sighing heavily and collapsing to the floor. "Let me see." He reached over and flicked through selecting a picture at random showing a young girl in a bikini and a man with shorts standing alongside her looking all-romantic.

"Oh that is so sad." He laughed, pointing at the couple. "This poor man has had his armour stolen. Although what does he expect with his hair all sticking up like that? Clearly, he has not been paying attention in knight school. I doubt he has ever held a sword."

Aradol laughed so much he hit his head on the wall behind him. "But what about her?" he asked pointing to the young woman.

"What about her?" Ives replied. "They all wear clothes like this where I am from and they shuffle their bellies when they dance in our tents."

"Shuffle their bellies." Aradol sat confused for a moment. "I can't see how they can do that."

"Have you never seen a belly dance?" Ives asked, amazed at the innocence of the man alongside him. "I will show you." He staggered back to his feet laughing and setting their current hiding place gently rocking at the movement. Then once steady, he lifted his robe and exposed an ample stomach. "Now you have to remember there is normally less magnificence to wobble." He remarked.

Ives made a clicking sound with his tongue; held one hand up high brushing the ceiling of the cabin and began to turn slowly on the spot singing a haunting melody and wobbling his belly as he swayed.

Aradol laughed so much he started coughing and found he could not stop. He reached for a small bottle unscrewed the lid and swallowed hoping it would ease his symptoms and instead sprayed the sickly sweet liquor out across the floor. Ives kept singing gently, rocking backwards and forwards, with an idiotic grin on his face. The ship rocked more around them with his movement.

"I think I'm in love." Aradol joked, resting his chin on his hands and fluttering his eyelashes suggestively, which only encouraged Ives to respond more, wobbling his belly and the ship with more energy as his infectious laughter filled the air.

There was a crash as something landed hard on the roof above them, causing squeaks and metallic pops to resonate throughout their hiding place. Clicking and scrabbling, amplified by the acoustics in the cylinder stopped Ives dancing in his tracks. He looked up at the skylight above him and watched as something darker than night glided over them, then circled and came back again.

An eye appeared, the iris contracting and expanding as the monster outside tried to focus on the two men. Ives moved closer to the skylight, and caught a glimpse of sharp yellow teeth, as clear liquid dribbled onto the glass.

"It's one of the hounds." Ives hissed. "But we don't need to worry. There is no way a dog could get in here." He started to straighten his attire, satisfied they would be fine.

There was a loud crack and the ship rocked again. Ives stared up open-mouthed as the hound appeared to move away from the skylight, before it brought both front paws down hard on the window again, encouraging another spider like crack to snake across the glass.

Aradol looked over in concern, his hand reaching for his sword, the magazine tumbling forgotten on the floor. A third crack followed, then another in short succession, the motion setting the ship rocking crazily, making Aradol consider that maybe drinking the alcohol wasn't such a good idea after all.

"Don't worry." Ives tried to reassure his colleague. "There is no way that creature could get in here. The window is too small. The only way it could get to us is if it opened the door." He turned to look towards the front of the strange ship as if to reassure himself that all was well and his jaw dropped.

Standing by the doorway was a young woman, dressed in a strange dark jacket, beige trousers; short hair, full figure, lips a slash of red across pale frightened skin. She was struggling with the hatch in the ceiling after apparently climbing out of the door they had been unable to open at the front of the ship.

"No..." Ives throat went dry, making it hard to shout. "No please don't open the..." The aircraft door dropped down above the mysterious young woman and cold night air flooded into the vessel.

"Please don't go outside." Aradol begged, realising this young woman was clearly terrified of them and that she was not yet aware of the dangers lurking outside.

The young lady screamed as she found herself mercilessly dragged from sight. There was a thump, then another and two large black images from nightmare dropped through the hatch and started advancing along the floor towards them, snarling and growling, daring them to try to make a run for freedom.

Ives sighed, looking down at Aradol, resigned with what had to follow.

"I guess this party was getting boring anyway." He joked grimly and drew his sword.

* * * * * *

"Clean this, clean that, catch that crab and scrub the decks!" Ashe muttered angrily to himself, clearly considering mutiny against his callous taskmaster. He had been chopping away at the seaweed all afternoon and was exhausted but pleased with the progress he had made but Commagin would not relent on the chores that needed doing to keep the ship running and refused to give him any praise. Now he was scrubbing the pink tubes of the white armour that allowed Barney to go under water, checking the seals for leaks or snags, anything that could cause the apprentice harm for when he went back under the water in the morning.

Life just was not fair! At least Sticks and Rauph all got a chance to go off and explore. He was stuck on this stupid ship and nothing exciting was going on here at all.

He grabbed the next length of tubing and resumed his scrubbing, removing little pink jelly lumps that seemed to be stuck all along the length and flicking them off over the side. He pulled the next section towards him and noticed some shuffling feet approaching.

"Watch the tube!" he warned, as a foot came down inches from it, followed by another that landed at a strange angle on the far side.

Ashe looked up and noticed the feet belonged to a bald man, who appeared drunk. His head lolled at a strange angle, as if he was really, really, relaxed. It rolled about on his shoulders, as if the man had no control over where it looked. He walked funny too! His hips displaying an exaggerated twist at each landing of his impossibly positioned feet. It reminded Ashe of a play he had seen when a creature from the grave came back to get revenge on a lost love.

He sat back, dropping the brush back into the bucket near his knee and looked on happy for the break in the monotony of ships life, a la, Ashe Wolfsdale!

Marcus came hurrying up onto the deck his head turning this way and that clearly searching for something or someone. Ashe waved but Marcus did not appear to be in the mood to pay attention and swept past the Halfling leaving him quite hurt at the rebuff. Ashe followed the monk's progress with a scowl, tempted to throw his brush after the grumpy scholar.

The monk placed his hand on the staggering figure and moved to turn him around, allowing Ashe to notice who it was.

Sherman turned towards Marcus with slow robotic movements, causing the monk to ease backwards warily. Little hairs began to stand up at the nape of Ashe's neck. Looking at the body language shown by Marcus, something was wrong. Sherman's head lolled forward as if he was a marionette with the strings cut and his eyes glowed green.

Ashe looked over to the navigation lights and then back to the scene. The green in Sherman's eyes was not like the green of the lamp. This was not a simple case of light reflection. The light was coming from within the bald head of the first mate.

There was a flurry of movement, Marcus's robes appearing to blur as he moved to block attacks from the shuffling first mate, delivered with a speed and strength that rocked Marcus back on his heels several times and made no sense to Ashe. He could not understand what he was seeing. Why was Sherman fighting Marcus? Had they fallen out?

Sherman hit him from below, snapping Marcus's head up and turning the monk's knees to jelly, dropping him to the deck. Ashe expected Sherman to offer his hand, help Marcus back to his feet but instead the first mate turned away and continued to shuffle across the deck towards where Colette remained in her magical trance.

Ashe let his brush drop to the deck and quietly stood up to walk over to Marcus. The monk was groaning on the floor his eyes rolling. Ashe shook him gently, his little eyes constantly monitoring the shuffling figure of Sherman heading towards the mage.

"That was poor sport." Ashe muttered, shaking Marcus slightly firmer this time. "Are you alright?" Marcus's eyes flickered open and he blinked repeatedly as he focused on Ashe.

"Where is he?" Marcus asked.

"Sherman's over there." Ashe indicated in the direction of the shambling first mate. "I think he wants to talk to Colette about something."

"Colette!" Marcus's eyes shot open. He rolled over and got unsteadily to his feet, shaking his head to clear the stars from his vision.

"Get help now." He hissed. "That isn't Sherman."

Ashe looked perplexed.

"Yes it is!" he hissed defiantly, taking in Sherman's clothes, his face and his bald head. Wait... Didn't Sherman always wear a hat?

Marcus took an unsteady step then centred himself.

"Get Mathius."

"Get Mathius, okay I'll go get Mathius." Ashe stood for several seconds, watching as Marcus set off across the deck after the shuffling figure who was apparently not Sherman, but looked like Sherman. Then a sudden thought occurred to Ashe.

Who the hell was Mathius?

* * * * * *

Thomas spun on one foot, bringing his blade down hard across the flank of a hound behind him, following through to slice across the nose of another as it tried to come in from the side. Although he appreciated the yelps of surprise, the captain knew he had to be quicker if he was to escape before further canine reinforcements arrived.

The creatures circled the observation deck, tails flicking, saliva dripping, eyes watching his every move, looking for the opening Thomas was sure to present for them to wear him down. He risked a quick look at Kerian's inert form, only to spot a fourth hound slinking along the edge of the deck, its mouth dribbling at the thought of locking its teeth into the lolling head of the comatose man. There was simply no time to think.

Thomas stamped his foot hard making the animals all start at his movement, one even issuing a loud nervous bark. Then he feinted as if to run away from Kerian, before moving back and reaching out for his companion's foot, dragging him away from the immediate threat.

The captain dropped Kerian's foot back to the deck his eyes disbelieving the fact that the old man's hair appeared to be growing before his eyes. Some mad thought in the back of Thomas's mind made him wonder if his crewmate was a secret werewolf, or a diabolical Mr Hyde but he had no time to consider these weird ideas and had to consider the Scintarn threat first.

From the corner of his eye, he noticed one brute moving forward preparing to lunge, just as another of his newly acquired fan club moved in from the other side. Thomas turned side on, circling his blade inches from the Scintarn's nose even as his hand reached out and grabbed something he had noticed hanging from the rail.

He thrust out with his sword, causing the animal to turn its head or risk losing an eye. His blade gouged a furrow out of the animal's forehead and nicked its ear. A scrabble from behind marked the second hound jumping forward but Thomas was ready, pirouetting to bring his hand around to smash the fiend over the head with the lifebelt he had collected. With a grunt of satisfaction, Thomas dropped the lifesaver down over the black dog, wedging it down hard to stop the animal from being able to move. The Scintarn dropped to the deck and tried to roll free of what contained it, yelping and howling in distress.

Another beast leapt forward, catching Thomas off guard, its weight crushing him down to the deck. He rolled with the blow, knowing that attempting to stand under such weight was useless, coming up on one knee to perform a classic *Neuvieme* parry, dropping his sword over his shoulder so the hound ran into the weapon's turned edge. It backed away rubbing its nose furiously, smearing its snout with blood.

Thomas allowed himself a second of satisfaction at the whining creature, before he found himself hit again, from another direction, this Scintarn grabbing his left arm in a vice like grip and dropping him back to the deck.

It began to shake him. Hard!

Teeth rattled in his head as the Scintarn dragged him first one way, and then the other, loud growls emphasising each shake as its teeth bit deeper. Thomas hung on tight, bashing the hilt of his sword against the brute's thick skull but it refused to yield to his blows and shook him all the harder. He tried to stab the creature but his sword glanced off its armoured hide, the length of the blade making it impossible to angle and use for stabbing whilst being thrown from side to side.

His head bounced off the railing making him see stars and then something grabbed one of his legs. Thomas was in trouble and he knew it. He gritted his teeth and tried to roll towards the Scintarn that had his arm, hoping his momentum would allow him to tear free of the creature grabbing his leg. He instinctively knew that if he remained on the floor he was done for.

As he rolled, Thomas became acutely aware of the fangs he was rolling towards, the snorts from the Scintarn as it breathed loudly through flared nostrils, the tang of blood in the air and the clinging stench of the animal's breath. The most ridiculous thought came into his mind of giving it some breath fresheners, a consideration swiftly dashed by the pain in his arm as he tried to pull it free from the razor sharp cage in which it found itself ensnared.

The hound realised what was happening and started to bite repeatedly, pushing its head and his trapped arm harder and harder against his chest. Thomas could not relent; he continued his roll, pushing the animal's head down onto the deck with his whole weight, trying everything to force the creature to release its grip. Its yelps indicated he was causing the animal some distress but then the hound at his leg decided to intervene, dragging him physically off the creature he was trying to overpower.

He slammed into the deck with a jolt, his left arm being wrenched painfully inside the first Scintarn's mouth, as he found himself dragged away, yanking the creature's snout sharply over. The pressure around his leg suddenly released but was swiftly followed by the brute that had dragged him, pouncing onto his back, its hot breath inches from his exposed spine.

Its squashed companion opened its jaw to get a better grip now the captain had shifted position. Thomas acted fast, pulling his mauled left arm free and whipping his sword around in a weak backward swing to slap it into the side of the animal pinning him to the floor.

Then he was rolling again, pushing up and dislodging the beast on his back with the unexpected move, causing it to dig in with its curved claws as it slid off his body. The scream Thomas heard did not sound like it belonged to him but he knew deep inside he was its origin.

Thomas rolled again, groaning as his ripped back squashed against the deck as he moved himself into clear space. He struggled to his knees and came face to face with his newfound friends, they growled as they advanced, hackles up, blood and saliva dripping from their jaws. The hound trapped by the life preserver flipped hard on the floor and finally wriggled free, then sheepishly moved away from the pack, as if embarrassed at how easily it had been contained.

The captain gasped, lowering his head, trying to get air into his bruised and battered lungs, feeling the hot trickle of something running across his back. He looked around for help, anything to give him an advantage.

The deck lit up with a soft violet hue.

The Scintarns turned as one to locate the source.

"Do you want me to leave you playing with your new friends or would you like me to step in?" Kerian asked.

Thomas looked over at his companion with confusion. Kerian leant at a jaunty angle against the wall, his leg crossed, magical sword held down low at his side and a cocky smile spread across his tired face.

"How...?"

The first animal leapt towards its new foe and met a well-timed lunge that plunged Kerian's sword deep into its chest. There was a howl of pain as the creature fell to the deck. A second beast charged in as Kerian withdrew his sword, leaving him with barely enough time to parry the charge; he turned as the hound flew by and followed up with a flick of his blade that raised a yelp from the creature sending it off balance, crashing over the rail, down between the ships into the cold waters below.

Thomas used the diversion to regain his feet and brought his sword down in a lethal blow that nearly severed the head from the third brute. The fourth Scintarn, previously trapped in the lifebelt, leapt away over the rail, its tail between its legs.

Kerian took in Thomas's haggard appearance and looked back over the ship they were on to see if there was anywhere that he could take the captain to treat his injuries.

If Thomas had not been so preoccupied with his saviour's appearance, he could have explained to Kerian that he was looking at a bulk carrier but this mortally wounded ship had snapped in the middle, her back broken, rendering her completely unseaworthy. Above the breach, Kerian could see the most likely place for the bridge and main decks. A large rusted structure of peeling paint and broken windows.

They currently stood at her stern, where a small block of living quarters were located but the likelihood of finding a place secure enough to make a fire and keep them warm had to be in the larger structure. Open cargo holds filled with loose black rock occupied the open spaces in the deck fore and aft of the assembly, passable by gantries that spanned the holds. He turned back towards Thomas as the man came alongside him.

Do you think you can make it?" Kerian asked, indicating where he thought they could find sanctuary.

"How...?" Thomas kept staring at Kerian as if he had grown a second head.

"Now is not the time." Kerian replied, leading Thomas gently by the arm as they started across the deck towards shelter.

"But you were having a heart attack." Thomas ranted. "You were dying!" He paused; taking in Kerian's dishevelled state and his noticeably long lanky hair. "...Did anyone ever tell you that you look like the actor *Sam Elliott* from the movie *Roadhouse*?"

Kerian looked at the life preserver on the deck, ignoring Thomas's ramblings as he read the faded name. How was he going to explain his way out of this one? He had aged again, another year crossed off the sparse few remaining to him. He felt well now, whatever ailed him having occurred over a year ago, not the mere moments Thomas had observed. His curse delivered the unique opportunity of having a year's convalescence in a few short heartbeats. Kerian no longer felt tired and he felt strong enough to protect the man beside him, which was all that counted right now.

"Can you say; I'll get all the sleep I need when I'm dead?" Thomas asked, his mind still pursing the tenuous link between the fighter before him and the film from his past.

Kerian looked to the heavens for support. This was going to be a long night. Thomas was appearing delirious following his near brush with death. Maybe he was going into some kind of battle shock. He prayed the *New Haven* would be a gentle host for the hours to come and tried to blot out the sound of Thomas singing off key about all his 'X's living in Texas' and how he now wanted to live in Tennessee.

* * * * * *

Rauph crashed into the bottom of a wooden lobster boat, having dropped from the vessel above, his huge weight smashing holes in the rotten deck. He struggled to extricate himself and looked up to see Scrave jump across the gap between the ships to land lightly on the grey slanted roof. There were times that Rauph wished he could be as graceful as his friend. He watched as Scrave ran to the main mast, climbing swiftly up it to look back along the path they had come.

The navigator knew Scrave's heat sensitive eyes would be scanning for the hounds on their trail. The grim look displayed on the Elf's lips told Rauph all he needed to know. The Scintarns were closing in from two directions, purposefully herding them in a specific direction. They had been slowly moving around the shipwrecks skirting the edge of the inlet, trying to work ever closer to the *El Conquistador* but the going was slow, every vessel an obstacle to climb over, every crumbling wreck something new to negotiate and throughout their passage the Scintarns had been drawing ever closer.

He took in the smoking hole in the deck that he had fallen into and the damaged metalwork. This ship looked like it had been on fire and had been flooded in the past; the stern was in pieces, as if something large had landed on the edge of the boat and pulled it down into the water. He pulled himself free and up onto the outside of the ship, moving along the boat towards its bow with a sureness that came from navigating treacherous decks at sea.

His huge size made squeezing past the row of yellow barrels lined up on the deck quite difficult but he finally sucked in enough stomach to get through, just as the first hound landed on the grey roof behind him. Rauph swiftly weighed up the situation, pulling free a rusty harpoon tied near the barrels and turned to throw it with bone splintering accuracy straight into the snarling animal.

Scrave slid down the fore gallant stay to perch on the walkway extending out from the prow of the boat, beckoning Rauph after him as he leapt through the air out onto the next shipwrecked vessel. He landed lightly, seawater spraying up and rushing over his boots as the hull settled beneath him. Scrave took in the sunken structure with a critical eye. It lay on its side submerged just beneath the level of the sea like a dead fish, green seaweed and slime coating the surface and making footfalls treacherous. The wreckage bobbed gently under his feet as he moved away from his companion.

"Steady with this one." He warned, as Rauph moved to follow him. The Minotaur climbed over the rail and tried to place his feet gently down on the submerged surface but as he placed his weight on it, the boat tilted alarmingly, threatening to plunge him into the sea.

"Hang on." Scrave advised, quickly sizing up the problem, before moving back to his colleague and using his huge hairy body as footholds to clamber back up onto the lobster boat and move back across the deck towards the barrels. A loud howl filled the air, echoed and repeated by several other Scintarns out in the darkness.

Rauph's feet slipped and slid beneath him, kicking up small splashes that sounded very loud in the darkness. He swung around trying to pull himself back up onto the lobster boat but could not find a foothold to do so. He looked along the hull he hung from, taking in the numerous breaches along her side. This lobster boat had seen some action in the past. He swung his head around to take in the ships name. *Warlock.*

He could hear Scrave grunting above, then a large splash that sent cold water across the navigator's back. Rauph raised an eye at his colleague as Scrave dropped back down into the water after the barrel he had freed and pushed it over towards the Minotaur.

"Grab on." He indicated the barrel and the length of rope he held in his hand. "I'll tow you. It's not that far now."

Rauph looked at his floatation device and snorted his concerns. Then gingerly let go of the *Warlock* and flung himself over the barrel, his legs on one side his head dangling near the water on the other. Satisfied the impromptu life raft would work, Scrave started taking up the slack in preparation of dragging his friend behind him.

"Don't you tell a soul about this!" Rauph warned, clearly embarrassed at his undignified position. Loud growls rose from behind, made Rauph's eyes go wide.

"Uh oh!" Scrave said.

"What do you mean, uh oh?" Rauph asked, trying desperately to look over his shoulder at the problem but the wobbling of his precarious perch made him freeze in place or risk a dunk in the cold dark depths beneath.

"Just hold on tight." Scrave shot back, looking back over Rauph's huddled form to the line of six hounds now sitting on the edge of the *Warlock*, their ears twitching, tails flicking and haunches quivering with anticipation for what was to come.

Scrave tied the rope securely around his waist; his movements slow and deliberate as he turned to survey the way ahead. Their path involved moving along the submerged side of the vessel and then on towards the shipwrecks ahead. Unfortunately, several Scintarns were already sitting there, patiently waiting for them.

They were cut off! If they went forward, the hounds would be on them in seconds, if they went back a similar fate awaited. Scrave frowned and reappraised the route, looked along the edge of the creaking maritime shells, searching for inspiration in the skeletal spars and beams, masts and booms and the rotting remains of canvas sails hanging from the yards of the sad ships that lay in silent decay.

The fraying shroud of one ancient vessel caught his eye. If he could use it to clamber along the hull of that ship, jump to the yard of the ship beyond.... It seemed possible. He tightened and watched the hounds tense with him.

"Really hold on tight." Scrave warned. "This could get bumpy." He took a slow step, then another, watching the ears of the hounds' tremble and their black bodies rigid. The barrel initially resisted, then bobbed along gently behind him.

"On three... okay?" He whispered. "One... Two..."

Scrave leant forward and tried to run as if his life depended on it, his feet slipped on the slime coated boat and the resistance of the water against his legs made his forward motion hard to start with but he dug in, displaying the true strength in his slight frame and started to pick up speed. The Minotaur let out a shocked 'moo' and gripped the barrel tightly as it jerked across the water.

Rauph bounced along for several agonising heartbeats before he dared to reopen his eyes and the first thing that he saw was the line of hounds ahead, waiting eagerly with drool coming from their mouths in long strings. What was Scrave doing? He was running right at them!

Scrave splashed his way along the hull of the ship picking up momentum as he put his head down and pumped his arms for all it was worth. He needed the speed right now or the weight of Rauph was going to pull him down. He waited until the last minute, his initial passage taking him right to the end of the submerged boat: then, instead of taking the logical course and heading back in towards the mass of shipwrecks and the waiting Scintarns, he turned and threw himself across the water, crashing heavily into the side of an abandoned freighter. His breath rushed out of him but his hands gripped the shroud tightly, not daring to let go.

Rauph skidded to a stop on the barrel behind him, his momentum tugging at the rope around Scrave's waist, nearly pulling him from his perilous perch. The

Elf took a deep breath and then before he could tell himself his idea was insane, he started to move hand over hand along the side of the ship, his feet searching for secure footholds as he dragged the bobbing Minotaur behind him.

The brutes on the lobster boat immediately jumped down to the hull of the sunken ship, determined to catch up and herd their fleeing prey back towards the shore. Their footfalls sending up splashes of water, claws scraping on the metal surface as they moved to close the gap. The Scintarns perched on the far ships started to peel off and work their way towards the wreckage that lined the inlet, jumping across the ruined vessels and appearing at the railings to see that each time the Elf and his cargo were frustratingly always just ahead of them.

Scrave leapt for the next ship, reaching out for a stay to feel it crumble beneath his fingers, he dropped like a stone, fingers scraping a slimy piece of canvas before he was out in thin air. He angled his body and caught a boom from a sailboat that swung him over its deck. There was a crunch as Rauph and his barrel smashed into the side behind him.

"What are you doing?" Rauph shouted angrily, trying to pull his horn from the side of the hull where it had pierced it.

"Sorry." Scrave shot back, already scrambling along the side of the next vessel. He risked a quick glance behind him to note the animals moving ever closer. Then he looked again, down at the sea and went pale. "Hold on again." He warned.

The barrel jolted upwards as something flicked along its underside and lifted the sailboat they had just left several feet from the water. The loud crack made Rauph twist his head in surprise only to see the sailboat sink below the water in a mass of gurgling bubbles.

"Did I do that?" he asked himself. The surface of the water split with a 'V' in answer, as something long and dark started to cut through the water towards him.

"Umm... Scrave can you go faster please."

The barrel jerked again as Scrave moved from one ship to another, the barrel bouncing and skipping across the surface of the water as something hit it... hard! Rauph held on tightly, eyes wide, teeth gritted together, chin bumping against the barrel at every jolt. Scrave put his hands on the edge of a ship to pull himself up then dropped down again as a Scintarn lunged at him, passing over his head to crash into the water just in front of the barrel.

Rauph lowed in alarm as the creature started to swim frantically towards him. The navigator started to splash water in the hound's direction hoping to scare it away but it just kept coming faster, teeth glinting in the darkness.

"Shoo doggy! Shoo!" Rauph tried to splash with both arms but nearly fell off his barrel. He started blowing as if he were extinguishing a birthday candle but the Scintarn simply splashed closer, its evil eyes indicating Minotaur tartare was soon to be on the menu.

"Scrave," Rauph brayed in vain.

The water erupted in a geyser of bubbles as something silvery, long and displaying very sharp teeth, flipped the Scintarn up into the air and then caught it with a mighty chomp, dragging it under the sea. One minute it was there, the next it was fish food. The barrel jerked again but this time because something nudged it from below.

"Scrave!" The navigator screamed.

"It's not as easy as it looks!" the Elf snapped back from above, struggling to find a way through the tangled mess of rigging and stays. "I'd like to see you do better! All you do is sit on your backside all day complaining. Why don't we swap places and see how you like it?"

"That's an excellent idea." Rauph shot back as the barrel bounced again. "Come down here quickly and we'll do that." The barrel nudged, harder. Making the Minotaur's knuckles turn white as he tensed, not daring to move.

Scrave looked at the next leap and judged if he could make it. One more and they would be on the ghostly ruined sister ship of the *El Defensor* and they could look to getting themselves home.

The sea erupted in foam, the barrel launching into the air, taking one horrified Minotaur with it. A massive head rose from the depths, serrated teeth snapping at the barrel.

Scrave watched Rauph catapult up past him, twist around a mast, snap through a stay and fly into a mouldy canvas sail. There was an explosion of spores as the Minotaur disappeared. The rope jerked tight at the Elf's waist threatening to drag him after his large companion and then mercifully something snapped free at the far end releasing the pressure, leaving the Elf gasping. His eyes followed a large lump slowly sliding down through the yards of folded sail then Rauph reappeared, crashing down in a heap onto the *El Conquistador's* aft castle.

"Well I'll be..." Scrave grinned like a schoolchild, amazed at his friend's apparent acrobatic skills. He sliced through the slack rope at his waist and slid down the same canvas chute to land in a much more dignified manner, before turning and offering a bow. "We hope you enjoyed your trip." He laughed, overjoyed that they had arrived safely at their destination.

The whole galleon shook as something crashed hard against its hull. Scrave ran over to the side, worried they had a new problem to contend with and watched as the battered yellow barrel cannoned along between the ship and the vessels alongside it. A monstrous eel, clearly in a high state of frustration, was vainly trying to get its teeth into the bobbing object, its long length smacking repeatedly against the hull sending shivers up through the ship. With a groan, the galleon finally came free from its resting place and slowly started to ease away from the surrounding wrecks.

Scintarns skidded to a stop along the railings of several nearby derelict ships, their glaring eyes showing dismay at the companions' lucky escape. Several looked down into the dark waters, wondering if they should risk pursuit but then backed away as the large eel resurfaced, chasing the bobbing barrel across the water and whipping the sea into white foam.

Rauph untangled himself and brushed imaginary cobwebs from his armour. He looked around, checking his swords were still secure and flicked water from his hide. Scrave wrinkled his nose. Something smelled like wet carpet! He turned to his friend and started laughing at how close they had come to disaster.

"Did you see that?" he joked. "I almost caught that fish but alas, it got away."

"It was an eel." Rauph reminded him with a raised eyebrow and a stern stare.

"It doesn't matter what it was." Scrave shot back. "Did you see the size of it?" He held his arms open wide, then ran across to the other side of the deck and repeated the gesture.

"It was this big!"

Chapter Forty

The creature that controlled the corpse of Sherman, first mate of the *El Defensor,* took another shuffling step across the deck, cursing the cracked spine and shattered pelvis that restricted such a simple task. There was no pain; it was the basic motor mechanics of aligning joints and muscles to move that was the problem.

It swung forward with alarming cracks and pops as cartilage and bone ground against each other, resulting in the strange shuffling walk required to move. Sherman's head lolled senseless, as if someone had cut the muscles and spine that held it upright, making visual progress restrictive and often causing the creature to gaze up at the sky rather than down to the deck beneath it.

Movement from the side indicated the approach of a sailor, his face showing sympathy, his concerned voice asking if Sherman should even be out of bed in his condition, that he should return to his cabin and rest. The ghoul sucked in half a lungful of air and tried to keep the bubbles of blood and reflux that flooded into its mouth from dribbling out and being seen, then it reconsidered. The powerful body it had just located was mere steps ahead. There was no need to continue with the charade that it was still alive, still breathing despite the horrific injuries clearly sustained and that it was still Sherman. Someone who cared for these people.

It swung out, catching the man around the throat and lifting him off his feet, staring on with icy detachment as the chill from its touch surged through his shocked features. The sailor tried to struggle, tried to scream but with the slightest twist of the creature's wrist, something snapped in his throat and he fell limp, his struggles now over.

The body dropped to the deck and for a brief second the demon within the animated corpse considered the fresh shell at its feet as an alternative to the ruined remains in which it resided. Then it looked towards the young mage glowing star bright in the night and decided the transformation from one body to another was not worth the energy when faced with the prize before it.

Just one tiny piece of pressure on her slim neck and her windpipe would collapse, she would asphyxiate and the body would be it's for the taking. There was so much power coursing through her! You could level mountains with such strength, rule worlds! Kerian Denaris would never stand a chance against her strength! This ridiculous hunt would soon be at an end; Isobelle's powerful spell, goading the creature to pursue its target, would finally be broken. The demon could then return to its own world in the mage's empty shell and destroy anything standing in its way. The cadaver opened its mouth to lick its lips in anticipation and felt wet gore drip from its chin.

The creature was now one of two instead of one of three, its brother's death felt keenly back in Catterick when both itself and its companion had been caught, in of all things, a bar glass. The corpse would have shaken its head in dismay at the ease of their capture, if it had been inclined but that was the past. The greedy barmaid, thinking that the glass contained some kind of exotic liquor had dropped their magical snare in shock, at discovering their misty remains; releasing them from their forced incarceration in an explosion of spinning glass shards.

Picking up the trail of Kerian Denaris had been relatively simple, the magical touch of Isobelle's enchantment always drawing them in the direction he lay but finding a way to follow him was far from easy. The man had taken to the water. Sailing away from the lands across which they so easily travelled. They had required a ship for the hunt to continue and this delay had frustrated their pursuit.

Until the *Quicksilver*! A ship rushed into service with the sole purpose of hunting down the very man they sought. It was almost too good to be true, too easy to acquire two fresh bodies, join a crew with their blood up and adventure in their souls. Too easy to slip undetected amongst a crew that resided on a ship, so called, due to her sleek lines and the silvery coloured timbers making up her streamlined hull.

As it happened, it really was too good to be true.

The captain, Atticus Couqran was a mad man, stalking the decks like a beast possessed, his face ruined, his nose a decomposing piece of flesh. He repeatedly shouted out the fact that he would never forgive Kerian Denaris for the slight against him, much to the chagrin of any unfortunate crew who found themselves in the path of his frantic pacing. Two sailors had dared to whisper aloud within earshot what this slight might have been and were keel hauled for their impertinence, left bleeding in the wake of the ship, towed on lines until the sharks had their way with them.

However, this was not the worst of it.

The captain had a puppy dog. Apparently, his last pet had disagreed with something it ate and this replacement liked nothing better than crapping all over the deck! It was with horror that the ghoul found his allotted task was to clean up after the creature, to scrub the decks and prevent stain marks, to feed the annoying puppy and exercise it when the captain's thoughts centred on all-consuming revenge.

When the storm had appeared on the horizon, Atticus Couqran had impressed the crew with his tenacious attitude. Where any sane man would have pulled back and skirted the storm, waiting patiently for the *El Defensor* to emerge from the far side, he ordered them to follow in mad pursuit. The

Quicksilver was to hound their prey to the ends of the earth, they would not escape and there would be no respite from his wrath!

The resulting damage to *Quicksilver* was extensive, the man's obsession his folly. When they had moved close enough to the *El Defensor* for the demon to sense Kerian Denaris was near, it had taken the chance, leaving its fellow spirit and that stupid puppy dog behind. It slipped overboard in the darkness, striking out on its own, departing from the corpse it animated when the *El Defensor* was close enough, allowing the animated cadaver to slip beneath the waves and its demon mist form to roll across the water's surface and ooze along the decks of the *El Defensor* looking for another unfortunate shell to fill.

It shook itself out of reminiscing, fighting the frustration of having to shuffle forwards to preserve this body, instead of walk normally. If it were not for its own great strength and speed, the encounter with the monk would have ended much differently. As it was, being in a corpse that felt no pain and which it could control and attack with speed was a distinct advantage when fighting something warm that felt pain and bled when injured.

The delicate mage sat cross-legged and oblivious to the ghoul's shuffling approach. This was almost too easy, all it needed to do was reach out a hand and she was as good as dea...

Something slammed hard into Sherman's head knocking the corpse off balance. It staggered to the side unaware that the blow had practically taken off the first mate's ear. The fleshy mass hung by a twisting length of skin, turning lazily one way then the other, the inner ear torn open, its raw cavity exposed and glistening.

Frustrated at the interruption, the creature turned from its goal and noticed that the annoying monk was back, standing guard, a wooden belay pin held in each tightly clenched fist, as if the wooden pegs were swords instead of devices used to keep the rigging tidy.

It tried to laugh at the absurdity of the sight but ended up simply gurgling, dribbling more ichor from its mouth, before lurching forwards to deal with the nuisance before it.

* * * * * *

Marcus centred himself as the creature advanced. The belay pins were about two feet long and weighed heavily in both hands. Although in his mind he knew this shambling horror was not Sherman, it was still the body of the man. Part of his mind told him the first mate was beyond caring but Marcus had never liked violence; it worried him that people could slip so easily into a frame of mind that dealt death as coldly as a deck of cards.

His split second hesitation cost him. The creature threw itself at him with a roar, closing the distance in seconds, its shambling walk forgotten as the damaged joints were forced to do the monster's bidding, despite the fact they would probably never function properly again. Teeth stained with blood and gore snapped together barely missing the monk's face, as he stepped backwards swinging the first pin in with all the force he could muster.

Sherman's head snapped back, his nose twisted obscenely over to the side, the injury making the nightmare creature even more terrifying to behold. Clawed hands shot out, one from the left the other from below with a speed that left Marcus hard pressed to counter. The belay pin in his left hand swept up to parry, snapping the wrist of the clawed hand as it swung in but the uppercut knocked him back off his feet and off balance. A follow up blow glanced off his ear making his head ring.

Marcus staggered, bringing up the belay pins to defend against two further brutal attacks, before swiftly turning in a spin of blue robes, his turning path taking in Colette's form and making him realise how close he was to her and how near to danger she was. He completed his turn, striking out with his right hand, smashing the belay pin he held right between Sherman's eyes, delivering a blow that would have killed most men.

The corpse shook it off, as if nothing had happened and seized hold of Marcus's right arm. The cold was so intense and unexpected that the monk's hand jerked as if struck, the belay pin falling to the deck from nerveless fingers as his whole arm went numb. Marcus looked on horrified as the fingers of his hand started to turn from warm pink to the grey of decay.

He screamed out in horror, stepping away, desperately sweeping out with his leg to try to trip the monster, to gain a safe distance and withdraw from the searing pain racing through his arm. His foot connected and he drew back, catching Sherman's leg and pulling it towards him as he shoved hard. The demon crashed to the deck like a felled tree. However, Marcus did not pause to congratulate himself on his success, turning instead to offer his left side to the creature as it struggled to regain its feet. He followed up hard, his left hand smacking the remaining belay pin down on Sherman's right shoulder, before following up with a snap kick that jerked the creature's head back with a crack. It appeared to laugh, before lurching up from the deck in a rush, arms outstretched and no outward sign of damage apparent.

"Why do you try to stop me?" It hissed. "You cannot win, no matter how much you struggle. I feel no pain; if you strike me down I will simply find another shell and come after you again."

Marcus tried to quell the fear rising in him and bit his lip nervously.

"You will not hurt her." He promised, turning once more to guard his right side, his arm hanging numb and useless behind him.

"Oh I think I will." The creature threatened. "After I have dealt with you".

The blows came fast and heavy, staggering Marcus with the speed they landed, crashing down on his shoulders, knocking him to his knees, his left arm batted away, the belay pin spinning across the deck, before those cold hands gripped tightly around his throat closing off his air.

Marcus gasped in shock, his windpipe closing despite him desperately clawing at the dead lifeless hands crushing his throat. He tried to prise the fingers away, using every pressure point attack, he knew but the creature knew no pain, its strength omnipotent.

A dead finger snapped under the pressure but by this time Marcus was beyond caring at this limited success, his right arm was still useless, his left-handed attacks weaker by the second, his left arm becoming heavy despite his struggles to hold it up. Numbing cold started to seep into his bones and muddle his mind. He batted at something swinging near his left hand, trying to push it away and when that failed, grabbing at it in an effort to knock it from his chest. As his hand closed around the cool metal and felt the detail of the engraved flames portrayed around a simple unblemished cross, he realised this was not a threat, just the symbol of his faith, a pewter pendant suspended on a leather string.

Marcus found himself hoisted bodily off his feet, his left hand closing tighter in reflex, the metal pendant now feeling warm in his palm. His teeth chattered uncontrollably, his breath labouring in his lungs as he opened his eyes against every instinct, watching horrified as the creature that held him opened its mouth, exposing Sherman's ghoulish, bloody maw. He tried to draw breath to scream but only the barest whisper escaped as it closed in to bite his neck.

The monk desperately tried to throw his head to one side, the creature's lips grazing his cheek, smearing sticky residue across his face as it slipped lower towards the rapid, terrified beat of the monk's carotid pulse. One deep bite and arterial blood would pump unchecked across the deck. Marcus knew he was dead. Nothing could save him now. All he had left was his faith.

Sherman's teeth bit down.

The warmth in Marcus's hand suddenly flared, coursing through his tired and frozen limbs. There was a scream and the battered monk found himself dropping down on his knees, his hand clenched firmly around his pewter cross.

Sherman staggered before him, his jaw smoking, hanging at an odd angle.

"What have you done to me?" The creature lisped, its jaw finding it hard to form the words.

Marcus barely heard the question; instead, he looked down at his left hand in astonishment. Could his holy symbol have caused the creature such damage? He slowly got to his feet, held the pendant up before him like a shield, and stepped forwards.

Sherman flinched back as he advanced, holding his hands up to ward off the advance, one finger of his left hand broken and sticking out at an obscene angle. The monk cocked his head and smiled.

"I told you that you would not hurt her." He affirmed, brandishing his symbol with newfound authority.

Small pieces of skin flared like embers then turned to ash, flaking away from Sherman's body as the monk pressed the advantage. The creature stepped back, tripping over the dead body from the earlier skirmish in its haste to escape and fell down onto its back. Marcus moved to stand over him bringing the holy symbol to bear and watched as Sherman's skin began to blister and burn.

Voices sounded behind him. Reinforcements at last. He stood in confidence, hearing fragments of words as a wail started to rise from the squirming figure at his feet. "Marcus... Sherman... Attacked."

He turned to face them and looked into faces filled with inexplicable anger. Burly hands reached out grabbing him roughly by the arms. This was not right, what were they doing?

"Help me!" wailed Sherman's animated shell. "Marcus has gone mad; he's attacked me like an animal. He's killed..." The demon had no idea of the slain guard's name but its hesitation served it well. The concerned men continued to pull Marcus away in the mistaken belief Sherman was grieving for his lost shipmate.

"Dear god Sherman. What has that bastard done to your ear?" Austen said in disgust. "Who would have thought a monk could do such a thing."

"No." Marcus could not believe it. "You've got it all wrong! That's not Sher..." The blow that hit him split the skin above his eye and drew blood instantly.

"That's for Sherman!" spat Abilene. Marcus found himself pinned between the men as Plano landed further blows to his midsection knocking the wind from him and another to his face, splitting his lip.

Sherman slowly got to his feet, the corpse shambling over drawing further words of disgust from the crew holding Marcus.

"Thanks lads." The corpse nodded his head in appreciation. "Hold him still for me will you."

Marcus tried to tense tried to absorb the blows Sherman's corpse landed but it was like trying to dodge an avalanche. The first gigantic blow stole his breath. The second ended with a dull snap like dried wood as Marcus's rib snapped. He sagged in the arms of the men holding him, his flaming crucifix swinging loose at his neck.

Someone grabbed him by the head and forced him to look up through a swelling eye.

"Guess what I'm going to do now?" the creature taunted in a whisper, blood stained drool oozing from its broken jaw. "I'm going to see Colette and check she is okay."

"No." Marcus sobbed. "No. You must not harm her." He tried to struggle free, tried to ignore the line of fire he felt inside his chest but a swift blow from Plano silenced him.

"Throw him overboard." Sherman ordered. "I don't know how to thank you boys. If you hadn't turned up I don't know what I would have done." He turned to begin shuffling back across the deck again, his movements slow and sure, his goal still oblivious to the danger that approached intent on ending her life.

"You've got it all wrong." Marcus wheezed. "You've got it all wrong."

* * * * * *

"So, this happens to you every month?" Thomas asked, his mind racing, filling in the gaps of the mystery that was Kerian Denaris like a man finishing the last pieces of a stubborn jigsaw puzzle with the lid of the box missing.

"Roughly," Kerian replied, striking tinder and lighting a pile of kindling within a wood burning stove. "However, this time it seems to have come sooner than expected, as if being here, wherever here is, has somehow made things change." He tossed in some small lengths of wood stacked near the stove, noting how dry and dusty they were with age and looked around the derelict cabin they had decided to call a temporary home.

Thomas looked in a cupboard on the wall and pulled out a bottle of *Camp* coffee. He wrinkled his nose, sloshed the contents around and wrestled with the brittle top. The cap fell to pieces in his hand but the contents of the bottle showed no signs of mould and smelt of the over powering chicory odour he expected. He delved further into the cupboard and brought out two battered tin cups and a small tin. He looked at the tin, smiled and then tapped the cups to evict a reluctant spider that was squatting within. A quick blow dispersed the cobweb, and they were ready to roll. Now where was the water?

"So why didn't you tell me about this?" Thomas asked.

"I tried to. Don't you remember? The night when we were attacked in your cabin by the invisible assassin."

Thomas cast his mind back and shrugged, realising that Kerian was indeed about to tell him something that night when they were sharing drinks.

"But why not try again later?" Thomas pushed, looking over and watching the flames illuminate his colleagues aged features.

"I couldn't." Kerian spoke to the flames. "Once I had passed the map to you, I simply could not face you. I felt my guilt too keenly, being near you made me feel uncomfortable and I had other distractions too."

"You mean Colette?" Thomas smiled, wanting to tease like a schoolchild in the yard but seeing Kerian's troubled visage he knew better than to poke. "But surely you can't see a future with her?" Kerian looked over at his captain with an intensity that spoke volumes.

"If I had the chance to live my time over, I would give my life for her." He said in a voice tinged with longing. "I hope this cure can be found, that this quest isn't all some pipe dream conceived by the Order of St. Fraiser to ensure I protected Marcus until he got what he wanted. If I can reverse my aging, then who knows? Are you looking for this?"

Thomas smiled as Kerian lifted a battered kettle from the floor.

"That's perfect." He replied. "Fill it up and we can get ourselves warmed through."

"With what?" Kerian looked about the cabin, then clicked his fingers and stood. "I know where to get some water." He smiled. "Wait right there."

Thomas watched him leave and thought hard about the revelations he had just heard. Could this be true? Was this man so haunted? Aging so rapidly. What would that do to a man? He struggled to imagine the pain yet to come if all of this adventure was for naught. It would crush the man's spirit; destroy his soul.

The door opened and Kerian walked back in again with several thick glass bottles. The labels were faded, yellow and white with black swirling script.

"See!" he beamed. "Water."

He fiddled with the bottle top and finally freed it pouring the water into the kettle. It appeared to fizz a little. Thomas smelt something metallic on the air. He moved over, wincing at each movement and picked up one of the empty bottles.

"Tonic water…" he pulled a face. "This…" something made him pause. This was not the time to be negative. "…will be fine." He wondered secretly what chicory flavoured tonic water would taste like and braced himself for the exciting experience to come. At least he had a secret weapon to even the taste up a bit.

He returned to the cupboard and pulled out a first aid box. He opened the lid and looked at the lint and bandages within. At the bottom of the box was a small bottle of red iodine.

"This brings back memories." He winced at the thought of a misspent youth, when falling from a push bike and skinning your knee held more terror than embarrassment at falling in front of your friends. Even now, he could smell the antiseptic and the sting iodine would bring. He considered what he needed to do to the scratches and tooth marks he had contained. Surely, it would not hurt as bad as he remembered. He looked over at Kerian for assistance then reconsidered. What if he flinched like a baby? No, he would do it himself.

Kerian was looking out the window out into the darkness and the piles of wrecked ships beyond. He was a million miles away wishing things could be different, imagining what life would be like if he could lift the curse, if he could let Colette see him as he really wanted to be seen.

"Son of a..." Kerian snapped around and saw Thomas waving his arm around like crazy. Thomas looked up and realised he had broken his colleague's reverie. "I'm sorry I never meant to... bloody hell this stings like shit!"

Kerian offered a sad smile, then realised the kettle was steaming. He lifted the kettle from the stove and gestured Thomas over with the cups. Thomas poured in the chicory solution and dropped two white cubes into the water. Kerian raised a questioning eyebrow.

"What is that?" he asked.

"Magic!" Thomas grinned, spinning a battered spoon and whipping the hot liquid into a much faster simulation of the spinning waters that currently moved around them.

Kerian grabbed the spoon and moved it in the cup, his eyes going wider. He vainly fished for a moment longer before looking up at Thomas again.

"Where have they gone?"

"I told you... It's magic." Thomas smiled, enjoying the innocence that the old man showed before him.

"So how old are you really?" he asked, nursing his cup of coffee and blowing on the dark steaming surface.

"At least fifty-eight, maybe sixty-one." Kerian looked up at the ceiling as if considering the question and mentally trying to tally the score.

"No I mean how old are you...?"

"Thirty-four." Kerian mouthed quietly. He tallied the numbers again. Had he actually had a real birthday? "Yes, I'm sure I was thirty-four a few weeks ago."

"Oh well. In that case. Happy belated birthday." Thomas lifted his mug and clunked it against Kerian's. "Cheers."

They took a drink of their bitter coffee and looked at each other's faces as they winced, then burst out laughing together.

"That's how I like it." Thomas laughed, licking his lips and pretending to relish the foul concoction they had created. "Dark as a devil's heart, sweet as a stolen kiss."

"I'm not too sure on the sweet part." Kerian winced.

"I can fix that." Thomas opened the tin and unwrapped some more sugar cubes, plopping them into Kerian's drink.

Kerian took another tentative sip and paused mid slurp to voice his support for the additives. Then he frowned as if something had just occurred to him.

"What happened to the people we were trying to save?" he asked, suddenly serious.

"The hounds took them." Thomas replied, his jaw set firm at his failure to help.

"Well now you are all patched up we should go and save them." Kerian replied. "I've been resting for a year. I think it is time I put my rested body to good use. Where will they be?"

"You do realise we will be going into the heart of this place. There is something truly evil there that you have not met yet. I barely escaped with my life the last time I encountered him."

"So where are they?" Kerian prompted once again.

"That's the easy part." Thomas replied looking at Kerian with his steely gaze.

"If they are still alive. They're on the *Neptune*."

* * * * * *

Marcus's sandaled feet squeaked with protest as the three crewmen moved him towards the ships rail. He struggled to breathe, Colette was going to die and he was powerless to save her. He tried to turn his head, desperate to see what was going on.

A shadow fell across the group.

"Let Marcus go." The voice, tinged with ice, left no room for argument.

"Yeah! Let him go." Came Ashe's squeaky nervous voice, adding nothing to the argument, destroying the effect.

"It's kind of late for a swim." Mathius continued, trying to hide his annoyance at the interruption from his four-foot sidekick and moving over to stop the men in their tracks.

"He's going over." Abilene snapped. "He's beaten poor Sherman to pulp."

"Sherman is a dead man." Mathius shot back "I've seen his wounds. His back is broken. Marcus tried to save him. You don't know what you are talking about."

"He's not dead but this bastard gave him a right battering." Austen butted in.

"He can barely walk from what the monk has done to him." Plano added.

"I just told you his back was broken." Mathius interrupted. "He can't walk. If he had recovered he would have been paralyzed."

Austen burst out laughing.

"Are you serious? Of course he can walk."

"And I can fly in the moonlight." Mathius replied.

"No seriously..." Abilene continued. "He's over there." The sailor turned to gesture, his fellow colleagues turning to look in Sherman's direction as the man let his grip lessen. It was the opening Mathius wanted; he attacked as fast as the snake he used to represent.

Mathius grabbed Abilene's neck and yanked him down towards his already rising knee, bouncing the crewman's head off his kneecap and dropping him senseless to the deck. His right arm shot up as soon as he felt Abilene go limp, grabbing Plano by the shirt and turning to drag him over Marcus's drooped body, throwing the man off balance to smack his head soundly against the side.

Austen dropped Marcus in shock and watched as the assassin advanced on him, murder in his eyes. The animal handler stepped backwards and fell over Ashe's kneeling form, smacking his head off the deck. Before he could move, Mathius was on him his hand pulled back to deliver a punch with two fingers extended to rip the man's eyes from his sockets.

A bloodied hand stopped the assassin from landing the blow. Mathius spun in anger and took in Marcus's blooded and beaten figure.

"Remember... you wanted a fresh start." The monk slurred the warning through swollen lips.

Mathius dropped Austen's head back to the deck then prepared to run across the deck towards the shambling figure of Sherman. Marcus stopped him again.

"He's mine." Marcus snapped, setting off unsteadily in the direction of his undead foe.

Mathius watched as the monk struggled to bring his right arm forward and wrap it around the holy symbol at his neck. There was a soft glow as his numbed hand held tightly to the small lifeline of his rekindled faith.

"Are you sure." Mathius shouted after him, bouncing Austen's head off the deck one more time to be sure he stayed down. "These people don't seem to have much fight left in them."

"He's mine!" the monk replied. "You stay away."

"I can respect that." The assassin responded, holding out his hand and stopping Ashe from going against the monk's wishes.

Warmth flooded into Marcus's wounded limb as he advanced across the deck, the pain of the pins and needles as exquisite as the reassurance in his mind that he would not lose his miscoloured hand. He swiftly closed the gap, grabbed the back of Sherman's jacket, stopping his advance and making the monster spin around.

"Don't you ever quit?" the corpse hissed, amazed at the battered monk's resilience.

"By the power of St Fraiser, I bid you be gone." Marcus focused his will with an intensity that cut like a blade.

Sherman's shambling corpse wobbled on its feet as if hit by an invisible wall. It lowered its head and took another faltering step forwards. Light flared from the monk's hands, moving outwards towards the creature. Where it touched the animated corpse of the first mate, his skin started to smoulder, then ignite and turn to ash.

"You will not harm her!" Marcus yelled.

There was a flash of bright searing light, then Sherman's body exploded; bone, sinew and rotting entrails blasted apart in an explosion of green mist and stinking gore. The foul remains sprayed across the deck, steaming droplets landing all over the diving suit and tubing.

Marcus dropped to the deck groaning as the darkness rushed back in. He nursed his ruined hand as the pain continued to pulse searing agony back into his numbed fingers.

"You will not harm her." He reassured himself, his smile, despite his wounded appearance proving he was well aware he had kept his promise and that his faith had not deserted him after all.

A hand closed on his leg.

The numbing cold shooting through his limb made him arch his back in agony as he struggled to turn towards the source of his pain. The body of the sailor Sherman had killed looked back at him with a look of pure malice. Green light flickering in the depths of its eyes.

"I told you. You will never win." It hissed.

Marcus struggled to bring his holy symbol around but it was tangled and at an awkward angle. The creature reached out with its other hand, sinking its fingers into his left shoulder making the monk scream out anew. The pain was unbearable. Marcus could not stand it much longer. His arm started to jerk sharply, his pendant pulling tightly against his neck.

The leather string snapped. The holy symbol flew through the air, landing on the deck a distance away. Marcus tried not to cry out in despair. He fell forward, the creature's grip coming mercifully free from his shoulder, as his hands reaching out blindly, scrabbling for anything that could help save him.

His hand closed around something in the darkness, and he turned and threw it with all his might, smacking Ashe's discarded scrubbing brush off the ghoul's head. The creature jerked in astonishment, soap bubbles running into its eyes and blurring its vision. The demon let go of Marcus's leg in shock.

Marcus kicked out, smashing his foot into the side of the monster's head, before he turned and scrabbled across the deck after his lost cross. With a snarl, the demon chased after him, intent on finishing the monk by ripping him limb from limb.

The monk's hand fell upon the holy symbol, flaring it back to life, just as the animated corpse fell across his back, smashing him prone on the deck. Marcus gritted his teeth and willed himself to move, his breathing labouring after the punishment he had taken. He turned cross in hand, and presented it straight at the sailor's face.

"Get off this ship." Marcus snarled.

The monster shrieked as the symbol came near, skin bursting into flames, ash blowing away as Marcus focused his faith to cleanse the abomination before him. The cadaver joined Sherman's, exploding in a shower of gore that splattered widely across the area.

Marcus slumped to the deck exhausted, his faith clutched close to his chest.

"You will not harm her." He cried, rocking himself where he knelt. "You will not harm her."

Ashe ran across the deck, Mathius in tow and stopped short when he saw Marcus rocking. His little eyes raced to Colette and confirmed she was fine and then he looked for Sherman and came up blank. His eyes looked down, then did a double take at the state of the deck and groaned aloud.

"Just look at this mess!" he shouted, holding his hands up in the air in horror. "I just cleaned this up."

* * * * * *

"I'm definitely getting tired of this party," Ives confessed aloud. "The guests are boring, and the entertainment is substandard at best."

He looked across at the sorry group of people around him; Aradol mopping at a wound on his arm, the young woman with no name, who got them into this mess and three other men that appeared to know each other and wore similar uniforms embroidered with the words *Canyon Tours* on their khaki green shirts.

One of the men was clearly unwell. He rambled and paced, bumping against the bars of the cage they found themselves penned in, his head banging against the metal bars and drawing growls of warning from the Scintarns gathered outside.

Ives shook his head, not happy with their situation at all. He looked through the bars towards a large pile of items clearly collected over a considerable length of time. His ivory sword gleamed faintly in the darkness along with caskets, boxes and items of clothing gathered from doomed passengers who had found their way to this vile place.

The whole area reeked of dog and something else, not mould but a strong miasma of decay clung to everything nonetheless. There was a taste to the air, which lingered cloyingly on his tongue. It even penetrated his nasal passages. Ives knew he would remember this smell for as long as he lived. The wandering man bumped into the bars alongside him startling the merchant and making him curse aloud.

"Can someone please take this man away and calm him down." He snapped.

"Where would you like me to take him to?" the nameless woman snapped back. "I'm afraid we don't have any other cell to choose."

"Oh please shut up, temptress." Ives shot back, marvelling once again at the feistiness of her strong character. "If it wasn't for you letting those hounds in I could have spent the evening with Jack and Gordon and been looking at pictures of women with very little clothes on with my friend Aradol."

Ives watched as she moved over to the agitated man, trying to calm him, offering reassuring words. Her hand stroked the man's face but he moved his own hand up to pull hers away, a flash of a platinum wedding band on his ring finger, as his agitation grew. The hounds outside the cage suddenly stiffened. Growls and snarls became whimpers. A faint light glowed from the darkness as something glided towards them.

"What have we here?" Ives asked, reaching into his sash and gripping the handle of a short bladed fruit knife for reassurance.

The ghostly figure moving towards them wore a robe that appeared almost translucent, but at the same time hazy. There was movement within, but it was not clear if it was the creature's body moving or the robes. A wizened old face hovered within the robes hood, eye slits tight as if the creature were squinting, its gaze intense and knowledgeable.

Floating all around the figure were ornamental fans that glowed softly in the darkness. Pastel colours of peach, mauve, cobalt blue and corn yellow appeared to dance around, the vanes of the fans opening and closing like bellows. Click clack, click clack.

The strange old man moved closer to the cage and although his eyes did not appear to open Ives felt naked and vulnerable under the scrutiny. The creature continued to study the group, then seemed to gesture at one of the hounds.

Several Scintarns got to their feet and advanced on the cage door, one grabbing the latch in its jaws and tugging the door open. The others pushed into the cage in a group, snarling and growling a warning that all the prisoners needed to be wary of their approach. With movements that appeared long practised, they encircled the confused man, teeth bared at the woman, growling and making her move back or risk injury. Once they had corralled their target, they began to herd him from the cage.

"No. You can't take him." The woman shouted. A large Scintarn raised its hackles and backed her into a corner pushing her further away from the agitated man.

"Where are you taking him?" she demanded, knowing the hounds could never actually answer her questions. Her shoulders slumped powerless. Whatever was going to happen there was nothing she could do to prevent it.

The confused man staggered from the cage and moved to follow the glowing man. The fans continued to click clack, their lights turning on and off in a dazzling, mesmerising display of colours. The creature glided away out of sight, the hounds crowding in behind, pushing the man before them, taking him out of sight as well. The hounds began to whine in excitement, small barks escaping from their forms as they followed the strange creature that was their master.

Suddenly the multi-coloured lights stopped swirling and flashing, then began to wink out and change to a more menacing red. Click clack, click clack. The hounds became more frenzied, jumping around in excitement, nipping at any other hound that got too close.

Click clack, click clack. Snap! Snap! Snap!

The terrified scream from the crimson-lit darkness made everyone in the cage jump. The scream came again, louder more drawn out, painting a picture of agonising pain. Then the hounds began to fight, snapping, snarling, sounds of material ripping, of savage wrenching and then wet sounds that could mean only one thing.

Ives stood with his eyes wide, his hand held tightly to the handle of his fruit blade. What had he just witnessed? What had just happened to that man?

Click clack. The sound made Ives shudder. What was that creature?

A Scintarn padded over something pale in its hand, it dropped down near the cage and began to chew heartily at its hard-won prize. Ives felt the gorge rise in his throat. He saw the flash of platinum, the fingers crunching beneath the hound's serrated teeth.

Click clack.

He knew whose hand it was. Suddenly thoughts of his forced marriage were no longer something terrible to consider.

Click clack.

What in the world, did Thomas Adams have him into now?

Chapter Forty-One

"Welcome to the *Neptune*." Thomas gestured, standing at the top edge of a battered schooner, allowing time for Kerian to scramble up the slick deck and join him to take in the view. The captain of the *El Defensor* took in the scene before him and remembered the last time he was here as if it were yesterday. The local geography was slightly different; the constant movement of the shipwrecks having altered the makeup of the low area before him, there were even some Chinese Junks out in the wreckage he had not seen before but the *Neptune* remained a silent sentinel looming over all the other maritime vessels, brooding, pensive and filled with potential menace.

Kerian shared the vista, looking out across the remains of several unusual boats, some with sails that looked like ornate fans, some with huge wheels at their sterns; others were in pieces, a snapped hull lying derelict and forgotten, a barge listing on its side. Then he saw the ship that loomed over them all and he stared open mouthed.

Thomas could have told him that the *Neptune* was a cruise liner, used to entertain vast numbers of wealthy patrons across the waves in her halcyon days. This had once been a cruiser where one-upmanship was common, where the guests sized each other up by the weight of their property portfolio, not necessarily the glittering baubles on their model like wives. At her height, she was capable of carrying over three thousand passengers served by over one thousand crew. Now, the tormented screams of the damned, and the howls of the Scintarn hounds had replaced the excited conversation of wealth.

The faded gold livery along her side displayed a trident held triumphantly in the fist of an old man rising from the waves. She stood seventeen decks high and from his vantage point, Kerian could see the cracked windows and the rust eating her structure away. Weeds and shrubs had sprouted in long neglected corners of her superstructure, draping the ship in veils of lush green and yellow. Her standard hung limp, her four tall stacks pointing silently into the sky, no longer issuing the smoke of old but still impressive and brooding.

Kerian slowly raised his head, taking in the majesty of the spectacle before him, his amazement at her sheer size clear for Thomas to see.

"Did that thing actually sail on the high seas?" Kerian asked in disbelief. "Surely, nothing that large can float."

"Oh yes she did." Thomas replied, his eyes registering that the sky was finally starting to lighten. He gestured down along her port side where a jagged scar ran along her length. "Until she hit rocks and supposedly sank, with the loss of all on board."

Kerian followed Thomas's gaze and noticed several small dark shapes running in and out of the hole the captain had indicated. From this distance, they looked like ants scurrying from a nest, searching for food and carrying it back for consumption. A loud bark put paid to his initial speculation and confirmed that it was Scintarn hounds doing the scavenging.

"So what do we do now?" Kerian asked. "I mean we can't just walk in there without a plan."

"I'm not sure yet." Thomas replied, his voice lowering as he saw a lone Scintarn patrolling down below them. He brought a finger up to his lips and gestured that they should duck down. "If they do as I remember, the majority will be returning and going to sleep now. Only a few patrol during the daylight." He gestured at the sickly cloud cover above which was slowly assuming its rank mustard tone.

"If we are really quiet we should be able to slip inside and check out the place, rescue anyone that needs rescuing and get clean away before he realises we are even there." Thomas risked another look at his goal and ran his fingers nervously through his hair.

"You don't look entirely convinced with this great idea." Kerian commented, lightening to the man alongside him. Thomas turned and looked as if to ask 'what would you do then' but Kerian stopped him in his tracks.

"It's no good asking me for advice, I don't know the lay of the land, the weak points for entry, the most likely place for the prisoners, or more importantly where 'he' is. Speaking of which, who exactly is 'he'?"

"That's a story for when we get far away from here." Thomas replied, visibly repelled by the thought of even talking about the creature he knew lay in the depths of the haunted vessel.

"So where is he most likely to be?" Kerian asked.

"Where he always is." Thomas confessed. "By the food."

"Should we go and get reinforcements?"

"There's no time." Thomas replied. "The longer we wait the more likely there will be no one alive to rescue. Are you ready to do this? Sneak into the ship, tiptoe past hundreds of sleeping hounds, avoid the scary monster and collect anyone that needs rescuing?"

"Not really." Kerian replied, his face now wearing a mischievous grin. "But I'm always looking to start a new hobby."

* * * * * *

The shriek of stressed metal put Scrave's teeth instantly on edge; he instinctively held his arms over his head as pieces of rotten sail fell across the decks of the *El Conquistador.* The whole of the foremast vibrated in time with the sound, the wooden structure stressed to breaking point as the stays ground against the hull of the rusty fishing trawler it had just collided with, leaving fresh scars of bright metal to mark its trail. The galleon responded to hitting the larger ship by shuddering away, beginning a lazy spin out into the centre of the channel they sailed.

Scrave cringed, frozen to the spot, until he was convinced nothing else was going to come free and plummet towards the deck, then turned to offer a frustrated stare at his Minotaur companion struggling at the helm.

"Are you steering this thing at all?" he shouted. "The idea is we get her back to the others in one piece."

Rauph shrugged his shoulders and gestured at the ruined sails above.

"We have no wind." He remarked. "We are just drifting wherever the current takes us. What do you expect me to do about it?"

"Well try not to hit things for a start!" Scrave returned, his eyes suddenly going wide as he realised that they were closing on another teetering tower of wreckage on the starboard side. He started waving his arms wildly.

"Can't you see it?" he yelled. "Take evasive action!"

Rauph looked rapidly around the deck, noticed a hatch in the floor and set off for it leaving the helm spinning lazily behind him. He lifted the hatch and prepared to go below, only to have Scrave slam the opening down with his foot.

"I didn't mean for you to take evasive action; I meant the ship you fool!"

The inevitable collision knocked Scrave from his feet, crashing down onto Rauph's head as he struggled to get his balance back. It took several uncomfortable moments and a large hand from Rauph before the flustered Elf was back on his feet again.

"Are we evading or not?" Rauph asked, clearly believing that Scrave had tried to join him below decks. Scrave's raised eyebrow spoke volumes.

"I'll just go back to the helm then." Rauph offered standing back up to his full height. "Oh, the doggies are back."

Scrave turned in the direction the Minotaur indicated and noted how the current was drifting them closer to the outside passage but the path they were taking meant passing between two ships that formed an artificial span ahead. The archways lined up across the horizon beyond, beckoning the Elf home but standing on the wreckage of the ships were several large hounds, hunched and ready to pounce.

"Not again!" Scrave cursed. "Do they ever give up?" He pulled his sword free and set off down the length of the ship, dropping to the main deck before climbing the ladders to the foredeck, his Elven mind weighing up the odds as he calculated the best way to address the threat.

Scrave noted eight of them. Eight against one. He had beaten more! He slid to a stop in the centre of the foredeck, confident he had chosen the right ground and assumed the position he felt comfortable in; right foot slightly forward of the left, sword in his right hand pointing straight down at the deck. He would see them now when they came for him.

The galleon started edging through the gap, pieces of wreckage falling free at the larger ship's passage, pieces spinning across the deck and bouncing off the hull before crashing into the sea below. Growls from the Scintarns filled the air as they negotiated the wreckage and jumped onto the *El Conquistador.*

The Elf showed no worry. He was not scared. He let the hounds come to him and prepared to show no mercy.

The first hound attacked from the left and Scrave brought his sword across and down, stabbing the animal through the skull as it lunged. Even as the animal dropped to the deck, Scrave was stepping up onto its body, neatly sidestepping a lunge from another Scintarn, before turning and bringing his sword down onto the second creature's back, making it yelp in pain.

As he hit the creature, he followed his blade's path of travel, flipping himself physically over his target to regain his feet on the open deck. His sword came up, then down, his blade biting deeply into the hound's spine. The Scintarn made a pitiful howl and then flopped to the deck its back legs useless, its front claws scrabbling at the deck, trying to get away from the prey that had suddenly turned against it.

Scrave did not spare the creature a look, turning instead to face the other six hounds circling him. They backed off slightly, gathering their courage. Teeth bared, strings of drool hanging from their mouths.

The Elf lifted his sword from the deck, leaving himself open on purpose to see if any of the beasts would be foolish enough to attack. The nearest Scintarn leapt up at him, its jaws snapping, front feet trying to push him down. Scrave's blade shot up under its chin, pushing the snapping snout up so that its teeth clashed together on air instead of flesh.

He decided to let the creature's weight push him down, sliding his feet out ahead of him as he dropped, slipping underneath the hound's soft underside, his blade drawing a slash of crimson to mark its passing.

The next two hounds attacked together, coming in from either side. Scrave acted instinctively, pushing his sword blade into the deck and flipping up, pushing his body clear off the ground and using the sword to boost his height. The hounds smashed together below him, yelping in pain before backing off shaking their heads and sneezing from their collision.

Rauph stomped over from the stern and grabbed one unsuspecting Scintarn by its tail dragging it yelping towards him before he tossed it over the side. Scrave used his sword to intercept some weaker attacks, causing more yelps and snarls.

"Did you see my move?" He boasted, congratulating himself on his agile aerobatics.

"Can you do it again? I must have blinked."

Scrave's stern scowl broke as he noticed the grin slowly forming on his friend's bovine face.

Scrave's leg shot out behind him, clipping another snout with his boot as he plunged his blade forward into another hound. Rauph jumped onto its partner, smashing the creature's skull onto the deck. Its teeth cracked together to painfully trap its lolling tongue.

The Elf's blade swung out up high catching another jumping Scintarn, before swinging down to slice across another coming in from the right. He hacked at its feet with a backward swing, moving to face another threat as Rauph pile-dived the animal, knocking it senseless.

Scrave spun on his feet kicking out at another beast, then continued the spin bringing his sword down two handed onto the skull of another fiend, before turning to face the last Scintarn that still had an element of fight left in it.

The Scintarn lunged forward with a growl, only to have Scrave's foot snap across the left side of its snout, loop back, snap into the right side of its jaw and then kick upwards knocking it back onto its haunches.

Rauph waded in, making the creature bolt for safety and throw itself over the side in a desperate bid to escape, despite the danger of the eels in the water below.

Scrave dusted himself down as Rauph stomped around the deck clearing the dazed hounds from the area by flinging them over the rail.

"I didn't really need your help."

"Of course." Rauph agreed, grabbing the last yelping Scintarn and swinging it over his head to sail out across the water.

Scrave turned to take in the view and stopped.

"Who's steering the ship?"

"Not me." Rauph confessed his hands wide as if to say, 'why ask such a silly question?'

He turned to look at what Scrave was worried about and saw the towering ring of arches closing fast.

"Get back to the helm." Scrave snapped, leaving no room for argument.

Rauph set off at a clip, realising that this time, speed was the only option.

The archways were becoming more distinct; Scrave could make out the moss between the stones, identify the colours of the individual blocks and note the crumbling mortar holding it all together. He looked up at the rapidly advancing inactive gateways and suddenly felt the ship start to respond beneath his feet. Whatever happened, this was going to be close.

The *El Conquistador* moved into the turn but it was laboriously slow. Scrave winced as the prow of the ship smashed into the column between two gateways, and then started to slide painfully along the brickwork, sending up exploding splinters of wood and causing crumbling stonework to fall into the water.

The gateways shuddered and groaned at the abuse, suddenly flickering and becoming active. The closest one grew opaque then suddenly cleared, revealing an ice-covered tundra. The sea along the hull started to freeze as an icy blast tore through the opening, sheeting ice across the aged rigging and making Scrave hold his hand to his face to protect his eyes from the sudden wintery glare.

The Elf caught the impression of something huge and white thundering across the plain towards them, teeth snapping. It opened its maw to scream out it had discovered prey, then at the last minute, the gateway distorted and went dormant.

Scrave blinked several times in astonishment as the galleon continued its agonising slide across the next archway, triggering this opening just as it had the one before. This time the heat blazing through the door drew the Elf's gaze to an endless desert, flying beetles of huge size with shining emerald carapaces zoomed over massive stone carvings lying half buried in the wind rippled dunes. Faces of ethereal beauty stared with sightless eyes giving a glimpse into a civilization long past.

The image flickered and disappeared, as the stone column between the two arches caught another impact. The stern of the *El Conquistador* clipped the column hard, sending vibrations up the stonework. The ancient blocks of stone started gradually tilting before overbalancing and crashing into the sea. The galleon rocked heavily as plumes of spray washed across the deck, and falling debris cannoned off the side. The wash created by the fall of the massive stone blocks pushed the galleon back in towards the shipwrecks.

Rauph tried to compensate for the sudden shift, his manic turning of the helm resulting in sending the ancient ship into another wide circle. The galleon continued its crazy turn until her bow faced back towards the chaos they had caused.

Scrave looked at the hole in the archways and winced. He hoped none of the worlds he had just seen was Thomas's, or they were both in real trouble. He looked over the side of the ship and took in the destroyed paintwork, ruined carvings and smashed cannon ports along the hull. Thank goodness, they were only using this ship for spares! The Elf looked at the archways one more time and then back at the shipwrecks his eyes desperate to identify a feature to show where they were but nothing looked familiar.

Then he realised what was wrong. They were heading away from the *El Defensor*. The ship was going in the wrong direction.

* * * * * *

Rowan Bishop was living a nightmare. The brunette pilot looked at the cell around her and tried to hold back the tears. How had everything gone so wrong? How could any of this be real?

She closed her eyes tightly, imagining she had a pair of ruby slippers like Dorothy that she could knock together but knowing inside that this would never solve the problems she now faced. There was no place like home and her home was back in Arizona during the pleasant spring months of 1977. *The Eagles* were playing *Hotel California*, snow had fallen in Miami for the first time that year, *Gerald Ford* was the president and *George Lucas* had continued to surprise the world with his box office takings for the movie *Star Wars.* Rowan knew that the spaceships on the screen were nothing like flying for real.

Rowan had scraped together every cent she had, to throw in with three currently unemployed aviation mechanics, purchasing an old Cessna and entering into the dumbest business deal ever. One-quarter shares in a flying guide service called *Canyon Tours,* with Rowan as the pilot, Rodriguez, Vieira and Carlos as the ground support. The plane had problems with the engine and the flaps and it had taken some time, working late into the night to identify and remedy the faults before taking the plane on a test flight.

They had planned to launch *Canyon Tours* as soon as possible, dependant on ironing out the remaining issues and arranging the somewhat extortionate loan from Marty the bank manager. Just a few days remained before they could start taking clients on flights over the Grand Canyon. Money was desperately low and with equal shares, they needed something to go their way, as the remaining funds evaporated on permits, fuel and other fees.

The storm had come out of nowhere, lightning forks ripping through the sky, one striking their engine and causing a fire. The plane had started to dive but Rowan had wrestled with the controls, levelling the plane, only for the sky to tear open like fabric before her eyes, sending the Cessna Stationair spluttering through to this god-forsaken place.

An emergency bail out; the plane and their investment gone in a ball of flame, then those evil dogs, Rodriguez ripped apart and just now, Vieira. This could not be happening; it just could not be.

The hounds around the cage started to get restless again and Rowan stifled her panic with a low moan. The Scintarns agitation meant only one thing. The creature was coming back. The others in the cage tensed alongside her: Carlos, wringing his hands as he always did when he was nervous. The fat man in the robes who had been pacing the cage until the sound had stopped him in his tracks. Finally, the young one with the injured arm, who had been sitting quietly contemplating some great plan he permitted no one else to know.

They all understood how the selection process worked. The monster would glide in select his next victim then tear them apart and feed the hounds with the remains. Rowan had also discovered the point of the glowing fans circling the wizened figure. Initially they had made no sense, seemingly random, floating in the air like some illusionist trick. Colours flashing in no particular order. Opening, shutting, spinning and turning.

Click clack.

Vieira had solved the enigma for her, resisted his selection, and earning a serious mauling from the hounds. He had tried to fight them off, to escape, by crawling up to the feet of the hideous figure so he would call the sleek black creatures off. His thoughts of flight had disappeared the moment he had looked up and seen the flickering fans up close. It was as if the swirling pattern of colours had taken his resistance away. Flicking a switch and killing all anxiety. Almost like a case of powerful hypnosis.

His screams had been all too real when the creature started dismembering him. She remembered how she had jumped when the sound split the air, how she had tried to block her ears as the sounds became weaker, his pleas more urgent, until he was begging at the end.

Click clack, snap, snap.

The hounds moved forwards into the cage, teeth bared, herding them and splitting the group at a silent signal from their master. Resistance received the punishment of sharp bites and torn bleeding flesh, so they all moved away as the creatures focused in on Carlos.

Rowan hated herself for the feeling of relief that flooded through her mind, her guilt crushing her spirit as her last true friend was taken to be eaten alive.

The lights glowed softly in the darkness, the pastel colours slowly changing from their warm welcoming colours into the crimson that had only one end. The hounds moved away from the cage, their attention firmly on the food readied for them. Then the screams began.

She threw her hands over her ears, trying to blot out the sound but knowing it was futile. Then she walked as far away from the cage door as possible and sank down onto the dank floor, backing herself into a corner, emotionally drained as her feelings fought the terror within.

The cage seemed much larger now there were less of them in here. The man in the robes had stopped pacing and was now looking around as if he had lost something. What was he looking for?

Then it dawned on her. They were the only two people left in the cage.

The younger man had gone.

* * * * * *

Kerian held his breath and gently placed his leather boot down between two sleeping Scintarns. The hounds continued to snore, content now they had fed. He tried to find the funny side to this situation, looking up at the far end of the room and the fifty slumbering creatures that lay between him and the exit.

Movement to the side showed Thomas in an equally perilous position. He stood astride two hounds that were too close to slip a leg between, his wide stances so exaggerated that he could have sat comfortably across Saybier if the horse had been here. A soft lump formed in Kerian's throat. He fought to swallow it down and tried to understand why Thomas was waving his arms about. Was he about to over balance? Thomas's glare seemed to indicate that Kerian had the problem.

He looked behind him and froze, noticing his cloak was dragging across the nose of one of the slumbering animals and as he watched, was moving up and down with the beast's breathing. He carefully tried to lift the edge of the cloak, hitching up the dark material, unaware that the far end of his cloak dipped down in response.

Kerian moved forwards and felt his neck pull backwards, almost overbalancing him and dropping him onto the creatures he was stepping over. He looked about in horror to see what his cloak had snagged on, noting that the paw of one of the Scintarns was now lying across its edge.

He rolled his eyes at his colleague and tried to make light of the absurd situation but Thomas looked like he was practically having a fit from all the arm waving and jerking he was sending his way. Kerian carefully unclasped his cloak from his throat and started to gather it in, desperately trying to ignore the snores from the first fiend as his cloak settled across its nose again. He was damned if he was going to leave his cloak behind! It was a part of his uniform and he was not prepared to give it up.

Gathering the slack material up, Kerian lifted the trailing edge from 'Snuffles', before looking at the trapped edge of the cloak with a critical eye. How was he going to get out of this one?

Thomas continued to dance about in the background but Kerian ignored him. He had seen this done before; all he had to do was snap his wrists. He gripped the material tightly, slightly lifting the Scintarn's paw from the floor then counted inside his head.

One... Two... Three.

Kerian snapped the material away with all the grace of a bull dancer from *Folicia*. The cloak shot up and the hound's paw came down. He held his breath as the animal shifted into a more comfortable position and resumed its measured breathing then looked up at Thomas's thunderous face.

What was he so mad about? It was his stupid idea to come in here in the first place. He looked forwards towards the exit, judging his next move, stepping lightly down between three other Scintarns, only to feel a warm squelch under his boot.

Oh, this was just getting better and better!

* * * * * *

Aradol had noticed a weakness in the creatures that held them captive.

They were totally attentive and thorough as guards, until feeding time. He had watched it happen twice, both times, when they ate the first two unfortunate victims, they had herded and separated the prisoners but as soon as the prey moved away, the hounds' attentions followed the food.

Timing was everything.

When the creatures had taken the last man in uniform, Aradol had been quietly waiting, showing no resistance when the hounds came in to select their victim, keeping his head down, being non-adversarial.

As the Scintarns had turned to follow the latest victim, he had simply stood up and walked calmly out of the cage, straight through the open door. His heart had beat in his chest so loud that he thought it would give him away but he had managed to hide behind the cage and get a better idea of his surroundings.

The beasts had turned back to the cage once they had received the prize of fresh food, pushing the cage door closed. It took all of Aradol's nerves to tip-toe away towards the piles of trophies, getting down behind them and out of sight, before he allowed himself to breathe and try to calm the hammering in his chest.

The piles of belongings also gave Aradol an unexpected bonus. His father's sword lay discarded like a piece of junk amongst the collection and it had been relatively easy to slide the weapon from its resting place and instantly feel that little bit safer.

He hated leaving Ives behind but he needed to figure out how they were to escape from here. The young adventurer, who had once hidden in plain sight as a waiter, turned his green eyes towards the small stairwell in the back wall and slowly eased himself towards the opening, pausing for the smallest moment to check the way was clear before setting off up the darkened steps.

The terrace above was devoid of any hounds, enabling Aradol to slip silently along the open space and risk a quick glance down below.

The cage was where he left it; Ives was pacing in an agitated fashion, clearly disturbed at Aradol's unannounced departure. He could do nothing about this now without betraying his location and Aradol did not intend to yield such an advantage.

He was going to find the monster that held them and he was going to explain to it the reasons why Aradol of Deane was not to be crossed. He scurried over to the opposite side of the terrace and looked down onto the area where the monster had always come from. The sight froze him in his tracks. It was like a slaughterhouse. There was blood everywhere, some long dried, some still glinting wetly in the flickering multi-coloured lights. Piles of picked clean bones had been pushed away to clear the floor before a mockery of a throne.

There were areas of slime on the floor that could have only been rotting offal, discarded by even the hungry Scintarns. The stench was simply overpowering.

Aradol focused his attention on the throne, looking down at the creature perched there, loud slurping sounds coming from its lap. The hovering fans glowed brightly with each fresh wet sound, the colours racing from the wide ends of the fans, briefly flashing along fine translucent tubes, back into the main body of the monster they circled. He noticed that the fans were actually part of its body, not floating freely around as he had first thought.

The loud slurping continued; its source not yet apparent. Aradol leaned further forward to get a better view and noticed a thicker tube coming out of the hideous creature's back. He followed the tube as it curled up over the monster's shoulder and down into what appeared to be a sleeker but definitely longer fan.

This fan remained folded closed; the end plunged into something currently hidden in the folds of the strange pale body. As he looked, another jagged pulse ran in time with a fresh slurping sound, a ripple of pink colour rising up from the fan, along the tube and back over into the creature's back.

The slurping suddenly stopped and Aradol observed the figure shaking the object its fan inserted into. Then it lifted the pale object up high and Aradol thought he was going to be sick. It held the head of Carlos in its hands, the pulsing fan firmly embedded in the left eye socket, wiggling around and sucking at the remains of his brain tissue inside.

Aradol jerked away from the railing in horror, his hand coming up to his mouth to stop the gorge threatening to spill from his suddenly dry lips. What in the name of Adden was this thing?

The clatter from below made him cautiously approach his viewpoint once more. The empty skull bounced and skittered across the bones to come to rest against the back wall and the monster below giggled, uttering the first proper sound Aradol had ever heard it make. It rose to its feet, the translucent body floating down around it, its old wizened face looking around the room with eyes that appeared sightless. The fans started to glow anew, apparently invigorated by their latest feast and they started to open and shut in the intricate pattern Aradol had come to recognise.

Open close, click clack.

With a speed that surprised the observer, it started to glide from the room heading back towards the cage. The hounds started to howl in excitement as several began moving into the throne room to sit patiently in a routine that was clearly commonplace.

Aradol suddenly realised the implications of the sound. They were about to feed again and there was only Ives and the young woman left to choose from. The hounds may not have noticed his absence but this monstrosity would not be fooled so easily. It would see he was gone and it would come looking for him. His time was up. If he wanted to rescue his friend, it was now or never.

Chapter Forty-Two

"Are you sure there is nothing more we can do for you Marcus?" Abilene asked meekly, Plano and Austen standing alongside him, all three looking extremely ashamed and sporting bruises from their run in with Mathius several hours before.

They had been shocked to discover that what they had taken for Sherman had instead been a monster and were even more horrified at the thought of what their mistaken actions had almost led to. As such, they were looking to make amends and ease their guilty minds. They had extended the shaded area beside Colette, getting blankets and pillows to prop the monk up and let him lounge on the deck like an exotic prince. Marcus had made it clear he had no intentions of sitting in the darkness below decks. He wanted to have the light around him no matter how poor the quality of that light was.

Marcus stared out from a swollen face that sported bruises of several impressive hues from black to violet and to yellow. His swollen lips causing his words to be slurred, his eye half closed but despite the facial pain, the pain in his hand and the discomfort he felt on breathing, Marcus felt epic.

His faith had sustained him in his hour of need, moved him to do the right thing, to save a life and become a stalwart foe against evil. He felt vaguely amused by the attention shown by the three men, who had assaulted him but he bore no ill will, it was simply a case of misreading the situation and he understood they were trying to remedy it in their own clumsy way.

"I'd like something to read." Marcus slurred. "Anything you can find that will occupy my mind whilst we wait here." The three men looked at each other blankly, trying to think where any books were located on the ship.

"I know!" Austen clicked his fingers. "I'll be right back." He headed off along the ship running the walkway to head below decks, and passed another bandaged member of the crew coming up on deck.

* * * * * *

Weyn Valdeze breathed in deeply, trying to expand his chest and finding it only slightly uncomfortable to do so. The dressings to the arrow wounds on his chest were quite restrictive but Violetta had been fussing over him and had worked her magical touch, so he was healing faster than expected. He was desperate to get in some bow practice and loosen some of the stiffness he felt in his shoulders. He looked over at the profile of the *Rubicon* and noticed some life belts, faded with age at various stations along her deck. Yes... They would do nicely.

He wandered over to where Marcus sat propped up and whistled at the different colours of Marcus's face.

"That must hurt!" he remarked, sliding his bow from its leather case and setting about stringing his bow by putting one end into his instep and bending the polished wood behind his leg to slide the string up and give the bow its normal form and tension. "You look worse than me, and I managed to shoot myself several times with my own bow and arrow! Let me tell you, that takes some doing."

Marcus tried to crack a smile but it simply hurt too much. He looked on as Weyn pulled an arrow from his quiver, spun the arrow in his palm and then set it to his bow.

The archer turned, checked his target and drew in one smooth motion, letting his arrow fly. The bow hummed as his arrow spun away, arcing high into the sky to slam down into the nearest lifebelt. Weyn smiled despite the discomfort across his chest. It felt good to be shooting again. He repeated the motion, drawing again and sighting at the next lifebelt station further along the *Rubicon's* railing.

Again, the arrow flew true, slamming into the target.

Weyn reached for the next shaft and sighted at a dark object right at the far end of the deck. This lifebelt was a good distance away, one hundred and fifty yards easily and a much harder target to define. He let loose, his arrow speeding unerringly towards the mark but just before it hit, the target moved, dropping down to let the arrow fly harmlessly overhead.

The archer blinked in surprise; lifebelts did not move! He squinted trying to figure out where the life preserver had gone. As he looked, the dark shape returned to its stationary position and stared back at him.

"I do believe there is a dog watching us from that ship." he remarked, turning to discuss his discovery with anyone who cared to respond.

Abilene and Plano continued fussing over Marcus, Colette was in some spell-induced trance and Ashe was operating a set of bellows and pumping fiercely, whilst Commagin was staring over the edge of the ship at the sea.

Did anyone know there was a dog up there? The arrows slowly returned to his quiver, one by one, as he set off to voice his discovery.

He wandered over to join Ashe and Commagin and looked over the engineer's shoulder at the stream of bubbles rising from the water and then he took in the patched pipe Ashe was pumping the bellows into, as it jerked and moved along the side of the ship as if being pulled by something under the sea.

"Are they biting?" Weyn asked, attempting to start a conversation.

"Are what biting?" Ashe asked, pausing in his frantic pumping. "There isn't a crabby thing on my head is there?"

"What are you doing?" Weyn asked Commagin, ignoring the mad reaction of Ashe rubbing his hands through his hair and whipping around as if something was crawling on his back. "What's on the end of that tube?"

"My apprentice of course." Commagin replied deadly serious, his normal scowl turning into a troublesome frown as the air bubbles suddenly stopped popping to the surface of the seawater.

Weyn laughed. They had to be playing a joke on him... Weren't they?

Commagin started yelling at Ashe, calling him a buffoon and that he needed to get pumping again. Ashe started yelling back that it was not fair and he had not signed up for this, reluctantly picking the bellows up and pumping once more, whilst the patched pipe jerked and wiggled as if something was agitated on the far end.

Weyn decided to slide slowly away and look for someone with a little more sense. He wondered where Thomas or Scrave and his hairy bodyguard were. He decided to try his luck below decks to find out where everyone was and headed for the cabins below, just as Austen came back above decks with a pile of books in his arms.

"Do you know where Thomas is?" Weyn asked the rushing sailor.

"Can't stop now!" Austen replied, flustered and panting from his run to collect the books Marcus wanted. "Have to give these to Marcus."

Weyn watched him run by and shrugged his shoulders. Was no one going to give him a straight answer today? He wondered what was for lunch. Maybe he would talk to Violetta. She always seemed to know what was going on.

* * * * * *

Marcus allowed himself a painful smile as Austen skidded to a stop before him, a pile of books teetering in his arms. The sailor carefully placed them alongside Marcus so they were in easy reach. Some of the books were quite large, faded, dog-eared, and the titles long worn away by loving hands.

"Where did you get these from?" Marcus enquired through his swollen lips, his mind already relishing the opportunity to learn from the written word again.

"Thomas's cabin." Austen replied shyly. "He won't be happy to know they are out here as he is very protective of his books but if you are careful with them and we put them back before he returns it should be fine."

Marcus voiced his thanks and shooed the men away, feigning his need for some much-needed peace and quiet and reached for the pile.

He deserved some time on his own, a few moments to catch his breath, to recoup from the terrors of the night before. He picked up the first book and raised his eyebrow at the title. *The History of Piracy by Philip Gosse*.

"Well Mr Gosse. Let's take some time to get acquainted." He settled back into the cushions opening the faded book and took in the black and white illustration inside showing two ships involved in combat and a man in a tunic observing. The title informed Marcus he was looking at a Captain Avery. The ship with the upper hand looked very similar to the *El Defensor*. He licked his lips in anticipation, wincing slightly at the discomfort and then turned the page.

'Piracy, like murder, is one of the earliest of recorded human activities.'

Marcus sighed in pleasure and continued to read.

* * * * * *

"I think we need to turn around." Scrave remarked, sarcasm dripping from his voice.

"Why?" Rauph replied, struggling to straighten the *EL Conquistador*'s erratic passage as it drifted along the edge of the shipwrecks.

"Well you didn't manage to hit that last ship, and I would hate for it to feel left out."

"This is harder than it looks." Rauph replied, hurt showing in his eyes. "I'm also tired and I haven't had anything to eat in ages. It's no wonder I'm finding it hard to concentrate." The Minotaur raised himself up to his full height and looked straight ahead. "I don't think I want to talk to you anymore."

"Oh, don't be like that." Scrave replied. "I was only joking. Can't you take a little jo..."

Scrave's hands shot up to either side of his head, touching the golden band running through his hair. Was it his imagination or did it just tighten?

"You could be a little nicer." Rauph continued. "I'm doing my best."

Scrave winced as pain started to build above his right eye; he started rubbing the spot making the skin pink with the friction.

"Are you even listening to me?" Rauph asked.

"Yes." Scrave replied, rubbing his brow harder. "It's just that I have a headache and I'm tired too." He looked towards the front of the ship, his eyes scanning the line of arches running to the left and the twisted hulls to the right. Up ahead one archway was open, a thin golden thread of magic snaking its way out from the stonework to trace along the waters before them.

"I'll be." Scrave whispered. "We've sailed all the way around."

They drew level with the opening and looked through to a scene of blue sky and calm waters. Scrave squinted as fresh pain assailed him, curling his toes even as he acknowledged the fact the view held something more than simply endless ocean. There was an island out there. One with twin peaks, just like on the map Marcus had given to Thomas.

It had to be Stratholme. They had been so close all this time.

"Keep your eyes open." Scrave rubbed his brow again. "We should come up on the *El Defensor* soon and will need to weight anchor. Be prepared to move closer to the wrecks when I say.

Rauph nodded his understanding as Scrave moved the length of the ship. Why was his head hurting so much? It did not make sense. At least they would soon be back on the *El Defensor* and they could finally sail away from this cursed place.

* * * * * *

Aradol ran for the stairs, his heart beating loud in his throat. He needed to get back down the stairwell before they realised that he was gone. He had to save Ives and if possible, the young woman.

He slid to the opening and started to take the steps two at a time, turning around in the tight spiral, his breath coming in quick gasps. A huff from below made him halt his helter-skelter descent in horror as something started clattering up the stairs towards him.

The waiter turned and started back up the stairs, cursing the delay each second was costing him. He came out onto the terrace and slid to one side of the opening, just as the Scintarn ascending the steps burst out after him.

His sword flashed in the darkness. The blade came down on the creature's neck and actually sparked as it encountered the ridge of armour there. Aradol let loose a snarl of fury and whipped the sword around to deliver yet another two-handed blow. The Scintarn fell to the deck lifeless as the sword bit deep.

A chilling laugh started from somewhere below, the sound echoing up the stairwell and changing into something sinister and terrifying. For a second Aradol considered if his own actions were causing the merriment and then dismissed the idea as stupid, even though spectral fingers of doubt were stroking the back of his neck, causing shivers to race up and down his spine. He gripped his sword tighter, trying to reassure himself that his father would never act this way when facing such a foe, then gritted his teeth and set off down the stairwell.

* * * * * *

The cage opened and the hounds surged forwards. They showed no concern that there was one less person in the cell. They simply understood that they had to carry out this action to feed and that once the cage was empty they would go hungry again.

Rowan looked on frozen as the monster that had taken her friends glided eerily across the floor, his body appearing to billow softly as he approached, his wizened old face turned towards the cage, eyes closed, nose sniffing the air as it decided which delicacy to taste next.

The fans opened and closed, the colours flickering through different pastel hues.

Click clack, click clack.

The hounds waited expectantly and then with a gesture, moved in to separate Rowan from the only other prisoner in the cage. The pilot realised with desperate horror that she was going to be next.

She looked towards the fiend that was going to be her nemesis and watched the lights from the hovering fans change its facial features as they opened and closed, their hues accenting creases and making the horror even more demonic.

Her throat tightened. She wanted to scream out defiance but something had stolen her voice. Her resistance had deserted her.

However, the hounds did not expect resistance in another form.

Ives stood as the hounds approached and instead of backing away, began to move to stand alongside her. Rowan initially felt panic, was this man going to throw her to the wolves... literally? She tensed determined to fight her ground but instead the strange person who she had barely shared a dozen words with, turned and stood guard in front of her, a small fruit knife in his hand.

"I won't let you face this alone." Ives stated calmly, his hand slashing out as the hounds tried to shove them apart, giving the creatures' bloodied snouts that they instantly dropped and tried to hide under their paws. "You take us both or none." He snapped in defiance.

The Scintarns looked confused but then their master began to laugh.

The laugh was like something from a musty old tomb, dry and rasping, as if the voice was seldom required or used. It looked up, sightless eyes cracking open to issue yellow slime that tracked down alongside its small nose and dripped from its dry lips.

"It's been a long time since I have witnessed chivalry. It's a dying art and will only get you killed," it wheezed. "It's touching, but pointless. Why use charm to flirt with someone, when you will never experience a favourable outcome?"

Ives looked at the flashing fans and tried to concentrate on a witty reply but instead found himself walking slowly towards the cage door. His mind knew it was wrong but he felt compelled to advance towards the monster as it mocked him.

He felt fingers interlock with his own and in the back of his mind realised that the young woman was holding his hand. He had to protect her, he had to stand up to this thing that appeared to tower above him but the flashing, clicking fans seemed to fascinate him and they demanded all of his attention.

Click clack, click clack.

He watched as the fans twisted and turned, opened and closed spun and danced. How peach turned to cyan, pink turned to lime.

Click clack, click clack.

Although he knew it was wrong, he took another step forwards just as the monster turned and moved away from the cage. He was powerless to resist, he wanted to watch the fans, wanted to see the pretty colours.

Rowan held onto Ives hand tightly and followed his mesmerised steps. She realised what was going on, that her saviour was hypnotised, that he could not resist but she also knew that if she tried to run the hounds would have her and she knew she did not want to die alone.

* * * * * *

Aradol could not believe his eyes! What was Ives doing? Why was he getting out of the cage? How could he rescue his friend if he was intent on walking towards his doom?

His mind practically screamed at Ives to stop and turn around but his telepathic suggestion did not have the desired result. Not that he expected much but it would have been very handy to suddenly have the power to communicate using his mind so he could kick his friend hard, where it hurt and make him snap out of the stupid behaviour he was displaying!

He looked around at the piles of belongings he hid behind, hoping to find something he could throw and hit Ives on the head with. Instead, he noticed Ives ivory blade sticking out like a legendary sword from a fairy tale. The engraved handle resplendent with depictions of warriors fighting creatures among the clouds.

Aradol knew he was going to need that blade if he was to stage an escape attempt. He gritted his teeth and set off low, scooting across the deck, using the debris to block himself from the view of the creatures beyond.

His soft leather boot came down on a pale object in the darkness; as his foot crushed the soft item, it squeaked loudly, making the waiter jump and almost drop his own sword. He fell face first onto his front and grunted as his body quelled the noise. Several hounds turned in his direction but Aradol held his breath and froze, his heart racing, his mind expecting something to bite him hard at any instant.

The moment stretched on forever, the sounds of the fans magnified in his ears. Aradol moved his hand under his body and pulled forth the squeaking item. It was a baby doll but made of a material he had never seen before, incredibly soft, smooth and shiny. In the centre of its back was a small hole. Aradol lightly squeezed the toy and felt air whistling through the opening.

This was the worst rescue attempt in history. His friend was in trouble and all he could do was play with toys!

* * * * * *

Rowan looked around Ives shoulder and watched as the monster they were following suddenly stopped walking. It sniffed the air again, tilting its head, first one way and then the other. Its face turned towards her and cracked a toothless smile, before it decided to walk ahead, leading them into a room that was like a butcher's abattoir.

The smell of copper was heavy in the air. The scent of dried blood. There were bones everywhere, the remains of other victims who had come to the same grisly end she was about to face.

She tried to be brave but still felt the incriminating hot tears start to track down her face. Rowan mentally kicked herself. She was stronger than this. There had to be a way to turn this in their favour, to escape. She looked around searching for inspiration, her eyes frantically scanning the area, her soul becoming more horrified at the sights she was having to witness.

Then she saw the fruit knife in Ives hand. The blade was barely three inches long, stained with blood from the wounds inflicted on the hounds in the cell. Ives still held it tightly in his grasp but seemed to be unaware he held it. She moved closer and bumped purposefully into her mesmerised guardian, one goal in mind.

* * * * * *

Aradol moved closer to the procession of hounds and master, Ives ivory sword now held down at his side. He was nearly in position to act; he just needed to see an opening. The young woman seemed to fall forward into Ives, sending his friend bumping into the billowing monster before him. Something flashed in the darkness but Aradol was intent on saving his friend and focused instead on the fans clicking and clacking in the air before him.

He ran forwards, almost silent, the hounds unaware of his approach due to their focus being entirely centred on the thought of another meal. He ran through the surprised group and went to swing his sword, dropping Ives blade onto the floor, near at hand for his friend to grab.

The creature immediately sensed his approach and gestured to the hounds, they instantly dropped to the floor, trained to recognise this as a challenge to their pack leader, one that he alone would deal with. A fan shot out, the opening and closing instantly stopped, the colours flashing to yellow and black in a heartbeat, the closed end of the fan twisting around in mid-air and flying like a dart at his face.

Aradol barely missed a beat, ducking below the attack, swinging his sword in hard and watching as the fan severed from the gossamer thin thread that held it and spun off lifeless into the shadows. The effect was instant and horrifying.

An angry buzz filled the air, several fans flipping, turning black veined through with yellow and whipping towards him. Aradol parried two, dodged a third and lifted his sword to plunge it into the monster threatening his friends. Before the blade could hit its target, something whipped around his hand, tiny barbs latching onto his flesh like a thorny rose. He looked up in shock, watching the blood trickling down his arm and realised that one of the fans thin filaments had wrapped around his arm.

He dropped the sword from his trapped hand, spinning under his confined limb to catch his father's glittering blade as it fell and then went to thrust the sword back through the gap under his arm, intending to inflict a fatal blow on the creature that held him.

Another fan whipped in, buzzing angrily, its end glancing painfully off his forehead and making him see stars. He moved his free hand, abandoning his sword lunge to check the damage to himself and felt another filament loop in to restrain his left leg.

"Ives." Aradol snapped. "Wake up and fight!" Ives stared at him blankly and then something seemed to cut through the fog holding him in his stupor.

"Aradol?" He asked as if hung over. "What are you doing here?"

"It's a rescue, you idiot!" Aradol snapped back, parrying furiously as yellow and black fans buzzed him. Another fan flew away in a spray of fluid, causing a grunt of pain from the monster and for just a split second, the pastel colours stuttered in their pulsating mesmerising pattern.

Ives came to in a second, the hold of the fans gone. He looked around and spotted his sword on the floor. He dived for the blade as barbed fans slammed down into the deck around him vibrating angrily, barbs extending and contracting, writhing and wriggling as they tried to strike true.

He started to slide the ivory sword from its scabbard, as a fan came down yellow black and angry, spiking straight through Ives tunic pinning his hand to the floor. Another came down into his other arm, this time drawing blood, whilst another fan slammed down into the material at his neck, smashing his face into the floor.

Aradol continued to fight desperately but his lack of mobility was seriously hampering him. Another fan whipped in wrapping around his free hand and he suddenly knew his attempt had failed. He spun in the air as the monster moved him, splaying his arms and legs wide so he could not possibly fight back and only then did it decide to turn its terrifying gaze fully upon him. This revelation was more painful than the despair flooding through the young fighter. All this time, through all the fighting, it had not deemed him a big enough threat to even turn and face.

The waiter felt his bladder go weak. The face closing towards him was terrifying. Eye sockets dripped yellow pus on the carpet, the sightless eyes within, milky with some sort of cataract. Puckered, parched lips breathed dry festering air; the toothless mouth they encircled a void of unspoken horrors. The high forehead was dry, skin flakes like bad dandruff sticking to the surface, hair withered, long dead and colourless served as a reminder of where the creature's hair had once existed in the past, but did little to cover the red weeping sores that clustered behind its ears. It moved closer to his face, so bare inches separated them, sniffing the air, as if tasting his scent. Its overpowering presence emanated pure evil.

"Well," it wheezed. "The observer from the balcony. I smelt you watching me. Did you like what you saw?" It started to chuckle again, a laugh that was so lacking and devoid of joy that it seemed a travesty.

"Now you can experience me first-hand."

"This is some rescue!" came Ives muffled voice from the floor. "I can't wait to see what happens next!" The creature's face moved closer as Aradol found himself lifted higher. Then its features changed from one of amused taunting to shocked surprise.

Rowan plunged the fruit knife she held into the creatures back, not really sure what she was trying to do but determined to hurt the monster and pay it back for all the pain it had inflicted upon her. The speed of the response was truly staggering; fans whipped about like mad hornets, their trailing filaments lashing her hands as the creature slowly turned to bring all its horrid malevolence to bear upon her.

"You dare to strike me!" it wheezed, incredulous at such an insult. The wizened head moved forward, breathing heavily as it savoured her scent, sniffing her neck, rubbing her cheek and leaving a trail of slime upon her skin.

"I was going to save you until last." It snarled. "Now your friends can see you die first."

The fans swung around, pastels flashing angrily, the change of colours almost stunning in their rapid change. Rowan tried not to look, knowing that to look at these things meant her death but she could not help herself. The fans opened and closed. Her resistance started to drain from her body. She could hear Aradol screaming at her to snap out of it and could see Ives wriggling on the floor in the corner of her eye.

Click clack, click clack. Something dark started to rise behind the wizened old face. She looked at the colours racing across its surface, it was a larger fan, older, more weathered and the barbs looked well-worn and often used. She could not help but be fascinated as red colours started to race along its length from the tip up into the fan, the red slowly spreading to the smaller fans spinning, opening and closing around her.

Click clack, click clack. There was a loud snap as the large fan flicked open and then it shut again, the end turning, the sharp point moving in towards her face. The fan opened again. Snap, snap! She watched unable to believe her lack of worry as the fan reared up and prepared to plunge into her eye and strike deep within her brain.

Click clack, click clack. The fan shot forwards. There was a sharp crack! Something smashed into the appendage, snapping it and soaking Rowans face in gore. The creature howled with rage spinning to face its newest threat, allowing Rowan to glimpse the silhouette in the doorway to the room, standing side on, a .38 service revolver in his hand, smoke curling lazily up from the barrel.

The horror holding her sniffed at the air, head tilting one way and then the other as it compared what it smelt with memories long past. The snarl of hatred as it made the connection had the hounds on the floor shying away suddenly scared for their own welfare. Their master knew this person well and his hatred was almost tangible.

"Malum Okubi." Thomas Adams stated coldly. "Long time didn't want to see."

Chapter Forty-Three

"Thomas Adams." Malum hissed in pain, his voice filled with venom as he struggled to retract the ruined fan Thomas's bullet had just shattered.

"Let my crew, and the girl go." Thomas ordered. "Or the next one goes right between your eyes."

"Go Thomas!" came Ives muffled cry from the floor, his mouth half filled with mouldy carpet. "See Aradol. That's what you call a rescue!"

"So, I see." Aradol replied, hanging upside down, suspended by Malum's fans. "I have to agree he does display a certain finesse."

"You should know better than to come between me and my food." Malum warned, lifting Rowan up to place her struggling body directly between himself and Thomas. An evil smile slid across his face. It knew Thomas and how to manipulate him. "These people are none of your concern. They landed here so they are mine to do with as I please."

The fans flickered and spun, colours racing out, sending a signal to the agitated Scintarns, preparing them to attack at Malum's command. Satisfied the hounds would act, it then sent another yellow and black fan darting out to fly about Rowan's head, the thin trailing filament wrapping around her throat, pulling taut, making her struggle to draw breath.

"I won't warn you again." Thomas threatened.

"Or you will do what?" Malum mocked; confident the struggling woman he held would force Thomas to lower his guard. "She's going to die if you don't lower your weapon."

"It's not me you need to worry about..." Thomas replied confidently.

The cold steel of a sword tip suddenly rested besides Malum's ear, the blade giving off a soft violet light.

"...It's me." Came the voice by its ear.

Malum started in surprise, amazed someone could sneak up on him so successfully. It sniffed and initially could only smell hound waste matter. It turned its head, its milky eyes trying unsuccessfully to make out the figure standing beside it.

"Who are you? You... It's impossible." it sniffed again. "You have the stink of magic about you."

"Drop her!" Thomas ordered, stepping closer, the gun still held out before him.

"As you wish." Malum tensed, considering whether to flick his struggling meal aside into the hounds and let Thomas watch her be torn apart but the man behind him seemed to be prepared for such an action, edging his blade in closer, killing the entertaining thought with the gesture.

"Nice and slow now." Kerian warned.

Malum lowered Rowan gently to the carpet, the yellow and black fan releasing its grip from round her neck like a slowly uncoiling python. She started to cry hot tears as the air flowed freely into her lungs.

"Are you okay?" Thomas asked, warily approaching, one eye watching the deadly hovering fans as they flashed bright bursts of colour in agitated displays, the other on the kneeling woman who was struggling to breathe at his feet. He took in her tear streaked face and realised he had never seen anyone so breathtakingly beautiful.

"Are you going to introduce me to your friend?" Malum asked, his features confused as if the creature was struggling to try and understand something only he was aware of. "Or shall I just make a name up for him, like Spot?"

"My name is Styx." Kerian replied. "Now let our friends go!"

"What... all of them?" Malum teased, wriggling Aradol like a worm on a hook and pushing Ives head back into the carpet. "Let me at least keep the fat one."

"Aradol's not fat." came a muffled voice from the floor.

Malum retracted the fans with a snap, dropping Aradol to the carpet and allowing Ives to get up onto his knees.

Thomas held out his hand taking Rowan's protectively in his own.

"Can you walk?" he whispered, moving her gently behind him so that he stood between her and his rival.

"Show me the way and I'll run." Rowan gasped, rubbing her bruised throat and wiping the tears from her cheek with her sleeve.

She took in Thomas's worn face, his kind eyes, and open body language. "You're a cop right? And here's me thinking there's never one around when you need one."

"Oh you know us," Thomas whispered back, his eyes never moving from the swaying clicking fans. "We aim to protect and to serve."

"I haven't seen you serve yet." Rowan remarked, the colour returning to her cheeks.

"Aradol's the server. I'm the sophisticated company." Thomas replied, slowly backing away and easing her along with him.

"Is that a dinner date?" Rowan shot back. "I'll have you know I'm not that kind of woman!"

The growls from behind stopped them in their tracks. The Scintarns had slowly moved across the carpet cutting them off from the door.

"Where do you think you are going Thomas?" Malum hissed. "You interrupted my dinner but I'm a gracious host, there's always room for two more."

"It's always a sign of a bad eating establishment when you don't have to book ahead." Ives remarked, still on his knees, his hand reaching out for his ivory blade.

Aradol brushed himself down, a muffled squeak coming from within the folds of his shirt. He gripped his sword firmly and took his stance recognising from the tension in the air that this scenario was far from finished.

"Tell the hounds to back off." Kerian warned. "It's time for us to leave. There is no need for things to get nasty."

Thomas watched Malum carefully, taking in the flashing lights dancing across the fans, knowing from bitter experience, not to let his gaze linger on them.

"No... I don't think I am going to let you leave this time." Malum slowly shook his wrinkled head in emphasis, yellow slime dripping free from his chin to pool into the fetid carpet. "I let Thomas go once too. I won't make that mistake again."

A fan flicked over, diving into the folds of the creature's body, fumbling as if in a pocket before withdrawing something small that glinted in the light as a sly grin slid across Malum's face.

"I still have your souvenir Thomas." The fan curved out flowing like seaweed in a current, the small object secured by the tiny barbs on the fans flashing surface. "Don't you remember when you came to me? How you wouldn't let this go?"

Thomas could feel the tension building, could see the hounds stiffening as if anticipating the order to attack. He knew he had to be alert, to tackle this monster cleanly and then run for his life but the object in the fan called to something in his mind, a long forgotten memory tugging at his consciousness.

The colours on the fan flashed from peach to mauve and then green.

Click clack. Click clack.

"Yes Thomas, you remember this don't you." Malum hissed his voice rising and falling like a cobra swaying and readying to strike.

Thomas found himself stretching out his hand even as his mind screamed at him not to do so. The child's toy appeared to fall in slow motion towards him, Thomas's eyes drawn to the chipped paintwork of a *Matchbox* toy police cruiser, the blue and white colours flashing as the toy turned end over end, the dayglow orange decal spelling G12 still visible on its roof.

Pictures flashed through his mind, as he stood paralysed. Images of work colleagues, long forgotten eating doughnuts and drinking coffee. A packet of cigarettes, police tape around a shallow grave, a child's lifeless hand and then the same child playing with the toy police car now tumbling across his vision, running it across a bay window sill in a faded VHS home movie.

Malum knew the distraction he had created and the hypnotic flashing of the fans in Thomas's direction had halted the greatest danger he faced. Fans whirled out, flashing red and yellow, clicking, snapping, buzzing and seeking the exposed flesh of the other members of Thomas's party. There were yelps of surprise as the fans darted in and the sound of metal parrying the appendages that attacked from high and low.

Ives yelled in shock as three fans plunged down on his shoulders, knocking him back to the floor just as his hand closed around the hilt of his white blade. Aradol parried and blocked but knew his reactions were only stopping a strike from landing and his swordplay was merely defensive.

Kerian swung his violet blade in hard, glancing off Malum's flaking skull and raising a yelp of pain from the creature before fans whirled in knocking the blade aside. Malum turned with a look of red-hot anger and despite the milky slime filled eye sockets indicating the creature was blind, Kerian believed for that moment this nightmare could see him very clearly indeed.

Thomas struggled to respond to the cries around him, knowing in his mind that something was wrong but the images triggered by the spinning police cruiser were also turning violent and it was hard to tell if the noise was a memory or the reality of the chaotic scenes unfolding around him.

His colleagues were shouting at him, his locker was open, the police car found. They said he did it, that he was the one responsible. This could not be! It had to be a lie! He was running, running for his life, the toy car held tightly in his grasp, as if by holding it, he could will the truth to be known. Then two figures, people he knew and trusted, offering him a way to turn himself in. The shotgun blast, the burning pain in his chest; a fall from the pier into the freezing harbour water. Something touching his hand.

The toy landed in his palm. He closed his hand around it, the world snapping back to reality and Thomas suddenly recognised how quickly the tables had turned.

The hounds charged as a pack, barking and snarling, claws skidding across the floor, teeth flashing and saliva dripping from their jaws, eager to serve their master and earn a tender morsel of warm flesh in return.

Malum looked at the chaos around him, threw back his withered head and laughed.

* * * * * *

"I see..." Commagin nodded his head in understanding staring down at the semi-submerged figure of his apprentice Barney. The Dwarven engineer turned and shouting back across the decks. "Prepare to brace! We are about to re-float the ship."

He turned back to Barney, gave him a thumbs up for reassurance and watched as the apprentice resealed his helmet and submerged back under the surface of the sea with barely a bubble to mark his passing.

Commagin had to admit the suit had worked a charm. If they ever got out of here, he could set up shop repairing ships whilst they still floated instead of putting them in dry dock. He would make a fortune. Now where was Ashe? He turned taking in the ship as people ran to and fro, grabbing up loose items in preparation for the jolt to come, his thick muscular arms never ceasing to pump the bellows that supplied air to his submerged colleague.

He could not see Ashe anywhere. He yelled at Plano drawing the sailor away from his rigging duties and asked him if he could grab a few crewmen and go below decks to check for leaks once they settled back fully in the water. The sailor nodded agreement and whistled at his colleagues indicating that they follow him below.

* * * * * *

"See." Austen indicated, pointing into the shady cage at the bird of prey within. "She's laying eggs. With luck your baby bird Cinders will be one of them." He tried to suppress the chuckle in his throat as he continued to make fun of Ashe by calling the bird this way.

Ashe stood on tiptoe staring in through the bars of the cage his eyes wide with excitement. He took in the piercing yellow intelligent eyes staring out from within a mass of silvery white and blue-black plumage. Nevertheless, he could not see any eggs no matter how he tried to look.

"Really? Can I see them?"

"Not yet." Austen stated calmly. "You can see your bird only when it has been hatched, but it shouldn't be long now."

"I bet Sinders will be the biggest fastest bird ever." Ashe beamed. "Maybe she will take me flying through the clouds. Oh... can I teach Sinders to talk?"

Austen rolled his eyes. How was he going to tell the Halfling that the bird would never, ever get that big and why would he want to teach it to talk? Its job would be to catch fish for the crew not to sit on a ship's rail talking all day like a stupid parrot.

"I don't believe anyone has ever tried to make one talk." He confessed, feeling slightly exhausted at the ongoing discussion and wondering how he would get out of it.

"Well Sinders will be really sharp. I'm sure it will pick this up in no time."

They both paused as the warning to brace rose from the front of the ship.

"Oh, what a shame." Austen announced in relief. "There will be lots of things to do now, so off you go and find out how you can help!" He shooed the Halfling away, secretly feeling a silent glee at the timing of the announcement and no guilt at all that the little man was loose to wreck chaos on other members of the crew.

* * * * * *

Barney had to confess he was enjoying being under the water. It was like being in a strange forest where there were no bird sounds, just your own breathing ringing in your ears. He looked around at the softly swaying stalks rising from the bed of the sea beneath the ship and believed he would like to stay here forever if he could.

Small fish darted about around him, some rushing in where he had disturbed the sediment searching for submerged organisms uncovered by the apprentice's passing, whilst others came in close to peer through his helmet and look at the strange creature that was inside the glass globe with their curious round yellow eyes. The colours were breath-taking, reds, yellows, sandy grey and black stripes. Colours that changed depending on whether the fish were in the shade of the weed mat or darting through the feeble rays of light that passed for day. This experience was one he would never forget. He only wished it could last longer.

He looked up at the last thick vestige of weed holding the *El Defensor* out of the water and sighed loudly from within his helmet. It had to end now. He would be back to sweeping the lab floor before he knew it.

The apprentice bounced across the bottom, puffs of sand and silt rising behind him marking his trail. He came to the base of the thick weed and stared up at the dark shape of the ship above. It was quite a unique perspective looking at it this way. He could see the pink tube supplying his air spiralling up towards the *El Defensor* in soft whorls and could see the little fish nibbling at the surface where small air bubbles escaped through the material.

He took in the thick stem before him and decided where it would be best to start sawing. It was like trying to cut down a miniature tree and Barney knew it would take him a while to sever the stalk from its base and bring the ship safely back down into the water. He bent to the task, carefully lining up the sawblade with the rubbery stem of the weed and set to work, the teeth of the dulled blade bouncing off the trunk a couple of times before finally biting and starting to work. Barney blew hard within the helmet, it got very warm when he did this and he could feel the sweat starting to bead on his brow.

The swaying forest of reeds behind him started to part, revealing the snub-nosed snout of a gigantic eel. The creature had been stalking its prey for a while now, creeping forwards with slow deliberate flicks of its fins, its sleek silver body threading its way laboriously through the stalks of vegetation moving undetected, finally getting close enough to strike.

Barney continued to saw away at the weed, blissfully unaware of the encroaching danger, his little bottom wiggling as he got into the sawing motion. The eel slowly moved out from its cover, the floor beneath it growing dark as it cast a shadow. The little apprentice was just the right size for a juicy morsel. It opened its mouth, displaying an array of needle fine razor-sharp teeth as it moved closer and prepared to strike.

A darker, much larger shadow crossed the sandy bottom making the eel freeze, its predatory nature over-ruled by the risk of becoming prey itself. With a flick of fins, it backed up and settled to the floor, making itself one with the murk.

Barney paused in his sawing as he suddenly felt a chill and noticed it had become darker. He looked up and saw off behind the *El Defensor* a second ship, similar in size, was drawing close. As he looked on, an ancient anchor fell through the water to hit the floor and start scraping up sediment as the galleon slowed to a halt.

Barney tried to scratch his bottom through the padded suit wondering for a moment what the arrival of this other ship could mean, then he turned back to the job he was supposed to do and set to sawing again.

The eel stayed stock still, waiting to see if the shadow cast from above was a threat, before tentatively moving forwards again. It started to pick up speed, jaws opening wide.

With a grunt, Barney sawed through the last part of the stem and watched in satisfaction as it shot upwards, the weight of the *El Defensor* now pushing down onto the freed weed, making the base of the plant rush towards the surface.

The pink tubing curling freely above rotated into the path of the weed, becoming ensnared and yanking the apprentice up after the rocketing underwater flora. One minute, Barney was looking up in wonder, the next his legs were up and his head was down, as he shot towards the surface at speed, just as the eel snapped its jaws closed on the space he had recently occupied.

* * * * * *

Marcus looked up at the cheer that ran across the deck, tearing himself away from a large ledger that detailed the story of the *El Defensor* under her previous captain. It was quite fascinating and he really wanted the crew to be quiet but they were all clapping and cheering.

He pulled himself to his feet and looked out over the railing towards the strangest sight. A battered version of the *El Defensor* looked back at him, Rauph waving manically from the helm as Scrave released the anchor and sent it clattering into the waters below. It was as if looking into a mirror, except the ship he looked at was showing signs of neglect and was much the worse for wear. By the scrapes along her barnacle-covered hull, she had clearly seen some action.

Marcus's first thoughts were whether there was another ship's log somewhere within that he could compare, to see if this seaweed covered vessel, with her sails rotted away, held as interesting a set of secrets as this crew seemed to hold. It was like looking at a future picture of the ship on which he sailed, as if someone plucked it from the waters, packed it away and hid it in a dusty cobwebbed vault for hundreds of years. It was quite fascinating.

The sudden drop of the ship caught Marcus unawares. He fell backwards, his legs giving out, his pile of books scattering across the deck. His thoughts went from the amazement of seeing the ancient galleon to his concern for the volumes in his care. He clambered across the deck, trying to scoop the books up and tidy them again but his injuries made it hard going. He lifted one very large ledger and froze as it caught on a book beneath and pulled the canvas cover, tearing it.

Marcus tried to blot out the second round of cheers around the deck as the *El Defensor* creaked and groaned, settling in the sea as if she had never left its embrace. Commagin was roaring out that they needed to fish Barney out of the water and demanding to know where Ashe was but Marcus could not focus on any of it. He was horrified that he may have inadvertently damaged one of Thomas's collection. Books were precious, something to treat with respect. The thought that he had damaged one tore at his heart.

He placed the ledger gently to one side and examined the canvas, sighing in relief. The canvas covering served to stop damage occurring to the book at sea, simply a wrapping for the volume it protected. He lifted the torn material and froze in wonder.

Staring up at him was his charge. The book sat there quite innocent, looking slightly damp and battered at the corners but it was there and it was real. He closed his eyes breathed deeply and cracked them open again. The leather-bound book reflected his gaze.

At that second, Marcus vowed he would never doubt his faith again.

* * * * * *

"Thomas!" Kerian screamed over the laughter of Malum. "We need to get out of here and we need to do it now!" He swung his violet hued blade, severing the fans pinning Ives to the floor and drawing a scream from the creature as its filaments spurted pinkish fluid into the air.

The response was immediate, angry fans swept in trying to latch onto any exposed flesh and tear bleeding strips away. Kerian parried furiously, battling for his life against an enemy that seemed to be everywhere at once.

"Just shoot him!" Rowan shouted, pulling Thomas's arm not realising she was backing away into the hounds.

Thomas turned, his eyes still taking in everything, the gun useless in his hand. What did those images he had just witnessed mean?

Rowan slapped him hard across the face, tugging furiously on his arm and Thomas looked over her head to see the first hound jumping for her unprotected back. His response was instinct. He raised the gun, Rowan's eyes going wide in shock, her feelings clear that she thought the bullet was for her because she had dared to slap him.

She threw up her arms as he fired and the bullet passed over her shoulder and ploughed into the hound's skull, taking the Scintarn down in a crashing heap.

Thomas immediately regretted the action. He now had only one bullet left.

He drew his sword, turning back to his friends and the buzzing angry swarm of clicking fans. The blade slicing through the air and making Malum retreat.

"This way," Aradol shouted, spearing one animal and batting away two fans as he withdrew the thrust. "Back to the cage."

"Back to the cage." Ives grunted, swinging his sword to make three Scintarns duck and back away snarling in frustration. "Are you serious? We just got..." He swung his sword in hard making one hound retreat with a laceration on its flank. "...away from the cage."

Kerian tried to see where Aradol was gesturing and missed an attacking fan that latched onto the back of his hand and ripped a strip of flesh away. Blood immediately bloomed across the wound and he swore in anger, pushing forward towards the nightmare, the pain fuelling his ferocious response.

He slammed the hilt of his sword into Malum's head twice, making the creature shy away, and shower putrid pus on the carpet but Kerian continued the press, swinging his rune etched blade around his head and bringing it down towards Malum's skull.

Fans buzzed in left and right trying to wrap around the sword and stop its downward path, the creature giving ground as the violet blade sliced through the filaments like a knife through butter, sending fans flapping and jerking to the carpet at his feet.

Malum threw up a stunted arm from the folds of his body and caught the blade on his upturned wrist. The withered fist flew away and landed among a group of hounds who initially took it for an attack and turned on each other, not sure, where the source of the panic came from.

"Not so tough now eh?" Kerian continued to press, as Malum screamed in rage and pain. "Keep your hands off my friends."

"Oh, I will kill you so slowly." The creature hissed; his slime filled eyes burning with hatred. "You will rue the day you crossed me old man Styx."

"Less of the old." Kerian snapped back. "Haven't people told you looks can be deceiving?" He swung his sword in hard, the blade tracing arcs of violet as it passed through the air.

Malum roared and backed off with a speed that left Kerian unexpectedly standing in free space. The creature hit the wall and then used the glowing fans to grip the surface and lift itself clear from the floor like some horrendously enlarged grotesque spider.

Aradol was waving dramatically indicating they needed to follow him and Kerian took one look at the ranting monster scrabbling along the wall before deciding he had nothing to lose but oblige!

Thomas was pushing the young woman in the same direction as Aradol, pausing only to swing his blade wildly at any Scintarn close enough for his steel to reach, missing more times than he connected but keeping the hounds wary and allowing himself and Rowan to make leeway.

"Where are you taking us?" Thomas shouted as Aradol skidded around the corner back to where the holding area lay. "We need to go the other way. This is not right; you are leading us further into the *Neptune*."

"Yes, please tell." Ives requested, spinning on one foot and lashing out with his ivory blade. "I worked really hard to get out of the cage and you appear to be leading me straight back to it."

"Just follow me okay. I know a way out of here." Aradol threaded his way through the piles of discarded belongings alongside the cage and ran to the stairwell he had found earlier. He took the steps two at a time determined to leave the monsters as far behind him as possible.

The others piled into the stairwell in pursuit, Thomas letting them through first before standing and fending off the snarling snapping jaws of the Scintarns fast behind. With the narrow confines of the stairwell working in his favour, he was able to back slowly up the stair, lunging repeatedly with his blade to inflict wounds on the hounds, filling the stairway with pained howls.

Aradol exploded from the top of the stair jumping over the corpse of the Scintarn he had killed earlier, his eyes darting left and right to see a way out. He noticed another flight of stairs beyond and went to run along the terrace towards them.

Malum clambered over the edge of the balcony with a scream, using his fans to propel himself with such speed that it caught Aradol off guard. The monster slammed into him with such power that the young man fell to the floor, his sword flying from his hand. The fans buzzed in, landing on his back like suckers and then ripping off, taking strips of flesh from his bones. He screamed with agony as Malum laughed with glee.

Ives burst from the stairs and tripped over the dead Scintarn, his ivory blade flying free from his grasp, flipping end over end to plunge straight into Malum's pale torso. The monster dropped to the deck gasping, Aradol crawling desperately away from the flailing fans clicking and buzzing angrily on the floor behind him.

Rowan came out of the stairwell next, took one look at the thrashing figure on the floor and stopped dead. Kerian came up behind her and rather than push her away politely picked her up and moved her to one side before running over to Aradol and looking down at the wounds the youth had received. It did not look good. Blood was dripping freely from two large wounds on his back and running down the back of his tunic and legs.

Thomas appeared at the top of the stairs battling the hounds and making them pay for every yard. He took a quick glance over his shoulder and realised the momentum of their exit had slowed to a standstill.

"I can't hold them forever!" he yelled, slashing with his sword. "We need to keep moving."

Ives walked over to retrieve his blade and looked down at the creature he had inadvertently speared. It appeared to be drawing into itself like a spider as it dies. He gripped the sword hilt and pulled it free with a wet squelch.

"Come on," he gestured, sweeping his arm under Aradol's left side as Kerian took the right. "Let's get out of here."

Aradol moaned anew as they tried to walk him towards safety. Rowan ran up nervously alongside them, leaving Thomas fighting the hounds until he was sure they had a good lead. Then the captain turned and ran as fast as he could, leaping over the curled-up form of Malum, wishing he had kept himself in better shape.

They all ran for the stairwell and ascended another deck, even as Thomas tried to orientate himself as to where they needed to go. Up was no good. They needed to go down. The signs on the wall indicated paths to the *Moonlight Club,* a market café and the *Pinnacle restaurant.* There was an atrium, a salon and shopping on deck seven, signs for *Lucky Luke's casino* and even an *Oasis Spa*.

"Everyone just stop." Thomas yelled, trying to make sense of a pastel coloured chart that showed rows upon rows of accommodation stretching from one end of the ship to the other. The numbers stretched into the thousands and the key was faded and indistinct.

Where were the elevators? Howls rose from behind indicating the Scintarns were moving in.

"Elevators... Elevators. Yes!" Thomas turned and ran past his colleagues slamming through a huge set of glass doors and running into a boulevard that was so huge it emphasised the list at which the liner lay. Dirty crystal chandeliers served as resting places for errant birds that had made their way into the structure through holes in the hull. Pale beams of light filtered down making the whole setting beautifully surreal.

A faded mural ran along the wall behind a rather decrepit reception desk, the figure of Neptune standing proud from a cascade of foaming sea. Thomas scanned the walls frantically looking for a sign to show their escape route.

Scintarns slammed into the glass doors, paws squeaking on the crystal surface. Sheer weight of numbers moved the doors open enough for scrabbling paws to get into the gap and exploit it, pushing the door further ajar. They had mere moments.

Thomas noted the signs for the *Mermaid Explorer's Club* and clicked his fingers. This was it. It was all flooding back now. He gestured for his colleagues to follow him and turned a corner to a large bank of elevators. The power was out but Thomas knew enough about elevators to open a door. He wedged the flat of his blood-soaked blade up the streaked mirrored surface and clicked the safety latch so the door would slide open.

A yawning abyss stared back at him.

"I don't want to go down that fast!" Thomas muttered, moving to the next elevator and repeating the action to open the door.

"Hurry" Rowan screamed, "The dogs are getting closer!" The door squeaked open to reveal an elevator car. Thomas breathed a sigh of relief.

"Come on." He gestured. "In here now!"

They all piled in as the doors slid slowly together, leaving them breathless, wrapped in shadows and darkness, lit only by Kerian's softly glowing sword.

"Hold on a moment." Ives remarked his eyes wide in disbelief as he turned about in the small space. "Where's the door out?" The plump trader raised his eyes to the heavens and turned to face Thomas. "You seem to have made a mistake. There is no way out from this little room. Aradol all is forgiven; it appears your rescues are better planned than our illustrious captain's."

"Shush!" Thomas warned, encouraging them all to be quiet.

Loud sniffing along the door froze them in place. The Scintarns were looking for them. In the darkness, the sniffing seemed so much louder than a hound should be able to make. The doors to the elevator squeaked loudly as something pushed up against them whining in frustration.

The scrabbling at the base of the door slowly eased and then silence descended. Thomas still refused to move, waiting to see if the hounds would return. He knew keeping silent was hard, especially in a highly stressed situation like theirs, even so, when Aradol groaned in pain they all jumped.

"I think they have gone." Ives opened. "So how do we get out of here?"

The door to the elevator dented in towards them with a scream of tortured metal. Red glowing light filtered through the crack and Malum's haunting voice echoed into the shaft.

"You cannot hide from me. I can smell your fear!"

"But... But he's dead." Ives exclaimed. "How can he be alive?"

The doors squealed again and a fan wriggled through the gap, clicking and clacking, scenting the air. Kerian's sword slammed down on the fan, severing it from the filament making Rowan squeal as it flopped about on the floor of the elevator snapping and quivering.

"That's enough of that!" Kerian stated. "Come on Thomas, you got us into this where is the way out?"

Thomas started frantically pulling up the carpet in the floor, searching for a seam that he knew would lead to the emergency hatch. Most elevators usually had hatches in the roof, but with the nature of disabled and elderly passengers, the Neptune's hatches would have been too high for the majority of their clients to reach. Hatches set into the floor meant any age could access them in an emergency no matter what their height. He grunted as he pulled the hatch up, revealing the darkness below.

"Come on, one at a time." He pointed at a ladder set into the side of the shaft. "Do you think you can make it Aradol?"

"I'll make it." He replied through gritted teeth. "You aren't leaving me here with that thing!"

Ives went first, finding the rungs and starting down. He took a few steps then waited for Rowan to follow ensuring she was secure before he set off.

"Could have been worse." He joked, descending into the darkness. "We could have been going up instead of down."

Kerian slid onto the ladder and waited until Aradol had a firm grip then whispered into his ear.

"One rung at a time okay. I'm here with you every step of the way." Thomas went to follow as the elevator door ripped from its runner, bending completely out of shape as several fans rushed in working the hole wider. Malum's terrifying figure filled the doorway.

"Where are you hiding? You know I shall find you." He sniffed, turning his head from side to side scenting his prey. Thomas froze half in and half out of the hatch, afraid to move in case he gave away their location. He held his breath not daring to breathe.

"Boom, boom, boom." Malum bobbed his head in time with the words. "I can hear your heart Thomas. Are you scared? Come out and join me for dinner." Something slimy dribbled onto Thomas's face and he winced, knowing it was the disgusting slime from Malum's eye sockets tracking across his skin.

"There you are." Fans snapped into the elevator shaft, filling it with a crimson light as Malum's head swung down to where Thomas was hiding.

Thomas dropped through the hole in the floor and gripped the top of the rungs hoping against all hope that the others had a suitable lead. He wedged his feet against the edge of the ladder and slid down it like a firefighter, his hands used as a guide as he dropped into the darkness. The elevator rattled and shook above him as Malum started attacking the floor in a frenzy of anger. Pieces of the car flipping and clanging as they dropped down the shaft.

"I am going to kill you Thomas. You and your friend Styx will pay for what you have both done to me."

The elevator groaned then something snapped. There was a metallic clang and the elevator dropped, the emergency brakes corroded from years of neglect. It shrieked down the cables whistling by Thomas and the group, plummeting with such speed, that they were nearly torn from the ladder as the draft pulled at them. The elevator came to a stop far below with a crash that echoed up from the darkness, reverberating in the shaft and almost deafening them within its narrow confines.

Acrid clouds of disturbed mould, mildew and grit made breathing difficult but Thomas kept on descending the ladder. Hoping that Malum had been a passenger on the cars one-way trip but knowing in his heart that evil did not die so easily.

Especially something as evil as Malum Okubi.

Chapter Forty-Four

The light was virtually blinding when they finally found their way outside, having spent so long in the darkness feeling their way down the elevator shaft rung by rung, so it took a few moments to adjust to the putrid mustard coloured sky.

The *Neptune* stared down at them in judgement and found them wanting. Thomas looked about him, consciously aware of the scrutiny, that every second they wasted was another moment their enemy could organise pursuit and catch them. He took in the landmarks and pointed.

"I think the ship is that way. Let's go!"

"We need to stop." Kerian confessed. "Aradol is not fit to scramble over these wrecks and the rest appear to be winded. Just a few moments okay?"

Thomas shook his head, not happy at any delay.

"Malum isn't dead. He is also really pissed at us! I mean you chopped off his hand!"

"Oh yes." Ives chuckled as he sank down onto a large metal overhang. "I heard him say hands off and off it came. You are very funny for an old guy and pretty good in a fight."

Kerian hung his head, embarrassed at receiving such a compliment.

"And humble too. Good qualities. I am honoured to call you my friend."

Rowan looked at the two men talking and then over at Thomas who was becoming more agitated at each moment passed. She knew he was upset but also wanted to thank him for saving her life.

"My name is Rowan." She extended her hand, walking over and smiling through a face covered in dirt and grit. Thomas took her hand and tried to smile, despite his increasing concerns. He pointed at Kerian, introducing him, and making Rowan's face frown in confusion.

"I thought he said his name was Styx?" She took in the stern face of the old man with hazel eyes and long white hair, a million questions forming in her mind.

"It's a long story." Thomas replied. "I believe you have already made the acquaintance of Ives and Aradol."

"I have." She replied, brushing her hair from her face, steadily warming to the gentleman before her. "I haven't forgotten my date you know."

"Hold that thought." Thomas grinned. "Now if we have all caught our breath. It really is time to go."

The howls that echoed across the ship's graveyard made the hairs stand up on Rowan's arms.

"I do believe you are right," she smiled, making Thomas realise he was going to get these brave souls to his ship or die trying.

* * * * * *

"I thought I told you to stay on the *El Defensor?*" Commagin snapped, pulling the canvas cover off the front of their last remaining dinghy to find Ashe smiling sweetly up at him. "We don't have time for any of your messing about. We need to get the parts and secure the ships together."

"Well I can do that!" Ashe replied indignantly. "I'm very good at finding things. Just tell me what part you need and I will find it."

Austen continued to row down the channel through the weed towards the ghostly sister ship, keeping his head down and not wanting to get involved with Commagin's wrath at the Halfling stowaway. He had heard the tales of when Commagin last became upset and did not intend to suffer a bite on the leg.

The other ship came closer at each pull of the oars and before long they came alongside. Commagin threw up a thick coil of rope and asked Rauph to secure it firmly so they could draw the ships closer and start the work of transferring parts and getting the *El Defensor* ready to sail, away from this awful place.

Ashe pulled himself up on deck ignoring the gruff remarks from the chief engineer and ran over to Rauph, giving him a reassuring hug.

"I have missed you so much!" he exclaimed. "There was a monster in Sherman but then he blew up and then Barney went under water to save our ship and shot into the air. Wheee!" He mimicked a hand motion of something arcing through the air. "And I'm going to have a baby bird called Sinders and he is going to fly with me!"

Rauph looked down at the tiny Halfling babbling excitedly away and wondered whether to tap him sharply on the head to make him shut up but found he did not have the heart. If only he felt as energetic as this. Speaking of which he was hungry.

"Did you bring any food?" he asked.

"I don't know." Ashe confessed. "I was hiding in the boat because I wanted to come across and see your spooky ship. Commagin told me not to come so I didn't let him know I was there and now it is too late for me to go back. Where's Scrave?"

Rauph wrinkled his nose and wondered how Ashe managed to keep talking so long without drawing a breath. Maybe if he kept nodding his head the Halfling would talk so much he would pass out?" He tried to look attentive and nodded his head several times, throwing in a shake or two for good measure.

"Well I'm going to find Scrave." Ashe waved. "It was good catching up. Ooh! This boat is so spooky; I wonder if it's haunted?" He shot off heading for the cabins leaving Rauph still shaking his head attentively and wondering when he was going to eat.

* * * * * *

Ashe tiptoed into the darkness below decks, only pausing to light a candle he found in a dusty lantern along the way. This was so exciting. A completely new ship to explore! He tried to ignore the bangs and crashes from above decks as the crew set about securing the ship and allowed his imagination to run away from him.

Captain Ashe of the galleon *Indomitable*, rogue of the high seas! He chuckled. First port of call for a captain, checking the sleeping quarters and the grog. He turned the corner and approached the cabin that he knew belonged to Thomas on the *El Defensor*.

The locked door denied Captain Ashe his rightful entry but not for long!

Ashe stuck his tongue out the side of his mouth and bent to examine the door. His pick slid smoothly into the lock, flicking the catch aside with a skill acquired from years of trespassing. The door squeaked open, revealing a deserted cabin. Chills ran up Ashe's spine and he chuckled mischievously as he walked into the room. He took in the cobweb-covered furniture and the worn desk that was even more impressive than that of Thomas's back on the *El Defensor*.

He blew a ragged end of cobweb away and slipped around to the far side of the desk, before considering the chair that was rightfully his in his make-believe world. It looked a little uncomfortable to be honest. All gold gilt and velvet. Not practical at all.

Ashe pushed the chair to one side, ignoring the squeals it made as it scraped across the floor. The Halfling moved up to the desk, standing on tiptoe and peering over the edge, his little nose imprinting in the dust. He sniffed and then sneezed repeatedly his eyes watering but there was nothing of interest on the desktop.

Captain Ashe frowned. As master of the seven seas and all he surveyed he was bound to have treasure squirrelled away to shower on wenches he had wooed in the ports he had visited. So where would he put his fortune?

Tapping his foot and sending up further little plumes of dust, the Halfling checked the underside of the desk and then started feeling the engraved designs, looking for something that turned clicked or popped out. Still nothing.

What was the point of being captain of the high seas when you had no loot?

He leant forwards; his head resting on the edge of the desk, feeling something click under the pressure of his forehead. Ashe looked up at the little button, cunningly designed to look like one of many studs running around the edge of the desk and pressed it again. A small drawer popped open near his right knee and Ashe leaned forward to see what riches he had discovered.

"Oh my!" he gasped and leant forward for a better look. "That is absolutely perfect!"

* * * * * *

Scrave felt so ill. His head hurt and he had no idea why. The pain had steadily worsened as they had closed on the *El Defensor*; it was as if the cause of his distress directly related to his proximity to the vessel.

He rubbed his forehead, feeling the cold metal of the headband beneath his fingers.

"Where was it?"

Scrave stopped short, his fingers dropping from the golden jewellery. Whatever did he say that for? He shook his head. Maybe being in the ship's graveyard was causing the problem. Maybe if he had some rest, some water and food, he would feel better and this stubborn headache would relent.

He turned to look for Rauph and realised that the Minotaur was at the far end of the ship, a good distance away from where Scrave had last seen him greet Commagin. They seemed to be wrestling with a fixture from the ship, trying to get it free and from the looks of them, they had been struggling for some time.

How long had he been standing here staring at nothing?

Scrave shivered, rubbed his headband then set off to see how he could help.

* * * * * *

Justina cursed anew, pushing the scrying bowl away from her in disgust.

Where was the *El Defensor*? She knew it had not sunk. If it had, her little demon apprentice would have returned to let her know and would have demanded she release its brittle preserved corpse. Not that she ever would of course.

However, it was clear the ship had disappeared somewhere and she had no idea where. Even scrying was useless. She had thought, for just a fleeting moment, that she had located The Raven again but the contact was so quick and ethereal that she almost convinced herself that she had imagined it.

This was driving her to distraction. She needed to know what was going on and why her spell was not working. Maybe Hamnet, her little sorcerous pet, could find out. If she gave the creature explicit instruction, maybe it could use its own magic to enhance the connection between the serpent circlet and herself. Justina scowled, she did not like relying on others to do her work for her.

What she needed was a distraction to take her mind off her problems.

She thought about how withered and frail Pelune had become and a wicked smile came to her lips. Maybe spending a bit of time teasing Pelune and laughing at his impotence and lack of stamina would help her to feel better.

Justina grabbed her silken robe around her smooth curves and set off for her victim's chambers, whistling softly as she did so.

* * * * * *

Weyn counted the dark shapes now appearing along the rail of the *Rubicon*, there were more dogs there now, large ones by the looks of them. As he looked, another animal joined the others, ears up and alert, looking down on the two galleons as they drew together. Something about the scrutiny raised the hairs at the back of Weyn's neck. This was not right. It was not right at all.

As if in agreement, the beasts chose that moment to raise their heads to the sky and howl, a long mournful note that stopped everyone on board, heads turning as one to identify the source of the sound.

Weyn tagged a sailor as the man stopped to observe the display.

"Do we have an armoury?" The archer asked, unslinging his bow case from his shoulder. The sailor nodded in reply. "Get whoever is in charge to hand out weapons. We may be about to have visitors."

He turned his attention back to his bow and strung the weapon in one practiced move before starting to make his way towards the prow of the ship. He needed a good vantage point if he was to be of use in the attack that he expected was mere moments away.

* * * * * *

Thomas was reaching down to help Rowan scramble across the deck of an old fishing skiff and just started pulling her up when the howl sounded ahead. The *Rubicon* was close now, its profile, clear to see. She was within five wrecks then they would be able to reach her deck and return to the *El Defensor* but from the howls, it was clear the way ahead would not be a simple walk in the park.

Aradol continued to look unwell, his face ashen, every step clearly causing him great pain but Thomas had to admire the man, as he never voiced a complaint and simply kept placing one foot resiliently in front of another, although he was using Kerian and Ives more noticeably for support as they progressed.

Thomas looked back the way they had come, tracing their route, looking for signs of pursuit indicating that they would have to press ahead even faster. Answering howls rose from the direction of the *Neptune* and suddenly the dark shapes of tracking hounds became visible. They moved from ship to ship, their path matching the one that had taken the group so long to traverse, the beasts heading unerringly towards them.

Rowan suddenly raised her hand pointing back, a tremor on her lips.

"He's coming."

Two words Thomas dreaded to hear.

Ives looked up at Rowan, his scared facial expression asking for a confirmation he did not need to hear. Kerian stopped helping Aradol and looked in the same direction. Sure enough, bobbing lights indicated the pursuit of Malum and his terrifying evil presence. The monster scrabbled and jumped across the ruined wrecks, heading towards them with a pace that they would be hard to match. The race was doomed from the start. There was no way they would be able to keep ahead if Malum maintained his rapid spider-like speed.

"Time to move!" Thomas shouted, despite his colleagues all being able to hear him quite clearly. He winced inwardly as they jumped realising his nerves were showing. "Come on, last one back makes the coffee!"

Ives and Kerian turned to Aradol and lifted him bodily up the slanting deck.

"We better hurry," Ives joked to his numb friend. "I have heard stories of how bad Kerian's coffee is. We must make haste!"

They faced the next vessel with determination in their hearts but each step caused another groan from Aradol and the distance between them and their pursuers narrowed noticeably. By the time they reached the superstructure of the *Rubicon,* it was a matter of when rather than if Malum would catch them. It was a straight run now. Thomas found himself torn between putting his head down and fleeing or standing with his friends and he knew that the latter was the only thing he could do.

He turned to see how Kerian and Ives were coping with their charge and watched as Malum started to cross the last few ships behind them, Scintarns pacing the monster on either side, running in formation, their flanks rising in and out as they kept pace with their master.

The captain turned back to the group and noticed they had made some ground across the wide-open deck but then Thomas saw the dark silhouettes of the hounds appearing ahead and his heart sank. They were heading into a trap and there was nothing he could do about it.

Malum shrieked in perverse pleasure, making Thomas turn his head and look back at him, wanting to run for his life but unable to tear his gaze away. The creature's limbs propelled it across the uneven ground as sure footed as if each appendage adhered perfectly to the deck. With a lunge, the creature threw itself across the gap between ships and caught hold of the ladder Thomas had used to climb but moments before.

"Run Thomas, run." Malum teased, his voice cracking into another malicious laugh. "I will have you soon. You can't get away." Thomas had seen enough, he turned and ran after his colleagues, aware that Malum would gain the deck in seconds and start scuttling across it at a speed he could never hope to match, let alone outpace.

He ran between some fallen cargo containers and straight into his colleagues knocking Aradol to the floor with a groan of anguish and another strange squeak. Thomas fell to his knees behind him, winded, his hands reaching to help his colleague up even as his lungs tried to suck in air. He lifted his head and realised the others had stopped too. The reason all too clearly apparent.

Many hounds stood before them, hackles up, fangs bared, slowly advancing across the deck. Kerian stepped forwards, sword drawn, his walk one of a man resigned to meet his fate as he purposefully placed himself between his friends and the grisly destiny awaiting them.

Ives looked back through the cargo containers behind Thomas, his widening eyes confirming that Malum was closing rapidly, as Rowan moved across and grabbed the merchant's hand for reassurance.

It could not end like this.

Thomas straightened Aradol up and pressed against his side. The squeak came again. What was that? He fumbled with the waiter's soaked shirt and pulled out a small doll.

"Why?" Thomas asked, temporarily bemused at his crewmates motives.

"I was going to give it to Violetta's daughter." Aradol smiled painfully.

Thomas suddenly had an idea. A cocky grin appearing on his face.

"Everyone stand to the side." He shouted. "Kerian move back and get ready to help Aradol run. We may have only one shot at this."

A Scintarn ran forward, breaking formation and Kerian whipped his sword down, whistling through the air to catch the beast painfully on the snout. Angry barks and snarls rose from the rest of the closing pack. Behind them further answering barks, confirmed enemy reinforcements were closing.

Thomas surprised everyone and ran forward towards the hounds, making the pack stop in surprise. He held out his hand towards the beasts but to Kerian's surprise, he was not holding his sword. Instead, he held out the item he had taken from Aradol and squeezed it tightly making the toy give out the same silly squeak they had heard several times before.

The hounds stopped in their tracks as Thomas started to talk to the animals in a high-pitched excited voice. Barking and growling died instantly, hound eyes wide, heads cocked at an angle tilting from side to side trying to identify the source of the squeaking sound.

Thomas repeated the action, waving his arm about, squeaking the toy and still talking in his exaggerated tones. The hounds tilted their heads comically trying to understand what this man was doing. Tails started to flick from side to side with excitement.

"Are you ready?" Thomas spoke calmly to his friends, squeaking the toy as if his life depended on it. "When I say *now,* you run like hell for the stern of the ship. Do not stop, do not look back and just keep going until you run out of deck.

Ives looked back through the gap in the containers at Malum, now mere feet away, the monster's movements slowing as he listened to the calls from his pack, his cautious sniffing showing his recognition that his prey were trapped. The merchant turned anxiously back to Thomas who was now waving his arms at the hounds and squeaking the toy. The Scintarns were starting to bob their heads up and down as they followed his exaggerated arm swings, punctuated at each turn by another excited squeak. It was quite clear that Ives had put his trust in the hands of a mad man.

"Now!" Thomas screamed, turning and throwing the toy doll as hard as he could, right back through the containers, arcing high into the air before falling directly down onto Malum's head. The doll squeaked as it collided with his skull, then squeaked again as it hit the deck. It was more than the Scintarn's could stand.

They ran straight at their master, chasing the squeaking toy, leaving the passage ahead open, their excitement and speed so fast that they barrelled the monster over, jumping, pouncing and wrestling with each other, trying to grab the little doll. Malum roared with rage, slapping the hounds off their feet, knocking them to the floor with his fans, his limbs struggling to get back under his frame and bring him to his feet. He finally regained his footing, his head turning from side to side sniffing the air urgently. Somehow, in the confusion Thomas had made good his escape.

* * * * * *

Thomas ran along the railing of the *Rubicon*, his mind racing as fast as his beating heart, his cocky grin plastered across his face. He could not believe that hair-brained plan had worked. He would have laughed aloud but his breath was coming in such laboured gasps that he knew he would have to stop running if he did. The rest of his companions were heading towards the end of the deck as fast as they could but Thomas was acting as decoy, ensuring he was in line of sight and weaving to draw the hounds' attention away from them.

He looked down at the sea and the reed beds below. It was a long way down. They were never going to get Aradol to climb down the line fired up from the *El Defensor*. That meant they would have to jump and then swim to safety. He was not even sure he would be able to manage that himself.

Lifebelt stations were set at regular intervals along the railing. This seemed to be his day for having bright ideas! He ran for the first one, his colleagues continuing to race ahead as he peeled off towards his goal. Excited howls and barks indicated the Scintarns had recovered from the earlier distraction and were now back in 'dogged' pursuit.

Thomas lifted the first lifebelt and slung it over his shoulder, running full pelt for the next one. His chest felt like it was bursting. He had never run as fast in his life! He slid to a stop at the next station, snatching up the belt and turning to run, only to hear the hammering of paws on the deck behind him. He took off for the third lifebelt hearing the paws hitting ever closer, the growls getting louder and louder.

As the ship curved, Thomas finally made out the shape of the *El Defensor* and his heart soared, the adrenaline giving him an extra spurt of energy as the Scintarns bounded towards him. He risked a quick look over his shoulder.

Dear lord... the hound was too close.

He turned to the front and tripped, falling face first onto the deck. The Scintarn leapt onto him, snarling loudly, before yelping once and appearing to deflate before his eyes as something punched it hard in the side, knocking it to the floor. Thomas scrabbled back to his feet not believing his luck, spotting the polished wooden shaft that had sprouted from the animal's side.

Weyn Valdeze.

He was going to give that man a raise!

Thomas ran for the next station, hearing cheers rising from the ship below at his show of athletic prowess. As the curve in the Rubicon's deck continued to lead him around, Thomas noticed a ghostly ship coming into view, drawn up close alongside his home.

Rauph and Scrave had pulled through! His breath was gasping now, sweat running into his eyes. Another hound charged in from the side, snarling and snapping at his heels, only to collapse in a lifeless heap as another shaft struck home with deadly accuracy.

Thomas allowed himself one last quick look at the *El Defensor* and noticed that she was free of the weeds. Thankful for small mercies he lowered his head and piled on the speed, the lifebelts whipping around him.

* * * * * *

Commagin sized up the unfolding situation with a keen eye, watching as Weyn fired shaft after shaft into the mass of barking howling animals chasing his captain down. He noticed the remainder of the landing party arriving at the railing high above, looking down at the rope but no one was even considering making the descent.

"Get a boat into the water!" he ordered. "Get over to that ship now!"

Austen and Plano leapt to obey, tearing their gaze from the pursuit and recognising the sense in the Dwarven engineers command. They ran for the side of the *El Defensor* and swiftly climbed into the dinghy, pushing off the larger vessel and rowing as if it was themselves pursued and not their crewmates.

"Weigh anchor! Unfurl the sails! Let's get this girl moving!"

The ship galvanised into action, sailors leaping to their tasks, ropes pulling taut, sails dropping down to take advantage of any draught or slight breeze that could help ease their great ship from her resting place.

Commagin looked back up at the figure of Thomas running along the rail, then down at the dinghy rowing madly through the reeds before he factored in the snail-like pace at which *the El Defensor* was moving and tried to estimate the unknown displacement of her sister ship that they had no choice but to tow.

This was going to be close!

* * * * * *

"Get these on!" Thomas yelled, dropping the lifebelts at the feet of his colleagues.

"But we aren't sinking!" Rowan stated confusion clear on her face. "How are we going to get down to your ship? It's a long way and Aradol is in no fit shape to climb."

"We jump!" Thomas replied.

"We what!" Ives screamed, looking down over the side and shaking his head vehemently. "There is no way I'm jumping from here!"

"Fine by me." Thomas shot back, throwing a belt to Kerian as he tried to assist Rowan into hers. "If you wish to end up as dog food that's your choice."

Ives looked across the deck as the hounds closed, pink tongues lolling out of the sides of their mouths, drool dripping on the deck. Then he looked further back at the figure of Malum racing across the deck towards them, his fans flashing black and yellow in agitation. He took another terrified look at the sea far below and shook his head.

"I'm sorry I can't," he wailed, gripping his lifebelt firmly to his chest.

Thomas bit back a curse and forced his face into a reassuring smile.

"It's okay. Don't worry we will find another way." He moved over to Ives, his hand held out, dropping it onto Ives shoulder, patting him, reassuring the trader that all was well. "I'm sorry..." he paused, "but I know you will thank me later." Ives looked up at Thomas in confusion as the captain shoved hard, sending Ives through the gap in the rail.

"Thomas... you... son... of... a... whore!" Ives screamed as he plummeted to the sea below.

Kerian moved over to the opening in the rail, supporting Aradol on his arm, looking down at Ives thrashing in the water far below.

"Not bad," he smiled. "The triple somersault at the end was a nice touch!"

"It was more of a belly flop." Thomas acknowledged. "And with that belly he will be feeling it for hours!" He looked up, taking in the swiftly advancing hounds and smiled at his friend. "See you back on deck."

Kerian nodded without replying, grabbed Aradol securely and jumped into space.

"It's just us now." Thomas remarked, turning to grab Rowan's hand. He could not help but notice how she shook. "Don't worry. I'm here to protect you remember." He tried to disarm her worries with a smile but instead found himself leaning forward and kissing her firmly on the lips.

"What was that for?" she asked, catching her breath.

"I saw it in a movie once." Thomas smiled. "It's for luck."

Then he jumped and took Rowan screaming over the side with him.

They hit the water like rocks, the force of entry crushing the air from their lungs and plunging them deep below the surface. Thomas tried to quell the panic in his chest as he felt millions of bubbles brush up from around his body. He waited until his downward momentum eased, before striking out for the surface.

He broke through the weed covering gasping loudly, hearing shouts from the left and blinked his eyes clear to see the dinghy closing. His next thought was for Rowan but she was already making for the boat. Ives was already sitting in the small vessel shivering and looking miserable but thankfully still alive.

Kerian was swimming with some difficulty, trying to keep Aradol's head free of the water, so Thomas struck out for him, powerful strokes moving him through the water in moments to help share the load of his wounded crewmate.

Blood seeped slowly into the water from Aradol's wounds as they struggled to keep him afloat, awaiting the slowly approaching dinghy to pull them to safety.

Ives noticed the disturbance in the weeds first.

"Something is coming." His voice wavered, indicating the 'v' pattern visible on the water's surface as a submerged creature started swimming towards them.

Hands moved under Aradol's frame pulling him up into the boat and clear of the water. Thomas struggled to get up, levering himself into the dinghy but his efforts swung the boat side up and down leaving Kerian struggling; the toll of running across the ships and carrying Aradol had clearly exhausted him.

Something long and silver started to break the surface of the sea as the monster picked up speed.

"Hurry." Ives shouted.

Kerian tried to pull himself up and slipped, plunging back under the surface. Hands followed him grabbing at his clothes and bringing him gasping to the surface.

"Come on!" Rowan screamed. "Get him out."

They pulled in unison, dragging Kerian's exhausted frame from the sea, his legs kicking and scrabbling for a foothold where there was none. His boots just cleared the water as the biggest eel Thomas had ever seen slammed into the side of the dinghy, skipping the boat across the reed bed with the force of its strike. They all collapsed into a heap in the bottom of the boat laughing with relief.

Thomas wiped his face, pushing the hair back from his eyes and looked up the side of the *Rubicon* from his prone position in the bottom of the boat. He threw a salute he knew Malum would not be able to see but felt it was only fair to give the creature a parting wave.

Malum was screaming down at him in fury.

"Where are you Thomas?" He cried, his pale head sniffing the air repeatedly. "Come here and let me kill you."

"Oh, I think I'm quite comfortable down here." Thomas shouted back, making Malum turn his head sharply towards the sound.

"You are still alive!" the creature questioned, clearly surprised at the revelation.

"You don't sound happy for me." Thomas shot back, indicating to the others that they should start to row after the departing galleons. "I'd like to say it's been fun catching up and all but don't be upset if I don't call for a while."

Malum shrieked in fury, pacing up and down the railing edge, his glowing lights flashing with agitation.

"I'm going to kill you!" it hissed.

"As you keep telling me." Thomas shouted. "Now I really must be going."

"No!" Malum screamed. Then he did the one thing Thomas did not expect. Malum stepped over the side of the ship and started to run and skid down the sheer surface of the *Rubicon's* hull.

"Shit!" Thomas struggled to sit up from the bottom of the boat, his jibes and insults forgotten, his mirth replaced with terror. "Row! Row now!" Austen and Plano bent to the task, the oars cutting into the water taking the dinghy slowly away from the massive cargo ship.

Malum hit the water with a crash, seawater splashing up as he landed. His head turned towards the sound of the oars and with a roar, he was off, his spindly flashing limbs displacing his weight and allowing him to run across the top of the weed. Like a spider pursuing its struggling prey across the surface of its web.

"Row faster damn you!" Thomas yelled, his mind hardly comprehending the speed at which Malum was closing, limbs flicking out to grab impossible purchases on the undulating carpet beneath him.

Thomas struggled to his feet, drawing his sword, taking his stance, knowing that the chance of fighting to any degree of accuracy in this situation was absurd. Malum barrelled on towards him, his rage obvious to every terrified member of crew in the dinghy. His sheer presence radiating pure malevolence.

The sea erupted in spray as the monster eel attacked, jaws closing on the running object passing above it. Malum screamed as needle sharp teeth came together trapping some filaments and tugging the monster down under the water with a mighty splash.

The reed bed calmed impossibly for a few seconds, before exploding again in a burst of spray. Malum rose from the sea, his fans wrapped around the eel's head, ripping flesh from its snout in spurts of blood and gore, pulling one large eye clear from the socket. The water foamed crimson as shredded eel flesh and muscle tore free. The eel coiled defensively about the monster attacking it, sinuous lengths of its body attempting to crush the cause of its pain.

The eel twisted and turned, rolling Malum and repeatedly plunging the fiend beneath the weeds, then up in the air again as his spiderlike form crawled up and down its length, barbs whistling out and inflicting further deep wounds. The thrashing created a swell that aided their small rowboat in making headway towards the *El Defensor.* Thomas struggled to remain standing and looked on in stunned amazement at the raw power of his enemy. Sheets of spray cascaded down on them as if they were out in a monsoon.

Scintarn hounds bayed to the heavens, aware that their Master was in trouble but powerless to do anything about it. Their agitated forms running backwards and forwards along the *Rubicon's* deck. The crew of the dinghy could not clear the area fast enough, pulling at the oars for all their worth. The *El Defensor* moved near as she started to commence a wide turn towards the open archway and Thomas was relieved to find the crew were ready to receive them.

Sailors armed with boathooks leaned out from the side of the galleon, desperate to fasten on to the fleeing crew as their path came near, the surge from the thrashing battle thrusting the boat hard into the *El Defensor's* hull and jarring all the passengers aboard. Thomas kept looking over his shoulder terrified that Malum would win his battle with the eel at any moment and set off after them, spitting his defiance and wrath but the eel was tenacious, despite its grievous wounds, teeth flashing and coils tightening as it tried to rend and crush the creature wounding it so badly.

Kerian felt he was on a bucking stallion, trying to grip the side of the ship and hoist himself aboard. Ives slipped twice but with a helping hand from the others, managed to find his footing and clamber aboard. It was harder to move Aradol but a makeshift harness swung from the main stay allowed them to hoist the valiant crew member and Rowan aboard.

Thomas felt relief flood into him as he finally placed his feet on the *El Defensor's* deck. He was back on his ship and back in command! He turned to watch the battle, the giant eel continuing to thrash, weaker than before, the sea a slick of red as its struggles started to slow. Malum still clung on, screaming with rage, the barbed extensions of his frame slashing, gouging and ripping the eel to quivering shreds.

"Take us out of here," Thomas ordered, hands on his knees gasping for breath. "Warp speed!"

"We can do a couple of knots and that's it!" Commagin shot back, his face showing the confusion he felt at such a command. "You will just have to settle for that." He turned and started ordering the crew, trying to squeeze any more speed he could out of the sails and the choppy sea conditions beneath them, the *El Conquistador* wallowing along behind.

Kerian stood on the deck, looking back towards the shipwrecks they had just traversed. He vowed to himself that he would never, ever, return to this place. Malum was terrifying, a force of pure evil. Kerian shivered, unsure if he would ever sleep soundly again.

It took some time for the eel to die, some time for Malum to painfully extricate himself from its crushing coils. He dragged his wounded body from the water, crawling up onto a dry piece of listing deck and looked out towards where he surmised his fleeing enemy must lie. Scintarns scrabbled over to stand as silent sentinels either side of him as he slowly got to his feet, water and blood dripping from his body, rage lighting a fire within his blackened heart.

The *El Defensor* slowly navigated her way through the archway and to the world beyond, towing the *EL Conquistador* behind her. As the two ships safely negotiated the arch, the opening closed, leaving the swirling mists as the only sign of their passage, the gateway becoming inert as the magic required to keep it open ceased. Malum found himself marooned with just the company of his baying Scintarn hounds.

The creature's pale chest rose and fell, slight tremors racing through his body. His hand was lost, severed at the wrist, his main feeding tube shattered, numerous fans severed. It would take time to recover and lick these wounds but Malum knew he had all the time in the world.

Time to let his anger fester, let his rage grow.

He knew Thomas needed to come back through the archways again if he wanted to access a passage to go home, him and his accursed companion Styx.

Malum let his remaining hand settle on the head of a nearby hound, rubbing the hair on its head, letting the animal become reassured before gripping its skull hard and making it squeal with pain.

Oh, they would come back... and he would be waiting for them.

Part Four:- Stratholme

I worry for the man who has achieved his heart's desire.
For few remain contented with what they have, whilst others
lose direction when there is nothing left to motivate them.
People once friends can find envy in their souls
and seeing happiness will seek to take it and keep it for their own.

A wise man's proverb.

Chapter Forty-Five

Richard Perrot looked out from the observation deck set within the opulent gardens of his church and stared down across the calm mirrored surface of the bay below. He was truly content, his mind at peace, his heart and soul in a place few men would ever find themselves.

His steel blue eyes took in the volcanic island of Stratholme and the abundance of life that grew here in the rich fertile soil; the vivid green trees that cloaked the shoulders of the twin peaks behind him cascaded down the mountainside and covered every inch of the land not worked on by the islanders below. It was like an opulent carpet, broken by ribbons of white water from high falls in the peaks and the sporadic terracotta rash of clay-tiled houses where dwellings stood proud of the greenery nearer to the bay.

The village gardens were home to luscious vegetables of exquisite taste and fruits of vibrant colour and sweetness. Tended lovingly by the villagers who tried to work in harmony with the world around them. Fruits grew vertically to use less space, whilst vines clung to the trees themselves, fashioned into bowers that added to the richness of the living canvas Richard could see.

He ran his hand through his dark hair, feeling its length and realising it would need cutting soon if he were to keep it tamed. There was a time in the past when his hair was shorn ridiculously short, giving him no sense of style or identity. He disregarded the dark thought. He was never going to think of that place again. It was an ocean away, a different world of a different time.

He tried to centre his thoughts, return to a balanced state of rest and poise but something was not right. Something was worrying him, a small feeling of unease that was slowly worming its way into his mind.

Bright scarlet and yellow birds flew from carefully constructed nests, trilling their ownership to all that would listen and bringing distraction from Richard's troubles. A small blue bird zipped past his ear, its wings whistling as it passed, busy looking for nectar from the *Jangro* flowers that grew in the rough bark of some of the more mature trees. Thin needle like beaks dipped in and out of the little pools of energy the flowers offered freely, before they took flight again at frenetic speed, whilst lime and orange frogs hopped around the edge of the ornamental pond, disappearing with small plops that made the brightly coloured fish swimming in the depths shoot away defensively.

Richard felt the warmth of the sun kissed stone railing beneath his hands and smiled at the beauty behind him. This was anything a man could ask for. It truly was paradise.

His gaze wandered down the switchback cobblestone trail, from the church down to the port. A large windmill spun lazily below, its movement catching the observer's eye, smoke rising from the attached extension that held the only public house the village had. Richard licked his lips, fleeting thoughts considering what would be on the menu this evening to excite the senses and tantalise his taste buds, before his eyes continued their journey down to the waterfront where several foreign ships remained at dock.

Maybe it was the strange design of the ships that worried him? The congregation had talked of nothing else this morning. The current story circulating was that this crew were lost souls, caught in the storm he had witnessed from this very spot but two nights ago.

The sky had ripped apart that night, red lightning danced angrily across the clouds. The strange portent was just the beginning; an eerie yellow light had appeared far out on the horizon, as if someone had left a candle unattended in a window. Everyone had seen it; the fishermen had kept their boats in the harbour worried by the faint and mysterious light that grew more ominous and threatening by night.

Richard allowed himself a small private laugh, taking in the harbour and the two wrecked ships at dock. The repetitive bashing of hammers and rasping of saws echoed up the mountain to him. He could see figures moving about the two strange ships, stripping parts from one ship to patch extensive damage on the other and wondered why the crew even bothered. From seeing the ruined deck smashed mast and rigging, it would have been easier to simply transplant the crew to the other ship. Someone clearly had deep emotional ties to the vessel to carry out such a labour-intensive exercise.

Gossip about the crew was rife throughout the village. There was even talk of a giant horned creature working amongst them!

Richard shook his head. He really needed to have a word with the village gossips and get them to tone down their descriptions, as they would only serve to scare the children. He turned from the ships, his eyes tracing the opaque surface of the sea, his ears trying to blot out the sounds of construction and concentrate on the soothing sounds of the waves. Seagulls bobbed up and down on the surface of the sea and from this distance, they looked just like apple blossom floating on the pond.

He felt for the sleeve of his robe and started to rub it, reassuring himself with the comforting feeling and repetitious action, blissfully ignorant of the green moss streaks that marked his clothes and the areas showing wear and holes that required repair. Richard had never been a confident man; his actions unintentionally showed the anxiety he was trying to convince himself he did not have.

The thing was that this was not the only visitors the island had received.

He set off across the well-tended lawn, aiming for a tunnel of weeping willow through which the bright colours of his church beckoned. As he entered the cool shade, he tried to reassure himself that his imagination was running wild. They were not used to having guests at the island. At least not this many all in one go.

He exited the tunnel, looking up at his church and felt elation flood through him. The domed construction was terracotta and white, clean and compact, butting up against the stone of the mountain peaks behind. Richard still found it amazing how the villagers had constructed the church and the gardens to such exquisite detail. Everything was just as he had imagined it to be. It was everything he had ever desired.

A disturbance in the underbrush caught his attention, he wandered over, parting the grass to find a delicate violet bird in distress and a smoke grey kitten with oversized ears and clumsy white paws toying with the bird as it struggled to escape the cat's clutches.

He reached in and pulled the cat away, gently squeezing the paw to retract the claw caught in the bird's wing and scolded the cat, tapping it firmly on the nose.

"No Socks. You know the rules. No one hurts anyone here." He gently scooped the bird up in his hand and lifted it back into its nest, a glimmer of heat radiating from his palm as he healed the bird's wounds.

Socks was not happy and struggled to free itself from the priest's clutches but he held firm, despite the claws inserted into his forearm.

"Now, now!" Richard continued to scold, walking away with the cat in his arms. "If you are hungry, we can see if aunty has anything for you."

He walked over to the doors of the church, debating whether to go inside now or stand for a few moments longer on the steps, his view of the village now including an extra building, not visible from his old vantage point.

An old jetty, complete with a covered dock also held visitors who had arrived a day before the newest arrivals. Richard had watched the ship sail into port, she was sleek, her wooden hull made of silvered wood, clearly shaped with speed in mind but she had not fared well navigating the storm. Her splintered bow buckled by the force of the waves she had sailed through, her sails in tatters, hanging limp and useless as the fishermen had used their own boats to carefully bring the vessel in to shore.

However, the captain commanding the ship caused Richard the most consternation. This was the very type of individual the priest had worked so hard to get away from in his old life. Something about the man, even If his looks had not telegraphed his character so clearly, marked a man used to violence and hatred.

He hoped the man would be on his way, the sooner the better.

Socks finally wriggled its floppy body out of his arms and dropped to the floor, shooting away back in the direction of the bird's nest and Richard allowed himself another smile. It was no good having such dark thoughts on such a beautiful day.

He turned and walked into the shaded nave of the church, his sandals clicking upon the tiled floor, his eyes slowly adjusting to the low light within. Coloured beams of light through the stained-glass windows illuminated his path towards the altar and he paused there for a few moments allowing the serenity of his surroundings to seep into his being.

Richard prayed silently, then turned to the right, past a small table where candles lit to signify times of remembrance, flickered gently in the draft from his passing. He arrived at a stout wooden door and pushed it open, moving in to his sanctuary, his living quarters and his study where he could read peacefully in the sitting nook near the gothic window and gaze out across the gardens that brought him so much peace.

He paused before the window taking in the view, trying to calm his feelings of unease, and then heard the clearing of a throat behind him.

Richard did not mean to jump but his tension betrayed him, his heart leaping in his throat. He turned to take in his desk and the man sitting at his seat.

It was a face from the past, a face that turned the blood in his veins to ice.

His eyes darted for the door to consider a path of escape but someone stood in the entryway a sword held blade down. It took Richard seconds to realise the armour was from the Order he thought he had escaped from. His eyes swept the room to notice other knights standing silently in the shadows.

His head turned slowly back to the man sitting at his desk, even as his heart sank at the realisation of what was before him.

"How can I help you?" he tried not to stammer the question, tried not to show the signs of defeat crashing into his soul.

"Brother Richard." Marcus replied solemnly. "By decree of Abbot Brialin and on behalf of the Holy Order of St Fraiser, we have come to bring you back home."

* * * * * *

Ashe finished sweeping up the rubbish from the floor of the lab, whistling as he worked in a way that anyone knowing him would have recognised as a signal he was up to no good.

Commagin waved as he walked out the door, relying on Ashe to close shop and leaving him alone at last. The Halfling whistled a few strained notes, then ran over to the door of the lab and opened it a crack making sure Commagin had really left for the mess hall. The Dwarven engineer was gone, Violetta's gumbo his siren call.

Ashe looked down at the dustpan in his hand, filled with bits of metallic flash, screwed up papers with plans for new inventions long abandoned and other assorted detritus. What was he going to do with this? He looked about the room, discounting the one chair in the lab as it was already at a strange angle and the rug that looked more like a minor mountain range.

The Halfling clicked his fingers. There was a store cupboard on the far side of the lab. He set off walking through the congested walkways, past bubbling test tubes filled with multi-coloured liquids. Squeezed by a pile of books and narrowly avoided backing into some glass jars filled with strange preserved creatures. He reached the cupboard door, threw it open and went to throw his rubbish inside.

"Whatcha doing in there Rauph?" Ashe asked, stopping himself mid-swing from throwing the dustpan, complete with swept up rubbish into the cupboard.

"I'm hiding." Rauph stated sheepishly back at him. "Thomas told me I need to hide and not be seen because I scared the lady on the dock."

Ashe cast his mind back and vaguely remembered something about a fisherwoman dropping some fish and pointing at Rauph and screaming demon when they had first come into port. Their arrival in Stratholme had caused quite a stir but Ashe was pre-occupied at the time, visiting the caged birds, trying to get a glimpse of his baby egg and find out if it had hatched yet.

"You did scare her good." Ashe confirmed laughing. Then he realised Rauph being in the cupboard did not help his master plan. "You don't need to hide in the cupboard Rauph." The Halfling sighed in frustration, putting the dustpan down on a pile of dirty dishes left over from meals Commagin had taken when working late and then had forgotten to clean up after himself. "Let me help you out of there."

Rauph slowly clambered out of the cupboard, amazing Ashe that he had even been able to fit in there in the first place.

"I'm sure it will be fine if you just stay in your cabin." Ashe suggested. "I think Thomas just wants us to keep a low profile until the *El Defensor* is fixed and we move on. He even told me we have had enough adventures recently to last us a long while. He won't even let me go wandering about." Ashe paused mid-conversation. Did Thomas really ask that of him? As if he, a humble Halfling would cause any trouble.

"Okay Ashe. If you think so." Rauph started to smile his scary smile, all teeth and snorts. "I'll go and hide in my cabin then."

"Um that's fine," Ashe nodded his head, still lost in thought and not really interested in the Minotaur's predicament. He was still amazed that he had actually done what he was asked without putting up a fight. Maybe he was feeling unwell, coming down with a cold or something.

Ashe started to shepherd Rauph's huge form out of the lab, herding the Minotaur towards the door when Rauph stopped dead in his tracks, effectively running Ashe into a hairy wall. The Minotaur turned around and bent down so his head was near Ashe's.

Ashe flushed, this was it, the Minotaur was onto him, somehow he had realised the Halfling had an ulterior motive for being here alone.

"I just want to say what a great friend you are." Rauph snorted. "If you are ever passing my cabin and want to come in for some time, just knock on the door."

"Oh, that's fine I've already been in..."

Rauph turned and left Ashe in mid-conversation, the lab door swinging shut behind him.

Silence descended around Ashe, broken only by the odd 'blob' and 'blip' sounds of experiments going on in the background. He located a stool and dragged it towards the workbench then climbed up, grabbing several tools before reaching inside his jerkin to pull out Colette's necklace. His other hand fumbled in his pocket and pulled out the treasure he had discovered on the *El Conquistador.*

The smoky grey pearl was slightly larger than the cracked one currently in the setting but Ashe liked fixing things and he knew this would be a simple case of working the setting until it was open enough to accept the replacement glistening sphere. He pulled over a magnifying glass, set his elbows firmly on the surface of the worktop and set to work.

* * * * * *

"I'm sure that this is wonderful honey." Kerian tried to interrupt, "but it's not honey that I'm after." He looked over the counter at the proprietor of the village grocery store and took in Constance's stern gaze from over the top of her glasses. Clearly, his interruption of her sales pitch was not a way to get on the good side of the village busy body.

"As I was saying." She continued. "Any of these pots of honey are excellent to sweeten oatmeal, add flavour to drinks and they also help stave off colds. At your age, you need to look after yourself." The flutter of eyelashes and tilt of her head made Kerian blink several times in surprise.

Kerian flushed and tried to remain calm. She was old enough to be his mother! Then he remembered how he looked and his heart sank again.

"Listen," Kerian started again, "I am sure your honey is excellent and that I can benefit from having it but I'm really after information. Have you heard any tales about this place, any legends or bedtime stories? I am looking for a long-abandoned temple and a dragon."

Another stern gaze and a stack of candles joined the pot of honey, a crusty loaf of bread and a chunk of blue veined cheese. Kerian realised he would have no choice but to buy the lot if he wanted to get anything from this woman. He fished into his pocket and placed several coins onto the counter.

Her smile reassured him that he had read the situation correctly and as she started wrapping up his purchases he tried again.

"So... a dragon and a lost temple?"

Constance leaned forward on the counter and stared up into his hazel eyes as she started to talk in a low conspiratorial tone.

"There are tales..." she began, offering him a sweet to suck on. "...Of a temple that used to be under the mountain. There are numerous tunnels running through the mountain and it is possible people once lived in them long ago but no one can get down there now to find out. The heat gets too much and there are noxious vapours."

"Noxious vapours?" Kerian furrowed his brow. "What do you mean?"

"Well," Constance beckoned, indicating that he should bring his head closer. "The air isn't very good down there. People go in and then have to be dragged out again. No one has ever found a temple that I know of. However, let us be serious, what good is a temple if everyone passes out before they get there. Personally, I think it's all baloney. Just an excuse for people to slip away for a while and have a good time." She planted a kiss on Kerian's cheek and he nearly dropped his honey jar.

Kerian flushed and started to back out of the shop, just missing the basket of fresh eggs alongside the counter and banging his head on the bell hung above the door.

"You've been very helpful." Kerian tried to smile but Constance had a veracious look in her eye now and he was starting to feel like a staked goat used as bait to catch a man eating purple striped *Tagir*. "Is there anyone that could have records of the old times? Do you have a library or..." Kerian thought back to the monks in Catterick, "Maybe a priest?"

"You mean Richard." Constance's demeanour changed in an instant, suddenly guarded but there was also something else, a sense of fear rippling just beneath the surface of her bustling exterior. "Richard the priest. He's either up at the church, or he will be down at the *Vane Arms* eating."

"Good day to you now."

Kerian was not sure what had just happened to their conversation but he recognised when he was no longer welcome. He left the grocery store, found himself out on the main street through the town and noticed Colette standing out in the street talking to Thomas and Rowan.

He stepped clear of the shop awning and looked down towards the port from where sounds of construction could clearly be heard, before turning his head the other way and looking up the street watching it wind lazily into the trees and climb the mountainside all the way to the terracotta and cream church nestled high above. That looked to be some climb!

"Are you hungry or something?" Colette nudged his arm, trying to suppress a smile. "Violetta's food not good enough for you anymore?"

Kerian blushed again. He always felt a fool when he was alongside her.

"I don't suppose you'd like to join me for some bread and cheese... or I have honey if you prefer?" Colette looked up into Kerian's eyes and beamed at the invitation.

"I would love to." She smiled. "The gardens are open over there; we can sit and take some time to relax. Then we can discuss your inability to go into a shop and not buy something. It's a very poor habit to get into."

"Where are they going?" Kerian asked, pointing at Thomas and Rowan who were walking away.

"The Vane Arms." Colette gestured towards the windmill turning lazily in the breeze from the harbour. "Apparently it's the in place to be around here. Now about the shopping problem. You know what you need is someone to shop for."

* * * * * *

"Table for two." Thomas held up two fingers on his hand to emphasise the need for a cosy table rather than a large one. He wanted to spend some time getting to know Rowan and the *Vane Arms* served the bill nicely.

He took in the wooden beams and the layout of the main meeting place in the town. The *Vane Arms* was incredibly a working mill and the internal workings of cogs and gears intermeshed and turned as they were powered by the tall canvas vanes circling slowly around outside. The sails creaked comfortingly as they turned, the sound echoing around the tall structure and matched by a low rumbling sensation beneath Thomas's feet. In its own way, the vibration was also comforting, akin to being on board ship. As he looked around, he soaked up the ambience of the place, and had to admire the thought that had gone into this unique and comforting hostelry.

The actual mill tower rose from one end of the building, a staircase spiralling upwards with broad landings set at several levels offering seating and tables for customers. In the past, this walkway was little more than a method of access to the sails outside at times of breakdown. However, with foresight and adjustment, the widened walkway allowed secluded nooks and crannies, providing space to eat and socialise in privacy, with an incredible view of the bar and the dance floor below.

The actual working millstones were set at a level out of sight below the restaurant area, and Thomas had already remarked to the proprietor on the rumblings beneath his feet as he had walked in. The milling area needed to be separate from the rest of the building due to the dust that built up, as the flour was ground for the bread and rolls freshly baked on the premises. The captain wondered just how long the place would remain open if checked over by a modern-day health and safety inspection.

The wandering bar ran from around the central spindle of the tower out into the extension, where an open fire pit complete with a large boar slowly crisping on a spit and banked hot coals sizzled under an enormous grill. An elaborate pulley system behind the bar allowed the hoisting of baskets containing ordered drinks up to the seating above, adding another element of uniqueness to this beautiful establishment. Shelving set up around the moving parts of the mill contained bottles of various hues and shapes, promising delights for the taste buds and a hangover to match.

The kitchen area located on the far side of the fire pit sent tantalising aromas wafting out across the seating area, setting Thomas's mouth watering in anticipation. He decided he instantly liked this place and stole a glance over at his demure dining companion, confirming to himself that the pleasant company helped as well.

The proprietor, a large man, aged somewhere in his late fifties, with a neatly trimmed white beard and a jovial smile pulled out a table for Rowan and indicated Thomas take the seat opposite.

"You the captain of the new ship in harbour?" he jerked his head in the direction of the port.

"Thomas Adams." Thomas replied and then indicated his dining companion. "Rowan."

"Charmed. Charleton." With introductions over, he produced a menu and laid it in front of Rowan to examine first. "To be honest it's all good," he grinned, patting his stomach "How else do you think I got this way? The steak and cold sausage comes highly recommended. Just make sure you leave space for the lime and chocolate pie at the end." Thomas watched as Charleton moved away and busied himself behind the bar, leaving the two of them alone.

Rowan leant forward, staring deeply into Thomas's dark eyes.

"Well you certainly know how to impress a lady." She opened. "This place is incredible."

"If the food is as good as he says we should do fine." Thomas grinned, his eyes wandering past Rowan to take in the small rooms set off from the main building, curtains tied back showing tables where people could sit in larger groups away from the main floor.

Above on a second floor a railing ran around with further rooms set off the balcony but Thomas had a feeling they were for sleeping in and not for eating and entertaining. Several other customers were sitting at the bar, one talking quietly to Charleton and pointing in their direction. Thomas did not like the fact he and his crew had become instant celebrities, nevertheless it was clear that strangers were rare in this unspoilt place.

Charleton made his excuses and came back over to their table with a bottle of bright red wine and two glasses, poured a small amount and then stepped back for Thomas to voice his approval.

"All grown locally." Their proprietor boasted. "Are you ready to order mam?"

"Chef's choice." Thomas intercepted, starting to like the honestly charismatic man and his overt attempts to flatter his female guest.

"Coming right up."

Thomas watched as Charleton walked over to the fire pit and the large metal grill. He lifted two huge steaks from somewhere out of Thomas's line of sight and slammed them down onto the grill then dropped a large amount of plant onto the hot coals, sending up a thick cloud of fragrant smoke that was clearly intended to flavour the meat. Thomas thought he could detect a scent not unlike the herb Rosemary.

"Hey you." Rowan teased, her finger touching Thomas's cheek and bringing his eyesight back in line with hers. "I'm over here."

"I'm sorry." Thomas confessed. "My attention can wander. Part of the old job I'm afraid."

"Well you can stop that." Rowan lifted the wine glass to her mouth, her eyes widening as she tasted the fruity strawberry vintage. She licked her lips savouring the taste. "Umm, well you are not a cop any more. I mean what could possibly happen around here?" She sat back in the chair her arms wide in comic emphasis.

Thomas smelt something burning. He wanted to focus more on the beautiful woman before him but the smell was starting to get stronger. He looked around over to the fire pit and realised Charleton was gone and the steaks were smoking. He reluctantly got to his feet, walked over to the kitchen area and shouted through the smoke.

"We didn't want the steak that well done!" he joked, peered through the smoke, turning his head to see where everyone was. The kitchen area appeared deserted. Thomas reached out and grabbed a pair of tongs, rescuing the steaks and putting them onto two plates laid to one side, already dressed with crispy cubes of peppered potato and some sort of salad leaf. Maybe this was a quirk of the place. A do it yourself thing? He walked back over to Rowan shrugging, placing the food before her.

"Are you going to sit?" she asked politely.

"Umm?" Thomas looked back down at his dinner date and winced. "I'm sorry I'm doing it again aren't I?"

"Just slightly." Rowan tried to smile but Thomas could sense she was getting uptight with his lack of attention.

"It's just hard to take the detective out of me." He confessed. "I have no idea where Charleton has gone." Thomas glanced around the room and noticed the empty bar; the customers had apparently disappeared too. He went to sit down, tried to smile and then stopped, slowly shaking his head.

"I'm sorry." He gritted his teeth getting back to his feet again. "Something is wrong here." He walked over to the bar and looked at the tankards placed there. Several vessels were still three quarters full.

"Now I know something is wrong." Thomas turned back to Rowan who sat barely controlling her frustration. "I'm sorry but in all my years as a cop, I have never known someone to leave a full drink at the bar."

He walked to the door and cracked it open, then stood there open mouthed.

"Rowan, you have to see this." He whispered.

Rowan rose from her chair and walked over; preparing to slap him for his impudence and set off back for the ship but when she got to the door, she could not help but agree with his assessment that something was wrong.

The whole village stood quiet, the only people moving about the street were the crew from the *El Defensor* and they were all looking in the same direction. Thomas followed their gaze, taking in toys left dropped in the street, open doors and windows, curtains blowing freely in the harbour breeze, baskets of wares simply discarded on the floor and left unattended. Mathius stood at the blacksmiths forge, his hand holding a new sword but there was no smith to discuss terms of sale. Kerian and Colette stood at the entrance of the gardens their picnic unattended on the seat behind them.

Beyond them, walking up the long trail to the church was every villager Thomas had seen in his time ashore. Every child, every elderly frail person, tackling a slope that made Thomas breathless just thinking about it. As he looked, he made out the shape of villagers who had been working the fields, their rakes and hoes, scythes and spades forgotten, as they heeded a summons Thomas could not hear.

However, the most eerie aspect of the scene was the silence. No one spoke, no child cried at the indignity of having to go to church, no one argued, no one smiled. No one held their back, complained at the climb, or stopped to catch their breath.

It was like looking at a scene from a zombie movie, the extras shambling determinedly after the last few survivors of the human race. They moved in slow deliberate steps, some barefoot, some in a state of undress, all heading towards the church at the end of the trail. Mathius held his arms out, looking perplexed. He noticed Thomas and shouted over, pointing at the mass exodus they were witnessing.

"They sure seem to take their religion seriously here. Either that or their priest must put on one hell of a show!"

Thomas looked back up at the steep climb and tended to agree and then he looked down at Rowan and tried to give his best cheeky smile.

"Shall we go and see what all the fuss is about?"

Rowan took a deep breath. "Is it always this strange travelling with you?" she asked.

Thomas's smile grew broader.

"Stick with me and you'll soon find out."

"Stick with you!" Rowan punched Thomas in the arm. "You bet I will. You still owe me dinner!"

Chapter Forty-Six

Marcus looked on amazed as Brother Richard delivered his sermon to an audience that hung onto every word, silently digesting his passages of wisdom, singing psalms and bowing their heads in prayer as he preached peace and respect for his fellow man. He had never seen anything like this. Not a single person showed disinterest, no one whispered to the person sitting alongside them, no child cried, or ran rampaging through the aisles. It was the perfect rapturous audience and this was what made it feel so contrived.

Something else failed to add up as well. The timing of this gathering was all wrong. Mid-afternoon, no one went to church in the afternoon unless it was a special religious festival, wedding, funeral or similar. It was as if Richard had somehow summoned the people in answer to the threat of Marcus's arrival.

What was clear however was the fact they could not forcibly restrain and remove Brother Richard when streams of his faithful villagers were coming in to attend service. Marcus was naturally low key and did not want to cause more fuss than necessary. He studied Richard from the shadows, listening to the man continue with his sermon, pausing only occasionally, to risk a quick nervous glance in Marcus's direction then return to the scriptures in front of him, or to wipe his sweating brow.

"We can take him now if you wish, *Bearer*."

Marcus turned to the knight standing alongside him and brought a finger to his own lips signalling silence. He was not prepared to cause a disturbance and upset all these people, possibly turning the whole village against them. No, he would wait until the end of the service and then gently escort Richard away, transport him back to Catterick and whatever punishment Abbot Brialin had awaiting him there.

The doors of the church creaked open and Marcus moved further back into the shadows as he recognised the new arrivals. The unmistakable shapes of Kerian, Colette, Thomas and the new female crewmember Rowan entered, quietly taking seats at the back of the church. He could not allow them to see him here! They would not understand the importance of the *Bearer* role and would easily become confused seeing the twelve knights that had materialized from nowhere. He also had worries they would fail to comprehend the importance of carrying out Abbot Brialin's edicts and that Brother Richard had strayed so far from the righteous path he needed reminding of his transgressions.

Marcus backed further into the study and pulled the door to, leaving the slightest crack so he could continue to monitor Brother Richard from afar. The knights moved uncomfortably behind him.

"Why are we hiding?" asked one, "We are Knights of the Order of St Fraiser. We do not hide!"

"You are knights under my command," Marcus shot back with more authority than he felt. "You will do what I say."

The knight stepped away, bristling with barely controlled rage but Marcus was too pre-occupied to notice. This situation was messy and had the potential for spiralling out of control. He needed to bide his time and deal with the situation as calmly as possible. He returned to the opening in the doorway and waited for the service to conclude.

* * * * * *

Scrave was in pain.

His head hurt badly, waves of pain rushing up from the back of his neck, over his head to just above his eyes. He felt sick, dizzy and even delirious. The circlet on his brow now felt too tight to remove but every time he considered doing something about it, the pressure in his head made him forget the problem.

Putting it down to dehydration, lack of rest and food, he had eaten a large meal, drank copious amounts of fresh water and retired to his cabin to attempt to get some sleep. However, try as he might, sleep would not come, his restless nature making him toss and turn, the sheets of his bunk wrapping around him like the coils of the snake in Catterick.

Indeed, snakes seemed to be slithering throughout his dreams, as he kept replaying the image of Kerian Denaris being given his golden dagger. He really wanted to take the blade back. The thought of Kerian having it riled him in ways he could not explain. The weapon was rightfully his, all he had to do was go into Kerian's cabin and take it.

A part of Scrave's subconscious knew it was wrong to feel this way. It was only a dagger. He could always get another one. Nevertheless, something about the blade called to him, something was telling him he needed to reclaim what was rightfully his.

He awoke but some sixth sense warned him not to move. Something told him he was not alone. He instinctively decided not to open his eyes in case he warned whoever or whatever was in the room.

What was wrong? He gently wiggled his toes, the same with his fingers. All present and correct. He swallowed and felt a slight constriction around his throat, making him suck in his breath by reflex, his chest rising as the air inflated his lungs. There was a slight increase in pressure through the sheets.

Something had him around the throat and was sitting on his chest!

He slid his right hand slowly over the side of the bed, easing his fingers under the mattress to a small knife he kept there. As his hand felt the cool metal of the weapon, he dared to crack open his eyes and wished at that instant he had not done so.

Something horrific sat on his chest, skeletal, with a head too big for its body, eyes glowing softly in the dimmed light of the darkened cabin. It was similar to a dead monkey, complete with a grin emphasised by the lips being pulled up and shrivelled away, exposing a worn set of stained teeth. It looked heavier than it felt, making him wonder if the creature had hollow bones or was partly magical by design. The creature shifted its weight and leaned towards him, whispering strange words like some sort of mantra. As it moved the tightness at his throat increased and he realised with horror that it was the creature's tail wrapped around his neck.

Scrave tried to calm the terror growing within him, tried to focus, even his breathing to fool the creature into believing he was still asleep. He had to learn as much about the skeletal horror as he could, identify if it was a threat to him or the crew. The Elf inhaled deeply, taking in an aged smell of sweet spices mixed with something sour, bitter, like embalming fluid. He moved gently and felt the creature's dry skin crackle as it repositioned itself. Had this monster been mummified or preserved? His pulse started to quicken despite his best efforts to quell it then he realised he had seen this creature before!

The realisation hit him hard. He *had* seen this creature before. Now where was it?

It took a moment and then it came to him. The skull like face he had glimpsed in a reflection on the water, off the side of the *El Defensor,* the night when he fought the invisible assassin! He had passed it off as a distortion of the moon at the time but now here it was again, closer, more real and more terrifying.

The monster continued to chant, as if casting a spell. Scrave could feel the circlet on his head becoming warm but did not know for sure if it was due to the sweat breaking out on his brow or something the creature was attempting to do. Either way, he was not going to simply lie there and let it happen.

His arm shot up, dagger in hand, the short blade slicing through the air, its point angled directly for the side of the creature's enlarged grinning skull. It turned, sensing the attack and shrieked, its head dropping forward to over balance and bounce back off his chest. Scrave's blade missed its mark but his forearm connected with the side of the monster knocking it from his chest. The tightness around his neck released as the tail uncoiled, the skeletal monkey turning to throw itself from the bed. With a frustrated chatter, it leapt away but the Elf was faster, his free hand catching the sinuous tail as it slipped by, snapping the creature back down onto the bed.

It turned, slashing and biting in fury at being held. Tugging relentlessly to escape from Scrave's grasp.

"Oh no you don't!" Scrave shouted, snapping the tail down and bouncing the monster off the mattress, jarring its teeth together, before he buried it under the blanket from his bed. The shrieks of outrage from the thrashing bundle made holding onto it hard, especially when he had one hand still gripping the tail and the other still trying to aim the dagger for a suitable attack.

Scrave gritted his teeth and threw the bundle across the cabin, smashing it off the wall and letting the whole heap crash to the floor. He was up and after it like a flash, his dagger flipping across his right hand, blade turning down for the coup de grace.

The blade pierced the blanket and plunged into the dried flesh and bone beneath with a crack like an axe going through ice. The monster shrieked louder then disappeared in a small implosion of smoke and ozone, leaving Scrave holding an empty blanket and blinking rapidly to adjust his vision. What had he witnessed? Had he just woken from some twisted nightmare? He looked at the scratches down the lengths of his arms and the scorched blade still held in his hand, noticing it was now several inches shorter than it should have been.

If that was a nightmare, it was a very real and troubling one.

* * * * * *

The priest finally started winding down and with it, Kerian's growing fascination with a list of several unpleasant things that could happen to the man delivering it; an acute attack of laryngitis the tamest of the options imagined. The man had droned on and on, as if he was intentionally trying to extend the length of the sermon. He had also appeared to develop a fascination with a closed door partially hidden in the shadows at the back of the church and kept casting fearful glances in its direction, as if he expected it to suddenly fly open at any moment.

Throughout it all, the villagers remained eerily attentive. No children fidgeting or asking to go to the toilet, no whispers, no gossip and now that the sermon was finished, everyone got silently to their feet and headed for the large door that led outside.

Finally, now Kerian could find out more information about the lost temple and pursue his quest; he could enquire about accessing the church archives. The wait was unbearable now he was this close. He rose, intending to head towards the priest, only to find Richard was walking slowly up the aisle towards him, having a one-sided conversation with a villager that chose to walk at the same pace. It was as if he the monk were talking to a marionette for all the emotional response he was getting in return but Richard seemed unbothered by this and continued to make idle banter.

Kerian considered stepping out and interrupting the priest's path but the woman sitting in the pew in front of him decided to get to her feet, blocking his view as she turned to head for the door. Kerian stepped back in surprise as she turned. The voracious Constance stared right through him and then, looking blankly ahead, walked past him without any comment, a single tear gently rolling down her face.

Thomas nudged Kerian, asking him to move aside so that the others could exit the church. Kerian stepped out into the aisle as Thomas squeezed by. The captain had recognised the proprietor of the Vane Arms walking silently by.

"Charleton," Thomas opened, stepping towards him. "You walked out on us mid-meal, and despite the fact I had to finish serving it, I would not want you to think we left without paying."

Charleton paused, considering his blocked path then took a step to the side like some bizarre automaton and continued out the door, leaving the confused captain standing behind him. Thomas followed the innkeeper with his eyes and then frowned. This man had been kind and courteous to him, he owed him this much to find out what was going on, make sure the man was safe and get to the bottom of this strange mass hypnosis that was affecting the whole village.

Kerian watched Thomas go, followed by Rowan and then felt a nudge from Colette as she rolled her eyes in the direction of the priest who had somehow bypassed him and was also exiting the church. He kicked himself realising he had missed the opportunity to catch the priest as he had planned and set off in determined pursuit, Colette in tow.

"Excuse me sir!" he shouted as they exited the church. "Excuse me; I wonder if I can have a moment of your time."

Richard turned his head in shock, at hearing someone talking to him, his face initially a mask of fear until he noted that the man calling to him was not who he expected. He faltered in his walk, confusion washing over his features, glancing nervously at the people walking silently away as Kerian closed the ground between them.

"I thought I had missed you for a second." Kerian grinned catching up. "My name is Styx; I wanted to ask you if you know anything about the myths and lore of this island. I am looking for some information on a lost temple and a mythical dragon. I wanted to know if I could access your records and see if there is any mention of such."

"I...I," Richard's eyes widened slightly and he flushed, before he appeared to gather himself as he comprehended what this stranger was asking him. "I'm sorry but I don't think I can help you." He replied, his gaze now hard and defensive. "There is a problem with the archives... there was a storm... Yes, a storm, a few nights ago and all the records were soaked, totally ruined. I am also certain that I have no recollection of seeing anything about a lost temple in the caves below. I'm afraid it's impossible for you to see the archives right now."

Kerian stood stunned, as if slapped in the face as Richard turned and continued off across the lawn, his tunic held in his hands so he could move at a faster speed, his sandals flapping as he practically sprinted towards the cover of the gardens ahead.

"What do you think he meant by that?" he asked, turning to Colette.

"Oh, I know what he meant." She replied, her intelligent gaze tracking the fleeing priest. "And he appears to be in a hurry to go somewhere."

"I can't believe this." Kerian shouted, suddenly angry and frustrated. "I came all this way for there to be no record of the myth of this island. I cannot believe it. I won't believe it!" Kerian shook his head, suddenly crestfallen.

Colette gently took Kerian by the hand and stared coolly in the direction of the departing priest.

"Don't you think it odd that he didn't want to stop and talk to us? Did you notice how he flushed when you mentioned the dragon?"

Kerian followed Colette's gaze towards the gardens where the priest had fled and now disappeared into. Villagers continued walking silently past the couple, heading back down the hill towards the village below; where the sounds of distressed voices were starting to rise through the air.

"I also don't remember you telling him that the temple was supposed to be in any caves. Do you?"

Kerian looked back at the young charge beside him, his face set in a suddenly stony frown.

"I could kiss you!" he said, meaning every word, despite his thunderous appearance.

* * * * * *

"I told you I should have taken him." The knight shouted, making Marcus flush. "This could have all been over by now. Instead, Brother Richard has run and we now need to waste valuable time tracking him down. I am sorry but as a *Bearer* I find you somewhat lacking."

"How dare you!" Marcus snapped back, eyeing the knight, his armour and his gleaming blade and subconsciously deciding that maybe he should have been more open with the crew of the *El Defensor*. "You speak out of turn Tobias. You have eleven other men, send them out, track him down, how far can one monk run? However, I order you to remain hidden from the villagers. I will not cause distress to these people. They have done nothing wrong and it goes against all our teachings as followers of St Fraiser to threaten innocent people."

"Abbot Brialin would not see it this way. He would not let a few peasants stop us from doing our holy work." Tobias retaliated; his eyes narrowed with contempt. "Lukas, Cameron, Bartholomew, search the grounds. The rest of you with me." He turned in a swirl of blue cloak and headed for the study door but Marcus was not finished with him yet. His hand came down on Tobias's shoulder spinning the man around to face him once more.

"Just remember I called you from the book. I can just as easily put you back in it again." Marcus warned.

"Of course, *Bearer*." Tobias practically bristled but placed his lips tightly together and left the room, his eleven men at arms moving with him as he shouted out further orders to hunt Brother Richard down and bring him back to the church.

Marcus watched the door close and then sank down onto the nearest chair, his body trembling with the stress of the confrontation. This was not how it was supposed to be. He had never heard of the knights questioning their *Bearer*! Abbot Brialin said the knights were his to command. This wasn't right. He suddenly felt uneasy. Was there something that the Abbot had neglected to disclose in their hurried meeting all those months ago?

He looked out the gothic window into the opulent gardens beyond then pulled back as he noticed Kerian and Colette walking by, the two of them walking side by side, heads turning from side to side, clearly taking in the rich sights and exotic scents of the visual spectacle. If only he, Marcus, could be so carefree. If only his life were as simple as the man outside who had one goal to focus on and saw everything in shades of black and white.

The monk suddenly wished he could tell Kerian what was going on but Kerian was so volatile and from experience, attracted danger like a magnet. He knew deep down that if he had confided in the man, before Marcus knew it, the island would be reduced to rubble and the church and town destroyed by flame. It was better if he just saw this whole thing through by himself and returned to the monastery in Catterick as quickly as possible, where he could return to his studies and regain his sense of inner peace.

He took a deep breath, looking around Brother Richard's place of sanctuary and shook his head in realisation. This was Richard's place of peace, a place where he had found a home and contentment. Just by sitting here, Marcus felt he was violating it. He needed to get out and mingle with the crew and villagers. They would recognise him from the *El Defensor* and not question his comings and goings, unlike the knights he travelled with.

Marcus steeled himself and then got to his feet. He would take a slow walk, order his own thoughts and consider the actions of the knights. Then he would return here by dusk to see how the search was progressing. He was still in control. He had to be in control.

He was the *Bearer* and he had trained for this all his life. He would not fail the Abbot, or more importantly himself in this moment of achieving his potential.

* * * * * *

Brother Richard's breath was coming in rapid bursts as he slipped under the shadow of a great oak and paused with his back against the gnarled bark to see if he was being followed.

How could Brialin have found him so easily? How had he realised this would be the place he would go? He cast his mind back to the monastery and his studies all that time ago. He was always so careful with the books he examined, always ensured they were placed safely away. Brialin must have become suspicious somehow; started to watch his comings and goings before he decided to flee.

It had to be Brother Paul; he was Brialin's lackey, brown nosing and being sly. Oh, wait a moment...What about Brother Anthony, or for that matter, Brother Ivan? Ivan always looked at him in a funny way and had been caught going through his post and Anthony was always slow in replying to his work, hovering in the background at meals, listening in to conversations but never openly offering anything to the discussions. Maybe he had let something slip, maybe one of his notes had fallen into the wrong hands? He could send himself mad mulling this over. Whatever or whoever was responsible there was no doubt the *Bearer* and his knights were here now and he had to do something to resolve the situation fast!

Rosalyine would know what to do. He needed to get to her and ask her advice.

Richard stole a quick glance to the left and right, listened intently for footsteps approaching and then gathered up his faded robes and set off through the wandering flower borders, keeping his head low. Dozy bees bumbled along from flower to flower, rainbow hues tantalised the eye and the scent of honeysuckle wafted across the manicured lawns but the monk ignored all of these things. His heart was hammering too fast in his chest and his eyes were too busy looking for threats to appreciate the beauty around him.

He ran over to the pond and skirted around the edge, his reflection mirrored on the surface alongside him. Brightly coloured fish sensed his approach and set off in pursuit, swimming after his hurried steps expecting to be fed, only to face disappointment when he stopped at the stone fountain raised at the far end.

A dragon, immortalised in stone, captured gracefully leaping into the air, wings spread wide, signified mankind's fight to break free from the bonds of the mundane and soar the heavens: the sculptor emphasising the sleek lines and raw power of the magnificent creature for all who would take the time to sit back and absorb it. However, this was all lost on Richard, whose fevered gaze lay not on the fountain but what was hidden far beneath it.

He reached out over the water, his robes touching the surface, sending the fish into further inquisitive mouth gaping forays of disappointment and touched a stud under the dragon's outstretched wing. There was a soft click, then just as the manuscripts had foretold back in Catterick, a small scale started to rise from the pattern of hide engraved across the creatures back leg. Richard reached over, swivelled the scale aside and revealed another small stud in a recess. He pushed down hard and a grating vibration started to rise from the ground at his feet.

The water started to move away from the fountain, the entire structure where the fish swam, shifting with some major surface turbulence and a loud ominous rumble, to slip under the lip of the pond on the far side. The fish darted away scared, as a flight of stairs started to emerge from under the edge of the manicured lawn by Richard's feet and over into the space recently filled by hungry fish. The grating stopped as suddenly as it occurred, water spilling over the sill into the submerged stairwell as the pond suddenly stopped its sideways motion.

Richard took one quick look around and then slipped down into the stairwell, pressing another stud that was level with the fourth stair down. With an answering rumble, the pond started to roll back into its rightful place and bury him deep under the ground. He stood there in the darkness breathing heavily, his ears listening for any sign of pursuit, any shouts of alarm that his whereabouts had been detected but nothing befell his ears.

Confident he was safe, he reached a niche at the top of the stair and fumbled for a moment before sparks cut the darkness and a flickering lantern lit the spiral pathway down into the earth. It was cooler here, deep beneath the earth, far away from the light of the sun. Richard took the steps confidently, having travelled this route into the subterranean temple many times before. The lantern light traced the history of the temple, highlighting the murals on the wall as he descended.

There were skilfully carved bas-reliefs of the island, its twin peaks instantly recognisable. A Lord and Lady much in love, an island of peace and tranquillity. Then another plaque showed invaders burning the villages, killing the people. The Lord deposed and slain before his wife and unspeakable atrocities carried out upon her person. The next panel showed the Lady gathering herself, releasing great magic and wreaking terrible bloody vengeance on her enemies, delivering pain to her oppressors. Striking out, killing those who had taken her husband's life. The final mural showed the building of the gardens and the temple and the Lady choosing to defend the island and keep the people safe. Using magic to make the ultimate sacrifice, ensuring in her new form, she would live long enough to save her people and that no one would ever harm them again.

Richard kept shuffling on as the scenes unfolded, already knowing the story he had spent so many hours in Catterick's archives to uncover. He came away from the stairway, aware that the darkness was stretching out around him and onto a large platform that held numerous other openings at the perimeter of his flickering light. He had tried to explore several of them, finding some passages ending in collapsed piles of masonry, blocked and impassable, others winding further into the earth, some possibly to the other side of the island. One tunnel descended to the docks, probably used in the past as a way of transporting goods to the temple when ships came into port. However, it remained dark, dusty and as disused as the rest; no one had been there for a very long time.

The deep rasp of a breath drawn in and the sudden drop in temperature that accompanied it, made Richard reach into his robes and clutch his holy symbol close to his heart. When the breath expelled, in an equally impressive blast, he closed his eyes to counter the bright sparks illuminating his form as a toxic fog encountered his protective magic shield.

"Rosalyine." Richard broke the silence. "It is only me; there is no need for you to breathe your spells."

"Richard." The voice came out of the shadows, everywhere and nowhere all at once. "What brings you here this fine day? I sense you are nervous and worried."

"I have a problem." The monk began. "Travellers have come to take me away from your people. To take away all I have been granted. I need you to make them go away or let me use the gem so that they never threaten us again."

"You know the rules Richard. The gem can be used only once per user." Her voice had a cold edge to it, her response to his question harsh as if she were annoyed in his being here. "You have already been granted your heart's desire. You asked for a church of your own and an attentive congregation that would come at your call. You have been granted all of this and more. If I had foreseen what your desire would result in, the distress it is causing my people, I would never have allowed you access to my husband's heart."

"But I have never harmed your people." The monk replied shuffling his feet uncomfortably. "I am there for them in their hour of need; I offer guidance, a sense of belonging. I have harmed no one."

"How dare you." Rosalyine's voice rumbled from the darkness. "How can you have the gall to stand before me and even suggest such a thing? I may live in the darkness but I am not blind. Do you not see the harm you do when you take away their free will, their right to choose? Open your eyes Richard. Your heart's desire is killing them."

"There are others here that will do much worse." Richard replied. "They are coming to take me away with them, coming to punish me for running away from the order. Abbot Brialin's wrath will be immense. I am afraid Rosalyine and I do not know what to do."

There was a rattle in the darkness, a sense of something huge sliding across the floor.

"Afraid." Rosalyine scoffed. "You know nothing of being afraid."

"What can I do?" Richard moaned. "How can I get away from the *Bearer* and his knights?"

The voice from the darkness took her time replying, having listened, considered and judged the request before her.

"You will do what all men do Richard. You will be selfish and fickle; you will look after your own interests and you will die."

"I will what!" Richard screamed, walking into the shadows towards the sounds of the movement he heard. "I will not accept that. I need to use the gem. I need to make them go away. That is my heart's wish now, not what I asked for before."

"As I predicted." Rosalyine replied. "Fickle." There was a louder rasp of scale on tile, as the creature moved and then an unexpected flare of red light from below the far side of the platform cast a warm ruddy glow over the entire area bathing the monk in its crimson light.

Richard felt the heat despite the protection gained from his holy symbol but he continued to walk resolutely towards the shimmering light, only to watch something ripple and slide across the front of it like sunlight through a warped glass window.

A huge crash to the left indicated the creature was shifting position again but Richard was determined. He approached the edge of the platform, watching the ripple reduce in size as it slid before him. He knew it was Rosalyine's crystal tail and chose to ignore it. The monk looked down over the edge of the platform at the lava fields below and the series of tall magical pillars that hovered above the liquid magma churning there. He marvelled anew at how the massive monoliths reduced in height and acted like a giant flight of stairs, winding gently down towards the ruined temple that stood at their end, surrounded by liquid fire.

The heat was uncomfortable from this vantage point but Richard knew it would get worse before he reached the bottom of the causeway. He moved to step out onto the stone, only to feel something cold, curved, and extremely sharp land on his shoulder.

"You will not take another step." Rosalyine warned.

"Or you will do what?" Richard snapped back. "I know the rules as well as you do. No one is to be harmed on this island. I bring no weapon and I am unarmed. You cannot hurt me I am one of your people."

"You are not one of *my* people Richard." She replied. "You never have been and you never will be. You have hurt my people with your wish. You could have had a congregation that loved you over time, respected you and used you as their confidant in times of strive. Instead, you wanted your recognition and position right away, no matter what the cost. I cannot take back the wish my husband's heart granted but I will be damned if I will let you use the gem again."

The stones of the floor shook as something large and heavy slammed into them. There was a warning growl and a shriek from the floor as something clawed across the surface. Pieces of masonry crashed down around the monk as something unseen hit the high ceiling many feet above.

Richard moved to step forward but the pressure on his shoulder increased as the massive claw pushed determinedly downwards. He had the unpleasant choice of bending over to the side or risk losing his arm as the crystal bit into his flesh. His eyes went wide at the sudden realisation that Rosalyine was actually considering harming him. The fear flared inside him, real and terrifying.

"Be gone from here Richard. You are no longer welcome. You made your choices in life, now live with them."

* * * * *

Ashe was bored.

Well not exactly bored per se. He had finished his work on the necklace and had been all excited to return it to Colette, only to discover that she had gone wandering into the village. Therefore, determined to seek her out, he had gone to look for her, leaving her repaired necklace on her pillow for her to find later. Only when he got to the village there were no villagers there, just groups of the crew looking up at the church perched on the hill and muttering amongst themselves.

He had been about to ask one of the crew if they had seen Colette when he had come across an open door. Clearly the owner of the establishment would not have been happy at this clear lapse of security, so Ashe had wandered in purely to have a kind word, check that the door lock was working and suggest security upgrades to prevent any future break ins.

After several minutes of examining some beautiful kiln blasted pottery and little ceramic animals, several of which, shaped like cute bunnies, decided to hop into his pocket and come along for an adventure, Ashe decided the owner of the shop was not home. He had politely left, locking the door behind him only to discover the shop next to it was also open and left shockingly unattended. What was it with these people? Had they no conception of the terrible things that could happen to shop merchandise if there was no one there to make sure things were safe?

The sweet rolls were very tasty and would have probably spoilt or been eaten by passing stray dogs, so Ashe was very glad he could put them to their full potential. The little dagger he found in the blacksmiths was clearly too valuable to leave lying around and in another shop there were some sweet candies on the counter that were just to die for.

A loud cry of distress froze the Halfling in place just as he was about to try on a set of clothes for size and he realised that time simply had slipped away from him. He exited the latest shop with serious security issues, only to notice the villagers had all considered the error of their ways and were now coming back down the hill along the main street. This was a good thing, because Ashe simply was not able to act as a guard for all these establishments at once, so he was relieved that he could now walk away and let them take care of their properties for themselves.

Another wail tore his gaze from a particularly fetching scarf that had been carelessly left unattended, to observe a villager crying in horror at the state of her basket of overturned goods lying crushed in the street. She fell to her knees sobbing, as if she had suffered some ailment or great grief and tried to pick up her belongings but her smashed eggs were dripping yolk and shell through the weave of the basket and her produce ruined where it had rolled in the gutter.

The Halfling could not understand why the woman was complaining. What did she expect when she left her food in the middle of the street? Of course, it would be ruined! Ashe knew as well as anyone that you should never carry all your eggs in one basket!

He watched for a few moments more as the woman looked around her, apparently confused as to why her items were in this state and as he watched other villagers completed their own journeys down the mountain and started to get upset too.

This was not a good sign. Ashe was aware that when people got upset and he was around, they normally always looked in his direction and decided that he was to blame, even when all he was trying to do was help. As such, he removed a pair of long black gloves from his arms, kicked his way free from a large pair of boots several sizes too big for him and decided that it was time to explore the sea front and put these people well behind him.

The sea front had held only a few minor distractions. A big spindly crab that popped in and out of its shell as it slid across the sand and got agitated when Ashe poked it with a big stick. A few deep green pebbles worn clear by the motion of the waves and some seaweed that when split and blown through, made strange noises like Marcus did when he slept after eating Violetta's bean stew.

Now, where was he? Oh yes, he was bored.

The Halfling looked behind him back towards the village and the hubbub that was only just starting to ease, then along the coastline and the pale yellow strip of sand at his feet towards an old boathouse that looked like one good puff of air would send the whole structure falling into the sea. It did not look promising for a place of high adventure. Nothing in there but dust and mouldy fish!

A large seagull landed on an exposed groyne and cawed loudly in warning at the Halfling's trespass on its territory. Ashe looked at the webbed leathery feet, the huge sharp beak and the wide powerful wings. An excited thought came to him.

"Hi." He opened, walking towards the bird and extending his hand. "My name is Ashe and I am going to have a bird soon just like you called Sinders. I am very excited abou..."

The seagull squawked in annoyance as the little man moved too close for comfort and took to the sky with a sharp beat of its wings, soaring a few feet before landing on the yellow sand. Ashe stood hands on hips indignant at the lack of communication and set off to continue his conversation.

"As I was saying my bird Sinders will be this bi... Oh mouldy carrots. I just want to ask your advice on some baby bird rearing matters. Won't you sit still and let me finish?"

The seagull tilted its head watching Ashe run towards it after another brief escape from gravity ensured the proper respectful distances were kept. Ashe refused to give up and gave chase, running this way and that all over the beach, before he realised the gull was not a good conversationalist and did not really care about his imminent new avian arrival.

He stopped running, putting his little hands on his legs and hanging his head to catch his breath, then looked up and realised the boathouse was now a lot closer. Very close in fact and if he was not mistaken, he could hear some building work going on inside.

Putting the seagull from his mind, Ashe pootled across the sand and walked up to the nearest window, he dropped to his knees, putting his nose up against the glass and peered inside. There was a ship in there, another ship! Instant thoughts of Ashe the pirate captain sprang to mind, more treasure to find, more wenches to seduce. Then he paused. This was unfortunate, just when he thought he had found something to pass the day he realised people were walking about inside the shed doing the repairs

So much for a life of excitement. He pulled himself to his feet. It was time to get back to the *El Defensor* and see the crew. Maybe Colette had come back? Something came down over the Halfling's head plunging him into darkness.

"What in the world!" he exclaimed, coughing at the taste of mouldy fish and dust that was lining the bottom of the sack that was over his head. A swift kick to the mid-section whooshed the air from the little thief and he sank back to the floor wheezing for breath.

"That wasn't nice." He gasped, getting another swift kick as a reward for his opinion.

"Shut up!" came a voice made all of gravel and broken glass.

"That's not very nice either." Ashe confirmed, gaining an additional smack to the back of the head that made him see stars. He felt himself lifted into the air and hoisted over someone's shoulder.

This was not the kind of adventure Ashe had been looking for. There were several steps up and down, the banging and sawing got louder and suddenly he found himself deposited roughly into a chair and his hands tied behind his back. The sack came off his head leaving the Halfling coughing and squinting in the light.

Another chair was opposite him and in it sat a large man with something metallic on his face where his nose should be. Ashe took in the sight of the man, the rings on his fingers, the pudgy jaw, the swept over hair. If he did not know better, he would have sworn that he was looking at Atticus Couqran, the guild master from Catterick, except for the metal nose that was. That man was a danger to doing business in Catterick and had been a constant concern to the Halfling in his old life a world away. Indeed, there had been some real close scrapes when Atticus had almost caught him poaching on guild territory. Then there was the incident with the statue of the silver ship. Well, he was sure that was long forgotten by now. Ashe knew Atticus actively discouraged 'incidents', often with broken limbs and accidental falls onto sharp objects.

The man grinned wickedly in his direction, as a little puppy dog padded over to Ashe's chair, cocked its leg and deposited a stream of urine down the chair leg. Several laughs from unseen figures behind him, meant observers were finding this animal's antics amusing. Ashe just hoped none of it was dribbling into his shoes.

"Hello," Ashe started. "I'm Ashe..."

"Wolfsdale." Answered the man who looked really, really like Atticus the mad evil guild master who Ashe had always tried to stay as far away from as possible.

"So, you know my name." Ashe shrugged, his mind trying to put it all together and not liking the answer he was getting. The figure in the chair got to his feet and moved closer. The resemblance to Atticus was uncanny. Who would have thought the man had a twin on the other side of the ocean? The man reached into his pocket and brought out a long-handled dagger that he pointed at Ashe in the most unfriendly way.

"Have you broken any more statues recently?" He asked, making the Halfling's innocent face crease with confusion. "Why are you so far from home, Ashe?"

"Do I know you?" Ashe replied, trying desperately to understand what was going on. "I once knew someone just like you but they didn't have that lump of metal where their nose should be."

"Don't get sharp with me lad." The man threatened, waving his blade and moving it closer to Ashe's chest. "Tell me what you know about the *El Defensor*. What is she doing here and what is her crew and complement?"

"I'm sorry but I do not think that is something Thomas Adams would like you to know." Ashe shot back adamant in the fact. "Now put the knife down and let me go before my friend Sticks finds out, or you will wish you had never been born." Laughs echoed around the open space as the man leaned forward and a foul smell wafted over the Halfling.

"Oh boy!" Ashe wrinkled his nose in disgust. "Can you back up a bit? Something smells a little ripe around here." The cut was delivered so quick Ashe never realised until a few seconds after the injury was administered.

"What are you? Hey, I'm bleeding what did you do that for?"

"Now I have your undivided attention, why don't you tell me all about the *El Defensor*," Atticus Couqran leant forward, filling the little thief's vision as he spoke with a voice filled with menace and the promise of more pain to come. "Tell me about her crew, why she is here and especially about Styx. I *really, really* want to know where Styx is, as we have so much unfinished business to talk about."

Chapter Forty-Seven

If Thomas found himself impressed by the ambience of the *Vane Arms* during the day, in the evening it simply stole his breath away. The inn hummed with energy, laughter and a nurturing warmth. The tantalising aromas of the food set his mouth watering. Villagers packed the mill to the rafters, from the youngsters sitting by the fire listening to magically spun folk tales, to the eldest spinster's toe tapping to folk tunes from musicians close around. Tonight, the inn was especially boisterous, as the majority of the crew of the *El Defensor* were invited as guests of honour, an open invite from Charleton to make up for the poor service, he believed, he had shown earlier.

Lantern lights set within the mill illuminated everything with a warm welcoming glow, reflecting off bottles hoisted to customers in the rafters and glinting off brass ornaments that added to the sparkling image before his eyes. It made Thomas think fondly of the fairy stories he had heard as a child. The whole place looked like something from one of these stories, mysterious welcoming and intriguing all at once.

Thomas had left a skeleton crew manning the ship. Rauph had stayed for obvious visible reasons and Scrave was apparently unwell and had remained in his cabin. The captain made a mental note to send Violetta to check on him when they returned.

Rowan was delighted to accompany Thomas to the inn that evening but as they entered, the ladies of the village intercepted her, whisking her away and out of sight behind one of the larger curtained alcoves in a fit of giggles. Thomas found himself looking at his newly vacant hand with a fond longing, wishing he could have extended the pleasure of her company. From the sounds behind the curtain, Rowan seemed to be enjoying herself but when Thomas tried to look, he encountered a stern wagging finger from the shopkeeper Constance and recognising an offensive weapon when he saw one, he wisely stepped away.

His eyes scanned the bar, a lifetime habit Thomas felt he would never break. He took in the scowls from the villagers as Charleton informed them of what had happened earlier in the day. Their blood was up that was for sure. The captain had felt it was his place to tell the proprietor what had occurred when the man had finally regained his senses. Then when Charleton declared he had no recollection of the time he had spent at the church the whole scenario took on a distinctly more sinister feel. When the proprietor informed him that all the villagers had been suffering from lapses over the last few months and that they had all felt it was simply a prolonged virulent virus, difficult to shake off, Thomas realised more and more he had stumbled into something terrible and the finger of blame was pointing directly at Richard.

Now, as the tale unfolded and the people took in the news with angry gestures and clenched fists, Thomas started to ponder if he could have handled his disclosure better. He had a feeling this was one step away from an angry mob forming, waving pitchforks and storming up the hill to burn the church to the ground. It appeared Richard had a lot of explaining to do.

A tankard of ale appeared on the polished mahogany bar he approached, Charleton nodding his head to indicate it was for the captain. Thomas reached into his pocket to find some coin but a scowl from the landlord left him feeling any attempt at considering payment would be an insult to the proud man before him.

"Your money is no good here." Charleton confirmed. "The drinks and food are on us tonight for what you and your crew have discovered."

"It's very kind of you to offer," Thomas replied. "But I feel I can't accept this generous offer."

"I'm sorry." Charleton smiled, holding his hand up to his ear as if he had a hearing problem. "I can't seem to make out what you are saying." He turned away with a good-natured warm smile and moved to serve another customer, leaving Thomas to nurse his ale and his thoughts. He turned around, taking a sip of the dark nutty brew, before leaning up against the bar, the better to take in the bustling establishment around him. Villagers came up to thank him, some with nods, some with nervous smiles, others with hugs, tears and warm slaps on his back. He flushed at all the unwanted attention, realising that there would be no warm welcome for the priest if he wandered in here this evening.

Thomas noticed Kerian stepping through the door, Colette sauntering close alongside him and shared a secret smile with her across the room. He had taken the young mage to one side and explained some of the mystery behind her elderly companion. Colette had surprised him by explaining that she had already picked up some clues regarding Kerian's true nature and was not surprised at his revelation. Thomas would bet good money, based on her smile that Kerian had no idea of the gossip passed about him. Equally, he was sure the gruff adventurer had not opened up to Colette yet. If only he knew the speed at which gossip spread on ship. The whole crew probably knew about it by now.

As before, the hawk like ladies of the village swooped on fresh prey and Colette was bustled behind the same curtained alcove where laughter from many excited voices appeared to be growing. Kerian looked lost without his companion and turned slowly in place, unsure where to go, before he spotted his friend and used his location as a means to escape the thanks showered upon him. It appeared Kerian was as humble as Thomas when it came to accepting appreciation for his work.

The captain continued scanning the room as he waited for Kerian to arrive. He took in the open fireplace where all the children of the village sat, eyes wide, attention rooted on a thin man wearing a wide brimmed hat and a scarf around his neck despite the warmth of his position in the overstuffed ragged chair in which he sat. A lanky Irish wolfhound, its faded coat peppered with wiry grey, sat patiently at his side, looking up at its master with sad dark eyes. The man was telling stories to the attentive children but his method for telling them was unique. As Thomas watched, the man inhaled smoke from his long pipe and blew it into the air where it magically formed into rampaging monsters, heroic knights, ships sailing across tempestuous seas and even a dragon that flew around one boy's head before dissipating in front of his sparkling eyes.

"Where have they taken the girls?" Kerian asked, arriving alongside.

"Hang on just a moment" Thomas waved his hand in annoyance, upset at having the magic of the moment broken. He stepped away from the bar to watch the smoke form into a cat playing a fiddle, then a cow swaggered into the scene, took a long gallop around and in-between the young spectators before jumping high in the air and over a pale smoky moon. He could not help but smile; knowing that before long a dog would be rolling around in laughter and a feeding bowl and spoon would elope looking for better times in the future. He turned to Charleton beckoning him over.

"Why doesn't he speak his stories?" he asked, finding it hard to tear his eyes away as a smoky canine threw its head back to howl silently at the moon.

"Sad story," the barman replied at his shoulder. "He was involved in a terrible accident when he was young; nearly found himself hung as a result. He can't speak now, even if he wanted to. Therefore, he uses the smoke to tell his tales. I'm sure after tonight's revelations there will be little stories of your ship and crew to add to his repertoire."

Kerian tugged on Thomas's arm drawing his attention away from Charleton.

"Have you seen Ashe or Marcus?"

"No..." Thomas asked, instinctively checking his pockets to see if anything was missing. "Why do you ask?"

"Well that's just it. No one has seen them and it's unusual for Ashe to be missing an evening's entertainment and spectacle such as this."

"I'm sure Marcus has wandered up to the church by now. Maybe he's examining some religious icons, digging through dusty archives or sharing religious gossip." Thomas laughed, noticing other villagers bringing in baskets of food for a huge already overloaded table at the back of the room, as Ives, Aradol, Weyn and Commagin came in through the door.

"Apparently the archives are flooded." Kerian replied, his frustrated tone bringing Thomas back to face his friend.

"Well I'm sure Marcus is big enough to look after himself doing whatever things monks do." he replied, trying to reassure Kerian and reduce his concern. "I mean what's the worst thing he could be up to?"

"You have no idea." Kerian whispered to himself thoughtfully.

* * * * * *

Marcus walked back into the church and immediately picked up that the atmosphere was different. The building had taken on a more sinister nature in the dark, especially as no one had thought to light the candles within, leaving several areas cloaked in darkness as the final rays of the sun sank below the horizon. He slowed his walk, aware that his sandal footsteps were much louder to his ears and paused to listen to the sounds around him.

Raised voices came from within the sacristy, come study area, to the right of the altar but they were muffled at this distance. It almost sounded like chanting. Were the knights taking a rare opportunity to pray together? He moved closer, aware that his walk around the village had tired him. He was hungry, thirsty and conscious that he had not found any sign of the errant Brother Richard. Candlelight flickered from under the study door, showing the knights had the sense to illuminate one room of the church.

Marcus opened the study door and froze as he took in the scene. The twelve knights stood in a circle chanting, their swords laid in a circular pattern on the floor, tips towards the centre and hilts circling around. Hastily moved furniture, rugs rucked up and items pushed aside allowed clear space for the knights to occupy.

The sound of the raised voices hit him like a wave, the sounds now clear, concise and ominous in their content. It took Marcus seconds to link the phrases in his mind and realise this was some sort of summoning spell.

He glared at Tobias but the knight was deeply into his chanting. What were they doing? This made no sense. The chanting grew more intense, voices rising to a crescendo before something started to glow directly above the prone blades. A bright flash forced Marcus to look away and when he finally found the courage to look up his heart almost skipped a beat.

Abbot Brialin's vulture like features glared down at him.

"I understand things have not been going according to plan." The Abbot opened, the malice and threat in his voice clearly intentional.

Marcus tried to meet the Abbot's probing gaze but found it hard to do so. The Abbot could be terrifying when he was displeased. He looked past Brialin's robed form looking for some form of inspiration and noted the smug face of Tobias looking back at him.

"I find it bothersome that I have to come here to ensure my orders are obeyed." The Abbot continued, his comments drawing Marcus back to looking into the man's hooded eyes, as goose bumps raised across his arms causing him to grasp himself or risk shivering in front of his Master.

"But I forget myself..." The Abbot stepped away from the circle of knights and moved to sit down, his fighters pulling a chair up behind him. He sat carefully, tucked his robes about him, slowly crossed his legs and placed his hands together in a mockery of prayer, before slowly interlocking the fingers in a deliberate act to have Marcus hanging on his every move.

"So tell me Marcus." Brialin smiled like a cat about to eat a mouse. "Did you have a good trip? And when you are ready, please tell me where I can find Brother Richard?"

* * * * * *

"Zap. I'm turning you into a frog." Shouted a clearly excited voice.

Kerian and Thomas turned towards a nearby alcove where a bunch of youths appeared to be playing some elaborate game with multi-sided dice, paper and charcoal sticks. There were eight of them, all intent on the table and the sketched sheets before them as if their very lives depended on the smudged rushed strokes scribbled across their surfaces.

"Crossbows at the ready!" shouted another, making Kerian stifle a chuckle as he took in the youth in question, clearly a brother to the frog sorcerer and a confident member of the group.

The latest crew members arrived at the bar, picking seats along its length and commandeering a taller stool so that Commagin could clamber up it and assume his traditional position near the liquid refreshments. Thomas tugged on Charleton's sleeve as he headed over to serve them, bringing the landlord up short and causing a grumpy look from the engineer.

"What's that all about?" Thomas enquired, pointing at the youths.

"Oh, that's the lads. They come in once a week, eat me out of banana fritters, spicy potatoes, chilli and pints of prawns, play their game and are totally harmless."

"I'm going to rule the world." Shouted another, rising to his feet to proclaim his right to all who would listen, his face intelligent and his imagination clearly visiting places the others were yet to see. "You should all know your place and bow before me. I am the master here."

Thomas turned to take in the rest of the group. They looked like a group of geeky university students, minus the mobile phones and the laptops. Apart from the brothers and the aspiring megalomaniac, there were five other individuals in the group. Two were thin and lanky; one sporting blond spiky hair, more intent on eating, drinking and looking longingly at the girls on the dance floor. Whilst his darker haired associate sat tapping his feet, spinning a charcoal stick around in one hand and placing the fingers of his other on the table as if pretending to play on a piano.

"I'm the doctor." Stated another youth, who towered over his friends, his swept back blond hair adding to his height. "We just need to reverse the polarity of the neutron flow." Thomas stared at the youth's musculature in awe, even as he struggled to understand the meaning behind the words he had just uttered. This man would have been awesome as a wingman in the university bars of old. In a few years, he could even be a match for Rauph.

His friends were all groaning but seemed to understand completely what the tall youth said and started scribbling anew, dice rattling across the wooden table in frantic rolls resulting in some painful moans as the random dice throws decided their fates. A smaller blond-haired lad threw his dice and smiled as they landed, clearly using loaded dice to ensure his fate was better than that of his colleagues. Thomas felt his gaze drawn to the boy at the back, struggling to be heard, sporting the worst case of acne the captain had ever seen.

"I'm going to nail his character's head to the floor." Shouted the youth threatening to crossbow everyone. The boy at the back sat in shock at this revelation.

"I don't think that's keeping in character." He stammered, much to the enjoyment and mirth of all those around him. It appeared this was something of a regular occurrence by his crestfallen face.

Thomas felt a pull on his arm again and turned to look at Kerian, leaving the boys to enjoy their fun.

"What?" Thomas asked; too busy enjoying himself taking in the sights, sounds, and goings on of the bar to worry about Kerian's concerns.

"I was asking about Ashe." Kerian's eyebrow arched in annoyance. "I've just quizzed the others and they also haven't seen him. I'm telling you he would not have missed this!" Kerian said spreading his arms wide. A cheer went up from the crowd and the curtains slid open to reveal the women of the town all dressed in their finery, hair in braids, long flowing dresses and skilfully applied makeup.

"I'm sure Ashe is just poking his nose into everyone's business whilst we are all in here." Thomas tried to reassure Kerian, even as his eyes scanned the rainbow of bright free flowing dresses tumbling out from the alcove onto the dancefloor in search of the lady that he now found so fascinating. He identified Violetta and her daughter laughing and admiring each other's beautiful gowns gifted by the townsfolk and he smiled at their happiness before continuing his visual search for Rowan.

"We need to find him." Kerian continued to push, interrupting Thomas's quest. "What if he's broken in somewhere and is taking the villager's things? They seem to like us here. I'd prefer to leave without flaming torches pursuing us to the docks for a change."

Thomas continued scanning the crowd, as the words finally sank in about their diminutive problem. Just as he was about to address his colleague's concerns his eyes finally caught sight of Rowan. She smiled demurely at him and he felt his jaw drop. Her oversized working clothes and boots cobbled together from spares gathered on the *El Defensor* were gone. She now stood in a full-length flowing terracotta dress with the most delicate embroidery, braid, gold stitching and small pearls sewn onto the wide flowing skirt. The bodice was tight, accentuating her figure, her hair piled up onto her head with a few choice soft curls cascading to frame a face bright with sparkling mischievous eyes. The captain realised he definitely wanted to see that face when he awoke the following morning.

Kerian stood beside him looking like another gasping fish on dry land as Colette ran over and planted a kiss on his left cheek, her long blond hair piled in a similar style to Rowan's and her coltish smile lighting fires within the man that were clear for all to see as his cheeks lit rosy red. She stood in a similar gown but of moss green, tiny intricate stitching all over the flowing dress pulling it in to hug her shape. Tiny silver shells stitched across the hem glittered in the lamp light. She laughed infectiously as Rowan walked up beside her and they examined each other in ways only true friends can.

"Steady old chap." Thomas nudged Kerian in the ribs. "You need to think of your blood pressure."

Kerian shook his head snapping himself out of the daze. Colette looked stunning. He wanted to think of nothing else but what about the absent Ashe? The ship's mage winked one of her deep blue eyes and gestured that Kerian accompany her over to a table and Ashe slid down Kerian's mental priority list. The Halfling was more than capable of looking after himself. There was clearly nothing dangerous to worry about here?

"Would you like to dance?" Rowan asked. "I don't wish to be forward but if we dance now I'll have more room for the food." She laughed grabbing Thomas's hand as she started to pull him from the bar.

"Hang on... Hang on." Thomas held up his tankard, gesturing he had to put it down and turned to tap Commagin on the back.

"Duty calls." He stated, taking in Commagin's raised bushy eyebrow and smile. "You need to send someone back to the *El Defensor* to find the Halfling. It would be a shame to mess this up just because of his light fingers."

Rowan pulled hard, spinning Thomas out after her and onto the floor as the band picked up the tempo. Kerian found himself similarly sucked up in the whirling mass of dancers and simply hung on to his young charge. Commagin looked down at Thomas's tankard on the bar and then over at the men sitting beside him. He tapped Weyn on the shoulder.

"You need to go back to the ship and find Ashe." He stated gruffly.

Weyn was about to ask for a drink and had his arm outstretched to gain the barman's attention. He looked down at Commagin in frustration at the interruption.

"What, right now?" he asked disappointment clear on his face.

"Well someone needs to." Commagin stated. "And I'm the senior crewman here." The Dwarven engineer pulled hard on Thomas's drink and let out a contented sigh.

Weyn took in the engineer's comment, thinking for a moment, then turned to the crewman alongside him, reaching past his bow case he had leaning up against the bar, to tap the merchant on the shoulder. Ives turned from drooling at the huge buffet table filling with a multitude of exotic dishes and frowned.

"Why do you disturb me when I am about to become one with the bounty before me?" he asked.

"We need to send someone back to the *El Defensor* to find the thief." Weyn stated. "And as I am more senior than you, you have to go."

"Well can't you tie a message to one of your arrows and let the ship know that way? My feet are aching and my stomach is critically ill, listen to the sounds it is making? I'm sure I will die unless I have sustenance." Ives pleaded, looking longingly back at the table of food and then back at the archer.

"You are more junior in rank than I." Weyn replied. "And as you say, I am a very good shot with a bow and arrow."

Ives turned to the loud snort alongside him and noticed Aradol laughing into his drink. He went to voice his disappointment then paused, a smile sliding across his face.

"Aradol my friend." He opened, grinning broadly. "As you have heard, my colleagues need the most junior member of the crew to return to the ship and find the little man Ashe. As I am your senior crewmember, I am telling you it is your job to undertake this very important role."

"What!" Aradol spluttered indignantly. "How are you my senior? We joined the crew at the same time."

"Oh no my friend, you are sadly mistaken." Ives replied. "I was a crewman before the inn burnt down. You did not join us until after the festivities had finished." He beamed a smile at his reckoning, leaving his colleague grasping for a possible comeback.

Aradol frowned at the injustice of the situation and turned to look down the bar at the next crewman who sat there nursing his drink. He tapped on the man's shoulder to draw his attention, unaware that this person had been listening intently to their conversation all the way along its journey.

"Excuse me." Aradol opened.

Mathius Blackraven turned slowly around and leaned back against the bar, smiling innocently as he flipped a newly brought dagger across the back of his hand and danced the blade through his fingers.

"Yes..." he replied in a voice that dripped theatrical menace. Aradol took one look at the man, the deadly confidence he showed with the knife and the thinly veiled threat the spinning blade implied before swallowing hard.

"Don't worry..." He spluttered. "It was nothing. I'm... I'm just heading back to the ship... Do you want anything?"

"No." Mathius replied trying hard to hold in his laugh. "I think I'm fine thank you."

* * * * * *

Scrave looked at the newly hung door before him and paused to consider his actions. Was this right? Should he really be doing this? He took a second and then shook his head. No, he was right to do this. The dagger was his.

He pushed open the door to Kerian's cabin and looked at the wreckage before him. There were lengths of wood lying everywhere, nails and tools scattered on the floor. A snapping sheet of canvas flapped above his head, fastened there to try to keep the room dry whilst repairs continued. How could he have been so stupid! The storm destroyed Kerian's cabin. Clearly, taking in the contents of the room it was still inhabitable. His eyes scanned the floor, hoping against all odds that the man's belongings were still stored here but even as he searched, he knew the outcome was clear. He racked his brains, struggling to concentrate as the tension inside him threatened to make him burst.

He had to find his dagger. Had to get it back. Now where would Kerian have put his belongings in the meantime?

Scrave knew he could not simply come out with it and ask the crew where the man had put his things. It would look too suspicious if something turned up missing. Maybe he should just give this all up. The pain lanced through his forehead making him stagger against the doorframe. He rubbed the headband again, it felt so tight and it hurt so much.

"Where is it?" he muttered, biting his lip.

A second wave of nausea flooded over the Elf. He leant against the wall panting as he struggled to gather himself. A haze seemed to descend over Scrave and as he looked up, his eyes took on a determined look. If the serpent dagger was not in this cabin, it had to be somewhere else on the ship.

He would not stop until he had found it, even if he had to tear the ship apart with his bare hands.

* * * * * *

Loud laughter filled the air as Kerian spun around, the *Vane Arms* flashing before his eyes. He was intoxicated with the young woman who he was supposed to be leading although he knew it was in fact himself playing catch up. Colette's eyes sparkled in the light and Kerian wished he could preserve the moment forever, although he knew no artist would ever do it justice.

The music wound down, leaving him flushed, his heartbeat loud in his ears. People were laughing and clapping. It was almost too much for him to take in. He stood still and closed his eyes, letting the room slowly stop spinning. When he opened his eyes the first thing that he noticed was the sight of a busty woman, spectacles perched on the end of her nose, hair pulled back in a bun, taking on Commagin drink for drink and appearing to be winning. Her laughter rang again as another draught disappeared much to the astonishment of the Dwarf beside her.

"You won't beat Aunty." Charleton laughed, as he drew another tray of drinks. "Once she had Richard so drunk in here, he forgot to give service..." The barman paused, brows furrowing as he considered what he had said. He slammed the tray down, drinks slopping over the sides, aware that people had stopped to watch him.

"Bridget," he called out to a young woman with a violin under her chin. "Let's get them dancing again." She nodded her head, drew her dark hair back from her face and closed her eyes, tapping a foot to a rhythm only she could hear. With a flourish, she drew an ornate bow across taut strings and a mournful tone filled the air, drawing everyone's attention to her skill on the instrument. The violin responded to her actions, tones, rising up and down with its rich timbre.

Thomas tried to judge the style; it was similar to Gaelic folk music, the beat slow as other musicians joined in. The crowd of dancers spread out, linking arms in a massive circle that swept up the dancing couples. Step to the left, the circle turned, then to the right, the tempo slowly picking up, a drum started somewhere in the crowd, followed by a flute. Feet began to pound the floor, the circle turned faster as Thomas struggled to step with them.

The beat perceptively picking up speed, the music working its magic around the inn. The ladies split from the circle, turning and spinning into the centre of the room, skirts flaring up, obscuring faces, flashing toned calves. Kerian stood clapping as the girls turned and then found himself grabbed by the males in the wider circle, their steps increasing in speed to match the music, right feet landing with exaggerated stamps adding to the rich tapestry of sound.

Flute and violin were leading the dance, the tempo rising and falling as the bow danced across the strings and the wind instrument floated up and down the musical scale. Thomas scanned the turning dancers before him, trying to see over the spinning dresses and spot Rowan; she twirled by, laughing head held back, hair flying free. Colette a few steps behind looking as radiant as ever. The crowd were roaring approval now, the inn starting to spin around them. Feet tapping loudly, drinks hoisted high, clapping and cheering encouragement as the music flowed through the crew and washed their troubles and fears away. It was as if the music was rushing through their veins, lifting their troubled hearts, soothing worried brows, rolling into them all and leaving blessings in its wake.

Thomas laughed deeply and let down his guard. He turned with the crowd, watching the walls of the inn pass him by. The girls started to turn in the opposite direction, dresses twirling to hide and expose faces, flashes of smiles dancing before his eyes. He noticed the door of the inn opening and saw a figure staggering inside. More faces passed before him, more brightly coloured dresses. Then Rowan was there, breathing excitedly, her cheeks flush as she moved in to kiss him on the lips.

Thomas kissed her back hard, taking in her scent, finding it intoxicating. They spun in each other's arms; two people destined to be together. Someone crashed into them, causing gasps of dismay and shouts of anger. The captain looked up, checking Rowan was okay before turning to whoever had collided with them.

Scared eyes looked out of a dirty streaked face. A blue robe torn and stained covered the man who had fallen to his knees before them, a bottle of opened spirits slopping out onto the floor where he had dropped it. He kept saying the same thing repeatedly and it took a moment to make out the drunken man's words and figure out who this individual was due to his dishevelled state.

"I'm sorry. I'm so sorry." Richard shook his head tears streaming down his face. "I never meant it to be this way."

* * * * * *

"Have you seen Ashe?" Aradol asked, poking his head into Rauph's cabin intending to simply shout the question and move on so he could get back to the party. Instead, the man stopped short to take in Rauph looking up at him from under a blanket. "What are you doing Rauph?"

"I'm hiding." Rauph replied. "Thomas said to keep out of sight."

"I'm sure that won't be a problem tonight." Aradol laughed. "Everyone is in the *Vane Arms* partying. No one is going to see you tonight." He shook his head and pulled the blanket from his friend's head then remembered what he had been asking. "Hey, have you seen Ashe?"

Rauph paused to consider it.

"Not since this morning." He confessed. "Ashe was in Commagin's lab."

"Well he's not there now." Aradol confirmed. "I've just been there and it's all locked down tight. No one's in there now."

"Umm." Rauph snorted, getting to his feet and towering over his fellow crewman. "Do you think he's in trouble?"

"I think Thomas is more worried we could all be in trouble if he isn't found." Aradol smiled. "Sorry to have worried you." He turned to leave but Rauph stopped him with a massive hand.

"Everyone's at the party, right?"

"Everyone of importance." Aradol confirmed.

"So, no one will see me if I go out looking?" Rauph started to adjust his armour, tightening straps before reaching behind the smaller man to lift his swords over and fasten them to his back.

"It's unlikely now it is dark." Aradol replied, watching the gentle navigator transform himself into a warrior with a mission.

"Then don't worry." Rauph stated calmly, looking down and rolling his shoulders as if working out kinks. "Tell Thomas I'll find him."

Aradol looked back at his colleague and tried to think of a way to explain that the thought of an eight-foot tall chestnut-haired Minotaur stomping around town under cover of darkness was probably just as much a worry. Then he shrugged his shoulders. Something about how Rauph looked just seemed to quash any thought of argument clear out of his mind.

"Just make sure you are careful." He emphasised.

"Oh, it's not me you have to worry about," Rauph replied pushing the man gently aside. "If anyone has hurt Ashe, they are the ones that need to be careful."

Aradol stood and watched Rauph head off down the corridor and decided the Minotaur had never said a truer word.

* * * * * *

"Give him space." Thomas yelled, adopting his role as peacekeeper and keeping the angry villagers from dragging Richard outside and lynching him. He turned to Charleton and took in the barman's thunderous face.

"Listen we can all have our say later but I need to take this man somewhere we can sober him up and talk to him. Have you got such a place?"

"Stick him in an alcove." Charleton replied gruffly. "I'm not letting him out of this inn until he and I have had words."

"That will be fine." Thomas replied, lifting Richard under his arm and winced at the smell of the liquor. How many times had he done this in his past life? Some things never change. Kerian moved in on the other side and between the two of them they carried the priest over to an alcove and placed the man behind the table there, sliding in on either side, Colette slipping in alongside Kerian, Charleton and Rowan on the other, making the alcove hot and near claustrophobic.

Richard looked up at the faces around him, thankful that the thin covering hid him from the most accusing stares.

"So, Richard." Thomas opened. "I'll make this simple. The game is up. Your goose is cooked. We know what you have been doing and the only way out of this that keeps you alive is if you spill the beans."

Kerian, Colette and Charleton all looked at Thomas confused. He realised instantly that he had slipped back into modern speak, even as Richard looked up at him.

"I have no beans here to spill." He confessed, making Rowan burst out laughing as the only other member of the group that understood the joke.

"We need to know how you did it. How did you control the people of this village and how can we make sure this never happens again?"

Richard cleared his throat and started to talk. Thomas simply sat back and let him pour his story out, knowing that during an interrogation once someone started to open up it was better to let them say their piece and not butt in and risk them clamming up. The others listened alongside him, hearing of the tyranny of living a life in fear under the eyes of Abbot Brialin. How the man used his position to corrupt those of influence in Catterick. How Richard had found out about his connection with a local crime lord and how he realised he would never be more than the Abbot's pawn. How he had always dreamed of having his own church and congregation and how he had found a secret to a treasure in the monastery archives he felt no one knew about.

The escape plan was rather too easy, as Richard told it and Thomas immediately started to realise the man before him had been used in more ways than he knew. By the sounds of it Brialin had known about the treasure and the way it supposedly granted a heart's desire. The power from such a prize would be staggering in the wrong hands. He had to interrupt despite his desire to let the sad monk continue talking.

"Did you not think he may have let you run with the information just to see if it was possible to find the island?" Thomas asked. "I mean what are the chances of finding such a treasure, especially as it was based on a fairy tale. It was a slim prospect at best."

"I suppose that could have been the case." Richard confessed. "Although it is also feasible that the crew who bought me here could also have successfully sailed back to Catterick and told him I was still here."

He rambled on, telling of the statue he had found in the overgrown and neglected gardens, how he had followed the manuscript and found Rosalyine asleep in her magnificent form, forever guarding the jewelled heart of her lost love. He told how he had used his religious icon's power to survive the heat and gas from the creature. How he found the gem in a temple surrounded by molten lava, before using its power to grant his deepest desire. It was then a simple matter to think of his church and watch the magic of the wish build it. With a thought, he tamed the gardens and the villagers worked long hours alongside him helping to complete his dreams.

Then one day, as he looked at his empty church, he thought about the villagers below and how he wished to offer them his words of advice. Richard had almost fallen over when the doors of the church opened and the villagers poured in attentive and ready for his teachings. It did not take him long to realise that all he had to do was call and they would attend service, no matter what time of day it was. It was that simple to have all the attention he desired. He knew it was false, knew it was wrong but the excitement of the corrupting power swept him away and it was too tempting to have instant gratification rather than earn it through respect and example.

"You cold bastard." Charleton snarled. "We ought to kill you where you stand."

Richard withdrew into himself like a tortoise going back into a shell. Rowan suddenly jumped and looked under the table before smiling and reaching under to lift a small cat up into her lap where it commenced to sharpen its claws on her leg.

"Socks, stop that." Richard scolded, reaching over and extracting the cat claw by claw from her lap. He hugged the animal close and its purrs reverberated around the enclosed space.

"So what do we do now?" Rowan asked.

"That's simple." Colette stood up from her place at the table and took Kerian's hand in her own. "Kerian and I are heading back to the ship. We need some things and then we are heading up to that fountain."

"Now?" Kerian asked incredulously. "Aren't we going to wait until daylight?"

"Now." Colette replied staring directly into his eyes, leaving no room for argument. "I'm not prepared to wait any longer to see you young again."

"How did you know about that?" Kerian asked mouth agape as if he were catching flies.

"Really Kerian." She replied, "You are my soulmate. I already know everything there is about you. Oh... and Thomas also cracked under my questions."

"He did!" Kerian raised an eye and turned to his friend. "That's the last time I..."

The curtain flew aside and a breathless villager stood there.

"Come quickly." He gasped. "The church is on fire."

* * * * * *

Ashe was not sure what was real or not anymore. Sounds and feelings all blurred into red. He remembered starting out defiant and loyal to the crew of the *El Defensor* but then these men had started hurting him. Atticus, oh it was Atticus all right, took great delight in ordering his thugs to beat Ashe to a pulp.

He had lost teeth; one eye had swollen shut and the other showed images tinged with red and had an alarming dark spot over to one side. Something had come loose inside and it did not take a genius to realise this was not a good sign. Punches landed with sounds like bags of wet washing falling to the floor but Ashe became numb to the punishment after a while.

At that point, Atticus had suggested they started breaking parts of him.

Ashe shuddered as his mind patched together the events leading up to him passing out. He remembered talking, remembered talking a lot. All about Kerian how he was old and looking to get young, how he was after a magical treasure that would remove his curse and that it was somewhere on the island.

They broke two fingers just to make sure he was telling the truth. The first and second fingers of his right-hand snapping like kindling as they used tools from the boat shed to make good on their threats.

Ashe remembered saying other stuff then. Most of it made up. That there was a dragon on the island and that the dragon had more than just the gem, it actually had a massive hoard of treasure. The Halfling had warned it was a strange looking dragon. Kerian had shown him a picture and it actually looked like a large duck, so they needed to be careful around anything feathered.

The third finger snapping made Ashe pass out with a shriek of pain. This state did not help him however as he had faced flashbacks of his youth. His abandonment at the age of three. His father walking away and leaving him under the care of a mother who had to work all hours and was often too tired to offer much more than her love, leaving him for periods with a kindly lady who used to wash him in a faded red bucket in front of a roaring fire.

He recalled facing his father; this much was true, walking up to him in a shop at the age of seven, only to be told he was mistaken. The man stood with others, clearly embarrassed, part of another family, he certainly did not have a previous son and had asked him to walk away and leave him alone. It was then Ashe decided love was a weakness, that to trust someone was to leave him vulnerable and exposed. He vowed never to let himself be vulnerable again. It had coloured the decisions he had made for the rest of his life.

Ashe recollected turning to the streets to survive, being badly beaten one day for stealing a glass of milk and a biscuit before slowly realised he was coming back awake again and the stale milk smell was actually the stench from Atticus's nose as he had moved in close to ensure the Halfling was still alive.

He remembered a man coming in and excitement mounting at the discovery of a cave nearby that had carvings inside on the walls showing a temple and a dragon. It appeared to be a way into the caves used by the people of this place. Voices had raised, a group of men armed and Ashe had finally hoped his luck was starting to improve.

Atticus had moved to leave and had then stopped as if in afterthought. He walked over to his beaten captive and sneered at him before moving closer, his breath whistling in and out of his decaying nose.

"I'm going to find Kerian now. I'm going to find him and I'm going to kill him." He had informed Ashe. "You had better not have lied to me. If Kerian is not up there I will come back and do even worse things to you than I already have."

Thinking back on it, Ashe reflected, being smart at this moment had probably not been the wisest of actions for him to take. He remembered trying to think of a witty response but had instead come out with the lame comment that he did not think there was much more the crime lord could do to him.

Atticus had smiled, picking up a set of shears and testing the edge of them on his finger. He had then explained to Ashe there were a great many things he could still do. Then he had laughed aloud before slipping the shears under Ashe's struggling hand severing his right thumb with a crunch like pulling the wing off a chicken. Then he had turned and callously thrown Ashe's thumb across the room, laughing further as he left.

Oh, dear god!

They had taken his thumb!

* * * * * *

"There is something so beautiful in a naked flame." Abbot Brialin commented standing before the roaring pyre that Richard's church had become. "Don't you agree Marcus?"

Marcus looked up at his Master and nodded in agreement even though inside he was horrified at the wanton destruction he observed. The knights were laughing at his obvious discomfort but Brialin feigned not to notice.

The Abbot turned his head and listened as Tobias whispered into his ear. He walked over to Marcus; the large blue ledger that had once been Marcus's proud badge of honour tucked into a bag slung from his shoulder.

"Tobias tells me Richard had a congregation." Brialin tutted. "You neglected to tell me this Marcus. We can't have that can we?" He dragged Marcus with him to the observation point that looked down over the village below, the flickering flames lighting up the mountain at their back. Marcus noticed people running out of the *Vane Arms* and gesturing up at the conflagration lighting up the night sky.

"All of those people listening to his vitriol and lies." The Abbot continued. "We all know there is only one true religion don't we Marcus?" Marcus nodded mutely.

"Anything else is an affront to St Fraiser's teachings and must be eradicated." Brialin gestured down at the village below. "All of these people are heretics; blasphemers and they must be punished. Every man, woman and child." He turned to the twelve knights as Marcus suddenly realised what was going to happen, his blood turning to ice in his veins.

"Cleanse this outrage with fire. Scour it from the earth. No survivors, no witnesses."

Chapter Forty-Eight

"Come on." Colette gasped, pulling at Kerian's hand and rushing him from the inn. "There's no time to lose."

"But what about the others?" Kerian asked, looking over his shoulder at the people streaming out of the inn to gaze at the fire roaring high on the mountain above them. "What about the fire?"

"There are more than enough villagers to handle the fire. We can always send others from the ship to help but we also need to consider that the entrance to the temple is somewhere up there; the longer we leave it, the more chance there is the entrance may become impassable." Colette shot back. "Richard said something about heat and toxic gas so we will need some items from my cabin to keep us safe if we are to be successful. Just think, molten rock, now that will be something to see."

"Yes... I suppose so." Kerian tried to stop a smile spreading across his face. Despite the chaos on the mountain and all the dangers they still faced, he could not deny that being swept up in Colette's excitement was enchanting. He could not believe that things were moving so fast. It was like being on a galloping stallion with no way to steer. He had never felt so alive or so young. "Thank you for helping me."

"Wouldn't miss it." Colette grinned. "Now race you to the ship."

* * * * * *

"Do you have a system for fighting fires?" Thomas asked Charleton. "You know a water source, lots of buckets, human chain, that sort of thing?"

"For down here maybe but up on the mountain, not really." Charleton confessed. "The only water source up there is the fountain and I am sure Richard would not like all his fish to die."

"Well that depends on what he values more." Thomas grimly replied. "His church or his fish."

The villagers were looking concerned, confused and unsure if they should be rushing to save the church. Torn between the anger they felt towards Richard and their love of their community building. Thomas realised he had to take charge quickly.

"Weyn, go high. I need eyes from a higher point of elevation. I need to know what is happening. See if you can spot who our arsonist is. Ives, put down the pie and start getting some men together with shovels and picks. We may need a fire break if the wind fans the flames this way." Ives swiftly hid his hands behind his back but the attempt to act innocent and conceal the apple and blackberry pie he had been eating failed, mainly because he had the evidence smeared all around his mouth. Weyn ran over to the slowly turning windmill vanes and timed his leap to take him onto the edge of the lowest sail. He swung there as the windmill turned, lifting him slowly up into the darkening sky above.

"How many people are up there?" Thomas turned to Richard, the words almost dying on his lips as he saw the tears flowing down the priest's face. He was vanquished, broken hearted at the loss of the one thing he had yearned for and had held for the briefest of moments. In that instant, Thomas could almost forgive the man for the misguided actions he had taken against the villagers. No one with a heart would take any enjoyment from the crushing pain this priest was experiencing.

"Who else is up there?" Thomas shouted, trying to snap a response from the man.

"M... M... Marcus and his knights." Richard gasped.

"Marcus. Oh hell!" Thomas thought of the timid monk up there somewhere on the side of the mountain, possibly in danger of being caught up in the fire. "Where was he when you last saw him?"

"In the sacristy chambers where I have my study." Richard replied, slowly sinking to his knees, his moist eyes reflecting the flames on the mountain, as his hopes and dreams were dispatched to the heavens on billowing clouds of acrid smoke.

"Damn." Thomas looked at the people beside him, discarding possible candidates and weighing up possibilities before his eyes came to rest on Mathius.

"Mathius I need you to find Marcus. Make sure he's safe and bring him down to us."

"Consider it done." Mathius nodded and stepped backwards cloaking himself in the shadows where he belonged.

Thomas then turned to the villagers, glad of his previous training and drawing on his inborn leadership ability as he addressed them.

"Do any of you know if someone has gone up the mountain, a family member, friend or neighbour? Someone who could have started that fire?" Heads shook all around, the faces of the people not showing any sign of hiding a guilty secret.

"Take the women and children back into the Vane Arms. We were having a party remember." He smiled, trying to lift the dark mood of the people before him. Silently, they began to gather their children and ferry them back under shelter. Charleton walked up alongside Thomas and watched as everyone traipsed inside.

"I don't believe anyone has set that fire." He stated. "We may have considered it but no one harms anyone here. It is an unspoken rule. Don't worry I'll see to settling everyone." The landlord promised before following the crowd. The captain of the *El Defensor* turned from Charleton to watch Ives lead a group of men off in search of spades, digging implements and buckets, then swung his head up towards the roof of the *Vane Arms*.

"Weyn what's the weather like up there?"

"It looks like we are in for a hot and sultry night." came down Weyn's reply. "I'll keep you posted if there is any change."

Thomas found himself standing alone and turned, feeling momentarily lost, his mind racing. Rowan stepped out from the shadows and into the pool of light cast through the doors of the inn, gently placing her hands on his shoulders and leaned in close to kiss him lightly on the cheek.

"There's nothing more you can do for now." she told him. "Let's go inside in the warm, you can climb up and talk to him through one of the windows."

She traced a hand down his arm and lightly gripped his hand, dragging him after her into the inn. Thomas tried to smile as he allowed himself to be moved but something was niggling in the back of his mind. Then he remembered.

What did Richard mean by Marcus's knights?

* * * * * *

Rauph knelt down on the sand, his fingers tracing the indentation of little footprints that appeared to belong to an over-excited child. He watched as they ran this way and that across the beach, with no sense in direction or any logical destination. Granted, these could be the footprints of village children but Rauph did not think so.

Children were more direct in his opinion and tended to tear directly towards their intended target. This was the footsteps of someone new to the area, someone who did not know this shoreline, someone who was only now discovering the hidden rock pools, starfish and crabs.

He sniffed the air, tracking the small prints away from him as his mind filtered the scents of dead fish, brine and something faint, indistinct, something... Violetta's gumbo? No... that was what he had to eat last night. He breathed on his hand and inhaled, confirming he was going to have to take his oral hygiene more seriously. The Minotaur shook his head and continued following the meandering tracks, not realising that his quarry lay only a few feet away in the old boathouse behind him.

* * * * * *

Scrave swung the door of Rauph's room open and stepped into the shadows. He had checked the galley, Thomas's cabin and most of the empty crew berths and it had suddenly occurred to him that the navigator's quarters might be the place to look.

The room had a musty odour to it, mainly of moist cattle but Scrave knew that before the navigator took possession of this room it belonged to the ship's mage Lucas Sumnar. It was quite eerie knowing the man's corpse sat in the corner of the room permanently pinned to the ship's destroyed magical helm.

Scrave knew that before the tragic boarding incident the *El Defensor* did much more than simply sail the high seas. Unfortunately, access to another helm was like many things on this ship, dependant on finding the right gate through the ship's graveyard and the Elf knew their luck in such matters was sorely pressed of late.

His eyes darted around the room, taking in the chart table, sextant, callipers and rolled up charts. Then he looked beside Rauph's bed. The Minotaur's blanket was on the floor, thrown as if in haste. Clearly, the Navigator had decided to leave in a hurry. Glancing near the door he noted the absence of Rauph's twin swords and confirmed his friend was definitely not going to interrupt his searching. He turned to the shelves, his eyes scanning the dusty archives for any sign of a gleaming piece of serpent gold.

"Where is it?" he asked himself. "Where is it?"

Footsteps in the corridor froze him in place. He had left the door open! Scrave ran lightly across the room and pushed the door close, leaving a slither of light to see through.

Kerian and Colette walked by and Scrave's blood boiled. It was all Kerian's fault, all of this. He ought to just walk right out and demand the dagger from him. Rational thought tempered his action. If Kerian were here, maybe he would lead Scrave to his dagger.

Scrave calmed his inner turmoil and hissed his breath between clenched teeth, realising he was clenching his hands so tightly the nails were digging into his palms. Now was a time for patience. He needed to think clearly, take his time and then if Kerian did not lead him to the dagger, he would beat the elderly man to a pulp and force it from him.

* * * * * *

Colette threw open her cabin door and walked confidently into her room. The quilted bed was the centrepiece of furniture, accompanied with a small dresser and a wooden rocking chair that completed the set. The walls held shelves practically groaning with books and magical paraphernalia. Some shelves bowed so much that they looked as if one more page or magical component would cause the complete lot to collapse to the floor.

Kerian moved to follow, only to stop short, blocked by a serious stare from the mage.

"Do you always walk into a lady's room so confidently Kerian Denaris?" Colette asked, catching Kerian as he was about to cross the threshold. "I'll have you know I don't invite gentleman of your type into my private chambers."

"Oh..." Kerian stammered. "So, what kind of men do you allow in then?"

"Only tall dark and handsome ones. Preferably with lots of money and a castle I could make my own." She smiled back.

"Umm, those kind of men are hard to find." Kerian replied, recognising the tease for what it was. "I'll keep my eye out and let you know when I find one, preferably a short fat one or a tall thin one with no hair."

"I don't need any of those." Colette turned, eyes flashing with mischief. "Just someone I can learn to love."

Kerian stood and took in the beautiful eyes that held his heart captive and blushed.

"I... I..." his throat was dry and the words refused to come. He knew what he wanted to say. To tell Colette he would guard her and love her for the rest of his life, no matter what the world threw at them. That he would build her the castle of her dreams and shower her in all the riches he could ever discover if it were her wish but the words refused to come. He thought back to Isobelle and how she had said she loved him. He could not bring himself to say he loved Colette, not yet, at least not until he was sure he had the curse beaten, until he knew his future was secure and he could be with this woman. What if she did not like how he looked once the curse was undone? What if the curse was too strong to be lifted? What if he could not live up to her expectations?

He looked up and saw Colette was blushing too, awaiting her reply and not getting what she expected. If Kerian had been able to rewind time, he would have done so at that moment after recognising the hurt that flashed briefly across her features. The moment was now lost, never to be reclaimed.

Colette turned away from him making out she was intently scanning the bookshelves before her, then with a cracked voice she reached out and pulled a dusty tome free. She flicked through the aged parchment and turned back to face him her eyes bright and sparkling with barely concealed tears. She cleared her throat as if words were stuck, then began to describe the enchantment she planned to cast.

* * * * * *

Scrave paused outside Colette's cabin and listened intently as she described the fountain in the church gardens and the methods it required for opening. She talked about the gas and the heat that Richard had described and the steps required to prevent these environmental hazards from affecting them. It was a simple piece of magic, something Scrave could duplicate easily.

He watched Kerian grabbing lengths of wire from the shelf to start fashioning them into twisted wristbands. The Elf listened intently as Colette explained the principle and the fact that the wires would glow once activated and then flare with light running around the bracelet length like a fuse until the spell completed the circle and burnt out. This meant that timing was an issue. They had to be quick, in and out, or the repercussions of exposure to the heat and gas would have only one rather grisly ending, the thought of which Scrave found somewhat appealing.

* * * * * *

"How hot do you think molten rock is?" Kerian asked.

"About as hot as you can imagine." Colette replied, coolly professional in her reply.

"Hot enough to destroy something magical?" he asked.

"If the item was not protected from heat as part of its abilities then yes. Why do you ask?"

"Just a moment. I'll be right back." he replied, heading out the cabin door.

Kerian swung to the left and heard a clatter from behind him. He turned and looked down the passage but could not find the source of the sound, maybe they had a rat running about the ship. He resumed his forward heading, eager to seek out Austen who was acting as watch commander and had the key to the armoury, where Kerian knew a certain object was safely ferreted away under a pile of armour plate and rusted pikes. Safe behind the only locked door on the ship.

* * * * * *

Scrave untangled himself from the hammock he had fallen over and brushed himself down. That was close! Kerian had almost seen him. He stood considering the options available to him. Why was the old man asking about the heat of molten rock, what item did he intend to destroy? The revelation hit him hard.

He was talking about the dagger! Kerian was going to throw the serpent dagger into the lava. It was like a physical blow to the gut, almost making Scrave gasp. He could not let this happen. He would not let this happen. He had to get there first and stop this.

His mind raced, thinking the unfolding scenario through even as his hand subconsciously shot to his ear. He needed magic. His earrings had new gems in them. He knew the spells required to keep him safe from the heat and gas. He did not need a prop to focus the spell on as he could focus it on himself. The gem in his earring would power the barrier spell, probably for much longer than Colette's magical bracelets could.

He needed to ensure he was at the temple first to stop Kerian from destroying the dagger. That meant leaving now. He thought about where his sword lay back in his cabin but Kerian had headed off in that direction and he could not risk a confrontation below decks, there were too many crew about, it would lead to too many questions, he needed a new weapon fast.

Then he realised he knew exactly where to find one.

* * * * * *

Thomas looked up the inside of the windmill, judging whereabouts Weyn had positioned himself and ran up the staircase to the nearest window, opening a small casement that was more for ventilation than for any view.

"Are you out there Weyn?" he whispered, hearing something shifting suddenly above him.

"I'm sitting just above you." The archer laughed nervously. "You scared me half to death when you opened the window."

"Can you see anything out there? Is there any sign of Marcus?"

"I can see people moving about up by the church if that is what you mean." came Weyn's ominous reply. "But there is more than just one person up there and I'm not sure which one is Marcus."

Thomas strained to see through the small window but the angle was all wrong. Something started to churn in his gut; he felt goose bumps on his arms and a little voice that had kept him alive all those years on the force started to whisper in his ear.

"There's something not right about this. It's damned peculiar."

"That's not all that's strange." Weyn replied shifting himself above Thomas's head to get a better view and scattering disturbed moss down onto the sill. "Twelve of them look like they are wearing something metallic. Are they knights?" he asked aloud.

There was that word again. Knights.

"Can you be more certain?" Thomas asked, the little voice in his mind getting louder, clamouring for attention.

"Yup, definitely knights and they appear to be heading in our direction."

"Keep a bead on them." Thomas ordered. "If they do anything aggressive you have my permission to take them down." The captain turned from the window and shouted down over the railing at the Dwarven engineer who appeared to have passed out on the bar.

"Commagin get to the ship, round up the men and break out the armoury. I think we have trouble coming."

The Dwarf cracked an eye wincing, his limited field of vision in his prone state making it difficult to see where Thomas was speaking to him from.

"Trouble." The Dwarf groaned, feeling quite sick and disorientated. "I'll give you trouble. If I don't throw up first."

Richard sat hunched in a chair frantically stroking Socks. The cat was struggling to escape his frantic ministrations but the monk was not even aware of the cat squirming to escape from his hands. He had heard the archer mention the knights were coming but unlike the others, he knew keenly what the knights would do when they arrived. He had heard the tales, that they could not be killed by conventional means and that they carried out orders without question, no matter how dark those orders could be.

The Knights of St Fraiser were coming and everyone he knew, every man woman and child seeking shelter in the *Vane Arms* would be dead before dawn.

* * * * * *

Mathius ran from house to house, flitting from shadow to shadow, revelling in his newfound freedom and kinship with the crew he was starting to call his friends. Thomas's request to find Marcus was not a chore it was a pleasure. The fact that Marcus might need his help refreshing. Marcus was his friend and The Raven had very few of those.

He pushed himself, heading ever upwards, until he reached the outskirts of the village and the start of the long path leading up to the church. Some instinct told him to slow down and be cautious, so he headed over to the trees lining the path and slipped behind one better to see the trail ahead.

People were heading down the hill towards him, torches held aloft, marching in formation. Mathius ducked down making sure his shape was not discernible and his line broken by the vegetation. He reached for the double sheath at his side and drew his new daggers, flipping them to hold the hilts with the blades running up the underside of his arms, out of sight and unlikely to reflect back any of the flaming torches heading his way.

He peered through the plants and watched as a dozen armoured knights came clearly into view, wearing chainmail and plate, navy black coloured cloaks, gleaming swords and a burning torch to light the way. They continued to march past his hiding place, metal clanking loudly as they passed, exposing the backs of their cloaks to his eyes.

The symbol of Saint Fraiser stood emblazed in embroidered silver threads. These were the fabled knights of Abbot Brialin! His mind raced. What were they doing here so far from home? He went to duck lower down in the bushes, his memory filling in the stories of how these were the Abbot's deadliest weapon. Rumour had it they were unstoppable in battle. Ruthless killers that acted without mercy.

Mathius smiled. They did not look ten feet tall, nor did they shoot fire from their eyes and swing swords longer than their height. It appeared the rumours were as false as Pelune's serpent god. Which answered the question why the serpent cult had never had these men visit them. Maybe Brialin was too scared to let his knights face real competition; either that or he was worried about the political implications of causing trouble in his home town of Catterick.

He was about to turn and run back with the news of the knights when he noticed two figures following the parade. His eyes widened as he realised that Marcus was one of them and that he was walking alongside a tall man bedecked in flowing robes.

Was that? No... it could not be! Abbot Brialin was here too! Literally speaking, mention the devil and he was sure to arrive! This was almost too much. The fabled Abbot here outside of the safety of his monastery. Could these knights have burned Richard's church down? Why was Marcus walking with them? Had Marcus turned back to the fold or was he in trouble?

There was only one way to find out.

Mathius waited until the two walked by then slipped around the tree and into the open, leaning back against it, daggers still hidden, acting calm and cocky as if he had been in plain view the whole time.

"Marcus." He yelled, stopping the entire troupe in their steps. "Are you going to introduce me to your new friends?"

Marcus looked at Mathius with wide eyes and then held his head down, his gaze firmly on the floor.

"Who is this fool?" Abbot Brialin asked. "He seems to know you." Marcus appeared to mumble something in reply but refused to look up. Mathius could not understand this. The monk appeared to be upset but he was not moving away from the vulture like shadow of his previous master.

One knight moved up alongside the Abbot, nodded his head as if receiving orders and then stepped forward dropping his torch to the path and drawing his long gleaming sword.

So, that was how it was going to be. Mathius let his daggers slip more comfortably into his palms and moved away from the tree, sizing up the knight as he advanced. The man was roughly Mathius's height, a firm, probably glass jaw, short clipped black hair and a cold passionless gaze that followed every move Mathius made. The Raven had killed many a man with such obvious dedication.

"Are you going to play nice?" Mathius goaded, circling warily, his daggers twisting in his hands.

"Kill him quickly Cameron and catch us up." The Abbot shouted, turning to resume his descent towards the village as if the outcome of the battle were a foregone conclusion. Marcus lingered in place, his body language indicating he was struggling to know what the best course of action would be. Brialin noticed the hesitation shown by his aide and shouted at him.

"Come now, Marcus." He snapped. "There will be plenty of time to look at all the dead bodies when we have finished our cleansing." Mathius noted Marcus turn and follow, dragging his feet, his head bowed like a whipped hound with its spirit broken.

A loud grunt snapped Mathius back to the challenge at hand as the knight sent to dispatch him lunged with his sword. Mathius relaxed, ducked under the swing and focused on killing the poor idiot.

"I promise I will make this quick Cameron." He smiled coldly, stepping to one side as the knight's back swing cut the air where he had been standing. Mathius spun around the fighter's back and rapped him hard on the skull, not putting too much force into it but enough to stagger most men. Saint Fraiser's elite fighter did not tumble or fall; instead, he spun on one leg, his right foot whistling through the space where Mathius's head would have been if he had not ducked. Mathius retaliated, standing up straight and smacking the hilt of his dagger as hard as he could against Cameron's chin.

The Raven blinked in disbelief, as the knight appeared to shake off the attack, Cameron's chin appearing to ripple impossibly in the guttering light from the discarded torch, as if the construction of his face were like a book and someone had just thumbed quickly through the pages. What had he just seen?

He had no time to ponder the mystery as the fighter's sword continued to slam in from left and right, the keen edge of the silvery blade barely deflected with the honed skills that made Mathius a living legend. His daggers swept in, crossing to catch a downward slash from the knight's blade in a shower of sparks. Mathius took everything in as he parried and noticed the opening for his final thrust.

Cameron had not fastened his chain mail correctly. When he had lifted his arms up for the overhead swing, he had displayed an opening in the mail where his undershirt was exposed. A soft spot not armoured just over his right axilla. One deft thrust of a dagger, The Raven's steel would plunge into the man's heart and this game would be over.

He backed off, allowing the man to centre himself as The Raven thought through the right move to expose the weakness.

"Well, Cameron. It's been fun." Mathius smiled, circling, always looking for his opportunity. "I have to go and rescue my friend Marcus now. Thank you for sharing." He stepped in, watching the knight's blade predictably swing up to intercept, as he turned in place, the weapon's cold edge missing his narrower presented profile by inches. He dodged under the rising weapon and lunged with all his strength, slamming the steel dagger straight under Cameron's arm, piercing the undershirt and forcing the foot and a half of virgin steel deep into the torso beneath.

Cameron went up on tip-toe at the force of the attack, teetering on his feet as Mathius looked up into his face, expecting to see a visage of a man shocked into paralysis by the fatal attack. The knight hesitated for a moment then turned towards Mathius with a snarl.

"Marcus is a weak fool." The fighter stated impossibly. "Much like yourself."

Mathius's confident grin dissolved in an instant. This man should have been dead. He gritted his teeth and twisted the seated blade, expecting to hear bone cracking and feel blood jetting from the wound. He experienced neither and instead received a blow to the face that staggered him, forcing him to release his grip on the dagger and leave it in place, wedged beneath Cameron's arm.

The Raven hit the ground and rolled with the blow, getting back onto his feet in a move that displayed his great balance and poise. The recovery was fast but not fast enough. The knight's blade whistled down, catching Mathius's jerkin as it passed, sending buttons spinning into the air. The assassin spun in place closing the space between them in seconds and slammed his remaining dagger up under Cameron's chin, the penetrating steel actually making the knight's skull bulge upwards before there was a loud ripping noise and the tip of the blade came through.

Mathius stepped back, wiping his hand across his face and pushing his hair out of the way as Cameron fell to the ground. Now that was an unexpected turn of events! Fancy missing the man's heart. He could not believe he had fumbled such a textbook strike. Had to give Cameron credit though. Not many fighters would have been able to land a punch like that after being stabbed in the chest.

He breathed deeply and then noticed the warm tickle on his forehead. He put his fingers up to assess the damage and then sighed when they came back wet with his blood. Cameron was also faster than he looked. He had actually managed to land a hit!

The clink of chain signalled Cameron moving on the floor. This was incredible; the man did not know when he was dead. Mathius turned intent on finishing the fighter off and found himself routed to the spot.

Cameron was sitting up and struggling to remove the dagger from beneath his chin, wiggling it about and making the tip sticking out of the top of his head turn comically.

"Oh please, don't." Mathius said, shocked he had not been able to land the killing blow. "Let me take the blade out. You will just hurt yourself further. Don't worry it will all be over soon." He moved closer and gulped as Cameron finally yanked the blade clear and tossed it aside. Then before The Raven could register the fact that there was no blood or brain matter on the blade, Cameron gripped the blade under his right arm and tore it clear with another loud bizarre ripping sound.

The second blade went the same way as its partner, much to Mathius's astonishment and chagrin. Cameron regained his feet, initially unsteady, something ragged hanging from his chin. The Raven watched warily as the knight rolled his shoulders and swung his blade through the air, making it whistle at the speed of its passing. This was impossible! This could not be happening.

Mathius looked at his nearest dagger lying on the grass from the corner of his eye, judging if he could get to the blade before Cameron closed. He weighed up the options and lunged, intending to drop into a forward roll and scoop the weapon up but Cameron was faster, lashing out with his mailed foot and lifting Mathius up into the air as he dived, flipping him onto his side to crash into the ground and roll over and over on the gradient of the hill.

He slammed into something hard, shocked to find it was the closest house and looked up seeing double as Cameron advanced. Before he could even voice his surprise, the knight had him by his shirtfront, lifting him high before throwing him forwards to slam into the house wall.

Mathius grunted in pain as his body found itself dealt a double slam, once into the house wattle and daub walls and then again, when he landed heavily on the ground. He gasped, winded as the knight landed another kick, snapping his head back and almost making him pass out. Rough hands grabbed him and hoisted him back into the air.

The Raven swung above the ground dazed but refusing to give in, despite his ridiculous predicament. He slammed his clenched fist into the wound under Cameron's right arm, determined to take advantage of the opening he had made. He felt something dry and hard beneath his hands and gripped it hard, hoping it was a bone or something vital. He hung on as the knight threw him, his legs swinging out to collide with the wall, his trousers catching and ripping.

Cameron staggered into the side of the building as his balance was thrown off and The Raven found himself dropping to the floor. He ripped his hand free from under the knight's arm, as his other hand went for the knight's exposed throat, determined to try to choke the man into submission. His free hand slammed into something rough that flickered against his palm, making him lose grip and step back as if he had rubbed a particularly stiff feather.

He fell back, his eyes glancing down in shock at the mess of curled dry paper in his hand, ornate black script flowing across the surface in tightly scrawled passages that meant nothing to the assassin. What was this? He looked up in shock as the knight lunged again, grabbing him roughly and throwing his surprised frame back at the side of the house. He closed his eyes as his body slammed through the house window, glass and frame barely breaking his velocity before he fell into the room beyond in a shower of glass and splintered wood.

Mathius lay there struggling to figure out which way was up and which was down. He knew he had to get up and fight but it was simply too hard to do so. It would be better to just lie here and have a rest for a moment.

That would be nice... He would close his eyes for just a mom...

* * * * * *

"Thanks Austen." Kerian smiled as he reached into the armoury and lifted out the saddlebags he had hidden there. He plunged his hand into one pouch and felt for a soft velvet bag, inside of which he had wrapped the horrific dagger. He almost yanked his hand away as he felt the bag move beneath his fingers. The dagger was in there all right.

"No problems," Austen replied relocking the door and failing to notice the look of disgust and horror that had raced across Kerian's features.

The icy scream that wailed through the ship froze them both in place. Its deep tone sending chills racing up their spines. They turned as one and started heading for the source, both secretly wondering if they really needed to discover where such a ghostly wail had come from.

Other crew tumbled down from above decks or poked their heads out from under blankets where sleep had decided to flee. Lanterns held in shaking hands joined the group as the crossed from one side of the ship to the other shouting out to see if anyone needed help.

The door to Rauph's cabin was standing ajar when they arrived. Austen took a deep breath and walked in lantern held high, Kerian at his side, Aradol racing along the corridor behind them, a gaff hook in hand.

The sight in the cabin left them temporarily confused. A man was standing in the shadows and the screams seemed to be coming from him. He appeared indistinct, even vague, the robes he wore almost transparent as he turned in place and paced before the ruined chair.

Austen stared as if he could not believe his eyes.

"L...Lucas Sumnar?" he asked the ghostly figure. "Is that you?" The ghostly shape turned to take in the crew and wailed again, his pain and anguish turning the blood in their veins to ice.

Colette ran into the cabin and forced her way between them, taking in the sight of her bereft Master. She walked over, hesitation barely showing in her steps as she advanced.

"What are you doing?" Kerian hissed. "Get away from him. You don't know what he is going to do."

Colette turned eyes blazing.

"He is my Master and he would never do anything to harm me." She turned back, taking in the crumbling remains of the corpse on the floor where it had disintegrated after all these years. She scanned the debris frantically, her face suddenly going pale.

"Where is the wizard seeker?" she asked herself. "Where is the spear?"

Lucas Sumnar, long dead mage of the *El Defensor* turned and looked at his young student, his face a mask of pain. He opened his mouth, impossibly large and screamed anew.

"Sssssccccrrrrraaaavvvvveeee."

* * * * * *

Ashe could hear crashing and screams of pain. In a flash, he was back in his childhood, receiving yet another beating, his teeth throbbing in his head, his body on fire from the abuse he had taken. He vividly recalled the physical assault he had taken for the stolen glass of milk. He had been in a chair then too. He imagined the beaker being knocked from his hand, flying across the room in a doomed trajectory that trailed white liquid in its wake. His hands had been pinned and crushed, pain radiating from them up his arms as blows rained down on his defenceless body delivered by a man so much bigger than him.

That was until he had caught one passing hand in his mouth and bit down hard, making the coward shriek and fall away in horror, the salty tang of blood running down Ashe's lips.

He licked his lips and tasted the blood and then his probing tongue found a hole in his gum and wiggled inside to feel the jagged remains of a tooth.

This was a bit of a realistic dream.

He cracked one swollen eye and looked up realising he was actually tied to a chair. A wave of pain rolled over him, smothering, crushing, lighting every nerve and setting off red flashes in his vision. Everything hurt really bad.

A man flew through the air in front of him, smashing through two glass windows, slamming over a workbench and hitting the floor at an odd angle with a resounding snap. His neck lolled to one side. He was clearly dead. Something had hit him hard.

Screams followed, intermingled with clashes of steel and roars from some enraged beast. Ashe started to panic. He was tied to a chair and in no position to meet whatever was causing that tremendously scary noise. He started to rock the chair, trying hard to loosen his bonds but of all the luck, this seemed to be the sturdiest piece of furniture in the whole building. He knew this because the chair Atticus had sat in had no problems disintegrating into whirling splinters when another man's head came smashing down onto it.

A loud snorting and panting sound came from directly behind the struggling Halfling making him freeze in his violent rocking motions. Whatever it was stood right behind him and smelt like wet carpet.

"R...Rauph?" Ashe slobbered, suddenly discovering his ability to speak was sorely affected by the beating he had taken. The huge hulking figure of Rauph stepped into view, salty patches of foaming sweat coating his chestnut coat, splatters of blood and gore dripping from his horns.

"Oh Rauph. I'm so glad to see you." Ashe started to shake, the tears coming, his body wracked with sobs. "I'm so glad to see you."

Rauph's nostrils flared close to Ashe's one working eye and he moved closer, sniffing his wounded companion.

"Who did this?" he demanded. "I will make them pay."

Ashe looked around the room, taking in the bodies around him.

"Atticus Couqran and his men." He spluttered, "I think that person over there also helped but it is hard to tell as he has no face left."

Rauph snorted in agreement, nodding his head apparently happy with the justice meted out.

"So where is this Atticus?" the Minotaur demanded, with such ferocity Ashe almost forgot the monster was on his side.

"He went out to the caves." Ashe replied, jerking his head to one side to try and show the direction they went.

"Okay." Rauph stood thinking hard, then gripped his swords and headed for the door. "I'll go and get him for you."

Ashe sat there for a few moments, letting the dust settle, hearing the remains of the broken windows slipping from their frames and smashing on the floor, listening to the groans of the people around him slowly fade as they died. Then he decided to try to stand up and follow his friend.

He struggled to stand but then after a few moments futile effort collapsed back in the chair, quite disappointed at his lack of progress. He wiggled his arms and hands and confirmed his earlier discovery.

"Rauph!" he shouted after the departing Minotaur. "Come back here and untie me from this stupid chair!"

Chapter Forty-Nine

Rosalyine could not settle, no matter how hard she tried. No matter which way she turned or how she positioned herself on her bed of ancient coins and glittering gems, sleep still refused to come. She cracked open one massive yellow reptilian eye and stared at her lover's heart resting upon the worn stone pedestal, within the protective circle of her own curved body and felt a tear starting to form.

Why had Strathe been fated to die all those years ago? Why had he left her all alone for all these years so impossibly lonely? She shifted her weight again, coins rolling from the hoard she had accumulated over the years, creating a glittering metallic waterfall. Rosalyine looked at her lover's heart once more then closed her eyes remembering the good times they had experienced together. He was such a good man and had only wanted to share his power with others, never to hurt anyone. When he had been cut down before her eyes, his face had been one of shock, not quite believing people could be so callous and so cruel.

When she held him dying in her arms, she had demanded her own wish, her heart's desire, to be able to stay to protect him and keep him safe until the end of her days. Strathe had granted it at the moment of his death but somehow the wish became twisted, the meaning interpreted and manifested by her own painful transformation into the creature she now was. A transformation that ensured she would live and guard her fallen husband's remains for as long as she wanted.

Dragons aged slowly and rarely died, unless slain by some hair-brained knight on a quest to impress a damsel in distress or errant treasure hunters that would kill them trapped like rats in their lairs. Instead, she found most of the time she slept, knowing that these periods would increase more and more until one day, she would simply never wake up. She still loved her husband dearly and had looked forward to granting blessings to visitors to their place of rest but as each new selfish request came, each new materialistic wish granted, she started to resent the intrusions, breathing on seekers, knocking them out with the gases that she could produce from her massive lungs.

Maybe it was Richard that had caused this resentment? She had hoped, as he was a pious man, he would have put others first but as in all cases, his wish was a self-centred and selfish one. The monk had been so stupid, so greedy and had squandered her husband's magic on something for himself like all the other treasure seekers that had come before him. She shrugged, her scales lifting and then settling again, allowing the heat collected from the fires around her to be released. Maybe she was too hot to sleep?

She had hoped Richard would be different, had looked forward to his discussions in the darkness but he failed her just like the rest of them. He had abused the wish granted to him with repercussions for the whole village that Rosalyine watched over. Her frustration at his betrayal made worse because she could not break her husband's gift once it was bestowed.

Rosalyine stretched out her long translucent neck and inhaled the sulphurous fumes in the air, shading her crystalline body golden as the yellow gas passed deep into her lungs before she expelled it again.

Why could she not sleep?

She calmed herself, closing her eyes thinking about the island and the people living upon it, the people she had grown to view as her children. Her magical senses reached out through the mountain, seeking out those she protected. Nostrils flared and the scales along her back rippled as she detected the fear from her subjects and the threat of approaching violence, something that should never have occurred.

Rosalyine pulled herself to her feet, her eyes now fully open and her quick anger simmering just below the surface of her hard crystal body. The people of the village were not in danger of being hurt due to Richard's foolishness. There were other forces at play.

The dragon spread her massive wings, flapping them as her powerful legs helped her spring high into the air, her tail whipping across the pile of coins and sending several spinning around the temple floor as she headed up through the insides of the mountain towards the night sky above.

* * * * * *

"The knights are setting fire to all of the houses." Weyn reported, "It's like a trail is being blazed down the mountain towards us. They appear to have encountered Ives party and are engaging as we speak but they are still out of range, so I cannot strike back."

"Why would they do that?" Thomas asked himself, perplexed at this destructive behaviour. "These people have done nothing to them. It makes no sense."

The clash of weapons echoed eerily from the distant alleyways galvanising the captain into action. He moved from the casement and over to the railing, looking down into the interior of the *Vane Arms*. Charleton was waving his arms, trying to animate and reassure the villagers but from the pained look on his face, he was being anything but successful.

"Charleton." Thomas shouted down. "Can you come up here a moment?" The landlord looked up at Thomas with a look of relief at being called away from his duties and he headed for the stair, unaware that the captain's news was going to make matters so much worse. Thomas met him halfway.

"What's up?" Charleton asked, his face wearing a weary smile.

"We have trouble." Thomas replied. "There are people fighting out in the streets and I have a feeling they mean us all harm. We are sitting ducks here. Is there a way out that doesn't face towards the fire?"

Charleton took a moment weighing up the information Thomas was giving him and scarcely believing it, before he nodded his head.

"You can exit through the works of the mill beneath the floor, there is a ramp at the back to allow for the grain to be loaded into the mill and the flour sacks to be taken away but it is very noisy and dusty. Who is fighting us?"

Thomas looked down at the group of children clapping their hands excitedly to a tune played by Bridget on her violin. Rowan, Violetta and her daughter stood clapping their hands in accompaniment alongside the other women of the village. He needed to sort his priorities and get these people and their children to safety.

"Is there anywhere we can put everyone to keep them safe?" he asked, ignoring the question asked by his confidant. The landlord shook his head, his face clearly displaying the concerns Thomas felt.

"Not heading away from the inn. We usually head up to the church and gardens. The high ground as it were. You are asking us to flee in the opposite direction down to the harbour edge. Are you sure, someone is coming to hurt us? Rosalyine won't like that. No one is allowed to hurt people here."

"Thomas!" Weyn shouted from above. "They are advancing rather quickly. If we are going to do something, we need to do it now."

"The *El Defensor*." Thomas muttered to himself, mentally trying to calculate the amount of people below and the space he had on decks. "We can put everyone on the *El Defensor*." He took another look down at the clapping villagers and swallowed hard. Little feet, swaddling babes, timid individuals. This would not happen quickly. They were going to need to keep the approaching mysterious knights busy whilst these people made their escape through the streets. That meant creating a diversion.

"Right then..." Thomas turned to Charleton and began issuing orders. "Start getting the children into small groups and lead them quietly through the mill to the ramp. Then when we have gathered them all together wait for my signal and start leading them through the town directly to my ship. We need to do this smoothly, without upsetting the children, so it needs to look like a game." He looked back at Rowan clapping happily below and swallowed hard.

"Won't they see us all leaving?" Charleton asked.

"Not if the rest of us keep them occupied." Thomas replied.

Charleton bowed his head as if a weight had been dropped on his shoulders.

"I had a feeling you would say that."

Thomas turned from the landlord and raised his head to the heavens. They were taking a big risk. If anyone spotted the evacuation, if Rowan was hurt, he would never forgive himself. The captain of the *El Defensor* took in a deep breath and closed his eyes, silently praying Commagin and his reinforcements would soon arrive.

* * * * * *

Flickering torchlight announced the presence of the odious Atticus and his brigands long before they exited the tunnel leading from the cliff cave. Each thug bristled with weapons; torches held high in their free hands as they walked out onto the large open platform that was part of Rosalyine's home. They started to walk around the walls, checking each tunnel opening before returning to report to their guild master that everything appeared safe.

Atticus walked with slow purpose towards the centre of the open area and slowly turned, taking in the size of the floor and the frescos carved into the walls, their details visible due to the torches held by his loyal men.

"I don't see any dragon." He announced with bravado, his arms open as he turned around. "I don't see Styx either. That damn Halfling must have lied to us! Rafferty, go back to the boathouse and see that he is killed in a most painful way." His beady eyes continued to take in their surroundings, ignoring the grumbling from his reluctant lackey, who spun on his heel and headed back the way they had come. The fact that the wall with the tunnel entrances only encircled two thirds of the platform intrigued the guild master, so he turned towards the side furthest away from the tunnels and strode purposefully towards it.

His henchmen followed suit, jockeying for position, eager to glimpse some sign of the lost treasure hoard they had been promised. As the men advanced, they all noticed the deep red glow flickering up from below the platform's far edge. Several shot nervous looks, secretly wondering if the fabled dragon lay somewhere below and that its flames were what they were witnessing.

Atticus was the first to arrive at the lip of the platform and stared down into the fiery pit. The heat rose in waves that took his breath away. It was like standing too near to one of the ovens in his kitchens at home. His mouth felt dry as he breathed in the searing air and he started to believe his eyebrows would singe if he stood there for too long. He noticed the ruined temple far below, its appearance like some ancient coliseum, the roof long gone. Then he observed the large slabs of stone leading up from the crumbling entrance, a worn flight of steps to enable access.

"The steps are not supported by anything." One of his ruffians murmured to a companion. "They are just floating in the air. Its dark magic if you ask me."

"Look at all the treasure!" another exclaimed, pointing down through the open roof of the temple to the piles of gleaming wealth. The other thugs gathered closer, eager to see the prize they sought.

The guild master was a shrewd man. He took in the treasure, licking his parched lips at the thought of having such wealth for himself, then scrutinised the floating stairs and stepped back from the edge to consider the way forward and how to preserve his bushy eyebrows. Clearly, you did not leave such wealth simply unprotected. There would be a trap here; maybe the steps would drop away, or maybe the dragon was down there somewhere, waiting for the unwary to approach. He looked over the ten remaining men alongside him and gestured to the one he believed was the least intelligent.

"Douglas," he called. "I feel it's about time you earned your keep on this trip."

Douglas was a slightly portly man with bulging eyes and a stomach to match. He eyed his master suspiciously, as he advanced.

"The problem as I see it." Atticus continued, placing his arm around the shorter man. "Is that there is a lot of treasure down there in that temple. If we all go down and take it piecemeal there could be some misunderstandings as regards sharing out said loot afterwards. I need a man I can trust, a man who would be rewarded substantially for getting the best pieces."

Douglas shook his head in agreement; everything his master said so far made total sense.

"In truth, I need you to go down there first."

The mercenary's head slowly stopped nodding as he realised what the guild master had said.

"But it's hot down there." He stated nervously.

Atticus lead Douglas over to the edge of the platform. This man was not as stupid as he looked. He mentally decided he would have to go to a different supplier next time he rounded up a crew.

"Look," he gestured. "If it was as hot as it looks, all of the gold would have melted by now. It is obviously an illusion. You will be just fine."

Douglas looked down at the first step then back at Atticus's face. He went to say something but realised that it would be pointless to do so and instead simply nodded his head, recognising that it was better to take the first step down independently rather than end up being pushed. He took a deep breath and stepped from the platform, dropping down onto the first stone slab, eyes closed, body tensed, in case the step suddenly crumbled away from beneath him. Beads of sweat appeared on his brow as he breathed out a huge sigh of relief at not succumbing to a fiery end.

Douglas opened his eyes and then swiftly squinted them half closed again. The step down had been a matter of barely a foot but the level of heat was so much greater here than on the platform above. His clothes started to feel damp as he began to sweat.

"When you are ready." Atticus prodded from his position of safety.

The brigand took a deep breath as he walked over to the edge of the hovering slab of stone and looked down to the one below it, feeling the heat parching his mouth as he considered the distance. It was just a small drop of another foot. Another foot closer to the inferno of bubbling lava.

"Remember it's just an illusion." came the prompt from above. "Come on we don't have all day. The treasure is waiting."

Douglas took the next step down and felt as if he had walked into a desert landscape, where the only things that should be alive were hard and certainly not as fleshy and perspiring as himself. He could feel the hairs on his arms standing up and every nervous breath taken in through his nostrils smelled of burning hair. He cracked his eyes open, thankful that the step had remained as steady as its predecessor, before looking towards where his next drop would take him. He counted the continuing staircase through eyes that streamed. Dear lord there was at least another twenty-eight steps to go and that was just the ones he could see!

"Think of the rewards." The guild master jibed. "Keep going!"

The henchman took another step down to find he was now facing a furnace. The hairs on his arms started to curl and singe. His clothes had steam rising from them, as the moisture from his perspiration was wicked away before his eyes. He felt a wave of dizziness sweep over him and staggered forwards, his unsteady footing taking him over the edge of the step and down to the stone below.

"Now that's more like it." Atticus shouted encouragement. "Only about twenty five to go!"

Douglas turned unsteadily on the fourth step and looked up at the guild master, his hair curling and shrinking in on itself, his face a mask of pain.

"I don't think I can go any further." He croaked, as if the very act of taking in a breath was too much for him.

"Now, now!" his Master chided. "We can't have that kind of defeatist talk. Just look at the treasure. Think what you can do with your share."

"But it's so hot." Douglas wailed.

Atticus moved up to another lackey and held out his hand indicating he wanted the man's cudgel. This was taking too long. He needed to move things along. Douglas turned back to look down the stairs and hesitated on the far edge, his eyes barely focusing as the heat continued to dry them faster than his tears could lubricate. He blinked hard only to feel his left eyelid sticking for a second before pulling free from the surface of his eye. This was too much. He could not take this heat.

Atticus frowned angrily as the man hesitated, then took aim and threw the cudgel at Douglas's back. It hit with a resounding thwack, before spinning off the steps and igniting into a shooting star as it plummeted towards the lava.

Douglas was not as lucky. He fell forward, knocked of balance, stepping unsteadily to the sizzling hot slab below, arms wind-milling as he tried to catch himself but there were no railings here to hang onto. He continued stumbling forwards, tripped and fell onto the hot surface, then flopped down onto the next step, landing hard on his shoulder. Flames leapt into being as his tunic ignited. The man rolled clumsily over to try and extinguish the flames and rolled right over the edge to crash down onto the next step below that, his clothes smoking as he dropped.

He hit the seventh step on his hands and knees, trying to scream in terror but finding his lungs too scorched to even manage a squeak. The heat from the stone was intense, the pain excruciating. He tried to lift his hands free but they stuck to the surface, before tearing free in a rip of searing crisp flesh. Blisters rippled up his arms, popping and steaming, blood vessels bulged and exploded, pumping cool blood across his face, before this too dried in the intense heat, leaving a blackened scorched trail. He could not breathe, could not rise from his knees. His clothes fully ignited. Douglas struggled briefly and then fell forwards onto his face, dead before he even hit the step.

Atticus scowled at the crispy blackened remains of his initial volunteer as they sizzled like a steak on a skillet.

"That's very inconvenient." He muttered to himself, before turning to the rest of his crew of cutthroats. His gaze settled on another man near the back with a thin goatee and a mop of curly black hair.

"Keef," he pointed to the thug, watching the man's face turn pale. "You're up next."

* * * * * *

"So, Lucas was your mentor?" Kerian asked, still amazed at the ghostly scenes he had witnessed in Rauph's cabin. "And he was slain by a magical spear when the ship was boarded years ago and he has sat pinned in that chair all this time and no one thought to release him? Isn't that cruel, leaving him stuck on that spear like a prize butterfly in a collection?"

Colette nodded her head, having already informed Kerian of the facts on their walk back from Rauph's cabin, her hands nimbly packing her spell components into little pouches in her knapsack.

"You don't understand." She replied. "Lucas told us with his last breath, never to remove him from the chair. He was the only thing holding the spear in place."

"So?" Kerian asked, his mind still trying to fill in the blanks. "What was the spear going to do if it was pulled out? It's not as if it could move by itself."

"Actually it could." Colette replied, tugging a strap tight. "The spear is called *Wizardseeker*. Legend has it that when thrown, it hunts the strongest magic wielder and kills them. That is why Lucas would not let the spear go and remained, haunting the seat. If he had let himself be freed, the spear would have found me...." She paused in mid-explanation, her eye catching a glint of something that appeared to have slid down the side of her pillow.

"Did you leave this here?" Colette asked, turning from her bed with the retrieved pendant clutched in her hand.

Kerian looked up from securing his saddlebag, his face blank.

"Of course not." The ship's mage answered her own question, possibly a little more bluntly than she meant to, leaving Kerian looking even more confused. How could she have expected it to be Kerian who was responsible? Was she hoping it would be true? It had to have been Ashe. She initially felt annoyed that the Halfling had been in her room without permission but then she noticed the smoky grey pearl that had replaced the broken one she had held close all these years. Somehow, Ashe had managed to fix the necklace for her and the replacement pearl was beautiful. Tears sprang to her eyes, fiercely blinked away as she turned to grab the final items that they needed for the trip ahead.

"Is everything alright?" Kerian asked from the doorway, concerned about her sudden damp eyes. "Are you sure you are ready to go?" He took in Colette's slim petite form and attire, her suede leggings and tunic, high boots and knapsack, the dress from the evening packed away much like her earlier joviality. She was so small, so delicate. He found it hard to put her in harm's way.

Colette smiled weakly and then nodded, sliding a dagger into the sheath in her boot, whilst her free hand held up the two bracelets they had fashioned.

"These are really simple to use." She stated, slipping one on her wrist before throwing the other across the room for Kerian to catch. "Tap the bracelet three times and it will start to work. Remember it will glow when activated and you will have one full rotation of the bracelet before the enchantment runs out. If you are still down near the lava when this happens you will be burnt to a crisp."

"So how long will we have?" Kerian asked.

"About a third of an hourglass, not much more." Colette replied. "That should be ample for what we need."

A clamour started in the corridor as crewmen filed past, heading above decks. Kerian reached out grabbing one man as he headed past.

"What's going on?"

"Commagin is getting the crew together. He wants us to follow him back to the inn. Sounds like there is trouble." The man moved on before Kerian could ask for more information. In conflict, he turned to the ship's mage his face clearly showing his torn loyalties. Colette crossed the room and took Kerian's hand in her own, her piercing eyes locking on his own troubled ones.

"Now listen here Kerian Denaris." She lectured. "We have our own fight this evening. Commagin and the crew are more than capable of sorting out the problem at the inn. We will only get in the way."

"Are you sure?" he asked.

"Really Kerian. Sometimes I could box you on the ears. You don't need my permission to do anything. In fact, I find myself quite shocked that you would consider putting the welfare of the others first. This isn't the Kerian Denaris I know. You must be going soft."

Kerian stood in the doorway looking stunned as Colette squeezed gently past him. He realised the mage was right. Up until now, he would never have allowed anything to get in his way. By Adden! He had even killed people for less! Yet here he was, right at the end, when he was so close to finally finishing his quest and he was considering others first! Sailing on the *El Defensor* was changing him in ways that made him feel decidedly anxious.

"So what are you waiting for?" Colette asked, tapping him lightly on the chin. "We have a dragon to sweet talk and a curse to break."

* * * * * *

Rauph tracked his way along the weather worn cliff face, following the group of footprints in the sand that signified that Atticus's crew had passed this way. The Minotaur was on a mission, his face set in a resolute and grim stare. He held one of his huge swords comfortably in his right hand and a flaming torch high in the other, illuminating the trodden path ahead.

The sea crashed alongside him, casting shingle up onto the shore, then changed its mind and dragged it back in a clatter of stones. The breeze from the breakers carried a salty tang tinged with bitter smoke and ruffled his thick red fur as he stalked his prey. He was going to get the people that hurt Ashe and he was going to hurt them bad. No one hurt his friends and got away with it.

Rauph was going to set things right.

A little voice in the back of his mind tried to tell him that he had forgotten something or someone important. However, Rauph refused to let himself be side tracked. Vengeance was important and he was going to get some. What was it that Thomas had said to him about vengeance? That it was best served cold. He shook his head. No, nothing ever tasted nice served cold, apart from pizza! His vengeance would be hot, full of warm spraying blood and screams of pain.

He rounded the bluff and noticed the cave mouth ahead, checking the floor to confirm that the people he was shadowing had entered. A flickering light from within bobbed and danced, getting brighter by the second. Someone was coming this way.

Rauph placed his torch down against the cliff face and waited for his prey to come to him.

******

Rafferty was annoyed. Why did he have to go back to the boathouse? All the treasure was up in the cave, not back in the stinking boathouse. He had already helped torture the Halfling under Atticus's instructions and was frankly amazed the little man had it in him to not be entirely truthful, especially when he had broken the little man's fingers like thin sticks of wood. He was determined to dispatch the thief as soon as possible; slam a sword into his gut, or stick an axe in his skull and get back up to the cave and the treasure. They were probably passing the best bits out between them right now and chuckling that he was stuck down here! He rounded the corner and came face to face with a nightmare.

The creature towered above him, eyes glowing red, reflecting the torchlight Rafferty held in his suddenly shaking hand. Horns gleamed as the monster snorted loudly and a sword almost as long as Rafferty was tall, swung directly at him with painful accuracy. He screamed, feeling his bowels suddenly betray him, filling his pants with embarrassing warmth.

Rauph's first sword swing took the top off Rafferty's head, as if his skull was some morbid cookie jar. The second swing split the man practically in two, spraying his blood and entrails across the sand. Rauph looked down at the remains with no feeling of guilt. He watched the gore start to steam as it met the cool evening air and nodded to himself.

Vengeance was definitely hot.

He wrinkled his nose. Vengeance was apparently smelly too! The Minotaur snorted loudly, whipped his sword through the air to send any residual blood flying from the blade then retrieved his torch and stomped into the cave mouth.

One down, several more bad guys to go!

The sight of the ragged spider webs strewn across the tunnel entrance reduced Rauph's charge into a slow walk then a hesitant shuffle before he stopped cold. He could see where his prey had gone into the darkness directly below the dangling webs but the Minotaur had the disadvantage of his height placing him perilously close to the lairs of his greatest fear. What was more, Scrave had told him spiders could jump out from the shadows and get him when he was not looking. He shook his head, angry but at the same time not entirely sure, if Scrave was telling him the truth or if he was teasing him. Frustrated, he tried to walk forwards with his eyes closed, but ended up mooing nervously at each step, imagining little hairy legs touching his face, shiny beady eyes watching his every move, venom filled fangs sinking into his bovine flesh.

Rauph cracked open an eye in shock as something ran across his neck and found he had no hand free to brush himself off. Instead, instinct took over and he rubbed himself against the cave wall, realising as he did it just how stupid he had been. He leapt away, feeling something tickling across his back and skidded to a halt, his nose inches from one of his archenemies. It sat on a ledge bare inches from him, bright eyes gleaming, little legs twitching up and down as it considered his snorting face.

The Minotaur froze in terror, his breath coming in rapid shallow pants. He tried to step slowly away from the monster before him, not realising as he retreated that the creature was barely the size of a gold coin. To Rauph, in his agitated state, the spider was enormous! His task beckoned to him but he was too terrified to accept the challenge. He simply could not bring himself to pass the terrible guardian in the cave. His horn brushed another ragged cobweb, dropping an emaciated spider corpse down from a string to swing before his eyes. He knew the spider had to be dead but it still caused him to jump, shiver and spin in horror. The navigator suddenly found himself disorientated, loudly bellowing his fear, charging blindly about the tunnel before running headfirst into the cave wall, knocking himself out cold.

In the case of Rauph verses the spider, it appeared this time the spider had won.

* * * * * *

Ives parried desperately with his white blade, falling back against the sustained onslaught of three knights who attacked with a co-ordination that was almost supernatural. The villagers alongside him, armed with shovels, rakes and the odd small axe could not hope to fend off such determined and professional attacks, leaving Ives desperately trying to cover them as well as himself, as they were forced further back through the houses.

Groans of pain and anger came from behind him, as more and more of their dwellings succumbed to the torch in indiscriminate acts of arson and wanton destruction. Ives was powerless to stop the knights with only the low calibre of villagers acting as his men at arms.

The knights were more than just a wall of steel, pushing them resolutely back towards the inn. They also refused to die. Ives had seen one knight take a pitchfork to the chest and simply snatch the tool from the surprised villager's hands, plucking it free without any sign of injury whatsoever. Ives knew he had also managed to land a few telling blows but there was no sign of injury and no let-up in the attacks they faced from their relentless foes. He parried another overhead swing, feeling the vibration from the clashing blades numb his arm and hand.

Why were these people being attacked? They had never shown anything but kindness to the crew of the *El Defensor* and they cooked amazing food. To Ives it made no sense. He licked his lips nervously, wondering for a second if he would live to have another piece of lemon and herb drizzled chicken and took another step backwards. He needed a miracle if he was to survive here. The three knights continued to advance swords glinting.

Someone roughly pushed Ives aside, dropping the merchant to his knees. He looked up from his new vantage point to observe Scrave charging past him, a large black spear held tucked under one arm. The Elf did not stop and allow the knights to advance towards him but continued with his forward momentum, cutting his way through them like a scythe through ripe wheat, the spear whistling about his body as he used it like an elaborate quarterstaff. The wicked head of the blackened weapon cleaved arms and legs; separated fingers and even took one knight's head in an explosion of what looked like ancient manuscript, as Scrave spun and whirled his dance of death.

Two knights dropped to the floor, where they jerked and flopped about like fish out of water. The remaining knight gathered himself and managed several ferocious attacks and thrusts, slowing the Elf's passage down. A desperate lunge ended any thoughts of resistance as the man suddenly found himself literally disarmed; his sword catching on the edge of the spear point before his blade was flipped straight into the air, the weapon spinning end over end up into the darkness. A return sweep of the spear's fearsome edge took the knight's arm at the elbow in a move executed so fast it almost looked like a blur, the spear emitting an eerie hum as it passed through the air.

Ives could not believe his luck. He had wished for a miracle and one had arrived.

"That was incredible Scrave." He congratulated the Elf, getting himself to his feet. "Your skill with that spear is astounding. But we cannot dally, there are more of them coming, we need to form some sort of strategy for taking them all down..."

Scrave turned and looked at Ives, his form radiating a darkness that caused the merchant to shiver, his words of congratulation turning to ash in his mouth. The evil emanating from the Elf was staggering. His eyes were cold, emotionless, those of a killer who had no compassion. His penetrating gaze swept the trader up and down as if looking for something, then after apparently finding nothing to his liking, he turned away, pausing only to hold out his hand and deftly catch something as it fell back to earth. His move parodied actions perfected throwing daggers into the air on the *El Defensor's* main deck but this time he never even looked to check where the blade was, as if somehow he knew it would simply be there waiting for him to retrieve it. Armed with the black spear and now the knight's sword, Scrave continued to advance up the street towards the blazing church, moving with a confidence and purpose that made Ives seriously fear for whoever would be on the receiving end of his wrath.

The men around him started to shout and point, pulling the merchant's gaze away from the departing demonic Scrave and back to the immediate situation. The knights were impossibly reassembling themselves, limbs were reattaching, or elongating, forming out of curled tubes of paper. Loose sheets were firmly stuffed back into place, crumpling loudly as they were secured, whilst other pieces appeared to slide into wounds and then simply disappear as if absorbed magically into the knights' forms. The only fighter having problems was the one whose head had exploded. The torso continued to struggle to reassemble its head but without eyes was unable to find the parts.

What were these things? Ives seriously started to doubt his wisdom in signing on with Thomas and his crew. First, an elemental, then several spectral hounds, a spider like monster that ate human flesh and now knights made of paper that would not die. He knew he had asked for excitement and adventure but you could always have too much of a good thing!

The first knight regained his feet and whipped his sword around as he faced them. Ives took what felt like his thousandth step backwards this night and prepared for the next onslaught.

* * * * * *

"That looks a bit of a problem." Colette gestured at the main route up to the church, alongside which most of the houses now blazed, thick smoke and sparks rising to obscure the stars. She stood for a moment, considering the situation, then looked over at Kerian and shared her beguiling smile.

"Do you trust me?"

"What do you have in mind?" Kerian asked, his eyes scanning the area looking for any threats to his young charge.

"Let's just say you may soon be glad we never had any food at the party." She replied, cryptically reaching into her pocket and producing a small gem. "This should do the trick. Now hold my hand and whatever happens, don't let go."

Arcane words spoken in a dialect Kerian did not recognise raised goose bumps on his arms. He began to feel as if his skin were covered in static but he remained true in his faith and held tightly as the feeling intensified, trusting that Colette would never harm him. He felt himself stretching out like someone was pulling him across distances, the feeling becoming stronger and stronger until, like a piece of elastic held at full stretch and then let go, he found himself snapped forward at high speed to tumble out onto the gardens of the church they had walked in earlier that day.

His head spun at the sensation of speed and for a second Kerian thought he would vomit as the world around him grabbed hold and decided to slow him down. He felt himself go hot and cold, his eyes refusing to focus as the disorientation overcame him. Colette's laughter was like cool water.

"My teleport spell works!" She sounded somewhat relieved. "What a rush! I was not sure I could do it but because we had been here earlier, I knew where I wanted to go and could picture it clearly in my mind. It's such a shame it only works over short distances. Imagine, what if I could jump the whole ship this way? The speeds we could travel."

"I think everyone would be a lot thinner if you did." Kerian winced, his stomach still doing somersaults. Colette rubbed her hands together and let the remains of the destroyed gemstone she had used for her spell, fall to the grass. She looked around and saw the fountain right where she expected it to be.

"Now who wants to see a dragon?" she laughed.

"I was really hoping that part of the story was just made up." Kerian said coughing loudly, as a gust of errant wind fanned the columns of smoke rising from the village in their direction. He waved his hand energetically in front of his face while the air slowly cleared, noticing with some confusion that the prevailing wind appeared to be blowing in completely the opposite direction. It was as if something had just flown past them and physically battered the air away, although to do that, whatever it was, needed to be large.

They arrived at the fountain and swiftly found the mechanism to release the secret door hiding the way down into the temple. The fountain and pond grated loudly as it moved to one side revealing the worn steps leading down into the darkness.

Colette clapped her hands and a small globe of cool blue fire spun up into the air and bobbed ahead of her, lighting the way. She clicked her fingers, making the blue ball hover and then bob back towards her. She examined the light from all angles then drew a pinch of crushed lilac from her pocket and sprinkled it over the ball turning the light a violet hue.

"That's better." She smiled mischievously, sending the ball out again, down into the darkened stairwell. "I like this colour more; it matches my boots."

With the stairs illuminated, they were able to proceed swiftly via the passageway, Kerian electing to leave the fountain locked in its open position, just in case they needed to make a fast retreat from a large creature with claws, teeth and wings. He watched the ship's mage step fearlessly into the darkness. She did not seem to be at all concerned about meeting a mythical creature of legend. If anything, she appeared eager. His eyes took in her silhouette and he felt a wave of desire and love rush over him. His quest was nearly over. If everything worked out okay, he knew he would seriously consider spending the rest of his life with this woman if she would agree to have him.

A mural on the wall froze him in mid-step, the picture displaying the unmistakable image of a dragon circling a pedestal. Kerian turned to show his discovery to Colette but she appeared to have already exited the tunnel. He hurried to catch up, tripped over something as he passed through the entryway. He staggered forward out onto the large platform, his saddlebag falling free from his shoulder and found his entrance met with a chorus of mocking laughter.

His eyes went wide as he took in his surroundings. There were seven armed thugs standing all around him, weapons drawn, the odds boosting their confidence. He fumbled for his sword, turning to better assess the situation, before coming to a stop as he saw who held Colette in his arms and was holding a knife to her throat.

"Welcome Styx." Atticus sneered, as a maggot wriggled out from where his nose should have been and plopped down onto Colette's shoulder. "I am so glad you could join us. We have an annoying problem here and I think you are just the man to help us resolve it."

Chapter Fifty

"Are you alright?" Rowan asked, pushing the hair back from Thomas's face tenderly. "You look pensive."

"Oh, you know me," Thomas replied, trying to mask his nervousness with a forced smile. "I'm always alright."

"We will get through this." Rowan smiled, trying to reassure the concerned man she saw before her. "I feel there is a great future lying ahead for us."

"Really?" Thomas raised an eyebrow in surprise. "I... I wasn't sure. I mean the hours as captain are not sociable and I am prone to having low moods at times. I'm sometimes snappy and grumpy when I don't get my own way."

"Basically, you are high maintenance like a Steerman PT-17 Kaydet." Rowan interrupted, mentioning her dream plane from the 1930's that she would have sold her eye teeth to restore. "But I am sure the ride will be worth it."

The captain of the *El Defensor* stood stock still, his mind going over what had just been said, the implications slowly sinking in. Rowan smiled, leant forward and kissed him hard on the lips.

"Keep that picture in your mind." She whispered seductively. "I'll see you back on the ship soon." She turned in a whirl of dress and joined the women and children all gathered along the bar, each one instructed to hold the hands of the child or parent before and after, to form a long, disjointed human chain. Charleton raised the trapdoor in the floor and stepped back, allowing the dust from the working mill to billow up through the hole in a cloud.

"There we go! Now isn't this exciting?" he smiled at everyone. "Now remember what we said?"

"Don't touch anything." The children shouted back in unison.

"You all have your face masks to play bandits?" Rowan asked, taking the lead, lifting a hastily fashioned napkin up in front of her face."

"Yes." came the reply.

"Okay, Jon if you would be so kind." Rowan stepped back and allowed the tall man who was the children's storyteller to step to the front. It had been decided unanimously that Jon would lead the children, as they trusted him and he had a few ideas to keep things moving in the direction they needed to go. The man gestured with his hands showing the children how to hold their masks in place, held up his fingers to mime being as quiet as mice and then he sucked on his pipe and blew out a cloud of smoke. It magically transformed into the shape of a two-foot tall child's teddy bear, with the same bandit mask wrapped around the end of its nose. The bear bowed to his audience and bounced excitedly about, hopping from paw to paw, instantly capturing the attention of the children before leading the line in a stepping dance backwards and forwards around the room.

Thomas instantly thought of the pied piper rhyme from his childhood but there was no hidden malice from the piper in this instance. Jon appeared to be a kind and gentle soul who simply wanted to save the children and knew a magical way to do it. Some of the children were so engrossed that they mimicked the bear, taking little jumps from side to side as they followed the human snake chain around the room.

Some children giggled, only to be sternly shushed by the adults in the chain, as one by one, they took the steps down into the darkness. Thomas took one last lingering look at Rowan as she followed the chain into the workings of the mill. She turned to smile then was gone.

"Right!" Thomas stated to the villagers around him. "It's time we started making this place ready for a siege."

"How are we going to do that?" Charleton replied. "We have no weapons here. How will we fight?"

"I'm hoping it won't come to that." Thomas replied. "You must have kitchen knives or something behind the bar to deal with people who have outstayed their welcome."

"Kitchen knives, yes. Anything else, no." Charleton replied cutting him off. "I've told you already, we don't hurt anyone."

"Well I'm sorry to inform you that may have to change before the end of the evening." Thomas warned, turning to order the villagers about him. He paused as he looked at them all clearly for the first time. Nervous faces, looking like scared animals, some too old to be of use, too frail to hold a sword, others too young, all of them inexperienced and the greenest rookies he had ever seen. He tried to keep his face neutral but inside he worried the people around him would be the ones hurt this night.

* * * * * *

Mathius found his dream uncomfortably warm. He was in a meadow watching rabbits bouncing around and eating grass. He had no idea why, none of it made sense to him. One rabbit with a scraggly crooked ear wearing worn blue boots was talking to a wolf leaning on a fence. The wolf was smoking a pipe and kept tapping out the bowl, causing hot ash to fall out and roll over to where the assassin sat. Grasses exposed to the heat would wither and curl up as the ash rolled by. Each time the pipe emptied Mathius found himself coughing.

The fact this was so surreal and that a wolf would not normally smoke a pipe was not wasted on the dreamer. When the wolf pulled out a sheet of faded print, balanced a pair of spectacles on his nose and started discussing the headlines with the rabbit, Mathius really wanted to hear what they were talking about but all he could hear was an annoying pop and crackle that was rising in volume from no visible source.

The wolf tapped his pipe on the fence and another load of glowing embers fell near, causing Mathius to cough again and seriously consider going over to the wolf and explaining to the wolf that his pipe etiquette needed rethinking, especially near a man with a short temper. Although he had to admire the fact that his dream was so real, he could feel the heat and smell the burning. The assassin had a nagging feeling that the wolf was going to ask the rabbit to look closely at the sheet of paper. Then when the rabbit's guard was down, the wolf would open his mouth and there would be a spare pair of blue boots up for grabs. Mathius never had nice dreams but something about this one put him on edge.

His cough rattled in his throat. It actually hurt to breathe and he felt he was getting hotter!

His eyes snapped open. The room around him was a roaring inferno. Flames licked up the walls, blackening the ceiling, hungrily consuming the timber beams and structure with a voracious appetite. Furnishings and drapes fed the blaze, roaring to life as the fire took hold. It took the assassin moments to realise where he was, the fight rushing back to him in vivid levels of pain. Smoke cast a haze over everything in the room but Mathius identified the seat of the fire by the burning torch that still blazed near the window. A glass jar cracked loudly, its dry contents cascading down a dresser on the far wall. He turned his head toward the sound, wincing as pain shot up his back and then snapped back as a louder cracking sounded directly above him.

Mathius reacted by instinct, rolling to one side as a wooden beam engulfed by flame came away from the ceiling and crashed to the floor where he had lay seconds before. Smoke poured from the timbers, spreading out thickly across the room. The Raven kept his head low and drew in a deep breath that tickled his throat and launched him into spasms of coughing. He wiped his tear filled eyes and crawled painfully across the floor before he reached the door to the cottage and stood to kick it open, throwing himself outside and into the clear just as the roof of the house caved in with a whoosh of burning embers and smoke.

He staggered back over to the tree he had leant against earlier, however this time his demeanour was far removed from the cocky swagger he had previously shown. It took what felt like an eternity for the coughs to subside as he sucked in the sweet clean air of the mountainside and only then was he able to lift his head and take in the blazing houses around him.

It was like a scene from a painter's warped imagination. A vivid representation of one of the hells in Marcus's tales. Houses burnt everywhere, flames lighting up the street as if it were the middle of the day rather than late evening. The heat rippled off the flaming shells in waves that made the air shimmer and the brightness of the conflagration was such that he had to squint just to look at it.

His mind raced automatically, identifying the possibility of threats and eliminating them when it recognised there was no imminent danger. The fires were avoidable and the knight was gone. The torch previously dropped on the grass was missing; obviously Cameron had deposited the torch through the window after his vanquished foe had stayed down. The bastard had left him to burn!

The Raven's eyes continued to scan the area and he noticed two objects glinting in the firelight. He hobbled over, wincing as pain blossomed in every joint and took in his twin daggers lying discarded on the grass. The assassin picked up the blades and flipped them around in his hands before sheathing them. Cameron had made a tactical error. He had left Mathius alive.

Now The Raven would make him pay.

* * * * * *

"Do you realise why you make me so mad." Atticus ranted. "Without me you would have been nothing. I made you. If not for my painstaking efforts and genius, Styx would have been an unemployed street bum. I dragged you out of the gutter, made you the man you are today and your gratitude for all this was to cut off my nose."

Kerian remained frozen, his saddlebags at his feet, his eyes scanning the immediate area, desperately searching for some means to release Colette from the guild master's grasp. The violet light emanating from her enchanted spinning sphere cast a bizarre luminescence, making the mage appear pale and Atticus the more hideous.

Kerian had no idea what this mad man was rambling about. He had been Styx long before he had met Atticus. He had even been known as Styx back when he was in the Queen's army. It was his own actions which had made him into the man he was today. His own mistakes placing him into this ridiculous predicament. Atticus had not helped him; if anything, he had hindered him! The man had clearly lost more than his nose in the time since Kerian had last seen him. The metal cap fastened to Atticus's nose was almost mesmerising in the light and Kerian found it hard to stop his head bobbing up and down in mimicry of the man's actions as he ranted and raved before him.

Atticus had always been volatile, a man who was prone to episodes of rage, normally directed at items of furniture that he took a disliking to. However, Kerian had also seen him injure staff without a thought and with a level of callousness that bordered on the homicidal. The dagger held at Colette's throat was the only thing that made Kerian pause in leaping across the distance between them, drawing his sword and removing a larger part of the man's anatomy.

He could not see Colette hurt, not now that he had found her. Therefore, he decided to stand still, head lowered and non-threatening and hear the man out while he continued searching for a way out of this situation. Kerian flexed his hand frustratingly near his sword hilt, looking for an opening to draw the weapon and use it but a stern prodding from the thug behind him made him aware that his actions had been noted and were expected.

"Don't." he warned. Kerian did not honour the command with a reply and decided to ignore the man for now. He would just make sure he killed him later.

"The way I see it," Atticus drawled, "Is that you are the perfect person for this job. I need you to go down those steps..." Kerian turned and looked where Atticus was gesturing and just saw the platform stretching ahead of him to an edge tinged with red.

"...and I want you to retrieve the treasure down there and bring it back to me."

Atticus started walking with Colette towards the area he had been pointing towards, his henchmen closing in to assist Kerian in the same direction. They reached the edge of the platform and Kerian saw his future goal for the first time. It was real, the ancient ruined temple, the treasure, all of it! Then his eyes noticed the charred shapes of three bodies sizzling on the steps and his blood ran cold.

"Off you go then." Atticus prompted, over the enthusiastic giggling of the mercenaries behind him. "Oh, leave your sword here please. I don't want anyone having an unfortunate accident." Kerian frowned at this command but Atticus applied pressure on the blade at Colette's throat, so he reluctantly unbuckled his scabbard and passed the weapon over to the thug standing alongside him.

"Look after my sword." Kerian warned. "I will be back to claim it." He hated handing over his weapon. He felt naked and vulnerable without it and he had been missing a dagger since the events of the night back in Catterick. The only other weapon he knew of was safely wrapped up inside his saddlebags but they were on the floor back near the entrance. It might as well have been on another world! He needed to get those saddlebags if he was to have a chance of getting out of this.

The chorus of laughs at his earlier threat echoed in his ears as he took a step to the edge of the platform, his mind racing to put together a plan.

"Hang on a moment." He paused, causing the titters and laughs to stop. "What am I to put the treasure in? Do you have any bags or sacks? I can only carry so much in my pockets." Atticus looked at his hired thugs, his eyebrows rising in question. The men looked at each other, patted themselves down and all shook their shoulders.

"Are you telling me you forgot to bring the sacks?" Atticus roared, his face going scarlet with rage.

Kerian shook his head and tutted loudly. "Are you this lax when you go grocery shopping? I bet every time you go to pay you realise you have forgotten the bags."

"Rafferty had the bags." One man squealed as the guild master's frosty stare ran over him. Atticus's face turned thunderous and he grabbed Colette tightly causing her to squeal in pain. Kerian suddenly realised his comment could have put her safety in jeopardy.

"It's okay." He stated, holding his hands out and gesturing to try and calm the situation. "I have my saddlebags and Colette has a knapsack. Give them to me and I will fill them for you."

"Isn't this all a bit pointless?" asked one thug as he moved to take Colette's pack. "He'll be sizzling bacon by step five."

"He better not be." Atticus warned, or his lady friend will follow after him.

"There's no need for that." Kerian replied, trying to calm things down as he accepted the knapsack and his saddlebags. "Everything will be fine." He looked over at Colette and tried to smile as he slung the saddlebags over his shoulder and gripped the pack firmly by the strap.

"I'll be right back." he winked, looking directly at her. "Back before you know it and if any of you as much as hurt a hair on her head, I swear I will hunt you down, wherever you hide and I will kill you." He returned to the precipice and looked down the long flight of steps, unaware some of the men were looking decidedly disturbed by his threat. It appeared Styx reputation was more firmly established than Kerian recognised.

The heat radiating up off the stones made the flight of steps appear to be descending into a blacksmith's forge but Kerian knew his future lay somewhere down there and he would have to pass through the fires to get to what lay beneath him. He just hoped he would find something in the treasure horde, some weapon he could use to deal with these people and save Colette.

It was now or never, his destiny awaited.

He took a deep breath and stepped down into the furnace, his black cloak swirling around him like a set of wings. The strength of the heat wave he encountered astounded him. He almost dropped the saddlebags from over his shoulder at the shock. He turned to look back over his shoulder; his eyes wide with concern and watched Atticus push Colette closer to the edge, his body close up beside her and his dagger still pressing close to her flesh.

"Don't be too long." Atticus taunted staring down at him and willing him onwards with his insane eyes. "If I get bored waiting there is no telling what I might do."

"Not a hair, remember." Kerian stared back coldly.

He walked to the edge of the step, making a show of taking the end of his cloak and wrapping it around his arm as if he were trying to protect himself from the flames, before looking down at the next stone slab. Kerian took another breath and stepped off, tapping the bracelet at his wrist three times as he stepped down. Coldness swept over him as if he had stepped out into a winter storm. He felt goose bumps run up his arms at the change of temperature, mirroring the thrill racing through his veins that his spells protection had started and that he had about twenty minutes to get down to the temple below, break his curse and get back to rescue Colette. Salvation or cremation, it was a stark contrast.

In twenty minutes, this would end one way or another.

He took the next step and then the next, trying to ignore the crispy remains of the corpses littering the steps. The catcalls rose above him, the henchmen expecting a similar show of incineration, their enthusiasm showing the relief they felt that the person being burnt was not themselves. Kerian stepped gingerly over one burnt body, wrinkling his nose at the smell and descended to the next level. The ruined temple appeared closer at every step and he started to make out the details of the stonework. It was a beautiful building. How it remained intact under such extreme temperatures was a mystery he hoped to solve when he arrived there. The calls started to lessen as the thugs realised this time, it appeared, someone would actually be able to get down to the treasure below.

The lava bubbled and popped beneath his feet as he took the next step, the fumes and smoke rising into the air making it difficult to see up above with clarity. The fires around him generated so much heat that even with the protection offered by the bracelet he could feel himself starting to sweat. He looked up through the haze and tried to focus on Colette. She looked so small and vulnerable. If anything happened to her, he would never forgive himself. He hoped she would be safe whilst he was down here, prayed that Atticus would not simply decide to toss her into the fiery pit below as part of his warped view of revenge. Kerian had promised Colette he would be back soon. It was a promise he was determined to keep.

With one last longing look, he turned and took another step towards destiny.

* * * * * *

Marcus looked up at Abbot Brialin barely believing his eyes. The man was destroying everything around him. This was not the teachings of Saint Fraiser, it was anything but. The Abbot had a gleam in his eye bordering on the manic, his smile one of the damned. He looked, nodded and Marcus's knights, no, Brialin's knights cast flaming brands in through windows and consigned loving homes and pleasant lifestyles to flame.

The knights had not killed anyone yet, at least not to Marcus's knowledge but it appeared to be a simple matter of time. Instead, they appeared to be herding people down through the village towards the windmill that was lit up from the flickering flames raging all around it. The sails turned slowly, giving an illusion all was right with the world, whilst the villagers who lived here suffered their terrible losses.

Marcus was at a loss as to what to do. He looked longingly at the book hanging in the satchel at Brialin's side and thought about how the book had initially been his to carry. The honour he had felt at the position of *bearer* now felt like ash in his mouth as he realised what holding the book actually represented. Death by fire and sword. He briefly considered trying to stop the Abbot then swiftly reconsidered. How could he, a lowly novice, hope to tackle a man as powerful and ruthless as Brialin. The very thought was ridiculous.

The three knights leading the group moved apart as the road opened out to include the cobblestoned area around the windmill. Brialin pointed left and right and two of the knights stepped away to flank the structure and see if anyone were hiding beyond.

Marcus's heart sank as he stepped forward into the void left by the men. A rag tag assortment of villagers knelt in a line on the road before the windmill, hands held on their heads, a knight standing near them with a sword in hand. The third person from the end of the row had the unmistakable shape of Ives the merchant from the ship. He looked worse than the others, bruised, battered and decidedly downcast.

Abbot Brialin advanced towards the villagers he now had as hostages, nodding intently as a knight Marcus knew as Mitchellos, leaned in close and whispered into his ear. The Abbot turned to face the windmill and raised his head.

"Thomas Adams." He shouted over the roar of the flames. "I know you can hear me. You are harbouring the heretic Brother Richard. The man is an abomination to the teachings of the Church of Saint Fraiser. If you continue to shelter him, you will be judged guilty for harbouring a fugitive. The penalty for your indiscretion will be death."

Three arrows whistled down from the top of the windmill in answer to the charges, fired with such speed and skill they were barely inches apart when they hit. The arrows reached within a foot of Abbot Brialin's head then exploded into nothing, colliding with something unseen that prevented them from harming the thin man.

"You cannot hurt me with slings or arrows." Brialin lectured, walking slowly backwards and forwards in front of the prisoners kneeling before him. "For my faith protects me."

The prisoners watched in horror as the vulture like visage of the Abbot swept past them in his flowing robes. They looked into his eyes then swiftly looked away, his will stronger than anything they could muster.

"I am sorry it has come to this." The Abbot shouted. "You have left me no choice." He pointed to another knight that stood back observing the proceedings with religious fervour in his eyes.

"Atios. Choose one prisoner and kill him."

The knight stepped forwards. Picked the first prisoner in the row, drew his sword and calmly slid the blade through the man's chest and out his back. There were screams of outrage and fear from the other hostages as the man slumped to the floor, sliding free from the blood-streaked weapon.

"Thomas Adams. Let me make myself clear. I shall kill another prisoner for every minute you fail to supply me with Brother Richard. You can save lives here or condemn them all to death. The choice is yours."

More arrows rained down, fired from the same location as the previous failed attempt on the Abbot. Two exploded inches from his body causing the twisted man no harm. Then a barrage of shafts lanced out into the knights, some bouncing off chainmail, others striking home only to be calmly pulled free by the magical creations they hit with no apparent injury.

"I told you before." Brialin shouted. "You cannot kill me whilst my faith protects me. Bring out Brother Richard, or I will kill these people and when I am finished with them, I will burn you alive in your mill."

Marcus could not believe what he had just witnessed. He looked at the body lying lifeless on the floor, closed his eyes and prayed for the man's soul, tears welling in his eyes. Saint Fraiser would never have condoned this. These people were innocents, good people who had done no harm. By bringing the book here, he was responsible for unleashing this terror upon the villagers of Stratholme.

He could never forgive himself for what he had done.

* * * * * *

Thomas turned his head away from the window as the knight's sword slid home and the defenceless villager died. He knew it was senseless to blame himself for the outcome. It was clear the robed man outside intended to kill everyone regardless of whether Richard was surrendered or not.

The other villagers still present in the *Vane Arms* wore expressions of grief and shock. They were in no condition to stand and fight; it was a confrontation they could never hope to win. Weyn's arrows had failed to find their mark and from this range, there was not much Thomas could do to even the odds. He looked towards the bar where Charleton stood nervously polishing the surface off a tankard.

What Thomas would have given for a SWAT team right now. He called Charleton over and whispered hurried directions in his ear before turning back to see what was going on outside.

The captain cracked open the doors of the inn, staring out at the raging inferno sweeping through the town and the red-hot embers spiralling through the air. Then he lowered his gaze and took in the kneeling prisoners and his eyes alighted on Ives. Poor Ives looked as if he had been through a rough time. His face bruised, his lip bleeding. In front of Ives, the man dressed as some religious zealot who had ordered the death of the prisoner stalked up and down preaching to his terrified audience. Thomas tried to take a measure of the man, watching as he strutted backwards and forwards, his shadow moving across the faces of the kneeling men and the face of... Marcus! What was Marcus doing out there? In addition, if Marcus was out there what had happened to Mathius?

Then it dawned on Thomas what he was seeing. Marcus looked horrified to be there, his face an open book to a man that had spent many years reading body language. He was not outwardly a prisoner in the sense of the others kneeling on the floor but he was as much a prisoner in his mind. There would be no help coming from him.

Thomas took a deep breath and shouted out, hoping his training would pay off and delay further bloodshed.

"Who am I speaking to?"

The man pacing in front of the prisoners stopped mid stride and looked towards the sound of Thomas's voice, then his face cracked with a smile that would have given Malum Okubi a run for his money.

"My name is Abbot Brialin." He replied. "I assume you are Thomas Adams. I am pleased to make your acquaintance."

"I'm not." Thomas replied drawing a scowl from the Abbot that Thomas felt was entirely worth it. "Why don't you let those prisoners' go and then we can sit down and discuss this rationally."

"I don't think so." Brialin replied, resuming his pacing walk. "Why have you not given me Brother Richard? I know he is hiding in there; your friends have told me so."

"Why are you doing this?" Thomas shot back. "Why are you burning all these homes and hurting these people? They have done nothing to you. If it is Brother Richard you want, then let's deal directly with him. These people are innocent."

"They have accepted his blasphemous teachings." The Abbot snapped back. "They deserve to die."

Thomas looked back into the inn as a loud crash reached his ears. He gestured abruptly to keep the noise down as Charleton tried to stop the rest of the bottles on the bar from falling to the floor like a stack of dominos. He was stuffing the tops of the alcoholic bottles with rags as instructed by the captain but his nerves were clearly getting to him. The last remaining villagers were passing slowly down into the depths of the mill following the path of the children. Thomas could not allow these people to fight and be slaughtered; things were bad enough without that guilt resting on his shoulders. He had ordered a full evacuation and hoped he could delay the Abbot outside so that everyone could make their getaway to the relative safety of the ship.

"So, you actually have no intentions of letting any of us leave alive." Thomas shouted back, determined to keep the Abbot talking whilst the villagers continued to escape.

"We are both intelligent men." The Abbot replied. "The villagers sealed their fates when they took in Richard and his false religion. Your crew are not responsible for his vitriol and lies, you have not been subject to his teachings, therefore I see no reason why you should join them in death." The Abbot reached the end of the row and turned to sweep back past the prisoners, gesturing to another knight. "Providance, please kill another one."

"No!" Thomas screamed as the knight drew his sword and took the head from the prisoner's shoulders with one swing of his glittering blade.

"I warned you." Abbot Brialin snapped. "One prisoner for every minute. Bring Brother Richard to me."

"Over my dead body." Thomas muttered to himself, turning to look back at the bar and the progress Charleton was making. The last few villagers were queued at the opening to the trapdoor; the base of the mill was now dangerously full of people.

Brother Richard, sobered by the events unfolding before him, stepped out from the shadows of the alcove he had been sitting in and walked resolutely towards the door.

"What are you doing?" Thomas hissed.

"I'm going to surrender." Richard replied unsteadily. "I know he is going to kill me. That much is obvious. Use the time to get the others to safety.

"I'm getting bored." Brialin shouted from outside.

"I'd give good money to shut that man up." Thomas snarled, turning back towards the door. "I'm not letting you out there."

"Kill another one!" Brialin shouted from outside.

"That's not another minute!" Thomas shouted back; his fists clenched at his side.

"I am not a patient man." Brialin shot back. "My time keeping can be lapse in times of urgency. You can still stop this. All I need is Brother Richard and you can go."

Thomas bit his lip and felt Richard coming up alongside him.

"Let me go out." He pleaded. "I am ready to accept my fate."

"I'm not." Thomas replied wedging himself in the opening so the monk could not pass. He looked out towards the line of prisoners and watched as a knight stepped forward and calmly drew his sword. Then he realised who the next victim would be and closed his eyes as the warrior stepped towards Ives.

"Last chance." Brialin taunted.

"Please let me go." Richard begged.

"It will serve nothing." Thomas replied, "He's going to kill us all anyway."

"I will not have any more deaths on my conscious." Richard replied pushing Thomas aside.

"Wait!" Richard shouted. "I'm coming. You don't have to kill anyone else."

Abbot Brialin held up his hand stopping the knight with a gesture as the glittering blade rose to administer a deathblow to the kneeling merchant. Brialin's smile was lecherous and clearly displayed what he was about to do.

"Kill him anyway. View this as a lesson for Richard not to drag his feet in future."

"No!" Thomas screamed stepping through the door into the road, his sword in hand, knowing he would never get across the cobbles in time.

The knight's sword swung back and then came down, whistling through the air but the blow never landed.

One minute the knight was swinging his sword, the next, there was an explosion of what looked like parchment, as if someone had shot a sawn-off shotgun into a pile of old books. A wind blasted over everyone, knocking Thomas back towards the inn and sending a couple of knights falling onto their backs, as something massive passed between the line of prisoners and the windmill. An angry roar vibrated through the air.

Thomas staggered, his arm lifting to protect his face from the blast of whatever had just hit them. There was a shriek from above as the columns of black smoke rising from the houses appeared to fold in amongst themselves and then a crash as something immense smashed to the ground before them.

"How dare you harm my children!" The monster roared defiantly.

The captain could not believe what he was seeing. It was a dragon, towering forty feet high, with a wingspan to match. Claws gouged out the cobbles in the road as the monster opened its mouth and roared again, freezing everyone to the spot before it turned and fixed the Abbot with a vicious stare, its long neck rearing up as it opened its mouth and prepared to strike. A long serpentine tail coiled and flexed behind the creature; the end adorned with large spikes.

Thomas had seen a few dragons in his time but never anything like this. He knew there were tales of coloured dragons and metallic dragons, dragons that lived in ice, swamps and other inhospitable places but never in his years had he seen a dragon that appeared to be made of crystal and so very, very old.

Scales rippled impossibly, nostrils flared, as the creature scented its prey. Every inch of the monster was shifting, a kaleidoscope of colours as the light shone through its body and refracted. It was impossible that a creature like this could exist, that a creature like this could even move or flex but it did and it was here right in front of him.

The captain rubbed his eyes hard wondering if he had knocked his head somehow and that this was all some sort of dream or vision brought on by the stress of the moment but the creature remained before him its body practically emanating power.

Thomas started to smile. He could not help himself. Here before him was an actual dragon, all be it a very old, angry and pissed off dragon. A dragon with missing scales and scarred wings, twisted claws and fogged eyes. However, what made this dragon special was not that it was an impossibility made of crystal. Oh no... what made this dragon special is that for once the big, bad, monster appeared to be on the captain's side!

* * * * * *

Squeal, scrape. Squeal, scrape.

Oh, this was ridiculous! Ashe tried to blink the sweat from his eyes as he inched the chair holding him another painful inch across the floor. That stupid, stupid Minotaur! What kind of a rescue involved forgetting to actually rescue the person who needed rescuing! What kind of cretaceous crab cake would leave his friend tied to a chair?

Squeal, scrape. Squeal, scrape.

It would help if Ashe knew where he was heading but he could only shuffle the chair backwards and had no idea what was behind him. He did not even have a plan in his mind. He just wanted to get as far away from this boathouse and all the pain it signified and quickly before anyone came back and found him. Oh, Rauph why did you have to charge off like that?

Squeal, scrape. Squeal, clunk.

Clunk? That was different! Was that a door handle prodding the back of his left ear, or was someone happy to see... The door creaked open and the chair slowly started to overbalance on its back legs as its back slid down the door's surface.

"No... Oh no!" Ashe screamed, as the door opened fully, dropping him heavily onto his back. His teeth clacked together and his head bounced off the floor sending further stars dancing across his vision.

Oh, this was just great! He tried to look up from his horizontal position and figure out where he was. The silver-grey wood of the strange ship he had seen through the window was visible from the corner of his eye and he could now hear the sea lapping up alongside the vessel. Right, so he was where they repaired the ship.

The click clack of claws made Ashe freeze in place. Something was coming in his direction. He knew that sound and a groan escaped his swollen lips. Something wet and slobbery poked him in his ear.

"Urgh, get off!" he yelled but Atticus's dog was oblivious to such orders and took the resistance as something that needed quelling. A long rasping tongue dripped slobber across Ashe's face causing him to spit and stammer. "No please stop, please stop."

The scraggly dog finally stopped licking Ashe to death and then sniffed the Halfling more carefully and started to move around up and down past his head. Ashe had seen this behaviour too. The puppy paused in mid-circle and confirmed Ashe's darkest fears as it cocked its leg. When he got out of this, Ashe swore he was going to give the Minotaur a damned good talking to!

He swung himself from side to side, desperately trying to move the chair away from the puppy. The chair lifted, then crashed down again, lifted then crashed down harder, jarring him further. He gritted his teeth and swung himself as hard to the left as he could, the chair tilted then smashed down onto its left side, barely missing what was left of his shattered little fingers. Emboldened by the result, he turned again and found himself crashing down onto his face, the chair now above him.

So how was this position any better? Well, at least his face was so numb that it did not hurt any more than it already did! He tried to move back onto his knees, lifting his face gingerly from the floor. The puppy was waiting with an encouraging lick, causing Ashe to spit, splutter, and overbalance smashing his head into the floor again.

"Oww!" he moaned. "Will you keep away from me, you stupid dog." He gathered himself again, trying to ignore the growls of excitement coming from his left boot as the dog started trying to tug his laces and pull his shoe off. He lifted himself up, arching his back and tried to inch forwards on his knees, looking for some way to get up on his feet and get the chair off himself. He spotted a file hanging from the side of a workbench on the wall but it might as well have been a mile away instead of the few metres it actually was. He gritted his teeth in determination and started to shuffle inch by inch towards his goal, the puppy dragging behind him, growling and jumping excitedly as it tugged playfully at his lace.

He was definitely going to have words with Rauph when he got out of this!

Ashe continued to inch across the floor like some bizarre tortoise towing an excited puppy and finally got to the shelf, the file inches from his face. Then he realised he had no way to actually get the file. Both of his hands were securely tied to the chair! It was like opening a vault and then finding the owner had failed to stock it properly. Now what was he going to do?

A door creaked open somewhere behind him and loud footsteps started advancing in his direction. Ashe's worst fears had come true. Atticus had come back to kill him! He tried to merge in with the workbench, will himself invisible but the puppy continued to growl excitedly and repeatedly tried to eat his boot. The game was up. He was a dead Halfling!

"I'm so sorry I failed you, I couldn't..." boomed a deep shaggy voice. "Umm...Whatever are you doing playing with that puppy dog?"

Ashe closed his eyes in relief.

"Come over here." he yelled from his undignified position. "Come and untie me from this stupid chair so that I can punch you in the snout!"

Chapter Fifty-One

Kerian stood within the fiery depths of the volcano, molten rock bubbling all around him, flowing like a slow-moving river whose very touch would mean instant death. Gas pockets popped and exploded, vapours burned off and smoke spiralled upwards towards the platform high above. He could not help but draw parallels to his talk with Thomas all those weeks ago, when he had joked about his namesake. This truly was the river Styx and now here he was travelling it!

The hovering slabs of stone had twisted and turned as he had descended, weaving around rock outcroppings and passing through clouds of toxic fumes until they finally brought him here to his goal. He now stood at the entrance to the temple holding the magical artefact that would forever shape his future.

The stonework was ancient and pitted but surprisingly sound for being surrounded by liquid molten rock. Weathered and worn pillars rose up above him supporting a roof that appeared cracked and uneven. Murals carved into the fascia were faded and crumbled, some so badly damaged that it was impossible to see if they were pictures of men or women. A flight of three stairs led from his final stepping-stone and into the temple proper, where a piecemeal mosaic pathway directed visitors between the pillars and into the sanctum beyond.

Kerian's heart beat loudly in his chest as he tried to summon the courage to take the final steps towards his goal. He could not understand why he felt so insecure, why he stood here struggling to move forwards. Was he scared that after all of this, after all the adventures, all the suffering and pain he had experienced, that the story could be untrue; that when he walked into the temple there would be no artefact to save him and that all of this would have been for nothing.

He had to admit that he was truly terrified of this prospect.

What if he could not lift the curse and continued to age. He thought of the young woman he had come to care for so deeply and tried to suppress the chills that ran through him at the thought of losing her. Colette could never be happy to remain with him as a withered old man. He looked down at his wrist to check the progress of the protective bracelet glowing softly there and took in his thin skin and his age spots. Who was he kidding? He was already withered and old!

He looked through the rows of pillars at the glittering piles of wealth lying within the temple and took a deep breath. It was time to face his fears, not stand here wasting precious time second-guessing himself.

Kerian stood up straight, held his head up high and stepped off the final hovering stone onto the temple steps. As soon as his feet touched the ancient stone, he felt cooler, as if his protection spell was somehow working better or the heat from the lava had suddenly subsided. It appeared the temple was magically cooler than its surroundings. He walked along the mosaic pathway, taking in the scenes of village life displayed on the temple walls, his boots whispering across the floor as he followed footprints only visible through thick dust.

Coins, jewellery and small gem lay discarded in his path, some worth more money than he had ever seen in his lifetime. Currency from different realms reached knee high, half-burying ornate vases, wide goblets and intricately engraved armour plate in landslides of glittering discs. Just one handful would have allowed him to live the remainder of his life in luxury.

Statues of horses rearing, of men and women in various poses depicting sports, love, life, and death called to his eye but Kerian needed a weapon he could use competently, something to give him an advantage over the thugs above! He saw a shield with a mirrored surface, greaves of silver; helmets with huge ornamental plumes running along the top and golden arrows with swirling motes of black running through the shafts but he could find no bow to go with them.

He knew he had the dagger in his saddlebags but the very thought of touching the blade gave him the shivers. He knew he would only use that blade as a last resort. A sword, a sword, he would have given his kingdom for a sword. He stopped the thought dead. He needed to be careful. Richard had told him the wish only worked once. If he was not careful, he could inadvertently end up with the greatest sword in the world but it would be no good if he were too old and weak to wield it.

Kerian walked between two heaps of coin and found he was finally able to take in the specifics of the area around him. The open sky above showed the edge of the platform he had descended from and the small faces of his 'supporters' looking down. They could see him from their vantage point so he knew he had to be quick. The area was larger than he expected, the piles of coin and treasure having obscured the full size of the task he faced. The floor space measured well over one hundred feet by eighty feet, its surface covered in mounds of dragon hoard. All apart from the middle of the hall where the floor was clear and an area ten feet square seemed to have been cut away to reveal the lava bubbling and popping below. The molten liquid acted like a moat around a smaller portion of the floor measuring about three feet square that hovered in the middle of the lava expanse.

He moved closer, taking in the solitary pillar resting on the island, noting the pulsing object laying on its surface and the fact that the island was only accessible by the thinnest of stone spans. Kerian picked up a coin and threw it at the island, knowing his aim was long but doing it to confirm his fears. The coin dropped into the lava and melted instantly. It appeared that falling from the span would be a fatal experience.

His eyes continued to scan the treasure but there was simply too much of it. Where should he start? Where would they put weapons in this place? The bracelet at his wrist continued to shine brightly as the enchantment keeping him safe continued counting down. A quick glance confirmed that a fifth of his time had passed.

"Don't keep me waiting Styx." A voice shouted from far above. "I am not a patient man."

"You are going to be a dead man when I get out of here." Kerian vowed to himself, moving to the beginning of the span. He looked across to the pillar and the blood red artefact pulsing on the top of it. This was what he had been looking for. It was real, every bit of it. All he had to do was walk over and have his wish granted.

He placed his foot on the bridge and then stopped. What about Colette? What if whilst he was down here putting himself first, she was getting hurt? The thought stopped him cold and he stepped back. He looked down at the bracelet and mentally calculated his options.

The right thing to do was find a weapon, get back up the stairs and save Colette. If he moved fast enough, he could still return here and break the curse in time. It would be close but it was definitely possible.

What was he thinking! The cure was right there! Right in front of him! All he needed to do was cross the small bridge, break the curse and then, when he was cured, he could concentrate on rescuing Colette. He would be better placed to help her if he was fit and young again.

Indecision froze him to the spot.

The scream from above tore his thoughts back to reality and his head swung up in horror to watch a figure tumble from the platform. There was a flashing image of legs kicking and arms waving before the person flared brightly, igniting as they burnt up in the heat.

Kerian dropped the knapsack and the saddlebags in shock, his mind swiftly trying to replay the image, trying to identify if the person falling was Colette. He looked up furiously scanning the edge of the platform looking for a sign of Colette or Atticus but there was no longer anyone looking down at him. Where had they all gone? Something was definitely happening up there; Colette was in danger; she was all alone and she needed him. There was no time to find a weapon. He had to get back up those steps now!

He went to grab his saddlebags from the floor and as he lifted them, the velvet bag slipped free. A flash of golden scale glinted from the open neck of the bag.

He was out of time and out of options.

Kerian plunged his hand into the bag and felt the cool metal within wrap around his arm.

* * * * * *

Colette looked down at Kerian as he worked his way through the temple, silently willing him towards his goal and trying not to gag at the smell of rotten flesh over her left shoulder. Atticus's body felt hot and greasy against her and he constantly pulled her close as he leaned over to see her companion's progress.

Everything in this world seemed geared to the male of the species having the upper hand and it infuriated her when people felt she was unable to care for herself. When Atticus had first taken her as she stepped onto the platform, she had swiftly weighed up the situation in her mind. A fight was risky, especially seven against two. It had therefore been logical to simply act defenceless, pretend she was scared and let the thugs' macho behaviour work for her. Instead of having to fight their way to the temple the henchmen had simply stood aside and let Kerian go down to the temple below.

However, she could have hit Kerian at his earlier bravado. He had made things so much more difficult for her when he had asked for her knapsack. All of her spell components were in there!

Now she only had what she wore to her person to try to get out of the grips of this odorous man who had hands like an octopus. The stench from his nose was simply disgusting. Something was clearly rotting under the metallic cap he had placed over his nose and the smell was making it hard for her to concentrate.

She looked down into the temple and watched Kerian approach the centre of the treasure. This was it! Come on Kerian! Break the curse then come back to me, she willed.

What was he doing! The idiot had stopped!

"What is he doing?" Atticus echoed at her shoulder. "Why isn't he picking up the treasure?" He leant forward putting them dangerously off balance near the edge of the platform.

"Don't keep me waiting Styx." He shouted. "I am not a patient man."

Colette suddenly realised what the problem was. Her act at being helpless had been too real for Kerian. He genuinely thought she was in peril. She could not help but smile despite the frustration she felt. He was such a romantic fool.

She needed to act now.

"Excuse me." She opened; turning her head towards Atticus's sweating face. "We seem to be a bit close to the edge, do you mind stepping back a bit?"

"W...What?" Atticus replied, clearly confused by her interruption of his dreams of avarice. He took a step back and loosened his grip, moving the dagger slightly away from her throat as his eyes wandered down the curve of her breast. It was what Colette had been waiting for. She stamped down hard on his instep, her boot heel gouging into his leg.

"You bitch!" Atticus snapped, hopping away, as Colette reached up and pulled one of her violet ribbons from her hair. That was the predictable thing about men. They always looked down at your body first before looking up at your eyes and seeing your true intentions.

"Trappula!" she shouted, throwing the ribbon towards the guild master. The ribbon doubled, then tripled in size and whipped up around his body and arms as if it were alive. Colette knew the cantrip was only a temporary spell and that the ribbon would shrink back to nothing in a few minutes at most but it served to allow her to escape his grasp.

The other mercenaries were still looking over the side at Kerian's efforts and had not noticed Colette's escape. However, Atticus's loud insult did result in the nearest thug turning in their direction with an amused smile on his face, probably expecting to see Atticus put the prisoner in her place.

He was sorely mistaken.

Colette dropped to the floor and whipped out her legs, swinging them in behind the thug's knees and making him stagger backwards, straight off the ledge to fall screaming to the lava below.

The young mage did not stop to think about the other brigands. It was still five against one and she needed her own knapsack for the more powerful spells. Atticus would be free in moments and then the odds would worsen. She ran for the passageway back towards the gardens hoping that the thugs would follow her outside where she could lose them in the darkness and allow Kerian to come back from the temple and face no opposition when he reached the top of the steps. She just hoped he would be sensible enough to do what was needed to break his curse.

She lowered her head and pumped her arms running for all she was worth, the little violet ball bobbing along in her wake, its pale light pooling on the floor. Grunts and curses of surprise from behind her indicated that the thugs had realised she had broken free. Footsteps sounded indicating pursuit but she had a good start. The tunnel entrance was close, just a few more steps.

Darkness moved out from the opening. Colette skidded to a stop, her feet sliding out from beneath her, making her tumble to the floor as she looked up in horror into Scrave's twisted features. She had never seen such a look of hatred on her shipmate's face. His eyes seemed like dark voids sucking in the life of everything they gazed upon. A headband visible through his long black hair glinted in the violet light as if it was alive and moving. In his hand, he held Wizardseeker. The power from the spear made the air crackle; there was a scent of ozone and a real sense of evil emanating from the weapon.

"Oh Scrave." Colette voiced in shock. "What have you done to yourself?"

The blackened spear swung around as the Elf whipped it through the air, the point stopping inches from her chest. Colette felt herself under intense scrutiny, Scrave's eyes scanning her body as if he could see through her and identify everything she had about her person. Then he looked back into her eyes and spoke with a voice that was cold and unforgiving.

"Where is it?"

* * * * * *

The dragon lashed out to the left with its tail, sweeping two knights from their feet and smashing them hard against the buildings standing there. Her claw gripped one knight around the chest and lifted him high into the air before smashing him down hard into the cobblestones, practically squashing the man flat. Abbot Brialin stood frozen to the spot, staring in awe at the unbridled display of aggression and power before him.

Marcus edged away in terror, fearing for his own safety even as he started towards the line of prisoners thinking to start freeing them. Thomas had the same idea and had run towards Ives drawing his sword and meeting another knight head on, as the man rushed forward to complete his Master's bidding now that his comrade had been reduced to confetti.

Thomas slipped in under the knight's upraised sword and parried it, preventing a blow from landing, before pushing the man backwards and bringing his own cutlass up, whipping it in a figure eight before setting his feet and taking the hilt in two hands.

"I hope you are good." He opened, preparing to take the knight on. "I'll have you know I have studied the best, including Juan Sanchez Villa-Lobos Ramirez the Chief Metallurgist of King Charles V of Spain, Inigo Montoya slayer of the six fingered man and Obi wan Kenobi who fought in the Clone Wars."

Tobias smiled at the idiot in front of him. This was one of Marcus's stupid friends. He had no idea what the man was rambling about but it did not matter as he did not stand a chance.

He stamped his foot hard; the *Appel* move making his opponent think he was about to lunge forward. Thomas pulled his blade back in response, ready to parry only for the knight to smile again, tap his sword on the floor and start a slow circle of his opponent. Behind them, the scene was one of chaos. Ash fell from the sky; smoke filled the air; the dragon's wings flapped and fanned embers making them jump from houses already ablaze to lodge in the tightly packed thatch of houses yet to feel the fire's kiss.

"You didn't kill my father but prepare to die anyway." Thomas yelled, deliberately misquoting from the *Princess Bride*, moving forward and bringing his sword crashing down on Tobias's blade, angling his cutlass so that the edge ran down to the knight's hilt. The move surprised his opponent for an instant and Thomas made good on the advantage, punching with the hilt of his blade and bringing his knee up into the man's groin.

Tobias snapped his head forward; cracking it off his adversary's forehead and making Thomas stagger back. The knight's blade flicked out catching the captain under his chin and drawing blood. He lunged again, forcing Thomas to parry furiously leaving little time for any form of riposte. The man was simply too fast with his attacks.

Thomas staggered as Tobias pivoted on one foot kicking him squarely in the ribs and knocking the breath from him, forcing him backwards amongst the villagers who still knelt on the floor too terrified to move. His footing was unsteady and he found himself backpedalling hard before he fell, a huge dragon's claw smashing into the cobbles, inches from his head.

The captain hit the floor hard, rolling and grunting in shock just as Richard and Marcus ran up alongside him to grab the dishevelled group of prisoners and lead them away from the fighting. The dragon roared loudly, its tail whipping out and sending another knight crashing through a window.

"Get them into the *Vane Arms.*" Thomas shouted, gesturing wildly to indicate they should run for the doors. "Then tell the others to head for the ship now."

"What about you." Richard asked, looking over and noticing Tobias rapidly closing the distance.

"Don't worry about me." Thomas shot back. "Get the women and children to safety." He watched Tobias closing and groaned to himself. The *force* was definitely strong in this one.

The ragged band set off across the cobbles, running directly beneath the rampaging dragon, weaving between Rosalyine's stamping feet and swishing tail as they headed for safety. Thomas took one more look before Tobias was on him again.

"Seconds out. Round Two." Thomas goaded, knowing that it was the last thing in the world he actually wanted but the walking martial arts trained tin can appeared more than up for it. Cutlass hit longsword in a shower of sparks as the two fighters engaged, Tobias parrying and Thomas grunting hard and forcing through the parry with brute force. He struck repeatedly, actually gaining some ground and when Tobias moved to retaliate, Thomas was ready.

Tobias's silver blade swept up, forcing Thomas's sword out and high, leaving him open for a thrust but the captain expected the lunge and dropped down to perform a *Passata Sotto*, watching the knight's blade pass within inches of his head. He took in the symbol of the flaming cross, etched just below the hilt of the knight's blade as it passed right before his eyes, his own blade thrusting up and through Tobias's chest, the lunge strengthened by the knight's own forward motion.

His opponent grunted as the cutlass slid home, then incredibly lifted his head and smiled. Thomas stared in shock. The game was over. Had no one told this knight the rules of swordplay? Tobias stood up straight, his hands reaching for the captain's blade. Thomas saw something coming out of the corner of his eye, a flash of reflected fire on crystal and ducked as the dragon's tail whipped across and took the knight's head clean off his shoulders. Tobias staggered a few steps then sank to the floor, his arms shaking then dropping to his sides.

Thomas placed his foot on Tobias's chest and pulled his blade free before looking down at his opponent.

"Once your head comes away from your body, it's over." Thomas quipped, putting on a bad Scottish accent and quoting his favourite saying from the movie *Highlander*. "Remember, there can be only one."

* * * * * *

"Go, go, go!" Brother Richard shouted, shepherding the villagers into the *Vane Arms*. He pushed them through the door and shouted inside. "Thomas says make for the ship now." The monk counted the men inside, noting the man with the white sword was hesitating at the door as if torn between joining the others and waiting it out. He looked so weary that it was likely he would just step outside and be mistakenly squashed by the dragon or slain by the unstoppable knights.

"Look, Thomas will need a man to guard the end of the evacuation line. Stay here and make sure no one goes after them." Richard held his head, catching his breath. He felt a headache coming on, probably due to the excitement and all the alcohol he had consumed earlier. He hoped he was not going to be sick.

Ives looked up at Richard as if in shock, slowly nodding his head in agreement, despite looking like he had no idea what the monk had just said.

"What about Marcus and Thomas?" Ives asked.

Richard knew where Thomas was but suddenly realised that Marcus was unaccounted for. Where had he gone? He looked back out of the doors at the continuing chaos outside and noticed the young monk walking directly towards Abbot Brialin, his back straight, his body language indicating he intended to do more than just talk to the man.

Was he insane? Brialin would squash him like a fly!

He turned back to the shocked man in front of him just as Socks jumped up on the bar licking cream from its paw.

"Just stand guard here okay. I will go and get them. You look after the others and keep my cat safe." Brother Richard backed out the doors then turned and stepped straight into the havoc.

* * * * * *

Marcus stormed across the cobblestones, heading straight for Abbot Brialin. His eyes took in the man he had grown to despise who was throwing his head back and laughing as sulphur clouds billowed across him, blown by the crystalline dragon from a maw that, when opened, almost matched the height of some of the smaller buildings around them. Dagger like teeth, longer than a door's height, clashed around the Abbot's figure but could not gain purchase, deflected by something unseen that Brialin was calling his faith.

Marcus thought about the *Bearer's* book and started considering the inscription on the leather front. The pictures of the little monk with everyone bowing to him called to Marcus. It was as if the carrier of the book were a god. Someone immune to harm. Someone just like Abbot Brialin.

The book was the key. He had to get that book back but how was he going to get close enough? Brialin still seemed unaware of his approach, laughing at the dragon as it repeatedly attacked and tried to harm him, becoming more frustrated by the second at its failure. If he could just get close enough to get that book, Brialin's defences would be down and he would be vulnerable. He stepped closer, moving towards the Abbot his arm outstretched.

Something hard slammed into Marcus from the side, knocking the monk away. He shook his head, trying to figure out what hit him when something kicked him hard in the side. Marcus screamed as his injured ribs were slammed, lifting him off his knees and onto his side. He hugged his waist rocking and stared up, tears in his eyes to see the mocking face of the knight Cameron looking down at him.

"You are not permitted to touch the Master." Cameron warned. "You should know better."

The knight drew his long silver sword and stepped forward.

"I saw what you did." Brialin stated coldly. "Helping the heretics. You are a traitor! Just stay where you are. You are already in the perfect position." He turned to Cameron and nodded. "Kill him. He has served his purpose."

Marcus struggled to breathe; his ribs hurt so badly. He had not yet recovered from his beating on the *El Defensor* and the pain was excruciating. He tried to gasp a breath in but it felt like trying to suck water from a stone. His vision swam, his ears roared and Cameron stepped closer sword raised.

"Get away from my friend." A voice ordered from between two houses.

Cameron paused in mid-swing and turned towards the voice.

"Who are you to give me orders?" he demanded. "I only bend my knee to my Master the Abbot."

"I am The Raven." Came the sinister reply. "And tonight it is I you will kneel to before you die."

* * * * * *

The working mill beneath the *Vane Arms* was dark, dusty, noisy and every child's delight. It terrified Rowan that at any time one of these little children would place their hands into the machinery and touch something they should not to cause themselves terrible injury. The fact that they were all packed here in the darkness, not moving anywhere, only seemed to add to the mischief that was possible as the children grew bored.

When the order came to move out, she breathed a sigh of relief through her napkin as the large doors swung open to the night sky and everyone started heading up outside following the dancing bear. Children hopped and skipped from the mill, the long line snaking out into the darkened streets, child after child, lightly dusted in flour and looking like little ghosts, remaining tightly linked together under the close supervision of the adults who had joined to assist.

Jon and Charleton knew the streets well, turning down passageways where houses almost touched, the snaking line following with the barest of noises. They avoided all the main routes, checked and double-checked crossroads before they moved out. White ash fell from the heavens like snow and glowing embers danced across the rooftops as they continued their journey away from the mill and down towards the docks. The teddy bear continued to dance a path ahead and for a second Rowan allowed herself to believe they would make it clear.

Then the inevitable happened. Two young children started to argue over something and broke hands, stopping in mid-stride little voices rising indignantly as they strove to outdo the volume of each other. The line ahead of them walked off without a thought whilst the ones behind started to bunch up and wonder what all the fuss was about. As soon as they realised the bear was gone others started to lose interest and let go of each other's hands too.

Rowan walked over to the rebellious children and stared down at the instigators of the pile up. A rebellious four-year-old with freckles all over her face and her hair in pigtails stood with her hands on her hips and her tongue a good centimetre out of her mouth. Her little pink dress flared up behind her as she verbally accosted a five-year-old blonde child with a turned-up lip and a pudgy nose.

"What are you doing?" Rowan asked. "You need to be quiet."

"You are not my mother." The four-year-old shot back. "You don't get to tell me what to do."

"You don't have a mother stupid!" the five-year-old retaliated as only children could do. "Because she's dead. That's why you live with Ezzy the hag."

The four-year-old swung a roundhouse Rowan would have been proud of, smacking her taller adversary right in the face, then she turned and ran off into the darkness as the other child started to cry loudly.

"I've got her." Rowan stated, pointing at Violetta, "Get the line to catch up. I'll be with you in a moment." She set off in pursuit following the little footprints on the ground, determined no one would be left behind to face the terrible knights who were burning everything in their path.

Within a few twists and turns, she started to gain ground but the child was a resilient runner and dodged through openings that Rowan could not fit through. Sometimes she had to run wide, taking the long way around houses when her little charge had simply squeezed through openings, it was only because of the ash on the floor that she was able to pick up the trail and catch up.

She ran around the corner, came face to face with the little girl and found her talking to two knights who stood before her their swords gleaming cold in the night air.

"She's right there." She pointed. Her little finger directly aiming at Rowan's astonished face. "We are all following the teddy bear." Rowan tried to hide her horror at being found and held her hand out.

"Come here honey. We need to go now."

"I don't want to." came the indignant reply. Rowan bit her lip nervously and repeated her request that the child come over.

"I don't think she wants to come over." The first knight said. "Why don't you come over here instead and we can have a long talk about where you were taking everyone."

* * * * * *

Colette crabbed back across the floor as Scrave walked towards her, his spear setting all of the hairs on her arms prickling with the energy coming off the blade.

"Where is it?" he asked again shaking the spear threateningly. Footsteps came from behind her as two of the mercenaries ran over.

"We will take it from here." One said reaching down to take Colette by the arm.

"Thanks a lot." Said the other one. "Nice spear."

Scrave acted with a speed Colette would have thought impossible, the wickedly barbed spearhead plunging through the first man's throat with a wet crackle. The Elf withdrew the weapon, letting the corpse fall limply to the platform and then he flipped the staff of the spear around his body, the tip of the spear ripping through the side of the second man's face removing an eye and part of his nose as it completed its destructive arc.

He never even stopped to check if the men were dead. Instead, he strode past Colette as if she were of little consequence or meaning to his life; heading unerringly towards the far side of the platform where the other henchmen stood waiting, hands on swords.

Colette watched Scrave's back as he walked past, her head a whirl, initially happy that the Elf was going towards the men. Let them deal with him, see if she cared! Then she realised that Kerian was over there too. No... it was okay.

Kerian was deep into the temple. Scrave would be burnt to a crisp if he took the stairs after him without protection. She watched from a distance as the Elf approached the men and smacked a few with his whirling staff, dropping them senseless to the deck. Then he walked along the edge of the platform to where the floating steps began and simply stepped off the edge.

That was impossible! Colette blew the hair from her eyes. He would be dead within a matter of moments. She got to her feet and ran back across the platform, not noticing the blood flowing from the corpses behind her setting off little sparks from the floor as it pooled.

* * * * * *

Rosalyine roared in frustration, ripping the roof from a house and slamming it down onto the laughing Abbot, only to see him step through the debris and dust himself off still laughing. The knights about her continued to put themselves back together as fast as she was ripping them apart, attacking with their swords chipping her body, making hair thin cracks across her wing membranes and prising free scales trying to plunge their swords into the softer body beneath. She turned and fought with a fury but seemed to be making little headway.

The magical pulse that flared in her mind froze the mighty creature in mid-fight signalling a fresh assault from the knights much to the delight of the sniggering Abbot. The pulse meant one thing. Someone was in her inner sanctum; someone was trying to get into the temple and find her lover's heart and she was not there to protect him.

Three knights leapt onto her tail trying to climb onto her back but Rosalyine no longer cared, rearing up and flexing her legs, flapping her wings with a downdraft that knocked several people off their feet as she took to the skies. Her lover was alone and vulnerable. She could not be in two places at the same time and her priority was to *Strathe,* it was always to him.

* * * * *

Kerian took the steps as fast as he could but it was killing his legs. He was in such poor shape. His breath came in ragged gasps as he struggled to climb and the heat was so much greater outside of the cool temple interior. He felt sweat forming across his brow and the sensation of a droplet running into his eye. The bracelet on his left wrist glowed with its ghostly light showing he had now used a third of his time. This was going to be close. His mind kept replaying the falling figure he had glimpsed from down in the temple. It could not have been Colette. Atticus could not be that stupid as to push Kerian into a position where he knew he would be signing his own death warrant. The guild master may be insane but he was not suicidal. He was too cowardly for that.

On his right hand, the golden serpent dagger seemed to be adjusting to the flex of his wrist as he ran up the steps. The thing gave him shivers but he had already seen it could be a fearsome weapon. He just hoped it would be enough against Atticus's thugs. He tried to put the slithering feeling out of his mind, his skin crawling as he continued his relentless ascent.

He almost missed the dark figure standing above him but something made Kerian look up just as the Elf jumped through the air from the platform above and dropped five steps in an instant, landing three steps above him. The Elf looked evil. There was no other word for it. He was as a demon made real, black hair flying back from his forehead as he fell, his cloak billowing out behind him like a set of wings adorning the back of a nocturnal terror. In his hand, he held a large black spear that appeared to be humming. Kerian stopped his advance, knowing instinctively that Scrave meant him harm.

"That spear and the new dark and scary ensemble is a new look for you." Kerian quipped trying desperately to catch his breath. Scrave stared down at him with his dark intense eyes and lifted the spear up above his head with both hands, tip pointing downwards directly at Kerian's body.

"Where is my dagger?" Scrave asked without feeling.

"Is it like this one?" Kerian replied waving the weapon before the Elf's eyes, just as it sank in that he was facing a spear fight with of all things a dagger. He shrugged; realising things simply could not get worse. A resigned smile flitted across his lips. "Nope! Haven't seen it."

"I have been looking forward to this for a long time." Scrave snarled.

"Tonight, Kerian Denaris finally dies."

Chapter Fifty-Two

Thomas threw his hands up over his head as the dragon lifted into the sky, the downdraft flattening two burning houses and sending several knights and crewmembers sprawling. Debris, ash and embers blasted about the cobblestone area making the captain cough and splutter as he looked on with unbelieving eyes. Where did it think it was going? The battle was not finished here!

He turned from the knight scrabbling at his feet trying to find pieces of parchment to stuff them back into the wound at its open neck and took in the scene around him. There were still too many knights left to fight, even as he watched they were pulling themselves together and getting onto their feet, whilst the others continued to attack the people around him. He backed slowly towards the Vane Arms and heard something fall to the cobbles behind.

Thomas spun sword drawn but pulled his attack just in time as he came face to face with the shocked figure of Weyn who had just clambered down from the roof of the inn.

"Whoa!" The archer shouted, holding up his hands. "I'm on your side remember. Duck!" Thomas acted on instinct, ducking as Weyn fired two shots from his bow, putting the shafts clean through a knight's neck as he advanced to strike and dropping the man down onto his back.

"We are going to need to get out of here!" Thomas shouted, ash cascading down around him like snow. "We need to get everyone together and get out through the base of the inn like the others."

"I'm with you all the way." Weyn replied, firing off another couple of shots, his arrows re-materialising in his quiver as fast as he could fire them. "However, I don't think they want us to leave." He gestured at the knights standing up on the far side of the road and turning to look in their direction.

Thomas took in the disheartening view, his face turning grim. It seemed no matter what they tried the knights would not stay down. He looked over at the Abbot, standing out in the open, arms raised laughing manically. Why did people like this keep coming into his life? He needed to come up with a plan, something that would give them an edge, or a way of stopping these automatons from advancing. Somehow, he knew the answer lay with the Abbot. If he could figure out a way of taking him out, all of this would stop.

* * * * * *

Abbot Brialin threw his head back and laughed as the dragon left, clearly believing his magical powers had made the magnificent creature bolt. He turned to his scattered troops determined they should make good on this advantageous turn of events.

"You see, even a creature as mighty as a dragon cannot face me!" he screamed to the heavens, before turning to look down with distain at Marcus kneeling before him groaning and holding his chest. "I see you now realise your rightful place. I am your Master. Never forget it!" He lifted his hand to deliver a crushing blow to Marcus's exposed forehead but a figure stepped between him and his target causing Brialin to look up in surprise.

"Brother Richard." Brialin hissed. "So, the heretic has finally decided to come and face his punishment."

"If you are asking if I have come to answer for my actions, then you can see my punishment around you." Richard replied calmly. "There is nothing more you can do to harm me. I have lost everything. I have nowhere to go, nowhere to live. What more can you possibly do? All I have left is my faith."

"Your faith!" Brialin laughed. "There is no such thing. It is knowledge; riches and the terror you inflict on others that lets you rule the world. Not faith. It was never faith." Richard stepped back as if physically hit, his belief in the church rocked by the revelation that the Abbot was nothing more than a charlatan.

"I sent you out here to find the heart stone, to prove there was magic here that could grant a wish. Well I wish to be all-powerful, omnipotent, the very god you worship. Once I have destroyed you, removed all witnesses, I shall take my wish and the world shall know fear in the name Brialin."

"Not whilst I breathe." Richard replied.

"Nor I." Marcus groaned from the floor.

"That was the intention." The Abbot replied, his left hand sliding into the satchel and touching the surface of the blue book. "I shall grant you both a quick death."

The Abbot's right hand began to glow, as if he held a light source tightly in his fist. His fingers reddened as something pulsed within indicating the powers he was drawing to perform his conjuring. He opened his hand and a wall of force lifted the two monks crashing into them and sweeping them across the cobbles to smash them into the side of the *Vane Arms*. They hung there suspended above the floor, feet kicking, arms struggling but they were as bugs trapped in amber.

Brialin laughed again and started to walk towards them, his pacing slow and deliberate to build up the fear he knew they would both be feeling. He flexed his right hand and a ball of energy appeared, floating in the air, crackling ominously, its energy drawn from the electrical power that normally protected the bearer's book.

"I promise this will be very painful." He smiled.

* * * * * *

Scrave lunged with the spear, the barbed head missing Kerian's head by inches and catching on his cloak over his right shoulder. Kerian stepped to the side as the spear sliced past, his right hand coming up with the golden dagger, slamming against the crackling spear shaft, trying to force the weapon to the side and free himself. The dagger hissed angrily as its blades scored the dark surface, seemingly recognising this was a waste of its abilities and voicing its frustration.

The Elf tugged the spear back but the spearhead tangled with the dagger and Kerian continued his right turn, his left hand coming up to grab the shaft and halt his opponent's momentum. The two combatants found themselves tugging against each other, feet sliding on the slabs of stone as they sought to gain the advantage. Although Scrave held the higher ground, he was the lighter of the two and Kerian had fought against spear wielders before. With a roar Kerian yanked as hard as he could, pulling the Elf off balance and towards him.

Recognising his predicament, Scrave ceased all attempts to resist, his opponent suddenly finding Elf and spear flying towards him. Kerian tried to let go with his left hand and meet the charge as Scrave dropped to his step but he was already side on and the Elf slammed into him making his elderly opponent slide along the stone and teeter on the far edge. Kerian's feet struggled for purchase, determined to push his foe back but Scrave used his own momentum to angle further to Kerian's right before dropping to the floor, pulling his spear down with him and dragging Kerian awkwardly to the side, his cloak hopelessly tangled on the spearhead.

There was a loud rip and the spear suddenly came free. Scrave continued his slide, slipping off the stone slab and dropping down to the step below. Kerian turned trying to regain his balance and noticed his enemy now below him. Now Kerian held the high ground. Scrave whipped the spear around, the shaft whistling across the step above attempting to sweep Kerian's feet out from beneath him but the old man jumped and the spear slipped harmlessly past.

The serpent dagger continued to writhe in Kerian's hand, eager to enter the fray and taste the blood of his enemy, its movement unsettling to the fighter. He tried to ignore the feeling of cold scales sliding across his skin and focused on the crewman below. He knew Scrave was dangerous, had seen him fight several times now and knew there was a ruthlessness he could not ignore. This was not a practice bout. The Elf was out to kill him.

Kerian paused at the edge of the step trying to judge what he should do. Then it came to him. The Elf was volatile so why not feed on this?

"You missed me!" he goaded. "I thought you wanted your dagger?"

"I will have it back." Scrave glowered. "It is only a matter of time."

"Fighting like that?" Kerian remarked. "It's a good thing I have this weapon. You would only end up cutting yourself."

Scrave started to pace backwards and forwards along the step below, his face turning darker as he tried to figure out how to retrieve his blade, the insults from his opponent causing the reaction Kerian desired.

"I am so going to kill you." Scrave roared. "You came in, tried to push me out of favour with the captain, took my weapon and my position on board the *El Defensor*. You ruined everything."

"Aww! Scrave is upset. Don't you know you are supposed to share your toys?" Kerian replied, his smile at the end of this deadpan delivery putting the icing on the proverbial insult.

Scrave roared, running forward and planting the spear on his own step, vaulting himself up into the air as Kerian stepped to the side and lashed out as the Elf moved past. The serpent dagger bit deep, tasting Elven blood as Scrave's arm passed within its reach. Scrave screamed in fury as he landed on Kerian's stone, his hand instinctively feeling for the wound but his opponent had no such issues and charged in, the golden dagger seeking further nourishment dragging the old man's right arm for further telling attacks.

The spear whipped around in response but Kerian was in too close, his left hand forcing the weapon down as his own blade lunged for the Elf's head. Scrave's free hand swept up catching the blade inches from his face, the two men wrestling, slipping and sliding on the stone, aware that below them bubbling lava waited to reward the first person to make a mistake.

Something screamed in fury above them and a downdraft blasted the two men as they fought, buffeting them both and making them close their eyes at the dust and debris whipped up around them. It appeared that whatever had returned to its lair was not happy about the uninvited guests. As the massive creature crashed onto the platform above everything shook and then someone fell over the side of the platform and plummeted past screaming. Kerian turned to look and his foot slipped on the stone, his boot suddenly finding nothing below it.

At the same second the dagger hilt, eyes blazing struck Scrave's wrist, its golden fangs slicing into his flesh. Both screamed out, one in shock the other in pain as they fell towards the lava, crashing onto the stone step below before rolling along it and falling to the next step beneath. The air blasted out of Scrave's body as Kerian crashed down on top of him and then the positions reversed, as the Elf slammed down onto his rival on the following step.

Kerian kicked out, sending Scrave into the air and then down onto the adjacent step. His foe slid off the far edge of the stone, legs kicking desperately, hand still grasping the crackling spear. It took Kerian a moment to gather himself, lying prone on the stone slab, stars passing across his vision from the tumble but he felt invigorated somehow, as if by using the dagger to harm someone it had somehow transferred some energy to him. He pulled himself to his knees and looked down to where his Elven adversary was still trying to pull himself up and kept slipping back down again, his determination to maintain a grip on the spear apparently his undoing.

"Scrave I don't want to kill you." Kerian stated, his mind trying to blot out the pandemonium from the platform above. "I just need to get to Colette make sure she is safe and then leave here. You can have your stupid dagger but I need it right now and my need is greater than yours."

Scrave slipped again, his face red at the effort to pull himself up. Kerian dropped down to the stone and walked over, looking down at the bubbling lava. It was closer than Kerian had realised. He then noticed that they were almost back at the temple steps. Had they really fallen that far?

"Come on. Just give me your hand." Kerian reached out to offer some assistance but Scrave kept trying to touch his left ear, refusing Kerian's gesture, a darker intention in mind.

"Flossador" Scrave spat, the earring crumbling from its housing, the jewel within turned to dust.

"Is that anyway to talk to someone trying to help you?" Kerian joked, trying to defuse the tense situation. The Elf stopped scrabbling for purchase and looked up at his opponent and simply smiled, bringing Kerian up fast. He had a split second to understand why Scrave was smiling and then looked in horror as his rival pushed off from the stone and levitated in mid-air.

"Now that's cheating." Kerian shook his head in disbelief and watched as his opponent started to walk around him as if he were on solid ground instead of hovering several feet above molten lava and more disconcertingly out of reach of Kerian's dagger.

"You of all people should know..." Scrave replied whipping the spear slowly around his torso, the blackened spearhead crackling as it cut the air. "I never play fair."

* * * * * *

Twin daggers flashed in the night. Blades angling in high, sweeping in low, clashing on the gleaming steel sword held by the knight known as Cameron. Mathius was one with his weapons, his assassin persona coming to the fore as he fought with a ferocity that the knight struggled to repel. He knew Marcus was safe; this was not the issue at stake. This knight had beaten him and The Raven never lost. Ever!

He swung his left hand in, the dagger blade plunging into Cameron's right forearm, forcing the knight's arm down, his sword now out of play. His other dagger flew up straight for Cameron's neck but the knight's free hand intercepted the blade, taking the foot of steel through the centre of his palm. Instead of the usual human reaction of pulling away, the knight continued to bear down screaming his rage, his strength immense.

Mathius refused to yield, his muscles tensing in response, his knees trying to hold the weight of the two of them as the supernatural fighter continued to push down. The cobblestones were slippery with falling ash, his leather boots slid then regained traction and he grunted with effort as he tried to force the knight to yield ground. It was a struggle of titans but a struggle The Raven had no intention of losing.

His boot slipped again, allowing the knight extra leverage and making Mathius feel his back was about to break. He had no choice but to drop to the floor and as he did, he threw himself backwards, kicking out and flipping Cameron over him and into the flames of a burning building.

The dagger through Cameron's hand ripped free taking half of the knight's hand with it. The dagger through his forearm remained wedged and ended up in the flames with the fighter. The Raven flipped himself from his back up onto his feet, his one free dagger coming up in front of him, blade held down, his other arm ready to guard for the next attack. He noticed the knight lying in the flames and smiled. The creature was made of manuscript. Now he could see if it burnt like paper did.

Cameron sat up and then slowly stood to his feet, his ruined hand indeed on fire. The Raven watched intently, a cocky grin sliding across his face as he watched the flames licking the exposed manuscript tightly coiled within the knight's ruined hand. He remained balanced on his toes, expecting the knight to move from the flames, show some sign of pain and react accordingly. Instead Cameron looked calmly at his burning limb then took in an impossible breath and blew the flames out, leaving nothing but a few glowing embers.

The grin disappeared from Mathius's face like ice melting in the sun. What did you have to do to kill one of these things?

Cameron roared and lunged forward, his sword swinging, the silver blade sweeping through the air inches from Mathius's nose as The Raven stepped back and then moved in as the weapon sliced past. He battered the knight with his dagger, using the hilt, the pommel and the blade to inflict hit after hit on a face that refused to bleed, a body that refused to bruise and a target that simply refused to die.

The sword whistled in a returning arc, catching Mathius off guard and crashing into his side. He rolled with the blow, moving further into the burning house, the knight unconcerned for his own safety closing swiftly. The fire roared around them, the smoke making Mathius eyes smart, glowing embers dancing between the two fighters neither of which accepting defeat. Cameron tried to pull The Raven's dagger free from his arm but without fingers on his hand, he was unable to do so.

Mathius picked up a vase standing on a table not yet consumed by the inferno and threw it with dead accuracy smashing the ornament on Cameron's brow before he darted in, his dagger stabbing repeatedly in and out of the knight's side.

Cameron spat his defiance and battered Mathius to the floor with the hilt of his sword. As The Raven hit the charred rug, he kicked out with his legs, catching Cameron on the back of the knees and making the knight fall forward into a cupboard already aflame. The knight pulled himself from the wreckage then lunged at the assassin, who was already rolling away and into the clear.

A loud creaking sounded from above as the structure became unstable. Mathius finished his roll, got back onto his feet and noticed that the beams were sagging dangerously, crackles like lightning echoing through the house. Cameron charged in sword leading and Mathius spun in place, rolling along the outside of the knight's sword arm, plucking his dagger from the creature's arm before pushing off his back and sending the supernatural creation further into the building right under the burning timbers.

There was a roar and then the whole ceiling came down, smashing into Cameron slamming the knight to his knees. A large beam exploded at the stress placed upon it and crashed down upon the knight's head, the smouldering splintered end spearing through his neck and deep into the floor.

Mathius staggered, his breath whistling in and out in the smoky atmosphere. He looked down at the struggling creature, its arms jerking and moving spasmodically and then brushed the hair back from his own face.

"I told you I would make you kneel."

* * * * * *

"Come on, come on!" Aradol shouted from the deck of the *El Defensor*. "You all need to move faster." The ragged line of women and children filed up the gangplank, to find shelter under tarpaulins erected on deck. Other crewmembers stood in a thin line upon the dock, armed to the teeth, their nervous gazes ensuring that every straggler was safely aboard.

Violetta came up the gangplank with her daughter, her face instantly happy the second she felt the safety of the ship beneath her. She noticed Aradol and swiftly moved over to him.

"Have you seen Rowan?" she asked breathlessly.

"No, I don't think so." Aradol replied, looking over at Austen and seeing the same blank gaze. "She hasn't come in so far."

"She ran off after a stray." Violetta replied. "We had to take a wide path around due to the fire and I was hoping she would be here by now."

A little girl walked up the gangplank, her hand held firmly in the innkeeper's grasp.

"Charleton have you seen Rowan?" Aradol asked. "She appears to be missing."

"She went off after Violet." Charleton confirmed. "I'm sure she will catch up soon."

Aradol shared a look with Austen that spoke volumes.

"Get Commagin. We need to find her." He looked back at the blazing inferno the village had become and watched a couple of houses collapse as roaring flames engulfed them. "We need to find her now."

* * * * * *

Colette moved across the platform her heart in her throat. Scrave had jumped over the edge after Kerian and he had looked so evil. She had seen the Elf lose his temper before but he was way beyond that point. It was as if something had possessed him with a purpose that was terrifying and he was wielding *Wizardseeker*.

She noticed the thugs getting back to their feet near the edge of the platform, so moved away from them angling herself back to where Atticus lay on the floor wrapped in the lengths of her purple hair ribbon. He looked like a caterpillar stuck in a cocoon. She did not mean to laugh but seeing his feet wiggling from the end made her emit a nervous giggle as she reached the precipice.

The blast of heat rolled across her face as she looked over, her eyes darting to the stairs trying to focus through the rising fumes. Her pulse raced as she tried to spot Kerian. He had to be there somewhere. She moved along, suddenly recognising two figures struggling on the steps. Was that Kerian? One of them fell, making her breath stall in her throat as he tumbled. Was it Scrave? She had no choice, she had to get closer, had to see if she could help.

"You bitch!" screamed a voice. Colette snapped her head around and turned straight into the right hook thrown by Atticus. He shrieked his satisfaction, landing two more blows, the violet ribbon dangling ridiculously from his hair; now back to its normal size as Colette's spell dissipated.

Colette fell to the floor, stunned; realising that she had failed to consider the length of time her cantrip had remaining. Her spell was just short term, unfortunately too short term. Her head smacked off the floor making her bite her tongue. She tasted copper and looked up into the face of the raging guild master.

"I am going to kill you now." Atticus snarled, walking over to his dropped dagger and retrieving it. "I need to show you that you have to do as you are told. I don't like it when people disobey me. I also don't like it when people make me look foolish. You should have known better."

He lifted his dagger high in the air.

The roar of anger froze him in mid-strike. A blast of air slammed down into them both, forcing Atticus to use his arm to protect his eyes from the blast as a creature from legend crashed down onto the platform beside him.

Rosalyine's enormous head swooped down, maw open wide, crystal teeth like glass swords and bit down hard, Atticus's head disappearing into her mouth as her teeth plunged through his torso. The dragon shook him angrily from side to side, before she opened her mouth and smashed him forcefully into the cave wall. His body hit the wall with a sickening thud before he slid down it to come to rest on the floor, blood oozing from his shattered body.

Before Colette could voice her thanks, the dragon was turning, crystal tail whipping out catching one brigand and spilling him over the side to plummet to the lava below. The creature stomped angrily around the platform turning her attention on the four remaining thugs and advancing on them with murderous intent in her eyes.

One of them stepped back and calmly drew his weapon whilst the others stood frozen at the sight of crystalline death barrelling towards them. The dragon pounced like a cat, talons lancing through one man, blood spraying across the floor, her wing batting out and knocking another from his feet. The man who had calmly drawn his sword moved forward as the dragon turned, his eyes blazing green.

Colette picked herself up from the floor and ran back to the edge of the platform, her eyes frantically following the path down to the temple. It twisted backwards and forwards, her eyes following the same convoluted track, until she noticed the two tiny figures fighting right at the very bottom. Her foot kicked something discarded by the fleeing men and she tore her gaze from the temple to notice it was Kerian's sword and scabbard.

The dragon roared again, the ceiling shaking high above them, pieces of rubble falling free and crashing to the platform making Colette stagger. She sensed the danger before she saw it, dropping to the floor as the dragon's tail swept above her and smashed into another mercenary sending him spinning end over end to slam into a wall. She scooped up the blade, went to fasten it around her slim waist then laughed at the absurdity of it. Kerian was a lot wider than she was! Shrugging, she tucked her head and one shoulder through the belt and positioned the blade so it nestled comfortably between her shoulder blades. She knew she had no way of drawing the weapon from this position but she had no intention of using it, just keeping it secure whilst she made her way down to the temple.

Another brigand disappeared into the dragon's mouth; well the top half did. The bottom half just flopped onto the floor, legs twitching. The dragon looked down in shock as one thug lunged with his sword, the weapon cracking off her crystalline armoured hide. This one was different. She turned to look at him more closely, her nostrils flaring, taking in the man's scent.

"A demon!" she snarled. "What are you doing here?"

"That's none of your business." The ghoul snapped. "Why did you have to arrive and spoil everything? Styx was in my grasp. I would have been free when he came back up those steps. Do you know what I have had to put up with, remaining on the ship with that crime lord cretin and his stupid dog? I'm the last one in this world of three and I will not fail in my task."

"Steps?" Rosalyine roared, turning to look back where Colette stood at the rim of the platform. The scoundrel used the distraction to his advantage, moving in with his sword and levering the edge under an exposed flexed scale and snapping the crystal free to reveal a weak spot below.

The crystalline dragon realised instantly what she had done and moved back, her feet smashing down onto the platform attempting to crush the upstart that had tried to harm her. The thug twisted and turned, running between the dragon's legs making her twist and turn in frustration. With an angry snarl, she slammed down onto him, crushing the re-animated body he now possessed.

Rosalyine got back to her feet and pounced on the body a few more times, agitated at the green mist oozing from the body. It slithered across the floor eager to escape the dragon's wrath and sank into the mosaic floor.

Colette watched the dragon smash the last man's body into the ground. The noise of the battle was so intense that although she thought she heard the man speak to the dragon she had not been able to make out any words. No one was left standing out of Atticus's henchmen, which meant that once the dragon had finished playing with her food, she was going to turn her attention on one trespassing ship's mage.

She was not going to wait around for that to happen. Colette tapped her bracelet three times, waited for the metal to glow in response and then stepped down into the abyss.

* * * * * *

"You know what Rauph. Someone's got a bonfire going out there over by the village." Ashe remarked, his nose squashed up against a dirty window that looked out across the harbour towards where the *El Defensor* lay at anchor. "I wish I could see better..."

Rauph came over, took one look at the smeary glass and the rotten frame and pushed, sending the whole window straight out of its housing with a loud crunch. The frame sailed through the air before crashing into the black waters of the harbour, allowing a cold breeze to rush inside the boathouse setting everything rattling behind the two observers.

"They have got a bonfire!" Ashe exclaimed, his view now unrestricted, revealing the reflected flickering light of the flames upon the mirrored surface of the sea. "Oh, do you think they have sausages and fireworks. Can we go and see?"

The Minotaur looked down at his sorely beaten, swollen and mutilated companion and shook his head, amazed the Halfling could still have such enthusiasm for life despite all of the pain and suffering he had been through. His freshly bandaged little hand hid mangled fingers and an absent thumb under a relatively clean rag. Furthermore, despite his mottled face, Ashe's smile, absent a few key teeth, still managed to beam through the muck and gore.

"We can't go." Rauph explained sadly. "Thomas said I have to stay away from the villagers in case I scare them." Ashe looked up at his towering companion, all his hair sticking up, a large bump on his forehead, horns gleaming and swords poking out from the scabbards on his back.

"Scary, not a chance." the thief replied, making Rauph attempt a smile in that terrible way only Rauph knew, instantly transforming him into a monster looking like he was about to eat someone up. "Oh, no...hang on... I can see it now." The Halfling laughed aloud.

Ashe always tried to remain positive. If he could not go to the bonfire maybe there was something in the boat house that he could do. He looked around, taking in the sleek, silver lines of the sailing ship that now stood abandoned, her repairs clearly not completed. The cool wind rushed in over the Ashe's shoulder, making the lines and the canvas of the ship ripple and jangle, before it passed out the far side of the shed through a broken window, where an unfortunate member of Atticus's crew still hung after coming face to face with an enraged Minotaur.

The Halfling's eyes lingered on the ship and a little light came on in Ashe's mind, allowing his aches and pains to move to the back of his thoughts.

"Rauph, can we have a look on board the ship?" he asked. "Maybe there is some treasure or equipment we can take back to the *El Defensor*. Can we Rauph, can we?" He fluttered his eyelashes and tilted his head in an exact imitation of the puppy dog sitting behind him, so that both Halfling and dog were looking up at the Minotaur.

The navigator threw his hands up in resignation, at least this way he could keep an eye on the little man and make sure he came to no harm.

"Okay." he replied. "But we must get back before it's light, so that Thomas doesn't get angry with me." Ashe had already gone, hobbling off across the gangplank. His keen eyes taking in the smooth lines of the vessel as his mind escaped into his persona of Captain Ashe scourge of the seas.

"You know we could steal this ship!" Ashe declared, his overactive imagination already having him pillaging ships and being a name spoken in hushed fearful voices by those who dared to navigate the shipping lanes. "We can sail up alongside the *El Defensor* instead of walking all the way back along the beach. Ooh... that would make us partners in crime."

Rauph looked at the rigging with a critical eye and then moved forward to check out the hull. The ship did appear salvageable and they were looking for a few choice parts for the *El Defensor*. It actually was an idea worth considering. He looked to the front of the shed where the barred doors stretched down to the water, and then he took in the lines where Atticus's crew had tied the ship off. He tutted aloud, noting the lax way the lines had been coiled. The ship could have easily floated away from the buoys if the tide had been strong, especially with the amount of slack lying on the stone floor. It appeared that the locked doors were the only things keeping the vessel in place. He moved to have a closer look, noting the rub marks on the wood where the boat had been nudging up and down but then Ashe jumped up enthusiastically in front of him again waving his arms about.

"I want to open the sails." He gushed excitedly. "I know I can do it. I have seen the others do it on the *El Defensor*. It's this line here isn't it?"

"No!" Rauph yelled. "Don't touch that yet we haven't opened the..."

There was an explosion of cream canvas, sails catching in the cross wind from the open windows and billowing to their maximum, snapping taut, obscuring both Ashe and Rauph's vision. The *Quicksilver* jumped forwards, the prow of the ship smashing at full force into the barred door, splintering wood like a cannonball fired at close range. Her sails and rigging pulled to one side, catching on the wooden beams and walkways of the building, tearing and slamming the boat into the stone jetty. Creaks, groans and agonising screeches filled the air.

The building shivered in protest as the lines snapped this way and that across the floor, as if they were alive. Anyone watching the boathouse from the shore would have seen it literally leap forwards from its foundations, before the whole building started collapsing in on itself with a groan, planks of wood and terracotta tiles piling into the water. The *Quicksilver* continued to crash its way through the opening it had made and out into the harbour, everything above the main deck swept off by the bottom edge of the destroyed doors as if the rough splintered timbers were part of an enormous broom. The ship's bottom half surged out before the lines securing her came taut with a twang and any part of the boathouse that remained standing finally succumbed to gravity and crashed in on top of all the other debris.

"Oops!" A little voice stated from somewhere beneath the billowing clouds of dust and debris. There was a cough and a splutter then a huge shape lifted out of the rubble alongside him.

"Did anyone see us?" Rauph asked, looking frantically from side to side as wooden beams and tiles continued to rain down about them. "Thomas said we were not to be seen."

"I don't think so," Ashe coughed loudly, taking in the destruction they had both caused with his one working eye that was not swollen shut. "I think if we leave now, maybe no one will notice all of this."

"I guess we are walking back to the *El Defensor* after all." Rauph commented, shaking his head and dislodging a piece of crumbled tile from his fringe.

"Ooh! Can we look at the bonfire on the way?" Ashe asked, his mind instantly looking for another exciting diversion.

"No!" the Minotaur replied, leaving no room for argument. "We cannot!"

Chapter Fifty-Three

"Out of my way you fool!" Justina snapped, pushing the young acolyte from her path as she swept along the shadowy passageways of the Serpent temple in Catterick. She held her scrying bowl in her arms like a young babe, the surface flickering and highlighting her face in warm oranges and yellows.

The priestess arrived at Pelune's bedroom chamber, barged in, her black robes flowing about her offering a glimpse of shapely thigh and curved breast to anyone who dared look. Pelune gasped at the shock of the interruption, breath rasping from his frame his body shrunken and emaciated since the loss of his dagger and the unnatural sustenance it used to supply him.

Justina charged over to the bed and lowered her bowl into Pelune's lap so he could stare deep within and share the vision she beheld. Two men were fighting in what looked like the heart of a volcano. It took a moment for the High Priest to spot his golden dagger, wielded by an old man Pelune had never seen before. As they looked on a black spear tip entered the scene and scored a hit across the old man's brow drawing blood and making him step back staggering.

"My lord," Justina purred. "We have found it!"

* * * * * *

Kerian fell backwards his hand reaching up to check the spear wound on his forehead. Fingers came back marked with scarlet but he had no time to recover as Scrave's attacks were relentless, darting in scoring hits with his crackling spear and then stepping away across thin air, well out of reach of Kerian's dagger.

Things were getting uncomfortable. Scrave had hit him on the left leg, the right arm and now his head, the spear whistling in and catching him because he had nowhere to manoeuvre on the stone slab. Everywhere he stepped the Elf was there, lunging, stabbing and wearing him down.

The spear tip shot forwards and Kerian turned with inches to spare, grabbing the shaft in desperation as it moved past him. Scrave yanked the weapon back, leaving him with the only option to release his grip or fall from his precarious perch. The blade whipped through his hand and sliced cleanly across his palm making Kerian cry out in pain.

"Who's upset now?" Scrave taunted, stepping across in front of him, moving between the steps and the temple entrance. "Are you ready to die Denaris? I'm ready to help yo... Where is it?" Scrave stood stock still as if suddenly in a trance and Kerian saw his chance and acted running forwards and throwing himself directly at his opponent. He closed his eyes, knowing this was going to hurt but also aware that staying where he was would only result in one outcome.

The two fighters smashed into each other, Kerian's momentum pushing the Elf back through the air towards the huge temple steps. The serpent dagger hissed angrily, trying to adjust to the unexpected actions of its wielder, trying to adjust to his wrist and score a strike, but Scrave's clothing saved him from the worst of the damage.

They smashed into the pillars of the temple, jarring together and falling onto the steps in a disorganised heap. Kerian rolled away, his body crashing down the steps, his arms reaching out desperately, trying to find any means to halt his descent. He hit the last step just as his cursed blade realised the imminent danger it was in and acted on its own accord or risk being plunged into the lava. The dagger slid into a crack in the masonry bringing him to a halt that nearly tore his arm from his socket and left him hanging out over nothing, legs kicking in thin air.

Kerian looked up at the snake writhing at his wrist and realised that if the weapon wanted it could simply let him go and he would plunge to his doom. The ruby eyes gleamed in the light, golden coils curling around his wrist, adjusting its tenuous grip. He hung there, the moment stretching out as the snake slowly manoeuvred its way around and started to draw him up from the drop. Clearly, it had considered the options and felt it still needed him.

He swung a boot up over the edge of the last step and pulled himself to his knees, trying to ignore the tremors of tension in his arm. He took a deep breath and looked up to where he had last seen Scrave but the Elf was no longer there.

This was not good! Tactically he had an advantage of knowing the territory but Scrave was clearly not himself and completely unpredictable. He advanced slowly up the steps, checking every shadow, his heart in his mouth, unaware that above him Colette was slowly making her way down towards him.

He stepped onto the mosaic path and started to make his way through the pillars. It was dark here before the temple opened to the wide area beyond, the darkness now a potential ambush site, every creak, crack or sound magnified to a threat. Kerian inched forwards his palms sweating. Where was he?

His boot came down on some loose coins that had spilled into the passageway and his boot shot forward making his head move up as he fell and the black spear whistled across his vision, right where his head should have been. Kerian could not control his fall and slid onto his back as the barbed spearhead slammed into the pillar across from him cutting deep into the masonry and leaving little to the imagination as to what damage it could have done to his head if it had connected.

Scrave cursed loudly, the weapon momentarily trapped and started to tug it free as Kerian rolled and scrabbled forward on the loose surface trying to give himself much needed space. He ran up to the statue of the rearing horse and slid behind it, putting a barrier between him and his foe. The Elf yanked his weapon free and turned with spittle on his lips and death in his eyes. He ran blindly across the coins, his Elven heritage maintaining his balance and making the journey in a much more dignified manner than his opponent had.

The spear lunged through the gap in the horse's legs and Kerian brought up the golden dagger, screaming out with the effort as he tried to push the shaft up and snap the weapon using the statue's legs as leverage. There was a dull twang and the front leg of the stallion snapped free, spinning Kerian around and making Scrave bellow in surprise.

Kerian fell hard into the coins, disorientated, dizzy, his hair coming free and moving in front of his eyes. A river of gold slid towards him, washing over his body, half-burying him as the mirrored shield he had seen earlier slid down towards him.

Scrave screamed out in triumph and plunged his spear down, slamming the tip into Kerian's leg. The fighter cried out in pain as the barbed head crunched through bone and grated on the gold coins beneath. It felt like fire was running up and down his limb. He lashed out with his dagger but it was useless, Scrave stepping back out of reach and viciously twisting the head of the spear crunching the barbed weapon inside his limb.

Kerian threw his head back against the coins in shock, screaming out in agony, teeth clenched, veins bulging in his forehead but Scrave was not content to let him writhe on his blade and yanked it free, tearing the hole even larger, letting blood shoot from the wound. The old man almost passed out with the pain but realised to do so was to die. He grabbed the shield from the pile of coins and swung it with all his might, clipping the spear and knocking Scrave to the side.

The Elf recovered in seconds, whipping the spear back around his body and jumping forward, the spear angled for Kerian's chest. The shield swung in deflecting the blow, then again as Scrave continued to try to pin him to the floor. Kerian batted the spear away but his strength was ebbing, the pain in his leg making it hard to concentrate.

Scrave stepped back, amused at the distress his opponent was showing. It was time to end this. He hefted the magical spear to his shoulder and threw it as hard as he could; knowing instinctively that the enchanted weapon would pierce the shield and strike true.

The spear shrieked towards its target, energy crackling along the length of the shaft. Kerian threw up the shield in desperation, knowing that his attempt to deflect the weapon was wishful thinking at best, especially at such close range and he closed his eyes tightly waiting for the inevitable. Instead, it shot past him, its path so close that his hair moved. Then the spear headed towards the exit of the temple, howling loudly as it sought out the very thing it was created to destroy, the strongest wielders of magic.

******

"Violet please come over to me." Rowan pleaded.

"I'm afraid we cannot allow that." the knight replied, pulling the small child closer to him and making her cry out in concern.

"Please don't hurt her." Rowan stated.

"Then come over here!" the knight replied ominously, his colleague swinging his sword and adding to the threat.

Rowan bowed her head apparently in defeat, whilst her mind raced trying to figure out how she would deal with this. She had dealt with her fair share of bullies in a male orientated world but these men were armed with swords! To make matters worse she was standing here in a ball gown like a lost princess from a child's cartoon.

She briefly considered showing a generous piece of leg in the hope of distracting these terrifying men but then she reconsidered. These people did not intend to look at her as a sexual object, they wanted information on where the villagers were taken and they looked more than capable of using their weapons to extract such knowledge.

With a swish of dress, she stepped forwards hoping that some sort of inspiration would head her way. The first knight gripped Violet tighter making her wail, his expression threatening much worse if she did not get over to him quickly.

"Okay I'm coming, I'm coming." She stated mouth dry.

"Oh, Rowan dear, there you are!" a voice shouted, some exasperation evident in the tone. "Gentlemen thank you for so kindly keeping her safe from all these fires." Everyone turned to see a young man walking calmly towards them an ancient sword held lightly in his hand.

"Aradol." Rowan whispered to herself, her heart soaring at the sight of a proverbial knight in shining armour coming to rescue her. She raised her voice.

"I lost Violet," she stated turning back to the knights. "These kind men seem to have found her."

"Oh Rowan." Aradol sighed, shaking his head. "How many times have I told you to do your boots up properly."

Rowan stood open mouthed. What was Aradol on about? Indeed, how could he even tell her boots were untied, she could not even see them herself in this flowing dress.

"Please do your boots up." Aradol stated again. "I don't want you to have any accidents." His eyes were wide and he seemed to be gesturing with small nods that she needed to tie her boots. It did not make any sense.

The knights moved closer dragging Violet along with them. Aradol closed the distance as well, his hand gripping the hilt of his sword tightly.

"Duck." He whispered and then shouted. "I won't tell you again. Do up your boots!"

Rowan finally understood what he was asking her to do and she dropped to the floor as a loud roar sounded from behind Aradol and he too dropped to the ground. The air filled with whirring quarrels passing just overhead, missing Aradol, Rowan and Violet by inches and slamming into the knights lifting them from their feet and throwing them back against the houses at the far end of the alleyway.

The quarrels continued to fire stitching up the wall into the thatch of one cottage and then out into the sky clipping the wing of an errant seagull that loudly squawked its annoyance at the loss of a couple of tail feathers.

Rowan lifted her head and looked back past Aradol as the quarrels ceased filling the air. The silhouetted figure of the Dwarven engineer Commagin stood in the entryway, a large crossbow in his hands.

"Well done Janet!" he exclaimed to the weapon, kissing the silver engravings.

Aradol ran for Violet, picking her up from the floor and dusting her down.

"Are you okay?" he asked. Violet shook her head crying loudly. Rowan moved over trying to hush her but Aradol put his hand on her arm, drawing her attention to the fact that the knights were slowly pulling the quarrels from their bodies.

"Run." He stated calmly, "follow Commagin back to the ship now!"

"What about you?" She asked.

"What about me." Aradol smiled back. "I'm going to be the one running in front of you!"

* * * * * *

Colette judged the next step and dropped down unsteadily. These steps were so big! The drop was also a little worrying. She moved to the edge and heard a strange sound rising from below. It seemed to be a scream or a shriek or...

Something black and menacing streaked from the temple and changed direction to shoot up the steps towards her. Colette did not need any further information. She knew what that thing was and she knew what it was looking for. She turned around heart in her throat and struggled to take a step back up. Kerian's stupid sword was making it hard for her to move freely but she knew she was not going to drop it for anything.

She ran across the step and moved to take the next one the shriek getting louder and louder in her ears. There was nothing she could do, no shelter to be found, she was out in the open and *Wizardseeker* was bearing down on her. She looked back over her shoulder and almost swooned. It was so close!

Colette ran for the next step and tripped, sprawling headfirst across the step as the spear shot towards her. This was it. She was going to...

The spear shrieked overhead and kept going whipping up over the edge of the platform and striking true at the target it had sensed.

Rosalyine screamed in pain as the black spear slammed into her chest, right where the crystal scale had been levered away. The blade had identified her area of weakness and acted on it, piercing her hide at just the right angle. The wickedly barbed head of the spear spun as it entered, tearing its way towards her heart. The crystal guardian roared one last defiant bellow then crashed to her knees, her talons trying desperately to stop the spear from digging any deeper. Blood jetted down her front, making her crystal claws slick and her grip tenuous. She crashed to the floor of the platform and then she lay still, her breath slowing, aware she had been brought down protecting the person she loved.

* * * * * *

Mathius ran from the burning building and out into the street, instantly noticing the figures of Richard and Marcus pinned up against the wall of the *Vane Arms* jerking and jumping as arcs of electrical lightning danced across their bodies, the thin figure of the Abbot waving his arm and directing the energy to do the most effective damage to the struggling crewmen. He put his head down and pumped his arms, daggers leaping into his hands as he threw himself through the air to collide with the thin man.

It was like hitting a wall. He smashed into something that felt like stone, bounced off and slammed into the base of the wall to find himself looking up the tunics of Richard and Marcus.

“Gentlemen! Please!” he groaned. “Can’t you at least wear pants if you are going to hang around like this?”

Thomas skidded to a stop beside him. Weyn guarding his back, bow drawn, arrow knocked for all the good it was going to do them.

Marcus stopped shaking as the electrical ball dissipated, the Abbot’s concentration broken by the full-on collision.

“G...G...Get the book!” he stammered.

“What book?” Mathius replied, looking back up at Marcus and getting another eyeful. He rolled over, shaking his head, looking back at the Abbot and noticed the book hanging from the bag at his side. “Oh, that book. Now how exactly are we supposed to do that? I can’t even get near him.”

Thomas looked over at the book and nodded in agreement equally unsure until he saw a knight come up and stand alongside the abbot. He was a lot closer than they had managed to be.

“Come with me!” Thomas shouted. “I have an idea.”

"How did I know he was going to say that?" Mathius groaned, shaking his head and leaping up after the departing captain.

The two men ran across the cobbles, splitting up to outflank the knight alongside Brialin. He acted predictably, moving forward, away from his Master, bringing his sword up in preparation to fight.

"Weyn now!" Thomas shouted. The air filled with arrows streaking between the two running crewmen, blasting into the knight, knocking his sword from his hand. "Now get him!"

"Get him?" Mathius yelled. "Are you serious?"

Thomas and Mathius jumped as one colliding with their armoured foe and bringing him down in a crash that reverberated from the houses around them. Fists flailed, feet kicked and with a roar of triumph Thomas and Mathius stood up swinging the unfortunate knight between them. They turned around and ran towards the Abbot, the knight kicking and screaming in their arms.

The Abbot's eyes widened at the sight and his hand reached for the book at his side to draw power for another spell. The four of them slammed into each other and paper manuscript filled the air like snow in a blizzard. Brialin fell over backwards as the knight collided with him, his teeth clacking together, his robes flying up as he fell to the floor with a crash. The spell holding Richard and Marcus to the wall of the *Vane Arms* fizzled and then died, freeing the two men to fall to the floor, where they quickly dusted themselves down.

The Abbot roared in fury, struggling to get to his feet, only to watch his assailants flee into the *Vane Arms*, the doors slamming shut as he set off in angry pursuit. He would make these men pay. He gestured to the knights gathering around him and ran ahead confident his shield would keep him from harm. These men would suffer dearly for their impudence.

The doors were not bolted and Brialin crashed through without resistance, his face a mask of hatred. He walked into the centre of the inn and looked around him, his eyes taking in the food on the tables, the upturned seats, the drinks left on the counter. Where were they? He advanced further into the room checking the kitchens and the alcoves, the knights filing into the inn silently behind him.

Where were they? Had they climbed up into the rafters? He swung his head up then down again. They were not there either.

A loud noise was coming from behind the bar.

He walked around, his knights coming to a sluggish halt behind him.

"Mitchellos." He snapped. "Find out what that noise is."

The knight stood still and did not move to obey. What was it with people these days when he had to do everything himself? He stormed around the bar and noticed the open trapdoor, flour dust clouds wafting up into the room. Hanging above the opening was a lantern, the flame safe and secure behind the glass. Strangely, the lantern appeared suspended on an arrow shot into the cabinet above. The shaft gleamed black and gold in the light from the torches around it.

"Bartholomew get down there, see where it leads." Brialin ordered.

The knight refused to move. What was wrong with these knights? Brialin slid his hand to the bearer's book, ready to use the magic of the tome to compel the knight to do his bidding. The book was not in the bag. He must have dropped it when those stupid men threw the knight at him. Without the book, his shield spell would not function. He was vulnerable to harm. He turned towards the main doors of the inn determined to retrieve the book and continue after them.

The arrow holding the lantern suddenly winked out of existence and the lantern dropped into the base of the mill, the glass shattering on impact the flame igniting the tiny dust motes that filled the area and then raced along the spilt alcohol across the bar. The resulting explosion vaporized Brialin instantly.

* * * * * *

"You know I really liked that inn." Thomas remarked, turning to watch the top of the windmill fly up into the air, trailing sparks in its wake. Weyn paused alongside him clapping him on the back.

"You have to admit my idea with the arrow was amazing." He grinned.

"I really couldn't say," Thomas shot back, trying to hide his relief that the fight was over.

"See!" Weyn chuckled. "You were so amazed you are lost for words!" The party of five burst out laughing.

"Marcus!" Mathius yelped, walking over to his friend his face grimacing at every step. "You...could have...warned me...about the protection spell...on the damn book." He reached into his shirt and withdrew the blue bound volume, his body jerking in time to electric shocks leaping from the cover. Marcus took the book away as Mathius looked down onto his chest and took in the scorched hairs there.

"That better grow back." He grumbled to himself.

"What about the knights?" Weyn asked, still concerned they would be in pursuit.

"You don't have to worry about that." Richard interrupted. "Without orders they slowly fade back into the Bearer's book. We are safe now." Marcus looked warily at the tome in his hands apparently not as convinced as his colleague.

"There is one thing I'd like to ask." Ives interrupted, struggling to hold onto the squirming clawed fur ball known as Socks "Wouldn't it be nice to actually leave a port without burning the inn down in the process. I mean every inn so far!" The laughter rose again as the men headed for the harbour, the cleansing flames roaring approval behind them.

* * * * * *

Scrave watched in astonishment as the enchanted spear flew away from his outstretched hand and out of the temple. He took a few moments, looking around as if expecting the weapon to magically return. It was only when he heard Kerian groan in pain that he turned back to his opponent and the angry glower returned to his features.

"You seem to have lost your spear." Kerian laughed through the pain. "You can surrender any time now." The Elf charged across the coin littered floor and for a second his wounded opponent thought he was simply going to throttle him with his bare hands. Then Scrave stopped just short of him, reached under his cloak and slowly drew out the sword he had liberated from the knight at the church.

Kerian's face fell and he groaned anew as Scrave tested the blade for weight. Why was it that everyone but himself had managed to find a sword? He staggered slowly to his feet, wincing as he tried to bear weight on his ruined leg, clenching the shield tightly in his left hand and flexing his right, feeling the serpent dagger respond by coiling tighter around his skin. It all came down to this. A fight to the death in a dragon's lair deep beneath the earth.

The warm tracking of fresh blood down his leg was a distraction. Kerian realised he needed to attend to his wound but there was simply no time. He had seen Scrave fight with a sword and it was scary how fast the Elf could be. He knew his own melee skills were good in a fight but that was when he was on top form, not when he had a shattered leg and multiple lacerations from his earlier encounter with his opponent. He gritted his teeth and tried to spread his weight, his leg screaming in protest

Scrave charged, sword whistling through the air, the attack coming from up high. Kerian moved his shield to intercept the blow, the force of it pushing him down, sending vibrations along his arm to his elbow, his leg instantly giving up and dropping him to the floor as the blows rained down. He retaliated by lashing out with the golden dagger determined to score the Elf's leg and stop the attack but Scrave seemed to sense his lunge and his vulnerable legs seemed to disappear as he balanced perfectly on one hand on top of the shield his weight pushing Kerian even lower.

Kerian tilted the shield to one side with a grunt, tipping his opponent onto the floor where he rolled a few meters and then flipped gracefully up onto his feet. Kerian did not stop to check his opponent's actions but set off, moving as rapidly as his injured leg allowed to scramble over the pile of gold and jewels nearest him and slide down the other side. He was determined to put as much distance between himself and his attacker as possible, even though he knew he was leaving a trail of blood smeared gold coins in his wake. Scrave whipped the sword blade around in his hand and set off in pursuit.

"You won't get away that easily." He taunted, running up the shifting mound of coins as easily as if he were running on a flat surface. Kerian tried to run but his leg would not let him on the shifting surface of treasure. He sensed his opponent's approach and spun, bringing up the dagger just in time to catch Scrave's downward swing. The sword slid down between the twin dagger blades and clashed loudly when it encountered the weapons hilt, leaving the two foes face to face and much closer than Kerian would have liked.

The Elf tried to extract his larger blade as Kerian frantically twisted the dagger, trying to find a weakness in the long sword's length and shatter the gleaming steel but both weapons were forged from magic and neither would yield, much to both fighter's frustrations.

Kerian gritted his teeth and shoved as hard as he could, making Scrave lean forward to counter, then he head-butted the Elf as hard as he could, only to find himself staggering backwards, shocked at how hard Scrave's head was. His forehead started to swell as blood rushed to the site of the blunt injury.

Scrave found himself staggering backwards as well, equally stunned. However, the headband beneath his hair had taken most of the blow and he recovered more quickly, his sword now free allowing him to come back at his foe, the steel glittering as it moved through the air. Kerian parried blow after vicious blow; some on his shield and some with the serpent blade. He always lost ground, forever moving backwards towards the open space in the centre of the temple floor. The Elf's attacks came in high and low, sparks raining down on the fighter like rain as the edges of their weapons grated against each other.

The sword swung in low towards Kerian's wounded leg and as he swept his shield down to counter the blow, Scrave turned and delivered a mighty kick to its reflective surface, pushing Kerian backwards to sprawl across disturbed coins and gems right to the edge of the gap in the temple floor where the lava bubbled enthusiastically, mere feet away.

The Elf was on him in seconds, bludgeoning Kerian with the hilt of his sword, striking him repeatedly before catching the edge of the shield and spinning it away. Kerian wrestled with his opponent, desperately trying to avoid the razor-sharp edge of his foe's weapon. They struggled, sword against dagger, man against Elf, their movements more frantic and bestial as first one, then the other, threatened to roll their adversary into the molten rock below.

Kerian tried to push the Elf off balance but it was like fighting a berserker whose battle fury had taken full control of his body. Scrave appeared to have no concern for his own safety, intent on delivering as many possible injuries to his foe as possible. He lifted his sword high, determined to land a fatal blow but Kerian was fighting on instinct now, his dagger sweeping up to slice deeply into Scrave's wrist making the Elf jerk his arm back up, the sword flying from his hand to skate across the ancient treasures on the floor.

Scrave's eyes followed the sword and Kerian used the distraction to kick out as hard as he could, knocking Scrave from his feet and making him backpedal towards one corner of the pit. The Elf's heel slipped on the edge but incredibly, he flipped backwards, twisting his body like a cat falling from a tree to land on the adjacent edge, teetering precariously before he carefully regained his balance and stepped away from the danger of the lava. Kerian staggered in place as Scrave recovered, realising instantly that it was now a race for the sword. He spotted it further along the edge of the pit and tried to sprint but Scrave was faster, throwing himself back over the lava and tucking into a roll to pass harmlessly under Kerian's futile slash with his dagger.

The Elf bounced back to his feet, spun to a stop above the sword then slammed his foot down hard on the hilt making the blade jump up from the floor as he spun in place to catch it in the move he had practiced repeatedly in his drills.

"You are too slow." He taunted, his hand sweeping out to catch the spinning blade but he forgot to account for his off-balance foe. Kerian bulled full power into him, making Scrave miss the catch as the knight lashed out with the dagger, knocking the sword back up into the air. Scrave fumbled forwards, surprised at the speed his opponent had arrived, his hand snatching at thin air as he skidded on the coins.

The sword fell between them and they ran together, hands reached out blindly, scrabbling, fumbling striking each other, until Scrave gasped out in shock as both the long sword and the golden dagger slid into his chest. Kerian stared into the Elf's eyes and watched the awareness slowly drain from them, then he let go of the sword and let Scrave fall in a heap on the floor.

"Not as slow as you." Kerian replied, tossing the long sword to one side. The knight heaved in great gasps of breath, the serpent dagger still writhing at his wrist, amazed that he was even able to stand after their titanic struggle. Kerian had not wanted this. He had not wanted to kill Scrave. He did not even know why the Elf had wanted this cursed dagger in the first place. He groaned as waves of pain assaulted him. Blood dripped from his forehead into his eyes, his face hurt, his body hurt and his leg was on fire. He had been fighting on adrenaline alone and he was exhausted.

The bracelet at his wrist still flared brightly but it was nearly all the way around. There was five minutes remaining and no physical way that he could get back up the stairs to Colette and then back down again. His choice was made for him. He needed to make his wish and escape before the heat from the lava fried him. He turned his attention back to the small platform out over the lava and staggered towards it, wheezing and spluttering, his breath still struggling to get down into his bruised and battered lungs. The walkway was quite tricky to negotiate yet somehow he managed and finally he stood before his prize.

Kerian placed his hands on either side of the pillar and stared down at the jewelled heart trying to gather his thoughts. He had only one shot at this. One chance to make this right. The facets of the great jewel glittered as he looked on and he drew a breath in to make his important demand.

Something dark flickered across the surface of the stone. Several coins slid free and chinked against each other behind him. Kerian froze, pretending not to notice as the shadowy reflection in the mirrored surface moved closer. It appeared Scrave was not dead after all.

Kerian clenched his fist and slowly raised the serpent dagger, his eye not daring to blink from the indistinct shape moving closer in the jewel. If Scrave wanted the serpent weapon so damned much, he could have it! He took a deep breath to calm his shaking hand then turned and threw the dagger with all the strength he could muster.

...And Kerian's world shattered.

Chapter Fifty-Four

"No!" Pelune screamed, his body jerking, spasmodically as he thrashed about weakly on the bed. Spittle flew from his lips as he shook, his face drooping to one side as his body responded to the shock of the vision in the seekers bowl. He had failed again. The dagger was lost once more. He could not cope with such a thought and his mind shut down leaving him rocking slowly back and forth a shell of the man he once was.

Justina pulled away and gathered her things, trying not to smile as the priest reaped what he had sown. She cast her eyes over the man she had hated for so long and knew inside that her time to strike would be soon.

She walked to the doors of his room and opened them just as Vill ran up his face one of concern.

"I hear the Master is unwell." He stated. "I have come to see if I can be of help."

Justina placed a hand on the man's chest and pushed him back out into the hallway.

"Don't worry about him," she ordered. "He needs to be left alone to sleep. He has just had a bad dream. Nothing to worry about at all. It will all be over soon."

* * * * * *

"Get us out of here!" Thomas yelled, running up the gangplank, his eyes scanning the deck to see that everyone was well. His fellow adventurers raced up after him and lines were thrown as the crew jumped up into the rigging to free the sails and fill them with the ocean breeze.

"Not too far out." Thomas ordered thinking of the young children on board and not wanting the smell of vomit all over his ship. He took in the lines of her, the way the firelight from the shoreline reflected on her and thought he had never seen a more beautiful sight. Then a hand touched him on the shoulder and he turned to see Rowan and all the poetic feeling he had for his ship evaporated away in her beauty.

"You are safe." He beamed, sweeping her up into his arms.

"Of course!" she replied. "And so it appears, are you." Rowan teased away some debris in his fringe and tried to wipe away a line of soot on his face.

"Slightly singed but not overdone." She laughed.

"Wait for us, wait for us!" yelled two characters charging down the dock towards them. Thomas gestured quickly as the gangplank was lowered again allowing the two contrasting figures of Ashe and Rauph to gain access.

Constance looked up and screamed as Rauph charged on board, dropping to the deck in a swoon.

"What's wrong with her?" Ashe asked bemused. "I'm not that ugly!"

The crew laughed at the Halfling's obvious confusion, as Thomas continued to scan the decks doing a hurried head count.

"Kerian, Scrave or Colette?" he asked, turning to Commagin. The Dwarven engineer sadly shook his head.

"We've seen neither hide nor hair of them." He confessed.

"Let's just ease out far enough we are not at risk of the fire then drop anchor and give them a little more time. Okay?" the Captain ordered, failing to hide the concern on his face. "They just need a little more time."

* * * * * *

Time appeared to stop...

Kerian looked on powerless as Colette's eyes went wide in shock and disbelief as the serpent dagger struck her hard in the chest. She seemed to deflate before his eyes, falling backwards in slow motion to crash down amongst the coins like a discarded doll, limp and broken.

"Oh, by Adden no!" Kerian screamed, turning from his salvation and struggling back across the walkway, trying to run and close the gap, knowing in his heart that he would never be fast enough. The serpent writhed and twisted on her chest as she tried vainly to push the cursed snake away making Kerian sick to his heart.

There was no strength in her actions anymore, no future in her life.

Kerian crashed to his knees alongside her, ignoring his wounds over his concern for the woman he had come to love. He reached out trying to cradle her head whilst his other hand grabbed the serpent dagger and pulled it from her, hurling the cursed weapon away, not caring where it came to rest.

There was so much blood. Oh, by Adden, there was so much of it. He tried to stem the flow from her chest, tried to stop it with his cloak but the material simply became saturated.

"No, Colette. No!" Hot tears filled Kerian's eyes as he tried to brush the hair from her face and hold her tight. "Don't you leave me! Don't you dare! No, not now!" He rocked her gently and watched her eyes flicker open.

She tried to speak, blood tainted spittle coating her lips.

"K...Kerian." She said weakly, trying to focus and gather strength even as it ebbed out of her. "Are we going home now?"

"Yes Colette, we are." He said softly holding her tightly as his heart broke inside.

"Are you coming as well?" she smiled.

Kerian looked away, desperate to choke back the tears and then looked back down at her, brushing her hair away with fingers that felt numb. "I'll be right behind you." He cried.

Colette struggled to move her hand towards her chest and initially Kerian became confused, not sure what she was trying to do.

"No, don't touch it." He warned, trying to stop her hand, thinking she was going to touch her wound.

"My... my pendant," she gasped. "You can use it to find me if we get lost. Just hold it up in the rays of the sun at dawn and we will always find each other."

Kerian helped slip the pendant free and wrapped it firmly around his hand, continuing to rock Colette in his arms.

"Okay I've got it now." He smiled sadly. "Now we will always find each other."

"I was really looking forward to seeing you young... again." Colette smiled.

Then she slipped away in his arms.

* * * * * *

There was a huge drawn out sigh, a rasp of breath and then Rosalyine's eye cracked open. The pain from the spear was almost overpowering but she wanted to get back to her husband. With a gargantuan effort, she stretched out a claw and speared the floor then she gritted her teeth and pulled hard, her body sliding slowly across the floor. The pain almost made her pass out but she steeled herself and reached out again.

Nothing was going to stop her from being where she wanted to be.

* * * * * *

Kerian looked up, hot tears running freely down his cheeks. Had he just heard a noise from above? He looked down at Colette's body and fresh tears sprung to his eyes, he did not want to leave her, could not even consider it. He had no more time.

It did not matter anyway. Without Colette, there was no point in living. He glanced at the bracelet on his arm and noticed he now had a few minutes at most. He would stay at her side until the end. As long as they had some time left together, this was not goodbye.

He looked across at the jewel that he had travelled so far to find and then it occurred to him there was another answer to all of this. A way to make something good out of the tragedy he had found himself in.

"I'll be right back." He whispered to her, lowering her gently to the floor. Then he stood up, clenched his fists and strode towards the walkway.

He would never let this be goodbye.

* * * * * *

Rosalyine drew herself painfully to the edge of the platform and regarded the steps leading down to the temple below. She could never fly down, that much was obvious. She pulled herself further forward and the spear caught on the lip pushing even deeper into her making the large crystal dragon almost swoon with the pain. She had to remain focused. Had to keep trying.

She dug in and started to slide her huge body inch by inch over the edge.

* * * * * *

"Come on. Come on!" Thomas spoke to himself standing up by the helm alongside Rauph. Something was very wrong. They had been too long. He paced the deck and pulled the spyglass from his jacket to scan the dockside.

There was no one to be seen.

"Where can they be?" he asked.

For once, Rauph recognised the question for what it was, remaining silent and ever hopeful for his friend's return.

* * * * * *

Kerian lifted the jewel from the pillar and carried it back to where Colette lay, looking for all the world like she was sleeping on a bed of gold and jewels. He tried to smile but the tears threatened to overwhelm him. She had everything he had ever promised her. All the riches in the world.

He looked around and found her knapsack then glanced down at his bracelet. He was running out of time and had to be quick. He scooped in as many jewels as he could, as many coins and trinkets, filling the pack to capacity, then he swiftly returned to her side and placed the pack in her hands. He noticed the hilt of his sword sticking out from behind her shoulder, moved to retrieve it, then stopped. Where he was going he did not need it.

Dropping back to his knees, he lifted the jewel and looked deep inside not quite sure how to make it work.

"Jewel of the dragon." He began. "I am here to request my wish. I am here to have my heart's desire granted." For a second he thought nothing was happening and then he felt a presence near to him and turned to see a ghostly figure of a wise man standing nearby.

"I am Strathe, it is my heart you hold in your hands." The sage spoke solemnly. "Understand that you can have but one wish granted. There is no second chance. Speak freely and unburden your secrets, whisper to me your heart's desire and I shall grant it if it is within my power."

Kerian bowed his head trying to form his words, picturing Colette well and safely back on the *El Defensor*.

"I have my wish." He said, trying to hold back the tears. "I want her well again, safe aboard our ship, free from harm, free from pain."

"Are you sure this is your desire?" the sage asked, confusion and uncertainty on his face. "Are you sure you would not rather have something for yourself?"

Kerian considered his own predicament and fleeting thoughts of deliverance whispered to him. He gritted his teeth and held his head up high, tears flowing freely.

"No." he replied. "All I wish is for Colette to be well."

"So be it." The wise man nodded his head. "I will grant your heart's desire as I see this is truly what you seek and as it is a selfless wish at that, I can finally rest in peace." The ghostly image faded and glowing motes of twinkling light started to appear all over Colette's body as the jewel cracked cleanly in two, the light fading from its interior as Strathe granted his final wish.

Kerian leaned over and kissed her tenderly on the lips as the light grew brighter about her. There was a gasp and a deep intake of breath and Kerian stared into her beautiful eyes once more.

"K...Kerian what's happening to me."

"Don't worry." Kerian replied sadly. "Everything is going to be alright now. Just remember I love you. I always have, I always will. Look after my sword. I'll be along soon to collect it."

"What do you mean?" Colette jerked up, now fully aware. "What's going on? What do you mean you love me? Kerian your bracelet, you have no time left. Kerian I..."

Then she was gone.

* * * * * *

Thomas swept the dock for what felt like the thousandth time, still with no signs of his friends. A gasp made him look up quickly and several voices raised in horror as a light appeared in the middle of the main deck.

Villagers backed up scared, wondering what new terror this night held. Ashe took advantage of the fact to limp closer and see what new wonder was occurring. The light got brighter and brighter and then a figure started to appear.

"Kerian!" Colette screamed out; her hand outstretched to a figure no one else could see. "Kerian! Oh, dear god take me back. Send me back to him." She wailed bereft.

Violetta rushed over to take Colette in her arms, the mage's knapsack falling to the floor spilling gold and jewels across the deck. Ashe moved to place his foot over a spinning coin to prevent people pocketing it and then looked at Colette's face and the haunted gaze she returned. It stopped him in his tracks and he turned away, leaving the coin still spinning, forgotten on the floor. He met Thomas anxiously making his way down to her and stopped the captain with a raised palm, reaching into his pocket as Colette screamed Kerian's name again, even though she knew he could no longer hear her.

"I think you better give Colette this when she feels better." Ashe said, dropping something smooth and cool into his hand. "It's Kerian's. I think he would want her to have it."

Thomas looked down at the solemn Halfling and patted him gently on the shoulder.

"I will do that." He said, a lump forming in his throat. "I will do that."

* * * * * *

Kerian staggered slowly to the edge of the great temple, blood dripping from his wounds, his leg on fire but his heart as light as the clouds above. He sat down wearily and stared at his hands; looking at the rips and tears, the dripping blood and the liver spots on his skin and then froze. He had seen this sight before. It took him a moment and then he remembered. It was in a dream, when he was back in Catterick at Abbot Brialin's monastery.

How bizarre that his destiny had been revealed to him all those months ago. He looked down at the bracelet as it fizzled and crackled towards the end of its enchantment. It would not be long now. All his pain and suffering would soon be over.

"Where is Strathe?" a feminine voice gasped.

Kerian looked up and froze as he regarded the crystalline reptile before him. She was so old, so tired and in so much pain. He smiled as he considered the fact he was looking into a bizarre mirror. Did he look so old? Was he also so tired?

"If you mean the wise man from the gemstone," Kerian began. "He has gone now. His gem is broken. There are no more wishes to be granted."

"How did this happen." The dragon wheezed. "Are you responsible?" She growled in pain, her breathing so laboured it was painful to hear.

"I asked for a wish to be granted." Kerian confirmed, nodding his head. "Then the gem cracked."

"You asked for wealth, women and power I shall not wonder." The dragon wheezed closing her eyes. "You are all the same."

"No," Kerian replied. "I asked for my true love to be made well and sent somewhere safe."

"You what?" the dragon asked, her eye cracking open in surprise. "A selfless wish. Then Strathe is finally at peace."

"That's exactly what he said." Kerian confirmed looking down at the edge of his cloak and watching in fascination as a small spiral of smoke started to curl up from its edge.

"Then I can rest as well." The dragon sighed as if a huge weight had lifted from her shoulders.

"It's good you can be together." Kerian replied. "No such luck for me."

Rosalyine eased down another step taking in the old man sitting despondently on the steps before her with eyes, which despite being clouded with age; saw more than most people would know.

"And why, dear sir, can you not have the same thing?" she asked.

"I have run out of time." Kerian replied, feeling the heat starting to build in the soles of his boots. "I was cursed, doomed to age a year for every month I lived. Your jewel was the cure for that curse and I used it up. I can never be young again; can never find another love like the one I have just lost. In a few moments this bracelet charm will fail and I will cease to be."

"You are so sure about that are you?" The dragon gasped. "I sense magic about you."

"That's just the curse." Kerian replied, looking up at the magnificent creature before him. "But you know, I would not have lived these last months in any other way. The time I had with her was precious and I am a better man because of her."

"Would you go after her if you had the chance?" Rosalyine asked slyly, giving an exhausted smile.

"Of course I would." Kerian replied sadly.

"Then so be it." The dragon replied. "Let this be my parting gift to you."

Kerian sat back and laughed loudly.

"That's really funny." He smiled. "Thank you for making me smile at the end." He looked down at the bracelet one final time and the light finally completed its circuit and fizzled out.

So, this was it. This was how Kerian Denaris died.

The heat rushed in as the spell failed and from his chest the world flared green.

Chapter Fifty-Five

The pain of heartbreak is illogical; it makes no sense. Yet when I see those affected by it, clenching their chests as if suffering the most mortal of blows, eyes hollow and faces wracked in torment, I cannot deny the anguish and hurt that it causes.

I have only suffered heartache twice in my life; both times the pain was intense, sharper than a thrust of a rapier and leaving a wound deeper than could be seen with the eye. It left me not wanting to eat, not wanting to drink, wishing the pain would leave me but fearing that if it did I would learn nothing valuable from it. Lying awake all night staring at the ceiling, thoughts of insecurity running through my head, torturing me with what was, what could have been, if only I had made different choices, turned left instead of right, let an argument end before it began.

I see this in the eyes of Colette now.

Something has happened deep beneath the earth, below the church at Stratholme. Something between Colette and Kerian Denaris. Something earth shattering. She returned to us heart broken, carrying Kerian's sword and would let none of us take it away from her. Maybe...

Thomas paused in his musings, re-dipping his quill to continue his narrative in his personal log. He looked across his desk at where Rowan sat, relaxing as she looked through the pages of one of his favourite novels and cast her a reassuring smile before returning his attention to his log entry. His eyes lingered on the two items sitting beside the logbook and a fresh wave of sadness swept over him as he picked up his quill and began to write.

...In time Colette may reveal what happened, answer my gentle questions with answers I can understand. For now, the pain in her heart is too dark to share. Instead, she throws herself into her studies; she tells me that she has found an entry in Lucas Sumnar's old journals suggesting there is a possibility that using a prism can enhance the power from magical gemstones but it requires more exploration. Maybe we can find a less dangerous way to power the ship than the elemental. Maybe in time we can leave the ocean altogether and sail the heavens like this ship used to in her halcyon years. Maybe in time the ghostly mage will stop his wailing below decks and speak to us of these things, unlocking the mysteries that face us. Colette believes the extra power will open multiple doorways in the ship's graveyard, making the opportunities to find home faster than before.

I feel we are close to something here that I had long thought impossible, yet I dare not push for fear Colette may crack under the strain lurking behind her haunted eyes. Scrave and Kerian are clearly lost to us. Colette has confirmed they are gone but she has been sparse with details. The enchantments protecting them from the deadly heat in the temple have most certainly expired and Brother Richard informed us all how dangerous the vapours were within the dragon's lair.

I am sad to lose two valued members of my crew but as in all things, time moves on. We have taken on new crew members. Charleton helps Violetta in her kitchen, a tempestuous arrangement at best and probably not longstanding whilst Brother Richard has deemed he will join us along with his cat Socks. His skills of healing will be most useful on this ship and our little crewman Ashe requires serious attention from the torture he was subjected to. It has always been this way, the fluidity of the crew.

We set a fresh course early yesterday, heading due north looking for new ports in which to call, our dependence on gemstones dictating that we continue to search for stones powerful enough to navigate the ship's graveyard, although the treasures Colette returned with could be used at a push. Those refugees who requested it have been safely set ashore in a settlement capable of supporting them whilst the village at Stratholme is rebuilt. I shudder to think what would have happened if we had not been able to evacuate them all. When the time is right, we shall brave the terrors of the graveyard again and see if Colette can use her gems to get us where we all desperately wish to be. There are also more important matters to attend to. Demanding questions that need to be answered.

Thomas paused again and reached over to pick up the toy police cruiser sitting on the edge of his desk alongside Kerian Denaris's ring, turning the toy over in his hands, searching for a clue that would unlock the repressed memories in his mind. He needed to go back to the graveyard. There were answers there he desperately needed. Had Malum hypnotised him when they last met? Had he used his powers to gain the upper hand in the fight when they faced each other?

He had suggested Thomas was a killer. That this toy car was a trophy taken from a child victim.

The captain shook his head angrily; it was absurd to even consider such a thought! He did not kill unless it was self-defence. Malum really had got inside his head. He picked up the quill again, determined to finish his musings and put such dark thoughts from his mind.

J.M Barrie tells us to pick the second star on the right and head straight on until morning to find home. I do not have this luxury. I have no chart, no directions, just a will to go on and do the right thing. Until then I shall stand my watch, listening to my crew when needed, offering a comforting touch or word when allowed. Broken hearts can heal; it just takes time, understanding and a little patience.

I pray I have enough patience for all my crew in whatever troubled waters lie ahead.

Thomas stopped writing. His mind was not on this chore. He needed to walk the decks, mix with the people that relied on him, put on a brave face and lift their spirits, set an example, even though his own confidence felt so low. Rowan watched over the top of her book as he cleaned his quill and she smiled at him, flooding his heart with warmth.

Maybe a breath of sea air would do him some good. He would walk around the ship with Rowan and mix with the crew.

He scooped up Kerian's ring and the toy police cruiser, determined to put Malum's evil twisted thoughts to rest. A killer indeed. A collector of morbid trophies. He slid open his desk drawer to put the toy safely away and stopped dead, the realisation hitting him like a hammer blow, leaving him stunned as his eyes glanced over the contents within and the colour drained from his face.

"What's wrong Thomas?" Rowan asked noticing his sudden change in demeanour. Thomas could not bring himself to answer, horrified at what lay before him. He buried his face in his hands as Rowan hurried over, his trophy collection staring accusingly back at him.

* * * * * *

"There, there," Justina reassured Pelune, gently whispering into his cold ear. "Everything is going to work out just fine. You'll see."

She stroked his greasy hair, her eyes matching her lover's by staring off into space before she gently replaced the goose down pillow that she had used to smother him back onto the bed. She took in his haemorrhaged eyes with a deep sigh at her own stupidity at leaving such an obvious clue to his cause of death, then waved her hand over his face and made the crimson disappear with magic.

"Vengeance is mine!" she stated to her silent witness before sliding from the bed, her mind in a whirl of emotion as the sheets held around her finally fell forgotten to the floor.

Something did not feel right. What did she expect? A fanfare of trumpets at Pelune's demise? An unbearable sense of grief, rage or happiness, or was she expecting some tangible feeling of fulfilment at a job well done?

At this moment in time, she felt decidedly unsure of herself. Found herself confused and without direction, much like the current leadership void facing both the serpent cult and the Order of St Fraiser.

There was a thought. She knew both organisations well. Why could a woman not rule as well as a man? Justina contemplated herself in the mirror on the wall and smiled. It would be a thankless task bringing both religions together. Forming something stronger and more powerful than either Pelune or Brialin had imagined. It would take someone of strong character, someone ruthless who knew what she wanted and would stop at nothing to achieve it.

She looked at herself again with a critical eye and fluttered her eyelashes in an attempt to look demure. Something scurried across the floor and ran lightly up her back to perch on her naked shoulder chattering away in a language only Justina could understand.

"It's a tough one to call." She said to her reflection, looking at the monkey shaped skeletal demon perched on her shoulder. "But we think we know the perfect person for the job."

* * * * * *

Colette tossed and turned before finally looking around her cabin from sleep deprived swollen eyes. She still could not believe Kerian had sacrificed his life for hers. That he had made the decision to throw his future away so that she could live.

He had told her he loved her. Tears stared to well up in her inflamed eyes. How could life be so cruel? She slowly got to her feet and walked over to where her clothes sat neatly folded on her chair. Dressing was a numb affair, devoid of feeling, an automatic act of putting one hand in front of the other until she felt suitably attired to pass as someone civilised.

She stood looking down at the last item leaning against the chair and with a deep breath reached out to hold it, clutching the scabbard close to her chest as fresh tears flowed freely. The weapon was so heavy. The scabbard worn and aged with constant use.

Kerian's sword.

The One of Swords. A legendary blade with powers barely touched on by her owner.

The belt was too long to secure around Colette's waist and the blade too cumbersome to sit comfortably at her hip without hitting the floor at every step. She slipped the weapon up onto her back in the manner of how she had worn it in the dragon's lair and cinched the belt tight as if she were wearing a satchel about her, rather than a rune etched, enchanted blade.

Kerian had given her this weapon and told her to her to keep it safe until he came for it. Whilst she held it, despite the fact she knew he would never come to relieve her of her charge; she felt a strange sense of comfort. The blade was an enigma. Its runes had to mean something and Colette had the best reference library available near to hand. She wiped her eyes with her sleeve and took several deep cleansing breaths. She now had a purpose. She would discover the secrets of this sword and preserve the memory of the man who had sacrificed his life to save her.

* * * * * *

"The book is linked to you now." Brother Richard touched the blue leather binding of the bearer's book and then looked up at Marcus. "Its power is yours to access; you just need to know how to unlock it."

"What about the knights within?" Marcus asked. "They turned against me before. What's to stop them doing so again?"

"I can't answer that, Brother. Only time will tell." Richard replied. "Maybe it was the corrupting influence of Abbot Brialin? Maybe they were never really yours before. However, the Abbot is dead now; the book no longer has a Master. It is up to you to claim that power now and control it for the good of others."

"I'm scared to open it." Marcus confessed. "What if it's power gets loose and I can't control it?"

"We can take that journey together." Richard smiled, leaning forward and tapping the holy symbol hanging at Marcus's neck. "You, me and our faith."

Marcus picked up the book, held it close to his chest and closed his eyes, praying that his colleague was right. That he would have the strength to control the book and use it in the ways he wished but deep down in the back of his mind he worried that when the time came and his strength was needed the most, he would be found wanting.

"Do not worry." Richard commented, noticing his companion's concerned look. "You won't be alone. We are 'Brothers' for a reason. Not because we are related through blood but because we are brothers through life and I shall always be here to advise you."

* * * * * *

"I miss Scrave," Rauph confessed to his little friend as he stood at the helm. "I miss our shopping trips and all the fun we had." Ashe nodded his head in agreement, taking in the far-off look present in his giant friend's eyes.

"Don't be sad." He said clambering up onto the stool he had borrowed from someone's cabin so he could sit near his friend. He reached up, grabbing Rauph's horns, one with his normal hand and the other with his bandaged fingers and pulled the Minotaur's head slowly back towards him so their eyes met.

"I miss him too." Ashe said in a mature out of character tone. "But I also recognise that my friends are around me here on this ship and that although Scrave is gone there will be more shopping trips and adventures. More action, excitement and lost treasures to be found. I also know my best friend Rauph will be there to have those adventures alongside me and that I won't miss our future together for anything in the world."

Rauph lowered his head and rested his nose on Ashe's tiny button one snorting softly.

"Do you really think we will have more shopping trips?"

"Undoubtedly!" Ashe confirmed. "Can you move your nose away? You are slobbering on my face!"

"Ashe come quickly!" Austen yelled, running over towards him and gesturing that he got down from the stool and followed him immediately. "Your egg is about to hatch!"

He pushed Ashe along before him, threatening to bowl the Halfling over in his determination to get back to the caged birds in time.

"Is it really coming now?" Ashe babbled, a thousand questions on his excited swollen lips. He tried to fumble the cage open but his hands were so thickly swaddled in bandages that he was unable to manage.

Austen moved him aside, opened the door and reached gently into the cage, withdrawing the last solitary egg from the clutch. He handed it carefully to the little Halfling, standing close in case Ashe was unable to hold the egg with his wounded hands. The hen bird of prey was nestled over the rest of her recently hatched brood and had apparently abandoned this final egg.

"Ooh! It's so warm." Ashe commented, turning the egg carefully in his bandaged hands. There was a dull crack and a split appeared in the egg's surface, almost causing the Halfling to drop the egg to the floor. "Oh, it's opening," he shrieked excitedly. "It's really opening!"

Austen looked on carefully observing the handling of the fragile object and reached forward to help remove some of the more resilient shell as the chick within fought to come out into the wide world.

"Oh my!" He exclaimed, as the side of the egg finally came away exposing the ugliest chick he had ever seen. Its head was excessively big for its body, what little down there was covering its pink wriggly skin seemed to be completely the wrong colour and in some places it was bald. Little stubby wings stuck out from its sides, all glued together with the residue from the egg.

The chick raised its head, eyes still tightly closed, and uttered an ear-piercing cry that immediately put Austen's teeth on edge.

This chick was wrong.

There was something not right with it and now he had gone and got the Halfling's hopes up about this being his personal chick. It would be better for everyone if the bird was destroyed in a humane manner and put out of its misery right now.

The bird shrieked again making Austen wince. He looked down at Ashe expecting to see clear disappointment on the Halfling's mottled and swollen face.

Instead, he saw eyes sparkling with excitement.

"Hello Sinders." Ashe crooned, gently stroking the bird's mangy head with his little finger. "I'm your daddy."

"Are you sure you want this one?" Austen asked, horrified at the unnatural bonding occurring before his eyes.

"Awwwwkkkk! Accckkk!" squawked Sinders, its big head jerking back at the effort, making it nearly drop from Ashe's hands.

"Are you kidding?" Ashe remarked, his eyes not moving from the ugly top-heavy creature wriggling in his hands.

"I love it!"

* * * * * *

The green mist twisted and swirled about the dragon's lair, slipping over piles of coins, pooling into cups adorned with polished gems. Tendrils weaved through the strings of enchanted instruments, circled weapons that vibrated at its evil presence. It knew there was something down here, something that could help it in its quest. It narrowed in on a silent shadow that lay on the floor, surrounded by coins tainted with blood. It took a few moments to take control of its new host, then, impossibly, a blood smeared hand jerked in the darkness.

Epilogue

The stranger came from beyond the hills, back where the fire had spread upon the mountain those weeks past and he wanted a boat.

He did not haggle at the price, just pointed at the small sad fishing boat tied at the end of the jetty, asking how much it would cost to have her made seaworthy and stocked with sufficient supplies for a voyage. Paying with a handful of small jewels, much more than the job and boat were worth, he left as mysteriously as when he had first arrived.

True to his word, he returned one week later, as the early dawn defined the line of the sea from the horizon with a ruddy glow. The broker was enthusiastic, throwing his arms wide and inviting his generous benefactor on board the newly transformed vessel, pointing out the newly sanded and stained deck, explaining how the freshly calked hull would be watertight for years to come. The craft gleamed with the lavished attention only money could buy; far removed from the neglected, listing, vessel she once was. Seaworthy for many Nautical miles.

The ship chandleries had made good on their promises and all supplies had been securely stored aboard. The stranger nodded from within the folds of his hooded cloak, lifting wax sealed jars to the light, shaking them and listening carefully to ensure all was safe and dry from the ravages travel at sea would bring.

He asked few questions regarding how the vessel handled, clearly having some experience at sea travel, adjusted her new cream canvas sail with a practiced hand, checked the lines were free of rot and the mast was sound. The anchor was new, the chain free of seaweed or rust. The broker was particularly proud of his achievements and looked for positive comments, although few came freely. There were just simple nods, shakes of the stranger's cloaked head and a long pause when the stranger saw the new name under which his ship would sail.

The Tulip, represented on her bow by a flowing and elegant hand underscored by a lifelike presentation of the spring flower and its perfect creamy white bowl at the tip of a delicate green stem and leaf. The stranger raised an eyebrow then continued his tour of his new acquisition.

Satisfied all was as asked, the broker gathered the necessary paperwork to record the sale of *The Tulip* and legally register the vessel. He looked up from smoothing the parchment to see the stranger standing on the prow of the ship, holding a pendant up to the dawn sun, turning this way and that as if checking for something in the half-light.

The stranger stared intently at a figure that appeared to be moving in the large smoky pearl set within the pendants design. Then as the sun rose, the enchantment faded and he lowered the necklace, staring out across the waves and the reddening horizon, as if he could see something out there in the early mists that the merchant could not. The cloaked figure nodded to himself, apparently satisfied and came over to sign the bill of sale and be on his way.

"Are you happy with what you saw?" The broker asked intent on ensuring his generous patron was happy. His customer looked whimsical, his head turning once more to stare out across the waves.

"She's my future." He muttered.

The merchant's face remained confused as he waited in an uncomfortable silence before he took the courage to clear his throat in embarrassment.

You have done well," the stranger confessed, his voice rasping as if at some point recently he had worked in a forge. He collected the offered bill of sale and folded it tightly before securing it into a saddlebag he had slung across one shoulder. The broker could not help but notice the bulge underneath the stranger's cloak, as if a round shield hung there.

"I wish to catch the tide, so if there is nothing else?"

The broker found himself propelled to the jetty, despite his bluster and he turned to voice his dismay at the hurried departure after all his fine work. Another small gemstone dropped into his astonished hand, helping to ease his hurt feelings.

"For all your excellent work. Please be kind enough to release the lines."

The broker swiftly pocketed the gemstone and moved to comply, freeing the bowline first, followed by that of the stern.

There was an audible snap and crack of canvas as the wind started to fill the sails.

"Are you sure you want to set sail now?" the merchant asked. "It looks like there is a storm brewing."

"I'm counting on it." came the cryptic reply.

"Wait sir," the broker shouted. "I need your name for the registration. I'm afraid it is the law."

"S..." The stranger caught himself as he started to mouth his reply and then paused as if making an important decision. He shook his head and then lifted his hood free, revealing warm hazel eyes set in a travel worn face framed by long grey hair streaked through with faint lines of black.

"My name..." he tilted his head towards the merchant, his lips forming a poetically tragic smile.

"My name... is Kerian Denaris."

-: The End :-

Be sure not to miss the sequel to Styx & Stones.

The Labyris Knight

Book Two from The Tales of the *El Defensor*

Out now ....

Here's a special preview.

The Labyris Knight

-: Tales of the *El Defensor* :-

Book Two.

Prologue

In that moment when a storm ends, time almost stands still; the air feels scrubbed, clean and fresh, hinting at new beginnings, endless possibilities and whispered promises of what the future has yet to bring.

In that moment, when nature pauses to catch its breath, many a sailor has looked to the heavens and thanked their gods that they are still alive to face the challenges of another day. Counted their blessings for surviving the terrors that have placed them on the very cusp of death and destruction, elated they could now return to their families and huddle together for warmth and comfort, promising never to take those feelings for granted again.

However, for Kerian Denaris, the passing of the storm signalled one thing.

It meant that he had failed. Colette, the woman he loved, was sailing further away on the galleon *El Defensor*; unaware that Kerian remained alive and was searching so desperately for her.

Each of his previous attempts had begun with such renewed vigour, buoyed by false hope, only to be crushed into silence, as each expedition failed to locate a window of calm on the horizon, tinged by a sickly mustard yellow light and a skyline dotted with the skeletal remains of many ships.

The sea's surface was as flat as a millpond, barely a ripple marking the movement of the twenty-one-foot fishing boat *The Tulip* as she rocked gently from side to side. The paintwork on the vessel, once gleaming, was now worn and shabby and the hull leaked slowly in several places; testament to the punishment the valiant vessel had endured chasing storms up and down the coast over the last few months.

A splash shattered the silence, followed by another, this time accompanied with a string of expletives as the owner of *The Tulip* set to bailing out his vessel as it sat low in the water. There was a crash as something fell inside the boat, a further oath and then the pail used to bail out the vessel, flew out over the side, skipping across the mirrored surface of the sea before sliding slowly under the surface.

Despairing sobs filled the air, heartfelt cries of agony in protest of failure and love lost. It signalled a momentary loss of control, a rare glimpse into the vulnerable side of the normally stoic man from which they came.

Kerian looked despondently about him with weary hazel eyes, cursing his own stupidity and lack of control in throwing away the only item left intact on his small boat with which he could try to remove the water slopping around his ankles. He stood up to his six-foot height, hands on hips, scanning the horizon for a sight of land or a passing ship from which he could hail assistance. However, he knew he was all alone out here. In fact, he could be on the very edge of the world for all he knew.

No one would have been that stupid to dare set sail into the tropical storm that had just lashed this region. Its ferocity would feed the imaginations and tales of elders in taverns up and down the coast. Fishermen would only consider navigating these waters now the storm had passed. Help could be hours away.

He brushed back his salt and pepper hair from his weathered face, pulling the length tight and fastening it with a thin strip of leather. His mind wandered back, thinking of the path that had led him to this place; the curse cast on him by an evil sorceress now burnt at the stake, its enchantment aging him a year for every month he had lived. His time spent looking for a remedy, the desperate acts he had undertaken, before finding a slim clue in the dusty archives of a monastery in Catterick, where a faded manuscript detailed the location of a magical gemstone that could grant your heart's desire.

Kerian chuckled at the absurdity of it all. The jewel had granted his heart's desire but the results had been far from what he had expected. He sloshed across the waterlogged deck of his boat searching for a container to continue bailing. Although his trousers were folded up to his knees to try and keep them from dragging in the water they were still soaked through, as was his grubby grey linen shirt which hung on a frame verging on the gaunt.

He had to admit, that had been some storm. Practically everything not nailed down on *The Tulip* had been thrown about, with several items swept overboard. A fleeting sense of panic suddenly struck him and his hand quickly moved to his chest to touch his shirt and the shape of two pendants hanging from his neck, their presence reassuring the warrior and calming his tortured mind. He did not know what he would do if he were to ever lose these personal treasures.

Kerian took another deep breath to calm himself and considered his position carefully. Thomas Adams, the captain of the *El Defensor,* had once told him that sailing on the ocean was like being on the surface of a mirror and that whilst you sailed upon its surface there was plenty of time to reflect. It was true, he had endured another storm but this time his vessel was in urgent need of repair. The damage was quite severe and he knew with a despairing heart that it would take valuable time to make *The Tulip* seaworthy again.

On a brighter note, he was still alive, with no broken bones or serious injury. His aging was slowly reversing, making him feel stronger every day but it was a slow process and definitely not for someone with a low patience threshold.

He sank down on the edge of the boat and sat there thinking hard, chewing his lip nervously in thought. He needed to make for land, in whatever direction it lay. Get *the Tulip* repaired, take stock and ask himself several serious and searching questions. Why was he still doing this? Why was he out here, in the middle of nowhere, chasing storms and facing death like a lunatic?

Colette was slipping through his fingers and there appeared to be nothing he could do to change this, no matter how much he wished otherwise. He had even lost his birthright at some point in his adventures. The pale band of skin where his golden ring used to rest was yet another blow to his fragile psyche. He had lost so much, in such a short time.

Kerian sighed heavily, then looked over to where he had stored his saddlebags and suddenly had an idea. He reached up and carefully pulled out an object wrapped in the charred remains of a long black cloak. The mirrored shield gleamed brightly as he exposed it to the sunlight.

He looked down at his reflection in its surface, noticing the slow re-emergence of facial features he felt he had lost long ago. His hair was slowly changing back, even some of the lines were starting to smooth from his face. He stared at the image of the haunted man before him for a long time, realising that he had lost a lot of weight since he had last gazed upon his own features. Possibly too much! Had he been so focused in his pursuit that he had started to neglect himself?

His obsession was leading him into situations no sane individual would contemplate.

A forlorn flapping from above roused him from his thoughts and made him angle the shield to take in the image of the shredded sails on the main mast. The storm had ripped the canvas apart. Even if the wind returned, he would gain little speed with them in this sorry state! He flipped the mirrored shield over, banishing the image of the man within and then started to bail the water from the deck. With luck, he would find support when the fishermen arrived in the area to trawl in the hope the storm had disturbed the waters enough to make the fishing worthwhile, or if not, he would have to use the shield to paddle in a random direction and hope he found the shore.

He bent his back to the task and tried to ignore the voice in his head that told him to give up, find the mainland, settle down and rebuild a life for himself.

The problem with that thought was that giving up was something Kerian Denaris was not prepared to do.

He bailed some water over the side, sending ripples out from the boat and letting his mind wander, trying to imagine how his friends were on the *El Defensor*. If he knew Thomas, he was probably sitting in his cabin, boots up on the table, savouring the orange tang of his favourite alcohol and soaking in the ambience of life at sea.

What he would give to be in Thomas's boots right now.

* * * * * *

Paranoia is a feeling you experience when you imagine people are out to get you; unfortunately, for Thomas Adams, captain of the Spanish Galleon *El Defensor,* this feeling was growing rapidly and he knew without doubt that they were.

The crimson flashing light blinking at his side confirmed his worst fears. The battered NV-07 handgun was nearly out of charge. There were maybe one or two blaster shots left, at best. The blue metal was cold against his sweating palm and his twitching finger nervously stroked the trigger looking for the reassurance the side arm could never give.

Thomas paused for breath beneath a spluttering lime green neon sign, advertising some type of futuristic drink and then checked behind him for the pursuit he knew was closing in.

At just under six-foot-tall and shy of his forty-eighth birthday, Thomas cut an imposing figure. His salt worn leather boots, trousers, loose cream shirt and braid waistcoat completed an outfit partially covered by a long dark trench coat that was soaked through by the persistent drizzle falling from the grey lifeless sky. His short dark hair was swept back from a rugged face sculpted and tanned by his time spent at sea. An assortment of fading bruises completed his profile and his breathing came in gasps as he considered the limited options open to him.

He could always return the gemstone to the giant lizards tracking him and hope they would not kill him too slowly! Thomas shook his head, he did not consider that a viable option, they required the gemstone to power open another gate, the small stones Colette had remaining in her collection were not large enough to channel sufficient power to safely get the *El Defensor* through the archways between worlds, making any attempt dangerous for both ship and crew.

Without the stone, they could not continue their search for home and were at risk of being stranded either here in this futuristic nightmare world, or worse, marooned in the ship's graveyard.

Shouts and snarls sounded behind him, signalling his pursuers were closing. Thomas set off along the edge of the street, moving from one shadowy alleyway to the next, slipping from cover to cover as he had been taught all those years before in the academy. He kept his back to the wall, checked all corners, and when he was sure, ran across the street dodging the sweeping searchlights from a hover car running a frantic search pattern and zipping close by overhead.

How did he keep finding himself in these situations?

This urgent need for a gemstone had led Thomas to consider the one world where he knew he could find one. A world where for a price, or more importantly a risk, a stone could be found to secure passage to their goal. Inside the ship's graveyard there was only one archway out of the hundreds that ringed the derelict ships stranded there that had lost its keystone, setting it apart from the others. The broken arch was one of the few that Thomas had journeyed through several times in the past. It was just that he had failed to consider the bad feelings he had left in his wake the last time he had come this way.

It was at times like these that the captain wished he had listened to the advice of his crew. When they had arrived in Maraket, this place of gleaming skyscrapers, loud neon signs and futuristic technology, his friends had warned him to leave the scavenging to other crewmen with attributes more appropriate to the task but Thomas would not listen. He had things to sort out in his mind; he needed the distraction the landing would give to find his own self-worth. He slipped his hand into his coat pocket and felt the reassuring shape of a small toy *Matchbox* car police cruiser, his hand closing protectively around it.

Just by holding the toy, the image of a withered creature that preyed on lost souls and ate the bodies of the marooned sprang to mind; Images of a flaky skeletal face, hovering lights that danced around his body hypnotising the unwary and luring them to their doom. Thomas shook his head and turned a corner, finding himself arriving at the end of the street and a choice that made him wince at its absurdity.

Somehow, he had taken a wrong turn. He knew the docks were roughly in this direction but this was definitely not the waterfront. Instead, a graveyard lay ahead, complete with spectral mist which held an ominous foreboding. He could turn in there and hope to hide from the pursuit or turn back and meet the lizards head on. The weight of the nearly empty gun in his hand confirmed a full-frontal assault was suicide. A blaster shot ricocheted off the stone façade of the building beside him dropped an awning into the street with a crash of sparks deciding the matter for him.

The graveyard it was.

Thomas ran for the gateway, shouldering the railing and for once having something go his way. The gate swung open on squealing hinges and he found himself running up the gravel pathway. Rows of gravestones and neglected obelisks stretched away to either side, inscriptions worn away by the elements or slowly smothered by lichen. Plinths leaned over towards tilting grave markers as if engaged in secret conversations and mausoleums stood cold and aloof with warped doors opened in sinister invitation for the unwary to step inside.

The captain ducked behind a tall monument and dropped to his knees, facing back the way he came. The crying face of an angel loomed protectively over him, her wings sheltering the captain from the worst of the rain. The stonework was exquisite but Thomas had no time to critique the work, as his mind continued to think about the monster that stalked him in his nightmares and how it had taunted him with the miniature police cruiser.

The toy car was a trophy from a serial killer. Thomas had a fractured memory of his own past and knew the car had connections to himself but the images haunting him, whether hypnotically suggested by his nemesis, or real memories from his past, had shaken the captain to his core. He was no serial killer. Was he?

The gates to the graveyard squealed open as his hunters followed into the cemetery and slid between the monuments. Hisses and clicks signalled communication between the hunting party as they split and started to hunt him through the field of remembrance. Thomas clenched his gun tighter. He felt the damp start to seep through the material of his trousers and trickle down the inside of his leather boot.

Thomas raised his head and peered into the darkness beyond his cold marble shelter, his free hand touching the cool surface for a sense of reality as well as support. This marker was something real, something he could relate to, whilst somewhere out there, his enemies were seeking him.

A searchlight flickered across the graveyard, sending shadows slipping and sliding between the markers and putting Thomas further on edge. The lizards could be anywhere. The annoying hover car zoomed by on the right, its lights picking out the blackened ruins of a cathedral standing tall at the far end of the graves, a mere skeleton compared to the majestic building it once was. The drizzling rain, coupled with the briefness of the illumination made it difficult to make out the fine details of its crumbling structure, so Thomas turned back to the tombs around him and cursed how the grave markers gave cover to both himself and his pursuers.

Maybe he could hide in one of the crypts?

A flash of movement to the left caught his eye and he turned, focusing intently in the direction of the perceived threat. His gun hand swept up with a speed born from fear rather than professionalism as he balanced the muzzle of the weapon against the edge of the statue for stability and sighted through the luminescent twin v's along the top of the barrel.

Time stood still as the captain stared into the darkness, not daring to blink in case whatever he had seen moved again. His eyes strained hard to catch the smallest clue, the slightest hint of where his adversaries may be. They seemed to know his every move; huge reptilian creatures that walked on sturdy muscular hind legs that would kill him without mercy.

Sensing no further movement, Thomas began to slowly slide back down into the shadows, feeling the cool stone at his back despite the three layers of clothing he wore. He started to shiver, unsure if it was from the adrenaline coursing through his blood stream or the fact that he was so cold. He had a momentary wish to know whom the erected angel immortalised, fleeting thoughts suggesting he could be sharing the same resting place before morning.

He tried to calm his breathing, collect himself, slowing his breaths until he started to make out the sounds around him. It was strange that in the confines of the graveyard his breathing appeared to have an echo. That was ridiculous! How could his breathing be echoing? Thomas took a deep breath and held it, his heart hammering loudly in his ears.

The breathing continued heavily from directly behind his marble sanctuary!

"I know where you are." A voice shouted from near the cemetery entrance. "Come now Thomas, we can be reasonable. Give me back the stone and I'll call off Cornelius and Horatio."

Thomas gritted his teeth and bit his tongue, he dared not reply in case one of the walking designer handbags Miguel Garcia used as his 'hired muscle' realised where he was and by the sounds of the sniffing and scrabbling behind him one of them was about to find out anyway. He edged slowly along the base of the statue, feeling the water flooding more steadily into his boot at the movement and drawing a surprised gasp before he could stop himself. His free hand slipped from the stone and landed heavily on a hard, cobbled tube. Thomas winced as he suddenly realised what it was. The lizard man's tail slipped out from under his hand and a rumbling growl rose above him. The captain looked up into the shadows between the angel's wings and took in the blunt snout and cold eyes of Horatio staring back at him.

It was time to move!

The NV-07 spat a crimson bolt of searing energy straight up, fired practically by reflex. Horatio bellowed in pain as the blaster scored a furrow across his reptilian nose and deflected from the spiny ridge of bone running from between his eyes all the way down his seven-foot-long height and out along a further three feet of reptilian tail.

Marble chips exploded into the air as the lizard returned fire, his own weapon sending a withering barrage of bolts down into the space Thomas had just vacated. The captain caught a glimpse of a long sleek laser rifle, before he ran blindly from cover out across the graveyard. The air filled with crimson streaks of sizzling light, headstones that had resisted the elements for years exploding into rubble as the two lizards mowed down everything in their path.

He ran up to a mausoleum, briefly considering trying the door and grabbing the handle, only for the door to disintegrate under another stray laser bolt. Thomas dodged left, sprinting beneath a monolith with an urn on the top. The urn went the way of the door; granite chips whistling across the captain's path like shrapnel.

Thomas held his arm above his head, protecting his face from the whistling debris and ran towards the cathedral. If he could get into the building, maybe, just maybe, he could shake the gruesome twosome from his trail. He turned around to see how close they were to catching him and the ground fell away from beneath him.

The breath crashed out of his body as he hit the floor and it took Thomas a few seconds to extricate himself from the mud that now plastered him from top to toe. He staggered back to his feet, sludge dripping heavily from his clothes and realised he had fallen into a freshly dug grave. He wiped the mud from his face then frantically looked about the ground for his gun that he had somehow dropped in the fall but it was nowhere to be found.

It appeared this night was getting better and better!

Hissing grunts from above signalled the arrival of Horatio and Cornelius and they stared down at him with their cold reptilian eyes, their tails flicking excitedly. Thomas blinked to clear the rain from his eyes and noted that both creatures were armed with 326-CZ laser carbines. Thick tongues squelched from between armour scaled lips as the reptiles regarded their cornered prey with a hungry look in their eyes. A lighter set of footsteps arrived and walked slowly around the edge of the grave before moving forwards to reveal a silhouette Thomas knew only too well.

"I see you are still dressing up for the occasion." Miguel Garcia commented, pausing to light up a cigar and puff on it several times until the end glowed red. "You never had good dress sense. Now, I believe you have something that belongs to me." The privateer, standing slightly smaller than Thomas, wore a long frock coat which had bandoliers over his chest. Large buckles on his belt and coat added to the look of a stereotypical pirate from the high seas, which was exactly the look Miguel was trying to convey. The fact that his flintlock pistols were blasters only served to reinforce his authority in this situation. Thomas frantically turned, checking both ends of the grave. Where was his damned handgun? He needed to put a shot right between the shifty man's eyes.

"Looking for this?" Miguel asked, holding up Thomas's gun. "Sloppy Thomas, real sloppy. Now hand it over."

Thomas reached into his coat and lifted out a fist-sized amethyst. Even in the dull light from the hover car searchlight wobbling about erratically overhead, facets gleamed alluringly. Thomas knew he had no choice but to comply. It was Miguel's gemstone after all. Maybe if he were lucky Miguel would just shoot him in the leg as a warning and spare his life.

"You know I'm going to have to kill you?" Miguel informed him, rolling the cigar backwards and forwards in his lips and blowing out a cloud of smoke as he beckoned Thomas to come closer to his end of the grave. "It's nothing personal."

"Sure it is." Thomas replied, considering his unpleasant fate. "It's always personal with you." So much for the blaster bolt in the leg theory!

"That's because you always make it so!" Miguel screamed down at him, his control slipping as it had countless times in the past. "Every time our paths cross you make me a laughing stock! Remember how you tricked me into marrying the Twinwood Ambassador's daughter?"

"Oh yes." Thomas replied, stopping as if a sudden thought had occurred to him and lowering the jewel gently back down by his side near to his coat pocket "What was her name again." He clicked his fingers. "I remember. Tess. How is the old battle-axe?"

Miguel ignored the jibe continuing to spout bile, pacing the edge of the grave in growing agitation as he remembered the slights against him.

"Remember when you sold me that treasure map? The sure thing? The legendary Eaglestone treasure? The map that led to that island of cannibal frogs?"

Thomas tried to hide the grin sliding across his face. Now that had been a funny one.

Miguel shook with rage, brushing his hand nervously through his dark greasy hair. "And then there was the DeParys incident."

"Oh yes." Thomas could not help but laugh this time. "The DeParys incident."

"Don't talk about the DeParys incident." Miguel snarled, pointing Thomas's gun straight at him. "No one must ever mention the DeParys incident again." Thomas observed the diode on the sidearm pointed at him and smiled to himself, even as he gently slid the amethyst back into his jacket. He also noticed that the hover car had swung around behind Miguel and his reptilian heavies and was now heading their way, wobbling unsteadily in flight as if the pilot was new to the machine. The captain suddenly had a sneaky suspicion who was at its controls.

"I guess you've got me." Thomas confessed, hoping to hold their attention for just a bit longer. "Just pull the trigger. Let's get this over with."

"I have been looking forward to this." Miguel smiled, stroking the end of his bushy moustache theatrically. He pulled the trigger...

...and nothing happened.

"It's empty." Thomas confessed. "I used the last shot when I re-fashioned Horatio's nose."

Thomas surprised everyone as he dove towards their end of the grave. The hover car suddenly accelerated directly towards the group at high speed. It clipped a monument, teetered unsteadily then flipped; a large figure dropping from the driving seat as the car crashed to the ground, rushing straight over them, practically knocking the three thugs off their feet before exploding in a ball of flame. Miguel found himself teetering unsteadily on the edge, only for Thomas to take advantage and grab his feet, pulling the buccaneer into the grave with him where they grappled fiercely, each desperate to gain the upper hand.

Thomas's remaining lizard captors turned as one, as a creature from mythology smashed straight into them. Eight-foot-tall, horns gleaming wickedly in the light, red hair stuck up in every direction and slobber foaming from the end of its nose.

Horatio met an uppercut that lifted the lizard off his back legs and rattled his brains. As the reptile fell senseless to the floor, his laser rifle was snatched up by the roaring hover car pilot, who set about brandishing the carbine with devastating effect. He pummelled Cornelius repeatedly about the body, microchips, circuit boards, sparks and smoke coming from the ruined weapon, as the massive Minotaur navigator from the *El Defensor* protected his captain the only way he knew how; by hitting things really hard.

Miguel went to draw a blaster as he grappled with Thomas in the mud but a right hook from the captain stopped him in his tracks, making his teeth clash painfully together and catching his lip, which bloomed crimson droplets of blood.

"Give me your weapons." Thomas snarled, dripping mud down on his opponent.

"Now, now!" Miguel held up his hands showing he was unarmed. "I wasn't really going to shoot you Thomas. Old buddy, old pal." He reluctantly passed over his two blasters, his dismay at doing so quite evident in his facial expression.

The Minotaur stomped over to the edge of the grave and looked down at the two men covered from head to foot in mud. It took him a few seconds to recognise the man he sought and he gripped Thomas's hand securely and hoisted the captain clear from what Thomas had fleetingly thought could have been his final resting place.

"In the nick of time Rauph." Thomas laughed, addressing his rescuer. "Just in the nick of time." He turned to look down at the bedraggled figure in the open grave and smiled, his confidence returning in a rush now the tables had turned.

"Come on Rauph, aren't you going to help me out too?" Miguel asked holding up his hand. The navigator glared, snorting angrily down at the man, staring him down. Thomas tried not to laugh as the Minotaur continued to appear menacing, despite the fact, Thomas had never known a more loyal and gentler companion. "So, you want me to stay down in the grave?" Miguel gestured miserably. Rauph simply glared as intimidatingly as he could and turned away, his opinion on the matter clear to see.

"Thank you for your kind hospitality, and of course for the amethyst." Thomas bowed his head theatrically, his sodden clothes clinging to his skin. "We have to leave now. I suggest you stay down there until we are gone, otherwise Rauph may not be as understanding as I."

"I am going to get you for this." Miguel threatened.

"I will look forward to it." Thomas replied. "But it won't be here. I have a great dislike for science fiction. Put a sword in my hand, the wind at my back and the *El Defensor* beneath my feet and I am happy. Until another time then?" Thomas turned to leave, moving up alongside his massive rescuer.

"Let's get back to the ship as quickly as possible." Thomas suggested to his bovine friend. "Miguel has many friends. I would rather not be here when he gets out of that grave and gathers his hired muscle." Horatio started to stir on the floor, his tail curving out sinuously. Rauph responded by smashing the remainder of the laser rifle onto his head, knocking the lizard out cold.

Thomas slipped and slid along the path towards the exit of the graveyard and only when he felt they had put enough space between him and his adversary did he stop to consider his ruined wardrobe.

"You know Rowan is never going to let me in my cabin looking like this. I'm going to be in real trouble. I am glad you came after me Rauph, despite my telling you to stay on the ship. Come to think of it, where did you get the hover car from? You know if you had driven it properly, we could have saved ourselves this walk."

Thomas flung Miguel's blasters away as far as he could, the weapons sailing off into the lengthening shadows amongst the gravestones. It was all well and good having such futuristic blasters but once you passed beyond the ship's graveyard, they ceased to function as anything more exciting than a paperweight with an amusing story behind it.

"You know..." Thomas turned to his companion, as an afterthought struck. "Those Laser rifles work so much better if you pull the trigger." Rauph wrinkled his snout in confusion and turned to his captain.

"Which part was the trigger?"

Acknowledgements

This fantasy adventure has a tale all of its own, of a journey spanning years and of numerous people who encouraged me to stick with my story, showing a belief in my ability to write, even when I felt like giving it all up.

Styx & Stones started life in the late 1980's. I submitted it for publication in May 1990 as a short story under the name *Crossed Paths* to an American role-playing magazine called *Dragon*. The *DragonLance Chronicles* by Margaret Weis and Tracy Hickman were causing waves through the fantasy worlds of literature and the story was originally set in this TSR trademarked world. Kerian was a deserting lieutenant from the *Dragonwing* armies and Ashe adopted the *Kender* traits as was appropriate for that style of story. However, as the story grew, both characters became more three dimensional, reflective and sombre to match the darkness of the unfolding tale and my own life pathway. The editor of *Dragon* magazine did not send the standard rejection letter, instead they felt the story was too much of a cliff-hanger and wanted to know where the rest was.

There was a small problem with this request. I knew the characters. I had an ending and a beginning. What happened in between was a journey I had yet to travel. The commencement of my medical career found me scribbling chapters on scrap medical record sheets during the obligatory night shifts every trainee endures. On breaks, others went to sleep, whereas I travelled in a realm where a young man, trapped in an old man's body, fought injustice atop a white stallion whilst searching for a cure for old age.

One colleague informed me that '*Crossed Paths*' was a stupid title. The hero was Styx and he was searching for a magical gemstone... so why not *Styx & Stones*? Mr Jay Eales, of Factor Fiction, I know it is 25 years late but my thanks go out to you.

Others commented on my work as the months and years trickled by like individual grains of sand passing through an invisible timer I could never reset. Some of my dearest friends, from the most unlikely of places, gave advice and guided me through life, encouraging me to believe in a story some would never see completed. In no particular order, Dr R. Baldry, A Inman, J. Maxwell, J. Reid, Charles & Mark Southwell, D. Stear, R. Wilson, E. Worthy all kept me hammering away at the keyboard well into the early hours of the morning, when the chaos of life took a rest and allowed me time to catch my breath and free my mind to think. I tried to keep up the work but life kept getting in the way. Marriage, children, constant training and my own insecurities meant shelving the project repeatedly.

Every time I tried to submit for publication, I became mired in the editor, publisher and agent triangle with no one willing to take a chance on a writer who had no experience in the field. One publishing house even went so far as to suggest readers would never identify with a book whose main hero was an old man. Today fantasy movies and books abound with grey haired grizzled fighters, so on reflection I was actually ahead of the game.

Karen Sanderson, a charming editor who normally worked with science fiction and tales involving the Pegasus galaxy, started a painstaking editing process, dissecting my first few chapters with the skill of a surgeon, informing me that aspects of my earlier drafts were 'never going to happen in real life'. Whole segments required restructuring, others a stake through the heart or a ritual burning to make the unfolding scenarios believable. The finished result shows just how right she was.

Armed with this wealth of advice and manuscripts of various ages, covered in more red corrections than my own typed script, I did the only sensible thing open to me. I shelved it again! Until March 2015, when my colleague C. Mukundan pushed me to dust off the folder one last time, squash the spiders who had set up residence within and begin again from page one. I correlated all the various versions, sat back, taking in why earlier drafts had not worked and began to slowly rebuild my self-confidence from a point when I felt nothing but doubt. I went back into my imaginary world during my lunch breaks and decided to give my best, with a self-set deadline of twelve months to make my dream of publication a reality, or consign the lot to the refuse bin and never mention it again.

My new proof-readers pointed out the mistakes I would never have noticed. A clay pipe will not roll across a ship's deck... no matter how hard I wanted it to. A Cessna Skylane 5 cannot easily carry four passengers and four parachutes; H. Ewart's comments made me smile and continue to motivate me. My thanks to him is eternal. The eagle eyes of D. Lowe spotted a marble table that magically transformed to one of carved wood in the space of a page. Something five previous readers had failed to spot. I thank him for the delight he took in wiping that smile from my face every time he noticed another plot hole, normally just after I assumed the book was in the bag!

Finally, I need to thank my family for the support they have shown me in bringing this dream to life. Ryan, for his help with *Photoshop* and allowing me to use the clone and eraser tool only when I behaved! Owain for his keen eye and photographic skills, my author photograph is his work. Lastly, my wife Nicola who designed the cover concept. She is my inspiration, and my life and lets me babble on about little characters in my imagination without ever suggesting I seek medical help.

So my tale is finished... It is out there now, free from its cage, open to the criticism of the world. I can put my feet up and close my eyes, my life goal finally complete. There is just one problem: In my dreams, I am watching a new tale. There is a jungle full of tombs, set around a large maze. A twisted matriarch and a Minotaur Prince who needs to find a huge Labyris axe to gain his birth right.

His name is Rauph... and he wants to go home.

Adam Derbyshire
May 1st, 2016.

About the Author

Adam Derbyshire has always wanted to write stories...

But real life and utility bills kept getting in the way.
Swiftly approaching his mid-life crisis, he decided it was time to either buy the luxury sports car, or tell
the world about the ghostly ship and crew that sail
throughout his dreams.

He lives in Northamptonshire with his wife and children and sadly could not afford the Aston Martin.

Styx and Stones is his first novel.

Printed in Great Britain
by Amazon